By Terry Brooks

THE SHANNARA CHRONICLES
The Elfstones of Shannara
The Wishsong of Shannara

BEFORE THE CHRONICLES THERE WAS . . .
The Sword of Shannara
The First King of Shannara

TO FULLY EXPLORE THE WORLD OF SHANNARA VISIT:

terrybrooks.net/novels

The Wishsong of Shannara

THE SHANNARA CHRONICLES

THE WISHSONG OF SHANNARA

TERRY BROOKS

DEL REY • NEW YORK

2015 Del Rey Trade Paperback Edition

Copyright © 1985 by Terry Brooks
Map on p. viii by the Brothers Hildebrandt copyright © 1977
by Penguin Random House LLC
All other interior art by Darrell K. Sweet copyright ©
1985 by Penguin Random House LLC

ISBN 978-1-101-96561-0
eBook ISBN 978-0-345-44462-2

Printed in the United States of America on acid-free paper

randomhousebooks.com

2 4 6 8 9 7 5 3 1

For Lester del Rey
Expert

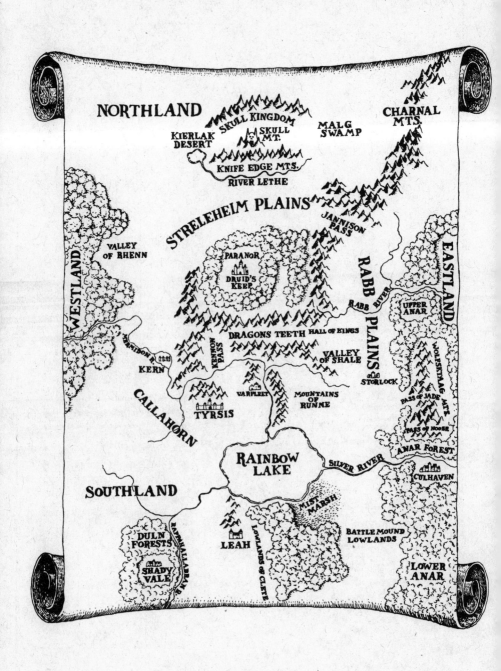

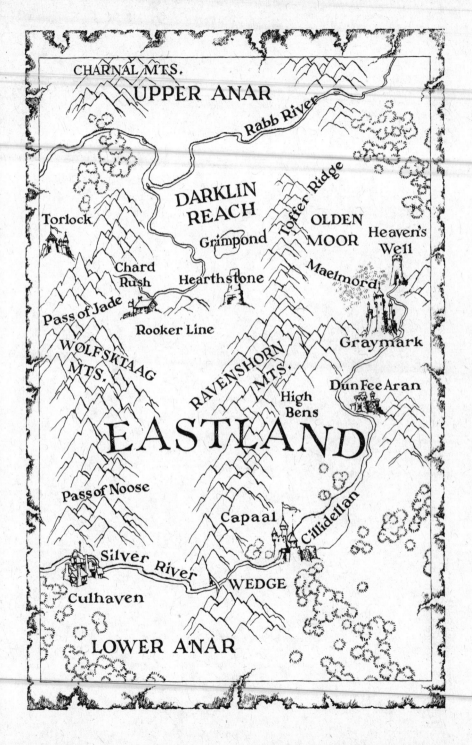

The Wishsong of Shannara

I

A CHANGE OF SEASONS WAS UPON THE FOUR LANDS AS LATE
summer faded slowly into autumn. Gone were the long, still days
of midyear where sweltering heat slowed the pace of life and there
was a sense of having time enough for anything. Though summer's
warmth lingered, the days had begun to shorten, the humid air to
dry, and the memory of life's immediacy to reawaken. The signs of
transition were all about. In the forests of Shady Vale, the leaves had
already begun to turn.

Brin Ohmsford paused by the flowerbeds that bordered the
front walkway of her home, losing herself momentarily in the crimson foliage of the old maple that shaded the yard beyond. It was a
massive thing, its trunk broad and gnarled. Brin smiled. That old
tree was the source of many childhood memories for her. Impulsively, she stepped off the walkway and moved over to the aged tree.

She was a tall girl—taller than her parents or her brother Jair,
nearly as tall as Rone Leah—and although there was a delicate look
to her slim body, she was as fit as any of them. Jair would argue the
point of course, but that was only because Jair found it hard enough
as it was to accept his role as the youngest. A girl, after all, was just
a girl.

Her fingers touched the roughened trunk of the maple softly,
caressing, and she stared upward into the tangle of limbs overhead.
Long, black hair fell away from her face and there was no mistaking

whose child she was. Twenty years ago, Eretria had looked exactly as her daughter looked now, from dusky skin and black eyes to soft, delicate features. All that Brin lacked was her mother's fire. Jair had gotten that. Brin had her father's temperament, cool, self-assured, and disciplined. In comparing his children one time—a time occasioned by one of Jair's more reprehensible misadventures—Wil Ohmsford had remarked rather ruefully that the difference between the two was that Jair was apt to do anything, while Brin was also apt to do it, but only after thinking it through first. Brin still wasn't sure who had come out on the short end of that reprimand.

Her hands slipped back to her sides. She remembered the time she had used the wishsong on the old tree. She had still been a child, experimenting with the Elven magic. It had been midsummer and she had used the wishsong to turn the tree's summer green to autumn crimson; in her child's mind, it seemed perfectly all right to do so, since red was a far prettier color than green. Her father had been furious; it had taken almost three years for the tree to come back again after the shock to its system. That had been the last time either she or Jair had used the magic when their parents were about.

"Brin, come help me with the rest of the packing, please."

It was her mother calling. She gave the old maple a final pat and turned toward the house.

Her father had never fully trusted the Elven magic. A little more than twenty years earlier he had used the Elfstones given him by the Druid Allanon in his efforts to protect the Elven Chosen Amberle Elessedil in her quest for the Bloodfire. Use of the Elven magic had changed him; he had known it even then, though not known how. It was only after Brin was born, and later Jair, that it became apparent what had been done. It was not Wil Ohmsford who would manifest the change the magic had wrought; it was his children. They were the ones who would carry within them the visible effects of the magic—they, and perhaps generations of Ohmsfords to come, although there was no way of ascertaining yet that they would carry within them the magic of the wishsong.

Brin had named it the wishsong. Wish for it, sing for it, and it was yours. That was how it had seemed to her when she had first discovered that she possessed the power. She learned early that she could affect the behavior of living things with her song. She could change that old maple's leaves. She could soothe an angry dog. She could bring a wild bird to light on her wrist. She could make herself a part of any living thing—or make it a part of her. She wasn't sure how she did it; it simply happened. She would sing, the music and the words coming as they always did, unplanned, unrehearsed—as if it were the most natural thing in the world. She was always aware of what she was singing, yet at the same time heedless, her mind caught up in feelings of indescribable sensation. They would sweep through her, drawing her in, making her somehow new again, and the wish would come to pass.

It was the gift of the Elven magic—or its curse. The latter was how her father had viewed it when he had discovered she possessed it. Brin knew that, deep inside, he was frightened of what the Elf-stones could do and what he had felt them do to him. After Brin had caused the family dog to chase its tail until it nearly dropped and had wilted an entire garden of vegetables, her father had been quick to reassert his decision that the Elfstones would never be used again by anyone. He had hidden them, telling no one where they could be found, and hidden they had remained ever since. At least, that was what her father thought. She was not altogether certain. One time, not too many months earlier, when there was mention of the hidden Elfstones, Brin had caught Jair smiling rather smugly. He would not admit to anything, of course, but she knew how difficult it was to keep anything hidden from her brother, and she suspected he had found the hiding place.

Rone Leah met her at the front door, tall and rangy, rust brown hair loose about his shoulders and tied back with a broad head-band. Mischievous gray eyes narrowed appraisingly. "How about lending a hand, huh? I'm doing all the work and I'm not even a member of the family, for cat's sake!"

"As much time as you spend here, you ought to be," she chided. "What's left to be done?"

"Just these cases to be carried out—that should finish it." A gathering of leather trunks and smaller bags stood stacked in the entry. Rone picked up the largest. "I think your mother wants you in the bedroom."

He disappeared down the walkway and Brin moved through her home toward the back bedrooms. Her parents were getting ready to depart on their annual fall pilgrimage to the outlying communities south of Shady Vale, a journey that would keep them gone from their home for better than two weeks. Few Healers possessed the skills of Wil Ohmsford, and not one could be found within five hundred miles of the Vale. So twice a year, in the spring and fall, her father traveled down to the outlying villages, lending his services where they were needed. Eretria always accompanied him, a skilled aide to her husband by now, trained nearly as thoroughly as he in the care of the sick and injured. It was a journey they need not have made—would not, in fact, had they been less conscientious than they were. Others would not have gone. But Brin's parents were governed by a strong sense of duty. Healing was the profession to which both had dedicated their lives, and they did not take their commitment to it lightly.

While they were gone on these trips of mercy, Brin was left to watch over Jair. On this occasion, Rone Leah had traveled down from the highlands to watch over them both.

Brin's mother looked up from the last of her packing and smiled as Brin entered the bedroom. Long black hair fell loosely about her shoulders, and she brushed it back from a face that looked barely older than Brin's.

"Have you seen your brother? We're almost ready to leave."

Brin shook her head. "I thought he was with father. Can I help you with anything?"

Eretria nodded, took Brin by the shoulders, and pulled her down next to her on the bed. "I want you to promise me something, Brin. I don't want you to use the wishsong while your father and I are gone—you or your brother."

Brin smiled. "I hardly use it at all anymore." Her dark eyes searched her mother's dusky face.

"I know. But Jair does, even if he thinks I don't know about it. In any case, while we are gone, your father and I don't want either of you using it even a single time. Do you understand?"

Brin hesitated. Her father understood that the Elven magic was a part of his children, but he did not accept that it was either a good or necessary part. You are intelligent, talented people just as you are, he would tell them. You have no need of tricks and artifices to advance yourselves. Be who and what you can without the song. Eretria had echoed that advice, although she seemed to recognize more readily than he that they were likely to ignore it when discretion suggested that they could.

In Jair's case, unfortunately, discretion seldom entered into the picture. Jair was both impulsive and distressingly headstrong; when it came to use of the wishsong, he was inclined to do exactly as he pleased—as long as he could safely get away with it.

Still, the Elven magic worked differently with Jair . . .

"Brin?"

Her thoughts scattered. "Mother, I don't see what difference it makes if Jair wants to play around with the wishsong. It's just a toy."

Eretria shook her head. "Even a toy can be dangerous if used unwisely. Besides, you ought to know enough of the Elven magic by now to appreciate the fact that it is never harmless. Now listen to me. You and your brother are both grown beyond the age when you need your mother and father looking over your shoulder. But a little advice is still necessary now and then. I don't want you using the magic while we're gone. It draws attention where it's not needed. Promise me that you won't use it—and that you will keep Jair from using it as well."

Brin nodded slowly. "It's because of the rumors of the black walkers, isn't it?" She had heard the stories. They talked about it all the time down at the inn these days. Black walkers—soundless, faceless things born of the dark magic, appearing out of nowhere.

Some said it was the Warlock Lord and his minions come back again. "Is that what this is all about?"

"Yes." Her mother smiled at Brin's perceptiveness. "Now promise me."

Brin smiled back. "I promise."

Nevertheless, she thought it all a lot of nonsense.

The packing and loading took another thirty minutes, and then her parents were ready to depart. Jair reappeared, back from the inn where he had gone to secure a special sweet as a parting gift for his mother who was fond of such things, and good-byes were exchanged.

"Remember your promise, Brin," her mother whispered as she kissed her on the cheek and hugged her close.

Then the elder Ohmsfords were aboard the wagon in which they would make their journey and moving slowly up the dusty roadway.

Brin watched them until they were out of sight.

Brin, Jair, and Rone Leah went hiking that afternoon in the forests of the Vale, and it was late in the day when at last they turned homeward. By then, the sun had begun to dip beneath the rim of the Vale and the forest shadows of midday to lengthen slowly into evening. It was an hour's walk to the hamlet, but both Ohmsfords and the highlander had come this way so often before that they could have navigated the forest trails even in blackest night. They proceeded at a leisurely pace, enjoying the close of what had been an altogether beautiful autumn day.

"Let's fish tomorrow," Rone suggested. He grinned at Brin. "With weather like this, it won't matter if we catch anything or not."

The oldest of the three, he led the way through the trees, the worn and battered scabbard bearing the Sword of Leah strapped crosswise to his back, a vague outline beneath his hunting cloak. Once carried by the heir-apparent to the throne of Leah, it had long since outlived that purpose and been replaced. But Rone had always admired the old blade, borne years earlier by his great-grandfather

Menion Leah when he had gone in search of the Sword of Shannara. Since Rone admired the weapon so, his father had given it to him, a small symbol of his standing as a Prince of Leah—even if he were its youngest prince.

Brin looked over at him and frowned. "You seem to be forgetting something. Tomorrow is the day we set aside for the house repairs we promised father we would make while he was away. What about that?"

He shrugged cheerfully. "Another day for the repairs—they'll keep."

"I think we should do some exploring along the rim of the Vale," Jair Ohmsford interjected. He was lean and wiry and had his father's face with its Elven features—narrow eyes, slanted eyebrows, and ears pointed slightly beneath a thatch of unruly blond hair. "I think we should see if we can find any sign of the Mord Wraiths."

Rone laughed. "Now what do you know about the walkers, tiger?" It was his pet name for Jair.

"As much as you, I'd guess. We hear the same stories in the Vale that you hear in the highlands," the Valeman replied. "Black walkers, Mord Wraiths—things that steal out of the dark. They talk about it down at the inn all the time."

Brin glanced at her brother reprovingly. "That's all they are, too—just stories."

Jair looked at Rone. "What do you think?"

To Brin's surprise, the highlander shrugged. "Maybe. Maybe not."

She was suddenly angry. "Rone, there have been stories like this ever since the Warlock Lord was destroyed, and none of them has ever contained a word of truth. Why would it be any different this time?"

"I don't know that it would. I just believe in being careful. Remember, they didn't believe the stories of the Skull Bearers in Shea Ohmsford's time either—until it was too late."

"That's why I think we ought to have a look around," Jair repeated.

"For what purpose exactly?" Brin pressed, her voice hardening. "On the chance that we might find something as dangerous as these things are supposed to be? What would you do then—call on the wishsong?"

Jair flushed. "If I had to, I would. I could use the magic . . ."

She cut him short. "The magic is nothing to play around with, Jair. How many times do I have to tell you that?"

"I just said that . . ."

"I know what you said. You think that the wishsong can do anything for you and you're sadly mistaken. You had better pay attention to what father says about not using the magic. Someday, it's going to get you into a lot of trouble."

Her brother stared at her. "What are you so angry about?"

She was angry, she realized, and it was serving no purpose. "I'm sorry," she apologized. "I made mother a promise that neither of us would use the wishsong while she and father were away on this trip. I suppose that's why it upsets me to hear you talking about tracking Mord Wraiths."

Now there was a hint of anger in Jair's blue eyes. "Who gave you the right to make a promise like that for me, Brin?"

"No one, I suppose, but mother . . ."

"Mother doesn't understand . . ."

"Hold on, for cat's sake!" Rone Leah held up his hands imploringly. "Arguments like this make me glad that I'm staying down at the inn and not up at the house with you two. Now let's forget all this and get back to the original subject. Do we go fishing tomorrow or not?"

"We go fishing," Jair voted.

"We go fishing," Brin agreed. "After we finish at least some of the repairs."

They walked in silence for a time, Brin still brooding over what she viewed as Jair's increasing infatuation with the uses of the wishsong. Her mother was right; Jair practiced using the magic whenever he got the chance. He saw less danger in its use than Brin did because it worked differently for him. For Brin, the wishsong altered appearance and behavior in fact, but for Jair it was only an illusion. When he used the magic, things only seemed to happen. That gave him greater latitude in its use and encouraged experimentation. He did it in secret, but he did it nevertheless. Even Brin wasn't entirely sure what he had learned to do with it.

Afternoon faded altogether and evening settled in. A full moon hung above the eastern horizon like a white beacon, and stars began to wink into view. With the coming of night, the air began to cool rapidly, and the smells of the forest turned crisp and heavy with the fragrance of drying leaves. All about rose the hum of insects and night birds.

"I think we should fish the Rappahalladran," Jair announced suddenly.

No one said anything for a moment. "I don't know," Rone answered finally. "We could fish the ponds in the Vale just as well."

Brin glanced over at the highlander quizzically. He sounded worried.

"Not for brook trout," Jair insisted. "Besides, I want to camp out in the Duln for a night or two."

"We could do that in the Vale."

"The Vale is practically the same as the backyard," Jair pointed out, growing a bit irritated. "At least the Duln has a few places we haven't explored before. What are you frightened about?"

"I'm not frightened of anything," the highlander replied defensively. "I just think . . . Look, why don't we talk about this later. Let me tell you what happened to me on the way out here. I almost managed to get myself lost. There was this wolfdog . . ."

Brin dropped back a pace as they talked, letting them walk on ahead. She was still puzzled by Rone's unexpected reluctance to make even a short camping trip into the Duln—a trip they had all made dozens of times before. Was there something beyond the Vale of which they need be frightened? She frowned, remembering the concern voiced by her mother. Now it was Rone as well. The highlander had not been as quick as she to discount as rumors those stories of the Mord Wraiths. In fact, he had been unusually restrained. Normally, Rone would have laughed such stories off as so much nonsense, just as she had done. Why hadn't he done so this time? It was possible, she realized, that he had some cause to believe it wasn't a laughing matter.

Half an hour passed, and the lights of the village began to appear through the forest trees. It was dark now, and they picked their way along the path with the aid of the moon's bright light. The trail dipped downward into the sheltered hollow where the village proper sat, broadening as it went from a footpath to a roadway. Houses appeared; from within, the sound of voices could be heard. Brin felt the first hint of weariness slip over her. It would be good to crawl into the comfort of her bed and give herself over to a good night's sleep.

They walked down through the center of Shady Vale, passing by the old inn that had been owned and managed by the Ohmsford family for so many generations past. The Ohmsfords still owned the establishment, but no longer lived there—not since the passing of Shea and Flick. Friends of the family managed the inn these days, sharing the earnings and expenses with Brin's parents. Her father had never really been comfortable living at the inn, Brin knew, feeling no real connection with its business, preferring his own life as a Healer to that of innkeeper. Only Jair showed any real interest in the happenings of the inn and that was because he liked to go down to listen to the tales carried to Shady Vale by travelers passing through—tales filled with adventure enough to satisfy the spirit of the restless Valeman.

The inn was busy this night, its broad double-doors flung open, the lights within falling over tables and a long bar crowded with travelers and village folk, laughing and joking and passing the cool autumn evening with a glass or two of ale. Rone grinned over his shoulder at Brin and shook his head. No one was anxious for this day to end.

Moments later, they reached the Ohmsford home, a stone and mortar cottage set back within the trees on a small knoll. They were halfway up the cobblestone walk that ran through a series of hedgerows and flowering plum to the front door when Brin brought them to a sudden halt.

There was a light in the window of the front room.

"Did either of you leave a lamp burning when we left this morning?" she asked quietly, already knowing the answer. Both shook their heads.

"Maybe someone stopped in for a visit," Rone suggested.

Brin looked at him. "The house was locked."

They stared at each other wordlessly for a moment, a vague sense of uneasiness starting to take hold. Jair, however, was feeling none of it.

"Well, let's go on in and see who's there," he declared and started forward.

Rone put a hand on his shoulder and pulled him back. "Just a moment, tiger. Let's not be too hasty."

Jair pulled free, glanced again at the light, then looked back at Rone. "Who do you think's waiting in there—one of the walkers?"

"Will you stop that nonsense!" Brin ordered sharply.

Jair smirked. "That's who you think it is, don't you? One of the walkers, come to steal us away!"

"Good of them to put a light on for us," Rone commented dryly.

They stared again at the light in the front window, undecided.

"Well, we can't just stand out here all night," Rone said finally. He reached back over his shoulder and pulled free the Sword of Leah. "Let's have a look. You two stay behind me. If anything happens, get back to the inn and bring some help." He hesitated. "Not that anything is going to happen."

They proceeded up the walk to the front door and stopped, listening. The house was silent. Brin handed Rone the key to the door and they stepped inside. The anteway was pitch black, save for a sliver of yellow light that snaked down the short hallway leading in. They hesitated a moment, then passed silently down the hall and stepped into the front room.

It was empty.

"Well, no Mord Wraiths here," Jair announced at once. "Nothing here except . . ."

He never finished. A huge shadow stepped into the light from the darkened drawing room beyond. It was a man over seven feet tall, cloaked all in black. A loose cowl was pulled back to reveal a lean, craggy face that was weathered and hard. Black beard and hair swept down from his face and head, coarse and shot through with streaks of gray. But it was the eyes that drew them, deep-set and penetrating from within the shadow of his great brow, seeming to see everything, even that which was hidden.

Rone Leah brought up the broadsword hurriedly, and the stranger's hand lifted from out of the robes.

"You won't need that."

The highlander hesitated, stared momentarily into the other's dark eyes, then dropped the sword blade downward again. Brin and Jair stood frozen in place, unable to turn and run or to speak.

"There is nothing to be frightened of," the stranger's deep voice rumbled.

None of the three felt particularly reassured by that, yet all relaxed slightly when the dark figure made no further move to approach. Brin glanced hurriedly at her brother and found Jair watching the stranger intently, as if puzzling something through. The stranger looked at the boy, then at Rone, then at her.

"Does not one of you know me?" he murmured softly.

There was momentary silence, and then suddenly Jair nodded.

"Allanon!" he exclaimed, excitement reflected in his face. "You're Allanon!"

II

———————————◆———————————

BRIN, JAIR, AND RONE LEAH SAT DOWN TOGETHER AT THE
dining room table with the stranger they knew now to be Allanon.
No one, to the best of their knowledge, had seen Allanon for twenty
years. Wil Ohmsford had been among the last. But the stories about
him were familiar to all. An enigmatic dark wanderer who had
journeyed to the farthest reaches of the Four Lands, he was philoso-
pher, teacher, and historian of the races—the last of the Druids, the
men of learning who had guided the races from the chaos that had
followed the destruction of the old world into the civilization that
flourished today. It was Allanon who had led Shea and Flick Ohmsford and Menion Leah in quest of the legendary Sword of Shannara
more than seventy years ago so that the Warlock Lord might be destroyed. It was Allanon who had come for Wil Ohmsford while the
Valeman studied at Storlock to become a Healer, persuading him
to act as guide and protector for the Elven girl Amberle Elessedil as
she went in search of the power needed to restore life to the dying
Ellcrys, thereby to imprison once more the Demons set loose within
the Westland. They knew the stories of Allanon. They knew as well
that whenever the Druid appeared, it meant trouble.

"I have traveled a long way to find you, Brin Ohmsford," the big
man said, his voice low and filled with weariness. "It was a journey
that I did not think I would have to make."

"Why have you sought me out?" Brin asked.

"Because I have need of the wishsong." There was an endless moment of silence as Valegirl and Druid faced each other across the table. "Strange," he sighed. "I did not see before that the passing of the Elven magic into the children of Wil Ohmsford might have so profound a purpose. I thought it little more than a side effect from use of the Elfstones that could not be avoided."

"What do you need with Brin?" Rone interjected, frowning. Already he did not like the sound of this.

"And the wishsong?" Jair added.

Allanon kept his eyes fixed on Brin. "Your father and your mother are not here?"

"No. They will be gone for at least two weeks; they treat the sick in the villages to the south."

"I do not have two weeks nor even two days," the big man whispered. "We must talk now, and you must decide what you will do. And if you decide as I think you must, your father will not this time forgive me, I'm afraid."

Brin knew at once what the Druid was talking about. "Am I to come with you?" she asked slowly.

He let the question hang unanswered. "Let me tell you of a danger that threatens the Four Lands—an evil as great as any faced by Shea Ohmsford or your father." He folded his hands on the table before him and leaned toward her. "In the old world, before the dawn of the race of Man, there were faerie creatures who made use of good and evil magics. Your father must have told you the story, I'm certain. That world passed away with the coming of Man. The evil ones were imprisoned beyond the wall of a Forbidding, and the good were lost in the evolution of the races—all save the Elves. There was a book from those times, however, that survived. It was a book of dark magic, of power so awesome that even the Elven magicians from the old world were frightened of it. It was called the Ildatch. Its origin is not certain, even now; it seems that it appeared very early in the time of the creation of life. The evil in the world used it for a time, until at last the Elves managed to seize it. So great was its lure that, even knowing its power, a few of the Elven magicians dared tamper with its secrets.

As a result, they were destroyed. The rest quickly determined to de-
molish the book. But before they could do so, it disappeared. There
were rumors of its use afterward, scattered here and there through
the centuries that followed, but never anything certain."

His brow furrowed. "And then the Great Wars wiped out the old
world. For two thousand years, the existence of man was reduced to
its most primitive level. It was not until the Druids called the First
Council at Paranor that an effort was made to gather together the
teachings of the old world that they might be used to help the new.
All of the learning, whether by book or by word of mouth, that had
been preserved through the years was brought before the Council
that an effort might be made to unlock their secrets. Unfortunately,
not all that was preserved was good. Among the books discovered
by the Druids in their quest was the Ildatch. It was uncovered by a
brilliant, ambitious young Druid called Brona."

"The Warlock Lord," Brin said softly.

Allanon nodded. "He became the Warlock Lord when the
power of the Ildatch subverted him. Together with his followers,
he was lost to the dark magic. For nearly a thousand years, they
threatened the existence of the races. It was not until Shea Ohmsford mastered the power of the Sword of Shannara that Brona and
his followers were destroyed."

He paused. "But the Ildatch disappeared once more. I searched
for it in the ruins of the Skull Mountain when the kingdom of the
Warlock Lord fell. I could not find it. I thought it was lost for good;
I thought it buried forever. But I was wrong. Somehow it was preserved. It was recovered by a sect of human followers of the Warlock Lord—would-be sorcerers from the races of men who were not
subject to the power of the Sword of Shannara and therefore not
destroyed with the Master. I know not how even yet, but in some
fashion they discovered the place where the Ildatch lay hidden and
brought it back into the world of men. They took it deep into their
Eastland lair where, hidden from the races, they began to delve into
the secrets of the magic. That was more than sixty years ago. You
can guess what has happened to them."

Brin was pale as she leaned forward. "Are you saying that it has begun all over again? That there is another Warlock Lord and other Skull Bearers?"

Allanon shook his head. "These men were not Druids as were Brona and his followers, nor has the same amount of time elapsed since their subversion. But the magic subverts all who tamper with it. The difference is in the nature of the change wrought. Each time, the change is different."

Brin shook her head. "I don't understand."

"Different," Allanon repeated. "Magic, good or evil, adapts to the user and the user to it. Last time, the creatures born of its touch flew . . ."

The sentence was left hanging. His listeners exchanged quick glances.

"And this time?" Rone asked.

The black eyes narrowed. "This time the evil walks."

"Mord Wraiths!" Jair breathed sharply.

Allanon nodded. "A Gnome term for 'black walker.' They are another form of the same evil. The Ildatch has shaped them as it shaped Brona and his followers, victims of the magic, slaves to the power. They are lost to the world of men, given over to the dark."

"Then the rumors are true after all," Rone Leah murmured. His gray eyes sought Brin's. "I didn't tell you this before, because I didn't see any purpose in worrying you needlessly, but I was told by travelers passing through Leah that the walkers have come west from the Silver River country. That's why, when Jair suggested that we go camping beyond the Vale . . ."

"Mord Wraiths come this far?" Allanon interrupted hurriedly. There was sudden concern in his voice. "How long ago, Prince of Leah?"

Rone shook his head doubtfully. "Several days, perhaps. Just before I came to the Vale."

"Then there is less time than I thought." The lines on the Druid's forehead deepened.

"But what are they doing here?" Jair wanted to know.

Allanon lifted his dark face. "Looking for me, I suspect."

Silence echoed through the darkened house. No one spoke; the Druid's eyes held them fixed.

"Listen well. The Mord Wraith stronghold lies deep within the Eastland, high in the mountains they call the Ravenshorn. It is a massive, aged fortress built by Trolls in the Second War of the Races. It is called Graymark. The fortress sits atop the rim of a wall of peaks surrounding a deep valley. It is within this valley that the Ildatch has been concealed."

He took a deep breath. "Ten days earlier, I was at the rim of the valley, determined to go down into it, seize the book of the dark magic from its hiding place, and see it destroyed. The book is the source of the Mord Wraiths' power. Destroy the book, and the power is lost, the threat ended. And this threat—ah, let me tell you something of this threat. The Mord Wraiths have not been idle since the fall of their Master. Six months ago, the border wars between the Gnomes and the Dwarves flared up once more. For years the two nations have fought over the forests of the Anar, so a resumption of their dispute surprised no one at first. But this time, unknown to most, there is a difference in the nature of the struggle. The Gnomes are being guided by the hand of the Mord Wraiths. Scattered and beaten at the fall of the Warlock Lord, the Gnome tribes have been enslaved anew by the dark magic, this time under the rule of the Wraiths. And the magic gives strength to the Gnomes that they would not otherwise have. Thus the Dwarves have been driven steadily south since the border wars resumed. The threat is grave. Recently the Silver River began to turn foul, poisoned by the dark magic. The land it feeds begins to die. When that happens, the Dwarves will die also, and the whole of the Eastland will be lost. Elves from the Westland and Bordermen from Callahorn have gone to the aid of the Dwarves, but the help they bring is not enough to withstand the Mord Wraiths' magic. Only the destruction of the Ildatch will stop what is happening."

He turned suddenly to Brin. "Remember the stories of your father, told him by his father, told to his father by Shea Ohmsford, of the advance of the Warlock Lord into the Southland? As the evil one came, a darkness fell over everything. A shadow cast itself across the land and all beneath it withered and died. Nothing lived in that shadow that was not part of the evil. It begins again, Valegirl—this time in the Anar."

He looked away. "Ten days ago, I stood at the walls of Graymark, intent upon finding and destroying the Ildatch. It was then that I discovered what the Mord Wraiths had done. Using the dark magic, the Mord Wraiths had grown within the valley a swamp-forest that would protect the book, a Maelmord in the faerie language, a barrier of such evil that it would crush and devour anything that attempted to enter and did not belong. Understand—this dark wood lives, it breathes, it thinks. Nothing can pass through it. I tried, but even the considerable power that I wield was not enough. The Maelmord repulsed me, and the Mord Wraiths discovered my presence. I was pursued, but I was able to escape. And now they search for me, knowing . . ."

He trailed off momentarily. Brin glanced quickly at Rone, who was looking unhappier by the minute.

"If they're searching for you, they'll eventually come here, won't they?" The highlander took advantage of the pause in the Druid's narration.

"Eventually, yes. But that will happen regardless of whether or not they follow me now. Understand, sooner or later they will seek to eliminate any threat to their power over the races. Surely you see that the Ohmsford family constitutes such a threat."

"Because of Shea Ohmsford and the Sword of Shannara?" Brin asked.

"Indirectly, yes. The Mord Wraiths are not creatures of illusion as was the Warlock Lord, so the Sword cannot harm them. The Elf-stones, perhaps. That magic is a force to be reckoned with, and the Wraiths will have heard of Wil Ohmsford's quest for the Bloodfire." He paused. "But the real threat to them is the wishsong."

"The wishsong?" Brin was dumbfounded. "But the wishsong is just a toy! It hasn't the power of the Elfstones! Why would that be a threat to these monsters? Why would they be afraid of something as harmless as that?"

"Harmless?" Allanon's eyes flickered momentarily, then closed as if to hide something. The Druid's dark face was expressionless, and suddenly Brin was really afraid.

"Allanon, why are you here?" she asked once more, struggling to keep her hands from shaking.

The Druid's eyes lifted again. On the table before him, the oil lamp's thin flame sputtered. "I want you to come with me into the Eastland to the Mord Wraiths' keep. I want you to use the wishsong to gain passage into the Maelmord—to find the Ildatch and bring it to me to be destroyed."

His listeners stared at him speechlessly.

"How?" Jair asked finally.

"The wishsong can subvert even the dark magic," Allanon replied. "It can alter behavior in any living thing. Even the Maelmord can be made to accept Brin. The wishsong can gain passage for her as one who belongs."

Jair's eyes widened in astonishment. "The wishsong can do all that?"

But Brin was shaking her head. "The wishsong is just a toy," she repeated.

"Is it? Or is that simply the way in which you have used it?" The Druid shook his head slowly. "No, Brin Ohmsford, the wishsong is Elven magic, and it possesses the power of Elven magic. You do not see that yet, but I tell you it is so."

"I don't care what it is or isn't, Brin's not going!" Rone looked angry. "You cannot ask her to do something this dangerous!"

Allanon remained impassive. "I do not have a choice, Prince of Leah. No more choice than I had in asking Shea Ohmsford to go in search of the Sword of Shannara nor Wil Ohmsford to go in quest of the Bloodfire. The legacy of Elven magic that was passed first to Jerle Shannara belongs now to the Ohmsfords. I wish as you do that it were different. We might as well wish that night were day. The wishsong belongs to Brin, and now she must use it."

"Brin, listen to me." Rone turned to the Valegirl. "There is more to the rumors than I have told you. They also speak of what the Mord Wraiths have done to men, of eyes and tongues gone, of minds emptied of all life, and of fire that burns to the bone. I discounted all that until now. I thought it little more than the late-night fireside tales of drunken men. But the Druid makes me think differently. You can't go with him. You can't."

"The rumors of which you speak are true," Allanon acknowledged softly. "There is danger. You may even die." He paused. "But what are we to do if you do not come? Will you hide and hope the Mord Wraiths forget about you? Will you ask the Dwarves to protect you? What happens when they are gone? As with the Warlock Lord, the evil will then come into this land. It will spread until there is no one left to resist it."

Jair reached for his sister's arm. "Brin, if we have to go, at least there will be two of us . . ."

"There will most certainly not be two of us!" she contradicted him instantly. "Whatever happens, you are staying right here!"

"We're all staying right here." Rone faced the Druid. "We're not going—any of us. You will have to find another way."

Allanon shook his head. "I cannot, Prince of Leah. There is no other way."

They were silent then. Brin slumped back in her chair, confused and more than a little frightened. She felt trapped by the sense of necessity that the Druid created within her, by the tangle of obligations he had thrust upon her. They spun in her mind; as they spun, the same thought kept coming back, over and over. The wishsong is only a toy. Elven magic, yes—but still a toy! Harmless! No weapon against an evil that even Allanon could not overcome! Yet her father had always been afraid of the magic. He had warned against its use, cautioning that it was not a thing to be played with. And she herself had determined to discourage Jair's use of the wishsong . . .

"Allanon," she said quietly. The lean face turned. "I have used the wishsong only to change appearance in small ways—to change the turning of leaves or the blooming of flowers. Little things. Even that, I have not done for many months. How can the wishsong be used to change an evil as great as this forest that guards the Ildatch?"

There was a moment's hesitation. "I will teach you."

She nodded slowly. "My father has always discouraged any use of the magic. He has warned against relying upon it because once he did so, and it changed his life. If he were here, Allanon, he would do as Rone has done and advise me to tell you no. If fact, he would order me to tell you no."

The craggy face reflected new weariness. "I know, Valegirl."

"My father came back from the Westland, from the quest for the Bloodfire, and he put away the Elfstones forever," she continued, trying to think her way through her confusion as she spoke. "He told me once that he knew even then that the Elven magic had changed him, though he did not see how. He made a promise to himself that he would never use the Elfstones again."

"I know this as well."

"And still you ask me to come with you?"

"I do."

"Without my being able to consult him first? Without being able to wait for his return? Without even an attempt at an explanation to him?"

The Druid looked suddenly angry. "I will make this easy for you, Brin Ohmsford. I ask nothing of you that is fair or reasonable, nothing of which your father would approve. I ask that you risk everything on little more than my word that it is necessary that you do so. I ask trust where there is probably little reason to trust. I ask all this and give nothing back. Nothing."

He leaned forward then, half-rising from his chair, his face dark and menacing. "But I tell you this. If you think the matter through, you will see that, despite any argument you can put forth against it, you must still come with me!"

Even Rone did not choose to contradict him this time. The Druid held his position for a moment longer, dark robes spread wide as he braced himself on the table. Then slowly he settled back. There was a worn look to him now, a kind of silent desperation. It was not characteristic of the Allanon Brin's father had described to her so often, and she was frightened by that.

"I will think the matter through as you ask," she agreed, her voice almost a whisper. "But I need this night at least. I have to try to sort through . . . my feelings."

Allanon seemed to hesitate a moment, then nodded. "We will talk again in the morning. Consider well, Brin Ohmsford."

He started to rise and suddenly Jair was on his feet before him, his Elven face flushed. "Well, what about me? What about my feelings in this? If Brin goes, so do I! I'm not being left behind!"

"Jair, you can forget . . . !" Brin started to object, but Allanon cut her short with a glance. He rose and came around the table to stand before her brother.

"You have courage," he said softly, one hand coming up to rest on the Valeman's slender shoulder. "But yours is not the magic that I need on this journey. Your magic is illusion, and illusion will not get us past the Maelmord."

"But you might be wrong," Jair insisted. "Besides, I want to help!"

Allanon nodded. "You shall help. There is something that you must do while Brin and I are gone. You must be responsible for the safety of your parents, for seeing to it that the Mord Wraiths do not find them before I have destroyed the Ildatch. You must use the wishsong to protect them if the dark ones come looking. Will you do that?"

Brin did not care much for the Druid's assumption that it was already decided that she would be going with him into the Eastland, and she cared even less for the suggestion that Jair ought to use the Elven magic as a weapon.

"I will do it if I must," Jair was saying, a grudging tone in his voice. "But I would rather come with you."

Allanon's hand dropped from his shoulder. "Another time, Jair."

"It may be another time for me as well," Brin announced pointedly. "Nothing has been determined yet, Allanon."

The dark face turned slowly. "There will be no other time for you, Brin," he said softly. "Your time is here. You must come with me. You will see that by morning."

Nodding once, he started past them toward the front entry, dark robes wrapped close.

"Where are you going, Allanon?" the Valegirl called after him.

"I will be close by," he replied and did not slow. A moment later he was gone. Brin, Jair, and Rone Leah stared after him.

Rone was the first to speak. "Well, now what?"

Brin looked at him. "Now we go to bed." She rose from the table.

"Bed!" The highlander was dumbfounded. "How can you go to bed after all that?" He waved vaguely in the direction of the departed Druid.

She brushed back her long black hair and smiled wanly. "How can I do anything else, Rone? I am tired, confused, and frightened, and I need to rest."

She came over to him and kissed him lightly on the forehead. "Stay here for tonight." She kissed Jair as well and hugged him. "Go to bed, both of you."

Then she hurried down the hall to her bedroom and closed the door tightly behind her.

She slept for a time, a dream-filled, restless sleep in which subconscious fears took shape and came for her like wraiths. Chased and harried, she came awake with a start, the pillow damp with sweat. She rose then, slipped on her robe for warmth and passed silently through the darkened rooms of her home. At the dining room table she lighted an oil lamp, the flame turned low, seated herself, and stared wordlessly into the shadows.

A sense of helplessness curled about Brin. What was she to do? She remembered well the stories told her by her father and even her great-grandfather Shea Ohmsford when she was just a little girl—of what it had been like when the Warlock Lord had come down out of the Northland, his armies sweeping into Callahorn, the darkness of his coming enfolding the whole of the land. Where the Warlock Lord passed, the light died. Now, it was happening again: border wars between Gnomes and Dwarves; the Silver River poisoned and with it the land it fed; darkness falling over the Eastland. All was as it had been seventy-five years ago. This time, too, there was a way to stop it, to prevent the dark from spreading. Again, it was an Ohmsford who was being called upon to take that way—summoned, it seemed, because there was no other hope.

She hunched down into the warmth of her robe. Seemed— that was the key word where Allanon was concerned. How much of this was what it seemed? How much of what she had been told was truth—and how much half-truth? The stories of Allanon were all the same. The Druid possessed immense power and knowledge and shared but a fraction of each. He told what he felt he must and never more. He manipulated others to his purpose, and often that purpose was kept carefully concealed. When one traveled Allanon's path, one did so knowing that the way would be kept dark.

Yet the way of the Mord Wraiths might be darker still, if they were indeed another form of the evil destroyed by the Sword of Shannara. She must weigh the darkness of one against the darkness of the other. Allanon might be devious and manipulative in his dealings with the Ohmsfords, but he was a friend to the Four Lands. What he did, he did in an effort to protect the races, not to bring them harm. And he had always been right before in his warnings. Surely there was no reason to believe that he was not right this time as well.

But was the wishsong's magic strong enough to penetrate this barrier conceived by the evil? Brin found the idea incredible. What was the wishsong but a side effect of using the Elven magic? It had not even the strength of the Elfstones. It was not a weapon. Yet Allanon saw it as the only means by which the dark magic could be passed—the only means, when even his power had failed him.

Bare feet padded softly from the dining room entry, startling her. Rone Leah slipped clear of the shadows, crossed to the table, and seated himself.

"I couldn't sleep either," he muttered, blinking in the light of the oil lamp. "What have you decided?"

She shook her head. "Nothing. I don't know what to decide. I keep asking myself what my father would do."

"That's easy." Rone grunted. "He would tell you to forget the whole idea. It's too dangerous. He'd also tell you—as he's told both of us many times—that Allanon is not to be trusted."

Brin brushed back her long black hair and smiled faintly. "You didn't hear what I said, Rone. I said, I keep asking myself what my father would do—not what my father would tell me to do. It's not the same thing, you know. If he were being asked to go, what would he do? Wouldn't he go, just as he went when Allanon came to him in Storlock twenty years ago, knowing that Allanon was not altogether truthful, knowing that there was more than he was being told, but knowing, too, that he had magic that could be useful and that no one other than he had that magic?"

The highlander shifted uneasily. "But, Brin, the wishsong is . . . well, it's not the same as the Elfstones. You said it yourself. It's just a toy."

"I know that. That is what makes all of this so difficult—that and the fact that my father would be appalled if he thought even for a minute that I would consider trying to use the magic as a weapon of any sort." She paused. "But Elven magic is a strange thing. Its power is not always clearly seen. Sometimes it is obscured. It was so with the Sword of Shannara. Shea Ohmsford never saw the way in which such a small thing could defeat an enemy as great as the Warlock Lord—not until it was put to the test. He simply went on faith . . ."

Rone sat forward sharply. "I'll say it again—this journey is too dangerous. The Mord Wraiths are too dangerous. Even Allanon can't get past them; he told you so himself! It would be different if you had the use of the Elfstones. At least the Stones have power enough to destroy creatures such as these. What would you do with the wishsong if you came up against them—sing to them the way you used to do to that old maple?"

"Don't make fun of me, Rone." Brin's eyes narrowed.

Rone shook his head quickly. "I'm not making fun of you. I care too much about you to ever do that. I just don't feel the wishsong is any kind of protection against something like the Wraiths!"

Brin looked away, staring out through curtained windows into the night, watching the shadowed movements of the trees in the wind, rhythmic and graceful.

"Neither do I," she admitted softly.

They sat in silence for a time, lost in their separate thoughts. Allanon's dark, tired face hung suspended in the forefront of Brin's mind, a haunting specter that accused. You must come. You will see that by morning. She heard him speak the words again, so certain as he said them. But what was it that would persuade her that this was so? she asked herself. Reasoning only seemed to lead her deeper into confusion. The arguments were all there, all neatly arranged, both those for going and those for staying, and yet the balance did not shift in either direction.

"Would you go?" she asked Rone suddenly. "If it were you with the wishsong?"

"Not a chance," he said at once—a bit too quickly, a bit too flip.

You're lying, Rone, she told herself. Because of me, because you don't want me to go, you're lying. If you thought it through, you would admit to the same doubts facing me.

"What's going on?" a weary voice asked from the darkness.

They turned and found Jair standing in the hall, squinting sleepily into the light. He came over to them and stood looking from face to face.

"We were just talking, Jair," Brin told him.

"About going after the magic book?"

"Yes. Why don't you go on back to bed?"

"Are you going? After the book, I mean?"

"I don't know."

"She's not going if she possesses an ounce of common sense," Rone grumbled. "It's entirely too dangerous a journey. You tell her, tiger. She's the only sister you've got, and you don't want the black walkers getting hold of her."

Brin shot him an angry glance. "Jair doesn't have anything to say about this, so quit trying to scare him."

"Him? Who's trying to scare him?" Rone's lean face was flushed. "It's you I'm trying to scare, for cat's sake!"

"Anyway, the black walkers don't scare me," Jair declared firmly.

"Well, they ought to!" Brin snapped.

Jair shrugged, yawning. "Maybe you should wait until we have a chance to talk with father. We could send him a message or something."

"Now that makes good sense," Rone added his approval. "At least wait until Wil and Eretria have a chance to talk this over with you."

Brin sighed. "You heard what Allanon said. There isn't enough time for that."

The highlander folded his arms across his chest. "He could make the time if it were necessary. Brin, your father might have a different slant on all this. After all, he's had the benefit of experience—and he's used the Elven magic."

"Brin, he could use the Elfstones!" Jair's eyes snapped open. "He could go with you. He could protect you with the Elfstones, just as he protected the Elven girl Amberle!"

Brin saw it then; those few words gave her the answer that she had been looking for. Allanon was right. She must go with him. But the reason was not one she had considered until now. Her father would insist on accompanying her. He would take the Elfstones from their hiding place and go with her in order that she should be protected. And that was exactly what she must avoid. Her father would be forced to break his pledge never to use the Elfstones again. He probably wouldn't even agree to her accompanying Allanon. He would go instead in order that she, her mother, and Jair be kept safe.

"I want you to go back to bed, Jair," she said suddenly.

"But I just got . . ."

"Go on. Please. We'll talk this all out in the morning."

Jair hesitated. "What about you?"

"I'll be only a few minutes, I promise. I just want to sit here alone for a time."

Jair studied her suspiciously for a moment, then nodded. "All right. Good night." He turned and walked back into the darkness. "Just be sure you come to bed, too."

Brin's eyes found Rone's. They had known each other since they were small children, and there were times when each knew what the other was thinking without a word being said. This was one such time.

The highlander stood up slowly, his lean face set. "All right, Brin. I see it, too. But I'm coming with you, do you understand? And I'm staying with you until it's finished."

She nodded slowly. Without another word, he disappeared down the hallway, leaving her alone.

The minutes slipped by. She thought it through again, sifting carefully the arguments. In the end, her answer was the same. She could not permit her father to break his vow because of her, to risk further use of the Elven magic he had foresworn. She could not.

Then she rose, blew out the flame of the oil lamp and walked, not in the direction of her bedroom, but to the front entry instead. Releasing the latch, she opened the door quietly and slipped out into the night. The wind blew against her face, cooling and filled with autumn's smells. She stood for a moment staring out into the shadows, then made her way around the house to the gardens in back. Night sounds filled the silence, a steady cadence of invisible life. At the edge of the gardens, beneath a stand of giant oak, she stopped and looked about expectantly.

A moment later, Allanon appeared. Somehow, she had known he would. Black as the shadows about him, he drifted soundlessly from the trees to stand before her.

"I have decided," she whispered, her voice steady. "I'm going with you."

iii

◆

MORNING CAME QUICKLY, A PALE SILVER LIGHT THAT SEEPED through the predawn forest mist and chased the shadows westward. Their restless sleep broken, the members of the Ohmsford household stirred awake. Within an hour, preparations were under way for Brin's departure to the Eastland. Rone was dispatched to the inn to secure horses, riding harness, weapons, and foodstuffs. Brin and Jair packed clothing and camping gear. In businesslike fashion, they went about their tasks. There was little conversation. No one had much to say. No one felt much like talking.

Jair Ohmsford was feeling particularly uncommunicative, trudging through the house as he went about his work in determined silence. He was more than a little disgruntled that both Brin and Rone would be going east with Allanon while he was to be left behind. That had been decided first thing that morning, practically moments after he was out of bed. Gathering in the dining area as they had gathered last night, they had discussed briefly Brin's decision to go into the Anar—a decision, Jair thought, of which everyone but he already seemed aware. Then came the determination that, while Brin and Rone would make the journey, he would not. True, the Druid had not been pleased by Rone's insistence that if Brin were to go, then he must go as well, because Brin needed someone she could depend upon, someone she could trust. No, the Druid had not been pleased with that at all. In fact, he had agreed to Rone's coming only after Brin had admitted she would feel better with Rone along. But when Jair suggested that she would feel better still with him along as well—after all, he had the magic of the wish-song, too, and could help protect her—all three had abruptly and firmly told him no. Too dangerous, Brin said. Too long and hazard-ous a journey, Rone added. Besides, you are needed here, Allanon reminded him. You have a responsibility to your parents. You must use your magic to protect them.

With that, Allanon had disappeared somewhere and there was no further opportunity to argue the matter with him. Rone thought the sun rose and set on Brin, so naturally he would not go against her wishes on this, and Brin had already made up her mind. So that was that. Part of the problem with his sister, of course, was that she didn't understand him. In fact, Jair was not altogether certain that she really understood herself a good deal of the time. At one point during their preparations, with Allanon still gone and Rone still down in the village, he had brought up the subject of the Elfstones.

"Brin." They were packing blankets on the floor of the front room, wrapping them in oilskins. "Brin, I know where father hides the Elfstones."

She had looked up at once. "I thought that you probably did."

"Well, he made such a big secret of it . . ."

"And you don't like secrets, do you? Have you had them out?"

"Just to look at," he admitted, then leaned forward. "Brin, I think you should take the Elfstones with you."

"Whatever for?" There was a touch of anger in her voice then.

"For protection. For the magic."

"The magic? No one can use their magic but father, as you well know."

"Well, maybe . . ."

"Besides, you know how he feels about the Elfstones. It's bad enough that I have to make this journey at all, but to take the Elf-stones as well? You're not thinking very clearly about this, Jair."

Then Jair had gotten angry. "You're the one who's not thinking clearly. We both know how dangerous it's going to be for you. You're going to need all the help you can get. The Elfstones could be a lot of help—all you need to do is to figure out how to make them work. You might be able to do that."

"No one but the rightful holder can . . ."

"Make the Stones work?" He had been almost nose to nose with her then. "But maybe that's not so with you and me, Brin. After all, we already have the Elven magic inside us. We have the wishsong. Maybe we could make the Stones work for us!"

There had been a long, intense moment of silence. "No," she said at last. "No, we promised father we would never try to use the Elfstones . . ."

"He also made us promise not to use the Elven magic, remember? But we do—even you, now and then. And isn't that what Allanon wants you to do when you reach the Mord Wraiths' keep? Isn't it? So what's the difference between using the wishsong and the Elfstones? Elven magic is Elven magic!"

Brin had stared at him silently, a distant, lost look in her dark eyes. Then she had turned again to the blankets. "It doesn't matter. I'm not taking the Elfstones. Here, help me tie these."

And that had been that, just like the subject of his going with them into the Eastland. No real explanation had been offered; she had simply made up her mind that she would not take the Elfstones, whether she could use them or not. He didn't understand it at all. He didn't understand her. If it had been him, he would have taken the Elfstones in a moment. He would have taken them and found a way to use them, because they were a powerful weapon against the dark magic. But Brin . . . Brin couldn't even seem to see the inconsistency of her agreeing to use the magic of the wishsong and refusing to use the magic of the Stones.

He went through the remainder of the morning trying to make some sense of his sister's reasoning or lack thereof. The hours slipped quickly past. Rone returned with horses and supplies, packs were loaded, and a hasty lunch consumed in the cool shade of the backyard oaks. Then all at once Allanon was standing there again, as black in midday as at darkest night, waiting with the patience of

Lady Death, and suddenly there was no time left. Rone was shaking Jair's hand, clapping him roughly on the back, and extracting a firm promise that he would look out for his parents when they returned. Then Brin was there, arms coming tightly about him and holding him close.

"Good-bye, Jair," she whispered. "Remember—I love you."

"I love you, too," he managed and hugged her back.

A moment later, they were mounted, and the horses turned down the dirt roadway. Arms lifted in farewell, waving as he waved back. Jair waited until they were out of sight before he brushed an unwanted tear from his eye.

That same afternoon, he moved down to the inn. He did so because of the possibility voiced by Allanon that the Wraiths or their Gnome allies might already be searching for the Druid in the lands west of the Silver River. If their enemies reached Shady Vale, the Ohmsford home would be the first place they would look. Besides, it was much more interesting at the inn—its rooms filled with travelers from all the lands, each with a different tale to tell, each with some different piece of news to share. Jair much preferred the excitement of tales told over a glass of ale in the tavern hall to the boredom of an empty house.

As he went to the inn with a few personal items in tow, the warmth of the afternoon sun on his face eased a bit the disappointment he still felt at being left behind. Admittedly, there was good reason for his staying. Someone had to explain to his parents when they returned what had become of Brin. That would not be easy. He visualized momentarily his father's face upon hearing what had happened and shook his head ruefully. His father would not be happy. In fact, he would probably insist on going after Brin—maybe even with the Elfstones.

A sudden look of determination creased his face. If that happened, he was going as well. He wouldn't be left behind a second time.

He kicked at the leaves fallen across the pathway before him, scattering them in a shower of color. His father wouldn't see it that way, of course. Nor his mother, for that matter. But he had two whole weeks to figure out how to persuade them that he should go.

He walked on, a bit more slowly now, letting the thought linger in his mind enticingly. Then he brushed it away. What he was supposed to do was to tell them what had happened to Brin and Rone and then accompany them into Leah, where they were all to remain under the protection of Rone's father until the quest was finished. That was what he was supposed to do, so that was what he would do. Of course, Wil Ohmsford might not choose to go along with this plan. And Jair was first and foremost his father's son, so it was to be expected that he might have a few ideas of his own.

He grinned and quickened his step. He would have to work on that.

The day came and went. Jair Ohmsford ate dinner at the inn with the family that managed the business for his parents, offered to lend a hand the following morning with the day's work, and then drifted into the lounge to listen to the tales being told by the drummers and wayfarers passing through the Vale. More than one made mention of the black walkers, the dark-robed Mord Wraiths that none had seen but all knew to be real, the evil ones that could burn the life from you with just a glance. Come from the earth's dark, the voices warned in rough whispers, heads nodding all around in agreement. Better that you never encountered such as they. Even Jair found himself feeling a bit uneasy at the prospect.

He stayed with the storytellers until after midnight, then went to his room. He slept soundly, woke at daybreak and spent the morning working about the inn. He no longer felt quite so bad about being left behind. After all, his own part in all of this was important, too. If the Mord Wraiths did indeed know of the magic Elfstones and came looking for the holder, then Wil Ohmsford was in as much danger as his daughter—possibly more so. It was up to Jair, then, to keep a sharp eye open, in order that no harm befell his father before he could be properly warned.

By midday Jair's work was finished and the innkeeper thanked him and told him to take some time for himself. So he walked out into the forests in back of the inn where no one else was about and experimented for several hours with the wishsong, using the magic in a variety of ways, pleased with the control he was able to exercise. He thought again about his father's continual admonition to forgo use of the Elven magic. His father just didn't understand. The magic was a part of him, and using it was as natural as using his arms and legs. He couldn't pretend it wasn't there any more than he could pretend they weren't! Both his parents kept saying the magic was dangerous. Brin said that on occasion, too, though she said it with a whole lot less conviction, since she was guilty of using it as well. He was convinced they told him that simply because he was somewhat younger than Brin and they worried more about him. He hadn't seen anything to suggest that the magic was dangerous; until he did, he intended to keep using it.

On the way back to the inn, as the first shadows of early evening began to slip through the late afternoon sunshine, it occurred to him that perhaps he ought to check the house—just to be certain that nothing was disturbed. It was locked, of course, but it wouldn't hurt to check anyway. After all, the care of the house was a part of his responsibility.

He debated the matter as he walked, finally deciding to wait until after dinner to make the inspection. Eating seemed more imperative to him at the moment than hiking up to the house. Using the magic always made him hungry.

He worked his way along the forest trails that ran back of the inn, breathing in the smells of the autumn day, thinking of trackers. Trackers fascinated him. Trackers were a special breed of men who could trace the movements of anything that lived simply by studying the land they passed through. Most of them were more at home in the wilderness than they were in settled communities. Most preferred the company of their own kind. Jair had talked with a tracker once—years ago now, it seemed—an old fellow brought down to the inn with a broken leg by some travelers who had chanced on him.

The old man had stayed at the inn almost a week, waiting for the leg to mend sufficiently that he might leave again. The tracker hadn't wanted to have anything to do with Jair at first, despite the boy's persistence—or anything to do with anyone else, for that matter—but then Jair had showed him something of the magic—just a touch. Intrigued, the old man had talked with him then, a little at first, then more. And what tales that old man had had to tell . . .

Jair swung out onto the roadway beside the inn, turning into the side entry, grinning broadly as he remembered what it had been like. It was then that he saw the Gnome.

For an instant he thought his eyes were playing tricks on him and he stopped where he was, his hand fastened to the inn door handle as he stared out across the roadway to the stable fence line where the gnarled yellow figure stood. Then the other's wizened face turned toward him, sharp eyes searching his own, and he knew at once he was not mistaken.

Hurriedly, he pushed the inn door open and stepped inside. Leaning back against the closed door, alone now in the hallway beyond, he tried to calm himself. A Gnome! What was a Gnome doing in Shady Vale? A traveler, perhaps? But few Gnomes traveled this way—few, in fact, beyond the familiar confines of the Eastland forests. He couldn't remember the last time there had been a Gnome in Shady Vale. But there was one here now. Maybe more than one.

He stepped quickly away from the door and went down the hall until he stood next to a window that opened out toward the roadway. Cautiously he peered around the sill, Elven face intense, eyes searching the innyard and the fence line beyond. The Gnome stood where Jair had first seen him, still looking toward the inn. The Valeman looked about. There appeared to be no others.

Again he leaned back against the wall. What was he to do now? Was it coincidence that brought the Gnome to Shady Vale at a time when Allanon had warned that the Mord Wraiths would be looking for them? Or was it not chance at all? Jair forced his breathing to slow. How could he find out? How could he make certain?

He took a deep breath. The first thing he must remember to

do was to stay calm. One Gnome presented no serious threat. His nose picked up the scent of beef stew simmering, and he thought about how hungry he was. He hesitated a moment longer, then started toward the kitchen. The best thing to do was to think matters through over dinner. Eat a good meal and decide on a plan of action. He nodded to himself as he walked. He would try to put himself in Rone's boots. Rone would know what to do if he were here. Jair would have to try to do the same.

The beef stew was excellent and Jair was starved, yet he found it difficult to concentrate on food, knowing that the Gnome was standing just outside, watching. Halfway through the meal, he remembered suddenly the empty, unguarded house and the Elfstones hidden within. If the Gnome was here at the bidding of the black walkers, then he might have come for the Elfstones as well as the Ohmsfords or Allanon. And there might be others, already searching . . .

He shoved his plate away, drained the remainder of his ale, and hurried from the kitchen back down the hallway to the window. Carefully, he peered out. The Gnome was gone.

He felt his heart quicken. Now what? He turned and raced back down the hall. He had to get back to the house. He had to make certain that the Elfstones were secure, then . . . He caught himself in midstride, slowing. He didn't know what he would do then. He would have to see. He quickened his step once more. The important thing now was to see whether or not there had been any attempt to enter his home.

He passed the side door through which he had entered and went on toward the rear of the building. He would leave by a different way just in case the Gnome was indeed looking for him—or even if he wasn't, but had become suspicious at the Valeman's furtive interest. I shouldn't have stopped to look at him, he told himself angrily. I should have kept going, then doubled back. But it was too late now.

The hallway ended at a door at the very rear of the main building. Jair stopped, listening momentarily, chiding himself for being foolish, then eased the door open and stepped out. Evening shadows cast by the forest trees lay dark and cool across the grounds, staining the inn walls and roof. Overhead, the sky was darkening. Jair looked about quickly, then started toward the trees. He would cut through the forest to his home, staying off the roadways until he was certain that . . .

"Taking a walk, boy?"

Jair froze. The Gnome stepped silently from the dark trees in front of him. Hard, rough features twisted with a wicked-looking smile. The Gnome had been waiting.

"Oh, I saw you, boy. I saw you quick enough. Knew you right away. Halfling features, Elf and Man—not too many like you." He stopped a half dozen paces away, gnarled hands resting on his hips, the smile fixed. Leather woodsman's garb covered the stocky form; his boots and wristbands were studded with iron, and knives and a short sword were belted at his waist. "Young Ohmsford, aren't you? The boy, Jair?"

The word *boy* stung. "Stay away from me," Jair warned, afraid now, and trying desperately to keep the fear from his voice.

"Stay away from you?" The Gnome laughed sharply. "And what will you do if I don't, halfling? Throw me to the ground, perhaps? Take away my weapons? You are a brave one, aren't you?"

Another laugh followed, low and guttural. For the first time, Jair realized that the Gnome was speaking to him in the language used by the Southlanders rather than the harsh Gnome tongue. Gnomes seldom used any tongue but their own; their race was an insular people who wanted nothing to do with the other lands. This Gnome had been well outside the Eastland to be so fluent.

"Now, boy," the Gnome interrupted his thoughts. "Let's be sensible, you and me. I seek the Druid. Tell me where he is, here or elsewhere, and I'll be gone."

Jair hesitated. "Druid? I don't know any Druids. I don't know what you're . . ."

The Gnome shook his head and sighed. "Games, is it? Worse luck for you, boy. Guess we'll have to do this the hard way."

He started toward Jair, hands reaching. Instinctively, Jair twisted away. Then he used the wishsong. There was a moment's hesitation, a moment's uncertainty—for he had never used the magic against another human—and then he used it. He gave a low, hissing sound, and a mass of snakes appeared, coiled tightly about the Gnome's outstretched arms. The Gnome howled in dismay, whipping his arms about desperately in an effort to shake loose the snakes. Jair looked around, found a broken piece of tree limb the size of a bulky walking staff, seized it with both hands and brought it crashing down over the Gnome's head. The Gnome grunted and dropped to the earth in a heap, unmoving.

Jair released the tree limb, his hands shaking. Had he killed him? Cautiously he knelt next to the fallen Gnome and felt for his wrist. There was a pulse. The Gnome was not dead, just unconscious. Jair straightened. What was he to do now? The Gnome had been looking for Allanon, knowing that he had come to Shady Vale and to the Ohmsfords, knowing . . . knowing who knew what else! Too much, in any case, for Jair to remain in the Vale any longer, especially now that he had used the magic. He shook his head angrily. He shouldn't have used the magic; he should have kept it a secret. But it was too late for regrets now. He didn't think the Gnome was alone. There would be others, probably at the house. And that was where he had to go, because that was where the Elfstones were hidden.

He glanced about, his thoughts organizing swiftly. Several dozen feet away was a wood bin. Seizing the Gnome's feet, he dragged him to the bin, threw back the lid, shoved his captive inside, dropped the lid down again, and put the metal bar through the catch. He grinned in spite of himself. That bin was well constructed. The Gnome wouldn't get out of there for a while.

Then he hurried back into the inn. Despite the need for haste, he had to leave word with the innkeeper where he was going— otherwise the whole community would be combing the countryside looking for him. It was one thing for Brin and Rone to disappear;

that had been easy enough to explain simply by saying they had gone for a visit to Leah and he had decided to stay in the Vale. It would be quite another matter entirely if he disappeared as well, since there was no one left to alibi for him. So feigning nonchalance and smiling disarmingly, he announced that he had changed his mind and was going over to the highlands after all early the next morning. Tonight he would stay at the house and pack. When the innkeeper thought to ask what had persuaded him to change his mind so abruptly, the Valeman quickly explained that he had received a message from Brin. Before there could be any further questions, he was out the door.

Swiftly, he melted into the woods, racing through the darkness toward his home. He was sweating profusely, hot with excitement and anticipation. He was not frightened—not yet, at least—probably because he hadn't stopped long enough to let himself think about what he was doing. Besides, he kept telling himself, he had taken care of that Gnome, hadn't he?

Tree branches slapped his face. He hurried on, not bothering to duck, eyes riveted on the darkness ahead. He knew this section of the forest well. Even in the growing darkness, he found his way with ease, moving on cat's feet, carefully listening to the sounds about him.

Then, fifty yards from his home, he melted silently into a small stand of pine, working his way forward until he could see the darkened structure through the needled branches. Dropping to his hands and knees, he peered through the night, searching. There was no sound, no movement, no sign of life. Everything seemed as it should. He paused to brush back a lock of hair, which had fallen down across his face. It should be simple. All he had to do was slip into the house, retrieve the Elfstones and slip out again. If there really wasn't anyone watching, it should be easy . . .

Then something moved in the oaks at the rear of the home—just a momentary shadow, then nothing. Jair took a deep breath and waited. The minutes slipped past. Insects buzzed about him hungrily, but he ignored them. Then he saw the movement a second time, clearly now. It was a man. No, not a man, he corrected quickly—a Gnome.

He sat back. Well, Gnome or not, he had to go down there. And if there was one, there were probably more than one, waiting, watching—but without knowing when or if he would return. Sweat ran down his back, and his throat was dry. Time was slipping away from him. He had to get out of the Vale. But he couldn't leave the Elfstones.

There was nothing for it but to use the wishsong.

He took a moment to pitch his voice the way he wanted, feigning the buzzing of the mosquitoes that were all around him, still lingering on in the warmth of early autumn, not yet frozen away by winter's touch. Then he glided from the pines down through the thinning forest. He had used this trick once or twice before, but never under conditions as demanding as these. He moved quietly, letting his voice make him a part of the forest night, knowing that if he did it all properly he would be invisible to the eyes that kept watch for him. The house drew steadily closer as he worked his way ahead. He caught sight again of the Gnome that kept watch in the trees behind the darkened building. Then suddenly he saw another, off to his right by the high bushes fronting the house—then another, across the roadway in the hemlock. None looked his way. He wanted to run, wanted to race as swiftly as the night wind to reach the dark of the home, but he kept his pace steady and his voice an even, faint buzz. Don't let them see me, he prayed. Don't let them look.

He crossed the lawn, slipping from tree to bush, eyes darting to find the Gnomes all about him. The rear door, he thought as he went—that would be the easiest door to enter, dark in the shadow of high, flowering bushes, their leaves still full . . .

A sudden call from somewhere beyond the house brought him to an abrupt, frightened halt, frozen in midstride. The Gnome at the rear of the Ohmsford house stepped clear of the oaks, moonlight glinting on his long knife. Again the call came, then sudden laughter. The blade lowered. It was from neighbors down the road, joking and talking in the warm autumn night, their dinner done. Sweat soaked Jair's tunic, and for the first time he was scared. A dozen yards away, the Gnome who had stepped from the oaks turned and disappeared back into them again. Jair's voice trembled, then strengthened, keeping him hidden. Quickly he went on.

He paused at the door, letting the wishsong die momentarily, trying desperately to steady himself. Fumbling through his pockets, he at last produced the house key, fitted it to the lock, and turned it guardedly. The door opened without a sound. In an instant, he was through.

He paused again in the darkness beyond. Something was wrong. He could sense it more than describe it—it was a feeling that ran cold to the bone. Something was wrong. The house . . . the house was not right; it was different . . . He stayed silent, waiting for his senses to reveal what lay hidden from him. As he stood, he grew slowly aware that something else was in the house with him, something terrible, something so evil that just its presence permeated the air with fear. Whatever it was, it seemed to be everywhere at once, a hideous, black pall that hung across the Ohmsford home like a death shroud. A thing, his mind whispered, a thing . . .

A Mord Wraith.

He quit breathing. A walker—here, in his home! Now he was really afraid, the certainty of his suspicion driving from him the last of his courage. It waited within the next room, Jair sensed, within the dark. It would know he was here and come for him—and he would not be able to stand against it!

He was certain for a moment that he would break and run, overwhelmed by the panic that coursed through him. But then he thought of his parents, who would return unwarned if he should fail, and of the Elfstones, the sole weapon that the black ones would fear—concealed not a dozen feet from where he stood.

He didn't think anymore; he simply acted. A soundless shadow, he moved to the stone hearth that served the kitchen, his fingers tracing the rough outline of the stone where it curved back along the wall in a series of shelving nooks. At the end of the third shelf, the stone slipped away at his touch. His hand closed over a small leather pouch.

Something stirred in the other room.

Then the back door opened suddenly and a burly form pushed into view. Jair stood flattened against the hearth wall, lost in the shadows, braced to flee. But the form went past him without slowing, head bent as if to find its way. It went into the front room, and a low, guttural voice whispered to the creature that waited within.

In the next instant, Jair was moving—back through the still open door, back into the shadows of the flowering bushes. He paused just long enough to see that it was the Gnome who kept watch within the oaks who had come into the house, then raced for the cover of the trees. Faster, faster! he screamed soundlessly.

And without a backward glance, Jair Ohmsford fled into the night.

IV

◆

İT PROVED TO BE A HARROWİNG FLİGHT.

Once before, Ohmsfords had fled the Vale under cover of night, pursued by black things that would harry them the length and breadth of the Four Lands. It had been more than seventy years now since Shea and Flick Ohmsford had slipped from their home at the Shady Vale inn, barely escaping the monstrous winged Skull Bearer sent by the Warlock Lord to destroy them. Jair knew their story; barely older than he, they had fled all the way eastward to Culhaven and the Dwarves. But Jair Ohmsford was no less able than they. He, too, had been raised in the Vale, and he knew something about surviving in unfamiliar country.

As he fled through the forests of the Vale, carrying with him little more than the clothes on his back, the hunting knife in his belt that all Valemen wore, and the leather pouch with the Elfstones tucked within his tunic, he did so with confidence in his ability to make his way safely to his destination. There was no panic in his flight; there was merely a keen sense of expectation. For just a moment, when he had stood within the kitchen of his home, hidden within the shadows of the great hearth, listening to the silence, knowing that only a room away there waited one of the Wraiths, and feeling the evil of the thing permeating even the air he breathed, there had been real fear. But that was behind him, lost in the darkness that slipped steadily back into the past as he raced ahead, and now he was thinking with clarity and determination.

The destination he had chosen in fleeing the Vale was Leah. It was a three-day journey, but one he had made before and so could make without danger of becoming lost. Moreover, help that could not be found in the Vale could be found in Leah. Shady Vale was a small hamlet, its people ill-equipped to stand against the black walkers or their Gnome allies. But Leah was a city; the highlands were governed by monarchial rule and protected by a standing army. Rone Leah's father was king and a good friend to the Ohmsford family. Jair would tell him what had befallen, persuade him to send patrols south in search of his parents so that they could be warned of the danger that waited in the Vale, and then all of them would take refuge in the city until Allanon returned with Brin and Rone. It was an excellent plan to Jair's way of thinking, and he could find no reason that it wouldn't be successful.

Still, the Valeman was not about to leave anything to chance. That was the reason that he had brought the Elfstones, taking them from their hiding place where they might have been found, though taking them meant revealing to his father that he had known all along where they were hidden.

As he ran, working his way steadily through the Vale forests toward the rim of the valley, he tried to recall everything that the old tracker had told him in their talks about disguising one's trail from pursuers. Jair and the old man had played at it like a game, each contriving new and different twists to the imaginary pursuits that made up their game, each delighting the other with a kind of grim inventiveness. For the tracker, experience was the touchstone of his skill. For Jair, it was an uninhibited imagination. Now the play adventure had turned real, however, and imagination alone was not going to be enough. A bit of the old man's experience was needed, and Jair called to mind everything he could manage to remember.

Time was his most pressing concern. The quicker he reached the highlands, the quicker those patrols would leave in search of his parents. Whatever else happened, they must not be allowed to return to the Vale unwarned. Therefore, no unnecessary time must be spent in disguising his trail eastward. This decision was reinforced by the fact that his skills were admittedly limited in any case and by the further fact that he could not be certain that the Gnomes and their dark leader would come after him. He thought that they would, of course, particularly after hearing from the Gnome he had locked in the wood bin. But they would still have to track him, and that would slow them down somewhat, even if they were to guess which direction he had taken. He had gained a head start on them, and he must take advantage of it. He would run swiftly and surely, his purpose fixed, and they must try to catch him.

Besides, even if they did catch up to him, he could still use the wishsong to protect himself.

By midnight, he had gained the eastern wall of the valley that sheltered Shady Vale, climbed the rock-strewn slope to its rim, and disappeared into the Duln. Using the moon and stars to mark his bearings, he made his way through the dark forest, slowing a bit to conserve his strength. He was tiring now, having had no sleep since the previous night, but he wanted to make certain that he crossed the Rappahalladran before he stopped to rest. That meant he must travel until dawn, and the journey would be a hard one. The Duln was a real difficult woodland to traverse, even under the best of conditions, and darkness often made the wilderness a treacherous maze. Still, Jair had traveled the Duln at night before, and he felt confident he could find his way. So with a careful eye for the forest tangle that stretched before him, he pushed on.

Time crawled past on leaden feet, but at last the night sky began to lighten into morning. Jair was exhausted, his slim body numb with fatigue and his hands and face cut and bruised by the forest. Still he had not reached the river. For the first time, he began to worry that perhaps he had misplaced his sense of direction and traveled too far north or south. He was still traveling eastward, he knew, because the sun was rising directly in front of him. But where was the Rappahalladran? Ignoring the weariness and a growing sense of concern, he stumbled ahead.

The sun had been up an hour when he finally reached the banks of the river. Deep and swift, the Rappahalladran churned its way southward through the dark quiet of the forest. Jair had already shelved his plans to cross the river now. The currents were too dangerous to attempt a crossing when he was not rested. Finding a stand of pine close to the water, he stretched out within the shaded coolness of their boughs and fell quickly asleep.

He came awake again at sunset, disoriented and vaguely uneasy. It took him a moment to remember where he was and what it was that had brought him there. Then he saw that the day was gone, and he became alarmed that he had slept so long. He had intended to sleep only until midday before continuing his flight east. A whole day was too long; it gave his pursuers too much time to catch him.

He went down to the river's edge, splashed cold water on his face to bring himself fully awake and then went in search of food. He hadn't eaten anything for the past twenty-four hours, he realized suddenly, and found himself wishing that he'd taken just a moment longer in making his escape to pack a loaf of bread and some cheese. As he searched through the trees, resigned to a meal of berries and roots, he found himself thinking again about his supposed pursuers. Maybe he was worrying about nothing. Maybe no one was giving chase. After all, what would they want with him anyway? It was Allanon they wanted. The Gnome had told him that much. What had probably happened was that, after he had escaped the Vale, they had gone on their way, looking elsewhere for the Druid. If that were true, then he was breaking his neck out here for nothing.

Of course if he were wrong . . .

Wild berries in autumn were a scarce commodity, so Jair was forced to make a meal principally of edible roots and a few wild rhubarb stalks. Despite his general dissatisfaction with the fare, he was feeling pretty good about things by the time the meal was finished. Rone Leah couldn't have done any better, he decided. He had overcome that Gnome, secured the Elfstones from under the noses of a walker and a patrol of Gnome Hunters, escaped the Vale and was now making his way successfully toward Leah. He took a moment to envision the surprised face of his sister when he told her all that had happened to him.

And then it occurred to him, suddenly, shockingly, that he really didn't know that he would ever see Brin again. His sister was being taken by Allanon into the very heart of the same evil that had invaded his home and driven him from the Vale. He remembered again what he had felt in the presence of that evil—the terrible, overpowering sense of panic. Brin was being taken to where that evil lived, where there was not just one of the black walkers, but many. Against them she had nothing more than the strength of the magic of the Druid and her wishsong. How could Brin hope to stand against something like that? What if she were discovered before she managed to reach the book . . . ?

He could not complete the thought. Despite their differing personalities and ways, Jair and his sister were close. He loved her and he did not like the idea of anything happening to her. He wished more than ever that he had been allowed to go with her to the Anar.

Abruptly he glanced westward to where the sun was slipping down into the treetops. The light was failing quickly now, and it was time to make his crossing and get on with the journey east. He cut a series of branches, using the long knife, and bound them together with pine bark strips to construct a small raft on which he could place his clothes. He had no desire to walk the chill autumn night in wet clothing, so he would swim the river naked and dress again on the far bank.

When the raft was finished, he carried it down to the river's edge and suddenly recalled one of the lessons taught to him by the old tracker. They had been talking of ways to throw off a pursuit. Water was the best disguise of one's tracks, the old man had announced in his cryptic way. Couldn't follow tracks through water—unless, of course, you were stupid enough to try losing a pursuer in water so shallow that your footprints left their mark in the mud. But deep water—ah, that was the best. The current always took you downstream, and even if your pursuer tracked you to the water's edge and knew you'd gone across—didn't have to go across, of course, but that was another trick—he'd still have to find your trail on the other side. So—and here was a glimmer of genius to the game—the very smartest quarry would wade upstream, then swim the deep water so that he would come out still above the point on the far bank where his tracks ended. Because the hunter knew you'd be carried downstream, too, didn't he—so where do you think he would be looking? He wouldn't think to look upstream right away.

Jair had always been impressed with that bit of trickery and resolved now to put it to the test. Maybe he wasn't being followed, but on the other hand, he couldn't be sure. He was still two days from Leah. If someone had come after him, this device of the old tracker would give him a bigger head start yet.

So he stripped off his boots, tucked them under one arm with the raft, then waded upstream several hundred yards to where the channel narrowed. Far enough, he decided. He took off the rest of his clothing, placed it on the raft and pushed off into the cold waters of the river.

The current caught him almost at once, pulling him downstream at a rapid pace. He let it take him, swimming with it, the raft held firmly in his trailing hand, angling as he swam toward the far bank. Bits of deadwood and brush swirled past him, rough and chill to the touch, and the sounds of the forest faded into the churning rush of the water. Overhead, the night sky darkened as the sun slipped below the treeline. Jair kicked steadily on, the far bank drawing closer.

Then at last his feet touched bottom, kicking into the soft mud, and he stood up, the night air chill against his skin. Snatching his clothes from the raft, he shoved it back into the river's current and watched it swirl away. A moment later he was back on dry land, brushing the water from his body and slipping back into his clothes. Insects buzzed past him, bits of sound in the dark. On the bank from which he had come, the forest trees were fading stalks of black in the night's deepening haze.

Within those dark stalks, something suddenly moved.

Jair froze, his eyes fixed on the spot from which the movement had come. But it was gone now, whatever it had been. He took a deep breath. It had looked—just for a moment—to be a man.

Carefully, slowly, he backed into the shelter of the trees behind him, still watching the other bank, waiting for the movement to come again. It did not. He finished dressing hurriedly, checked to be certain that the Elfstones were still tucked safely within his tunic, then turned and trotted soundlessly into the forest. He was probably mistaken, he told himself.

He walked all night, relying again on the moon and stars visible in small patches of forest sky to point him in the right direction. He traveled at a slow trot where the forest thinned, less certain than before that no one had come after him. When he had been alone with the memory of those few moments in his home with that black thing behind him, he had felt secure. But the idea that someone or something was back there, following him, brought back the sense of panic. Even in the cool autumn night, he was sweating, his senses sharp with fear. Time and again, his thoughts wandered back to Brin, and he found himself imagining her to be as alone as he— alone and hunted. He wished she were there with him.

When sunrise came, he kept walking. He was not yet clear of the Duln, and the sense of uneasiness was still with him. He was tired, but not so tired that he felt the need to sleep just yet. He walked on while the sun rose before him in a golden haze, thin streamers of brightness slipping down into the forest gray, reflecting rainbow colors from the drying leaves and emerald moss. From time to time he found himself glancing back, watching.

Several hours into morning, the forest ended and rolling grasslands appeared, a threshold to the distant blue screen of the highlands. It was warm and friendly here, less confining than the forest, and Jair felt immediately more at ease. As he walked further into the grasslands, he began to recognize the countryside about him. He had come this way before on a visit to Leah just a year ago when Rone had brought him to his hunting lodge at the foot of the highlands where they had stayed and fished the mist lakes. The lodge lay another two hours eastward, but it offered a soft bed and shelter for the remainder of the day so that he might set out again refreshed with nightfall. The idea of the bed decided him.

Disregarding the weariness he felt, Jair continued to march east through the grasslands, the rise of the highlands broadening before him as he drew closer. Once or twice he looked back into the countryside through which he had come, but each time the land lay empty.

It was midday when he reached the lodge, a timber and stone house set back within a tall stand of pine at the edge of the highland forests. The lodge sat upon a slope overlooking the grasslands, but was hidden by the trees until approached within hailing distance. Jair stumbled wearily up the stone steps to the lodge door, turned to locate the key that Rone kept concealed in a crevice in the stones, then saw that the lock was broken. Cautiously he lifted the latch and peered in. The building was empty.

Of course it was empty, he grumbled to himself, eyes heavy with the need for sleep. Why wouldn't it be?

He closed the door behind him, glanced briefly about at the immaculate interior—wood and leather furniture, shelves of stores and cooking ware, ale bar, and stone fireplace—and moved gratefully down the short hallway at the rear of the main room that led to the bedrooms. He stopped at the first door he came to, released the latch, pushed his way in, and collapsed on the broad, feather-stuffed bed.

In seconds, he was asleep.

It was almost dark when he came awake, and the autumn sky was deep blue, laced with dying silver sunlight through the curtained bedroom window. A noise brought him awake, a small scuffling sound—boots passing over wooden planking.

Without thinking, he was on his feet, still half-asleep as he walked quickly to the bedroom door and peered out. The darkened room at the front of the lodge stood empty, bathed in shadow. Jair blinked and stared through the dusk. Then he saw something else.

The front door stood open.

He stepped out into the hallway in disbelief, sleep-filled eyes blinking.

"Taking another walk, boy?" a familiar voice asked from behind.

Frantically he whirled—far too slowly. Something hammered into the side of his face, and lights exploded before his eyes. He fell to the floor and into blackness.

V

IT WAS STILL SUMMER WHERE THE MERMIDON FLOWED down out of Callahorn and emptied into the vast expanse of the Rainbow Lake. It was green and fresh, a mix of grassland and forest, foothill and mountain. Water from the river and its dozens of tributaries fed the earth and kept it moist. Mist from the lake drifted north with each sunrise, dissipated, and settled into the land, giving life beyond the summer season. Sweet, damp smells permeated the air, and autumn was yet a stranger.

Brin Ohmsford sat alone on a rise overlooking the juncture of lake and river and was at peace. The day was almost gone, and the sun was a brilliant reddish gold flare on the western horizon, its light staining crimson the silver waters that stretched away before her. No wind broke the calm of the coming evening, and the lake's surface was mirrorlike and still. High overhead, its bands of color a sharper hue against the coming gray of night where the eastern sky darkened, the wondrous rainbow from which the lake took its name arched from shoreline to shoreline. Cranes and geese glided gracefully through the fading light, their cries haunting in the deep silence.

Brin's thoughts drifted. It had been four days since she had left her home and come eastward on a journey that would take her to the deep Anar, farther than she had ever gone before. It seemed odd that she knew so little about the journey, even now. Four days had gone, and she was still little more than a child who gripped a mother's hand, trusting blindly. From Shady Vale they had gone north through the Duln, east along the banks of the Rappahalladran, north again, and then east, following the shoreline of the Rainbow Lake to where the Mermidon emptied down. Never once had Allanon offered a word of explanation.

Both Rone and she had asked the Druid to explain, of course. They had asked their questions time and again, but the Druid had brushed them aside. Later, he would tell them. Your questions will be answered later. For now, simply follow after me. So they had followed as he had bidden them, wary and increasingly distrustful, promising themselves that they would have their explanations before the Eastland was reached.

Yet the Druid gave them little cause to believe that their promise would be fulfilled. Enigmatic and withdrawn, he kept them from him. In the daytime, when they traveled, he rode before them, and it was clear that he preferred to ride alone. At night, when they camped, he left them and moved into the shadows. He neither ate nor slept, behavior that seemed to emphasize the differences between them and thereby widen the distance. He watched over them like a hawk over its prey, never leaving them alone to stray.

Until now, she corrected. On this evening of the fourth day, Allanon unexpectedly had left them. They had encamped here, where the Mermidon fed into the Rainbow Lake, and the Druid had stalked off into the woodlands bordering the river's waters and disappeared without a word of explanation. Valegirl and highlander had watched him go, staring after in disbelief. At last, when it became apparent that he had indeed left them—for how long, they could only guess—they resolved to waste no further time worrying about him and turned their attention to preparing the evening meal. Three days of eating fish pulled first from the waters of the Rappahalladran and then from the waters of the Rainbow Lake had blunted temporarily their enthusiasm for fish. So armed with ash bow and arrows, a weapon Menion Leah had favored, Rone had gone in search of different fare. Brin had taken a few minutes to gather wood for a cooking fire, then settled herself on this rise and let the solitude of the moment slip over her.

Allanon! He was an enigma that defied resolution. Committed to the preservation of the land, he was a friend to her people, a benefactor to the races, and a protector against evil they could not alone withstand. Yet what friend used people as Allanon did? Why keep so carefully concealed the reasons for all he did? He seemed at times as much enemy, malefactor, and destroyer as that which he claimed to stand against.

The Druid himself had told her father the story of the old world of faerie from which all the magic had come along with creatures who wielded it. Good or bad, black or white, the magic was the same in the sense that its power was rooted in the strength, wisdom, and purpose of the user. After all, what had been the true difference between Allanon and the Warlock Lord in their struggle to secure mastery over the Sword of Shannara? Each had been a Druid, learning the magic from the books of the old world. The difference was in the character of the user, for where one had been corrupted by the power, the other had stayed pure.

Perhaps. And perhaps not. Her father would argue the matter, she knew, maintaining that the Druid had been corrupted by the power as surely as the Dark Lord, if only in a different way. For Allanon was also governed in his life by the power he wielded and by the secrets of its use. If his sense of responsibility was of a higher sort and his purpose less selfish, he was nevertheless as much its victim. Indeed, there was something strangely sad about Allanon, despite his harsh, almost threatening demeanor. She thought for a time about the sense of sadness that the Druid invoked in her— a sadness her father had surely never felt—and she wondered how it was that she felt it so keenly.

"I'm back!"

She turned, startled. But it was only Rone, calling up to her from the campsite in the pine grove below the rise. She climbed to her feet and started down.

"I see that the Druid hasn't returned yet," the highlander said as she came up to him. He had a pair of wild hens slung over one shoulder and dropped them to the ground. "Maybe we'll get lucky and he won't come back at all."

She stared at him. "Maybe that wouldn't be so lucky."

He shrugged. "Depends on how you look at it."

"Tell me how you look at it, Rone."

He frowned. "All right. I don't trust him."

"And why is it that you don't?"

"Because of what he pretends to be: protector against the Warlock Lord and the Bearers of the Skull; protector against the Demons released from the old world of faerie; and now protector against the Mord Wraiths. But always, it's with the aid of the Ohmsford family and their friends, take note. I know the history, too, Brin. It's always the same. He appears unexpectedly, warning of a danger that threatens the races, which only a member of the Ohmsford family can help put an end to. Heirs to the Elven house of Shannara and to the magics that belong to it—those are the Ohmsfords. First the Sword of Shannara, then the Elfstones and now the wishsong. But somehow things are never quite what they seem, are they?"

Brin shook her head slowly. "What are you saying, Rone?"

"I'm saying that the Druid comes out of nowhere with a story designed to secure Shea or Wil Ohmsford's aid—and now your aid—and each time it's the same. He tells only what he must. He gives away only as much as he needs give away. He keeps back the rest; he hides a part of the truth. I don't trust him. He plays games with people's lives!"

"And you believe that he's doing that with us?"

Rone took a deep breath. "Don't you?"

Brin was silent a moment before answering. "I'm not sure."

"Then you don't trust him either?"

"I didn't say that."

The highlander stared at her a moment, then slowly settled himself on the ground across from her, folding his long legs before him. "Well, which way is it, Brin? Do you trust him or don't you?"

She sat down as well. "I guess I haven't really decided."

"Then what are you doing here, for cat's sake?"

She smiled at his obvious disgust. "I'm here, Rone, because he needs me—I believe that much of what I have been told. The rest I'm not sure about. The part he keeps hidden, I have to discover for myself."

"If you can."

"I'll find a way."

"It's too dangerous," he said flatly.

She smiled, rose, and came over to where he sat. Gently she kissed his forehead. "That's why I wanted you here with me, Rone Leah—to be my protector. Isn't that why you came?" He flushed bright scarlet and muttered something unintelligible, and she laughed in spite of herself. "Why don't we leave this discussion until later and do something with those hens. I'm starved."

She built a small cooking fire while Rone cleaned the hens. Then they cooked and ate the birds together with a small portion of cheese and ale. They ate their meal in silence, seated back atop the small rise, watching the night sky darken and the stars and gibbous moon cast their pale silver light on the waters of the lake.

By the time they had finished, night had fallen and Allanon still had not returned.

"Brin, you remember what you said before, about my being here to protect you?" Rone asked her after they had returned to the fire. She nodded. "Well, it's true—I am here to protect you. I wouldn't let anything happen to you—not ever. I guess you know that."

He hesitated, and she smiled through the dark. "I know."

"Well." He shifted about uneasily, his hands lifting the battered scabbard that housed the Sword of Leah. "There's another reason I'm here, too. I hope you can understand this. I'm here to prove something to myself." He hesitated again, groping for the words to explain. "I am a Prince of Leah, but that's just a title. I was born into it, just like my brothers—and they're all older. And this sword, Brin." He held up the scabbard and its weapon. "It isn't really mine; it's my great-grandfather's. It's Menion Leah's sword. It always has been, ever since he carried it in search of the Sword of Shannara. I carry it—the ash bow, too—because Menion carried them and I'd like to be what he was. But I'm not."

"You don't know that," she said quickly.

"That's just the point," he continued. "I've never done anything to find out what I could be. And that's partly why I'm here. I want to know. This is how Menion found out—by going on a quest, as protector to Shea Ohmsford. Maybe I can do it this way, too."

Brin smiled. "Maybe you can. In any case, I'm glad you told me." She paused. "Now I'll tell you a secret. I came for the same reason. I have something to prove to myself, too. I don't know if I can do what Allanon expects of me; I don't know if I am strong enough. I was born with the wishsong, but I have never known what I was meant to do with it. I believe there is a reason for my having the magic. Maybe I will learn that reason from Allanon."

She put her hand on his arm. "So you see, we're not so different after all, are we, Rone?"

They talked a while longer, growing drowsy as the evening lengthened and the weariness of the day's travel overcame them. Then at last their talk gave way to silence, and they spread their bedding. Clear and cool, the autumn night wrapped them in its solitude and peace as they stretched out next to the dark embers of the fire and pulled their blankets close.

They were asleep in moments.

Neither saw the tall, black-robed figure who stood in the shadow of the pines just beyond the fire's light.

When they awoke the following morning, Allanon was there. He was seated only a few yards away from them on a hollow log, his tall, spare form wraithlike in the gray light of early dawn. He watched silently as they rose, washed, and ate a light breakfast, offering no explanation as to where he had been. More than once the Valegirl and the highlander glanced openly in his direction, but he seemed to take no notice. It was not until they had packed their bedrolls and cooking gear and brought the horses in to be saddled that he finally rose and came over to them.

"There has been a change of plans," he announced. They stared at him silently. "We are no longer going east. We are going north into the Dragon's Teeth."

"The Dragon's Teeth?" Rone's jaw tightened. "Why?"

"Because it is necessary."

"Necessary for whom?" Rone snapped.

"It will only be for a day or so." Allanon turned his attention to Brin now, ignoring the angry highlander. "I have a visit to make. When it is finished, we will turn east again and complete our journey."

"Allanon." Brin spoke his name softly. "Tell us why we must go north."

The Druid hesitated, his face darkening. Then he nodded. "Very well. Last night I received a summons from my father. He bids me come to him, and I am bound to do so. In life, he was the Druid Bremen. Now his shade surfaces from the netherworld through the waters of the Hadeshorn in the Valley of Shale. In three days time, before daybreak, he will speak with me there."

Bremen—the Druid who had escaped the massacre of the Council at Paranor, when the Warlock Lord swept down out of the Northland in the Second War of the Races, and who had forged the Sword of Shannara. So long ago, Brin thought, the legendary tale recalling itself in her memory. Then, seventy-odd years ago, Shea Ohmsford had gone with Allanon into the Valley of Shale and seen the shade of Bremen rise from the Hadeshorn to converse with his son, to warn of what lay ahead, to prophesy . . .

"He can see the future, can't he?" Brin asked suddenly, remembering now how the shade had warned of Shea's fate. "Will he speak of that?"

Allanon shook his head doubtfully. "Perhaps. Even so, he would reveal only fragments of what is to be, for the future is not yet formed in its entirety and must of necessity remain in doubt.

Only certain things can be known. Even they are not always clear to our understanding." He shrugged. "In any case, he calls. He would not do so if it were not of grave importance."

"I don't like it," Rone announced. "It's another three days or more gone—time that could be spent getting into and out of the Anar. The Wraiths are already searching for you. You told us that much yourself. We're just giving them that much more time to find you—and Brin."

The Druid's eyes fixed on him, cold and hard. "I take no unnecessary risks with the girl's safety, Prince of Leah. Nor with your own."

Rone flushed angrily, and Brin stepped forward, seizing his hand. "Wait, Rone. Perhaps going to the Hadeshorn is a good idea. Perhaps we will learn something of what the future holds that will aid us."

The highlander kept his gaze locked on Allanon. "What would aid us most is a bit more of the truth of what we're about!" he snapped.

"So." The word was a soft, quick whisper, and Allanon's tall form seemed to suddenly grow taller. "What part of the truth would you have me reveal, Prince of Leah?"

Rone held his ground. "This much, Druid. You tell Brin that she must come with you into the Eastland because you lack the power necessary to penetrate the barrier that protects the book of dark magic—you, who are the keeper of the secrets of the Druids, who possess power enough to destroy Skull Bearers and Demons alike! Yet you need her. And what does she have that you don't? The wishsong. Nothing more, just that. It lacks even the power of the Elfstones! It is a magic toy that changes the colors of leaves and causes flowers to bloom! What kind of protection is that?"

Allanon stared at him silently for a moment and then smiled, a faint, sad smile. "What kind of power, indeed?" he murmured. He looked suddenly at Brin. "Do you, too, harbor these doubts the highlander voices? Do you seek a better understanding of the wishsong? Shall I show you something of its use?"

It was cold the way he said it, but Brin nodded. "Yes."

The Druid strode past her, seized the reins of his horse and mounted. "Come then, and I will show you, Valegirl," he said.

They rode north in silence along the Mermidon, winding their way through the rocky forestland, the light of the sunrise breaking through the trees on their left, the shadow of the Runne Mountains a dark wall on their right. They rode for more than an hour, a grim, voiceless procession. Then at last the Druid signaled a halt, and they dismounted.

"Leave the horses," he instructed.

They walked west into the forest, the Druid leading the Valegirl and the highlander across a ridge and down into a heavily wooded hollow. After several minutes of fighting their way through the tangled undergrowth, Allanon stopped and turned.

"Now then, Brin." He pointed ahead into the brush. "Pretend that this hollow is the barrier of dark magic through which you must pass. How would you use the wishsong to gain passage?"

She glanced about uncertainly. "I'm not sure . . ."

"Not sure?" He shook his head. "Think of the uses to which you have put the magic. Have you used it as the Prince of Leah suggests to bring autumn color to the leaves of a tree? Have you used it to bring flowers to bloom, leaves to bud, plants to grow?" She nodded. "You have used it, then, to change color and shape and behavior. Do so here. Make the brush part for you."

She looked at him a moment and then nodded. This was more than she had ever asked of herself, and she was not convinced she had the power. Moreover, it had been a long time since she had used the magic. But she would try. Softly, she began to sing. Her voice was low and even, the song blending with the sounds of the forest. Then slowly she changed its pitch, and it rose until all else had faded into stillness. Words came, unrehearsed, spontaneous and somehow intuitively felt as she reached out to the brush that blocked her passage. Slowly the tangle drew back, leaves and branches withdrawing in winding ribbons of sleek green.

A moment later, the way forward lay open to the center of the hollow.

"Simple enough, don't you agree?" But the Druid wasn't really asking. "Let's see where your path takes us."

He started ahead again, black robes drawn close. Brin glanced quickly at Rone, who shrugged his lack of understanding. They followed after the Druid. Seconds later he stopped again, this time pointing to an elm, its trunk bent and stunted within the shadow of a taller, broader oak. The elm's limbs had grown into those of the oak, twisting upward in a futile effort to reach the sunlight.

"A bit harder task this time, Brin," Allanon said suddenly. "That elm would be much better off if the sun could reach it. I want you to straighten it, bring it upright, and disentangle it from the oak."

Brin looked at the two trees doubtfully. They seemed too closely entwined. "I don't think I can do that," she told him quietly.

"Try."

"The magic is not strong enough . . ."

"Try anyway," he cut her short.

So she sang, the wishsong enfolding the other sounds of the forest until there was nothing else, rising brightly into the morning air. The elm shuddered, limbs quaking in response. Brin lifted the pitch of her song, sensing the tree's resistance, and the words formed a harder edge. The stunted trunk of the elm drew back from the oak, its limbs scraping and tearing and its leaves ripped violently from their stems.

Then, with shocking suddenness, the entire tree seemed to heave upward and explode in a shower of fragmented limbs, twigs, and leaves that rained down across the length of the hollow. Astonished, Brin stumbled back, shielding her face with her hands, the wishsong dying into instant stillness. She would have fallen but for Allanon, who caught her in his arms, held her protectively until the shower had subsided, then turned her to face him.

"What happened . . . ?" she began, but he quickly put a finger to her lips.

"Power, Valegirl," he whispered. "Power in your wishsong far greater than what you have imagined. That elm could not disentangle itself from the oak. Its limbs were far too stiff, far too heavily entwined. Yet it could not refuse your song. It had no choice but to pull free—even when the result meant destroying itself!"

"Allanon!" She shook her head in disbelief.

"You have that power, Brin Ohmsford. As with all things magic, there is a dark side as well as a light." The Druid's face came closer. "You have played with changing the colors of a tree's leaves. Think what would happen if you carried the seasonal change you wrought to its logical conclusion. The tree would pass from autumn into winter, from winter into spring, from seasonal change to seasonal change. At last it would have passed through the entire cycle of its life. It would die."

"Druid . . ." Rone warned and started forward, but a single dark glance from the other's eyes froze him in his tracks.

"Stand, Prince of Leah. Let her hear the truth." The black eyes again found Brin's. "You have played with the wishsong as you would a curious toy because that is all the use you saw for it. Yet you knew that it was more than that, Valegirl—always, deep inside, you knew. Elven magic has always been more than that. Yours is the magic of the Elfstones, born into new form in its passage from your father's blood to your own. There is power in you of a sort that transcends any that has gone before—latent perhaps, yet the potential is unmistakable. Consider for a moment the nature of this magic you wield. The wishsong can change the behavior of any living thing! Can you not see what that means? Supple brush can be made to part for you, giving you access where there was none before. Unbending trees can be made to part as well, though they shatter with the effort. If you can bring color to leaves, you can also drain it away. If you can cause flowers to bloom, you can also cause them to wilt. If you can give life, Brin, you can also take it away."

She stared at him, horrified. "What are you saying?" she whispered harshly. "That the wishsong can kill? That I would use it to kill? Do you think . . . ?"

"You asked to be shown something of its use," Allanon cut short her protestations. "I have simply done as you wished. But I think now you will no longer doubt that the magic is much more than you thought it was."

Brin's dusky face burned with anger. "I no longer doubt, Allanon. Nor should you doubt this—that even so, I would never use the wishsong to kill! Never!"

The Druid held her gaze, yet the hard features softened slightly. "Not even to save your own life? Or perhaps the life of the highlander? Not even then?"

She did not look away. "Never."

The Druid stared at the Valegirl a moment longer—as if to measure in some way the depth of her commitment. Then abruptly he wheeled away and started back toward the slope of the hollow.

"You have seen enough, Brin. We have to get on with our journey. Think about what you have learned."

His black form disappeared into the brush. Brin stood where he had left her, aware suddenly that her hands were shaking. That tree! The way it had simply shattered, torn apart . . .

"Brin." Rone was standing before her, and his hands came up to grip her shoulders. She winced at their touch. "We can't go on with him—not anymore. He plays games with us as he has done with all the others. Leave him and his foolish quest and come back with me now to the Vale."

She stared at him a moment, then shook her head. "No. It was necessary that I see this."

"None of this is necessary, for cat's sake!" His big hands drew back and fastened about the pommel of the Sword of Leah. "If he does something like that again, I'll not think twice . . ."

"No, Rone." She put her hands over his. She was calm once more, realizing suddenly that she had missed something. "What he did was not done simply to frighten or intimidate me. It was done to teach me, and it was done out of a need for haste. It was in his eyes. Could you not see it?"

He shook his head. "I saw nothing. What need for haste?"

She looked to where the Druid had gone. "Something is wrong. Something."

Then she thought again of the destruction of the tree, of the Druid's words of warning, and of her vow. Never! She looked quickly back at Rone. "Do you think I could use the wishsong to kill?" she asked softly.

For just an instant he hesitated. "No."

Even to save your life? she thought. And what if it were not a tree that threatened, but a living creature? Would I destroy it to save you? Oh, Rone, what if it were a human being?

"Will you still come with me on this journey?" she asked him.

He gave her his most rakish smile. "Right up to the moment when we take that confounded book and shred it."

Then he bent to kiss her lightly on the mouth, and her arms came up to hold him close. "We'll be all right," she heard him say.

And she answered, "I know."

But she was no longer sure.

VI

WHEN JAIR OHMSFORD REGAINED CONSCIOUSNESS, HE found himself trussed hand and foot and securely lashed against a tree trunk. He was no longer in the hunting lodge but in a clearing sheltered by closely grown fir that loomed over him like sentinels set to watch. A dozen feet in front of him, a small fire burned, casting its faint glow into the shadowed dark of the silent trees. Night lay over the land.

"Awake again, boy?"

The familiar, chiding voice came from out of the darkness to his left, and he turned his head slowly, searching. A squat, motionless figure crouched at the edge of the firelight. Jair started to reply, then realized that he was not only tied; he was gagged as well.

"Oh yes, sorry about that," the other spoke again. "Had to put the gag in, of course. Couldn't have you using your magic on me a second time, could I? Do you have any idea how long it took me to get out of that wood bin?"

Jair sagged back against the tree, remembering. The Gnome at the inn—that was who had followed him, caught up with him at Rone's hunting lodge, and struck him from behind . . .

He winced at the memory, finding that the side of his head still throbbed.

"Nice trick, that thing with the snakes." The Gnome chuckled faintly. He rose and came into the firelight, seating himself cross-legged a few feet from his prisoner. Narrow green eyes studied Jair speculatively. "I thought you harmless, boy—not some Druid's whelp. Worse luck for me, eh? There I was, sure you'd be so scared that you'd tell me right off what I wanted to know—tell me anything just to get rid of me. Not you, though. Snakes on my arms and a four-foot limb bashed up against my head, that's what you gave me. Lucky I'm alive!"

The blocky yellow face cocked slightly. "Course, that was your mistake." A blunt finger came up sharply. "You should have finished me. But you didn't, and that gave me another chance at you. Suppose that's the way you are, though, being from the Vale. Anyway, once I got free of that wood bin, I came after you like a fox after a rabbit. Too bad for you, too, because I wasn't about to let you escape, after what you'd put me through. Not by a whisker's cut, I wasn't! Those other fools, they'd have let you outrun them. But not me. Tracked you three days. Almost had you at the river, but you were already across and I couldn't pick up your trail at night. Had to wait. But I caught you napping at that lodge, didn't I?"

He laughed cheerfully and Jair flushed with anger. "Oh, don't be angry with me—I was just doing my job. Besides, it was a matter of pride. Twenty years, and no one's ever gotten the best of me until now. And then it's some nothing boy. Couldn't live with that. Oh, knocking you senseless—had to do that, too. Like I said, couldn't be taking chances with the magic."

He got up and came a few steps closer, his rough face screwed up with obvious curiosity. "It was magic, wasn't it? How'd you learn to do that? It's in the voice, right? You make the snakes come by using the voice. Quite a trick. Scared the wits out of me, and I thought there wasn't much left that could scare me." He paused. "Except maybe the walkers."

Jair's eyes glistened with fear at mention of the Mord Wraiths. The Gnome saw it and nodded. "Something to be scared of, they are. Black all through. Dark as midnight. Wouldn't want them hunting me. Don't know how you got past that one back at the house . . ."

He stopped suddenly and bent forward. "Hungry, boy?" Jair

nodded. The Gnome regarded him thoughtfully for a moment, then rose. "Tell you what. I'll loosen the gag and feed you if you promise not to use the magic on me. Wouldn't do you much good anyway trussed up to that tree—not unless those snakes of yours can chew through ropes. I'll feed you and we can talk a bit. The others won't catch up until morning. What about it?"

Jair thought it over a moment, then nodded his agreement. He was famished.

"Done, then." The Gnome came over and slipped free the gag. One hand fastened tightly to Jair's chin. "Your word now—let's have it. No magic."

"No magic," Jair repeated, wincing.

"Good. Good." The Gnome let his hand drop. "You're one who keeps his word, I'm betting. Man's only as good as his word, you know." He reached down to his waist for a hard leather container, released the stopper and brought it up to the Valeman's lips. "Drink. Go on, take a swallow."

Jair sipped at the unknown liquid, his throat dry and tight. It was an ale, harsh and bitter, and it burned all the way down. Jair choked and drew back, and the Gnome recapped the container and returned it to his belt. Then he sat back on his haunches, grinning.

"I'm called Slanter."

"Jair Ohmsford." Jair was still trying to swallow. "I guess you knew that."

Slanter nodded. "I did. Should have found out a bit more, it appears. Quite a chase you took me on."

Jair frowned. "How did you manage to catch up to me? I didn't think anyone could catch me."

"Oh, that." The Gnome sniffed. "Well, not just anyone could have caught you. But then I'm not just anyone."

"What do you mean?"

The Gnome laughed. "I mean I'm a tracker, boy. It's what I do. Fact is, it's what I do better than just about anyone else alive. That's why they brought me, the others. That's why I'm here. I've been tracking."

"Me?" Jair asked in astonishment.

"No, not you—the Druid! The one they call Allanon. It was him I was tracking. You just happened to cross my path at the wrong time."

A look of bewilderment crossed the Valeman's face. This Gnome was a tracker? No wonder he hadn't been able to escape him as he would have another man. But tracking Allanon . . . ?

Slanter shook his head helplessly and climbed to his feet. "Look, I'll explain it all to you, but first let's have something to eat. I had to carry you down from that hunting lodge two miles distant, and you may look small but you weigh better than your size. Worked up a pretty good appetite while you rested. Sit still, now—I'll put something on the fire."

Slanter retrieved a knapsack from the other side of the clearing, pulled clear some cooking utensils and within minutes had a beef and vegetable stew simmering over the fire. The smell of the cooking food wafted through the night air to Jair's nostrils, and his mouth began to water. He was beyond famished, he decided. He had not had a decent meal since he had left the inn. Besides, he needed to keep his strength up if he was to have any chance of escaping this fellow, and he had every intention of doing so at the first opportunity.

When the stew was finished, Slanter brought it over to where he was tied and hand-fed him mouthfuls, sharing the meal with him. The food tasted wonderful, and they ate all that there was, together with an end of bread and some cheese. Slanter drank more of the ale, but gave Jair sips from a cup of water.

"Not a bad stew if I do say so myself," the Gnome remarked afterward, bent next to the fire to scrape clean the pan. "Learned a few useful things over the years."

"How long have you been a tracker?" Jair asked him, intrigued.

"Most of my life. Began learning when I was your age." He finished with the cookware, stood up and came back over to the Valeman. "What do you know about trackers?"

Briefly Jair told him about the old tracker who had boarded at the inn, of their conversations, and of the tracking games they'd played while the man's leg had healed. Slanter listened quietly, obvious interest reflected in his rough yellow features. When Jair had finished, the Gnome sat back, a distant look in his sharp eyes.

"I was like you once, long time ago. Used to think about nothing but being a tracker. Left home with one finally—an old Borderman. I was younger than you. Left home, went right out of the Eastland into Callahorn and the Northland. Gone better than fifteen years. Traveled all the lands at one time or another, you know. As much of them in me as Eastland Gnome. Odd, but I'm kind of a homeless sort because of it. Gnomes don't really trust me, because I've been away too long, seen too much of what else there is ever to really be the same as them. A Gnome who's not a Gnome. I've learned more than they ever will, shut away in the Eastland forests like they are. They know it, too. They barely tolerate me. They respect me, though, because I'm the best that there is at what I do."

He glanced sharply at Jair. "That's why I'm here—because I'm the best. The Druid Allanon—the fellow you don't know, remember?—he came into the Ravenshorn and Graymark, tried to get down into the Maelmord. But nothing goes down into that pit, not Druid nor Devil. The Wraiths knew he was there and went after him. One walker, a patrol of Gnome Hunters, and me to track. Tracked to your village, then waited for someone to show. Thought someone would, even though it was pretty clear that the Druid had already gone elsewhere. And who should appear but you?"

Jair's mind was racing. How much does he know? Does he know the reason that Allanon came to Shady Vale? Does he know about the . . . ? And suddenly he remembered the Elfstones, tucked hastily within his tunic when he fled the Vale. Did he still have them? Or had Slanter found them? Oh, shades!

Eyes still fixed on those of the Gnome, he shifted cautiously against the ropes that bound him, trying to feel the pressure of the Stones against his body. But it was hopeless. The ties knotted his

clothing and gave him no sure feel for what he still had on him. He
dared not look down, even for an instant.

"Ropes cutting a bit?" Slanter asked suddenly.

He shook his head. "I was just trying to get comfortable." He
forced himself to sit back and relax. He changed the subject back.
"Why did you bother coming after me if you were supposed to be
tracking Allanon?"

Slanter cocked his head slightly. "Because I was tracking the
Druid to find out where he went, and I've done that. He went to
your village, to your family. Now he's gone back to the Eastland—
isn't that right? Oh, you needn't answer. At least not to me. But you
will have to answer to those who came with me when they get here
in the morning. A bit slow they are, but sure. I had to leave them to
be certain I caught you. You see, they want to know something of
Allanon's visit. They want to know why he came. And unfortunately
for you, they want to know one thing more."

He paused meaningfully, eyes boring into Jair. The Valeman
took a deep breath. "About the magic?" he whispered.

"Sharp fellow." Slanter's smile was hard.

"What if I don't want to tell them?"

"That would be foolish," the Gnome said quietly.

They stared at each other wordlessly. "The Wraith would make
me tell, wouldn't he?" Jair asked finally.

"The Wraith is not your problem." Slanter snorted. "The
Wraith's gone north after the Druid. The Sedt is your problem."

The Valeman shook his head. "Sedt? What is a Sedt?"

"A Sedt is a Gnome chieftain—in this case, Spilk. He commands the patrol. A rather unpleasant fellow. Not like me, you see.
Very much an Eastland Gnome. He would just as soon cut your
throat as look at you. He's your problem. You'd better answer the
questions he asks."

He shrugged. "Besides, once you've told Spilk what he wants
to know, I'll do what I can to see that you're released. After all, our
fight's not with the Vale people. Our fight's with the Dwarves. Not to
disappoint you, but you're really not all that important. That magic

of yours is what's interesting. No, you answer the questions and I think you'll be turned loose quick enough."

Jair eyed him suspiciously. "I don't believe you."

Slanter drew back. "You don't? Well, here's my word on it, then. As good as your own." Heavy eyebrows arched. "It means as much to me as yours does, boy. Now take it."

Jair said nothing for a moment. Strangely enough, he thought the Gnome was telling him the truth. If he promised he would seek Jair's release, he would do just that. If he thought Jair would be released on answering the questions asked, Jair probably would. Jair grimaced. On the other hand, why should he trust any Gnome?

"I don't know," he muttered.

"You don't know?" Slanter shook his head hopelessly. "You'd think you had a choice, boy. You don't answer, Spilk goes to work on you. You still don't answer, he turns you over to the walkers. What do you think happens to you then?"

Jair went cold to the bone. He didn't care to think about what would happen then.

"I thought you were smart," the Gnome continued, wizened yellow features twisting into a grimace. "Smart, the way you got past those others back there—even got past the walker. So stay smart. What difference does it make now what you tell anyone? What difference if you tell the Sedt why the Druid came to see you? The Druid's gone by now anyway—won't likely catch up to him this side of the Eastland. He wouldn't tell you anything all that important anyway, would he? The magic—well, all they want to know about the magic is how you learned it. The Druid, maybe? Someone else?" He waited a moment, but Jair said nothing. "Well, anyway, just tell how you learned it and how you use it—simple enough and no skin off your nose. No games, just tell the truth. You do that, and that's the end of your use."

Again he waited for Jair to respond, and again the Valeman stayed silent.

Slanter shrugged. "Well, think on it." He stood up, stretched, and came over to Jair. Smiling cheerfully, he replaced the gag in the Valeman's mouth. "Sorry about the sleeping accommodations, but I can't be taking many chances with you. You've shown me that much."

Still smiling, he retrieved a blanket from the far side of the clearing, brought it over to Jair and wrapped it about him, tucking in the corners where the ropes bound him to the tree so that it would stay fixed. Then he walked over to the fire and kicked it out. In the faint glow of the embers, Jair could see his stocky form as it moved off into the dark.

"Ah, me—reduced to chasing down Valemen," the Gnome muttered. "Waste of talent. Not even a Dwarf! At least they could give me a Dwarf to track. Or the Druid again. Bah! Druid's gone back to help the Dwarves and here I sit, watching this boy . . ."

He muttered on a bit more, most of it unintelligible, and then his voice faded away entirely.

Jair Ohmsford sat alone in the dark and wondered what he was going to do when morning came.

He slept poorly that night, cramped and bruised by the ropes that bound him, haunted by the specter of what lay ahead. Considered from any point of view, his future appeared bleak. He could expect no help from his friends; after all, no one knew where he was. His parents and Brin, Rone, and Allanon all thought him safely housed at the inn at Shady Vale. Nor could he reasonably anticipate much consideration from his captors. Slanter's reassurances notwithstanding, he did not expect to be released, no matter how many questions he answered. After all, how would he answer questions about the magic? Slanter clearly thought it something he had been taught. Once the Gnomes learned it was not an acquired skill, but a talent he had been born with, they would want to know more. They would take him to the Eastland, to the Mord Wraiths . . .

So the night hours passed. He dozed at times, his weariness overcoming his discomfort and his worry—yet never for very long.

Then finally, toward morning, exhaustion overtook him, and at last he drifted off to sleep.

It was not yet dawn when Slanter shook him roughly awake.

"Get up," the Gnome ordered. "The others are here."

Jair's eyes blinked open, squinting into the predawn gray that shrouded the highland forest. The air was chill and damp, even with the blanket still wrapped about his body, and a fine fall mist clung about the dark trunks of the fir. It was deathly still, the forest life not yet come awake. Slanter bent over him, loosing the ropes that bound him to the tree. There were no other Gnomes in sight.

"Where are they?" he asked as the gag was slipped from his mouth.

"Close. A hundred yards down the slope." Slanter gripped the Valeman's tunic front and hauled him to his feet. "No games now. Keep the magic to yourself. I've let you loose from the tree so that you might look the part of a man, but I'll strap you back again if you cross me. Understand?"

Jair nodded quickly. Ropes still bound his hands and feet, and his limbs were so badly cramped he could barely manage to stand. He stood with his back against the fir, the muscles of his body aching and stiff. Even if he could manage to break free, he couldn't run far like this. His mind was dizzy with fatigue and sudden fear as he waited for his strength to return. Answer the questions, Slanter had advised. Don't be foolish. But what answers could he give? What answers would they accept?

Then abruptly a line of shadowy figures materialized from out of the gloom, trudging heavily through the forest trees. Two, three, half a dozen, eight—Jair watched as one by one they appeared through the mist, bulky forms wrapped in woolen forest cloaks. Gnomes—rugged yellow features glimpsed from within hoods drawn close, thick-fingered hands clasping spears and cudgels. Not a word passed their lips as they filed into the clearing, but sharp eyes fixed on the captive Valeman and there was no friendliness in their gaze.

"This him?"

The speaker stood at the forefront of the others. He was powerfully built, his body corded with muscle, his chest massive. He thrust the butt of his cudgel into the forest earth, gripping it with scarred, gnarled fingers, twisting it slowly.

"Well, is it?"

The Gnome glanced briefly at Slanter. Slanter nodded. The Gnome let his gaze shift back to Jair. Slowly he pulled clear the hood of his forest cloak. Rough, broken features dominated his broad face. Cruel eyes studied the Valeman dispassionately, probing.

"What's your name?" he asked quietly.

"Jair Ohmsford," Jair answered at once.

"What was the Druid doing at your home?"

Jair hesitated, trying to decide what he should say. Something unpleasant flickered in the Gnome's eyes. With a sudden snap of his hands he brought the cudgel about, sweeping the Valeman's feet from beneath him. Jair fell hard, the breath knocked from his body. The Gnome stood over him silently, then reached down, seized the front of his tunic and pulled him back to his feet.

"What was the Druid doing in your home?"

Jair swallowed, trying to hide his fear. "He came to find my father," he lied.

"Why?"

"My father is the holder of the Elfstones. Allanon will use them as a weapon against the Mord Wraiths."

There was an endless moment of silence. Jair did not even breathe. If Slanter had found the Elfstones in his tunic, the lie was already discovered and he was finished. He waited, eyes fixed on the Gnome.

"Where are they now, the Druid and your father?" the other said finally.

Jair exhaled. "Gone east." He hesitated, then added, "My mother and sister are visiting in the villages south of the Vale. I was supposed to wait at the inn for their return."

The Gnome grunted noncommittally. "I've got to try to protect them, Jair thought. Spilk was watching him carefully. He did not look away. You can't tell that I'm lying, he thought. You can't.

Then a gnarled finger lifted from the cudgel. "Do you do magic?"

"I . . ." Jair glanced at the dark faces about him.

The cudgel came up, a quick, sharp blow that caught Jair across the knees, throwing him to the earth once more. The Gnome smiled, eyes hard. He yanked Jair back to his feet.

"Answer me—do you do magic?"

Jair nodded wordlessly, mute with pain. He could barely stand.

"Show me," the Gnome ordered.

"Spilk." Slanter's voice broke softly through the sudden silence. "You might want to reconsider that request."

Spilk glanced briefly at Slanter, then dismissed him. His eyes returned to Jair. "Show me."

Jair hesitated. Again the cudgel came up. Even though Jair was ready this time, he could not move fast enough to avoid the blow. It caught him alongside the face. Pain exploded in his head, and tears flooded his eyes. He dropped to his knees, but Spilk's thick hands knotted in his tunic and once more he was hauled to his feet.

"Show me!" the Gnome demanded.

Then anger flooded through Jair—anger so intense that it burned. He gave no thought to what he did next; he simply acted. A quick, muted cry broke from his lips and turned abruptly to a frightening hiss. Instantly Spilk was covered with huge gray spiders. The Gnome Sedt shrieked in dismay, tearing frantically at the great hairy insects, falling back from Jair. The Gnomes behind him scattered, spears and cudgels hammering downward as they sought to keep the spiders from their own bodies. The Sedt went down under a flurry of blows, thrashing upon the forest earth, trying to dislodge the terrible things that clung so tenaciously to him, his cries filling the morning air.

Jair sang a moment longer and then quit. Had he not been bound hand and foot or had he not been dizzy still from the blows struck by Spilk, he would have taken advantage of the confusion the wishsong's use had created to attempt an escape. But Slanter had made certain he could not run. As the anger left him he grew silent.

For a few seconds Spilk continued to roll upon the ground, tearing at himself. Then abruptly he realized that the spiders were gone. Slowly he came to his knees, his breathing harsh and ragged, his battered face twisting until his eyes found Jair. He surged to his feet with a howl and threw himself at the Valeman, gnarled hands reaching. Jair stumbled back, his legs tangling in the ropes. In the next instant, the Gnome was atop him, fists hammering wildly. Dozens of blows struck Jair's head and face, seemingly all at once. Pain and shock washed through him.

Then everything went black.

He came awake again only moments later. Slanter knelt next to him, dabbing at his face with a cloth soaked in cold water. The water stung, and he jerked sharply at its touch.

"You got more sand than brains, boy," the Gnome whispered, bending close. "You all right?"

Jair nodded, reaching up to touch his face experimentally. Slanter knocked his hand away.

"Leave it be." He dabbed a few more times with the cloth, then allowed a faint grin to cross his rough face. "Scared old Spilk half to death, you did. Half to death!"

Jair glanced past Slanter to where the remainder of the patrol huddled at the far side of the clearing, eyes darting watchfully in his direction. Spilk stood apart from everyone, his face black with anger.

"Had to pull him off you myself," Slanter was saying. "Would have killed you otherwise. Would have beat your head in."

"He asked me to show him the magic," Jair muttered, swallowing hard. "So I did."

The thought clearly amused the Gnome, and he permitted himself another faint smile, carefully averting his face from the Sedt. Then he put his arm about Jair's shoulders and raised him to a sitting position. Pouring a short ration of ale from the container at his waist, he gave the Valeman a drink. Jair accepted the ale, swallowing and choking as it burned clear down to his stomach.

"Better?"

"Better," Jair agreed.

"Then listen." The smile was gone. "I've got to gag you again. You're in my care now—the others won't have anything to do with you. You're to be kept bound and gagged except for meals. So behave. It's a long journey."

"A long journey to where?" Jair did not bother to conceal the alarm in his eyes.

"East. The Anar. You're to be taken to the Mord Wraiths. Spilk's decided. He wants them to have a look at your magic." The Gnome shook his head solemnly. "Sorry, but there's no help for it. Not after what you did."

Before Jair could say anything, Slanter shoved the gag back into his mouth. Then, loosing the ties that bound Jair's ankles, he pulled the Valeman to his feet. Producing a short length of rope, he looped one end through Jair's belt and tied the other end to his own.

"Spilk," he called over to the other.

The Gnome Sedt turned wordlessly and started off into the forest. The remainder of the patrol followed after.

"Sorry, boy," Slanter repeated.

Together, they walked from the clearing into the early morning mist.

VII

ALL THAT DAY, THE GNOMES MARCHED JAIR NORTH THROUGH the wooded hill country bordering the western perimeter of Leah. Embracing the shelter of the trees, forsaking the more accessible roadways that crisscrossed the highlands, they kept to themselves and to their purpose. It was a long, exhausting trek for the Valeman, made no less difficult by the way in which he was secured, for his bonds cut into and cramped his body with every step. His discomfort might not have gone unnoticed, but it went unrelieved. Nor did his captors evidence the slightest concern for the toll that the pace of their march was extracting from him. Rugged, hardened veterans of the border wars of the deep Eastland, they were accustomed to forced marches through the worst kind of country and under the least favorable of conditions—marches that at times lasted several days. Jair was fit, but he was no match for these men.

By nightfall, when they at last arrived on the shores of the Rainbow Lake and made their way down to a secluded cove to set their camp, Jair could barely walk. Bound once again to a tree, given a quick meal and a few swallows of ale, he was asleep in minutes.

The following day passed in similar fashion. Awake at sunrise, the Gnomes took him east along the shores of the lake, skirting the northern highlands that they might reach the concealment of the Black Oaks. Three times that day, the Gnomes paused to rest—once at midmorning, again at midday and a final time at midafternoon.

The remainder of the day, they walked and Jair walked with them, his body aching, his feet blistered and raw. Pushed to the limit of his endurance, he refused to give them the satisfaction of seeing him falter, even for a moment. Determination gave him strength, and he kept pace.

All the time they marched him through the highlands, he thought about escape. It never entered his mind that he wouldn't escape; it was only a question of when. He even knew how he would manage it. That part was easy. He would simply make himself invisible to them. That was something they wouldn't be looking for—not so long as they thought his magic limited to creating imaginary spiders and snakes. They didn't understand that he could do other things as well. Sooner or later he would be given the opportunity. They would free him just long enough so that he could make use of the magic one more time. Just a moment was all that he would need. Like that, he would be gone. The certainty of it burned bright within him.

There was added incentive now for his need to escape. Slanter had told him that the walker that had come into the Vale with the Gnome patrol had gone east again in search of Allanon. But how was Allanon to know that the Mord Wraith tracked him? There was only Jair to warn him, and the Valeman knew he must find a way to do so.

His plans for escape were still foremost in his thoughts when, later that afternoon, they passed into the Black Oaks. The great dark trunks rose about them like a wall. In moments the sun was screened away. They traveled deep into the forest, following a pathway that ran parallel to the shoreline of the lake, winding their way steadily eastward into dusk. It was cooler here, deep and silent within these trees. Like a cave opening downward into the earth, the forest took them in and swallowed them up.

By sundown, the highlands were far behind. Camped within a small clearing sheltered by the oaks and a long ridgeline that dropped away northward to the water's edge, the Valeman sat back against a moss-grown trunk a dozen times his girth—bound and gagged still—and watched Slanter scoop meat stew from a kettle that simmered over a small cooking fire. Weary and discomfited, Jair nevertheless found himself studying the Gnome, pondering the contradictions he saw in the tracker's character. For two days he had had ample opportunity to observe Slanter, and he was as puzzled by the Gnome now as he had been when he had first conversed with him that night following his capture. What sort of fellow was he? True, he was a Gnome—yet at the same time, he didn't seem like a Gnome. Certainly he wasn't an Eastland Gnome. He wasn't like these Gnomes he traveled with. Even they seemed to sense that much. Jair could see it in their behavior toward him. They tolerated him, but they also avoided him. And Slanter had acknowledged that to Jair. He was as much an outsider in his own way as the Valeman. But it was more than that. There was something in the Gnome's character that set him apart from the others—an attitude, perhaps, an intelligence. He was smarter than they. And that was due most probably to the fact that he had done what they had not. A skilled tracker, a traveler of the Four Lands, he was a Gnome who had broken the traditions of his people and gone out of the homeland. He had seen things they had not. He understood things they could not. He had learned.

Yet in spite of all that, he was here. Why?

Slanter ambled over from the fire with a plate of stew in one hand and squatted down beside him. Loosing the gag so that his mouth was clear, the Gnome began to feed him.

"Doesn't taste too bad, does it?" The dark eyes watched him.

"No—tastes good."

"You can have more if you want." Slanter stirred the stew on the plate absently. "How do you feel?"

Jair met his gaze squarely. "I hurt everywhere."

"Feet?"

"Especially the feet."

The Gnome set down the stew. "Here, let me have a look."

He pulled free the Valeman's boots and stockings and examined the blistered feet, shaking his head slowly. Then he reached over into his pack and pulled free a small tin. Loosening its cap, he dipped his fingers in and extracted a reddish salve. Slowly he began rubbing it into the open wounds. The salve was cool and eased the pain.

"Should take away some of the sting, help toughen the skin when you walk," he said. He rubbed on some more, glanced up momentarily, his rough yellow face creasing with a sad smile, and then looked down again. "Tough sort of nut, aren't you?"

Jair didn't say anything. He watched the Gnome finish applying the salve, then resumed his meal. He was hungry and had two plates of the stew.

"Take a drink of this." Slanter held the ale container to his lips when the food was gone. He took several swallows, grimacing. "You don't know what's good for you," the Gnome told him.

"Not that stuff." Jair scowled.

Slanter sat back on his heels. "I heard something a little while ago I think you ought to know. It's not good news for you." He paused, glancing casually over his shoulder. "We're to meet with a walker the other side of the Oaks. There'll be one waiting for us. Spilk said so."

Jair went cold. "How does he know that?"

Slanter shrugged. "Prearranged meet, I guess. Anyway, I thought you should know. We'll be through the Oaks tomorrow."

Tomorrow? Jair felt his hopes fade instantly. How could he escape by tomorrow? That wasn't enough time! He had thought he would have at least a week and maybe more before they reached the deep Anar and the Mord Wraiths' stronghold. But tomorrow? What was he going to do?

Slanter watched him as if reading his thoughts. "I'm sorry, boy. I don't care for it either."

Jair's eyes shifted to meet his, and he tried to keep the desperation from his voice. "Then why don't you let me go?"

"Let you go?" Slanter laughed tonelessly. "You're forgetting who's with whom, aren't you?"

He took a long swallow from the ale pouch and sighed. Jair

leaned forward. "Why are you with them, Slanter? You're not like them. You don't belong with them. You don't . . ."

"Boy!" The Gnome cut him off sharply. "Boy, you don't know anything at all about me! Nothing! So don't be telling me who I'm like and who I belong with! Just look after yourself!"

There was a long silence. In the center of the clearing, the other Gnomes were gathered about the fire, drinking ale from a heavy leather jug. Jair could see the glitter of their sharp eyes as they glanced in his direction from time to time. He could see the suspicion and fear mirrored there.

"You're not like them," he repeated softly.

"Maybe," Slanter agreed suddenly, staring off into the dark. "But I know enough not to cut against the grain. There's a change in the wind. It's shifted about and it's blowing straight out of the east, and everything in its path will be swept away. Everything! You don't begin to see the half of it. The Mord Wraiths are power like nothing I'd ever imagined, and the whole of the Eastland belongs to them. But that's only today. Tomorrow . . ." He shook his head slowly. "This is no time for a Gnome to be anything other than a Gnome."

He drank again of the ale, then offered it to Jair. The Valeman shook his head. His mind worked frantically.

"Slanter, would you do me a favor?" he asked.

"Depends."

"Would you take the ropes off my arms and hands for a few minutes?" The Gnome's black eyes narrowed. "I just want to rub them a bit, try to get some feeling back. I've had the ropes on for two days now. I can barely feel my fingers. Please—I give you my word I won't try to escape. I won't use the magic."

Slanter studied him. "Your word's been pretty good until now."

"It's still good. You can leave my legs and feet bound if you like. Just give me a moment."

Slanter kept looking at him for a few minutes longer, then nodded. Moving forward, he knelt beside the Valeman, then loosened the knots that secured the ropes about his arms and wrists and let them fall slack. Gingerly Jair began to massage himself, rubbing first his hands, then his wrists, his arms, and finally his body. In the darkness before him, he saw the glint of a knife in Slanter's hand. He kept his eyes lowered and his thoughts hidden. Slowly he worked, all the while thinking, don't let him guess, don't let him see . . .

"That's enough." Slanter's voice was gruff and sudden, and he drew the ropes tight again. Jair sat quietly, offering no resistance. When the ropes had again been secured, Slanter moved back in front of him.

"Better?"

"Better," he said quietly.

The Gnome nodded. "Time to get some sleep." He drank one time more from the ale pouch, then bent forward to test the bonds. "Sorry about the way this thing's worked out, boy. I don't like it any better than you do."

"Then help me escape," Jair pleaded, his voice a whisper.

Slanter stared at him wordlessly, blunt features expressionless. Gently he placed the gag back in Jair's mouth and rose.

"Wish you and I had never met," he murmured. Then he turned and walked away.

In the darkness, Jair let himself go limp against the oak. Tomorrow. One day more, and then the Mord Wraiths would have him. He shuddered. He had to escape before then. Somehow, he had to find a way.

He breathed the cool night air deeply. At least he knew one thing now that he hadn't known before—one very important thing. Slanter hadn't suspected. He had permitted Jair those few moments of freedom from the ropes—time to rub life back into his limbs and body, time to relieve them just a bit of the ache and discomfort.

Time to discover that he still retained possession of the Elf-stones.

Too swift, it seemed, the morning came, dawn breaking gray and hard within the gloom of the Black Oaks. For the third day, the Gnomes marched Jair east. The warming touch of the sun was screened away by banks of storm clouds that rolled down from out of the north. A wind blew harsh and quick through the trees, chill with the promise of winter's coming. Wrapped in their short cloaks, the Gnomes bent their heads against the swirl of silt and leaves and trudged ahead.

How can I escape?

How?

The question repeated itself over and over in the Valeman's mind as he worked to keep pace with his captors. Each step marked the passing of the seconds that remained, the minutes, the hours. Each step took him closer to the Mord Wraith. This one day was all the time he had left. Somehow during the day he must find an opportunity to get free of his restraints long enough to utilize the wishsong. A single moment was all it would take.

Yet that moment might never come. He had not doubted that it would—until now. But the time slipped so fast from him! It was nearing midmorning, and already they had been on the march for several hours. Silently he berated himself for not seizing the opportunity Slanter had presented him with the night before when he had agreed to free him from his bonds. There had been time enough then to escape his captors. A few seconds to freeze them where they stood, covered with something so loathsome they could think of nothing else as he worked loose the bindings about his ankles, then a few seconds more to shift the pitch of his voice to hide him from their sight, and he would have been gone. Dangerous, yes, but he could have done it—except, of course, that he had given his word. What difference, if that word had been broken when it was given to a Gnome?

He sighed. It did make a difference somehow. Even with a Gnome, his word was still his word, and it meant something when he gave it. One's word was a matter of honor. It was not a thing that could be bandied about when convenient or slipped on and off like clothing to match changes in the weather. If he went back on it even once, that opened the door to a flood of excuses for going back on it every time thereafter.

Besides, he wasn't sure he could have done that to Slanter, Gnome or not. It was strange, but he had developed a certain attachment for the fellow. He wouldn't have described it as affection exactly. Respect was more like it. Or maybe he just saw something of himself in the Gnome because they were both rather different sorts. In any case, he didn't think he could have made himself trick Slanter like that, even to escape whatever it was that lay ahead.

He kicked at the leaves that blew across his path as he walked onward through the dark autumn day. He supposed that Rone Leah, were he there, would have had a plan for escape by now. Probably a good one. But Jair didn't have a clue as to what it might have been.

Morning slipped away. The wind died with the coming of midday, but its chill lingered in the forest air. Ahead, the terrain grew rougher, the earth broken and rocky as the ridgeline slanted south and a series of ravines curved down across their pathway. Still the wall of oaks stretched on, immutable giants blind to the ages that had passed them by. Heedless of a small life like mine, Jair thought as he glanced upward at the great towering black monsters. Shutting me away, so that I have nowhere that I might run.

The path wound down a steep embankment, and the patrol followed its dark rut. Then the oaks gave way to a solitary stand of pine and fir, crowded close within the massive black trunks, hemmed like captives, stiff and frightened. The Gnomes trudged into their midst, grunting irritably as sharp-tipped boughs nipped and cut at them. Jair ducked his head and followed, the long needles raking his face and hands with stinging swipes.

A moment later he broke clear of the tangle and found himself in a broad clearing. A pool of water gathered at the base of the ravine, fed by a tiny stream that trickled down from out of the rocks.

A man stood next to the pool.

The Gnomes came to an abrupt, startled halt. The man was drinking water from a tin cup, his head lowered. He was dressed all in black—loose tunic and pants, forest cloak, and boots. A black leather pack lay beside him on the ground. Next to it rested a long wooden staff. Even the staff was black, of polished walnut. The man

glanced up at them briefly. He looked to be an ordinary Southlander, a traveler, his face brown and creased by sun and wind, and
his light hair turned almost silver. Flint gray eyes blinked once; then
he looked away. He might have been any one of a hundred journeyers who passed through this part of the land daily. But from the
moment he saw the man, Jair knew instinctively that he was not.

Spilk also sensed something unusual about the man. The Sedt
glanced quickly at the Gnomes on either side as if to reassure himself that they were nine to the man's one, then turned his gaze on
Jair. Clearly he was upset that the stranger had seen their captive.
He hesitated a moment longer, then started forward. Jair and the
others followed.

Wordlessly, the patrol moved to the far end of the pool, their
eyes never leaving the stranger. The stranger paid no attention.
Stepping forward from his companions, Spilk filled his water pouch
from the trickle that ran down off the rocks, then drank deeply. One
by one, the other Gnomes did the same—all but Slanter, who stood
next to Jair, unmoving. The Valeman glanced at the Gnome and
found him staring fixedly at the stranger. There was something odd
reflected in his rough face, something . . .

Recognition?

The stranger's eyes lifted suddenly and met Jair's. The eyes were
flat and empty. For just an instant, they were locked upon his own,
and then the stranger was facing Spilk.

"Traveling far?" he asked.

Spilk spit the water from his mouth. "Keep your nose to yourself."

The stranger shrugged. He finished his water in his cup, then
bent down to tuck the cup back into his pack. When he straightened again, the black staff was in his hand.

"Is the Valeman really so dangerous?"

The Gnomes stared at him sullenly. Spilk tossed aside his water
pouch, took a firm grip on his cudgel and came around the edge of
the pool until he stood at the forefront of his men.

"Who are you?" he snapped.

Again the stranger shrugged. "No one you want to know."

Spilk smiled coldly. "Then walk away from here while you still can. This doesn't concern you."

The stranger didn't move. He seemed to be thinking the matter through.

Spilk took a step toward him. "I said this doesn't concern you."

"Nine Gnome Hunters traveling through the Southland with a Valeman they've bound and gagged like a trussed pig?" A faint smile crossed the stranger's weathered face. "Maybe you're right. Maybe it doesn't concern me."

He bent down to retrieve his pack, slipped it across one shoulder and started away from the pool, passing in front of the Gnomes. Jair felt his hopes, momentarily lifted, fade again. For just a moment, he had thought the stranger meant to aid him. He started to turn toward the pool again, thirsty for a drink of the water, but Slanter blocked his way. The Gnome's eyes were still on the stranger, and now his hand came up slowly to grip Jair's shoulder, guiding him back several paces from the others in the patrol.

The stranger had stopped again.

"On the other hand, maybe you're wrong." He stood no more than a half-dozen feet from Spilk. "Maybe this does concern me after all."

The stranger's pack slid from his shoulder to the ground, and the flint gray eyes fixed on Spilk. The Sedt stared at him, disbelief and anger twisting the blunt features of his face. Behind him, the other Gnomes glanced at one another uneasily.

"Stay behind me." Slanter's voice was a soft hiss in his ear, and the Gnome stepped in front of him.

The stranger moved closer to Spilk. "Why don't you let the Valeman go?" he suggested softly.

Spilk swung the heavy cudgel at the stranger's head. Quick as he was, the stranger was quicker, blocking the blow with his staff. The stranger stepped forward then, a smooth, effortless movement.

Up came the staff, striking once, twice. The first blow caught the Sedt in the pit of his stomach, bending him double. The second caught him squarely across the head and dropped him like a stone.

For an instant, no one moved. Then, with a howl of dismay, the other Gnomes attacked, swords ripped from their sheaths and axes and spears lifting. Seven strong, they converged on the lone black figure. Jair bit into the gag that held him speechless when he saw what happened next. Cat-quick, the stranger blocked the assault, the black staff whirling. Two more Gnomes dropped in their tracks with shattered skulls. The remainder thrust and cut blindly as the stranger danced away. A glint of metal appeared from beneath the black cloak, and a short sword was gripped in the stranger's hand. Seconds later, three more of the attackers lay stretched upon the earth, their life blood seeping from their bodies.

Now there were but two of the seven still standing. The stranger crouched before them, feinting with the short sword. The Gnomes glanced hurriedly at each other and backed away. Then one caught sight of Jair, half hidden behind Slanter. Abandoning his companion, he leaped for the Valeman. But to Jair's surprise, Slanter blocked the way, a long knife in his hand. The attacker howled in rage at the betrayal, his own weapon sweeping up. From twenty feet away, the stranger was a blur of motion. Uncoiling with the suddenness of a snake, he whipped one arm forward, and the attacker went rigid in midstride, a long knife buried in his throat. Soundlessly, he collapsed.

That was enough for the remaining Gnome. Heedless of everything else, he bolted from the clearing and disappeared into the forest.

Only Jair, Slanter, and the stranger remained. The Gnome and the stranger faced each other wordlessly for a moment, weapons poised. The forest had gone silent about them.

"You, also?" the stranger asked quietly.

Slanter shook his head. "Not me." The hand with the long knife dropped to his side. "I know who you are."

The stranger did not seem surprised, but merely nodded. With his sword, he gestured at the Gnomes who lay stretched between them. "What about your friends?"

Slanter glanced down. "Friends? Not this lot. The misfortunes of war brought us together, and we'd traveled too far already the same road. Stupid bunch, they were." His dark eyes found the stranger's. "The journey's done for me. Time to choose another way."

He reached back with the long knife and severed the ropes that bound Jair. Then he sheathed the knife and slipped loose the gag.

"Looks like you've got the luck this day, boy," he growled. "You've just been rescued by Garet Jax!"

VIII

Even in a tiny Southland village like Shady Vale, they had heard of Garet Jax.

He was the man they called the Weapons Master—a man whose skill in single combat was so finely developed that it was said he had no equal. Choose whatever weapon you might or choose no other weapon than hands, feet, and body, and he was better than any man alive. Some said more than that—he was the best who had ever lived.

The stories were legend. Told in taverns when the drinks were passed about in the hours after work was finished, in village inns by travelers come from far, or about campfires and hearths when the night settled down about those gathered and the dark formed a bond that seemed strengthened somehow by the sharing of words, the stories of Garet Jax were always there. No one knew where he had come from; that part of his life was shrouded in speculation and rumor. But everyone knew at least one place that he had been and had a story to go with it. Most of the stories were true, verified by more than one who had been witness to its happening. Several were common knowledge, told and retold the length and breadth of the Southland and parts of the other lands as well.

Jair Ohmsford knew them all by heart.

One tale, the earliest perhaps, was of Gnome raiders preying on the outlying villages of Callahorn in the eastern borderlands. Smashed once by the Border Legion, the raiders had broken into small groups—remnants of fewer than a dozen men each in most cases—who continued to plague the less protected homesteads and hamlets. Legion patrols scouted the lands at regular intervals, but the raiders stayed hidden until they were gone. Then one day a band of ten struck a farmer's home just south of the Mermidon's joinder with the Rabb. There was no one there but the farmer's wife, small children, and a stranger—little more than a boy himself—who had stopped to share a brief meal and a night's sleep in exchange for chores that needed doing. Barricading the family in a storm cellar, he met the raiders as they tried to force their way in. He killed eight before the two remaining fled. After that, the raids slowed somewhat, it was said. And everyone began to talk about the stranger named Garet Jax.

Other tales were equally well known. In Arborlon, he had trained a special unit of the Home Guard to act as defenders of the Elven King Ander Elessedil. In Tyrsis, he had trained special units of the Border Legion, and others in Kern and Varfleet. He had fought for a time in the border wars between the Dwarves and Gnomes, instructing the Dwarves on weapons' use. He had traveled for a time in the deep Southland, engaged in the civil wars that raged between member states of the Federation. He had killed a lot of men there, it was said; he had made a great many enemies. He could not go back into the deep Southland anymore . . .

Jair cut short his thinking, aware suddenly that the man was staring at him, almost as if reading his thoughts. He flushed. "Thanks," he managed.

Garet Jax said nothing. Flint gray eyes regarded him without expression a moment longer, then turned away. The short sword disappeared back within the shadows of the cloak, and the man in black began checking the bodies of the Gnomes who lay scattered about him. Jair watched a moment, then glanced furtively at Slanter.

"Is that really Garet Jax?" he whispered.

Slanter gave him a black look. "I said so, didn't I? You don't for-

get someone like that. Knew him five years ago when he was training Legion soldiers in Varfleet. I was tracking for the Legion then,
passing time. Like iron I was, but next to him . . ." He shrugged.
"I remember once, there were some hard sorts, mad about being
passed over in training or something. Went after Jax with pikes
when his back was turned. He didn't even have a weapon. Four of
them, all bigger than he was." The Gnome shook his head, eyes distant. "He killed two of them, broke up the other two. So quick you
could barely follow. I was there."

Jair looked back again at the black-garbed figure. A legend,
they said. But they called him other things, too. They called him an
assassin—a mercenary with no loyalties, no responsibilities except
to those who paid him. He had no companions; Garet Jax always
traveled alone. No friends, either. Too dangerous, too hard for that.

So why had he helped Jair?

"This one's still alive."

The Weapons Master was bending over Spilk. Slanter and Jair
glanced at each other, then stepped over to have a look.

"Thick skull," Garet Jax muttered. He looked up as they joined
him. "Help me pick him up."

Together, they hauled the unconscious Spilk from the center of
the clearing to its far side, then propped him against a pine. Retriev-
ing the ropes that had been used to secure Jair, the Weapons Master
now bound the Sedt hand and foot. Satisfied, he stepped back from
the Gnome and turned to the two watching him.

"What's your name, Valeman?" he asked Jair.

"Jair Ohmsford," Jair told him, uneasy under the gaze of those
strange gray eyes.

"And you?" he asked Slanter.

"I'm called Slanter," the tracker replied.

There was a flicker of displeasure in the hard face. "Suppose you
tell me what nine Gnome Hunters were doing with this Valeman?"

Slanter grimaced, but then proceeded to relate to the Weapons
Master all that had befallen since the time he had first encountered
Jair in Shady Vale. Much to the Valeman's surprise, he even told the

other what Jair had done to him to escape. Garet Jax listened without comment. When the tale was finished, he turned again to Jair.

"Is what he says right?"

Jair hesitated, then nodded. It wasn't, of course—not entirely. A part of it was the fabricated story he had told to Spilk. But there was no reason to change that story now. Better that they both thought his father in Allanon's company with the Elfstones—at least until Jair knew whom he should trust.

A long pause followed as the Weapons Master thought the situation through. "Well, I don't think I should leave you alone in this country, Jair Ohmsford. Nor do I think it a good idea to leave you in the company of this Gnome." Slanter flushed darkly, but held his tongue. "I think you had better come with me. That way I'll know you're safe."

Jair stared at him uncertainly. "Come with you where?"

"To Culhaven. I have an appointment there, and you shall keep it with me. If this Druid and your father have gone into the Eastland, then quite possibly we shall find them there—or if not, at least we shall find someone who can take you to them."

"But I can't . . ." Jair started to say, then caught himself. He couldn't tell them about Brin. He had to be careful not to do that. But he couldn't go east either! "I can't do that," he finished. "I have a mother and sister in the villages south of the Vale who know nothing of what's happened. I have to go back to warn them."

Garet Jax shook his head. "Too far. I haven't time. We'll go east, then send word back when we get the chance. Besides, if what you've told me is right, it's more dangerous going back than going ahead. The Gnomes and the Wraiths know about you now; they know where you live. Once it's discovered you've escaped, they'll come looking for you there again. I didn't rescue you just to have you caught again the moment I'm gone."

"But . . ."

The flat gray eyes froze him. "It's decided. You go east." He glanced briefly at Slanter. "You go where you wish."

He strode back across the clearing to retrieve his pack and staff.

Jair stood looking after him, trapped by indecision. Should he tell
the man the truth or go east? But then, even if he told Garet Jax
the truth, what difference would that make? The Weapons Master
wasn't likely to take him back in either case.

"Well, luck to you, boy." Slanter was standing before him looking less than happy. "No hard feelings, I hope."

Jair stared at him. "Where are you going?"

"What difference does it make?" The Gnome shot a venomous
glance at Garet Jax. Then he shrugged. "Look, you're better off with
him than me. I should have gone my own way long ago."

"I haven't forgotten that you helped me, Slanter—all during the
journey," Jair said quickly. "And I think you would have helped me
again if I needed it."

"Well, you're wrong!" the Gnome cut him short. "Just because
I felt sorry for you doesn't. . . . Look, I'd have turned you over to the
walkers just as quick as Spilk, because that would have been the
smart thing to do! You and this Weapons Master don't begin to see
what you're up against!"

"I saw you stand there with that knife when the other Gnome
came at me!" Jair insisted. "What about that?"

Slanter snorted, turning away angrily. "If I'd had any brains at
all, I'd have let him have you. Do you know what I've done to myself? I can't even go back to the Eastland now! That Gnome who ran
off will tell them everything I did! Or Spilk, once he gets free!" He
threw up his hands. "Well, who cares? Not really my country anyway. Don't belong there; haven't for years. Wraiths can't be worried
about tracking one poor Gnome. I'll go north for a time, or maybe
south into the cities, and let this whole thing take its own course."

"Slanter . . ."

The Gnome wheeled suddenly, his voice a hiss. "But that
one—he isn't any better than me!" He gestured angrily at Garet Jax,
who was drinking again from the pool. "Treats me as if this was all
my doing—as if I was the one responsible! I didn't even know about
you, boy! I came here hunting the Druid! I didn't like chasing after
you, taking you off to the Wraiths!"

"Slanter, wait a minute!" Mention of the Mord Wraiths re-minded the Valeman of something he had almost forgotten in his relief at being freed. "What about the walker we were supposed to meet on the other side of the Oaks?"

Slanter was annoyed at having his tirade cut short. "What about him?"

"He'll still be there, won't he?" Jair asked quietly.

The Gnome hesitated, then nodded. "I see your point. Yes, he'll be there." He frowned. "Just go another way; go around him."

Jair stepped close. "Suppose *he* decides to go through him?" He motioned faintly toward Garet Jax.

Slanter shrugged. "Then there'll be one less Weapons Master."

"And one less of me."

They stared at each other in silence. "What do you want from me, boy?" the Gnome asked finally.

"Come with us."

"What!"

"You're a tracker, Slanter. You can get us past the walker. Please, come with us."

Slanter shook his head emphatically. "No. That's the Eastland. I can't go back there. Not now. Besides, you want *me* to take you to Culhaven. Me! The Dwarves would love that!"

"Just to the border, Slanter," Jair pressed. "Then go your own way. I won't ask for any more than that."

"I'm greatly appreciative of that!" the Gnome snapped. Garet Jax was coming back over to join them. "Look, what's the point of all this? That one wouldn't want me along anyway."

"You don't know that," Jair insisted. He turned as the Weapons Master came up to them. "You said that Slanter could go where he wished. Tell him then that he can come with us."

Garet Jax looked at the Gnome. Then he looked back at Jair.

"He's a tracker," Jair pointed out. "He might be able to help us avoid the walkers. He might be able to find a safe route east."

The Weapons Master shrugged. "The choice is his."

There was a long, awkward silence. "Slanter, if you do this, I'll show you a little of how the magic works," Jair said finally.

Sudden interest filled the Gnome's dark eyes. "Well now, that's worth a chance or . . ." Then he stopped. "No! What are you trying to do to me? Do you think you can bribe me? Is that what you think?"

"No," Jair answered hastily. "I just . . ."

"Well, you can't!" the other cut him short. "I don't take bribes! I'm not some . . . !" He sputtered off into silence, unable to find the words to express what it was that he wasn't. Then he straightened. "If it means this much to you, if it's this important, then all right, I'll come. If you want me to come, I'll come—but not for a bribe! I'll come because I want to come. My idea, understand? And just to the border—not a step farther! I want nothing to do with the Dwarves!"

Jair stared at him in astonishment for a moment, then quickly stuck out his hand. Solemnly, Slanter shook it.

It was decided that Spilk would be left just as he was. It would take him considerable time to free himself, but eventually he would do so. If worse came to worst, he could always chew his way through the ropes, Slanter suggested blackly. If he yelled for help, perhaps someone would hear him. He would have to be careful though. The Black Oaks were populated by a particularly vicious species of timber wolf, and the calls were likely to draw their attention. On the other hand, the wolves might drift in for water anyway . . .

Spilk heard the last of this, stirring awake as Jair and his companions were preparing to set out. Dazed and angered, the burly Gnome threatened that they would all meet a most unpleasant end when he caught up with them again—and catch up with them he would. They ignored the threats—though Slanter appeared somewhat uneasy at hearing them—and minutes later the Sedt was left behind.

It was strange company in which Jair found himself now—

a Gnome who had tracked him down, taken him prisoner, and kept him so for three days, and a legendary adventurer who had killed dozens more men than he had seen years on this earth. Here they were, the three of them, and Jair found the alliance thoroughly baffling. What were these two doing with him? Garet Jax might have gone his way without troubling himself about Jair, yet he had not done so. At risk to his own life, he had rescued the Valeman and then chosen to make himself temporary guardian. Why would a man like Garet Jax do such a thing? And Slanter might have rebuffed his request for help in avoiding whatever lay between them and the Anar, knowing the danger to himself and knowing that Garet Jax clearly didn't trust him and would watch his every move. Yet quite unexpectedly, almost perversely, he had chosen to come anyway. Again—why?

But it was his own motives that surprised him most of all when he began to consider them. After all, if their decision to be with him was baffling, what of his to be with them? Slanter, until just moments ago, had been his jailer! And he was genuinely frightened of Garet Jax, his rescuer. Over and over again, he thought of the Weapons Master facing those Gnomes—quick, deadly, terrifying, as black as the death he dealt.

For an instant, the picture hung suspended in the Valeman's mind; then quickly he thrust it aside.

Well, strangers on the road became companions for safety's sake, and Jair supposed that that was the way to view what had happened here. He must keep his wits. After all, he was free now and in no real danger. In an instant's time he could disappear. A single note of the wishsong, sung with the whisper of the wind, and he could be gone. Thinking about that gave him some sense of comfort. If he hadn't been so deep within the Black Oaks, if it weren't for the fact that the Mord Wraiths were searching for him, and if it weren't for his desperate need to find help somewhere . . .

He tightened his mouth against the words. Speculation on what might have been was pointless. He had enough with which to concern himself. Above all, he had to remember to say nothing about Brin or the Elfstones.

They had walked less than an hour through the Oaks when they came to a clearing in which half a dozen trails merged. Slanter, leading the way through the darkened forest, drew to a halt and pointed to a trail leading south.

"This way," he announced.

Garet Jax looked at him curiously. "South?"

Slanter's heavy brows knitted. "South. The walker will come down out of the Silver River country through the Mist Marsh. It is the quickest and easiest way—at least for those devils. They're not afraid of anything that lives in the marsh. If we want to take as few chances as possible, we'll go south around the Marsh through the Oaks, then turn north above the lowlands."

"A long way, Gnome," the Weapons Master murmured.

"At least that way you'll get where you're going!" the other snapped.

"Perhaps we could slip by him."

Slanter put his hands on his hips and squared his stocky frame about. "Perhaps we could fly, too! Hah! You haven't any idea at all what you're talking about!"

Garet Jax said nothing, his eyes fixing on the Gnome. Slanter seemed to sense suddenly that perhaps he had gone too far. Glancing hurriedly at Jair, he cleared his throat nervously and shrugged.

"Well, you don't know the Mord Wraiths like I do. You haven't lived among them. You haven't seen what they can do." He took a deep breath. "They're like something stolen from the dark—as if each were a bit of night broken off. When they pass, you never see them. You never hear them. You just sense them—you feel their coming." Jair shivered, remembering his encounter at Shady Vale and the invisible presence, just beyond the wall. "They leave no trail when they pass," Slanter went on. "They appear and disappear just as their name would suggest. Mord Wraiths. Black walkers."

He trailed off, shaking his head. Garet Jax looked over at Jair.

All the Valeman could think about was what he had felt when he had come back to his home that night in the Vale and found one of them waiting.

"I don't want to take the chance that we might stumble onto one of them," he said quietly.

The Weapons Master readjusted the pack across his shoulders. "Then we go south."

All afternoon they wound southward through the Black Oaks, following the pathway as it snaked ahead through the trees. Dusk fell over the forest, the gray light of midday fading rapidly into night. A faint mist began to seep through the trees, damp and clinging. It thickened steadily. The trail became more difficult to follow, disappearing at regular intervals as the mist settled in. Night sounds came out of the growing dark and the sounds were not pleasant.

Slanter called a halt. Should they stop for the night? he wanted to know. Both men looked to Jair. Stiff and tired, the Valeman glanced quickly about. Giant oaks rose about them, glistening black trunks hemming them in like a massive keep. Mist and shadows lay all around, and somewhere within them a black walker hunted.

Jair Ohmsford gritted his teeth against the aches and the weariness and shook his head. The little company went on.

Night also came to the clearing where Spilk sat bound to the great oak. All afternoon he had worked at his bonds, loosening the knots that held them and forcing them slack. Nothing else had passed through the clearing that day; no travelers had stopped to water; no wolves had come to drink. The crumpled bodies of his patrol lay where they had fallen, shapeless forms in the dusk.

His cruel features tightened as he strained against the ropes. Another hour or so and he would be free to hunt the ones who had done this to him. And he would hunt them to the very ends . . .

A shadow passed over him, and his head jerked up. A tall black form stood before him, cloaked and hooded, a thing of death strayed from the night. Spilk went cold to the bone.

"Master!" he whispered harshly.

The black figure gave no response. It simply stood there, looking down on him. Frantically the Sedt began to speak, the words tumbling over one another in his haste to get them out. He revealed all that had befallen him—the stranger in black, the betrayal by Slanter, and the escape of the Valeman with the magic voice. His muscled body thrashed against the bonds that held him fast, words inadequate to halt the fear that tightened about his throat. "I tried! Master, I tried! Free me! Please, free me!"

His voice broke, and the flood of words died away into stillness. His head drooped downward, and sobs wracked his body. For a moment, the figure above him remained motionless. Then one lean, black-gloved hand reached down to fasten on the Gnome's head, and red fire exploded forth. Spilk shrieked, a single, terrible cry.

The black-robed figure withdrew his hand, turned, and disappeared back into the night. No sound marked its passing.

In the empty clearing, Spilk's lifeless form lay slumped within its bonds, eyes open and staring.

IX

ACROSS THE TOWERING, JAGGED RIDGE OF THE DRAGON'S
Teeth, the night sky had gone from deepest blue to gray; the moon
and stars were beginning to fade in brilliance, and the eastern sky
began to glimmer faintly with the coming dawn.

Allanon's dark eyes swept the impassable wall of the mountains
that stood about him, across cliffs and peaks of monstrous, aged
rock, barren and ravaged by wind and time. Then his gaze dropped
quickly, almost anxiously, to where the stone split apart before him.
Below lay the Valley of Shale, doorstep to the forbidden Hall of
Kings, the home of the spirits of the ages. He stood upon its rim,
his black robes wrapped close about his tall, spare frame. There was
a sudden wistfulness on his face. A mass of black rock, glistening
like opaque glass, crushed and strewn blindly, stretched downward
to the valley floor, forming a broken walk. At the center of the rock
stood a lake, its murky waters colored a dull, greenish black, the
surface swirling sluggishly in the empty, windless silence—swirling
like a kettle of brew that some invisible hand stirred with slow, me-
chanical purpose.

Father, he whispered soundlessly.

A sudden scraping of booted feet on the loose rock caused him
to glance quickly about, reminded of the two who traveled with
him. They emerged now from the shadow of the rocks below to

stand beside him. Silently, they stared downward into the barren valley.

"Is this it?" Rone Leah asked shortly.

Allanon nodded. Suspicion cloaked the highlander's words and lingered in his eyes. It was always evident. There was no attempt to hide it.

"The Valley of Shale," the Druid said quietly. He started forward, winding his way down the rock-strewn slope. "We must hurry."

Suspicion and mistrust were in the eyes of the Valegirl as well, though she sought to keep them from her face. There was always suspicion in those who shared his travel. It had been there with Shea Ohmsford and Flick when he had taken them in search of the Sword of Shannara and with Wil Ohmsford and the Elven girl Amberle when he had taken them in search of the Bloodfire. Perhaps it was deserved. Trust was something to be earned, not blindly given, and to earn it, one must first be open and honest. He was never that—could never be that. He was a keeper of secrets that could be shared with no other, and he must always veil the truth, for the truth could not be told, but must be learned. It was difficult to keep close what he knew, yet to do otherwise would be to tamper with the trust that had been given to him and which he had worked hard to earn.

His gaze flickered back briefly to be certain that the Valegirl and the highlander followed him; then he turned his attention again to the scattered rock at his feet, picking his way in studied silence. It would be easy to forgo the trust he kept, to reveal all that he knew of the fate of those he counseled, to lay bare the secrets he kept, and to let events transpire in a fashion different from that which he had ordered.

Yet he knew that he could never do that. He answered to a higher code of being and of duty. It was his life and purpose. If it meant that he must endure their suspicion, then so it must be. Harsh though it was, the price was a necessary one.

But I am so tired, he thought. Father, I am so tired.

At the floor of the valley, he came to a halt. Valegirl and high-lander stopped beside him, and he turned to face them. One arm lifted from within the black robes and pointed to the waters of the lake.

"The Hadeshorn," he whispered. "My father waits there, and I must go to him. You will stand here until I call. Do not move from this place. Whatever happens, do not move. Except for you and me, only the dead live here."

Neither replied. They nodded their assent, eyes darting uneas-ily to where the waters of the Hadeshorn swirled soundlessly. He studied their faces a moment longer, then turned and walked away.

A strange sense of expectation swept through him as he ap-proached the lake, almost as if he were at the end of a long journey. It was always that way, he supposed, thinking back. There was that strange sense of coming home. Once Paranor had been the home of the Druids. But the other Druids were gone now, and this valley felt more like home than the Keep. All things began and ended here. It was here that he returned to find the sleep that renewed his life each time his journeys through the Four Lands were finished, with his mortal shell hung half within this world and half within the world of death. Here both worlds touched, a small crossing point that gave him some brief access to all that had been and all that would ever be. Most important of all, he would find his father here.

Trapped, exiled, and waiting to be delivered!

He blocked the thought from his mind. Dark eyes lifted briefly to the faint lightening of the eastern sky, then dropped again to the lake. Shea Ohmsford had come here once, many years ago, with his half brother Flick and the others of the small company who had gone in search of the Sword of Shannara. It had been prophesied that one of their number would be lost, and so it had happened. Shea had been swept over the falls below the Dragon's Crease. The Druid remembered the mistrust and suspicion the others had ex-hibited toward him. Yet he had been fond of Shea, of Flick, and of Wil Ohmsford. Shea had been almost like a son to him—would have been, perhaps, had he been permitted to have a son. Wil Ohmsford had been more a comrade-in-arms, sharing the responsibility for the search that would restore the Ellcrys and save the Elves.

His dark face creased thoughtfully. Now there was Brin, a girl with power that surpassed anything that her forebears had possessed in their time. What would she be to him?

He had reached the edge of the lake, and he came to a halt. He stood for a moment looking down into the depthless water, wishing . . . Then slowly he lifted his arms skyward, power radiating out from his body, and the Hadeshorn began to churn restlessly. The waters swirled faster, beginning to boil and hiss, and spray rose skyward. All about the Druid, the empty valley shuddered and rumbled as if awakened from a long, dreamless sleep. Then the cries rose, low and terrible, from out of the depths of the lake.

Come to me, the Druid called soundlessly. Be free.

The cries rose higher, shrill and less than human—imprisoned souls calling out in their bondage, straining to be free. The whole of the darkened valley filled with their wail, and the spray of the Hadeshorn's murky waters hissed with sharp relief.

Come!

From out of the roiling dark waters the shade of Bremen lifted, its thin, skeletal body a transparent gray against the night, shrouded and bent with age. Out of the waters, the terrible form rose to stand upon the surface with Allanon. Slowly the Druid lowered his arms, black robes wrapping tight as if for warmth; within his cowl, his dark face lifted to find the empty, sightless eyes of his father.

I am here.

The arms of the shade lifted then. Though they did not touch him, Allanon felt their cold embrace wrap about him like death. Slow and anguished, his father's voice reached out to him.

—The age ends. The circle is closed—

The chill within him deepened, froze him as ice. The words ran on together as one, and though he heard them all, each in painful detail, they were strung and tightened like knots upon a line. He listened to them all in silent desperation, afraid as he had never been afraid, understanding at last what was meant to be, must be, and would be.

In his hard, black eyes there were tears.

In frightened silence, Brin Ohmsford and Rone Leah stood where the Druid had left them and watched the emergence of the shade of Bremen from the depths of the Hadeshorn. Cold sliced through them, borne not on some errant wind, for there was none, but by the coming of the shade. Together they faced it, watched it stand before Allanon, tattered and skeletal, and saw its arms lift as if to embrace and draw the Druid's black form downward. They could hear nothing of its words; the air about them filled with the shrill cries let free from the lake. The rock shuddered and groaned beneath their feet. If they had been able, they would have fled and not looked back. At that moment, they were certain that death had been set loose to walk among them.

Then abruptly it was ended. The shade of Bremen turned, sinking slowly back into the murky waters. The cries surged higher, a frantic wail of anguish, then died into silence. The lake churned and boiled anew for a brief instant, then settled back, the waters swirling once again with placid calm.

In the east, the crest of the sun broke over the ragged edge of the Dragon's Teeth, silver gray light spilling down through the dying night shadows.

Brin heard Rone exhale sharply, and her hand reached over to grip his. At the edge of the Hadeshorn, Allanon dropped to his knees, head bowed.

"Rone!" she whispered harshly and started forward. The highlander seized her arm in warning, remembering what the Druid had told them, but she pulled free, racing for the lake. Instantly he was after her.

Together they rushed to the Druid, slid to a halt on the loose rock, and bent down beside him. His eyes were closed, and his dark face was pale. Brin reached for one great hand and found it as cold as ice. The Druid seemed to be in a trance. The Valegirl glanced hesitantly at Rone. The highlander shrugged. Ignoring him, she put her hands on the big man's shoulders and gently shook him.

"Allanon," she said softly.

The dark eyes flickered open, met hers. For an instant she saw clear through him. There was a terrible heedless anguish in his eyes. There was fear. And there was disbelief. It shocked her so that she moved back from him quickly. Then all that she had seen disappeared; in its place there was anger.

"I told you not to move." He pushed himself roughly to his feet.

His anger meant nothing, and she ignored it. "What happened, Allanon? What did you see?"

He said nothing for a moment, his eyes straying back across the murky green waters of the lake. His head shook slowly. "Father," he whispered.

Brin glanced hurriedly at Rone. The highlander frowned.

She tried again, one hand touching lightly the Druid's sleeve. "What has he told you?"

Depthless black eyes fixed upon her own. "That time slips away from us, Valegirl. That we are hunted on all sides, and that it shall be thus until the end. That end is determined, but he will not tell me what it is. He will only tell me this—that it will come, that you will see it, and that for our cause you are both savior and destroyer."

Brin stared at him. "What does that mean, Allanon?"

He shook his head. "I don't know."

"Very helpful." Rone straightened and looked away into the mountains.

Brin kept her eyes on the Druid. There was something more. "What else did he say, Allanon?"

But again the Druid shook his head. "Nothing more. That was all."

He was lying! Brin knew it instantly. Something more had passed between them, something dark and terrible that he was not prepared to reveal. The thought frightened her, the certainty of it an omen that, like her father and her great-grandfather before her, she was to be used to a purpose she did not comprehend.

Her thoughts snapped back to what he had said before. Savior and destroyer to their cause—she would be both, the shade had said. But how could that be?

"One other thing he told me," Allanon said suddenly—but Brin sensed at once it was not the thing he kept hidden. "Paranor is in the hands of the Mord Wraiths. They have penetrated its locks and broken through the magic that guards its passages. Two nights earlier it fell. Now they search its halls for the Druid histories and the secrets of the ancients. What they find will be used to enhance the power they already possess."

He faced them each in turn. "And they will find them, sooner or later, if they are not stopped. That must not be allowed to happen."

"You don't expect *us* to stop them, do you?" Rone asked quickly.

The black eyes narrowed. "There is no one else."

The highlander flushed. "Just how many of them are there?"

"A dozen Wraiths. A company of Gnomes."

Rone was incredulous. "And we're going to stop them? You and me and Brin? Just the three of us? Exactly how are we supposed to do that?"

There was a sudden, terrible anger in the Druid's eyes. Rone Leah sensed that he had gone a step too far, but there was no help for it now. He stood his ground as the big man came up against him.

"Prince of Leah, you have doubted me from the first," Allanon said. "I let that pass because you care for the Valegirl and came as her protector. But no more. Your constant questioning of my purpose and of the need I see has reached its end! There is little sense to it when your mind is already decided against me!"

Rone kept his voice steady. "I am not decided against you. I am decided for Brin. Where the two conflict, I stand with her, Druid."

"Then stand with her you shall!" the other thundered and wrenched the Sword of Leah from its scabbard where it lay strapped across the highlander's back. Rone went white, certain that the big man meant to kill him. Brin darted forward, crying out, but the Druid's hand lifted quickly to stop her. "Stay, Valegirl. This lies between me and the Prince of Leah."

His eyes fixed on Rone, harsh and penetrating. "Would you protect her, highlander, as I might myself? If it were possible, would stand as my equal?"

Rone's face hardened with determination across a mask of fear. "I would."

Allanon nodded. "Then I shall give you the power to do so."

One great hand fastened securely on Rone's arm, and he propelled the highlander effortlessly to the edge of the Hadeshorn. There he returned the Sword of Leah and pointed to the murky green waters.

"Dip the blade of the sword into the waters, Prince of Leah," he commanded. "But keep your hand and the pommel clear. Even the smallest touch of the Hadeshorn to mortal flesh is death."

Rone Leah stared at him uncertainly.

"Do as I say!" the Druid snapped.

Rone's jaw tightened. Slowly he dropped the blade of the Sword of Leah until it was completely submerged within the swirling waters of the lake. It passed downward without effort—as if there were no bottom to the lake and the shoreline marked the edge of a sheer drop. As the metal touched the lake, the waters about it began to boil softly, hissing and gurgling as if acid ate the metal clean. Frightened, Rone nevertheless forced himself to hold the blade steady within the waters.

"Enough," the Druid told him. "Draw it out."

Slowly Rone lifted the sword clear of the lake. The blade, once polished iron, had gone black; the waters of the Hadeshorn clung to its surface, swirling about it as if alive.

"Rone!" Brin whispered in horror.

The highlander held the sword steady before him, blade extended away from his body, eyes fixed on the water that spun and wove across the metal surface.

"Now stand fast!" Allanon ordered, one arm lifting free of the black robes. "Stand fast, Prince of Leah!"

Blue fire spurted out from the fingers of his hand in a thin, dazzling line. It ran all along the blade, searing, burning, igniting water and metal, and fusing them as one. Blue fire flared in a burst of incandescent light, yet no heat passed from the blade into the handle. While Rone Leah averted his eyes, he held the sword firm.

An instant later it was done, the fire was gone, and the Druid's arm lowered once more. Rone Leah looked down at his sword. The blade was clean, a polished and glistening black, the edges hard and true.

"Look closely, Prince of Leah," Allanon told him.

He did as he was asked, and Brin bent close beside him. Together they stared into the black, mirrored surface. Deep within the metal, murky green pools of light swirled lazily.

Allanon stepped close. "It is the magic of life and death mixed as one. It is power that now belongs to you, highlander; it becomes your responsibility. You are to be as much Brin Ohmsford's protector as I. You are to have power such as I. This sword shall give it to you."

"How?" Rone asked softly.

"As with all swords, this one both cuts and parries—not flesh and blood or iron and stone, but magic. The evil magic of the Mord Wraiths. Cut through or blocked away, such magic shall not pass. Thus you have committed yourself. You are to be the shield that stands before this girl now and until this journey ends. You would be her protector, and I have made you so."

"But why . . . why would you give me . . . ?" Rone stammered.

But the Druid simply turned and began to walk away. Rone stared after him, a stunned look on his face.

"This is unfair, Allanon!" Brin shouted at the retreating figure, angered suddenly by what he had done to Rone. She started after him. "What right have you . . . ?"

She never finished. There was a sudden, terrifying explosion and she was lifted off her feet and thrown to the valley floor. A whirling mass of red fire engulfed Allanon and he disappeared.

Miles to the south, his body fatigued and aching, Jair Ohmsford stumbled from night's shadows into a dawn of eerie mist and half-light. Trees and blackness seemed to fall away, pushed aside like a great curtain, and the new day was there. It was vast and empty, a monstrous vault of heavy mist that shut away all the world within its depthless walls. Fifty yards from where he stood, the mist began and all else ended. Sleep-filled eyes stared blankly, seeing the path of mottled deadwood and greenish water that stretched that short distance into the mist, yet not understanding what it was that had happened.

"Where are we?" he murmured.

"Mist Marsh," Slanter muttered at his elbow. Jair glanced over at the Gnome dumbly, and the Gnome stared back at him with eyes as tired as his own. "We've cut its border too close—wandered into a pocket. We'll have to backtrack around it."

Jair nodded, trying to organize his scattered thoughts. Garet Jax appeared suddenly beside him, black and silent. The hard, empty eyes passed briefly across his own, then out into the swamp. Wordlessly, the Weapons Master nodded to Slanter, and the Gnome turned back. Jair trailed after. There was no sign of weariness in the eyes of Garet Jax.

They had walked all night, an endless tiring march through the maze of the Black Oaks. It was little more than a distant, clouded memory now in the Valeman's mind, a fragmented bit of time lost in exhaustion. Only his determination kept him on his feet. Even fear had lost its hold over him after a time, the threat of pursuit no longer a thing of immediacy. It seemed that he must have slept even while walking, for he could remember nothing of what had passed. Yet there had been no sleep, he knew. There had been only the march . . .

A hand yanked him back from the swamp's edge as he strayed too close. "Watch where you walk, Valeman." It was Garet Jax next to him.

He mumbled something in response and stumbled on. "He's dead on his feet," he heard Slanter growl, but there was no response. He rubbed his eyes. Slanter was right. His strength was almost gone. He could not go on much longer.

Yet he did. He went on for hours, it seemed, trudging through the mist and the gray half-light, stumbling blindly after Slanter's blocky form, vaguely aware of the silent presence of Garet Jax at his elbow. All sense of time slipped from him. He was conscious only of the fact that he was still on his feet and that he was still walking. One step followed the next, one foot the other, and each time it was a separate and distinct effort. Still the path wore on.

Until . . .

"Confounded muck!" Slanter was muttering, and suddenly the entire swamp seemed to explode upward. Water and slime geysered into the air, raining down on the startled Valeman. A roar shattered the dawn's silence, harsh and piercing, and something huge rose up almost on top of Jair.

"Log Dweller!" he heard Slanter shriek.

Jair stumbled back, confused and frightened, aware of the massive thing that lifted before him, of a body scaled and dripping with the swamp, of a head that seemed all snout and teeth gaping open, and of clawed limbs reaching. He stumbled back, frantic now, but his legs would not carry him, too numb with fatigue to respond as they should. The huge thing was atop him, its shadow blocking away even the half-light, its breath fetid and raw.

Then something hurtled into him from one side, bowling him over, propelling him clear of the monster's claws. In a daze, he saw Slanter standing where he had stood, short sword drawn, swinging wildly at the massive creature that reached down for him. But the sword was a pitifully inadequate weapon. The monster blocked it away and sent it spinning from the Gnome's grasp. In the next instant one great, clawed hand fastened about Slanter's body.

"Slanter!" Jair screamed, struggling to regain his feet.

Garet Jax was already moving. He sprang forward, a blurred shadow, thrusting the black staff into the creature's gaping jaws and ramming it deep into the soft tissue of the throat. The Log Dweller roared in pain, jaws snapping shut upon the staff and breaking it apart. The clawed hands reached for the fragments caught in its throat, dropping Slanter back to the earth.

Again Garet Jax leaped up against the creature, his short sword drawn. So quickly that Jair could scarcely follow, he was upon the monster's shoulder and past the grasping claws. He buried the sword deep in the Log Dweller's underthroat. Dark blood spurted forth. Then swiftly he sprang clear. The Log Dweller was hurt now, pain evident in its wounded bellow. It turned with a lurch and stumbled blindly back into the mist and the dark.

Slanter was struggling back up again, dazed and shaken, but Garet Jax came instead to Jair, hauling him quickly to his feet. The Valeman's eyes were wide, and he stared at the Weapons Master in awe.

"I never saw . . . I never saw anyone move . . . so fast!" he stammered.

Garet Jax ignored him. With one hand fastened securely on his collar, he pulled the Valeman into the trees, and Slanter followed hurriedly after.

In seconds, the clearing was behind them.

Red fire burned all about the Druid, wrapping him in crimson coils and flaring out wickedly against the gray light of dawn. Dazed and half-blinded by the explosion, Brin struggled to her knees and shielded her eyes. Within the fire, the Druid hunched down against the shimmering black rock of the valley floor, a faint blue aura holding back the flames that had engulfed him. A shield, Brin realized—his protection against the horror that would destroy him.

Desperately she sought the maker of that horror and found it not twenty yards away. There, stark against the sun's faint gold as it slipped from beneath the horizon, a tall black form stood silhou-etted, arms raised and leveled, with the red fire spurting forth. A Mord Wraith! She knew immediately what it was. It had come upon them without a sound, caught them unawares, and struck down the Druid. With no chance to defend himself, Allanon was alive now only through instinct.

Brin surged to her feet. She screamed frantically at the black thing that attacked him, but it did not move, nor did the fire waver. In a steady, ceaseless stream, the fire spurted forth from the out-stretched hands to where the Druid crouched, whirling all about his folded body and hammering down against the faint blue shield that yet held it back. Crimson light flared and reflected skyward from the mirror surface of the valley rock, and the whole of the world contained within turned to blood.

Then Rone Leah rushed forward, springing past Brin to stand before her like a crouched beast.

"Devil!" he howled in fury.

He swept up the black metal blade of the Sword of Leah, giv-ing no thought in that moment to who it was he chose to aid or for whose sake he so willingly placed his own life in danger. He was in that moment the great-grandson of Menion Leah, as quick and reckless as his ancestor had ever thought to be, and instinct ruled his reason. Crying out the battle cry of his forebears for centuries gone, he attacked.

"Leah! Leah!"

He leaped into the fire, and the sword swept down, severing the ring that bound Allanon. Instantly, the flames shattered as if made of glass, falling from the Druid's crouched form in shards. The fire still flew from the Mord Wraith's hands; but like iron to a magnet, it was now drawn to the blade wielded by the red-haired highlander. It rushed in a sweep to the black metal and burned downward. Yet no fire touched Rone's hands; it was as if the sword absorbed it. The Prince of Leah stood squared away between Wraith and Druid, the Sword of Leah held vertically before him, crimson fire dancing off the blade.

Allanon rose up, as black and forbidding as the thing that had stalked him, free now of the flames that had held him bound. Lean arms lifted from beneath the robes, and blue fire exploded outward. It caught the Mord Wraith, lifted it clear off its feet, and threw it backward as if struck by a ram. Black robes flew wide, and a terrible, soundless shriek reverberated in Brin's mind. Once more the Druid fire flared outward, and an instant later the black thing it sought had been turned to dust.

Fire died into trailing wisps of smoke and scattered ash, and silence filled the Valley of Shale. The Sword of Leah sank, black iron clanging sharply against the rock as it dropped. Rone Leah's head lowered; a stunned look was in his eyes as they sought out Brin. She came to him, wrapped her arms about him and held him.

"Brin," he whispered softly. "This sword . . . the power . . ."

He could not finish. Allanon's lean hand fastened gently on his shoulder.

"Do not be frightened, Prince of Leah." The Druid's voice was tired, but reassuring. "The power truly belongs to you. You have shown that here. You are indeed the Valegirl's protector—and for this one time at least, mine as well."

The hand lingered a moment longer, then the big man was moving back along the path that had brought them in.

"There was only the one," he called back to them. "Had there been others, we would have seen them by now. Come. Our business here is finished."

"Allanon . . ." Brin started to call after him.

"Come, Valegirl. Time slips from us. Paranor needs whatever aid we can offer. We must go there at once."

Without a backward glance, he began to climb from the valley. Brin and Rone Leah followed in silent resignation.

X

IT WAS MIDMORNING BEFORE JAIR AND HIS COMPANIONS FI-
nally broke clear of the Black Oaks. Before them, rolling countryside stretched away—hill country to the north, lowlands to the
south. They took little time admiring either. Exhausted almost to
the point of collapse, they took just enough time to locate a sheltering clump of broad-leaf maple turned brilliant crimson by autumn's
touch. In seconds they were asleep.

Jair had no idea whether either of his companions thought to
keep watch during the time he slept, but it was Garet Jax who shook
him awake as dusk began to settle in. Wary of being so close yet to
the Mist Marsh and the Oaks, the Weapons Master wanted to find a
safer place to spend the coming night. The Battlemound Lowlands
were fraught with dangers all their own, so the little company turned
north into the hills. Somewhat refreshed by their half-day sleep, they
walked on almost to midnight before settling in to sleep until dawn
within a grove of wild fruit trees partially overgrown with brush. This
time Jair insisted at the outset that the three share the watch.

The following day, they traveled north again. By late afternoon,
they had reached the Silver River. Clear and sparkling in the fading
sunlight, it wound its way west through tree-lined banks and rocky
shoals. For several hours after, the three travelers followed the river
east toward the Anar, and by nightfall they were well away from the
Marsh and the Oaks. They had encountered no other journeyers

during their march, and there had been no sign of either Gnomes or black walkers. It appeared that for the moment, at least, they were safe from any pursuit.

It was night again by the time they found a small pocket sheltered by maple and walnut trees on a ridge above the river and made their camp. They decided to risk a fire, built one that was small and smokeless, ate a hot meal, and settled back to watch the coals die into ash. The night was clear and warm; overhead, stars began to wink into view, clustering in brilliant patterns across the dark backdrop of the sky. All about them, night birds sang, insects hummed, and the faint rush of the river's swift waters murmured in the distance. Drying leaves and brush gave a sweet and musty smell to the cool dark.

"Think I'll gather up some wood," Slanter announced suddenly after being silent for a time. He pushed himself heavily to his feet.

"I'll help," Jair offered.

The Gnome shot him a look of annoyance. "Did I ask for any help? I can gather wood by myself, boy."

Scowling, he trudged off into the dark.

Jair leaned back again, folding his arms across his chest. That typified the way things had been ever since the three of them had started out—no one saying much of anything and saying what they did without a great deal of warmth. With Garet Jax, it didn't matter. He was taciturn by nature, so his refusal to contribute anything in the way of conversation was not surprising. But Slanter was a garrulous fellow, and his uncommunicative posture was disquieting. Jair much preferred Slanter the way he had been before—brash, talkative, almost like a rough uncle. He wasn't like that now. He seemed to have withdrawn into himself and shut himself away from the Valeman—as if traveling with Jair had become almost distasteful.

Well, in a way it was, Jair supposed, reflecting on the matter. After all, Slanter hadn't wanted to come in the first place. He had only come because Jair had shamed him into it. Here he was, a Gnome traveling with one fellow who had been his prisoner before and another who didn't trust him a wink, all for the sole purpose of seeing to it that they safely reached a people who were at war with his own. And he wouldn't have been doing that, except that, in helping Jair, he had compromised his loyalties so that he was now little better than an outcast.

Then, too, there was the matter of the Log Dweller. Slanter had come to Jair's aid in an act of bravery that the Valeman still found mystifying—an act not at all in character for a fellow as opportunistic and self-centered as Slanter—and look what had happened. Slanter had failed to stave off the Log Dweller, had himself become a victim, and had been forced to rely on Garet Jax to save him. That must rankle. Slanter was a tracker, and trackers were a proud breed. Trackers were supposed to protect the people they guided, not the other way around.

Sparks shot out suddenly from the little fire, drawing his attention. A dozen feet away, stretched out against an old log, Garet Jax stirred and glanced over. Those strange eyes sought his, and Jair found himself wondering once more about the character of the Weapons Master.

"Guess I should thank you again," he said, drawing his knees up to his chest, "for saving me from that thing in the Marsh."

The other man looked back at the fire. Jair watched for a moment, trying to decide if he should say anything else.

"Can I ask you something?" he said finally.

The Weapons Master shrugged his indifference.

"Why *did* you save me—not just from the thing in the Marsh, but back there in the Oaks when the Gnomes had me prisoner?" The hard eyes suddenly fixed on him again, and he hurried his words before he had time to think better of them. "It's just that I don't quite understand what made you do it. After all, you didn't know me. You could have just gone your own way."

Garet Jax shrugged again. "I did go my own way."

"What do you mean?"

"My way happened to be your way. That's what I mean."

Jair frowned slightly. "But you didn't know where I was being taken."

"East. Where else would a Gnome patrol with a prisoner be going?"

Jair's frown deepened. He couldn't argue with that. Still, none of what the Weapons Master had said did much to explain why he had bothered to rescue Jair in the first place.

"I still don't see why you helped me," he pressed.

A faint smile crossed the other's face. "I don't appear to you to possess a particularly humanitarian nature, is that it?"

"I didn't say that."

"You didn't have to. Anyway, you're right—I don't."

Jair hesitated, staring at him.

"I said I don't," Garet Jax repeated. The smile was gone. "I wouldn't stay alive very long if I did. And staying alive is what I do best."

There was a long silence. Jair didn't know where else to go with the conversation. The Weapons Master pushed himself forward, leaning into the fire's warmth.

"But you interest me," he said slowly. His gaze shifted to Jair. "I suppose that's why I rescued you. You interest me, and not many things do that anymore..."

He trailed off, a distant look in his eyes. But an instant later it was gone, and he was studying Jair once more. "There you were, bound and gagged and under guard by an entire Gnome patrol armed to the teeth. Very odd. They were frightened of you. That intrigued me. I wanted to know what it was about you that frightened them so."

He shrugged. "So I thought it was worth the trouble to set you free."

Jair stared at him. Curiosity? Was that why Garet Jax had come to his aid—out of curiosity? No, he thought at once, it was more than that.

"They were frightened of the magic," he said suddenly. "Would you like to see how it works?"

Garet Jax looked back at the fire. "Later, maybe. The journey's not done yet." He seemed totally without interest.

"Is that why you're taking me with you to Culhaven?" Jair pressed.

"In part."

He let the words hang. Jair glanced over at him uneasily.

"What's the rest?"

The Weapons Master did not respond. He did not even look at the Valeman. He just leaned back against the fallen log, wrapped himself in the black travel cloak and watched the fire.

Jair tried a different approach. "What about Slanter? Why did you help him? You could have left him to the Log Dweller."

Garet Jax sighed. "I could have. Would that have made you any happier?"

"Of course not. What do you mean?"

"You seem to have formed an opinion of me as a man who does nothing for anyone without some personal benefit. You shouldn't believe everything you hear. You're young, not stupid."

Jair flushed. "Well, you don't like Slanter very much, do you?"

"I don't know him well enough to like or dislike him," the other replied. "I admit that for the most part I'm not particularly fond of Gnomes. But this one twice was willing to place himself in danger for your sake. That makes him worth saving."

He glanced over suddenly. "Besides, you like him and you don't want anything to happen to him. Am I right?"

"You're right."

"Well, that in itself seems rather curious, don't you think? As I said before, you interest me."

Jair nodded thoughtfully. "You interest me, too."

Garet Jax turned away. "Good. We'll both have something to think about on our way to Culhaven."

He let the matter drop and Jair did the same. The Valeman was by no means satisfied that he understood what it was that had persuaded the Weapons Master to aid either Slanter or himself, but it was obvious he would learn nothing more this night. Garet Jax was an enigma that would not easily be solved.

The fire had almost died away by now, causing Jair to remember that Slanter had gone in search of wood and not yet returned. He pondered for a moment whether or not he should do anything about it, then turned once more to Garet Jax.

"You don't think anything could have happened to Slanter, do you?" he asked. "He's been gone quite a while."

The Weapons Master shook his head. "He can look after himself." He rose and kicked at the fire, scattering the wood embers so that the flames died. "We don't need the fire any longer, anyway."

Returning to his spot next to the fallen log, he rolled himself in his travel cloak and was asleep in seconds. Jair lay silently for a time, listening to the man's heavy breathing and staring out into the dark. Finally he, too, rolled into his cloak and settled back. He was still a bit worried about Slanter, but he guessed that Garet Jax was right when he said the Gnome could look out for himself. Besides, Jair had grown suddenly sleepy. Breathing the warm night air deeply, he let his eyes close. For a moment, his mind wandered free and he found himself thinking of Brin, Rone, and Allanon, wondering where they were by now.

Then the thoughts scattered and he was asleep.

On a rise that overlooked the Silver River, lost in the shadows of an old willow, Slanter was thinking, too. He was thinking that it was time to move on. He had come this far because that confounded boy had shamed him into it. Imagine, offering him a bribe—that boy—as if he would stoop to accepting bribes from boys! Still, it was well meant, he supposed. The boy's desire to have his company had been genuine enough. And he did rather like the boy. There was a lot of toughness in the youngster.

The Gnome pulled his knees up to his chest and wrapped his arms about them thoughtfully. Nevertheless, this was a fool's mission. He was walking right into the camp of his enemy. Oh, the Dwarves weren't a personal enemy, of course. He didn't care a whit about Dwarves one way or the other. But just at the moment, they were at war with the Gnome tribes, and he doubted that it made a whole lot of difference what his feelings were about them. Seeing that he was a Gnome would be enough.

He shook his head. The risk was just too great. And it was all for that boy, who probably didn't know what he wanted from one day to the next, anyway. Besides, he had said he would take the boy as far as the border of the Anar, and they were almost there now. By nightfall of the coming day, they would probably reach the forests. He had kept his part of the bargain.

So. He took a deep breath and hauled himself to his feet. Time to be moving on. That was the way he had always lived his life—the way trackers were. The boy might be upset at first, but he would get over it. And Slanter doubted the boy would be in much danger with Garet Jax looking after him. Fact was, the boy would probably be better off that way.

He shook his head irritably. No reason to be calling Jair a boy, either. He was older than the Gnome had been when he first left home. Jair could look after himself if he had to. Didn't really need Slanter or the Weapons Master or anyone else. Not so long as he had that magic to protect him.

Slanter hesitated a moment longer, thinking it through once more. He wouldn't find out anything about the magic, of course— that was too bad. The magic intrigued him, the way the boy's voice could . . . No, his mind was made up. A Gnome in the Eastland had no business being anywhere near Dwarves. He was best off sticking to his own people. And now he could no longer do even that. Best thing for it was to slip back to the camp, pick up his gear, cross the river, and head north into the borderlands.

He frowned. Maybe it was just that the Valeman seemed like a boy . . .

Slanter, get on with it!

Quickly he turned about and disappeared into the night.

Dreams flooded Jair Ohmsford's sleep. He rode on horseback over hills, across grasslands, and through deep and shadowed forests, with the wind screaming in his ears. Brin rode at his side, her midnight hair impossibly long and flying. They spoke no words as they rode, yet each knew the other's thoughts and lived within the other's mind. On and on they raced, passing through lands they had never seen, vibrant and sprawling and wild. Danger lurked all about them: a Log Dweller, massive and reeking of the swamp; Gnomes, their twisted yellow faces leering their evil intentions; Mord Wraiths, no more than ghostly forms, featureless and eerie as they stretched from the dark. There were others, too—shapeless, monstrous things that could not be seen, but only felt, the sense of their presence somehow more terrible than any face could ever be. These beings of evil reached for them, claws and teeth ripping the air, eyes gleaming like coals in blackest night. The beings sought to pull Jair and his sister from their mounts and to tear the life from them. Yet always the things were too slow, an instant too late to achieve their purpose, as the swift horses carried Jair and Brin beyond their reach.

Yet the chase wore on. It did not end as a chase should end. It simply went on, an endless run through countryside that swept to the horizon. Though the creatures hunting them never quite managed to catch up to them, still there were always others lying in wait ahead. Exhilaration filled the pair at first. They were wild and free and nothing could touch them, brother and sister a match for all that sought to drag them down. But after a time, something changed. The change crept over them gradually, an insidious thing, until at last it lodged itself fully within them and they knew it for what it was. It had no name. It whispered to them of what must be: the race they ran could not be won for the things they ran from were a part of themselves; no horse, however swift, could carry them to safety. Look at what they were, the voice whispered, and they would see the truth.

Fly! Jair howled in fury, and urged his horse to run faster. But the voice whispered on, and about them the sky went steadily darker, the color faded from the land, and everything turned gray and dead. Fly! he screamed. He turned then to find Brin, sensing somehow that all was not well with her. The horror sprang to life before him and Brin was no longer there; she had been overtaken and consumed, swallowed by the dark monster that reached . . . that reached . . .

Jair's eyes snapped open. Sweat bathed his face, and his clothing was damp beneath the cloak in which he lay wrapped. Stars twinkled softly overhead, and the night was still and at peace. Yet the dream lingered in his mind, a vivid, living thing.

Then he realized that the fire was burning brightly once more, its flames crackling on new wood in the dark. Someone had rebuilt it.

Slanter . . . ?

Hurriedly he threw off the cloak and sat up, his eyes searching. Slanter was nowhere to be seen. A dozen feet away, Garet Jax slept undisturbed. Nothing had changed—nothing save the fire.

Then a figure stepped from the night, a thin and frail old man, his bent and aged frame clothed in white robes. Silver white hair and beard framed a weathered, gentle face, and a walking stick guided his way. Smiling warmly, he came into the light and stopped.

"Hello, Jair," he greeted.

The Valeman stared. "Hello."

"Dreams can be visions of what is to come, you know. And dreams can be warnings of what we must beware."

Jair was speechless. The old man turned and came about the fire, picking his way with care until at last he stood before the Valeman. Then he lowered himself gingerly to the ground, a wisp of life that a strong wind might blow from the earth.

"Do you know me, Jair?" the old man asked, his voice a soft murmur in the silence. "Let your memory tell you."

"I don't . . ." Jair started to say and then stopped. As if the suggestion had triggered something deep within him, Jair knew at once who it was that sat across from him.

"Speak my name." The other smiled.

Jair swallowed. "You are the King of the Silver River."

The old man nodded. "I am what you name me. I am also your friend, just as I once was friend to your father and to your great-grandfather before him—men with lives intertwined in purpose, given over to the land and her needs."

Jair stared at him wordlessly, then suddenly remembered the sleeping Garet Jax. Would not the Weapons Master waken . . . ?

"He will sleep while we talk," his unspoken question was answered. "No one comes to disturb us this night, child of life."

Child? Jair stiffened. But in the next instant his anger was gone, melted by what he saw in the other's face—the warmth, the gentleness, the love. With this old man there could be no anger or harsh feelings. There could be only respect.

"Hear me now," the aged voice whispered. "I have need of you, Jair. Let your thoughts have ears and eyes that you may understand."

Then everything about the Valeman seemed to dissolve away, and within his mind images began to form. He could hear the old man's voice speaking to him, the words strangely hushed and sad, giving life to what he saw.

The forests of the Anar lay before him and there was the Ravenshorn, a vast and sprawling mountain range that rose black and stark against a crimson sun. The Silver River wound through its peaks, a thin, bright ribbon of light against the dark rock. He followed its course upriver far into the mountains until at last he had traced it to its source, high within a single, towering peak. There stood a well, its waters spring-fed from deep within the earth, rising through the rock to spill over and begin the long journey west.

But there was something more—something beyond the well and its keep. Below the peak, lost in mist and darkness was a great pit hemmed all about by jagged rock walls. From pit to peak a long and winding stairway rose, a slender thread of stone spiraling upward. Mord Wraiths walked that causeway, dark and furtive in their purpose. One by one they came, at last gaining the peak. There they stood in a row and looked down upon the waters of the well. Then they advanced as one upon it and touched the waters with their hands. Instantly the water went foul, poisoned and turned from clearest crystal to an ugly black. It ran down out of the mountains, filtering west through the great forests of the Anar where the

Dwarves dwelt, then on to the land of the King of the Silver River and to Jair . . .

Poisoned! The word screamed suddenly in the Valeman's mind. The Silver River had been poisoned, and the land was dying . . .

The images were gone in a rush. Jair blinked. The old man was before him again, his weathered face smiling gently.

"From the bowels of the Maelmord the Mord Wraiths climbed the walk they call the Croagh to Heaven's Well, the life-source of the Silver River," he whispered. "Bit by bit, the poison has grown worse. Now the waters threaten to go bad altogether. When that happens, Jair Ohmsford, all of the life they serve and sustain, from the deep Anar west to the Rainbow Lake, will begin to die."

"But can't you stop it?" the Valeman demanded angrily, wincing with pain from the memory of what he had been shown. "Can't you go to them and stop them before it is too late? Surely your power is greater than theirs!"

The King of the Silver River sighed. "Within my own land, I am the way and the life. But only there. Beyond, I am without strength. I do what I can to keep the waters clean within the Silver River country, but I can do nothing for the lands beyond. Nor do I have power enough to withstand forever the poison that seeps steadily down. Sooner or later, I will fail."

There was a moment's silence as the two faced each other in the flickering light of the campfire. Jair's mind raced.

"What about Brin?" he exclaimed suddenly. "She and Allanon are going to the source of the Mord Wraiths' power to destroy it! When they have done that, won't the poisoning stop?"

The old man's eyes found his. "I have seen your sister and the Druid in my dreams, child. They will fail. They are leaves in the wind. Both will be lost."

Jair went cold. He faced the old man in stunned silence. Lost! Brin, gone forever . . .

"No," he murmured harshly. "No, you're wrong."

"She can be saved," the gentle voice reached out to him suddenly. "You can save her."

"How?" Jair whispered.

"You must go to her."

"But I don't know where she is!"

"You must go to where you know she will be. I have chosen you to go in my place as savior to the land and its life. There are threads that bind us all, you see, but they are knotted. The thread you hold is the one that will pull the rest free."

Jair didn't know what the old man was saying and he didn't care. He just wanted to help Brin. "Tell me what I have to do."

The old man nodded. "You must begin by giving to me the Elfstones."

The Elfstones! Again Jair had forgotten he had them. Their magic was the power he needed to break apart the Mord Wraith magic and any evil they might conjure up to stop him!

"Can you make them work for me?" the Valeman asked hurriedly, drawing them from his tunic. "Can you show me how to unlock the power?"

But the King shook his head. "I cannot. Their power does not belong to you. It belongs only to one to whom the magic has been freely given, and the magic was not given to you."

Jair slumped back dejectedly. "Then what am I to do? What use are the Stones if . . . ?"

"Of much use, Jair," the other interrupted gently. "But you must first give them to me. For good."

Jair stared at him. For the first time since the old man had appeared, the Valeman hesitated to believe. He had salvaged the Elfstones from his home at the risk of his life. Time and again, he had protected them, all for the sole purpose of finding a way to use them to aid his family against the Mord Wraiths. Now he was being asked to give up the only real weapon he possessed. How could he do such a thing?

"Give them to me," the soft voice repeated.

Jair hesitated a moment longer, wrestling with his indecision. Then slowly he passed them to the King of the Silver River.

"Well done," the old man commended. "You show character

and judgment worthy of your forebears. It was for these qualities that I chose you. And these qualities will sustain you."

He slipped the Elfstones within his robes and brought forth a different pouch. "This pouch contains Silver Dust—life restorer to the waters of the Silver River. You must carry it to Heaven's Well and scatter it into the poisoned waters. Do that, and the river will be clean again. Then you will find a way to give your sister back to herself."

Give Brin back to herself? Jair shook his head slowly. What did the old man mean by that?

"She will lose herself." The King of the Silver River again seemed able to read his thoughts. "Yours is the voice that will help her to find the pathway back."

Jair still did not understand. He started to ask the questions that would clear away his confusion, but the old man shook his head slowly.

"Listen to what I say." One thin arm reached out to him and the pouch with the Silver Dust was placed in his hands. "Now we are bound. Trust has been exchanged. So now it can be with magics. Your magic is useless to you, mine equally to me. I keep yours therefore and give you mine."

Again he reached into the robes. "The Elfstones are three in number, one each for the mind and body and heart—magics that entwine and form the power of the Stones. Three magics, then, shall you be given. First, this."

In his hand was a brilliant crystal on a silver chain. He passed it to Jair. "For the mind, a vision crystal. Sing to it, and it will show you the face of your sister, wherever she may be. Use it when you have need of knowing what she is about. And you *will* have need of knowing, for you must reach Heaven's Well before she reaches the Maelmord."

His hand lifted to Jair's shoulder. "For the body, strength to see you through on your journey east and to stand against the dangers that will beset you. That strength you shall find in those who will travel with you, for you shall not make this journey alone. A touch of the magic, then, to each. It begins and ends here." He pointed to the sleeping Garet Jax. "When your need is greatest, he shall always come. He shall be protector to you until you stand at last at Heaven's Well."

Once more he turned back to Jair. "And for the heart, child, the final magic—a wish that shall serve you best. *One time only* you may call upon the wishsong and it shall give you not illusion, but reality. It is the magic that will save your sister. Use it when you stand at Heaven's Well."

Jair shook his head slowly. "But how am I to use it? What am I to do?"

"I cannot tell you what you must decide for yourself," the King of the Silver River replied. "When you have thrown the Silver Dust into the basin at Heaven's Well and the waters are clear once more, throw the vision crystal after. You must find your answer there."

He bent forward then, his frail hand lifting. "But be cautioned. You must reach the Well before your sister enters into the Maelmord. It is written that she shall do so, since the Druid's faith in her magic is well placed. You must be there when that happens."

"I will," Jair whispered and clutched the vision crystal tightly.

The old man nodded. "I have placed much trust in you. The lands and the races depend now on you, and you must not fail them. But you have courage. You shall be true. Speak the words, Jair."

"I shall be true," the Valeman repeated.

Gingerly the King of the Silver River rose again, a ghost in the night. A great weariness stole suddenly over Jair, pulling him down into his travel cloak. Warmth and comfort seeped slowly through his body.

"You, most of all, are a part of me," he heard the old man say, the words faint and distant. "Child of life, the magic makes you so. All things change, but the past carries forward and becomes what is to be. Thus it was with your great-grandfather and your father. Thus it is with you."

He was fading, dissipating like smoke into the firelight. Jair peered after him, but his eyes were so clouded with sleep that he could not seem to make them focus.

"When you awake, all will be as it was save for this—I have come. Sleep now, child. Be at peace."

Jair's eyes closed obediently, and he slept.

XI

◆

When Jair awoke, dawn had already broken. Sunshine spilled down out of a cloudless blue sky and warmed an earth still damp with morning dew. He stretched lazily and breathed in the smell of bread and meat cooking. Kneeling next to the campfire, his back turned to the Valeman, Garet Jax was preparing breakfast.

Jair glanced about. Slanter was nowhere to be seen.

All will be as it was . . .

Abruptly he remembered everything that had happened the night gone past and sat up with a start. The King of the Silver River—or had it all been just a dream? He looked down at his hands. There was no vision crystal. When he had fallen back asleep, the crystal—if there really were one—had been clutched in his hands. He felt about the ground for it, then through the travel cloak. Still no crystal. Then it *had* been a dream. He felt hurriedly for the pockets of his tunic. A bulge in one pocket revealed the presence of the Elfstones—or was it the pouch that contained the Silver Dust? Quickly his hands flew over the rest of his body.

"Looking for something?"

Jair's head jerked up and he found Garet Jax staring at him. He shook his head hurriedly. "No, I was just . . ." he stammered.

Then his eyes detected a gleam of metal against his chest where the tunic opened in front. He looked down, tucking his chin back. It was a silver chain.

"Do you want something to eat?" the other man asked.

Jair didn't hear him. It hadn't been a dream after all, he was thinking. It had been real. It had all happened just as he remembered it. One hand felt down the front of his tunic past the length of the silver chain, touching upon the orb of the crystal fastened at its end.

"Do you want something to eat or not?" Garet Jax repeated, a touch of annoyance in his voice.

"Yes, I . . . yes, I do," Jair mumbled, rising and coming over to kneel beside the other. A plate was passed to him, filled with food from the kettle. Masking his excitement, he began to eat.

"Where's Slanter?" he asked after a moment, recalling once more the absent Gnome.

Garet Jax shrugged. "He never came back. I scouted around for him before breakfast. His tracks led down to the river and then turned west."

"West?" Jair stopped eating. "But that's not the way to the Anar."

The Weapons Master nodded. "I'm afraid your friend decided he had come far enough with us. That's the trouble with Gnomes— they're not very reliable."

Jair felt a twinge of disappointment. Slanter must indeed have decided to go his own way. But why did he have to sneak off like that? Why couldn't he at least have said something? Jair thought about it a moment longer, then forced himself to resume eating, pushing the disappointment from his mind. He had more immediate problems to concern himself with this morning.

He thought back over everything the King of the Silver River had told him last night. He had a mission to perform. He had to go into the deep Anar, into the Ravenshorn and the lair of the Mord Wraiths to the peak called Heaven's Well. It would be a long, dangerous journey—even for a trained Hunter. Jair stared hard at the ground. He was going, of course. There was no question about that. But as game and determined as he might be, he had to admit nevertheless that he was far from being a trained Hunter—or a trained anything. He was going to need help with this. But where was he going to find it?

He glanced curiously at Garet Jax. This man shall be your protector, the King of the Silver River had promised. I give to him strength to withstand the dangers that will beset you on your journey. When you have need of him, he shall be there.

Jair frowned. Did Garet Jax know all this? It certainly didn't appear that way. Obviously the old man hadn't come to the Weapons Master last night as he had come to Jair. Otherwise the man would have said something by now. That meant it was up to Jair to explain it to him. But how was the Valeman supposed to convince the Weapons Master to come with him into the deep Anar? For that matter, how was he supposed to convince him that he hadn't simply been dreaming?

He was still mulling the problem over when, to his complete astonishment, Slanter stalked out of the trees.

"Anything left in the kettle?" Slanter asked, scowling at them both.

Wordlessly, Garet Jax handed him a plate. The Gnome dropped the pack he was carrying, sat down next to the fire, and helped himself to a generous portion of the bread and meat. Jair stared at him. He looked haggard and irritable, as if he hadn't slept all night.

The Gnome caught him staring. "What's bothering you?" he snapped.

"Nothing." Jair looked away quickly, then looked back again. "I was just wondering where you'd been."

Slanter stayed bent over his plate. "I decided to sleep down by the river. Cooler there. Too hot by the fire." Jair's eyes strayed down to the discarded pack, and the Gnome's head jerked up. "Took the pack so I could scout upriver a bit—just in case. Thought I'd be certain that nothing . . ."

He broke off. "I don't have to account to you, boy! What's the difference what I was doing? I'm here now, aren't I? Let me be!"

He went back to his breakfast, attacking it with a vengeance. Jair glanced furtively at Garet Jax, but the Weapons Master seemed to take no notice. The Valeman turned again to Slanter. He was lying, of course; his tracks led downriver. Garet Jax had said so. Why had he decided to come back?

Unless . . .

Jair caught himself. The idea was so wild that he could barely conceive of it. But just perhaps the King of the Silver River had used his magic to bring the Gnome back again. He could have done that, Jair thought, and Slanter would never have been the wiser or realized what was being done to him. The old man could have seen that Jair would have need for the tracker—a Gnome who knew the whole of the Eastland.

Then suddenly it occurred to Jair that perhaps the King of the Silver River had brought Garet Jax to him as well—that the Weapons Master had come to his aid in the Black Oaks because the old man had wanted it so. Was that possible? Was that the reason that Garet Jax had freed him—all without realizing it?

Jair sat there in stunned silence, his food forgotten. That would explain the reluctance of both tracker and soldier-of-fortune to discuss the reasons for their actions. They didn't understand it fully themselves. But if that were true, then Jair, too, might have been brought here by similar manipulation. How much of what had happened to him had been the work of the old man?

Garet Jax finished his breakfast and was kicking out the fire. Slanter, too, was on his feet, wordlessly pulling on the discarded pack. Jair stared at them in turn, wondering what he should do. He knew that he couldn't just stay silent.

"Time to go," Garet Jax called over, motioning him up. Slanter was already at the edge of the clearing.

"Wait . . . wait just a minute." They turned to stare at him as he climbed slowly to his feet. "I've got something to tell you first."

He told them everything. He had not intended it to happen that way, but telling one thing led to telling another by way of explanation; before he knew it the whole story was out. He told them of Allanon's visit to the Vale and of his story of the Ildatch, of how Brin and Rone Leah had gone east with the Druid to gain entry into the Maelmord, and lastly of the appearance of the King of the Silver River and of the mission he had given to Jair.

When he had finished, there was a long silence. Garet Jax walked back to the fallen log and sat down, gray eyes intense.

"I am to be your protector?" he asked quietly.

Jair nodded. "He said you would be."

"What if I were to decide otherwise?"

Jair shook his head. "I don't know."

"I have heard some wild tales, but this is the wildest it has ever been my misfortune to suffer through!" Slanter exclaimed suddenly. "What are you up to with all this nonsense? What's the purpose of it? You don't think for a minute anyone sitting here believes a word of it, do you?"

"Believe what you want. It's the truth," Jair insisted, refusing to back away as the Gnome advanced on him.

"The truth! What do you know about the truth?" Slanter was incredulous. "You spoke with the King of the Silver River, did you? He gave you magic, did he? And now we're supposed to go traipsing off into the deep Anar, are we? And not just into the Anar, but right into the teeth of the black walkers! Into the Maelmord! You're mad, boy! That's the only truth there is in any of this!"

Jair reached into his tunic and brought forth the pouch containing the Silver Dust. "This is the Dust he gave me, Slanter. And here." He pulled the vision crystal on its silver chain free of his neck. "You see? I have the things he gave me, just as I said. Look for yourself."

Slanter threw up his hands. "I don't want to look! I don't want anything to do with any of this! I don't even know what I'm doing here!" He wheeled about suddenly. "But I'll tell you this—I'm not going into the Anar, not with a thousand crystals or a whole mountain of Silver Dust! Find someone else who's tired of living and leave me be!"

Garet Jax was back on his feet. He came over to Jair, took the pouch from the Valeman's hand, slipped the drawstrings open, and peered inside. Then he looked up again at Jair.

"Looks like sand to me," he said.

Jair glanced down hurriedly. Sure enough, the contents of the pouch looked exactly like sand. There was not a sparkle of silver to be seen in the supposed Silver Dust.

"Of course, the color might be a guise to protect against theft," the Weapons Master mused thoughtfully, a distant look in his eyes.

Slanter was aghast. "You don't really believe . . ."

Garet Jax cut him short. "I don't believe much of anything, Gnome." His eyes were hard again as they shifted to Jair. "Let's put this magic to the test. Take out the vision crystal and sing to it."

Jair hesitated. "I don't know how."

"You don't know how?" Slanter sneered. "Shades!"

Garet Jax didn't move. "This seems like a good time to learn, doesn't it?"

Jair flushed and looked down at the crystal. Neither of them believed a word he had told them. He couldn't really blame them, though. He wouldn't have believed it himself if it hadn't happened to him. But it had, and it had been all too convincing not to be real.

He took a deep breath. "I'll try."

He began to sing softly to the crystal. He held it cupped within his hands like a fragile thing, the silver chain dangling down through his fingers. He sang without knowing what it was he should sing or how he could bring the crystal to life. Low and gentle, his voice called to it and asked that it show him Brin.

It responded almost instantly. Light flared within his palms, startling him so that he nearly dropped the crystal. A living thing, the light shimmered a brilliant white, expanding until it was the size of a child's ball. Garet Jax bent close, his lean face intense. Slanter edged his way back from across the clearing.

Then abruptly Brin Ohmsford's face appeared within the light, dark and beautiful, framed by mountains whose slopes were stark and towering against a dawn less friendly than their own.

"Brin!" Jair whispered.

He thought for a moment she might reply, so real was her face within the light. Yet her eyes were far distant in their vision, and her ears were closed to his voice. Then the vision faded; in his excitement, Jair had ceased to sing, and the crystal's magic was spent. The light was gone in the same moment. Jair's hands cupped the crystal once more.

"Where was she?" he asked hurriedly.

Garet Jax shook his head. "I'm not sure. Perhaps . . ." But he did not finish.

Jair turned to Slanter, but the Gnome was shaking his head as well. "I don't know. It happened too fast. How did you do that, boy? It's that song, isn't it? It's that magic you have."

"And the magic of the King of the Silver River," Jair added quickly. "Now do you believe me?"

Slanter shook his head glumly. "I'm not going into the Anar," he muttered.

"I need you, Slanter."

"You don't need me. With magic like that, you don't need anyone." The Gnome turned away. "Just sing your way into the Maelmord like your sister."

Jair forced down the anger building within him. He shoved the crystal and the pouch with the Silver Dust back into his tunic. "Then I'll go alone," he declared heatedly.

"No need for that quite yet." Garet Jax swung his pack over his shoulder and started across the clearing once more. "First we'll see you safely to Culhaven, the Gnome and me. Then you can tell the Dwarves this story of yours. The Druid and your sister should have passed that way by now—or word of their passing reached the Dwarves. In any case, let's find out if anyone there understands anything of what you've been telling us."

Jair stalked after him hurriedly. "What you're saying is that you think I made this all up! Listen to me a minute. Why would I do that? What possible reason could I have? Go on, tell me!"

Garet Jax snatched up the Valeman's cloak and blanket and

shoved them at him as they went. "Don't waste your time telling me what I think," he replied calmly. "I'll tell you what I think when I'm ready."

Together they disappeared into the trees, following the trail that led east along the banks of the Silver River. Slanter watched them until they were out of sight, his rough yellow face twisting with displeasure. Then, picking up his own pack, he hastened after, muttering as he went.

XĬĬ

◆

FOR THE BETTER PART OF THREE DAYS, BRIN OHMSFORD AND
Rone Leah rode north with Allanon toward the Keep of Paranor.
The path chosen by the Druid was long and circuitous, a slow
hard journey through country made rugged by steep slides, narrow passes, and choking forest wilderness. But at the same time the
path was free of the presence of Gnomes, Mord Wraiths, and other
evils that might beset the unwary traveler, and it was for this reason
that Allanon had made his choice. Whatever else must be endured
on their journey north, he was determined that in the making of
that journey he would take no further chances with the life of the
Valegirl.

So he did not take them through the Hall of Kings as he had
once done with Shea Ohmsford, a march that would have forced
them to leave their horses and proceed afoot through the underground caverns that interred the kings of old, where traps could
be triggered with every step forward and monsters guarded against
all who trespassed. Nor did he take them across the Rabb to the
Jannisson Pass, a ride through open country where they might be
easily seen and which would take them much too close to the forests of the Eastland and the enemy they sought to avoid. Instead, he
took them west along the Mermidon through the deep forests that
blanketed the lower slopes of the Dragon's Teeth from the Valley of
Shale to the mountain forests of Tyrsis. They rode west until at last

they reached the Kennon Pass, a high mountain trail that led them far into the Dragon's Teeth to emerge miles further north within the forests that bound the castle of Paranor.

It was at dawn of the third day that they came down from the Kennon into the valley beyond, a dawn gray and hard as iron, clouded over and cold with winter's chill. They rode in a line, traversing the narrow pass through mountains bare and stark as they loomed against the morning sky, and it was as if all life had ceased to be. Wind swept the empty rock with fierce gusts, and they bent their heads against its force. Below, the forested valley that sheltered the castle of the Druids stretched dark and forbidding before them. A faint, swirling mist hid the distant pinnacle of the Keep from their eyes.

As they rode, Brin Ohmsford struggled with an unshakable sense of impending disaster. It was a premonition really, and it had been with her since they had left the Valley of Shale. It tracked her with insidious purpose, a shadow as murky and cold as the land she rode through, an elusive thing that lurked within the rocks and crags, flitting from one place of hiding to another, watching with sly and evil intent. Hunched down within her riding cloak, drawing what warmth she could from the bulky folds, she let her mount choose its path on the narrow trail and felt the weight of the presence as it followed after.

It had been the Wraith mostly, she thought, that fostered that premonition. More than the harshness of the day, the dark intent of the Druid she followed, or the newfound fear she felt for the power of her wishsong, it was the Wraith. The Druid had assured her that there were no others. Yet such a dark and evil thing, silent in its coming, swift and terrible in its attack, then gone as quickly as it had appeared, with nothing left but its ashes. It was as if it were a being come from death into life, then gone back again, faceless, formless, a thing without identity, yet above all, frightening.

There would be others. How many others she did not know nor care to know. Many, certainly—all searching for her. She sensed it instinctively. Mord Wraiths—wherever they might be, whatever their other dark purposes—all would be looking for her. One only, the Druid had said. Yet that one had found them; and if one had found them, others could. How was it that that one had found them? Allanon had brushed aside her question when she asked it. Chance, he had answered. Somehow it had crossed their trail and followed after, choosing its moment to strike when it thought the Druid weakened. But Brin thought it equally possible that the thing had tracked the Druid since his flight from the Eastland. If that were so, it would have gone first to Shady Vale.

And to Jair!

Odd, but there had been a moment earlier, a brief, fleeting moment as she wound her way down through the grayness of the dawn, alone with her thoughts, wrapped in the solitude of wind and cold, when she had felt her brother's touch. It was as if he had been looking at her, his vision somehow reaching past the distance that separated them to find her as she made her way out of the great cliffs of the Dragon's Teeth. But then the touch had faded, and Jair was as distant once more as the home she had left him to keep watch over.

This morning she was worried for Jair's safety. The Wraith might have gone first to Shady Vale and found Jair, despite what Allanon said. The Druid had dismissed the idea, but he was not to be trusted completely. Allanon was a keeper of secrets, and what he revealed was what he wished known—nothing more. It had always been that way with the Ohmsfords, ever since the Druid had first come to Shea.

She thought again of his meeting with the shade of Bremen in the Valley of Shale. Something had passed between them that the Druid had chosen to keep hidden—something terrible. Despite his assurances to the contrary, he had learned something that had disturbed him greatly, had even frightened him. Could it be that what he had learned involved Jair?

The thought haunted her. Were anything to happen to her brother and the Druid to learn of it, she felt he would keep it from her. Nothing would be allowed to interfere with the mission he had set for her. He was as dark and terrible in his determination as the enemy they sought to overcome—and in that he frightened her as much as they. She was still troubled by what he had done to Rone.

Rone Leah loved her; it was unspoken between them perhaps, but it was there. He had come with her because of that love, to make certain that she had someone with her whom she could always trust. He did not feel Allanon was that person. But the Druid had subverted Rone's intentions and at the same time silenced his criticism. He had challenged Rone's self-designated role as protector; when the challenge was accepted, he had turned the highlander into a lesser version of himself by the giving of magic to the Sword of Leah.

An old and battered relic, the Sword had been little more than a symbol Rone bore to remind himself of the legacy of courage and strength-of-heart attributed to the house of Leah. But the Druid had made it a weapon with which the highlander might seek to attain his own oft-imagined feats-at-arms. In so doing, Allanon had mandated that Rone's role as protector be something far more awesome than either she or the highlander had envisioned. And what the Druid had made of Rone Leah might well destroy him.

"It was like nothing I could ever have imagined," he had confided to her when they were alone that first night after leaving the Valley of Shale. He had been hesitant in his speech, yet excited. It had taken him that long just to bring himself to speak of it to her. "The power just seemed to explode within me. Brin, I don't even know what made me do it; I just acted. I saw Allanon trapped within the fire and I just acted. When the Sword cut into the fire, I could feel its power. I was part of it. At that moment, I felt as if there were nothing I could not do—nothing!"

His face had flushed with the memory. "Brin, not even the Druid frightens me anymore!"

Brin's eyes lifted to scan the dark spread of the forests below, still misted in the half-light of the harsh autumn day. Her premonition slipped through the rocks and across the twist of the pass, cat-quick and certain. It will show no face until it is upon us, she thought. And then we will be destroyed. Somehow I know it to be so. The voice whispers in my thoughts of Jair, of Rone, of Allanon, and of the Mord Wraiths most of all. It whispers in secrets kept from me, in the gray oppression of this day, and in the misty dark of what lies ahead.

We will be destroyed. All of us.

They were within the forests by midday. All afternoon they rode, winding their way through mist and gloom, threading needles of passage through massive trees and choking brush. This was an empty woods, devoid of life and color, hard as iron in autumn's gray, with leaves gone dusty brown and curled against the cold like frightened things. Wolves had once prowled these woods, great gray monsters that protected against all who dared to trespass in the land of the Druids. But the wolves were gone, their time long past, and now there was only the stillness and the emptiness. All about, there was a sense of something dying.

Dusk had begun to fall when Allanon at last bade them halt, weary and aching from the long day's ride. They tied their horses within a gathering of giant oaks, giving them only a small ration of water and feed so that they might not cramp. Then they went ahead on foot. The gloom about them deepened with night's coming, and the stillness gave way to a low, distant rumble that seemed to hang in the air. Steady and sure, the Druid led them on, picking his way with the sense of one familiar with the region; there was no hesitation in his step as he found the path. As silent as the shadows about them, the three slipped through the trees and brush and melted into the night.

What is it that we go to do? Brin whispered within her mind. What dark purpose of the Druid's do we serve this night?

Then the trees broke before them. Out of the gray dusk rose the cliffs of Paranor, steep and towering, and at their rim was the ancient castle of the Druids, called the Keep. It rose high within the darkness, a monstrous stone and iron giant rooted in the earth. From within the Keep and the mountain upon which it rested sounded the rumble they had heard earlier, and which had grown steadily louder as they approached, the deep thrum of machinery grinding in ceaseless cadence against the silence that lifted all about. Torches burned like devil's eyes within narrow, iron-barred windows, crimson and lurid against the night sky, and smoke trailed into mist. Once Druids had walked the halls beyond, and it was a time of enlightenment and great promise for the races of Man. But that time was gone. Now only Gnomes and Mord Wraiths walked in Paranor.

"Hear me," Allanon whispered suddenly, and they bent close to listen. "Hear what I tell you and do not question. The shade of Bremen has given warning. Paranor has fallen to the Mord Wraiths. They seek within its walls the hidden histories of the Druids so that their own power may be strengthened. Other times, the Keep has fallen to an enemy and it has always been regained. But this time that cannot be. This marks the end of all that has been. The age closes, and Paranor must pass from the land."

Highlander and Valegirl stared at the Druid. "What are you saying, Allanon?" Brin demanded fiercely.

The Druid's eyes gleamed in the dark. "That in my lifetime and yours—in the lifetime of your children and perhaps your children's children—no man shall set foot within the walls of the Druid's Keep after this night. We are to be the last. We shall go into the Keep through its lower passages that are yet unknown to the Wraiths and Gnomes who search within. We shall go to where the power of the Druids has for centuries been seated and with that power close away the Keep from mankind. We must pass quickly though, for all found within the Keep this night shall die—even we, if we prove too slow. Once the needed magic is brought forth, there will be little time left to escape its sweep."

Brin shook her head slowly. "I don't understand. Why must this be done? Why can no one again enter Paranor after tonight? What of the work that you do?"

The Druid's hand touched her cheek softly. "It is finished, Brin Ohmsford."

"But the Maelmord—the Ildatch . . ."

"Nothing we do here can help us in our quest." Allanon's voice was almost lost to her. "What we do here serves another purpose."

"What if we're seen?" Rone broke in suddenly.

"We shall fight our way free," Allanon answered at once. "We must. Remember first to protect Brin. Do not stop, whatever happens. Once the magic has been called forth, do not look back and do not slow." He bent forward, his lean face close to that of the highlander. "Remember, too, that you now possess the power of Druid magic in your sword. Nothing can stop you, Prince of Leah. Nothing."

Rone Leah nodded solemnly, and this time did not question what he was told. Brin shook her head slowly, and the premonition danced before her eyes.

"Valegirl." The Druid was speaking to her, and her eyes lifted to find his. "Stay close to the Prince of Leah and to me. Let us shield you from whatever danger we may encounter. Do nothing to risk your own life. You, most of all, must be kept safe, for you are the key to the destruction of the Ildatch. That quest lies ahead of you and it must be completed."

Both hands came up to grip her shoulders. "Understand. I cannot leave you here safely or I would do so. The danger is greater than it will be if you go with us into the Keep. Death flies all through these woods on this night, and it must be kept from you."

He paused, waiting for her response. Slowly she nodded. "I'm not afraid," she lied.

Allanon stepped back. "Then let us begin. Silently, now. Speak no more until this is done."

They disappeared into the night like shadows.

XIII

ALLANON, BRIN, AND RONE LEAH CREPT THROUGH THE FOR-est. Stealthy and swift, they traversed a maze of trees that jutted sky-ward like the blackened spikes of some pit-trap. All around them, the night had gone still. Between boughs half-shorn of their leaves by autumn's coming, bits and pieces of a clouded night sky rolled into view, low and threatening. The flames of torches high within the towers of the Keep flickered angrily with crimson light.

Brin Ohmsford was afraid. The premonition whispered in her mind and she screamed back at it in soundless despair. Trees and limbs and brush flashed all about her as she hurried on. Escape, she thought. Escape this thing that threatens! But no, not until we are done, not until . . . Her breath came in quick gasps, and the heat of her exertions turned quickly to chill against the skin. She felt empty and impossibly alone.

Then they were up against the great cliffs upon which the Keep stood. Allanon's hands flitted across the stone before him, his tall form bent close in concentration. He moved right perhaps a half dozen feet, and again his hands touched. Brin and Rone went with him, watching. A second later he straightened and his hands with-drew. Something in the stone gave way, and a portion of the wall swung clear to reveal a darkened hole beyond. At once Allanon mo-tioned them through. They groped their way forward, and the stone portal closed behind them.

They waited sightlessly for a moment within the dark, listening to the faint sounds of the Druid as he moved about close beside them. Then a light flared sharply and flames licked at the pitch-coated head of a torch. Allanon passed the torch to Brin, then lighted another for Rone and a third for himself. They stood within a small, sealed chamber from which a single stairway wound upward into the rock. With a quick glance back at them, Allanon began to climb.

They went deep into the mountains, one step after the other, hundreds of steps becoming thousands as the stairway went on. Tunnels bisected the passage they followed and split their path in two, yet they did not depart from the steps they were on, following the long twist and turn upward into the blackness. It was warm and dry within the rock; from somewhere further ahead the steady churning of furnace machinery rumbled through the stillness. Brin fought down the panic she could feel building slowly within her. The mountain felt as if it were alive.

Long minutes later, the stairway came to an end at a great iron-bound door whose hinges were seated in the stone of the mountain. There they halted, their breathing harsh in the stillness. Allanon bent close to the door, touched briefly the studs of the iron bindings, and the door swung back. Sound burst in on them—the pumping and thrusting of pistons and levers—rolling through their small passageway like the roar of some giant breaking free. Heat seared their faces, dry and raw as it sucked away the cool air. Allanon peered past the open portal momentarily, then slipped through. Shielding their faces, Brin and Rone followed.

They stood within the furnace chamber, its great black pit opening down into the earth. Within the pit the furnace machinery churned in steady cadence, stoking the natural fires of the earth and pumping their heat upward into the chambers of the Keep. Dormant since the time of the Warlock Lord, the furnace had been brought to life once more by the enemy that waited above, and the sense of intrusion was vibrant and oppressive. Quickly Allanon led them along the narrow metal catwalk that encircled the pit to one of a number of doors leading out from the chamber. A touch of its bindings and it swung inward into blackness. Clutching their torches before them, they stumbled from the terrible heat and pushed the small door shut behind them.

Again a passageway opened before them, and they followed it for a short time to where a stairway branched off to one side. Allanon turned onto the stairway, and they began their ascent. Slowly now, more carefully—for there was the unmistakable feel of others close at hand—the three wound upward through the dark, listening . . .

Behind them, below somewhere, a door slammed shut with a crash, and they froze motionlessly on the steps. The echo reverberated into stillness. There was nothing more. They went on cautiously.

At the head of the stairs, there was another door where they paused and listened. Allanon touched a hidden lock to slip the door open, passed through, and went on. Beyond was another passage with another door at its end, then another passage, a stair, a door, and another passage. Hidden corridors honeycombed the aged fortress and ran empty and black through the walls of the Keep. Must and cobwebs filled the air with the smell and feel of age. Rats scurried ahead through the blackness, small sentinels warning of their approach. Yet in the castle of the Druids, no one heard.

Then voices sounded from somewhere within the halls of the Keep that ran where the intruders crouched, furtive and hidden. The voices were deep and low, a muted mutter that rose and faded, but much too close. Brin's mouth was dry and she could not swallow. The smoke from the torches stung her eyes, and she felt the weight of the rock close down about her. She felt trapped. All about her, hidden in hazy half-light and shadow, the premonition danced.

And finally this newest tunnel ended. The gloom gave way suddenly before the light of their torches, and a stone wall blocked their passage. No portals opened to either side, and no corridors led away. Allanon did not hesitate. He went at once to the wall, bent close to its surface for a moment as if listening, then turned to Brin and Rone Leah. A finger lifted to touch his lips, and his head inclined slightly. Brin took a deep breath to steady herself. The Druid's meaning was clear; they were about to pass into the Keep.

Allanon turned back to the faceless wall. At his touch upon the stone, a small doorway hidden within swung silently back. In a line, the three passed through.

They stood within a small, windowless study filled with dust and smelling of age. The contents of the room lay scattered about in complete disarray. Books had been pulled from the shelves that lined the study's walls and strewn about the floor, their bindings broken and pages torn. Stuffed armchairs had been cut apart, and a reed table and high-backed chairs had been thrown over. Even pieces of the plank flooring had been ripped from their seatings.

Allanon surveyed the ruin through the smoky light of the torches, his dark face filled with rage. Then he moved wordlessly to the far wall, reached within the empty shelves and touched something he found there. Silently the bookcase swung back to reveal a darkened vault beyond. Motioning for them to wait without, the Druid stepped through the entryway, slipped his torch into an iron bracket fastened to a support, and moved to the wall on the right. The wall was constructed all of granite blocks, smooth and tightly sealed against air and dust. Lightly, the Druid began to run his fingers over the stone.

Still within the study, Brin and Rone watched for a moment as the Druid worked, then glanced suddenly away. A thin seam of light outlined a door in the blackness of the room, a door that led from the study into the halls of the Keep. From somewhere beyond that door came the sound of voices.

Within the vault, Allanon's fingers bridged against the granite wall and his head lowered in concentration. Abruptly a deep blue glow began to spread outward through the stone from where his fingers touched. The glow turned to fire that erupted soundlessly through the granite, flared and was gone. Where the wall had been, shelves of massive, leatherbound books stood revealed: the Druid histories.

In the corridor beyond the study, the voices were coming closer.

Swiftly Allanon lifted one of the massive volumes from its place upon the shelves and carried it to an empty wooden table that occupied the center of the chamber. Placing the book upon the table, he opened it. Still standing, he began to page through it quickly. He found what he was looking for almost at once and bent close to read.

Muted and rough, the voices without were joined by the sound of booted feet. There were at least half a dozen Gnomes beyond the door.

Brin mouthed Rone's name wordlessly, her eyes frightened in the glare of the torches. The highlander hesitated, then quickly passed her his torch and drew forth the Sword of Leah. Two steps carried him to the door, where he slipped tight the latch-lock.

The voices and the thudding feet passed and went on—all but one. A hand worked the latch, trying to open the door. Brin backed further into the shadows of the study, praying that whoever paused without could not see the light of her torch or smell its smoke, praying that the door would not open. The latch jiggled a moment longer. Then whoever was out there began to force it.

Abruptly Rone Leah drew back the latch, threw open the door, and dragged a startled Gnome inside. The Gnome managed a single yelp of surprise before the highlander's sword pommel hammered against his head and knocked him unconscious to the floor.

Hurriedly, Rone closed the open study door, locked it again and stepped back. Brin hurried to join him. In the vault, Allanon was returning the tome he had been reading to its place on the shelf. With a quick circular motion of his hand before the Druid histories, the granite wall was restored. Snatching his torch from its bracket, he hastened from the vault, pushed back into place the shelving that hid its entry, and motioned both Valegirl and highlander to follow as he slipped again into the passageway that had brought them. A moment later, the study was left behind.

They went back through the maze of tunnels, sweating now with fear and exertion. All about them was as before, bits and

pieces of voices appearing and fading in small snatches, and the deep thrum of the furnace rising up from somewhere far below like distant thunder.

Then again Allanon brought them to a halt. Another door stood before them, sealed with dust and cobwebs. Wordlessly the Druid motioned for them to extinguish their torches in the dust of the passageway. They were going into the Keep once more.

They stepped from the blackness of their passage into a hallway bright with torchlight and gleaming with brass and polished wood. Though dust lay over everything within the ancient Keep, still the trappings shone through its covering, small bits of fire in the dappled shadows. A great hallway disappeared into the dark, walls of oak hung thick with tapestries and paintings, fronted in tall niches by the ornaments of another age. Flattened against their small entry, Valegirl and highlander peered quickly about. The hall was empty.

Hurriedly Allanon led them left along the darkened corridor, slipping from one set of shadows to the next, past small pools of smoky torchlight and past glimmerings of night that shone deep gray through tall, latticed windows that arched skyward above the battlements without. A strange quiet hung across the halls of the ancient fortress, as if suddenly all life save their own had been stripped from the Keep. Only the constant hum of the machinery below broke the quiet. Brin's eyes darted from the darkened hall to the torchlit entry, searching. Where were the Mord Wraiths and the Gnomes they commanded? A hand gripped her shoulder and she jumped. It was Allanon, drawing her back into the shadows of an alcove that sheltered a tall set of iron doors.

Then suddenly, as if to answer Brin's unspoken question, a cry of alarm rang out, shrill and harsh in the silence of the Keep. The Valegirl whirled at the sound. It came from the study behind them. The Gnome that Rone had knocked unconscious had come awake.

There were footsteps everywhere then, thudding against the stone flooring and pounding through the stillness. There were cries all about them. Rone Leah's sword flashed darkly in the half-light, and the highlander pushed Brin behind him. But Allanon had the iron doors open now; and with a yank he pulled Brin and Rone from sight, slamming the doors behind them.

They stood upon a narrow landing, squinting through a haze of smoky torchlight given off by brands that burned along the length of a stairway coiling upward like a snake about the stone block walls of the massive tower that rose about them. Huge and black, the tower seemed to lift to impossible heights; yet at their feet, beneath the tiny landing that supported them, it dropped into the earth, a bottomless pit. Save for the landing and the stairway, there was nothing to break the smooth surface of the walls as they stretched away into impenetrable shadow with neither beginning nor end.

Brin shrank back against the iron doors. This was the tower of the Keep that guarded the sanctuary of the Druids. Those who had once come with Shea Ohmsford from Culhaven had believed it contained the Sword of Shannara. A monstrous thing, it had the feel of a giant's well made to bore through the whole of the earth.

Rone Leah took a step toward the edge of the landing, but Allanon pulled him back instantly. "Stand away, highlander!" he whispered darkly.

Without, the shouts and cries rose louder, and the running of feet scattered all about. Allanon started up the narrow stairs, his back to the tower wall.

"Stay clear of me!" he whispered down at them.

After a dozen steps, he moved to the stairway's edge. Lean hands lifted from within the black robes, fingers curling. Words slipped from his lips that Valegirl and highlander could not understand, low and muted with rage.

From within the pit of the tower, a sharp hiss sounded in response.

The Druid's hands lowered slowly, his fingers crooked like claws and his palms downward. Steam leaked from the corners of the hard mouth, from eyes and ears, and from the stone on which he stood. Brin and Rone stared in horror. Below, the pit hissed again.

Then the blue fire exploded from Allanon's hands, a huge burst of flame that flew downward into the blackness. Trailing sparks, it flared sharply far below, turned a sudden wicked green in color, and died.

The tower went suddenly still. Beyond the iron doors, the shouts of alarm and the thudding of feet sounded, faint and chaotic, but within the tower there were no sounds. Allanon sagged backward against the wall, his arms clutched tightly about his body and his head lowered as if in pain. The steam that had come from within him was gone, but the stone on which he stood and against which he leaned looked charred.

Then once more the pit hissed, and this time the tower itself shuddered with the sound.

"Look into its throat!" Allanon's voice was harsh.

Highlander and Valegirl peered downward from the edge of the landing into the pit. Deep within, a roiling green mist was stirring like liquid fire against the walls of the tower. The hiss it gave forth was like a voice, eerie and filled with hate. Slowly the mist fastened to the walls, weaving through the stone as if it were water. Slowly the mist began to climb.

"It's coming out!" Rone whispered.

The mist began to claw its way up the stone block walls like a thing alive. Foot by foot, it hauled itself closer to where they stood.

Now Allanon was beside them once more, pulling them away from the edge of the landing, drawing their faces close to his own. His dark eyes glinted like fire.

"Flee, now!" he ordered. "Don't look back. Don't turn aside. Flee from the Keep and from this mountain!"

Then he threw open the tower doors with a mighty thrust and stepped out into the halls of the Keep. There were Gnome Hunters everywhere, and they turned at his appearance, their rough yellow faces frozen with surprise. Blue fire burst from the Druid's outstretched hands and burned into them, flinging them back like leaves caught in a sudden wind. Screams rose from their throats as the fire caught them, and they scattered in terror from this dark avenger. One of the Mord Wraiths appeared, a black and faceless thing within its robes. Blue fire swept into it with stunning force as the Druid wheeled on it, and an instant later it was ash.

"Run!" Allanon called back to where Brin and Rone stood frozen within the empty doorway.

Quickly they followed after him, sprinting past the Gnomes that lay fallen across their path, racing through the smoky torchlight toward the passages that had brought them. The halls stayed empty for only a moment. Then the Gnomes reappeared, counterattacking, a solid wedge of armored yellow forms howling in anger, spears and short swords bristling from their midst. Allanon broke apart the assault with a single burst of the Druid fire, clearing the way. A second group surged at them from a cross corridor as they tried to push past, and Rone turned, the Sword of Leah lifted. Sounding the battle cry of his homeland as the Gnomes came at him, he launched himself into their midst.

Behind them, another Wraith appeared, and ahead still another. Red fire burst from their black hands, arcing toward Allanon, but the Druid blocked the assault with fire of his own. Flames scattered everywhere in a wild shower, and walls and tapestries began to burn. Brin shrank back against one wall, shielding her eyes, Rone and Allanon on either side of where she crouched. Gnomes came at them from every direction, and now there were more Wraiths as well, silent black monsters that lifted out of the dark and struck at them. Rone Leah broke off the battle with the Gnomes and sprang at one who had ventured too close. Down came the ebony blade of the Sword of Leah and shattered the Wraith into fragments of ash. Flames burned his own body from attacks all about him, but he shrugged them aside, the black blade absorbing the brunt of their force. With a howl of anger, he fought his way back to where Brin hunched down beside the wall. A fierce exhilaration lit his face, and lines of green mist swirled wildly within the black metal of the sword. Seizing her arm, he brought her to her feet and propelled her ahead. There Allanon battled to gain the door they had come through from the catacombs, his black form towering out of smoke, fire, and struggling bodies like death's shadow come to life.

"Through the door, highlander!" the Druid roared, flinging his attackers from his side as they fought to pull him down.

A sudden explosion of red fire engulfed them all, stunning them with its force. Allanon turned, and the Druid fire thrust from his own hands, a solid blue wall that shielded them momentarily from those who came after. Somehow they were through the Mord Wraiths' fire then, racing past a few scattered Gnomes who sought vainly to prevent their escape. Cries and screams echoed through the Druid's Keep as they reached the door they sought. They had it open an instant later and were safely through.

Sudden darkness closed about them like a shroud. The howls of their attackers faded momentarily behind the door through which they had come. Snatching up the discarded torches, Allanon quickly relighted them and the three companions began a race back through the catacombs. Down through passageways and stairwells they sped. Behind them, the cries of the pursuit grew strident once more, but the way ahead was clear now. They rushed downward into the furnace room once more, past earth's fire and the rumble of machinery, to where the stairs took them deep into the mountain's core. Still no one barred their way.

Then abruptly a new sound reached their ears, distant yet, but shrill with terror. It came to them in a single, endless wail, alive with horror.

"It begins!" Allanon called back to them. "Quickly now, run!"

They ran frantically as the wail grew more frenzied behind them. Something unspeakable was happening to those yet within the Keep.

Ah, the mist! Brin cried silently.

They fled down the stairs that led to the mountain's base, following the twists and turns of the passageway, hearing all the while the shrieks of those trapped behind them. Stairs came and went in countless number, and still they ran on.

Then finally the stairs ended, and the entry hidden in the rock of the cliff face loomed before them once more. Pushing through hurriedly, Allanon led them from the mountain into the cool dark of the forest beyond.

Still the screams followed after.

Night slipped away. It was nearing dawn when at last they walked their horses clear of the valley of Paranor. Weary and ragged, they paused on an outcropping of rock on high ground east of the pinnacle of the Keep and looked back to where green mist swirled wickedly about the aged fortress and hid it from their view. The sky lightened, and the mist burned away a little at a time, a shroud lifting. Silently they watched as it dissipated into air.

Then the dawn broke, and the mist was gone.

"It is finished," Allanon whispered in the stillness.

Brin and Rone Leah stared. Below, the pinnacle the Druid's Keep had once rested upon rose high into the light of the morning sun—barren and empty save for a scattering of crumbling outbuildings. The castle of the Druids had vanished.

"Thus was it written within the histories; thus was it foretold," Allanon continued quietly. "Bremen's shade knew the truth. Older than the time of the Keep was the magic conceived to close her away. Now she is gone, drawn back into the stone of the mountain, and with her all those she trapped within." There was a terrible sadness in the dark face. "So it ends. Paranor is lost."

But they were alive! Brin felt a fierce determination rushing through her, brushing aside the Druid's somber tone. The premonition had been wrong and they were alive—all of them!

"So it ends," Allanon repeated softly.

His eyes found those of the Valegirl then, and it was as if they shared some unspoken secret that neither quite fully understood. Then slowly Allanon turned his horse about. With Brin and Rone trailing after, he rode east toward the forests of the Anar.

XIV

LATE IN THE AFTERNOON, JAIR OHMSFORD AND HIS companions reached the Dwarf community of Culhaven. It was a
journey just as well over and done with in the Valeman's opinion.
Leaden skies and a chill wind had followed them east through the
Silver River country, and even the changing colors of the great Eastland forests had a gray and wintry cast to them. Geese flew southward over the land through threatening autumn skies, and the flow
of the river whose course they followed was rough and unfriendly.

The Silver River had begun to show signs of the poisoning foretold by its King. Blackish scum laced its waters, and its clear silver
color had turned murky. Dying fish, small rodents, and fallen birds
floated past, and the river was choked with deadwood and scrub.
Even its smell was bad, the fresh cleanness become a rank and fetid
odor that assailed their nostrils with each change in the wind. Jair
remembered his father's tales of the Silver River, tales told since the
time of Shea Ohmsford, and what he saw now made him sick at
heart.

Garet Jax and Slanter did little to improve his mood. Even without the constant reminder of the river's ill and the harsh cast of the
day, Jair would have found it difficult to keep a smile on his face or
cheerfulness in his voice with the Weapons Master and the Gnome
for traveling companions. Withdrawn and taciturn, they trudged

beside him with all of the enthusiasm of mourners at a death watch. Not a dozen words had been exchanged since the march had resumed early that morning, and not a smile had crossed either face. Eyes riveted on the path ahead, they went forward with a single-minded determination that bordered on fanaticism. Once or twice, Jair had ventured to speak, and the response each time had been little more than a muted grunt. The noontime meal had been a strained and awkward ritual of necessity, and even the silent march east had been preferable to that.

Thus their approach into Culhaven was more than a little welcome to the Valeman, if for no other reason than that it meant he would soon have a chance to talk to someone civil for a change—although there was some reason to doubt even that. Dwarves had sighted them as far west as the border of the Anar, silent watchers who had made no effort to make them feel welcome. All along the trail leading in, there had been patrols of Dwarf Hunters—hardened men wrapped in leather waistcoats and forest cloaks, armed and purposeful in their walk. None of these had given greeting, or paused for even the briefest chat. All had passed and gone their way without inquiry. Only their eyes had strayed over to view these visitors—and their eyes had not been friendly.

By the time Jair and his fellow travelers reached the edge of the Dwarf village, they were being studied openly by every Dwarf they passed, and there was more than a hint of suspicion in those looks. Still in the lead, Garet Jax seemed oblivious to the eyes that followed after them, but Slanter was growing increasingly edgy and Jair was almost as uncomfortable as the Gnome. Garet Jax led along the roadway that crisscrossed the village, clearly familiar with the community and certain of what he was about. Neatly kept homes and shops lined the pathways they walked, sturdily built structures fronted by immaculate lawns and hedgerows, and brightened by lines of flowerbanks and carefully tended gardens. Families and shopowners looked up as they passed, hands gripping tools and wares as they paused in their day's work. But there were armed men even here—Dwarf Hunters with hard eyes and belted weapons. This might be a community of families and homes, Jair thought to himself, but just at the moment it has more the look of an armed camp.

Finally, as they entered the central part of the village, they were brought to a halt by a foot patrol. Garet Jax spoke briefly with one of the sentries and the Dwarf disappeared on the run. The Weapons Master stepped back with Jair and Slanter. Together they faced the remaining members of the patrol in studied silence and waited. Dwarf children came to stand about them curiously, eyes fixed on Slanter. The Gnome ignored them for a time, then tired of the game and gave a sudden growl that sent the entire bunch scurrying for cover. The Gnome glowered after them, glanced irritably at Jair, and withdrew into a determined funk.

A few minutes later, the sentry dispatched by Garet Jax returned. With him was a rugged-looking Dwarf with a great curling black beard and mustache and a bald head. Without slowing, he went directly to the Weapons Master, his hand extended in welcome.

"Took your sweet time getting here," he growled as the other clasped the callused hand in his own. Sharp brown eyes peered out from beneath heavy brows, and the look of the man was hard and fierce. His stout, compact body was clothed in loose-fitting forest garb, belted and booted in soft leather, and he wore a brace of long knives at his waist. In one ear, a large gold earring dangled.

"Elb Foraker," Garet Jax introduced the Dwarf to Jair and Slanter.

Foraker studied them wordlessly for a moment, then turned back to the Weapons Master. "Strange company you're keeping, Garet."

"Strange times." The other shrugged. "How about a place to sit and something to eat?"

Foraker nodded. "This way."

He led them past the patrol to where the roadway branched right and from there into a building that housed a large eating hall filled with benches and tables. A handful of the tables were occupied by Dwarf Hunters absorbed in their evening meal. A few glanced up and nodded to Foraker, but no one this time showed any particular interest in the Dwarf's companions. Apparently it made a difference whom you were with, Jair thought. Foraker chose a table for them well back against one wall and signaled for food to be brought.

"What am I supposed to do with these two?" the Dwarf asked when they had seated themselves.

Garet Jax turned to his companions. "Direct sort of fellow, isn't he? He was with me ten years ago when I was training Dwarf Hunters for a border skirmish along the Wolfsktaag. He was with me again in Callahorn a few years back. That's why I'm here now. He asked me to come, and he doesn't take no for an answer."

He looked back at Foraker. "The Valeman is Jair Ohmsford. He's looking for his sister and a Druid."

Foraker leaned back frowning. "A Druid? What Druid? There aren't any Druids anymore. Haven't been any Druids since . . ."

"I know—since Allanon," Jair interjected, unable to keep still any longer. "That's the Druid I'm looking for."

Foraker stared at him. "That right? What makes you think you'll find him here?"

"He told me that he would be going into the Eastland. He took my sister with him."

"Your sister?" The Dwarf's brows were fiercely knit. "Allanon and your sister? And they're supposed to be here somewhere?"

Jair nodded slowly, a sinking feeling in his stomach. Foraker looked at him as if he were crazy. Then he looked at Garet Jax.

"Where did you find this Valeman?"

"On the way," the other replied vaguely. "What do you know about the Druid?"

Foraker shrugged. "I know that no one has seen Allanon in the Eastland for more than twenty years—with or without anybody's sister."

"Well, you don't know much, then," Slanter spoke up suddenly, the faintest hint of a sneer in his voice. "The Druid's come and gone right under your nose!"

Foraker's fierce countenance swung around on the speaker. "I'd watch my mouth if I were you, Gnome."

"This one supposedly tracked the Druid out of the Eastland," Garet Jax offered, gray eyes wandering off casually about the empty hall. "Tracked him from the Maelmord right to the Valeman's doorstep."

Foraker stared at him. "I'll ask again—what exactly am I supposed to do with these two?"

Garet Jax looked back at him. "I've been thinking about that. Does the Council meet tonight?"

"Every night, these days."

"Then let the Valeman speak to them."

Foraker frowned. "Why should I do that?"

"Because he has something to tell them that I think they're going to want to hear. And not just about the Druid."

Dwarf and Weapons Master eyed each other in silence. "I'll have to make a request," Foraker said at last, his lack of enthusiasm evident.

"Now seems like a good time to do it." Garet Jax rose to his feet.

Foraker sighed and stood up with him, glancing down at Jair and Slanter as he did so. "You two can eat your meal and stay put. Don't try wandering off." He hesitated. "I don't know anything about a Druid passing through, but I'll look into it for you, Ohmsford." He shook his head. "Come along, Garet."

The Dwarf and the Weapons Master left the eating hall. Jair and Slanter sat alone at the table, lost in thought. Where was Allanon? Jair asked himself in silent desperation, head lowered to study his hands as he clasped them before him. The Druid had said he was going into the Eastland. Wouldn't he come through Culhaven? If he hadn't, then where had he gone? Where had he taken Brin?

A Dwarf in a white bib apron brought them plates of hot food and cups of ale, and they began to eat. No one said anything. The minutes slipped past as they consumed the meal, and Jair felt his hopes fading with each bite he took—as if somehow he were consuming the answers his questions demanded. Pushing the plate

back from where he sat, he scuffed one boot against the plank flooring nervously and tried to decide what he would do if Elb Foraker
were right and Allanon and Brin had indeed not come this way.

"Stop that!" Slanter growled suddenly.

Jair glanced up. "Stop what?"

"Stop rubbing your boot against the floor. It's annoying."

"Sorry."

"And quit looking like you'd lost your best friend. Your sister
will turn up."

Jair shook his head slowly, still distracted. "Maybe."

"Humph," the Gnome muttered. "I'm the one who should be
worrying—not you. I don't know how I ever let you talk me into
this fool's errand."

Jair propped his elbows on the table and cupped his chin in his
hands. There was determination in his voice. "Even if Brin didn't
come through Culhaven, even if Allanon went another way, we've
still got to go into the Anar, Slanter. And we've got to persuade the
Dwarves to help us."

Slanter stared at him. "We? Us? You'd better take a moment and
rethink that 'we and us' nonsense! I'm not going anywhere but back
to where I came from before I got involved in this whole mess!"

"You're a tracker, Slanter," Jair said quietly. "I need you."

"Too bad," the Gnome snapped, his rough yellow face suddenly
dark. "I'm also a Gnome, in case you hadn't noticed! Did you see the
way they looked at me out there? Did you see those children looking at me like I was some sort of wild animal brought in from the
forest? Use your head! There's a war going on between Gnomes and
Dwarves, and the Dwarves aren't likely to listen to anything you
have to say so long as you persist in making me your ally! Which
I'm not, in any case!"

Jair bent forward. "Slanter, I have to reach Heaven's Well before
Brin reaches the Maelmord. How am I going to do that without
someone to guide me in?"

"You'll find a way, knowing you." The Gnome brushed the matter aside. "Besides, I can't go back there anymore. Spilk will have

told them what I did. Or if not him, then that other Gnome that ran off. They'll be looking for me. If I go back, someone will recognize me. When I'm caught, the walkers . . ." He stopped abruptly and threw up his hands. "I'm not going and that's that!"

He went back to eating his food, his head lowered to his plate. Jair regarded him silently, wondering if perhaps he were making a mistake in seeking Slanter's help in the first place; perhaps the King of the Silver River hadn't intended him as an ally after all. Slanter didn't really seem like much of an ally when you thought about it. He was altogether too clever, too opportunistic, and his loyalty changed as often as the wind. He wasn't one to be depended on, was he? Yet despite all that, there was still something about the Gnome that Jair liked. Maybe it was his toughness. Like Garet Jax, Slanter was a survivor, and that was the sort of companion Jair needed if he were to reach the deep Anar.

He watched as the Gnome drank down the last of the ale in noisy gulps, then said quietly, "I thought you wanted to learn about the magic."

Slanter shook his head. "Not anymore. I've learned all I care to know about you, boy."

Jair frowned in annoyance. "I think you're just scared."

"Think what you like. I'm not going."

"What about your people? Don't you care what the Mord Wraiths are doing to them?"

Slanter's eyes snapped up. "I don't have a people anymore, thanks to you!" Then he shrugged. "Doesn't matter, though. I haven't really had a people since I left the Eastland. I'm my own people."

"That's not true. The Gnomes are your people. You went back to help them, didn't you?"

"Times change. I went back because it was the smart thing to do. Now I'm not going back because that's the smart thing to do!" Slanter was growing angry. "Why don't you just give it up, boy? I've done enough for you already. I don't feel obliged to do anything further. After all, the King of the Silver River didn't give me any Silver Dust to help clean up his river!"

"That's fortunate, isn't it?" Jair flushed, a bit angry now himself. "A fat lot of good you'd be, changing sides every five minutes when things got a little rough! I thought you helped me back in the Oaks because you'd made a choice! I thought you cared what happened to me! Well, maybe I was wrong! What do you care about, Slanter?"

The Gnome was nonplussed. "I care about staying alive. That's what you'd care about, too, if you had any brains."

Jair went rigid with indignation. He came halfway out of his seat, arms braced on the table. "Staying alive! Well, just exactly how are you going to do that when the Mord Wraiths poison the Eastland and then move west into the other lands? That's what's going to happen, isn't it? That's what you said! Where will you run to then? Plan on changing sides one time more—become a Gnome again long enough to fool the walkers?"

Slanter reached up and shoved Jair back. "You have a big mouth for someone who understands so little about life. Maybe if you'd been out in the world looking after yourself instead of having someone do it for you, you'd not be so quick to point the finger at others. Now, shut up!"

Jair lapsed into immediate silence. There was nothing to be gained by pushing the matter any further. Slanter had made up his mind not to help, so that was the end of it. He was probably better off without the Gnome anyway.

The two were still glowering at each other when Garet Jax returned a few moments later. He was alone, and he came directly to where they sat. If he noticed the tension between them, he gave no indication of it. He took a seat next to Jair.

"You're to go before the Council of Elders," he said quietly.

Jair shook his head slowly. "I don't know about this. I don't know if this is the right thing to do."

The Weapons Master pinned him with his eyes. "You don't have a choice."

"What about Brin? And Allanon?"

"There is no news of them. Foraker checked, and they haven't been to Culhaven. No one knows anything about them." The gray eyes studied the Valeman intently. "Whatever help you're to find in this quest of yours, you'll have to find it on your own."

Jair glanced quickly at Slanter, but the Gnome refused to meet his gaze. He turned back to Garet Jax. "When do I go before the Council?"

The Weapons Master stood up. "Now."

The Dwarf Council of Elders had convened in the Assembly, a large and cavernous hall settled within the bowels of a squarish building that housed all of the offices governing the affairs of the village of Culhaven. Twelve strong, the members of the Council sat behind a long table on a dais at the head of the chamber and looked down upon rows of benches separated by aisles that ran back to a pair of wide double-doors leading in. It was through these doors that Garet Jax brought Jair and Slanter. Shadows cloaked all but the very forefront of the Assembly, where oil lamps cast their harsh yellow light across the dais. The three who entered made their way to the edge of the light and stopped. A gathering of others occupied seats on the benches closest to the dais, and heads lifted and turned at their approach. A haze of pipe smoke hung over the men gathered, and the pungent smell of burning tobacco filled the air.

"Come forward," a voice called.

They proceeded until they stood even with the foremost line of benches. Jair glanced around uneasily. The faces that stared back at him were not simply the faces of Dwarves. A handful of Elves sat immediately to his right, and half a dozen Bordermen from Callahorn far to his left. Foraker was there as well, black-bearded face dour and set as he leaned against the far wall.

"Welcome to Culhaven," the voice spoke again.

The speaker rose from behind the table on the dais. He was a gray-bearded Dwarf of some years, rough-faced and bluff, skin browned and lined in the harsh light of the lamps. He stood center-most among the Elders at the Council.

"My name is Browork, Elder and citizen of Culhaven, First at this Council," he informed them. His hand lifted and beckoned to Jair. "Come forward, Valeman."

Jair came toward him a step or two and stopped, glancing at the line of faces that looked down at him. All were aged and weathered, yet with eyes still quick and alert as they studied him.

"Your name?" Browork asked him.

"Jair Ohmsford," he replied. "Of Shady Vale."

The Dwarf nodded. "What would you say to us, Jair Ohmsford?"

Jair glanced about. The faces all about him waited expectantly—faces he did not know. Should he reveal what he knew to them? He looked back at the Elder.

"You may speak freely," Browork assured him, sensing his concern. "All gathered here are to be trusted; all are leaders in the fight against the Mord Wraiths."

He sat down again slowly and waited. Jair looked about once more, then took a deep breath and began to speak. Step by step, he revealed all that had happened since the arrival of Allanon in Shady Vale those many nights past. He told of the Druid's coming, of his warning of the Mord Wraiths, of his need for Brin, and of their departure east. He described his subsequent flight, the adventures that had befallen him in the highlands and the Black Oaks, his meeting with the King of the Silver River, and the prophecy foretold by the legendary King. It took him some time to tell it all. While he spoke, the men gathered about him stayed silent. He could not bring himself to look at them; he was frightened of what he might see in their faces. Instead, he kept his eyes fixed on the seams and hollows that molded Browork's weathered countenance and the deep-set blue eyes that stared fixedly back at him.

When at last he was finished, the Dwarf Elder leaned forward slowly, his rough hands folding on the table before him, his gaze still holding Jair's.

"Twenty years ago, I fought with Allanon to keep the Demon hordes from the Elven city of Arborlon. It was a terrible battle. Young Edain Elessedil—" He indicated with his hand a blond-haired Elf barely older than Brin. "—was not even born then. His grandfather, the great Eventine, was King of the Elves. That was when Allanon last walked the Four Lands. Not since that time has the Druid been seen, Valeman. He has not come to Culhaven. He has not come to the Eastland. What say you to that?"

Jair shook his head. "I don't know why he didn't come this way. I don't know where he has gone. I only know where it is that he goes—and my sister with him. And I know, too, that he has indeed been within the Eastland." He turned toward Slanter. "This Hunter tracked him from the Maelmord west to my home."

He waited for confirmation, but Slanter said nothing.

"No one has seen Allanon for twenty years," another Elder of the Council repeated quietly.

"And no one has ever spoken with the King of the Silver River," a third said.

"I spoke with him," Jair said. "And my father also spoke with him. He helped my father and an Elf girl flee the Demons to Arborlon."

Browork continued to study him. "I know of your father, youngster. He did come to Arborlon to aid the Elves in their fight against the Demons. It was rumored that he was the possessor of Elfstones, just as you have said. But you say that you took the Elf-stones from your home and then gave them up to the King of the Silver River?"

"In exchange for magic I could use," Jair affirmed quickly. "For a wish I could use to save Brin. For a vision crystal to find her. And for strength for those who would help me."

Browork glanced now at Garet Jax. The Weapons Master nodded. "I have seen the crystal of which he speaks. It is magic. It did show to us the face of a girl—one he says is his sister."

The Elf identified as Edain Elessedil came suddenly to his feet. He was tall and fair-skinned, his blond hair reaching to his shoulders. "My father has spoken to me of Wil Ohmsford many times.

He has said that he is an honorable man. I do not think a son of his would speak anything but the truth."

"Unless he mistook fantasy for truth," one of the Council suggested. "This tale is difficult to swallow."

"But the waters of the river are indeed fouled," another pointed out. "We all know that in some way the Mord Wraiths poison them in an effort to destroy us."

"As you say, common knowledge," replied the first. "Hardly proof of anything."

Other voices rose now, arguing the merits of Jair's tale. Browork raised his hands sharply.

"Peace, Elders! Give thought to what we are about!" He turned back to Jair. "Your quest, if it be true, requires that we give you aid. You cannot succeed without that aid, Valeman. Armies of Gnomes lie between you and the thing you seek—this place you call Heaven's Well. Understand, too, that none among us have ever been where you would go or seen the source of the waters of the Silver River." He glanced about for confirmation; heads nodded and no one spoke in contradiction. "For us to help you then, we must first be certain of what we do. We must believe. How are we to believe a thing of which we have no personal knowledge? How are we to know what you tell us is the truth?"

"I would not lie," Jair insisted, flushing.

"Not knowingly, perhaps," the Elder mused. "Yet all lies are not intended. Sometimes what we believe to be truth is but a falsehood which deceives us. Perhaps that is what has happened here. Perhaps . . ."

"Perhaps if we waste enough time talking about it, it will be too late to do anything to help Brin!" Jair lost his temper completely. "I have not been deceived in anything! What I spoke of happened!"

The voices murmured in dissatisfaction, but immediately Browork signaled for quiet. "Show to us this pouch of Silver Dust that we might gain some measure of belief in what you say," he ordered.

The Valeman stared at him helplessly. "It will not aid you. The dust appears as common sand."

"Sand?" One of the Council members shook his head in disgust. "We are wasting our time, Browork."

"Let us at least see the crystal, then," Browork sighed.

"Or prove to us in some other way that what you say is true," another demanded.

Jair felt his chance of convincing the Dwarves of anything slipping rapidly away. Few, if any, of the Council believed what he was telling them. They had seen nothing of Allanon or Brin; none of them had ever heard of anyone speaking with the King of the Silver River; for all he knew, they didn't even believe that such a being existed. Now he was telling them he had given away Elfstones for magics they could not even see.

"We waste time, Browork," the first Elder muttered once more.

"Let the Valeman be questioned by others while we get on with our business," another said.

Again the voices rose, and this time they drowned out Browork's pleas for silence. Almost to a man, the Dwarves of the Council and those gathered with them called for the matter to be disposed of without further delay.

"I could have told you this would happen," Slanter whispered suddenly from behind him.

Jair went crimson with anger. He had come too far and endured too much to be shoved aside now. Give us proof, they were telling him. Make us believe.

Well, he knew how to make them believe!

Stepping forward suddenly, he lifted his hands high, then pointed into the shadows of the aisle leading back from where he stood. So dramatic was the gesture that the voices went abruptly still, and all heads turned to look. There was nothing there, nothing but darkness . . .

Then Jair sang, the wishsong quick and strident, and a tall, black figure wrapped in cloak and cowl emerged from out of the nothingness of the air.

The figure was Allanon.

There was a sharp gasp from those assembled. Swords and long knives slipped from their sheaths, and men bounded from their seats to defend against this shade that had emerged from the dark. Within the cowl, a dark lean face lifted to the light, eyes fixing on the men of the Council. Then Jair's song faded and the Druid was gone.

Jair turned once more to Browork. The Dwarf's eyes were wide. "Now do you believe me?" the Valeman asked quietly. "You said you knew him; you said you fought with him at Arborlon. Was that the Druid?"

Slowly Browork nodded. "That was Allanon."

"Then you know that I have seen him," Jair said.

All assembled turned back now to stare at the Valeman, uneasy and shaken by what had happened. Behind him, Jair heard Slanter chuckle, a low nervous laugh. He caught a glimpse of Garet Jax from the corner of his eye. The Weapons Master had a curious, almost surprised look on his face.

"I have told you the truth," Jair said to Browork. "I must go into the deep Anar and find Heaven's Well. Allanon will be there with my sister. Now tell me—will you help me or not?"

Browork glanced at the other Elders. "What say you?"

"I believe what he says," one old man ventured quietly.

"But it could yet be a trick!" another said. "It could be the work of the Mord Wraiths!"

Jair glanced quickly about. A few heads were nodding in agreement. In the smoky light of the oil lamps, suspicion and fear clouded many eyes.

"The risk is too great, I think," yet another Elder said.

Browork rose. "We are pledged to give aid to any who seek the destruction of the Wraiths," he said, blue eyes quick and hard. "This Valeman has told us he is allied with others of like mind and purpose. I believe him. I believe we should do what we can to aid him in his quest. I call for a vote, Elders. Give me your hands in support if you agree."

Browork's hand lifted high. Half a dozen more from the Council lifted with it. But the dissenters were not to be silenced so easily.

"This is madness!" one shouted. "Who will go with him? Are we to send men from the village, Browork? Who is to go on this quest to which you have so unwisely given your blessing? I call for volunteers if this is to be done!"

A scattering of voices muttered in support. Browork nodded. "So be it." He looked about the chamber silently, his eyes shifting from one face to the next, searching, waiting for someone to accept the challenge.

"I will go."

Jair looked around slowly. Garet Jax had come forward a single step, gray eyes expressionless as he faced the Council.

"The King of the Silver River promised the Valeman that I would be his protector," he said softly. "Very well. The promise shall be kept."

Browork nodded, then looked about the room once more. "Who else among you will go?" he called out.

Elb Foraker pushed away from the wall against which he was leaning and walked over to stand with his friend. Again Browork looked out among those gathered. A moment later there was a stirring from among the men of Callahorn. A giant Borderman rose to his feet, black hair and beard close-cropped about his long, strangely gentle face.

"I'll go," he rumbled and came forward to stand with the others. Jair took a step back in spite of himself. The Borderman was almost as big as Allanon.

"Helt," Browork greeted him. "The men of Callahorn need not make this quest their own."

The big man shrugged. "We fight the same enemy, Elder. The quest appeals to me, and I would go."

Then suddenly Edain Elessedil came to his feet. "I would go as well, Elder."

Browork frowned. "You are a Prince of the Elves, young Edain. You are here with your Elven Hunters to repay a debt your father feels he owes from the time the Dwarves stood with him at Arborlon. Well and good. But you carry the price of the debt too far. Your father would not approve of this. Reconsider."

The Elven Prince smiled. "There is nothing to reconsider, Browork. The debt owed in this matter is not to the Dwarves but to the Valeman and his father. Twenty years ago, Wil Ohmsford went with an Elven Chosen in search of a talisman that would destroy the Demons who had broken free of the Forbidding. He risked his life for my father and for my people. Now I have a chance to do the same for Wil Ohmsford—to go with his son, to see to it that he finds the thing he quests for. I am as able as any man here and I would go."

Still Browork frowned. Garet Jax glanced at Foraker. The Dwarf merely shrugged. The Weapons Master looked over at the Elven Prince for a moment as if measuring the depth of his commitment or perhaps simply his chance of surviving, then slowly nodded.

"Very well," Browork acquiesced, "five, then."

"Six," Garet Jax said quietly. "An even half-dozen for luck."

Browork looked puzzled. "Who is the sixth?"

Garet Jax turned slowly about and pointed to Slanter. "The Gnome."

"What!" Slanter's jaw dropped. "You can't choose me!"

"I have already done so," the other replied. "You are the only one here who has been where we want to go. You know the way, Gnome, and you are going to show it to us."

"I'll show you nothing!" Slanter was livid, his face contorted with rage. "This boy . . . this devil . . . he put you up to this! Well, you have no power over me! I'll throw you all to the wolves if you try to make me go!"

Garet Jax came up against him, the terrible gray eyes as cold as winter. "That would be most unfortunate for you, Gnome, for the wolves would reach you first. Take a moment and think it through."

The Assembly went deathly still. Weapons Master and Gnome faced each other without moving, eyes locked. In the eyes of the man in black, there was death; in the eyes of Slanter, hesitation. But the Gnome did not back away. He stood where he was, seething with anger, trapped in a snare of his own making. Slowly his gaze shifted to find Jair, and in that instant the Valeman actually found himself feeling sorry for the Gnome.

Slanter's nod was barely perceptible. "I've no choice, it seems," he muttered. "I'll take you."

Garet Jax turned back once more to Browork. "Six."

The Dwarf Elder hesitated, then sighed in resignation. "Six it is," he declared softly. "Fortune go with you."

XV

◆

Late the following morning, their preparations completed, the little company departed Culhaven for the deep Anar. Jair,
Slanter, Garet Jax, Elb Foraker, Edain Elessedil and the Borderman
Helt, armed and provisioned, slipped quietly from the village and
were gone almost without notice. Only Browork was there to see
them off, his aged countenance reflecting a mix of conviction and
misgiving. To Jair, he gave his promise that warning of the Mord
Wraiths would be sent to the elder Ohmsfords before their return to
the Vale. To each of the others, he gave a firm handshake and a word
of encouragement. Slanter alone evidenced an understandable lack
of appreciation for the good wishes. No other fanfare accompanied
their departure; the Council of Elders and the other leaders, both
Dwarf and outlander, who had participated in last night's gathering
remained divided in their feelings as to the wisdom of this undertaking. More than not, were the truth to be made known, felt the
entire venture doomed from the start.

Yet the decision had been made, and so the company went. It
went alone, without escort, despite strenuous objection from the
Elven Hunters who had accompanied Edain Elessedil east from the
home city of Arborlon and who felt more than a little responsible
for the safety of their Prince. Theirs was but a token force, after all,
dispatched hurriedly by Ander Elessedil upon his receiving a call
for aid from Browork and, until a larger force could be mobilized,

dispatched in recognition of an obligation owed the Dwarves for their aid in the Demon-Elf struggle of twenty years earlier. Edain Elessedil had been sent in his father's place, but without any real expectation that he would see battle unless the Gnome armies advanced all the way to Culhaven. His offer to join the company on their quest into the heart of enemy country had been completely unexpected. But there was little that the Elven Hunters could do about it—since the Prince was free to make his own decision in the matter—other than to insist that they, too, be made a part of the undertaking. There were those among the Dwarves and Bordermen who would have gone as well, but all were refused. Garet Jax made the decision, and it was supported by the others who comprised the company of six, even Slanter. The smaller the group, the greater its mobility and stealth and the better its chances of slipping through the great forests of Anar unseen. With the unavoidable exception of Jair—and he had the magic to protect him, he kept reminding them—all were skilled professionals, trained in survival. Even Edain Elessedil had been tutored by members of the King's Home Guard during the years he had grown to manhood. The fewer they numbered, they all agreed, the better off they would be.

And so only six went—on foot, for the forest wilderness prevented any other form of travel—eastward from the Dwarf village into the darkened woods, following the bend of the Silver River. Browork watched them until they were lost from sight in the trees, then turned reluctantly back to Culhaven and the work that awaited him there.

It was a clear, cool autumn day, the air sharp and still and the skies bright with sunlight. Trees shimmered in myriad hues of red, gold, and brown, leaves falling to blanket the forest earth in a soft carpet that rustled beneath the feet of the six as they marched ahead. Time slipped quickly away. Almost before they knew it, the afternoon was gone, the evening settling in across the Anar in dark shades of gray and violet, and the sun sinking slowly from view.

The company made camp next to the Silver River in a small grove of ash, sheltered on their eastern fringe by an outcropping of rocks. Dinner was prepared and eaten, and then Garet Jax called them all together.

"This will be our route." It was Elb Foraker who spoke, kneeling in their midst to clear the leaves away, a broken stick tracing lines in the bare earth. "The Silver River flows thus." He marked its passage. "We stand here. East, four days or so, is the Dwarf fortress at Capaal that protects the locks and dams on the Cillidellan. North of that, the Silver River runs down out of the High Bens and the Gnome prisons at Dun Fee Aran. Further north still lie the Ravenshorn and Graymark."

He looked about the little circle of faces. "If we can do so, we must follow the river all the way into Graymark. If we are forced to leave the river, the path through the Anar becomes a difficult one—all wilderness." He paused. "Gnome armies hold everything north and east of Capaal. Once there, we will have to watch ourselves carefully."

"Questions?" Garet Jax glanced up.

Slanter's snort of derision broke the silence. "You make it seem a whole lot easier than it is," he growled.

"That's why we have you along." The Weapons Master shrugged. "Once beyond Capaal, you'll be the one choosing the path."

Slanter spit disdainfully on the drawing. "If we get that far."

The group broke up, each member moving off to make up his bed for the night. Jair hesitated, then started after Slanter. He caught up with the Gnome on the far side of the clearing.

"Slanter," he called. The Gnome glanced about momentarily, saw who it was and looked away at once. Jair stepped around in front of the Gnome and faced him. "Slanter, I just want to tell you that it was not my idea to bring you with us."

Slanter's eyes were hard. "It was your idea, all right."

Jair shook his head. "I wouldn't force anyone to come who didn't want to—not even you. But I'm glad you're here. I want you to know that."

"How very comforting," the Gnome mocked. "Be sure to remind the walkers of that when they have us all in their prisons!"

"Slanter, don't be like this. Don't . . ."

The Gnome turned away abruptly. "Leave me alone. I want nothing to do with you. I want nothing to do with any of this." Then he glanced back suddenly, and there was a fierce determination in his eyes. "First chance I get, boy, I'll be gone! Remember that—first chance! Now—are you still glad I'm here?"

He whirled and stalked away. Jair stared after him helplessly, both saddened and angered by the way things had worked out between them.

"He's not as angry at you as he seems," a low voice rumbled. Jair turned and found the Borderman Helt beside him, the long gentle face looking down. "He's mostly angry at himself."

Jair shook his head doubtfully. "It didn't look that way."

The Borderman moved over to a tree stump and sat, stretching his long legs. "Maybe not, but that's the truth of it. The Gnome's a tracker; I knew him in Varfleet. Trackers are not like anyone else; they're loners, and Slanter is more alone than most. He feels trapped in this, and he wants someone to blame for that. Apparently he finds it easiest to blame you."

"I suppose I am to blame in a way." The Valeman stared after the retreating Gnome.

"No more than he himself," the other said quietly. "He came into the Anar on his own, didn't he?"

Jair nodded. "But I asked him to come."

"Someone asked all of us to come," Helt pointed out. "We didn't have to come, though; we chose to come. It's no different with the Gnome. He chose to come with you to Culhaven—probably he wanted to come. It may be that he wants to come now, but can't admit it to himself. Maybe he's even a little frightened by the idea."

Jair frowned. "Why would he be frightened of that?"

"Because it means he cares about you. There isn't any other reason that I can think of that he would be here."

"I hadn't thought of that. I guess that I thought just the opposite from what he's been saying—that he didn't care about anything."

Helt shook his head. "No, he cares, I think. And that frightens him, too. Trackers can't afford to care about anyone—not if they expect to stay alive."

Jair stared at the Borderman a moment. "You seem pretty sure about all this."

The big man rose. "I am. You see, I was once a tracker, too."

He turned and walked away into the dark. Jair stared after him, wondering what it was that had prompted the Borderman to speak, but rather grateful nevertheless that he had done so.

Dawn broke gray and cheerless, and a mass of rolling dark clouds swept east across the morning sky. The wind blew chill and harsh out of the north, biting at their faces in fierce gusts, whistling through the skeletal limbs of the forest trees. Leaves and dirt swirled all about them as they resumed the march, and the air smelled heavily of rain.

Jair Ohmsford walked that day in the company of Edain Elessedil. The Elven Prince joined him at the start of the journey, conversing in his loose, easy manner, telling Jair what his father the King had told him of the Ohmsfords. There was a great debt owed Wil Ohmsford, the Elven Prince explained, as they bent their heads against the wind and trooped forward through the cold. If not for him, the Elven nation might have lost their war with the Demons, for it was Wil who had taken the Elven Chosen Amberle in search of the Bloodfire so that the seed of the legendary Ellcrys might be placed within its flames, then returned to the earth to be born anew.

Jair had heard the tale a thousand times, but it was different somehow hearing it from Edain, and he welcomed the retelling. He, in his turn, recounted to the Prince his own small knowledge of the Westland, of his father's admiration for Ander Elessedil, and of his own strong feelings for the Elven people. As they talked, a sense of kinship began to develop between them. Perhaps it was their shared Elven ancestry, perhaps simply the closeness in age. Edain Elessedil was like Rone in his conversation at times—serious and relaxed by turns, anxious to share his feelings and ideas and to hear Jair's—and bonds of friendship were quickly formed.

Nightfall came, and the little company took shelter beneath an overhang along a ridgeline that shadowed the Silver River. There they had their dinner and watched the sullen rush of the river as it churned past through a series of rocky drops. Rain began to fall, the sky went black, and the day faded into an unpleasant night. Jair sat back within the overhang and stared out into the dark, the fetid smell of the poisoned river reaching his nostrils. The river had grown worse since Culhaven, its waters blackened and increasingly choked with masses of dying fish and deadwood. Even the vegetation along the riverbanks had shown signs of wilting. There was a murky, depthless cast to the river, and the rain that fell in steady sheets seemed welcome, if only to help somehow wash clean the foulness that lay therein.

The members of the company began to fall asleep after a time. As always, one among them stood guard for the rest. This watch was Helt's. The giant Borderman stood at the far end of the outcropping, a massive shadow against the faint gray of the rain. He had been a tracker a long time, Edain Elessedil had told Jair— more than twenty years. No one ever talked about why he wasn't a tracker anymore. He'd had a family once, it was rumored, but no one seemed to know what had become of them. He was a gentle man, quiet and soft-spoken; he was also a dangerous one. He was a skilled fighter. He was incredibly strong. And he possessed night vision—extraordinary eyesight that enabled him to see in darkness as clearly as if it were brightest day. There were stories about his night vision. Nothing ever crept up on Helt or got past him.

Jair hunched down within his blankets against the growing cold. A fire burned at the center of the outcropping, but the heat failed to penetrate the damp to where he sat. He stared a while longer at Helt. The Borderman hadn't said anything further to him after their brief conversation of the previous night. Jair had thought to talk again with him, and once or twice had almost done so. Yet something had kept him from it. Perhaps it was the look of the man; he was so big and dark. Like Allanon, only . . . different somehow. Jair shook his head, unable to decide what that difference was.

"You should be sleeping."

The voice startled Jair so that he jumped. Garet Jax was next to him, a silent black shadow as he settled in beside the Valeman and wrapped himself in his cloak.

"I'm not sleepy," Jair murmured, struggling to regain his composure.

The Weapons Master nodded, gray eyes peering out into the rain. They sat there in silence, huddled down in the dark, listening to the patter of the rainfall, the churning rush of the river, and the soft ripple of leaves and limbs as the wind blew past. After a time, Garet Jax stirred and Jair could feel the other's eyes shift to find him.

"Do you remember asking me why I helped you in the Black Oaks?" Garet Jax asked softly. Jair nodded. "I told you it was because you interested me. That was true; you did. But it was more than that."

He paused, and Jair turned to look at him. The hard, cold eyes seemed distant and searching.

"I am the best at what I do." The Weapons Master's voice was barely a whisper. "All my life I have been the best, and there is no one even close. I have traveled all of the lands, and I have never found anyone who was a match for me. But I keep looking."

Jair stared at him. "Why do you do that?"

"Because what else is there for me to do?" the other asked. "What purpose is there in being a Weapons Master if not to test the skill that the name implies? I test myself every day of my life; I look for ways to see that the skill does not fail me. It never does, of course, but I keep looking."

His gaze shifted once more, peering into the rain. "When I first came upon you back in that clearing in the Oaks, bound and gagged, trussed hand and foot, guarded by that Gnome patrol— when I saw you like that, I knew there was something special about you. I didn't know what it was, but I knew it was there. I sensed it, I guess you'd say. You were what I was looking for."

Jair shook his head. "I don't understand what you mean."

"No, I don't guess you do. At first, I didn't understand either. I just sensed that somehow you were important to me. So I freed you and went with you. As we traveled, I saw more of what had intrigued me in the first place . . . something that I was looking for. Nothing really told me what I should do with you. I just sensed what I should do, and I did it."

He straightened. "And then . . ." His eyes snapped back to find Jair's. "You came awake that morning by the Silver River and told me of the dream. Not a dream, I guess—but something like it. Your quest, you called it. And I was to be your protector. An impossible quest, a quest deep into the heart of the lair of the Mord Wraiths for something no one knew anything about but you—and I was to be your protector."

He shook his head slowly. "But you see, I had a dream that night, also. I didn't tell you that. I had a dream that was so real that it was more . . . vision than dream. In a time and place I did not recognize, I stood with you as your protector. Before me was a thing of fire, a thing that burned at the touch. A voice whispered to me from within my mind. It said that I must do battle with the fire, that it would be a battle to the death, and that it would be the most terrible battle of my life. The voice whispered that it was for this battle alone that I had trained all of my life—that all of the battles that had gone before had been to prepare me for this."

His gray eyes burned with the heat of his words. "I thought after hearing of your vision that perhaps mine, too, came from the King of the Silver River. But whatever its source, I knew that the voice spoke the truth. And I knew as well that this was what I had been looking for—a chance to match my skill against power greater than any that I had ever faced and to see if I was indeed the best."

They stared silently at each other in the dark. What Jair saw in the other man's eyes frightened him—a determination, a strength of purpose—and something more. A madness. A frenzy, barely controlled and hard as iron.

"I want you to understand, Valeman," Garet Jax whispered. "I choose to come with you that I might find this vision. I shall be your protector as I have pledged that I would. I shall see you safely past whatever dangers threaten. I shall defend you even though I die doing so. But in the end it is the vision that I seek—to test my skill against this dream!"

Pausing, he drew back from the Valeman. "I want you to understand that," he repeated softly.

Silent again, he waited. Jair nodded slowly. "I think I do."

Garet Jax looked out into the rain once more, withdrawing into himself. As if alone, he sat and watched the rain fall in steady sheets and said nothing. Then, after a time, he rose and slipped back into the shadows.

Jair Ohmsford sat alone for a long time after he was gone, wondering if he really did understand after all.

The next morning, when they came awake, Jair brought forth the vision crystal to discover what had become of Brin since last he had sought her out.

Rain and gray mist shrouded the forest as the members of the little company crowded about the Valeman. Holding the crystal before him so that all could see, he began to sing. Soft and eerie, the wishsong filled the dawn silence with its sound, rising up through the patter of the rain on the earth. Then light flared from within the crystal, fierce and sudden, and Brin's face appeared. She stared out at the members of the company, searching for something their own eyes could not see. There were mountains behind her, stark and barren as they rose against a dawn as gray and dismal as their own. Still Jair sang, following his sister's face as she turned suddenly. Rone Leah and Allanon were there, haggard-looking faces lifted toward a deep, impenetrable forest.

Jair ceased to sing, and the vision was gone. He looked anxiously at the faces about him. "Where is she?"

"The mountains are the Dragon's Teeth," Helt rumbled softly. "No mistaking them."

Garet Jax nodded and looked at Foraker. "The forest?"

"It's the Anar." The Dwarf rubbed his bearded chin. "She comes this way, she and the other two, but farther north, across the Rabb."

The Weapons Master gripped Jair's shoulder. "When you used the vision crystal before, the mountains were the same, I think—the Dragon's Teeth. Your sister and the Druid were within them then; now they come out. What would they be doing there?"

There was a moment's silence, faces glancing one from the other.

"Paranor," Edain Elessedil said suddenly.

"The Druid's Keep," Jair agreed at once. "Allanon took Brin into the Druid's Keep." He shook his head. "But why would he do that?"

This time no one spoke. Garet Jax straightened. "We won't find out huddled here. The answers to such questions lie east."

They rose, and Jair slipped the vision crystal back into his tunic. The march into the Anar resumed.

XVI

♦

On the fourth day out of Culhaven, they arrived at
the Wedge.

It was late afternoon, and the sky hung gray and oppressive
across the land. Rain fell in steady sheets as it had fallen for three
days past, and the Anar was sodden and cold. Trees stripped bare
of autumn color shone black and stark through trailers of mist that
slipped like wraiths across the deepening dusk. In the empty, sullen
forest, there was only silence.

All day the land had been rising in a steady, gentle slope that
lifted now into a mass of cliffs and ridgelines. The Silver River
churned through their midst, swollen by the rains, cradled within
a deep and winding gorge. Mountains rose up about the gorge and
blocked it away with walls of cliffs that were sheer and stripped of
trees and scrub. Shadowed by mist and coming night, the Silver
River was soon lost from sight entirely.

It was the gorge that the Dwarves had named the Wedge.

The members of the little company came high upon its southern slope, heads bent against the wind, cloaks wrapped tightly
about their bodies as the cold and the rain seeped through. Silence
hung over everything, the roar of the wind sweeping from their ears
all sound save its own, and there was a deep and pervasive sense of
solitude in each man's mind. The company walked through scrub
and pine, making its way upward with slow, steady progress, feel-

ing the whole of the skyline close down about it as the afternoon
faded and night began to creep slowly in. Foraker led the way; this
was his country and he was the most familiar with its tricks. Garet
Jax followed, as black and hard as the trees they slipped through;
then came Slanter, Jair, and Edain Elessedil. Giant Helt brought up
the rear. No one spoke. In the stillness of their march, the minutes
dragged by.

They had passed over a gentle rise and come down into a stand
of glistening spruce when Foraker suddenly stopped, listened, then
motioned them all into the trees. With a word to Garet Jax, the
Dwarf slipped from them and disappeared into the mist and rain.

They waited in silence for his return. He was gone a long time.
When he finally reappeared, it was from a different direction en-
tirely. Signaling for them to follow, he led them deep into the trees.
There they knelt in a circle about him.

"Gnomes," he said quietly. Water ran from his bald head into
his thick beard, curling in its mass. "At least a hundred. They've
secured the bridge."

There was shocked silence. The bridge was in the middle of
supposedly safe country—country that was protected by an entire
army of Dwarves stationed at the fortress at Capaal. If there were
Gnomes this far west and this close to Culhaven, what had befallen
that army?

"Can we go around?" Garet Jax asked at once.

Foraker shook his head. "Not unless you want to lose at least
three days. The bridge is the only passage over the Wedge. If we
don't cross here, we have to backtrack down out of these mountains
and circle south through the wilderness."

Rain spattered down their faces in the silence that followed.
"We don't have three days to waste," the Weapons Master said finally. "Can we get past the Gnomes?"

Foraker shrugged. "Maybe—when it's dark."

Garet Jax nodded slowly. "Take us up for a look."

They climbed into the rocks, circling through pine, spruce, and
scrub, boulders damp and slick with rain, and mist and deepening

night. Silent shadows, they worked their way ahead, Elb Foraker in the lead as they crept cautiously into the gloom.

Then a flicker of firelight shone through the gray, its faint, lonely cast washed with rain. It slipped from beyond the rocks ahead of them. As one, they crouched from its eyes and crawled slowly on, up to where they could peek above the rim of a ridgeline and look down.

The sheer walls of the Wedge dropped away below, misted and rainswept as the night came down. Spanning the massive drop was a sturdy trestle bridge built of timber and iron, fastened to the cliff rock at a narrows, and pinioned with Dwarf skill and engineering against the thrust and bite of the wind. On the near side of the bridge, a broad shelf ran back to the ridgeline, thinly forested and covered now by Gnome watchfires in the shelter of makeshift lees and canvas tents. Gnomes huddled everywhere—about fires in shadowed knots, within the tents silhouetted against the firelight, and along the shelf from ridgeline to bridge. On the far side of the gorge, nearly lost in the dark, a dozen more patrolled a narrow trail that ran back from the drop over a low rise to a broad, forested slope that fell away a hundred yards further on into the wilderness.

At both ends of the trestle bridge, Gnome Hunters stood watch. The six who crouched upon the ridgeline studied the scene below for long moments, and then Garet Jax signaled for them all to withdraw into the shelter of a clump of boulders below.

Once there, the Weapons Master turned to Helt. "When it's dark, can we slip past?"

The big man looked doubtful. "Maybe as far as the bridge."

Garet Jax shook his head. "That's not far enough. We have to get beyond the sentries."

"One man might do it," Foraker said slowly. "Crawl under the bridge; crawl along the braces. If he were quick enough, he could slip across, kill the sentries and hold the bridge long enough for the others to follow."

"This is madness!" Slanter exclaimed suddenly, his rough face shoving into view. "Even if you manage somehow to make it to the far side—past those dozen or so sentries—the rest will be after you in a minute! How will you escape them?"

"Dwarf ingenuity," Foraker growled slowly. "We build things better than most, Gnome. That bridge is rigged to collapse. Pull the pins on either side and the whole thing drops into the gorge."

"How long to pull the pins?" Garet Jax asked him.

"A minute, maybe two. It's been expected for some time that the Gnomes would try to flank Capaal." He shook his head. "It worries me, though, that they've done it now and no one's stopped them. They're bold to seize the bridge as openly as this. And the way they've camped suggests they aren't much concerned about being caught from the other direction." He shook his head once more. "I'm worried for the army."

Garet Jax brushed the rain from his eyes. "Worry about them another time." He glanced quickly at the others. "Listen carefully. When it's dark, Helt will lead us through the camp to the bridge. I'll cross underneath. When I dispose of the sentries, Elb and the Gnome will cross with the Valeman. Helt, you and the Elven Prince use long bows to keep the Gnomes on this side of the bridge until the pins are pulled. Then cross when you're called and we'll drop the bridge."

Elb Foraker, Helt, and Edain Elessedil nodded wordlessly.

"There's more than a hundred Gnome Hunters down there!" Slanter pointed out heatedly. "If anything goes wrong, we won't have a chance!"

Foraker looked coldly at the Gnome. "That shouldn't bother you, should it? After all, you can pretend you're with them."

Jair glanced quickly at the Gnome, but Slanter turned away without comment. Garet Jax came to his feet.

"No sound from here forward. Remember what we have to do."

They climbed back onto the ridgeline, then huddled patiently within the rocks and watched as the night descended. An hour slipped away. Then two. Still the Weapons Master kept them where they were. Darkness fell over the whole of the gorge, and the rain and the mist passed across it like a veil. The cold began to deepen, settling through them with numbing bitterness. Below, the fires of the Gnome Hunters grew brighter against the black.

Then Garet Jax brought his arm up, and the little company rose. They slipped from the rocks like bits of scattered night and began their descent toward the Gnome encampment. They went one after another, Helt leading the way, slow and cautious as he picked his path downward. The fires burned closer, and then voices became audible in the rush of wind and rain—low, guttural, and sounding of discomfort. The six forms crept past fire and tent, bent low within shadows that spread from rock and trees into the night. The company circled left about the encampment, and only Helt's night vision kept them from wandering off the drop.

The minutes slipped away, and the slow crawl through the enemy camp dragged on. Jair could smell food cooking as the wind blew the odor back in his face. He could hear the voices of the Gnomes, their laughter and grunts, and see the movement of the toughened bodies passing in the faint light of the fires. He tried hard not even to breathe, willing himself to become one with the night. Then suddenly it occurred to him that if he wanted to, he really could become one with the night. He could use the wishsong to make himself invisible.

And then he realized that he had just stumbled on a better way to get them all across the bridge.

But how was he going to let the others know what it was?

They had crept to the edge of the gorge and were beyond the shelter of rocks and trees. Only the open face of the cliff stretched ahead. They edged forward, crouched low against the night. There were no fires here, and so they stayed hidden in the mist and the rain. Ahead, the bulk of the trestle bridge loomed through the dark, its wooden beams glistening with rain. Gnome voices came softly from above, brief and cryptic as the sentries hunched down within their cloaks and stared longingly at the warmth and cheer of the camp behind them. Silently, Helt took the company down beneath the bridge to where the supporting beams were anchored in the rock. Yards away, the empty depths of the Wedge opened in a monstrous chasm, wind howling through its cavernous stomach across the rock.

They crouched in a knot, and now Jair reached tentatively for Garet Jax. The hard face swung about. Jair pointed to the Weapons Master, then to himself, then to the sentries above them on the bridge. Garet Jax frowned. Jair pointed to his mouth and said soundlessly "Gnome" and pointed again to each of them. The wishsong can make the two of us appear as Gnomes to the sentries and we can cross without being stopped, he was trying to say. Should he whisper it? But no, the Weapons Master had said that no one was to speak. The wind would carry the sound of their voices; it was too dangerous. Again he made the same motions. The others crowded closer, glancing at one another uneasily as Jair continued to motion to Garet Jax.

Finally the Weapons Master seemed to understand. He hesitated for a moment, then took Jair's arm in his own, pulled him close and pointed to the others, then to the bridge above. Could the Valeman disguise them all? Jair hesitated; he hadn't considered that. Did he possess strength enough to carry the disguise that far? It was dark, raining, and they were all cloaked and hooded. It would only be for moments. He nodded that he could.

Garet Jax braced him firmly with both hands, gray eyes fixed upon his own. Then he motioned the others to follow them up. All understood. The Valeman was going to use the wishsong to get them across. They did not know how he was going to do that, but they had seen the power he commanded. Moreover, excepting only Slanter—and even he might have deferred to the other under those conditions—they trusted implicitly the judgment of Garet Jax. If he believed in Jair, so would they.

They rose in a knot from where they crouched hidden and walked boldly up the bluff rise toward the bridge. Before them, shadowed forms huddled in idle conversation. Aware suddenly of their approach, the Gnome sentries turned. There were only three. Jair was already singing, his voice blending into the wind in a harsh, guttural song that whispered of Gnomes. For an instant the sentries seemed to hesitate, and a few brought their weapons up guardedly. Jair pushed harder, probing with the wishsong to make them all appear as Slanter. The Gnome tracker would surely think I'm mad now, he thought fleetingly. Still he sang.

Weapons lowered then, and the sentries stepped aside. A changing of the watch? A relief for those on the far side of the gorge? Jair and his companions left them wondering, passing through their midst with faces lowered and cloaks wrapped close. They trooped onto the bridge, their booted feet thudding softly on the heavy wooden planks. Still Jair sang, shading them all in Gnome disguise.

Then abruptly his voice faltered, drained by the use to which he had put it. But they were past the line of sentries now, lost in a shroud of mist and rain to any eyes that might follow them. They reached the center of the bridge, the wind howling past them in stinging swipes. Hastily Garet Jax motioned for Helt and Edain Elessedil to drop back. For just an instant Jair had a fleeting glimpse of Slanter's face, filled with wonder as he stared at the Valeman. Then Garet Jax motioned both of them behind him, and with Elb Foraker at his side started forward once more.

They emerged from rain and night at the far side of the bridge, little more than hooded shadows to the Gnomes who kept watch there. Jair's throat tightened. This time there could be no wishsong to see them safely past; there were too many. A gathering of faces turned at their approach. For a few uncertain moments, the sentries simply stared at the figures who came at them, surprised by their appearance, yet certain that only Gnomes could come from the encampment they knew to hold the far cliff. Then before surprise could turn to alarm, or size and shape could properly register, Garet Jax and Foraker were upon them. Short sword and long knife glistened in the night. Half a dozen Gnomes lay dead before the others even realized what was happening. Their attackers swept into their midst, and now shouts of alarm broke wildly from their throats, calling to those on the far side.

Answering cries came back a moment later. Jair and Slanter crouched low at the far end of the bridge, watching the battle before them as it swept into the dark and hearing disembodied cries rise all about them. The sharp twang of Elven ash bows sounded above the rush of wind and rain, and more Gnome Hunters began to die.

Then a single Gnome burst from the darkness before them, bloodied and disheveled, his yellow face frantic in the dim light. He rushed onto the bridge, a two-edged axe in his hands. He saw Slanter and stopped, confused. Then he caught sight of Jair and sprang forward. The Valeman stumbled back, trying vainly to protect himself, so startled by the other's appearance that he momentarily forgot about the long knife he carried at his waist. The Gnome howled, weapon lifting, and Jair threw up his hands protectively.

"Not the boy, you . . ." Slanter cried out.

The Gnome screamed in rage, and again the axe came up. Slanter's sword swept down, and the attacker dropped to his knees, dying. Slanter drew back, a shocked look on his rough face. Then he had Jair by the arm, yanking him to his feet and pulling him ahead until they were clear of the bridge.

Abruptly Elb Foraker appeared. Without a word, he dropped below the trestle bridge to where the pins that held it fixed were concealed. With frantic motions, he began to pull them free.

Renewed cries sounded from the center of the bridge. Booted feet raced onto the wooden planks and from out of the mist and night Helt and Edain Elessedil burst. Still upon the bridge, they turned, and the great ash bows hummed. Gnomes howled in pain in the dark behind them. Again the bows hummed, and more cries rose. The sound of running feet disappeared back into the night.

"Hurry with those pins!" Helt bellowed sharply.

Garet Jax appeared now, joining Foraker beneath the bridge. Together they knocked the remaining pins free, one after the other—all but two. Again the thudding of booted feet rang out.

"Helt!" the Weapons Master called a moment later, scrambling back onto the ledge. Foraker was a step behind him. "Get off the bridge!"

The Borderman and the Elven Prince raced from out of the night, bent low against the wind. Spears and arrows flew after them.

Lighter and quicker, Edain was first off the bridge, springing past the crouched forms of Jair and Slanter.

"Now!" Foraker called over to Garet Jax.

They stood opposite each other, pry bars anchored in hooks fixed to the last of the concealed pins. As one, they pulled them free. In the same instant, Helt sprang clear of the bridge.

With a groan, the wooden beams wrenched free of their pinnings, and the bridge began to sink downward into the night. Screams rose from the throats of the Gnomes still caught upon its length, but it was too late for them. The bridge dropped away with a sudden heave, falling downward into the mist and the rain, spinning away against the cliffs until it broke free on the far side, dropped into the gorge, and was lost.

On the northern cliffs of the Wedge, six shadowed forms slipped swiftly into the darkness and were gone.

XVII

THE RAIN STOPPED THAT NIGHT, SOMETIME IN THE EARLY morning hours while the members of the little company from Culhaven lay sleeping within a shallow cavern half a dozen miles east of the Wedge. No one knew exactly when it happened—not even Edain Elessedil, who had been given the late watch. Exhausted by the harrowing flight across the Wedge, he had fallen asleep with the others.

So it was that dawn brought with the new day a change in the weather. North, almost lost in the horizon's bluish haze, stood the vast mountain range they called the Ravenshorn, and from down out of her giant peaks blew a wind chill with the promise of autumn's demise and winter's coming. Bitter and stiff, it swept the clouds, the rain, and the mist that had cloaked the Silver River southward, and once again the sky turned depthless blue. The damp and discomfort were gone. The sodden earth dried hard once more, the rain water evaporated in the wind, and the whole of the land came back into focus with stunning clarity, sharp-edged and brilliant in the sun's golden light.

Once more the company marched east, wrapped close in their still-damp woolen forest cloaks to ward off the wind's biting chill. Ridgelines and grassy bluffs flanked the Silver River now as she churned through her forested banks. As the six pushed ahead, the whole of the Anar spread away beneath them. All day the clustered peaks of Capaal loomed eastward of where they marched, jutting from out of the forest trees like massive spikes to pierce the fabric of the sky. Still distant when the day began, they grew steadily closer with the passing of the hours until, by midafternoon, the company had reached their lower slopes and begun the climb in.

They had not gone far, however, when Edain Elessedil brought them to a halt. "Listen!" he cautioned sharply. "Do you hear it?"

They stood silently upon the open slope, heads turned eastward toward the peaks as the Elven Prince pointed. Wind blew fiercely from out of the rocks, and there was no sound save its mournful howl.

"I hear nothing," Foraker murmured softly, but no one moved. The Elf's sense of hearing was much sharper than their own.

Then abruptly the wind seemed to shift and die, and a deep, steady booming came from far in the distance. It sounded faint and muffled, lost in the myriad twists and turns of the rock.

Foraker's black-bearded face went dark. "Gnome drums!"

They went forward again, more cautiously now, eyes scanning the cliffs and drops ahead. The pounding drums grew deeper and harder, throbbing against the rush of the wind, rumbling ominously through the earth.

Then, as the afternoon lengthened and the shadow of the peaks stretched farther down to where the six climbed, a new sound reached their ears. It was a strange sound, a kind of chilling howl that seemed almost a part of the wind at first, then grew distinct in its pitch and fury. Lifting out of the distant heights, it rolled down across the mountain slopes and gathered them in. Faces glanced one from the other, and at last it was Garet Jax who spoke, a hint of surprise in his voice.

"There is a battle being fought."

Foraker nodded and started ahead once again. "They've attacked Capaal!"

They climbed into the mountains, working their way through an increasingly jumbled maze of fragmented boulders, crevices, drops, and slides. The sunlight fell away as the afternoon died into dusk, and shadows lengthened over the whole of the southern exposure. The wind faded as well, and the chill it carried lost its edge. Silence descended across the land, its empty corners reverberating with the harsh echo of drums and battle cries. Far beyond where they climbed, through gaps in the barren peaks, great birds of prey circled in lazy sweeps—scavengers that watched and waited.

Then at last the company was atop the ridgeline of the nearest peak, turning into a deep and shadowed defile that ran through the rock into coming night. Cliff walls hemmed them in on all sides, and they squinted sharply through the half-light for signs of movement. But the way forward lay open, and all of the life among these rocks seemed to have been drawn to where the battle ahead was being fought.

Moments later they emerged from the defile and drew to a sudden halt. The cliff face dropped away before them and the whole of what lay beyond stood revealed.

"Shades!" Foraker whispered harshly.

Across a narrows, high within the peaks through which the waters of the Silver River flowed, stretched the locks and dams of Capaal. Huge, rough, and startlingly white against the dark rock, they rose high within the gathering of the mountains and cupped the waters of the Cillidellan in giant's hands. Atop their broad, flat crest, extending through three levels, was the fortress that served as protection, a sprawling mass of towers, walls and battlements. The greater portion of the citadel was settled upon the northern edge of this complex and faced onto a plain that ran back at a gentle slope into the sheltering peaks beyond. A smaller watch stood sentinel at the near end where the peaks ran down to the banks of the reservoir and only a series of narrow trails gave access to her walls.

It was here that the battle had been joined. The army of the Gnomes stretched all across the broad expanse of the far shelf and the slopes beyond, and all along the trails and rock slides running down. Huge and massive, it surged against the stone battlements of Capaal in a dark wave of armored bodies and thrusting weapons, seeking to breach the fortifications that held it out. Catapults flung huge boulders through the fading light, which smashed with crushing force into the armor and flesh of the Dwarf defenders. Screams and howls rose up through the ringing clash of iron, and men died all across the length and breadth of the fortress. Tiny, faceless beings, they struggled before the battlements, Dwarves and Gnomes alike, and were swept away in the carnage that resulted.

"So this is what the Gnomes have chosen for Capaal!" Foraker cried. "They have put her under siege! No wonder they were so bold in seizing the Wedge!"

Jair pushed forward for a better look. "Are the Dwarves trapped?" he asked anxiously. "Can't they escape?"

"Oh, they can escape easily enough—but they won't." Elb Foraker's dark eyes found the Valeman's. "Tunnels bore underground to the mountains on either side, secret passages built for escape should the fortress fall. But no army can breach the walls of Capaal, Ohmsford, and so the Dwarves within will stay and defend."

"But why?"

Foraker pointed. "The locks and dams. See the waters of the Cillidellan? The poison of the Mord Wraiths has blackened and fouled them. The dams hold back those waters from the lands west; the locks control the flow. Should the fortress be abandoned, the locks and dams would fall into the hands of the enemy. The Gnomes would open the gates and drain through the whole of the Cillidellan. They would flood the lands west with the fouled waters, poison as much of the land as they could, and kill as much of its life as they were able. The Wraiths would see to it. Even Culhaven would be lost." He shook his bearded face somberly. "The Dwarves will never permit that."

Jair stared down once more at the battle below, appalled by the ferociousness of the struggle. So many Gnomes besieged the defenders of the fortress; was it possible for the Dwarves to withstand them all?

"How do we get past this mess?" Garet Jax was studying the drop.

The Dwarf seemed lost in thought. "When it's dark, work your way east along the heights. That should keep you above the Gnome encampment. Once past the Cillidellan, come down to the river and cross. Then turn north. You should be safe enough then." He straightened and extended his hand. "Luck to you, Garet."

The Weapons Master stiffened. "Luck? You're not thinking of staying, are you?"

The other shrugged. "I'm not thinking of anything. It's decided."

Garet Jax stared. "You can't do any good here, Elb."

Foraker shook his head slowly. "Someone has to warn the garrison that the bridge at the Wedge has been dropped. Otherwise, if the worst happens and Capaal falls, they might try to escape back through the mountains and be trapped there." He shrugged. "Besides, Helt can lead you in the dark better than I. And after Capaal, I don't know the country anyway. The Gnome will have to guide you."

"We made a pact—the six of us." The voice of the Weapons Master had gone cold. "No one goes his own way. We need you."

The Dwarfs jaw tightened stubbornly. "They need me, too."

An unpleasant silence descended over the group as the two faced each other. Neither showed any intention of backing away.

"Let him go," Helt rumbled softly. "He has a right to choose."

"The choice was made at Culhaven." Garet Jax gave the Borderman an icy stare.

Jair's throat tightened. He wanted to say something—anything—to break the tension between the Dwarf and the Weapons Master, but he couldn't think of what it should be. He glanced at Slanter to see what the Gnome was thinking, but Slanter was ignoring them all.

"I have an idea." It was Edain Elessedil who spoke. All eyes shifted toward him. "Maybe this won't work, but it might be worth a try." He bent forward. "If I could get close enough to the fortress, I could tie a message to an arrow and shoot it in. That would let the defenders know about the Wedge."

Garet Jax turned to Foraker. "What do you think?"

The Dwarf frowned. "It will be dangerous. You'll have to get much closer than you'd like. Much."

"Then I'll go," Helt announced.

"It was my idea," Edain Elessedil insisted. "I'll go."

Garet Jax held up his hands. "If one goes, we all go. If we become separated in these mountains, we'll never find each other again." He glanced at Jair. "Agreed?"

Jair nodded at once. "Agreed."

"And you, Elb?" The Weapons Master faced the Dwarf once more.

Elb Foraker nodded slowly. "Agreed."

"And if we can get the message to the garrison?"

The other nodded again. "We go north."

Garet Jax took a final look down at the battle between Gnome and Dwarf armies, then motioned for the others to follow him back into the rocks. "We'll sit it out here until nightfall," he called back over his shoulder.

Jair turned to follow and found Slanter at his elbow. "Didn't notice him bothering to ask me if *I* agreed," the Gnome muttered and shouldered his way past.

The little company slipped down into a cluster of boulders, passing into the shadow of their concealment to wait until dark. Seated about the rocks, the six consumed a cold meal, wrapped themselves in their cloaks and settled back in silence. After a time, Foraker and Garet Jax left the cover of the rocks and disappeared down the slide for a closer look at the passage east. Edain Elessedil took the watch, and Helt stretched out comfortably on the rocky ground and was asleep almost at once. Jair sat alone for a few moments, then got up and walked over to where Slanter sat staring out into the empty dusk.

"I appreciate what you did for me back at the Wedge," he said quietly.

Slanter didn't turn. "Forget it."

"I can't. That's three times now that you've saved my life."

The Gnome's laugh was brittle. "That many, is it?"

"That many."

"Well, maybe next time I won't be there, boy. What will you do then?"

Jair shook his head. "I don't know."

There was an uncomfortable silence. Slanter continued to ignore the Valeman. Jair almost turned away again, but then his stubbornness got the better of him and he forced himself to remain. Deliberately, he took a seat next to the Gnome.

"He should have asked you," he said quietly.

"Who? Asked me what?"

"Garet Jax—he should have asked you if you were willing to go down to the fortress with us."

Now Slanter turned. "Hasn't asked me anything before, has he? Why should he start now?"

"Maybe if you . . ."

"Maybe if I sprout wings I'll be able to fly out of this place!" The Gnome's face flushed with anger. "In any case, what do you care?"

"I care."

"About what? That I'm here? Do you care about that? You tell me, boy—what am I doing here?"

Jair looked away uncomfortably, but Slanter gripped his arm and brought him about with a jerk.

"Look at me! What am I doing here? What has any of this got to do with me? Nothing, that's what! The only reason I'm here is because I was foolish enough to agree to guide you as far as Culhaven—that's the only reason! Help us get past the black walker, you asked! Help us get to the Eastland! You can do it because you're a tracker! Hah!"

The rough yellow face thrust forward. "And that stupid dream! That's all it was, boy—just a dream! There isn't any King of the Silver River, and this whole trek east is a waste of time! Ah, but here I am anyway, aren't I? I don't want to be here; there isn't any reason for me to be here—but here I am anyway!" He shook his head bitterly. "And it's all because of you!"

Jair pulled free, angry now himself. "Maybe that's so. Maybe it is my fault that you're here. But the dream was real, Slanter. And you're wrong when you say that none of this has anything to do with you. You call me 'boy' but you're the one who acts as if he hasn't grown up!"

Slanter stared at him. "Well, you are a wolf's cub, aren't you?"

"Whatever you want to call me, that's fine." Jair flushed. "But you better start thinking about who you are, too."

"What's that supposed to mean?"

"It means that you can't go on telling yourself that what happens to other people doesn't have anything to do with you—because it does, Slanter!"

Wordlessly they stared at each other. Darkness had fallen now, deep-shadowed and windless. It was strangely still, the booming of the Gnome drums and the clamor of the battle for Capaal silenced.

"Don't think much of me, do you?" Slanter said finally.

Jair sighed wearily. "As a matter of fact, that's not so. I think a lot of you."

The other studied him for a moment, then looked down. "I like you, too. Told you before—you got sand. You remind me of me in my better moments." He laughed softly, a hollow chuckle, then looked up again. "But you listen to me now because I'm not going to repeat this again. I don't belong in this. This isn't my fight. And whether I like you or not, I'm getting out of it the first chance I get."

He waited a moment as if to be certain that what he said had the intended effect, then turned away. "Now shove off and leave me be."

Jair hesitated, trying to decide if he should pursue the matter, then reluctantly climbed to his feet and walked away. He was passing close to the sleeping Helt when he heard the Borderman murmur, "I told you he cares."

Jair Ohmsford glanced down in surprise, then smiled and continued on. "I know," he whispered back.

It was drawing toward midnight when Garet Jax took the company out from the sheltering cluster of boulders and back onto the slide. Below, hundreds of Gnome watchfires ringed the fortress of Capaal, spread out across the cliffs on either side of the besieged locks and dams. The six began their descent, Elb Foraker in the lead. They proceeded down along the slide, then turned onto a narrow trail that ran forward into a series of defiles and rocky shelves. Cautiously, they worked their way ahead, silent shadows passing through the night.

It took them better than an hour to reach the perimeter of the watchfires on the near side of the encampment. Here the Gnomes were fewer in number; most were settled close to the edge of the Dwarf battlements. On the trails leading in, the fires were few and scattered. Beyond the siege lines on these southern slopes, a gathering of peaks thrust skyward, bunched at their base like bound and broken fingers, crooking from out of the earth. The six knew that beyond the peaks could be found a scattering of low hills that flanked the southern shores of the Cillidellan, and beyond these was the shelter of the forests that spread east. Once there, they could melt into the night and slip north without risk of being seen.

But first they must work their way close enough to the battlements of Capaal to permit Helt to use the ash bow so that Foraker's message could be delivered to the Dwarf defenders. It had been decided earlier that the Borderman would attempt the shot, for while the idea had been Edain Elessedil's, Helt was by far the stronger of the two. With the great ash bow to aid him, he need get no closer than two hundred yards from the fortress walls in order to place the arrow and its message within.

Step by step, the six made their way down from the mountain heights through the lines of the Gnome watch. Stretched upward along the broader paths from where the main encampment ringed the battlements of the fortress, the Gnomes gave little attention to the smaller trails and ledges that crisscrossed the cliff face. It was down these smaller trails and ledges that Foraker took his little group in a slow, cautious descent where the footing was treacherous and the cover thin. Pieces of soft leather bound each booted foot, and charcoal blackened each face. No one spoke. Hands and feet picked their way carefully, wary of loose rock or of any sound that would call attention to their passage.

Two hundred yards from the walls of the fortress, they were still just back of the forward siege lines of the Gnome army. Watchfires burned all about them—all along the trails leading back. Silently, they hunched down within a small gathering of scrub and waited for Helt. The giant Borderman removed the arrow with its message from his quiver, fitted it to the ash bow and slipped forward into the night. Several dozen yards ahead, at the edge of the scrub, he rose to a kneeling position, pulled back the bowstring, held it momentarily to his cheek and released it.

A sharp twang shattered the silence of the little company's shelter, yet beyond where they hid, the sound was lost in the routine clamor of the Gnome camp. Nevertheless, the six flattened themselves within the brush for long minutes, waiting and listening for any indication that they had been discovered. There was none. Helt slipped back through the darkness and nodded briefly to Foraker. The message had been delivered.

The little company crept back through the night and the lines of watchfires and Gnomes, this time working its way eastward about the dark girth of the peaks toward where the waters of the Cillidellan shimmered with the moon's soft light. Far away across the lake, where the dam joined with the broad slope of the mountains north, Gnome fires burned fiercely about the encircled locks and dams and along the shoreline of the Cillidellan. Jair glanced at the mass of watchfires and went cold. How many thousands of Gnomes had been brought to besiege this fortress? he wondered dismally. So many, it seemed. Too many. The fires reflected on the waters of the lake with a reddish glow, bits and pieces of flame dancing across the mirrored surface like droplets of blood.

Time slipped away. Stars winked into view far north, scattered and lost somehow in the vastness of the night. The company had gone back above the watchfires on the southern slope once more and worked its way south of where the Gnomes laid siege. High upon the cliff face, they were almost to where they might view the lowlands that flanked the southern bank of the Cillidellan—almost to where they could begin their descent into the forests below. Jair felt a distinct sense of relief. He felt uncomfortably exposed, caught like this upon the open slopes of the cliffs. They would be far better off when they could rely once more upon the concealment of the forestland.

Then they turned the corner of the cliff face, slipped downward through a mass of giant boulders, and came to an abrupt and startled halt.

Before them, the slope broadened toward the banks of the Cillidellan in a meandering passage through rock and cliff face. A mass of watchfires lay spread out across its entire length and breadth. Jair felt his throat tighten with fear. A second Gnome army blocked the way forward.

Garet Jax glanced quickly at Foraker, and the Dwarf disappeared ahead into the night. The five who remained crouched down within the shelter of the boulders to wait.

It was a long, tense wait. Half an hour passed before Foraker reappeared, slipping from the darkness as silently as he had gone. Hurriedly, he drew the others close about him.

"They're all across the cliff face!" he whispered. "We can't get through!"

In the next instant, they heard the sound of booted feet and voices on the trail behind them.

XVIII

---◆---

THEY FROZE FOR A SINGLE INSTANT WHERE THEY WERE, STAR-
ing back in startled silence into the dark. Sudden laughter blended
with the approaching voices, sharp and raucous, and a flicker of
torchlight appeared from out of the rocks.

"Hide!" Garet Jax whispered, dragging Jair with him into the
shadows.

They scattered at once, swift and silent as they bolted into the
rocks. Pushed roughly to the ground by the Weapons Master, Jair
lifted his head and peered out into the night. Torchlight reflected
off the dark surface of the boulders and the voices grew distinct.
Gnomes. At least half a dozen. Booted feet scraped against the stone
of the pathway and leather harness creaked. Jair flattened himself
against the earth and quit breathing.

A squad of Gnome Hunters marched into the cluster of boulders, eight strong, torches held before them to light their path down
out of the cliffs. Laughing and joking in their rough, garbled tongue,
they sauntered unseeing into the midst of the hidden members of
the company from Culhaven. Torchlight flooded the little clearing,
chasing shadows and night, brightening even the deepest recesses of
the company's concealment. Jair went cold. Even from where he lay,
he could see the shadowed form of Helt pressed against the rocks.
Surely there was no way that they could avoid being discovered.

But the Gnomes did not slow. Oblivious to the figures that

crouched about them, the members of the squad continued on. The foremost were already past the front line of boulders, their eyes drawn to the lights of the encampment below. Jair took a slow, cautious breath. Perhaps . . .

Then one of those who trailed slowed suddenly and turned toward the rocks. A sharp exclamation broke from his lips, and he reached quickly for his sword. The others in the squad turned, laughter dying into startled grunts.

Already Garet Jax was moving. He sprang from the concealing shadows, daggers in both hands. He caught the two members of the squad nearest him and killed both with a single pass. The others whirled, weapons coming up defensively, still confused by the unexpected attack. But by now Helt and Foraker had appeared as well, and three more fell without a sound. The Gnomes who remained bolted down the pathway onto the slide, yelling wildly. Springing onto the rocks, Edain Elessedil brought up his bow. The bowstring hummed twice and two more died. The final Hunter scrambled wildly from sight and was gone.

Quickly the members of the little company rushed to the edge of the boulders. Shouts of alarm had already begun to ring out from the mass of watchfires below.

"Well, we're in for it now!" Foraker snapped angrily. "Every Gnome on both sides of these cliffs will be looking for us in the next few minutes!"

Garet Jax calmly slipped the daggers back beneath the black cloak and turned to the Dwarf. "Which way do we run?"

Foraker hesitated. "Back the way we came. The heights, if we can gain them in time; if not, we find one of the tunnels into Capaal."

"You lead." Garet Jax motioned swiftly. "Remember—stay together. If we become separated, try to stay with someone. Now, go!"

They raced back up the narrow trail into the night. Behind them, the shouts and cries of the Gnome watch continued to sound, spreading across the whole of the slide. Ignoring the pursuit, the six scrambled along the empty pathway until they had rounded once more the side of the peak and the lights of the encampment behind them were lost in the dark.

Ahead, the watchfires of the siege flickered into view. Still far below the trail they followed, the main body of the Gnome army had not yet had time to discover what was happening. Torches wavered in the darkness as sentries scrambled up from their watchfires and began to spread out onto the cliffs, but the hunt was still well below the six. Foraker took them swiftly along the darkened ledge, down slides and drops, and through shadowed defiles. If they were quick enough, they might yet escape back the way they had come, through the peaks about Capaal. If they were not, the search to find them would spread upward into the rocks, and they would find themselves trapped between the two armies.

Shouts of alarm broke suddenly from somewhere ahead, lost in the darkness of the rocks. Foraker muttered a low oath, but didn't slow. Jair stumbled, sprawling wildly onto the rocks, scraping arms and legs. From behind, Helt lifted him back to his feet and pulled him roughly on.

Then they burst from the concealment of a defile onto a broad trail atop a slide directly into the path of an entire Gnome watch. Gnomes came at them from everywhere, swords and spears glinting in the firelight. Garet Jax spun into them, short sword and long knife cutting a path for the others. Gnomes fell dying all about the Weapons Master, and for an instant the entire watch shrank from the fury of this dark attacker. Desperately, the little company tried to force passage through, Elb Foraker and Edain Elessedil leading the way. But there were too many Gnomes. Rallying, they closed off the trail ahead and counterattacked. They surged down the cliff face, howling in rage. Foraker and Edain Elessedil disappeared from view. Helt stood against the assault for just an instant, his giant form flinging Gnomes aside as they sought to pull him down. But even the Borderman could not withstand so many. Sheer numbers forced him from the ledge, and he tumbled from sight.

Jair stumbled back in dismay, alone now. Even Slanter had disappeared. But then Garet Jax was there once more, a black form slipping past the Gnome Hunters who sought to slow him. In an instant he was next to Jair, sweeping the Valeman before him, turning him back into the defile.

Alone, the two retraced their steps hurriedly through the darkness. Shouts of pursuit followed after, and a flicker of torchlight chased their shadows. At the far end of the defile, the Weapons Master gave a quick glance upward at the sheer cliff face, then pulled Jair after him as he worked his way down a scrub-covered drop toward the mass of siege fires that twinkled below. Jair was too stunned by what had happened to the others of the company to question the decision. Slanter, Foraker, Helt and Edain Elessedil—all lost in an instant's time. He could not believe it.

Halfway to the bottom of the drop was a small pathway, barely wide enough for a single man. It was deserted—for the moment, at least. Crouching within a small bit of brush, Garet Jax searched quickly the land about him. Jair searched with him and saw no way out. The Gnomes were all about them. Torches flickered on the paths above as well as the broader ledges and trails below. Sweat ran down the Valeman's back, and his own breathing sounded harsh in his ears.

"What are we . . . ?" he started to ask, but the Weapons Master's hand clamped about his mouth instantly.

Then they were on their feet again, bent down within the rocks as they scrambled east along the narrow path. Boulders and jagged projections rose up against the faint light of the sky, thrusting out from the cliff face. They ran on, and the path ahead grew less easy. Jair risked a quick glance back. A line of torches was coiling up the slope from the siege camp below, up to where they had just knelt within the brush. Moments later, the torches were upon the trail.

The Weapons Master slipped down into the jumbled rocks, with Jair a step behind him, scrambling wildly to keep his feet. Ahead, the cliff face jutted far out into the night sky, and the slope beneath where they climbed began to drop away sharply. Jair felt a sinking sensation in his stomach. This was a dead end. They were not going to get through.

Still Garet Jax worked his way forward, easing downward through the rocks, climbing farther out onto the cliffs. Behind, the torches followed after, and all across the length and breadth of the chasm that sheltered the locks and dams of Capaal the cries of the Gnome Hunters rang out.

Then at last the Weapons Master drew to a halt. The trail fell away in a sheer cliff a dozen yards farther on. Far below, the waters of the Cillidellan reflected with firelight. Jair glanced quickly above where they stood. There, too, the cliff angled sharply out. There was nowhere left for them to go but back. They were trapped.

Garet Jax put a hand on his shoulder and led him forward to where the trail fell away completely. Then he turned.

"We have to jump," he said softly, his hand still gripping the Valeman. "Just lock your legs and pull in your arms. I'll be right behind you."

Jair glanced down to where the Cillidellan shimmered. It was a long, long way. He looked back again at the Weapons Master.

"It's the only choice we have left." The other's voice was calm and reassuring. "Hurry, now."

The torches grew closer on the pathway behind them. Guttural voices called sharply to one another.

"Hurry, Jair."

Jair took a deep breath, closed his eyes, opened them again and jumped.

So violent was the Gnome counterattack, as the six from Culhaven sought to break through the heights above Capaal, that the initial rush carried most of the attackers right past Foraker and Edain Elessedil. Thrown back against the cliff face as the assault swept on toward the others, Dwarf and Elven Prince scrambled upward into a stand of brush, a handful of Gnomes in desperate pursuit. They turned to fight at a small outcropping, the Elf swinging the sturdy ash bow, the Dwarf stabbing out with short sword and long knife. The Gnomes tumbled, howling with pain, and the pursuit fell back for an instant. The two companions peered down at the ledge and the steep slide below, swarming now with Gnome Hunters. There was no sign of the others.

"This way!" Elb Foraker called, pulling the Elven Prince after him.

They scrambled up the slope, scratching and clawing their way over the loose earth and rock. Cries of anger followed after, and suddenly arrows flew past them, a vicious hissing in their ears. Torches bobbed in the darkness, searching them out, but for the moment at least, they were beyond the light.

A roar sounded from somewhere below, and the pursued companions looked back apprehensively. The lights of the watchfires seemed to be spreading out across the cliff face, bits of fire darting about in the blackness. Hundreds more flickered into view on the dark line of the peaks south—torches from the army that lay camped along the banks of the Cillidellan. The whole of the mountainside now burned bright with flame.

"Elb, they're all around us!" the Elven Prince cried out, staggered by the number of the enemy.

"Keep climbing!" the other snapped.

Onward they went, fighting their way through the dark. Now a new cluster of torches appeared to their right, and shouts of discovery broke from the throats of the Gnomes who bore them. Spears and arrows whistled all about the two who climbed. Foraker scrambled away from them, eyes searching frantically across the dark cliff face.

"Elb!" Edain Elessedil screamed in pain and spun about, his shoulder pierced by a dart.

Instantly the Dwarf was at his side. "Ahead—another dozen feet to that patch of scrub! Hurry!"

Half carrying the injured Elven Prince, Foraker scrambled toward a broad thatch of brush that loomed suddenly out of the night. Torchlight flickered above them now as well, Gnome Hunters coming down from high off the slopes of the peak where the search lines cordoned off all escape. Edain Elessedil set his teeth against the pain in his shoulder and struggled forward with the Dwarf.

They tumbled into the brush, down into the concealing shadows to lie panting on the earth.

"They'll . . . find us here," the Elven Prince gasped, forcing himself to his knees. Across his back, blood and sweat mingled and ran.

Foraker yanked him down again. "Stay put!" Wheeling, he began groping his way through the brush until he found the slope against which it grew. "Here! A tunnel door! Thought I'd remembered right, but . . . have to find the trip lock . . ."

While Edain Elessedil watched, he began to fumble frantically about the slope face, through crumbling rock and earth, pulling and clawing in silent desperation. The cries of their pursuers were drawing steadily closer. Through faint breaks in the brush appeared the flicker of torchlight, bobbing and weaving against the black.

"Elb, they're almost here!" Edain whispered hoarsely. His hand reached down to his waist and drew forth the short sword belted there.

"Got it!" the Dwarf cried triumphantly.

A squarish chunk of rock and earth swung back, and an opening in the cliff face yawned before them. Frantically, they scrambled through into the darkness beyond, and Foraker pulled shut the rock behind them. It closed ponderously, sealing them away with a series of sharp clicks, the locks fastening in place.

They lay in the dark for long moments, listening to the faint sounds of the Gnomes without. Then the pursuit passed on, and there was only silence. A moment later Foraker began groping about in the dark. Flint and stone struck a spark, and harsh yellow torchlight filled the void. They sat within a small cave from which a stone stairway ran downward into the mountain.

Foraker slid the torch into an iron bracket next to the sealed door and began working on the Elven Prince's injured shoulder. In a few minutes' time, he had the arm bound and wrapped in a makeshift sling.

"That should do for now," he muttered. "Can you walk?"

The Elf nodded. "What about the door? Suppose the Gnomes find it?"

"Too bad for them if they do," Foraker snorted. "The locks should hold it; but if they don't, a break-in will trigger a collapse of the whole entrance. On your feet, now. We've got to go."

"Where do the stairs lead?"

"Down. Into Capaal." He shook his head. "Have to hope the others will find some different way to get there."

He helped Edain to his feet, pulling the Elf's good arm over his shoulder. Then he snatched the torch from its rack.

"Hold tight, now."

Slowly, they began their descent.

The Borderman Helt tumbled headlong down the steep slide, weapons flying from him as he fell, the maddened struggle on the cliff ledge left behind. Lights and sound whirled about him as he went, a jumble that spun and faded in his mind. Then came a jarring halt, and he found himself wedged within a mass of brush at the slide's bottom, sprawled in a tangle of arms and legs. He lay dazed for a minute, the breath knocked from his body. Gingerly he tried to extricate himself from the tangle. It was then that he realized that not all of the arms and legs were his own.

"Easy!" a voice hissed in his ear. "Half broke me in two already!"

The Borderman started. "Slanter?"

"Keep it down!" the other snapped. "They're all around us!"

Helt lifted his head carefully and blinked his eyes against the dizziness. Torchlight flickered close by, and there were voices calling back and forth through the darkness. He realized suddenly that he lay on top of the little Gnome. With great care, he lifted himself clear of the other, coming unsteadily to his knees within the shadow of the brush.

"Took me right off the ledge with you!" Slanter muttered, disbelief and anger mingling in his voice. The gnarled body straightened, and he peered carefully about through the scrub, the distant firelight reflected in his eyes. "Oh, shades!" he groaned.

Helt came to a low crouch, staring out into the dark. Behind them, the slide down which they had fallen loomed like a wall against the night. Before them, spread out for hundreds of yards in all directions in a mass of blazing yellow light, were the watchfires of the Gnome army that encircled the fortress of Capaal. Helt studied the fires wordlessly for a moment, then dropped back into the brush, Slanter beside him.

"We're right in the middle of the siege camp," he said quietly.

Already there were torches lining the ledge from which they had fallen, far distant yet unmistakable in their purpose. The Gnomes on the ledge were coming down after them.

"We can't stay here." Helt came to his feet once more, eyes peering out through the brush at the Gnome Hunters about them.

"Well, where do you suggest we go, Borderman?" Slanter snapped.

Helt shook his head slowly. "Perhaps along the slide . . ."

"The slide? Perhaps we can fly while we're at it!" Slanter shook his head. The Gnome Hunters were calling down into the camp from the ledge. "No way out of this one," he muttered bitterly. He cast about futilely for a moment, then paused. "Unless, of course, you happen to be a Gnome."

His rough yellow face swung about to find Helt. The Borderman stared back at him wordlessly, waiting. "Or perhaps one of the walkers," he added.

Helt shook his head slowly. "What are you talking about?"

Slanter bent close. "Must be mad even to consider this, but I guess it's no madder than anything else that's happened. You and me, Borderman. Black walker and Gnome servant. Pull that cloak about you, hood about your head, no one'll know. You're big enough for it. Walk right through them, you and me—right up to the gates of that fortress. Hope to all that's good and right that the Dwarves open up long enough for us to slip in."

Shouts rose from off to their left. Helt glanced over quickly, then back again. "You could do all this without me, Slanter. You could get out on your own a lot easier than if I'm with you."

"Don't tempt me!" the Gnome snapped.

The gentle eyes were steady. "They're your people. You could still go back to them."

Slanter seemed to think it over for a moment. Then he shook his head roughly. "Forget it. I'd have that black devil Weapons Master tracking me all through the Four Lands. I'm not risking that." The hard yellow face seemed to stiffen further. "And there's the boy . . ."

His eyes snapped up. "Well, do we try it or not, Borderman?"

Helt rose, pulling his cloak close about him. "We try it."

They strode clear of the brush, Slanter with his cloak thrown wide so that all could see it was a Gnome who led the way, Helt with his drawn close, a massive, hooded giant towering above the other. They passed boldly down through the spokes of the siege lines toward where the army massed before the fortress walls, staying carefully within the darkness between those lines so that they could not be clearly seen. They walked for nearly fifty yards, and no one gave challenge.

Then a cross line blocked their way forward, and there was no longer any darkness left through which to pass. Slanter never hesitated. He stalked toward the watchfires, the cloaked figure following. The Gnome Hunters who were gathered there turned to gape, weapons lifting guardedly.

"Stand back!" Slanter called out sharply. "The Master comes!"

Eyes widened and fear reflected in the harsh yellow faces. Weapons lowered quickly, and all stood aside as the two figures passed, slipping into a square of half-light between the lines. Gnomes were all about them now, heads turning, eyes staring in surprise and curiosity. Still no one challenged, the tumult of the search on the slope drowning out everything else in the autumn night.

Another siege line lay ahead. Slanter lifted his arms dramatically to the Gnome Hunters who turned. "Give way to the Master, Gnomes!"

Again the lines parted to let them through. Sweat was pouring down Slanter's rough face as he glanced back at the shadowed figure behind him. Hundreds of eyes followed after them, and there was a faint stirring within the ranks of the Gnomes. A few were beginning to question what was happening.

The last of the forward lines of the siege lay before them. Here the Gnome Hunters again brought up their short spears menacingly, and there were disgruntled mutterings. Beyond the watchfires the dark walls of the Dwarf citadel rose up against the night and on their battlements, torches burned in solitary patches of hazy light.

"Stand away!" Slanter bellowed, again throwing up his arms. "Dark magic runs loose this night and the walls of the enemy keep shall crumble before it! Stand away! Let the walker pass!"

As if to emphasize the warning, the cloaked figure following lifted one arm slowly and pointed toward the watch.

That was enough for the Gnomes on the siege lines. Breaking ranks, they parted hurriedly, most of them scurrying back toward the second line of defense, casting anxious glances over their shoulders as they went. A few lingered, frowns on their faces as the two figures passed, but still no one stepped forward to offer challenge.

The Gnome and the Borderman walked into the night, eyes riveted now on the dark walls ahead. Slanter raised his hands high above his head as they approached, praying inwardly that this simple gesture would be enough to stay the deadly missiles surely pointed in their direction.

They were two dozen yards from the walls when a voice rang out. "Come no farther, Gnome!"

Slanter drew to an immediate halt, arms lowering. "Open the gates!" he cried furtively. "We're friends!"

There was a low muttering on the walls, and a call down to someone below. But the gates remained closed. Slanter glanced about frantically. Behind where he and Helt stood watching, the Gnomes were stirring once more.

"Who are you?" the voice from atop the wall called out again.

"Open the gates, you fool!" Slanter's patience was gone.

Now Helt came forward to stand beside the Gnome. "Calla-horn!" he called out in a hoarse whisper.

Behind them, a chorus of howls rose up from the Gnomes. The game was up. The two broke for the fortress walls in a mad dash, calling to the Dwarves within. They dashed up against the iron-bound gates, casting desperate glances back as they ran. An entire line of Gnome Hunters swept toward them, torches bobbing wildly, cries of rage breaking from their throats. Spears and arrows launched through the dark.

"Oh, shades, open up in there, you . . . !" Slanter bawled.

Abruptly the gates swung open and hands reached out to yank them through. An instant later they were within the fortress, the gates slamming shut behind them as renewed howls of fury filled the night. They were thrown to the ground, and iron-tipped spears ringed them tightly.

Slanter shook his head in disgust and glanced over at Helt. "You explain it to them, Borderman," he muttered. "Even if I wanted to, I don't think I could."

Jair Ohmsford fell a long way into the Cillidellan. Downward he plunged, a tiny speck of darkness against the deep blue-gray of the night sky, the pit of his stomach dropping away, the rush of the wind filling his ears with its sound. Far below him the waters of the lake shimmered with bits of crimson light as the watchfires of the Gnomes reflected against their rippling surface, and all about him the vast sweep of the mountains and cliffs encircling Capaal rose up through the blur of his vision. Time seemed to come to a sudden standstill, and it felt as if he would never come to rest.

Then he struck with jarring force, breaking through the surface of the lake and plunging deep into the cold, dark waters. The breath left his lungs with stunning suddenness, and his whole body went numb with shock. Frantically, he clawed his way through the chill blackness that had closed about him, barely conscious of anything beyond his need to reach the surface once more so that he could breathe. The heat from his body dissipated in seconds, and he felt a crushing force pressing in against him, so terrible that it threatened to break him in two. He struggled upward, desperate with need. Lights danced before his eyes and his arms and legs seemed suddenly turned to lead. Weakly, he thrashed against their pull, lost in a maze of dark turns.

A moment later, everything slipped away from him.

He dreamed, a long, endless dream of disconnected feelings and sensations and of times and places both remembered and yet somehow new. Waves of sound and motion carried him through landscapes of nightmare and haunts of the familiar, through oft-traveled forest trails of the Vale, and through sweeps of black, cold water where life passed in tangled disarray in faces and shapes not fixed one to the other, but disjointed and free. Brin was there, come and gone in brief glimpses, a distorted form that combined reality with falsehood and begged for understanding. Words came at him from things misshapen and lifeless, yet her voice seemed to speak the words, calling to him, calling . . .

Then Garet Jax was holding him, arms wrapped tightly about his body, his voice a whisper of life in a dark place. Jair floated, the waters buoying him, and his face turned skyward into the clouded night. Gasping, he sought to talk and could not manage. He was awake again, come back from where he had slipped away, yet not fully conscious of what had befallen him or what he was about. He drifted in and out of darkness, reaching back each time he began to slide too far so that he might be grasped anew by the sound and color and feeling that meant life.

Then there were hands grasping him as well, pulling him up from the waters and the blackness, easing him down onto solid ground once more. Rough voices muttered vaguely, the fragmented words slipping through his mind like stray leaves blown by the wind. His eyes flickered, and Garet Jax was bending over him, lean brown face damp and drawn with the chill, fair hair plastered back against his head.

"Valeman, can you hear me? It's all right. You're all right now."

Other faces pushed into view—blocky Dwarf faces, resolute and grave as they studied his. He swallowed, choked and mumbled something incoherent.

"Don't try to talk," one said gruffly. "Just rest."

He nodded. Hands wrapped him in blankets, then lifted him up and began to carry him away.

"Sure has been a night for strays." Another voice chuckled.

Jair tried to look back to where the voice had come from, but he could not seem to focus his sense of direction. He let himself sink downward into the warmth of the blankets, eased by the gentle rocking of the hands that bore him.

A moment later, he was asleep.

XIX

◆

It was midday of the next day when Jair awoke again. He might not have come awake even then were it not for the hands that shook him none too gently from his slumber and the rough voice that whispered in his ear, "Wake up, boy! You've slept long enough! Come on, wake up!"

Grudgingly, he stirred within the blankets that covered him, rolled onto his back and rubbed the sleep from his eyes. Gray sunlight filtered through a narrow window next to his head, causing him to squint against its brightness.

"Come on, the day's almost gone! Been shut away the whole of it, thanks to you!"

Jair's eyes shifted to find the speaker, a stoutly familiar figure positioned at the side of his bed. "Slanter?" he whispered in disbelief.

"Now who else would it be?" the other snapped.

Jair blinked. "Slanter?"

Abruptly the events of the previous night recalled themselves to his mind in a flood of images: the flight from the Gnomes in the mountains about Capaal; the separation of the company; the long drop into the Cillidellan with Garet Jax; and their subsequent rescue from its waters by the Dwarves. You're all right now, the Weapons Master had whispered to him. He blinked again. But Slanter and the others . . .

"Slanter!" he exclaimed, now fully awake. Hastily, he pushed himself upright. "Slanter, you're alive!"

"Of course I'm alive! What does it look like?"

"But how did . . . ?" Jair left the question hanging and grasped the Gnome's arm anxiously. "What about the others? What's happened to them? Are they all right?"

"Slow down, will you?" The Gnome freed his arm irritably. "They're all fine and they're all here, so stop worrying. The Elf took a dart in the shoulder, but he'll live. Only one who's in danger at the moment is me. And that's because I'm shut up in this room with you, dying of boredom! Now will you climb out of that bed so we can get out of here?"

Jair didn't hear all of what the Gnome was saying. Everyone's all right, he was repeating to himself. Everyone made it. No one was lost, even though it had seemed certain that some of them must be. He breathed deeply in relief. Something the King of the Silver River had said recalled itself suddenly to his mind. A touch of magic for each who journey with you, the old man had told him. Strength for the body, given to others. Perhaps that strength, that touch of the magic, had seen each of them safely through last night.

"Get up, get up, get up!" Slanter was practically hopping up and down with impatience. "What are you doing just sitting there?"

Jair swung his legs out of the bed and glanced about the room in which he found himself. It was a small, stone block chamber, sparsely furnished with bed, sitting table, and chairs, its walls bare save for a broad heraldic tapestry hung from the far supports of its sloped ceiling. A second window opened out at the other end of the wall against which Jair's bed rested, and a single wooden door stood closed, opposite where he sat. In one corner, a small fireplace cradled an iron gate and a stack of burning logs.

He glanced at Slanter. "Where are we?"

Slanter looked at him as if he were a complete idiot. "Now where do you think we are? We're inside the Dwarf fortress!"

Where else? Jair thought ruefully. Slowly he stood up, still testing his strength as he stretched and peered curiously out of the window in back of him. Through its narrow, barred slot he could see the murky gray expanse of the Cillidellan stretching away into a day thick with mist and low-hanging clouds. Far distant, through this shifting haze, he could discern the flicker of watchfires burning along the shores of the lake.

Gnome watchfires.

Then he noticed how quiet it was. He was within the fortress of Capaal, the Dwarf citadel that stood watch over the locks and dams that regulated the flow of the Silver River westward, the citadel that one day earlier had been under assault by Gnome armies. Where were those armies now? Why wasn't Capaal under attack?

"Slanter, what's happened to the siege?" he asked quickly. "Why is it so still?"

"How should I know?" the other snapped. "No one tells me anything!"

"Well, what's happening out there? What have you seen?"

Slanter jerked upright. "Haven't heard a word I've said, have you? What's the problem—ears not working or something? I've been right here in this room with you ever since they dragged you out of the lake! Shut away like a common thief! Saved that confounded Borderman's skin out there and what do I get for my trouble? Shut in here with you!"

"Well, I . . ."

"A Gnome's a Gnome, they think! Don't trust any of us! So here I sit, mother hen to you while you slumber on like you don't have a care in the world. Waited all day for you to decide to wake up! You'd be sleeping still, I suppose, if I hadn't lost patience entirely!"

Jair drew back. "You could have woken me sooner . . ."

"How could I do that!" the other exploded. "How was I to know what was wrong with you? Could have been anything! Had to let you rest just to be sure! Couldn't be taking chances, could I? That black devil Weapons Master would have had me flayed!"

Jair grinned in spite of himself. "Calm down, will you?"

The Gnome clenched his teeth. "I'll calm down when you get yourself out of that bed and into your clothes! There's a guard on the other side of that door keeping me shut up in here! But with you awake, maybe we can talk him into letting the two of us out! Then you can be amused on your own time! Now, dress!"

Shrugging, Jair slipped off the night clothes that had been provided him and began pulling on his Vale clothes. He was surprised, though pleased, to find Slanter so vocal again, even if his discourse was, for the moment at least, limited to a tirade against the Valeman. Slanter seemed more his normal self again, more that voluble fellow he had been that first night after making Jair his prisoner in the highlands—that fellow Jair had come to like. He wasn't sure why the Gnome had chosen now to come out of his shell, but he was delighted to have the old Slanter back as company once more.

"Sorry you had to be locked in here with me," he ventured after a moment.

"You ought to be," the other grumbled. "They put me in here to look after you, you know. Must think I make a good nursemaid or something."

Jair grinned. "I'd say they're right."

The expression that crossed the Gnome's face then caused Jair to turn away quickly, his face a carefully frozen mask. Chuckling inwardly, he was in the process of reaching for his boots when he abruptly remembered the vision crystal and the Silver Dust. He had not seen either while dressing. He had not felt them in his pockets. The grin he had allowed to slip back over his face faded. He ran his hands over his clothing. Nothing! Frantically, he pawed through his bedding, his bedclothes, and everything in sight. The vision crystal and the Silver Dust were gone. Then he thought back to the night previous, to the long jump into the Cillidellan. Had he lost them in the lake?

"Looking for something?"

Jair stiffened. It was Slanter speaking, his voice laced with false concern. Jair turned. "Slanter, what have you done . . . ?"

"Me?" the other interrupted quickly, feigned innocence in the crafty face. "Your devoted nursemaid?"

Jair was furious. "Where are they, Slanter? Where did you put them?"

Now it was the Gnome's turn to grin. "Enjoyable as this is—and believe me, it is enjoyable—I have better things to do. So if it's the pouch and the crystal you're looking for, the Weapons Master has them. Took them off you last night when they brought you in here and stripped you. Wouldn't trust them to my care, of course."

He folded his arms across his chest contentedly. "Now let's put an end to this. Or do you need help dressing, too?"

Jair flushed, finished dressing, then wordlessly walked over to the wooden door and knocked. When the door opened, he informed the Dwarf standing guard that they would like to go out. The Dwarf frowned, told them to stay put, glanced suspiciously at Slanter, and pulled the door firmly shut again.

Growing curiosity over the absence of any sort of battle without and impatience with things in general notwithstanding, they had to wait fully an hour before the door to the room opened a second time, and the guard at last beckoned them to follow. Leaving the room hastily, they turned down a windowless corridor that ran past dozens of doors similar to the one they had just passed through, climbed a series of stairs, and emerged on battlements overlooking the murky waters of the Cillidellan. Wind and a faint spray blew off the lake into their faces, the midday air chill and hard. Here, too, the day was still and expectant, cloaked in mist and banks of low-hanging clouds that stretched between the peaks that sheltered the locks and dams. Dwarf sentries patrolled the walls, eyes shifting watchfully through the haze. There was no sign of the Gnome armies, save for the distant flicker of the watchfires, reddish specks of light in the gray.

The Dwarf took them down off the battlements, turning into a broad courtyard that spanned the center of the high dam where it walled away the Cillidellan. North and south of where they walked, the towers and parapets of the Dwarf fortress rose up against the leaden sky, stretching away into mist. It was an eerie, ghostly look that the day lent to the citadel, shrouding it in half-light and haze so that it almost seemed as if it were something strayed from a dream that threatened to be gone in a moment's time upon waking. Few Dwarves were in evidence here, the vast courtyard all but deserted. Stairwells burrowed down into the stone at regular intervals—black tunnels that Jair presumed must run to the inner workings of the locks below.

They had almost crossed the empty courtyard when a shout brought them up short, and Edain Elessedil came running to greet them. Grinning broadly, his injured arm and shoulder heavily wrapped, he went to Jair at once and extended his hand in greeting.

"Safe and sound after all, Jair Ohmsford!" He put his good arm about the other as they turned once more to follow their taciturn guide. "Feeling better, I hope?"

"Much better." Jair smiled back. "How is your arm?"

"Just a small scratch. A little stiff and nothing more. But what a night! Lucky that any of us got through safely. And this one!" He indicated Slanter, who trailed a step behind. "His escape was nothing short of miraculous! Did he tell you?"

Jair shook his head, and Edain Elessedil promptly informed him of all that had befallen Slanter and Helt during their harrowing walk through the Gnome encampment the previous night. Jair listened with growing astonishment, casting more than one glance back at the Gnome. Beneath a mask of studied indifference, Slanter was looking a bit embarrassed by all the attention.

"Simplest way out, that's all," Slanter announced gruffly when the effusive Elf had finished his tale. Jair was smart enough not to make anything more out of it.

Their guide took them up a stairway onto the battlement on the northern watch, then led them through a set of double-doors into an atrium filled with plants and trees, flourishing in an obviously transplanted bed of black earth beneath glass and open sky. Even here, within the high mountains, the Dwarves carried with them something of their home, Jair thought in admiration.

Beyond the gardens lay a terrace occupied by tables and benches.

"Wait here," the Dwarf ordered and left them.

When he had gone, Jair turned back to Edain. "Why is there no battle being fought this day, Elven Prince? What of the Gnome armies?"

Edain Elessedil shook his head. "No one seems certain what has happened. The locks and dams have been under siege for almost a week. Each day, the Gnomes attack both exposures of the fortress. But today, no attack has come. The Gnomes gather at their siege lines and watch us—nothing more. It appears as if they are waiting for something."

"I don't like the sound of that," Slanter muttered.

"Nor do the Dwarves," Edain said quietly. "Runners have been sent to Culhaven and scouts slip through the underground tunnels to the rear of the Gnome army to keep watch." He hesitated, then glanced at Jair. "Garet Jax is out there, too."

Jair started. "He is? Why? Where has he gone?"

"I don't know," the Elf shook his head slowly. "He said nothing to me. I don't think he's left us. I think he's simply out looking around. He took Helt with him."

"Scouting on his own, then." Slanter frowned. "He would do that."

"Who can say?" The Elf tried a quick smile. "The Weapons Master keeps his own counsel, Slanter."

"Dark reasons and dark purposes drive that one," the Gnome muttered, almost to himself.

They stood in silence then for a few moments, not looking at each other, lost in their private speculations of the actions of Garet Jax. Jair remembered Slanter telling him that it was the Weapons Master who had possession now of the vision crystal and the Silver Dust. That meant that if anything were to happen to Garet Jax, the magic of the King of the Silver River would be lost. And that meant that Jair's only chance of helping Brin would be lost as well.

The sound of the door opening brought them about, and Foraker appeared from out of the fortress. He came quickly to where they stood and greeted each with a handshake.

"Rested, Ohmsford?" he asked gruffly, and Jair nodded. "Good. I've asked that dinner be brought to us here on the terrace, so why don't we find a table and sit?"

He motioned to the table closest to them, and the other three joined him there. The trees and shrubs of the gardens darkened further the gray cast of the late afternoon, so candles were lighted against the gloom. Moments later, a meal of beef, cheese, bread, soup, and ale was brought, and they began to eat. Jair was surprised to discover how hungry he was.

When the meal was finished, Foraker pushed back from the table and began fishing through his pockets. "I have something for you." He glanced briefly toward Jair. "Ah-ha, here we are."

He held in his hand the bag of Silver Dust and the vision crystal on its silver chain. He pushed them across the table to the Valeman. "Garet said to give these to you. Said to keep them safe until you woke. He had a message for you, too. He said to tell you that you showed courage last night."

Surprise flashed over the Valeman's face, and he experienced a sudden, intense feeling of pride. He glanced self-consciously at Edain Elessedil and Slanter, then back to the Dwarf.

"Where is he now?" he stammered.

Foraker shrugged. "He's gone with the Borderman to explore a passage that will take us out from the fortress behind the Gnome siege lines north. He wants to be certain it's safe before we all go. And we go at nightfall tomorrow. Can't wait any longer on the siege; it may go on for months. We've been shut away too long already for his taste."

"Some of us have been more shut away than others," Slanter grumbled pointedly.

Foraker faced him, brows knitting fiercely. "We have vouched for you, Gnome—all those who came with you from Culhaven. Rad-homm, who commands this garrison, feels that our word is enough. But there are some within these walls who feel much differently— some who have lost friends and loved ones to the Gnomes who lay siege without. For them, our assurance may not be enough. You have been kept under guard not as a prisoner, but as a charge. Your safety is of some concern, believe it or not—particularly to Ohmsford here."

"I can look after myself," Slanter muttered darkly. "And I don't need anyone's concern—especially this boy's!"

Foraker stiffened. "That ought to come as good news to him!" he snapped.

Slanter lapsed into silence. He withdraws into himself again, thought Jair; he shields himself from everything happening about him. It is only when he is alone with me that he seems to be willing to come out of that protective shell. It is only then that he seems to recover even a bit of the old Slanter he showed when we first met. The balance of the time he is an outsider, a self-proclaimed loner, unaccepting of his role as a member of our little company.

"Did our message get through?" Edain Elessedil was asking Foraker. "About the destruction of the bridge at the Wedge?"

"It did." The Dwarf removed his dark gaze from Slanter. "Your plan was well conceived, Elven Prince. Had we known better the extent of this siege and the army that mounts it, we might have escaped in the bargain."

"Are we in danger here, then?"

"No, the fortress is secure. Stores are plentiful enough to withstand a siege of months if need be. And no army can bring the whole of its strength to bear with the mountains so close. Any danger to us will be found outside these walls when we resume our journey north."

At his elbow, Slanter muttered something unintelligible and drained the remainder of his ale. Foraker glanced at the Gnome and his bearded face tightened. "In the meantime, there is something that must be done—and you and I, Gnome, must do it."

Slanter's eyes lifted guardedly. "What is it we must do—Dwarf?"

Foraker's face darkened further, but his voice stayed calm. "There is someone within these walls who claims to know well the castle of the Mord Wraiths—someone who claims to know it better than anyone. If true, that knowledge could be of great use to us."

"If true, then you have no further use for me!" Slanter snapped. "What have I to do with this?"

"The knowledge is of use only if it is true," Foraker continued carefully. "The only one who can tell us that is you."

"Me?" The Gnome laughed mirthlessly. "You would trust me to tell you whether or not what you are being told is the truth? Why should you do that? Or do you think to test me? That seems more likely, I think. You would test what I tell you against what another says!"

"Slanter!" Jair admonished the Gnome, a flush of anger and disappointment stealing through him.

"You are the one who mistrusts," Edain Elessedil added firmly.

Slanter started to respond, then thought better of it and went still.

It was Foraker who spoke then, low and pointed. "If I thought to test you, it would not be against this one."

The table was silent. "Who is it?" Slanter asked finally.

The Dwarf's fierce brows knitted. "A Mwellret."

Slanter went rigid. "A Mwellret?" he growled. "A lizard?"

He said it with such loathing that Jair Ohmsford and Edain Elessedil looked at each other in astonishment. Neither had ever seen a Mwellret. Neither had even heard of one until now, and both, having witnessed the Gnome's reaction to the mention of one, wondered if perhaps they would have been better off remaining ignorant.

"One of Radhomm's patrols found him washed up at the edge of the lake a day or two before the siege," Foraker went on, his eyes holding Slanter's. "More dead than alive when they pulled him out. Mumbled something about being driven from the Ravenshorn by the black walkers. Said that he knew ways in which they could be destroyed. The patrol brought him here. Didn't have time to get him out before the siege." He paused. "Until now, there had been no way to test the truth of what he has to say."

"The truth!" Slanter spit. "There is no truth in the lizards!"

"Revenge against those he feels have wronged him may bring out the truth. We can offer him that revenge—a trade, perhaps. Think carefully. He must know the secrets of the Ravenshorn and Graymark. Those mountains were once his. The castle was his."

"Nothing was ever his!" Slanter came out of his chair with a lunge, stiff with anger. "They took it all, the lizards did! Built their castle on the bones of my people! Made slaves of the Gnome tribes living in the mountains! Used the dark magic like the walkers! Black devils, I would as soon cut my own throat as give them an instant's trust!"

Jair thought to intercede, rising as well. "Slanter, what . . . ?"

"A moment, Ohmsford," Foraker cut him short. The fierce countenance turned again to Slanter. "Gnome, I give the Mwellrets no more trust than you. But if this one can help, then let us take whatever help we find. Our task is difficult enough as it is. And if we find that the Mwellret lies . . . well, then we know what can be done with him."

Slanter glared down at the table in front of him wordlessly for a moment, then slowly reseated himself. "It is a waste of time. Go without me. Use your own judgment, Foraker."

The Dwarf shrugged. "I thought that this would be preferable to being left under lock and key. I thought you might have had enough of that." He paused, watching the dark eyes of the Gnome snap up to find his own. "Besides, my judgment is useless in determining whether or not the Mwellret speaks the truth. You are the only one who can help us with that."

For a moment, no one spoke. Slanter's eyes remained locked on Foraker. "Where is the Mwellret now?" he asked finally.

"In a storage room that serves as his cell," Foraker answered. "He never comes out, even to walk. Doesn't like the air and the light."

"Black devil!" the Gnome muttered in response. Then he sighed. "Very well. You and me."

"These two as well, if they choose." Foraker indicated Jair and Edain.

"I'm coming," Jair announced at once.

"And I," the Elven Prince agreed.

Foraker rose to his feet and nodded. "I'll take you there now."

XX

THEY WENT FROM THE TERRACE GARDENS DOWN INTO THE bowels of the locks and dams of Capaal. From the gray light of an afternoon rapidly fading into dusk, they descended stairwells and passageways that curled deep into stone and timber. Shadows gathered about small pools of hazy light given off by the flames of oil lamps dangling from iron brackets. The air trapped within the massive rock of the dam was stale and damp. Through the silence that pervaded the lower levels came the distant rush of waters flowing through the locks and the low grinding of great wheels and levers. Closed doors came and went as the four passed deeper, and there was the sense of a beast hidden somewhere within, stirring in response to the sounds of the locks and their machinery, caged and waiting to break free.

They came upon few Dwarves within these levels of the fortress. A forest people who had survived the Great Wars by tunneling within the earth, the Dwarves had long since emerged from their underground prison into the sunlight and in so doing had vowed never again to return. Their abhorrence of dark, closed places was well known among the people of the other races, and it was only with some difficulty that they managed to endure such closures. The locks and dams at Capaal were necessary to their existence, vital in the regulation of the waters of the Silver River as they flowed westward to their homeland, and so the sacrifice was made—but never for long and never more frequently than was required. Brief shifts to monitor the machinery that they had built to serve their purposes were followed by hasty exits back into the world of light and air above.

So it was that the few faces the four companions did come upon as they made their way downward bore a look of stoic endurance that barely masked an abiding distaste for this most unpleasant of duties.

Elb Foraker evidenced a trace of this, though he bore his discomfort well. His fierce, dark face was turned forward into the maze of corridors and stairwells, and his solid frame was erect and purposeful as he took his companions through lamplight and shadow toward the storage room yet farther down. As they went, he told Jair and Edain Elessedil the story of the Mwellrets.

They were a species of Troll, he explained in beginning his tale. The Trolls had survived the Great Wars above the earth, exposed to the terrible effects of the energies those wars had unleashed. Mutated from the men and women they had once been, they had altered in form, their skin and body organs adapting to the frightening conditions the Great Wars had created over almost the whole of the earth's surface. Northland Trolls had survived within the mountains, grown huge and strong, their skin toughened until it had taken on the appearance of rough tree bark. But the Mwellrets were the descendants of men who had sought to survive within forests that the Great Wars had turned to swamp, the waters poisoned, the foliage diseased. Assuming the characteristics of creatures for whom swamp survival was most natural, the Mwellrets had taken on the look of reptiles. When Slanter called them lizards, he was describing them in truth as they now appeared—scaled over where skin had once been, arms and legs grown short and clawed, and bodies grown as flexible as snakes.

But there was a greater difference yet between the Mwellrets and the other species of Trolls that occupied the dark corners of the Four Lands. The Mwellrets' climb back up the ladder of civilization had been more rapid, and it had been marked by a strange and

frightening ability to shape-change. Survival had made fearful demands upon the Mwellrets, as upon all of the Trolls; in the process
of learning the secrets of that survival, they had undergone a physical transformation that enabled them to alter body shape with the
pliability of oiled clay. Not so advanced in their art as to be able to
disguise their basic characteristics, they nevertheless could shorten
or elongate all of the parts of their bodies and could mold themselves in ways that would allow them to adapt to the demands of
any environment in which they found themselves. Little was known
as to how the shape-changing was done. It was enough to know
that it could be done and to know that the Mwellrets were the only
creatures who had mastered it.

Few beyond the borders of the Eastland knew of the Mwellrets,
for they were a reclusive and solitary people who seldom ventured
beyond the shelter of the deep Anar. No Mwellrets had come forth
in the time of the Councils at Paranor. No Mwellrets had fought in
the Wars of the Races. Withdrawn into their dark homeland, within
forest, swamp, and mountain wilderness, they had kept themselves
apart.

Except where the Gnome people were concerned, that was.
Sometime after the First Council at Paranor, a time more than
a thousand years earlier, the Mwellrets had migrated up from
swampland and broken forest into the wooded heights of the Ravenshorn. Leaving the dank and fetid mire of the lowlands to the
creatures with whom they had shared those regions since the destruction of the old world, the Mwellrets had drifted into the higher
forestlands inhabited by scattered tribes of Gnomes. A superstitious
people, the Gnomes had been terrified of these creatures who could
change shape and who seemed to command elements of the dark
magic that had been brought to life with the advent of the Druids.
In time, the Mwellrets began to take advantage of that fear and to
assert their authority over the tribes living within the Ravenshorn.
Mwellrets assumed the role of chieftains, and the Gnomes were reduced to slaves.

At first, there was resistance to these creatures—these lizards, as they were called—but after a time all resistance ceased. The Gnomes were not strong enough or organized enough to fight back, and a few terrifying examples of what would be done to those who failed to submit made a lasting impression on the others. Under the rule of the Mwellrets, the fortress at Graymark was constructed—a massive citadel from which the lizards governed the tribes inhabiting the immediate region. Years passed, and the whole of the Ravenshorn fell under the sway of the Mwellrets. Dwarves to the south and Gnome tribes to the north and west stayed out of those mountains, and the Mwellrets in turn showed no inclination to venture beyond their newly adopted home. With the coming of the Warlock Lord in the Second War of the Races, it was rumored that a bargain had been struck in which the lizards offered a number of their Gnome subjects to serve the Dark Lord—but there was never anyone who could prove it for a fact.

Then with the conclusion of the aborted Third War of the Races—the war in which Shea Ohmsford had gone in search of the mystic Sword of Shannara and the Warlock Lord had been destroyed—the Mwellrets had unexpectedly begun to die out. Age and sickness began to deplete their numbers and only a handful of young were born into the world. As their numbers declined, so did their sway over the Gnome tribes in the Ravenshorn. Bit by bit, their small empire crumbled away until at last it was limited to Graymark and the few tribes that still remained within that region of the world.

"And now it seems that these last few, too, have been driven back into the swamps that bred them," Foraker concluded his tale. "Whatever their power, it was no match for that of the walkers. Like the Gnomes they ruled, they would become slaves as well, were they to remain within the mountains."

"Better they had been wiped from the face of the earth!" Slanter interjected bitterly. "They deserve no less!"

"Do they in truth possess the power of the dark magic?" Jair asked.

Foraker shrugged. "I've never seen it. The magic is in the shape-changing, I think. Oh, there are stories of the ways in which they affect the elements—wind, air, earth, fire, and water. Maybe there is some truth to that simply because they have developed an understanding of how the elements react to certain things. But for the most part, it is just superstition."

Slanter muttered something unintelligible and gave Jair a dark look that suggested he wasn't in complete agreement with the Dwarf.

"You will be safe enough, Ohmsford." Foraker smiled gravely. The dark brows lifted. "If he were foolish enough to use the magic within these walls, he would be dead quicker than you could blink!"

Ahead, the darkened corridor grew suddenly light, and the four approached an intersecting passageway and a line of doors stretching down to their right. A pair of sentries stood watch before the closest door. Hard eyes turned to oversee their approach. Foraker spoke a quick word in greeting and ordered that the door be opened. The sentries glanced at each other and shrugged.

"Take a light," the first said, passing Foraker an oil lamp. "The lizard keeps it black as pitch in there all the time."

Foraker lighted the lamp from the wick of one hanging beside the door, then glanced over at his companions. "Ready," he told the sentries.

Latch bolts released and a crossbar lifted. With a mournful groan, the ironbound door swung open into total blackness. Foraker started forward wordlessly, the other three a step behind. As the faint circle of the oil lamp penetrated the gloom, the humped and shadowed forms of crates, packing cases, and sack stores came into view. The Dwarf and his companions stopped.

Behind them, the door swung closed with a bang.

Jair glanced about the darkened room apprehensively. A rank and fetid odor permeated the air, a smell that whispered of things dying and fouled. Shadows lay over everything, deep and silent about their little light.

"Stythys?" Foraker spoke the name quietly.

For a long moment, there was no answer. Then from the shadows to their left, from out of a corner of crates and stores, a stirring broke the silence.

"Who iss it?" something hissed.

"Foraker," the Dwarf answered. "I've come to talk. Radhomm sent word to you that I would come."

"Hss!" The voice rasped like chain being dragged over stone. "Sspeak what you would, Dwarf."

Something moved within the shadows—something huge and cloaked like death itself. A shape appeared, vague and shadowy, rising up beside the stores. Jair felt a sudden, overwhelming repulsion for what was there. Keep very still, a voice within him warned. Say nothing!

"Little peopless," the figure murmured coldly. "Dwarf and Elvess and Gnome. Musstn't be frightened, little peopless. Sstep closser."

"Step closer yourself," Foraker snapped impatiently.

"Hss! Don't like the light. Need darknesss!"

Foraker shrugged. "Then we'll both stay where we are."

"Sstay," the other agreed.

Jair glanced quickly at Slanter. The Gnome's rough face was twisted in a mask of hatred and disgust, and he was sweating. He looked as if he might bolt at any moment. Edain Elessedil must have seen the look, too, for all at once he moved around Jair and Foraker and placed himself almost protectively on the other side of the distraught Gnome.

"I'm fine!" Slanter muttered almost inaudibly, brushing with his hand at the darkness before him.

Then abruptly the Mwellret came forward to the edge of the light, a tall, cloaked form that seemed to materialize from out of the shadows. Essentially man-shaped, it walked upright on two powerful hind legs, crooked and muscled. Forearms reached out tentatively, and where there should have been skin and hair there was only a covering of toughened gray scales ending in crooked claws. Within its cowl, the Mwellret's face turned toward them, reptilian snout lifting into the light, scaled and split wide to reveal rows of sharpened teeth and a serpent's tongue. Nostrils flared at the snout's blunt end; further up, almost lost within the cowl's darkness, slitted green eyes glimmered.

"Sstythyss knowss what bringss you, little peopless," the monster hissed slowly. "Knowss well."

There was silence. "Graymark," Foraker said finally.

"Wraithss," the other whispered. "Sstythyss knowss. Walkerss that desstroy. Come from out of the pitss, from the black hole of the Maelmord. From death! Climbss to Heaven'ss Well to poisson the waterss of the Ssilver River. Poisson the land. Desstroy it! Comess into Graymark, doess the evil. Comess to drive uss from our homess. Ensslave uss."

"You saw it happen?" Foraker asked.

"Ssaw it all! Wraithss come from darknesss, drive uss forth and sseize what iss ourss. No match for ssuch power. Flee! Ssome of uss desstroyed!"

Slanter spit suddenly into the darkness, muttering as he shifted back a step and kicked at the stone flooring.

"Sstay!" the Mwellret hissed suddenly, an unmistakable tone of command in its voice. Slanter's head snapped up. "Gnomess have no need to fear uss. Friendss have we been—not like the Wraithss. Wraithss desstroy all that iss life becausse they are not life. Thingss of death! The dark magic ruless. All the landss will fall to them."

"But you have a way to destroy them!" Foraker pressed.

"Hss! Graymark belongss to uss! Wraithss tresspasss in our home! Think themsselvess ssafe with uss gone—but wrong. Wayss to get at them there! Wayss they do not know!"

"Passages!" Jair exclaimed suddenly, so intent on what the other was telling them that for an instant he forgot his vow.

At once the Mwellret's head snapped up, as if an animal testing the air. Jair went cold, a sense of something tremendously evil settling over him as he stood there in the sudden silence.

The Mwellret's serpent tongue snaked out. "Magicss, little friend? Magicss do you have?"

No one spoke. Jair was sweating violently. Foraker glanced

about at him sharply, momentarily uncertain as to what had happened.

"In your voisse, little friend?" the Mwellret whispered. "Ssense it in your voisse, I do. Ssense it in you. Magicss like my own. Do it for me, yess? Sspeak!"

Something seemed to wrap itself about Jair, some invisible coil that squeezed the breath from him. Before he could help himself he began to sing. Quick and sharp, the wishsong slipped from between his clenched teeth and waves of color and shape rode the air between them, dancing through the darkness and lamplight like living things.

An instant later Jair was free again, the coils that had bound him gone. The wishsong died into silence. The Valeman gasped in shock and dropped weakly to his knees. Slanter was at his side at once, pulling him back toward the door, yelling wildly at the Mwellret, grappling with his free hand for Edain Elessedil's long knife. Hurriedly, Foraker parted them, his own sword drawn free as he turned to face Stythys. The Mwellret had suddenly shrunk in size, withdrawing into the shadows of the cowled robes, stepping back again into darkness.

"What did you do to him?" Foraker snapped. The Mwellret shrank back further, slitted eyes gleaming in the black. Foraker wheeled abruptly. "That's enough. We're leaving."

"Sstay!" the Mwellret wailed suddenly. "Sspeak with Sstythyss! Can tell you of the Wraithss!"

"Not interested anymore," Foraker replied, banging his sword handle against the storage room door.

"Hss! Musst talk with Sstythyss if you wissh the Wraithss destroyed! Only I know how! Ssecretss mine!" the creature's voice was hard and impossibly cold now, all pretense of friendliness gone. "Little friendss will come back—musst come back! Be ssorry if you leave!"

"We're sorry we came!" Edain Elessedil threw back. "We don't need your help!"

Jair was walking through the open doorway now, supported on

one side by the Elven Prince and on the other by Slanter, who was muttering every step of the way. Shaking his head to clear it, the Valeman glanced back at the Mwellret, a cloaked and faceless shape squeezed deep within the shadows as Foraker took his small light from the room.

"Needss my help!" the creature said softly, scaled arm lifting. "Comess again, little friendss! Comess back!"

Then the Dwarf sentries were closing and barring the storage room door once more, latch bolts and crossbars snapping tightly into place. Jair took a deep breath and straightened himself, shrugging free of the supporting arms. Foraker stopped him, peering closely into his eyes, grunted, and turned back down the passageway that had brought them.

"Guess you're all right," he announced. "Let's get back up into the air."

"What happened, Jair!" Edain Elessedil wanted to know. "How did he make you do that?"

Jair shook his head. "I'm not sure." Still shaken, he began walking after Foraker, the Elven Prince and the Gnome on either side. "I'm just not sure."

"Black devils!" Slanter muttered heatedly, invoking his favorite epithet. "They can twist you."

The Valeman nodded briefly and walked on. He wished he knew how that twisting had been done.

XXI

Night swept down about Capaal, black, misted and still. Moon and stars lay screened away from the mountain heights, and only the oil lamps of the Dwarves and watchfires of the Gnomes gave light to the shadowed dark. Frost began to form on stone and scrub, moisture freezing white as the temperature fell lower. An unpleasant stillness lay over everything.

Atop the battlements of the Dwarf fortress, Jair and Elb Foraker looked down upon the locks and dams that spanned the gap between the mountains where the Silver River flowed.

"More than five hundred years old now," the Dwarf was explaining, his voice low and rough against the night's silence. "Built in the time of Raybur, when our people still had kings. Built when the Second War of the Races was ended."

Jair stared wordlessly over the parapets into the darkness below, tracing the massive outline of the complex against the faint light of torches and lamps that lit its stone. There were three dams, broad bands curving back against the flow of the Silver River as it dropped downward to the gorge below. A series of locks regulated that flow, the machinery seated within and concealed by the dams and the fortress that protected both. The fortress sat astride the high dam, sprawled end to end and guarding all passageways leading in. Behind the high dam, the Cillidellan stretched away into blackness, ringed by the red watchfires of the siege army, yet oddly opaque in the moonless shadows of this night. Between the high dam and its lower levels, the Silver River pooled in two small reservoirs on its passage downward from the heights. Sheer cliffs flanked both ends of the lower levels, and the only way down was across catwalks or through underground passageways that tunneled into the rock.

"Gnomes would love to have this," Foraker grunted, his arm sweeping over the complex. "Controls nearly the whole of the water supply for the lands west to the Rainbow Lake. In the rainy seasons, without this, there would be flooding, as there used to be before the locks and dams were built to guard against it." He shook his head. "In a bad spring, even Culhaven would be swept away."

Jair looked about slowly, impressed with the size of the complex, awed by the effort that must have been expended in its construction. Foraker had already taken him on a tour through the inner workings of the locks and dams, explaining the machinery and the duties of those who tended it. Jair was grateful for the tour.

Slanter was absorbed in reworking Dwarf maps of the lands north to the Ravenshorn—maps, the Gnome had been quick to point out when they were shown him, which were entirely inaccurate. Anxious to avoid the necessity of a return to the storage room where the Mwellret was caged and determined to establish his own expertise, Slanter had agreed to make notations on the maps so that the little company would be properly advised as to the geography of the lands they must pass through during the journey that lay ahead. Edain Elessedil had excused himself and gone off on his own. When Foraker, therefore, had offered to show Jair something of the locks and dams, the Valeman had been quick to accept. Part of the reason for the tour, Jair suspected, was to take his mind off Garet Jax, who had still not returned. But that was all right, too. He preferred not to think about the missing Weapons Master.

"Cliffs don't allow the Gnomes a way down to the lower dams," Foraker was saying, eyes turned back toward the distant watchfires. "The fortress guards all passage that way. Our ancestors knew that well enough when they built Capaal. As long as the fortress stands, the locks and dams are safe. As long as the locks and dams are safe, the Silver River is safe."

"Except that it's being poisoned," Jair pointed out.

The Dwarf nodded. "It is. But it would be worse if the whole of the Cillidellan were let loose into the gorge. The poisoning would be quicker then—all the way west."

"Don't the other lands know this?" Jair asked quietly.

"They know."

"You would think they would be here to help you, in that case."

Foraker chuckled mirthlessly. "You would think so. But not everyone wants to believe the truth of things, you see. Some want to hide from it."

"Have any of the races agreed to aid you?"

The Dwarf shrugged. "Some. The Westland Elves are sending an army under Ander Elessedil. It's still two weeks away, though. Callahorn promises aid; Helt and a handful of others already fight with us. Nothing from the Trolls yet—but the Northern territories are vast and the tribes scattered. Perhaps they will at least help us along the northern borders."

He trailed off. Jair waited a moment, then asked, "And the Southland?"

"The Southland?" Foraker shook his head slowly. "The Southland has the Federation and its Coalition Council. A bunch of fools. Petty internal bickerings and power struggles occupy all of their energies. And the new Southland has no use for the peoples of the other lands. The race of Man reverts to what it was in the time of the First War. If there were a Warlock Lord alive now, I fear the Federation would be a willing follower."

Jair winced inwardly. In the First War of the Races, fought hundreds of years earlier, the Warlock Lord had subverted the race of Man and convinced it to attack the other races. Man had been defeated in that war and had still not recovered from the humiliation and bitterness of their loss. Isolationist in policy and practice, the Federation had absorbed and become spokesman for the majority of the Southland and the race of Man.

"Still, Callahorn stands with you," Jair declared quickly. "The Bordermen are a different breed."

"Even the Bordermen may not be enough." Foraker grunted. "Even the whole of the Legion. You've seen the gathering of tribes without. United, they are a power greater than anything we can match. And they have the aid of those black things that command them . . ." He shook his head darkly.

Jair's brow furrowed. "But we have an ally of our own who can stand against the Mord Wraiths. We have Allanon."

"Yes, Allanon," Foraker murmured, then shook his head once more.

"And Brin," Jair added. "Once they've found the Ildatch . . ."

He trailed off, the warning of the King of the Silver River suddenly a dark whisper in his mind. Leaves in the wind, he had said. Your sister and the Druid. Both will be lost.

He shoved the whisper aside roughly. It won't happen like that, he promised. I'll reach them first. I'll find them. I'll throw the Silver Dust into Heaven's Well to cleanse its waters, throw the vision crystal after, and then . . . He paused uncertainly. What? He didn't know. Something. He would do something that would keep the old man's prophecy from coming to pass.

But first there was the journey north, he reminded himself glumly. And before that, Garet Jax must return . . .

Foraker was walking along the battlements once more, bearded face lowered into his chest, hands stuffed into the pockets of the travel cloak he wore wrapped about his stocky frame. Jair caught up with him as he started down a set of broad stone steps to a lower ramp.

"Can you tell me something about Garet Jax?" the Valeman asked suddenly.

The Dwarfs head remained lowered. "What would you have me tell you?"

Jair shook his head. "I don't know. Something."

"Something?" the other grunted. "Bit vague, don't you think? What sort of something?"

Jair thought about it a moment. "Something no one else knows. Something about him."

Foraker walked to a parapet overlooking the dark expanse of the Cillidellan, resting his elbows on the stonework as he stared out into the night. Jair stood silently beside him, waiting.

"You want to understand him, don't you?" Foraker asked finally.

The Valeman nodded slowly. "A little, at least."

The Dwarf shook his head. "I'm not sure that it's possible, Ohmsford. It's like trying to understand a . . . a hawk. You see him, see what he is, what he does. You marvel at him, you wonder at his being. But you can't ever understand him—not really. You have to be him to understand him."

"You seem to understand him," Jair offered.

Foraker's fierce countenance swung sharply about to face him. "Is that what you think, Ohmsford? That I understand him?" He shook his head once more. "No better than I understand the hawk. Less, maybe. I know him because I've spent time with him, fought with him, and trained men with him. I know him for that. I know what he is, too. But all that doesn't amount to a pinch of dust when it comes to understanding."

He hesitated. "Garet Jax is like another form of life compared to you, me, or anyone else you'd care to name. A special and singular form of life, because there's only one." The eyebrows lifted. "He's magic in his way. He does things no other man could hope to do—or even try to do. He survives what would kill anyone else, and he does it time after time. Like the hawk, it's instinct—it lets him fly way up there above the rest of us where no one can touch him. A thing apart. Understand him? No, I couldn't begin to understand him."

Jair was quiet for a moment. "He came to the Eastland because of you, though," he said finally. "At least, he says that is why he came. So he must feel some sort of friendship for you. You must share a kinship."

"Perhaps." The other shrugged. "But that doesn't mean I understand him. Besides, he does what he does for reasons that are all his own and not necessarily what he says they are—I know that much. He's here not just because of me, Ohmsford. He's here for other reasons as well." He tapped Jair on the shoulder. "He's here as much because of you as because of me, I think. But I don't know the reason why. Perhaps you do."

The Valeman hesitated, thinking. "He said he would be my protector because that was what the King of the Silver River had said he must be." He trailed off.

"Well and good." Foraker nodded. "But do you understand him any better for knowing that? I do not." He paused, then looked back out across the lake. "No, his reasons are his own and the reasons are not ones he would tell to me."

Jair barely heard him. He had remembered something, and a look of surprise flitted over his face. Quickly he turned away. His mind froze. Were the reasons that Garet Jax would not tell to Foraker ones that he would tell to the Valeman? Hadn't the Weapons Master done just that in the dark, chill rain that second night out of Culhaven when the two had crouched alone beneath that ridgeline? The memory stirred slowly to life. I want you to understand . . . That was what Garet Jax had told him. The dream promised a test of skill greater than any I have ever faced. A chance to see if I am truly the best. For me, what else is there . . . ?

Jair breathed deeply the chill night air. Maybe he understood Garet Jax better than he thought. Maybe he understood him as well as anyone could.

"There is one thing not many know." Foraker turned back suddenly. Jair shoved aside his musings. "You say he found you in the Black Oaks. Ever wonder why he happened to be there? After all, he was coming east out of Callahorn."

Jair nodded slowly. "I hadn't thought about that. I guess the Black Oaks are rather out of the way for one traveling from the borderlands to the Anar." He hesitated. "What was he doing there?"

Foraker smiled faintly. "I'm only guessing, you understand. He's not told me any more than you. But the lake country north, between Leah and the lowlands of Clete—that was his home. That was where he was born, where he grew up. Once, long ago, he had family there. Some, anyway. Hasn't said anything about it for a long time, but maybe there's still someone there. Or maybe just memories."

"A family," Jair repeated softly, then shook his head. "Has he told you who they were?"

The Dwarf pushed himself back from the parapet. "No. Mentioned it once, that was all. But now you know something about the man no one else knows—except me, of course. Does that help you understand him any better?"

Jair smiled. "I don't suppose so."

Foraker turned and together they started back across the battlements. "Didn't think it would," the Dwarf muttered, pulling his cloak close about him as the wind caught at them beyond the shelter of the wall. "Come back inside with me, Ohmsford, and I'll brew you a cup of hot ale. We'll wait for our hawk's return together."

Foraker's rough hand clapped his shoulder gently, and he hurried after.

The night slipped away, its hours empty and lingering and clouded with dark anticipation. Mist crept down out of the heights on cat's paws, thickening, shrouding the whole of the locks and dams, and draping Gnome and Dwarf armies alike in veils of damp, clinging haze until even the bright glow of the watchfires disappeared from view.

Jair Ohmsford fell asleep at midnight, still awaiting the return of Garet Jax. Slumped wearily in a high-backed captain's chair in a watch lounge while Foraker, Slanter, and Edain Elessedil talked in low voices over mugs of hot ale and a single candle lighted against the deepening gloom, he simply drifted off. One minute he was awake, listening in weary detachment to the drone of their voices, eyes closed against the light; in the next, he was sleeping.

It was almost dawn when the Elven Prince shook him awake.

"Jair. He's back."

The Valeman brushed the sleep from his eyes and pushed himself upright. Barely visible through the gloom of fading night, the embers of a dying fire glowed softly in the little hearth across the room. Without, the patter of rain sounded on the stonework.

Jair blinked. He's back. Garet Jax.

He stood up hurriedly. He was fully dressed save for his boots, and he quickly snatched them up and began to pull them on.

"He came in not half an hour ago." The Elf stood next to him, his voice strangely hushed, as if fearful he might wake someone else within the room. "Helt was with him, of course. They've found a path north beyond the tunnels."

He paused. "But something else has happened, Jair." The Valeman looked up expectantly. "Sometime after midnight, it began to rain and the mist to dissipate. When the light returned with dawn's approach, the Gnomes were there, too—all of them. They'd gathered close about the shoreline of the Cillidellan from one end of the high dam to the other, dozens deep, just standing there, waiting."

Jair was on his feet. "What are they up to?"

Edain Elessedil shook his head. "I don't know. No one seems to know. But they've been out there for hours now. The Dwarves are all awake and on the battlements. Come with me and you can see for yourself."

They hastened from the watch lounge down the maze of corridors beyond until they had passed through doors leading out into the courtyard that spanned the central section of the high dam. A chill wind blew across the Cillidellan, and the rain stung their faces as they hurried forward. It was still night, the predawn light a distant gray haze beyond the tips of the mountains east. The Dwarf defenders had taken their positions along the ramparts of the dam and fortress, cloaked and hooded against the weather, weapons in hand. The whole of Capaal lay shrouded in silence.

On reaching the fortress that protected the north end of the high dam, Edain took Jair up a series of stone stairs and across a line of battlements to a watchtower high above the complex. The wind seemed to grow stronger here, and the rain beat harder through the gray night.

As they paused before an ironbound oak door leading into the tower, a cluster of Dwarves pushed past them and started down the stairs adjoining. Foremost of these was a fierce-looking Dwarf with flaming red hair and beard, armored in leather and chainmail.

"Radhomm, the Dwarf commander!" Edain whispered to Jair.

Hurriedly, they pushed through the oak door into the tower beyond, shutting the weather behind them as they entered. A faint glow of lamplight barely penetrated the gloom within as a handful of cloaked forms seemed to materialize before them.

"Humph, he'd sleep all the time if you'd let him!" he heard Slanter grumble.

"Well met again, Jair Ohmsford," a deep voice greeted him, and Helt's massive hand extended to clasp his own.

Then Garet Jax was there, as black as the night about him, implacable and unchanging as the stone of the mountains. They faced each other, and no words were spoken. Lean face intense, the Weapons Master rested his hands gently on Jair's shoulders and within the eyes of ice there flickered a strange, unfamiliar warmth. Only for the briefest second was it there; in the next, it was gone. The hands slipped away, and Garet Jax turned back into the gloom.

The door burst open behind them, and a rain-soaked Dwarf hastened over to where Elb Foraker crouched above a pile of maps that rested on a small wooden table. They conversed in low, hushed voices; then as swiftly as he had come, the runner was gone again.

Foraker walked over at once to Jair, the other members of the little company gathering about them. "Ohmsford," he said quietly, "I've just been told that the Mwellret has escaped."

There was a stunned silence. "How could that happen?" Slanter snapped angrily, his rough face pushing forward into the light.

"A shape-change." Foraker kept his eyes on Jair. "He used it to fit himself into a small ventilation shaft that circulates air to those lower levels. It happened sometime during the night. No one knows where he might be now."

Jair went cold. There was no mistaking the Dwarf's intent in telling him this unpleasant piece of news. Even locked within that storage room, the Mwellret had been able to sense the presence of the Elven magic and to force Jair to reveal it. If he were loose . . .

"This was something he could have done anytime," Edain Elessedil pointed out. "There must be a reason that he chose to do it now."

And I could be that reason, Jair acknowledged silently. Foraker realizes it, too. That is why he made it a point to speak first to me.

Garet Jax reappeared from out of the gloom, sudden and purposeful. "We are leaving at once," he advised. "We have delayed too long already. The quest given us lies north. Whatever is to happen here, we need not be part of it. With the Gnomes gathered about the Cillidellan as they are, it should be easy enough to . . ."

OOOOOOMMMMMMMMMM!

Startled, the members of the little company looked hurriedly about. A monstrous wail assailed their ears, deep and haunting as it shattered the predawn silence. It grew louder, thousands of voices giving it life, rising up against wind and rain into the mountains about Capaal.

"Shades!" Slanter cried, his rough yellow face twisting in recognition.

All six broke for the door in a rush, burst through, and in seconds were clustered against the battlements without, rain and wind thrusting at them as they peered north across the choppy waters of the Cillidellan.

OOOOOOMMMMMMMMM!

The wail rose higher, one long, continuous howl that swept through the heights. All about the shoreline of the Cillidellan, the Gnomes joined in the dark chant, voices blended into one as they faced the murky lake, the air filled with the mournful sound.

Radhomm appeared on the battlements below, shouting orders, and runners scurried from his side as he dispatched them to his captains. Everywhere there was a frenzy of activity as the garrison braced for whatever was to come. Jair's hand moved to his tunic, searching out and finding the reassuring presence of both the Silver Dust and the vision crystal.

Garet Jax snatched Slanter by his cloak and hauled him close. "What is happening here?"

There was unmistakable fear in the Gnome's eyes. "A summons— a summons to the dark magic! Once before I saw it—at Graymark!" The Gnome twisted in the iron grip. "But it needs the touch of the walkers, Weapons Master! It needs their touch!"

"Garet!" Foraker pulled the other about roughly, pointing to the near shore of the Cillidellan, not a hundred yards from where the high dam arced away. The Weapons Master released his grip on Slanter. All eyes turned to where the Dwarf directed.

From out of the midst of the Gnomes gathered along the shoreline, three black-cloaked figures approached, tall and hard against the coming dawn.

"Mord Wraiths!" Slanter whispered harshly. "The walkers have come!"

XXII

---◆---

DOWN TO THE CILLIDELLAN THE MORD WRAITHS CAME,
gliding to the water's edge almost without seeming to move. Hooded
and featureless within the shadow of their cowls, they might have
been ghosts of no substance but for the black-clawed fingers slipped
from beneath their coverings to wrap with death grips about three
gnarled gray staffs of burnished witch-wood. The wail of their
Gnome believers rose all about them, shrieking into the whistle of
the wind; to those who watched from the battlements of Capaal, it
seemed as if the black ones had been born of its sound.

Then, without warning, the terrible wail died into silence as
the Gnomes grew suddenly still. The wind's strident shriek sounded
across the empty expanse of the Cillidellan, and the lapping of the
waves stirred with its passing.

The foremost of the Mord Wraiths lifted his staff high, his
skeletal black arm thrusting from its protective robe like blasted
deadwood. A strange and vibrant hush fell over the heights, and
it seemed to the defenders that for an instant even the wind had
gone still. Then the staff came slowly down, reaching toward the
blackened waters of the lake. The other staffs joined it, witch-wood
touching and becoming one as burnished tips slipped within the
waters of the Cillidellan.

For an instant, nothing happened. Then the staffs exploded
into lances of red fire, the flames ripping downward into the lake,

burning and scorching its cool darkness. The waters shuddered and heaved, then began to boil. Gnomes shrieked in a cacophony of glee and fear, stumbling back from the shore's edge.

"It is the summons!" Slanter cried.

The red fire burned through the murky, impenetrable blackness, down into the deepest recesses of the lake to where no light ever shone. Like a stain of blood, the light of those flames spread outward through the waters, reaching. Geysers of steam burst skyward with a violent hiss, and the whole of the lake began to churn.

The defenders on the ramparts of the Dwarf fortress stood frozen with indecision. Something was about to happen, something unspeakable, and no one knew how it could be stopped.

"We've got to get out of here!" Slanter snatched at Garet Jax urgently. There was fear in his eyes, but reason as well. "Quickly, Weapons Master!"

Abruptly the fire from the witch-wood staffs died away. The gray wood lifted from the Cillidellan, clawed hands drawing back within their robes. Yet still the waters boiled feverishly; the reddened stain had become a deep and distant glow that shone from far beneath the surface like an eye slipped open from sleep.

OOOOOOMMMMMMMMMM!

The wail of the Gnome siege army rose once more, shrill and expectant. Hands lifted and joined, stretching as the staffs of the Mord Wraiths signaled anew. Steam ripped from the lake in answer to the wail, and the whole of the Cillidellan seemed to erupt with a newfound fury.

Then something huge and dark began to rise from the depths.

"Weapons Master!" Slanter cried out.

But Garet Jax shook his head. "Stand fast. Helt, bring the long bows."

The Borderman disappeared back into the watchtower at once. Jair glanced after him momentarily, then turned back to the Cillidellan—back to the deafening wail of the Gnomes and to the black thing rising from the deep.

It came swiftly now, growing in size as it neared the surface.

An evil summoned by the Wraiths—but what manner of thing was it? Jair swallowed against the tightening of his throat. Whatever it was, it was monstrous, its bulk seeming to fill the whole of the lake bottom as it lifted free. Slowly it began to take shape, a great and hulking thing with arms that twisted and groped . . .

Then, with a thunderous surge, it broke the surface of the lake and burst free into the gray dawn. A misshapen black body wrenched clear of the confining waters and hung silhouetted for an instant against the light. Barrel-like in appearance, it was coated with bottom mud and slime, crusted over with sea life and coral. Four great fin-legs propelled it as it rose, clawed and spiny. Its head was a mass of writhing tentacles that surrounded a giant beak-shaped maw lined with razor teeth. Suckers coated the insides of the tentacles, each the size of a man's spread hand, the whole protected without by scales and spines. Immediately back of the tentacles and to either side, a pair of reddened eyes blinked coldly. Stretching as it rose, the thing was more than a hundred feet from tip to tail and forty feet across.

Cries of dismay sounded from the battlements of Capaal.

"A Kraken!" Foraker said. "We are done now!"

The wail of the Gnomes had risen to a shriek that forbore all semblance of anything human. Now, with the monster's appearance into the light, the wail dissipated into a battle cry that broke across the length and breadth of Capaal. Down into the waters of the lake the Kraken thundered, its black body twisting in response as it turned abruptly toward the wall of the dam and the fortress that protected it.

"It comes for us!" Garet Jax whispered in surprise. "A thing that cannot live within freshwater, a thing that comes from the ocean—yet here! Brought by the dark magic!" The gray eyes glittered coldly. "But it shall not have us, I think. Helt!"

Instantly the giant Borderman was at his side, three long bows clasped in one great hand. Garet Jax took one, left one with the Borderman, and passed the third to Edain Elessedil.

Slanter pushed forward. "Listen to me! You cannot stand against this thing! It is a monster summoned out of evil and too much even for you!"

But Garet Jax didn't seem to hear him. "Remain with the Valeman, Gnome. He is your charge now. See that he stays safe."

He went down off the watchtower, Helt and Edain Elessedil close upon his heels. Foraker hesitated only an instant, a mistrustful glance directed at Slanter; then he, too, followed.

The Kraken surged up against the wall of the Dwarf citadel, its giant bulk hammering into stone and mortar with stunning force as it breached. The giant tentacles swept from the water, reaching for the Dwarves that clustered on the battlements. Dozens were caught up, knocked from their feet into the waters of the lake, and wrapped in the suckers and spines of the thing that attacked them. Shrieks and howls filled the morning air as the Dwarves died. Weapons rained down upon the black thing, but its hide protected it from harm. Steadily it cleared away the small figures who sought to hold it back, tearing at them with its whiplike arms, breaking apart the battlements behind which they sought to keep safe.

Now the Gnomes joined in the attack as well, the siege army battering the gates at both ends of the high dam, scaling ladders and grappling hooks clutched in their hands as they came. Dwarf defenders rushed to the parapets, holding fast against this fresh assault. But the Gnomes seemed to have gone mad. Heedless of the losses being inflicted upon them, they flung themselves against the gates and walls to die.

Yet there was purpose to this seeming madness. While the Dwarf defenders were thus distracted, the Kraken worked its way north until it was up against the wall where it banked closest to the gates. With a sudden lurch, it rose from the waters of the lake, fin-legs braced upon the stone of the dam where it curved into the shoreline. Massive tentacles snapped forward along the walls, suckers fastened to the gates, and the monster heaved back. With a splintering of wood and iron, crossbars snapped and locks broke apart. The gates to the citadel tumbled down, ripped from their hinges, and the army of the Gnomes poured through with a roar of triumph.

On the battlements of the watchtower, Jair and Slanter viewed the struggle with growing horror. With the gates gone, the Dwarves could no longer hold back their attackers. In a matter of minutes the fortress would be overrun. Already its defenders were in retreat along the walls leading back, small clusters rallying about their captains, desperately trying to stand against the onslaught. But it was clear from where the Valeman and the Gnome stood watching that the battle was lost.

"We've got to escape while we can, boy!" Slanter insisted, a hand gripping the other's arm.

But Jair refused to leave, still searching for his friends, almost too horrified by what was happening to do anything else. The Kraken had slipped once more into the waters of the lake, dragging its bulk back along the sea wall toward the center of the dam. In its wake, the Mord Wraiths glided to the edge of the shattered battlements, gray staffs raised in exhortation as their Gnome followers surged forward. With implacable purpose, the Gnomes moved into the fortress of the Dwarves.

"Slanter!" Jair cried suddenly, pointing into the heart of the battle.

High atop the ramparts of the forward wall, Helt's giant form rose up through the smoke and dust, Elb Foraker at his side. Bow gripped tightly in one hand, the Borderman braced himself against the parapets, sighted downward to where the Mord Wraiths stood, slowly drew back the bowstring, and let it slip free. A shadowy blur, the long black arrow sped away to bury itself deep in the breast of the foremost Wraith. The creature straightened with a shudder, hammered back by the force of the blow. A second arrow followed close upon the first, and again the Wraith staggered back. Shrieks of dismay rose up from those closest to the black things, and for an instant the whole of the Gnome advance seemed to falter.

But then the Mord Wraith steadied. One clawed hand grasped

the arrows embedded within it and drew them free with effortless ease. Holding them high for all to see, the monster crushed them into splinters. Then the staff of witch-wood lifted and red fire burst from its tip. All along the battlements the fire burned, exploding into stone and defender alike. Helt and Foraker flew back as the fire reached them and disappeared in an avalanche of broken wall and dust.

Jair started forward in fury, but Slanter yanked him about. "You can't do anything to help them, boy!" Without waiting for any argument on the matter, he began dragging Jair along the ramparts toward the stone stairway leading down. "Better start worrying about yourself! Perhaps if we're quick enough . . ."

Then they caught sight of the Kraken. It had lifted itself out of the Cillidellan midway along the sea wall where the broad courtyard joined together the fortress that guarded the ends of the high dam, its tentacles and fin-legs gripping at the stone. Once clear, with only the hindmost portion of its barreled body still submerged within the lake, it pivoted slowly to where the Dwarf defenders were attempting to escape the north fortress. Tentacles stretched across the girth of the high dam in a writhing mass; in seconds, all passage out was blocked.

"Slanter!" Jair cried out in warning, falling back against the stairs as one giant feeler swept past his head.

They retreated back up the stairway, crouching down within the shelter of a balustrade where it curved back into the parapets. Spray from the monster's tail fin that thrashed within the lake mixed with dust and shattered stone to rain down about them. Below, the Kraken's tentacles groped and hammered about the fortress walls, clutching at anything that ventured within reach.

It seemed for a moment as if any chance of escape back across the courtyard had been lost. But then the Dwarves counterattacked. They rushed from the lower levels of the fortress, the darkened stairwells, and the tunnels that ran beneath. Foremost among them was the Dwarf commander Radhomm. Red hair flying, he led his soldiers into the tangle of giant arms, cutting and hacking with a broadax. Bits and pieces of the Kraken flew in a froth of blood, reddish ichor spilling down upon the dampened stone of the dam. But the Kraken was a monstrous thing, and the Dwarves were little more than gnats to be brushed aside. The tentacles came down, smashing the tiny creatures who swarmed about it, leaving them lifeless. Still the defenders came on, determined to clear the way for those trapped within the doomed fortress. But the Kraken swept them aside as quickly as they appeared, and they fell dying all about the monster.

Finally the Kraken caught Radhomm as the Dwarf commander fought to break past. The monster swung the red-haired Dwarf high into the air, unaffected by the broadax that still flailed in stubborn determination. The Kraken lifted Radhomm; then, with horrifying suddenness, it smashed him downward to the stone, broken, twisted, and lifeless.

Slanter was pulling vainly at Jair. "Run!" he screamed in desperation.

Tentacles swept past them, hammering into the battlements and smashing the stone so that it flew in all directions. A shower of jagged fragments struck the Valeman and the Gnome as they struggled, knocking them sprawling, half burying them in debris. Shaking his head dazedly, Jair regained his feet and staggered forward against the stone balustrade. Below, the Dwarves had fallen back within the besieged fortress, demoralized by the loss of Radhomm. The Kraken was still stretched across the littered courtyard, edging closer now to the walls upon which Jair crouched. The Valeman started to drop back, then stopped in dismay. Slanter lay stunned at his feet, blood oozing from a deep cut in his head.

Then far below, seemingly from out of nowhere, Garet Jax appeared. Lean and black against the gray light of the dawn, he darted swiftly from the shelter of the battlements on the sea wall, a short spear gripped in his hands. Jair cried out as he saw him—a sudden, wild cry—but the sound was lost in the wail of the wind and the screams of battle. Across the blood-soaked length of the high dam the Weapons Master raced, a small and agile figure—not away from the deadly tentacles of the Kraken, but directly into them. Weaving and dodging like a shadow without substance, he broke for the monster's gaping maw. The tentacles hammered down, swatting at him, missing him, sliding past him, far too slow for anyone so impossibly quick. But one slip, one mistake . . .

Up against the hooked beak, the Weapons Master leaped, against the very jaws of the beast. He struck with stunning swiftness, the short spear burying itself deep within the soft tissue of the open maw. Instantly, the tentacles collapsed, the giant body lurching. But Garet Jax was already moving, spinning sideways and diving clear of the trap that sought to snare him. On his feet once more, the Weapons Master caught up a new weapon, this one a lance fixed with an iron pike, the haft still clutched in the lifeless hands of its owner. With a quick scooping motion, Garet Jax had wrenched it free. Too late, the Kraken caught sight once more of this dangerous attacker, barely two yards from one lidded eye. The iron-tipped lance thrust upward at the unprotected eye, piercing through skin, blood, and bone into the brain beyond.

The stricken Kraken wrenched backward in obvious distress, fin-legs churning madly. Stone ramparts shattered all about it as it sought to regain the waters of the Cillidellan. Still Garet Jax clung to the lance embedded within the monster's brain, refusing to release it, grinding it deeper and deeper as he waited for the life force to expend itself. But the Kraken was impossibly strong. Heaving upward, it lifted free of the high dam, then fell ponderously into the Cillidellan and dove from sight. Hands still fixed upon the haft of the lance, Garet Jax was carried with it.

Jair stumbled back against the shattered balustrade in stunned disbelief, his cry of anger dying soundlessly in his throat. Below, the high dam lay clear again and the Dwarf defenders trapped within broke from their prison for the safety of the south watch.

Then Slanter was next to him once more, staggering back to his feet. Blood covered the wizened yellow face, but the Gnome brushed it aside wordlessly and yanked the Valeman down the stairs after him. Stumbling and falling, they gained the courtyard and started across in the direction taken by the fleeing Dwarves.

But already they were too late. Gnome Hunters had appeared on both sides of the battlements behind them. Howling and screaming, a mass of armored, blood-soaked forms, they poured across the crest of the high dam and streamed down into the court. Slanter took one quick look back and abruptly wheeled Jair into one of the dark stairwells. They raced down several flights of lamp-lighted stairs, deep into the shadowed dark of the lower levels that led to the inner workings of the locks. Above, the sounds of pursuit began to fade.

When the stairs ended, they found themselves in a dimly lighted corridor that disappeared down the length of the dam. Slanter hesitated, then turned north, pulling Jair after him.

"Slanter!" the Valeman howled, struggling to slow the Gnome. "This leads back the way we've come—away from the Dwarves!"

"Gnomes will be going the other way, too!" Slanter snapped. "Won't be hunting Dwarves or anybody else this way, will they! Now, run!"

They ran into the gloom, stumbling wearily along the empty corridor. The sounds of battle were far away now, distant and faint against the steady grinding of the machinery and the low rush of the waters of the Cillidellan. Jair's mind spun with the shock of what had befallen them. The little company from Culhaven was no more—Helt and Foraker struck down by the walkers, Garet Jax carried away by the Kraken, and Edain Elessedil disappeared. Only Slanter and he were left—and they were running for their lives. Capaal was gone, fallen to the Gnomes. The locks and dams that regulated the flow of the Silver River west into the homeland of the Dwarves were in the hands of their most implacable enemy. Everything was lost.

His lungs tightened with the strain of running, and his breathing was harsh and labored in his ears. Tears stung his eyes, and his mouth was dry with bitterness and anger. What was he to do now? How was he to reach Brin? He could never find her before she stepped down into the Maelmord and was forever lost. How was he to complete the mission given him by the King . . . ?

His legs went out from under him, knocked away by something he hadn't seen, and he went sprawling into the darkness. Ahead, Slanter ran on, unheeding, a dim shadow in the darkness of the tunnel. Hurriedly, Jair scrambled back to his feet. Slanter was getting too far ahead of him.

Then an arm shot out of the darkness and a hand clamped across his mouth, rough and scaled, sealing away his breath. A second arm encircled his body, hard as iron, and he was dragged back into the shadows of an open door.

"Sstay, little peopless," a voice hissed. "Friendss, we of magicss. Friendss!"

Jair's voice was a soundless scream in his mind.

It was midmorning when Slanter pulled himself clear of the Dwarf escape tunnel, exiting through a thick mass of scrub that concealed the hidden entrance, there to stand alone upon the windswept heights of the mountains north of Capaal. Gray, hazy light filtered down out of skies clouded and drenched by rain, and the chill of night still lingered in the mountain rock. The Gnome glanced about cautiously, then he hunched down against the scrub and moved forward to where the slope dropped away into the gorge.

Far below, the locks and dams of Capaal were swarming with Gnomes. All across the broad bands of stone block, about the battlements and ramparts of the fortress, and deep within the inner workings of the complex, the Gnome Hunters scurried like ants about the business of maintaining their hill.

Well, this was the way it had to end, Slanter thought. He shook his rough yellow face in silent admonition. No one could stand against the walkers. Capaal was theirs now. The siege was done.

He stood up slowly, eyes still fixed on the scene below. There was little danger of being discovered this high up. The Gnomes were all within the fortress and what remained of the Dwarf army had fled south to Culhaven. Nothing was left for him to do but to go his own way.

And that, of course, was exactly what he had wanted all along.

Yet he stood there, his mind adrift with unanswered questions. He still did not know what had become of Jair Ohmsford. One minute the Valeman had been right behind him; the next he had vanished just like that. Slanter had looked for him, of course; but there hadn't been a trace. So at last the Gnome had gone on alone—because, after all, what else could he do?

"Boy was too much trouble anyway!" he muttered irritably. But his words lacked conviction somehow.

He sighed, glanced upward into the graying skies, and turned slowly away. With the Valeman gone and the rest of the little company dead or scattered, the journey to Heaven's Well was finished. Just as well, of course. It was a stupid, impossible quest from the beginning. He had told them so time and again—all of them. They had no idea what they were up against; they had no idea of the power of the walkers. It wasn't his fault that they had failed.

The frown on his rough face deepened. Nevertheless, he didn't like not knowing what had happened to the boy.

He slipped back past the scrub guarding the hidden entrance to the tunnel and climbed to a rocky projection overlooking the Eastland and giving view to its sweep west. At least, he had been smart enough to plan his own escape, he thought smugly. But that was because he was a survivor, and survivors always took time to plan for an escape—except for the crazed ones like Garet Jax. Slanter's frown turned to a faint smile. He had learned long ago not to risk himself unnecessarily where there was no reason for it. He had learned long ago to keep one eye open for the quickest way out of any place into which he ventured. So when the Dwarf had been kind enough to provide him with maps showing the underground tunnels that would take them north behind the siege army, he had been quick to study them. That was why he was alive and safely out of there. If the rest of them hadn't been so foolish . . .

The wind blew against his face, harsh and bitter as it came out of the mountain rock. Far north and west, the forests of the Anar spread away into patches of autumn color, dampened by mist and rain. That was the way for him, he thought grimly. Back to the borderlands, to some semblance of sanity and peace, where his old life could be regained and all of this forgotten. He was free again and he could now go where he wished. A week, ten days at the outside, and the Eastland and the war that ravaged it would be left behind.

He scuffed his boot against the rock. "That boy had sand, though," he said quietly, his thoughts straying yet.

Undecided, he stared out into the rain.

XXIII

---◆---

LATE IN THE AFTERNOON OF THE DAY THAT MARKED THE DIS-
appearance of Paranor from the world of men, the whole of Callahorn from the Streleheim south to the Rainbow Lake was engulfed
in heavy autumn rains. The storms swept down through the borderlands, swept across forest and grassland, and over the Dragon's
Teeth and the Runne, falling at last across the broad expanse of the
Rabb Plains. It was there that it caught up with Allanon, Brin, and
Rone Leah as they journeyed eastward toward the Anar.

They camped that night, exposed to the downpour and huddled
within their sodden cloaks, beneath the sparse shelter of an oak broken and ravaged by years of seasons passing. Empty and barren, the
Rabb stretched away on all sides as the storms thundered overhead,
the glare of the lightning revealing in vivid flashes the starkness of
the plain. No other life could be found on its cracked and windswept surface; they were all alone. They might have pushed on that
night, ridden east until dawn, and thereby gained the Anar before
stopping to take their rest. But the Druid saw that the highlander
and the Valegirl were exhausted and thought it better not to press.

So they stayed that night upon the Rabb and rode on again at
dawn. The day stretched out to greet them, gray and rain-filled, the
sun's light a faint and hazy glow behind the storm clouds that blanketed the autumn skies. They rode east across the plains until they
reached the banks of the Rabb River, then turned south. Where the

river branched west out of its main channel, they crossed at a narrows close to the forest's edge and continued south until daylight
had slipped into a murky, sodden dusk.

They spent a second night unsheltered upon the Rabb, crouched
within cloaks and hoods, with the rain a constant, annoying drizzle
that drenched them to the bone and kept them from sleep. The chill
of the season settled in about them. While neither cold nor sleep-
lessness had an apparent effect upon the Druid, it wore with singular perseverance on the stamina of the girl and the highlander. On
Brin, particularly, it began to take its toll.

Yet at dawn of the following day, she was ready to travel once
more, her determination as hard as iron, reforged out of an inner
battle she had fought through the empty hours of the night to keep
herself sane. The rains that had followed them since their departure
out of the Dragon's Teeth were gone, turned now to a soft, feathery
mist. The skies were clearing into wisps of whitened clouds as the
sunlight began to slip above the forestline. The appearance of the sun
rekindled in the Valegirl a strength of mind and body that the rains
and the dark had done much to erode, and she fought valiantly to ignore the exhaustion that seeped through her. Back astride her horse,
she turned gratefully toward the warmth of the still hazy sunlight
and watched as it crept steadily out of the east.

But exhaustion was not so easily dispatched, she found. Though
the day brightened as they traveled on, a weariness still persisted
deep within, besieging her with doubts and fears that would not
fade. Faceless demons darted in their shadows—darted from her
mind into the forest they rode beside, laughing and taunting. There
were eyes upon her. As it had been within the Dragon's Teeth, there
was the sense of being watched, sometimes from far away through
eyes that were not bound by any distance, sometimes from eyes that
seemed very close. And again there was that insidious premonition.
It had come to her first in the rocks and shadows of the Dragon's
Teeth, following after her, teasing her relentlessly, warning her that
she and those she traveled with played a game with death they could
not win. She had thought it lost after Paranor, for they had escaped

the Druid's Keep alive and safe. Yet now it was back again, reborn in the gray and wet of the last two days, a familiar and haunting demon of her mind. It was evil, and though she sought to drive it from her thoughts with determination and a savage anger, still it would not stay gone.

The hours drifted aimlessly away in the course of the third morning's travel, and Brin Ohmsford's determination gradually began to drift with them. The drifting manifested itself first as an inexplicable sense of aloneness. Besieged by her premonition— a premonition that her companions could not even recognize—the Valegirl began to withdraw into herself. It was done in self-defense to begin with, a withdrawing from the thing that sought to ravage her with its viperous warnings and insidious teasings. Walls came up, windows and doors slammed, and within the shelter of her mind she sought to close the thing out.

But Allanon and Rone were closed out as well, and somehow she could not find a way to bring them back in. She was alone, a prisoner within her own self, chained in irons of her own forging. A subtle change began to overtake her. Slowly, inexorably, she began to believe herself alone. Allanon had never been close, a distant and forbidding figure even under the most favorable circumstances, a stranger for whom she could feel pity and for whom she could sense an odd kinship—yet a stranger nevertheless, impervious and forbidding. It had been different with Rone Leah, of course; but the highlander had changed. From her friend and companion, he had become a protector as formidable and unapproachable as the Druid. The Sword of Leah had wrought that change, giving to Rone Leah power that made him in his own mind equal to anything that sought to stand against him. Magic, born of the dark waters of the Hadeshorn and the black sorcery of Allanon, had subverted him. The sense of intimacy that had bound them each to the other was gone. It was the Druid to whom Rone was bound now and to whom the kinship belonged.

But the drifting of Brin's determination grew quickly beyond her sense of aloneness. It became a feeling that somehow, in some way, she had lost her purpose in this quest. It wasn't gone entirely, she knew—yet it had strayed. Once that purpose had been clear and certain; she was to travel into the Eastland, through the Anar and the Ravenshorn, to the edge of the pit they called the Maelmord and there descend into that pit's blackened maw to destroy the book of dark magic, the Ildatch. That had been her purpose. But with the passage of time, in the dark, cold, and discomfort of their travels, the urgency of that purpose had slipped from her until it now seemed distant and tenuous. Allanon and Rone were strong and certain—twin irons against the shadows that would stop them. What need had they of her? Could they not act as well as she in this quest, despite the Druid's words? Somehow she felt that they could, that she was not the important member of this company, but almost a burden, a thing not needed, her usefulness misjudged. She tried telling herself that this was not true. But somehow it was; her presence was a mistake. She sensed it, and in sensing it grew even more alone.

Midday came and went, and the afternoon wore on. The mist of early morning was gone now, and the day had become bright with sunlight. Bits of color reappeared on the barren plains. The cracked and ravaged earth turned slowly once again to grassland. Brin's sense of aloneness became for a time less oppressive.

By nightfall, the riders had reached Storlock, the community of Gnome Healers. An aged, famous village, it was little more than a gathering of modest stone and timber dwellings, settled within the fringe of the woods. It was here that Wil Ohmsford had studied and trained for the profession that he had always sought to follow. Here Allanon had come to find him so that he might accompany the Druid on his journey south to find the Chosen Amberle in the quest to preserve the Ellcrys tree and the Elven race—a journey that ended with the infusion of the Elfstone magic into Brin's father, thereby bequeathing to her the power of the wishsong. It had been more than twenty years ago, Brin thought in somber, almost bitter reflection. That was how the madness had begun—with the coming of Allanon. For the Ohmsfords, that was how it always began.

They rode through the tranquil, sleepy village, drawing to a halt behind a large, broad-backed building that served as the Center. The white-robed Stors appeared as if they had been waiting for the three to arrive. Silent and expressionless, a handful led away the horses while three more took Brin, Rone, and Allanon inside, down dark and shadowed hallways to separate rooms. Hot baths waited, clean clothes and food, and beds with fresh linens. The Stors spoke no words as they went about the task of caring for their guests. Like ghosts, they lingered for a few minutes and then were gone.

Alone in her room, Brin bathed, changed, and ate her meal, lost in the weariness of her body and the solitude of her mind. Nightfall slipped down across the forestland, and shadows passed over the curtained windows, the light of day fading into dusk. The Valegirl watched its passing with sleepy, languorous unconcern, given over to the pleasure of comforts she had not enjoyed since leaving the Vale. For a time, she could almost pretend that she was back again.

But when the evening deepened, there came a knock upon the door and a white-robed Stor beckoned for her to follow. She went without argument. She knew without asking that Allanon had called.

She found him within his room at the end of the hallway, Rone Leah seated beside him at a small table on which an oil lamp burned to cast away the night's shadow. Wordlessly, the Druid beckoned to a third chair, and the Valegirl moved to occupy it. The Stor who had brought her waited until she was seated, then turned and glided from the room, closing the door softly behind him as he left.

The three companions faced one another in silence. Allanon shifted in his chair, dark face hard and fixed, eyes lost in worlds that the Valegirl and the highlander could not see. He looked old this night, Brin thought and wondered that it could be so. No one had known Allanon to age, save for her father, and that had come about just before the Druid disappeared from the Four Lands twenty years earlier. Yet now she saw it, too. He had aged beyond what he had looked when first he had come to the Vale to seek her out. His long, dark hair was grayer in its tone, his lean face more lined and time-ravaged, his look more bent and rough. Time was working against the Druid, even as it worked against them all.

The black eyes swept up to meet her own. "I would tell you now of Bremen," he rumbled softly, and the gnarled hands folded before him.

"Long ago, in the time of the Councils of the Druids at Paranor, in the time between the Wars of the Races, it was Bremen who saw the truth about the coming of the magic. Brona, who was to become the Warlock Lord, had unlocked the secrets years before and fallen prey to their power. Consumed by what he had hoped to master, the rebel Druid became a slave. After the First War of the Races, the Council believed him destroyed, yet Bremen saw that it was not so. Brona lived, preserved by the magic, driven by its force and its need. The sciences of the old world were gone, lost in the holocaust of the Great Wars. In their place was reborn the magic of a world older still, a world in which only faerie creatures had existed. It was this magic, Bremen saw, that would preserve or destroy the new world of men.

"Thus Bremen defied the Council as Brona had before him— yet with greater care for what he was about—and began to learn for himself the secrets of the power that the rebel Druid had unlocked. Prepared for the Warlock Lord's eventual return, he saved himself when all the other Druids were destroyed. It became his mission, the sole and fixed purpose of his life, to regain the power that the evil one had let loose, to recapture it and seal it away where it could not again be tampered with. No easy task—yet a task to which he pledged himself. The Druids had unlocked the magic; now, as the last of those Druids, it was left to him to lock it away once more."

Allanon paused. "He chose to do this through the creation of the Sword of Shannara, a weapon of ancient Elven magic that could destroy the Warlock Lord and the Bearers of the Skull that served him. In the darkest hour of the Second War of the Races, with the whole of the Four Lands threatened by the armies of the evil one, Bremen forged, from magic and from the skills he had acquired and the knowledge he had gained, the fabled Sword. He gave it to the

Elven King Jerle Shannara. With that Sword, the King would face in battle the rebel Druid and see him destroyed.

"As you know, however, Jerle Shannara failed. Unable fully to master the power of the Sword, he let the Warlock Lord escape. Though the battle was won and the armies of the evil one driven forth, still Brona lived. Years would pass before he could return, but return he would. Bremen knew that he would not be there to face Brona again. Yet his pledge had been given, and Bremen would never forsake a promise."

The Druid's voice had slipped down to a whisper, and there was a look of intense pain within the black, impenetrable eyes. "He did three things, then. He chose me to be his son, the flesh and blood offspring of the Druid line who would walk upon the Four Lands until the time of the Dark Lord's return. He gave added life to himself first and to me later through the sleep that preserves so that, for as long as might be necessary, a Druid would stand as protector of mankind against the Warlock Lord. And finally, he did one thing more. When the time of his passing was at hand and he could not make himself let go, he used the magic in one last, terrible evocation. He bound his spirit to this world in which his body could not stay, so that he could reach beyond life's end to see fulfillment of the pledge that he had made."

Gnarled hands tightened into fists. "He bound himself, spirit out of flesh, to me! He used the magic to achieve that binding, father to son, his spirit exiled in a world of dark where past and future joined, where summons could be had when the need was there. That was what he chose for himself, a lost and hopeless being, never to be freed until it was done, until both had passed . . ."

He stopped suddenly, as if his words had brought him farther than he wished to go. In that instant, Brin caught sight of what had been hidden from her before—a quick, elusive glimpse of the secret that the Druid had withheld from her in the Valley of Shale when Bremen had risen from the Hadeshorn and spoken of what was to be, and which gave substance to the whisperings of her premonition.

"I thought it done once," Allanon went on, brushing past the sudden pause. "I thought it done when Shea Ohmsford destroyed the Warlock Lord—when the Valeman unlocked the secret of the Sword of Shannara and made himself its master. But I was wrong. The dark magic did not die with the Warlock Lord. Nor was it locked away again as Bremen had foresworn it must be. It survived, kept safe within the pages of the Ildatch, secreted away within the bowels of the Maelmord to await new discoverers. And, finally, the discoverers came."

"And became the Mord Wraiths," Rone Leah finished.

"Made slaves to the dark magic as had been the Warlock Lord and the Skull Bearers in old days. Thinking to be master, they became only slaves."

But what is the secret that you hide? Brin whispered in her mind, still waiting to hear it told. Speak now of that!

"Then Bremen cannot be freed from his exile within the Hadeshorn until the book of the Ildatch is destroyed—and the magic with it?" Rone was too caught up in the history of the tale to see what Brin saw.

"He is pledged to that destruction, Prince of Leah," Allanon whispered.

And you. And you. Brin's mind raced.

"All of the dark magic gone from the land?" Rone shook his head wonderingly. "It does not seem possible. Not after so many years of its being—of wars fought because of it, of lives expended."

The Druid looked away. "That age ends, highlander. That age must pass."

There was a long silence then, a hushed stillness that filled the night shadows about the flame of the oil lamp and crowded close about the three who huddled there. Wrapped by it, they thought their separate thoughts, eyes slipping past one another's faces to shield what whispered within. Strangers joined in common cause but without understanding, thought Brin. We strive for a common good, yet the bond is curiously weak . . .

"Can we succeed in this, Allanon?" Rone Leah asked suddenly.

His wind-burned face turned toward the Druid. "Have we strength enough to destroy this book and its dark magic?"

The Druid did not answer for a moment. His eyes flickered with hidden knowledge, elusive and quick. Then he said quietly, "Brin Ohmsford has the strength. She is our hope."

Brin looked at him and shook her head slowly. Her smile twisted with irony. "Hope and no hope. Savior and destroyer. Remember the words, Allanon? Your father spoke them of me."

Allanon said nothing. He simply sat there, dark eyes staring into her own.

"What else did he tell you, Allanon?" she asked him quietly. "What else?"

There was a long pause. "That I shall not see him again in this world."

The silence deepened. She was close now to the secret the Druid kept hidden, she realized. Rone Leah stirred uneasily in his chair, eyes shifting to find those of the Valegirl. There was uncertainty in those eyes, Brin saw. Rone did not want to know any more. She looked away. It was she who was the hope, and she who must know.

"Was there more?" she said.

Slowly Allanon straightened, dark robes wrapping close about him, and on his worn and haggard face, a small smile appeared. "There is an Ohmsford obsession with knowing the truth of all that is," he replied. "Not a one of you has ever been content with less."

"What did Bremen say?" she pressed.

The smile died away. "He said, Brin Ohmsford, that when I go from the Four Lands this time, I shall not come again."

Valegirl and highlander stared at him in shocked disbelief. As certain as the cycle of the seasons was the return of Allanon to the Four Lands when the danger of the dark magic threatened the races. There had never been a time in memory when he had not come.

"I don't believe you, Druid!" Rone insisted heatedly, unable to think of anything else to say, a trace of outrage in his voice.

Allanon shook his head slowly. "The age passes, Prince of Leah. I must pass with it."

Brin swallowed against the tightness in her throat. "When . . . when will you . . . ?"

"When I must, Brin," the Druid finished gently. "When it is time."

Then he rose, a tall and weathered form as black as night and as steady as its coming. The great, gnarled hands reached out across the table. Without fully understanding why, the Valegirl and the highlander reached to clasp them in their own, joining for just an instant the three as one.

The Druid's nod was brief and somehow final. "Tomorrow we ride east into the Anar—east until our journey is done. Go now and sleep. Be at peace."

The great hands released their own and dropped away. "Go," he said softly.

With a quick, uncertain glance at each other, Brin and Rone stood up and walked from the room. All the way out, they could feel the dark gaze following after.

They walked in silence down the hallway beyond. The sound of voices, distant and fragmented, wafted through the shadows of the empty hall and drifted disembodied from some unseen place. The air was thick with the smell of herbs and medicines, and they breathed in the aromas, distracted from their thoughts. When they reached the doors to their sleeping rooms, they stopped and stood together, not touching or looking at each other, sharing without speaking the impact of what they had been told.

It cannot be true, Brin thought, stunned. It cannot.

Rone turned to face her then, and his hands reached down to take hers. For the first time since their departure from Hadeshorn and the Valley of Shale, she felt close to him again.

"What he told us, Brin . . . what he said about not returning . . ." The highlander shook his head. "That was the reason we went to Paranor and he sealed away the Keep. He knew he would not be coming back . . ."

"Rone," she said quickly and put her finger to his lips.

"I know. It's just that I cannot believe it."

"No."

For a long moment they stared at each other. "I am afraid, Brin," he said finally, his voice a whisper.

She nodded without speaking, then wrapped her arms about him and held him close. Then she stepped back again, kissed him lightly on the mouth and disappeared into her room.

Slowly, wearily Allanon turned from the closed door and seated himself once more at the small table. Eyes shifting from the flame of the oil lamp, he stared fixedly into the shadows beyond, his thoughts drifting. Once he would not have felt the need to reveal the secrets that were his. He would have disdained to do so. He was the keeper of the trust, after all; he was the last of the Druids and the power that had once been theirs belonged now to him. He had no need to confide in others.

It had been so with Shea Ohmsford. Much of the truth had been kept from Shea, left hidden for the little Valeman to discover on his own. It had been so as well with Brin's father, when the Druid had taken him in quest of the Bloodfire. Yet Allanon's resolve for secrecy, for deliberate and iron-willed refusal to tell to any—even those closest—all that he knew, had somehow weakened through the years gone past. Perhaps it was the aging, come upon him at last, or the inexorable passing of time that weighed so heavily upon him. Perhaps it was simply the need to share what he carried with some other living soul.

Perhaps.

He rose again from the table, another of night's shadows floating beyond the reach of the light. A sudden breath of air, and the oil lamp went dark.

He had told so much more to the Valegirl and the highlander than to any of the others.

And still he had not told them all.

XXIV

DAWN BROKE OVER THE EASTLAND AND THE FORESTS OF THE
Anar, and the journey of the three who had come from Shady Vale
resumed. Supplied with fresh provisions by the Healers of Storlock,
they rode east out of the village into the woodlands beyond. Few
saw them depart. A handful of white-robed Stors, sad-faced and
voiceless, gathered at the stables behind the Center to lift their arms
in farewell. Within minutes, the three had disappeared into the
trees, gone as silently and as enigmatically as they had come.

It was the kind of autumn day fond memories conjure up of a
milder season's passing when winter snows lie deep about. It was
warm and sun-filled, with the colors of the forest trees radiant and
sprinkled with soft beams of light and the morning smells sweet
and pleasant. Dark and chill as the days gone by had been in the
wake of the passing of the late-year storms, this day was light and
comforting with its dazzling blue skies and sunshine.

The promise of the day was lost, however, to Brin Ohmsford
and Rone Leah. Haunted by Allanon's dark revelation and by a
tense expectation of what lay ahead, neither could share much of
the warmth that the day had to offer. Separate and withdrawn, each
within a dark covering of private emotions and secretive thoughts,
Valegirl and highlander rode forward in determined silence through
the dappled shadows of the great, dark trees, feeling only the cold
that lay buried within themselves.

"Our path hereafter will be a treacherous one," Allanon had told them as they gathered that morning before the stables where their horses had been tended, his voice low and strangely gentle. "All across the Eastland and through the forests of the Anar, the Wraiths will be watching for us. They know that we come; Paranor removed all question of that. They know as well that they must stop us before we reach the Maelmord. Gnomes will seek us, and where they do not, others who obey the walkers will. No path east into the Ravenshorn will be safe for us."

His hands had come up then to rest upon their shoulders, drawing them close. "Still, we are but three and not so easily found. The Wraiths and their Gnome eyes will look two ways for our approach—north above the Rabb River and south out of Culhaven. Safe and unobstructed but for themselves, these are the approaches a wise man would choose. We will choose neither, therefore. Instead, we will pass where it is most dangerous—not only to us, but to them as well. We will pass directly east into the central Anar—through the Wolfsktaag, Darklin Reach, and Olden Moor. Older magics than theirs dwell within those regions—magics that they will be hesitant to challenge. The Wolfsktaag are forbidden to the Gnomes, and they will not enter, even though the Wraiths command it. There are things there more dangerous than the Gnomes we seek to avoid, but most lie dormant. If we are quick and cautious, we should pass through unharmed. Darklin Reach and the Moor are the haunts of other magics yet, but there perhaps we shall find some more friendly to our cause than to theirs . . ."

They rode through the western fringe of the central Anar up into the high ground that formed the doorstep to the rugged, forested humps of the Wolfsktaag. As they traveled, they searched past sunlight and warmth and the brilliant autumn colors for the dark things that lay hidden there. By midday, they had reached the Pass of Jade and begun a long, circuitous climb along its southern slope, where trees and scrub hid them from view as they walked their horses in the deep shadow. Midafternoon found them well east of the pass, wending their way upward toward the high peaks. Timber

and rock stretched dark and silent about them as the daylight began
to wane. By nightfall, they were deep within the mountains. In the
trees through which they passed, the shadows slipped now like living things. All the while they searched, yet found no sign of other
life and felt themselves to be alone.

It was curious and somehow frightening that they could be so
alone, Brin thought as the dusk settled into the mountains and the
day came to an end. She should sense at least a touch of life other
than their own, yet it was as if these peaks and forests had been
stripped. There were no birds within these trees, no insects, no
living creatures of any kind. There was only the silence, deep and
pervasive—the silence, itself become a living thing in the absence
of all other life.

Allanon brought them to a halt in the shelter of a grove of
rough and splintering hickory to set their camp. When provisions
were sorted, the horses tended, and the camp at ready, the Druid
called them to him, ordered that no fire be lighted, and stalked off
into the trees with a quick word of farewell. Valegirl and highlander
stared after him wordlessly until he was out of sight, then sat down
to consume a cold meal of bread, cheese, and dried fruit. They ate in
darkness, not speaking, watching the shadows about them for the
life that never seemed to come. Overhead, the night sky brightened
with a great scattering of stars.

"Where do you think he has gone this night?" Rone Leah wondered after a time. He spoke almost as if he were asking himself the
question. Brin shook her head and said nothing, and the highlander
glanced away again. "Just like a shadow, isn't he? Shifts with every
change of sun and moon, appears, and then he's gone again—always
for reasons all his own. He wouldn't share those reasons with us,
of course. Not with mere humans like us." He sighed and set aside
his plate. "Except that I guess we're not mere humans anymore, are
we?"

Brin toyed with the bit of bread and cheese that remained on
her own plate. "No," she answered softly.

"Well, no matter. We are who we always were, nevertheless."

He paused, as if wondering how sure of that he really was. Then he leaned forward. "It's odd, but I don't feel the same way about him now that I did before. I've been thinking about it all day. I still don't trust him entirely. I can't. He knows too much that I don't. But I don't mistrust him either. He is trying to help, I think, in the best way that he can."

He stopped, waiting for Brin to agree with him, but the Valegirl stayed silent, eyes turned away.

"Brin, what's troubling you?" he asked finally.

She looked at him and shook her head. "I'm not sure."

"Is it what he told us last night—that we wouldn't see him again after this?"

"That, yes. But it's more than that."

He hesitated. "Maybe you're just . . ."

"Something is wrong," she cut him short, and her eyes locked on his.

"What?"

"Something is wrong." She said it slowly, carefully. "With him, with you, with this whole journey—but most especially with me."

Rone stared at her. "I don't understand."

"I don't understand either. I just feel it." She pulled her cloak tightly about her, hunching down within its folds. "I've felt it for days—ever since the shade of Bremen appeared in the Hadeshorn, and we destroyed that Wraith. I feel something bad coming . . . something terrible. And I don't know what it is. I feel, too, that I'm being watched; all the time I'm being watched, but there is never anything there. I feel, worst of all, that I'm being . . . pulled away from myself, from you and Allanon. Everything is changing from what it was when we started out at Shady Vale. It's all different, somehow."

The highlander didn't say anything for a moment. "I suppose it's because of what's happened to us, Brin. The Hadeshorn, Paranor—Allanon telling us what the shade of Bremen told to him. It had to change us. And we've been away from the Vale and the highlands for many days now, from everything familiar and comfortable. That has to be a part of it, too."

"Away from Jair," she said quietly.

"And your parents."

"But Jair most of all," she insisted, as if searching for a reason for this. Then she shook her head. "No, it's not that. It's something else, something besides what's happened with Allanon and missing home and family and . . . That's too easy, Rone. I can feel it, deep down within me. Something that . . ."

She trailed off, her dark eyes uncertain. She looked away. "I wish I had Jair here with me now—just for a few moments. I think he would know what was wrong. We're so close that way . . ." She caught herself, then laughed softly. "Isn't that silly? Wishing for something like that when it would probably mean nothing?"

"I miss him, too." The highlander tried a quick smile. "At least he might take our minds off our own problems. He'd be out tracking Mord Wraiths or something."

He stopped, realizing what he had said, then shrugged away his discomfort. "Anyway, there's probably nothing wrong—not really. If there was, Allanon would sense it, wouldn't he? After all, he seems to sense everything else."

Brin was a long time responding. "I wonder if that is still so," she said finally. "I wonder if he still can."

They were silent then, neither looking back at the other as they stared fixedly into the dark and pondered their separate thoughts. As the minutes slipped away, the stillness of the mountain night seemed to press in about them, anxious to wrap them in the blanket of its stark, empty solitude. It seemed more certain with the passing of each moment that some sound must break the spell, the distant cry of a living creature, the small shifting of forest wood or mountain rock, or the rustle of leaf or insect's buzz. But nothing did. There was only the quiet.

"I feel as if we are drifting," Brin said suddenly.

Rone Leah shook his head. "We travel a fixed course, Brin. There is no drifting in that."

She looked over at him. "I wish I had listened to you and had never come."

The highlander stared at her in shock. The beautiful, dusky face stayed turned toward his own. In the girl's black eyes there was a mix of weariness and doubt that bordered too closely on fear. For just an instant he had the unpleasant sensation that the girl who sat across from him was not Brin Ohmsford.

"I will protect you," he said softly, urgently. "I promise."

She smiled then, a faint, uneven smile that flickered and was gone. Gently her hands reached out to touch his own. "I believe that," she whispered in reply.

But somewhere deep inside, she found herself wondering if he really could.

It was nearly midnight when Allanon returned to the campsite, stepping from the trees as silently as any shadow that moved within the Wolfsktaag. Moonlight slipped through the boughs overhead in thin streamers of silver and cast the whole of the night in eerie brightness. Wrapped within their blankets, Rone and Brin lay sleeping. Across the broad, forested sweep of the mountains, all was still. It was as if he alone kept watch.

The Druid paused several dozen feet from where his charges slept. He had walked to be alone, to think, and to ponder the certainty of what was to be. How unexpected the words of Bremen had been when the shade had spoken them—how strangely unexpected. They should not have been, of course. He had known what must be from the beginning. Yet there was always the feeling that somehow it might be changed. He was a Druid, and all things were possible.

His black eyes shifted across the mountain range. The yesterdays of his life were far away, the struggles he had weathered and the roads he had walked down to reach this moment. The tomorrows seemed distant, too, but that was an illusion, he knew. The tomorrows were right before him.

So much had been accomplished, he mused. But not enough. He turned and looked down at the sleeping Valegirl. She was the one upon whom everything would depend. She would not believe that, of course, or the truth about the power of the wishsong, for she chose to see the Elven magic in human terms, and the magic had never been human. He had shown her what it could be—just a glimpse of the limits to which it could be taken, for she could stand no more, he sensed. She was a child in her understanding of the magic and her coming of age would be difficult. More difficult, he knew, because he could not help her.

His long arms wrapped tightly within the black robes. Could he not help her? There it was again. He smiled darkly. That decision that he should never reveal all, only so much as he felt necessary—that decision that as it had been for Shea Ohmsford in a time long past, truth was best learned by the one who would use it. He could tell her, of course—or at least he could try to tell her. Her father would have said that he should tell her, for Wil Ohmsford had believed the same about the Elven girl Amberle. But the decision was not Wil Ohmsford's to make. It was his own.

It was always his own.

A touch of bitterness twisted his mouth. Gone were the Councils at Paranor when many voices and many minds had joined in finding solutions to the problems of mankind. The Druids, the wise men of old, were no more. The histories and Paranor and all the hopes and dreams they had once inspired were lost, and only he remained.

All of the problems of mankind were now his, as they always had been his and would continue to be his for as long as he lived. That decision, too, had been his to make. He had made it when he had chosen to be what he was. But he was the last. Would there be another to make the same decision when he was gone?

Alone, uncertain, he stood at the edge of the forest shadows and looked down at Brin Ohmsford.

They rode east again at daybreak. It was another brilliant, sun-filled autumn day—warm, sweet, and alive with dreams of what could be.

As night fled westward from the Wolfsktaag, the sun lifted out of the eastern horizon, slipping from the forestline in golden streamers that stretched and spread to the darkest corners of the land and chased the gloom before them. Even within the vast and empty solitude of the forbidden mountains there was a feeling of comfort and peace.

Brin thought of home. How beautiful the Vale would be on a day such as this one, she thought to herself as she walked her horse along the ridgeline and felt the sun's warmth upon her face. Even here the colors of the season spread in riotous disarray against a backdrop of moss and groundcover still green with summer's touch. Smells of life filled her nostrils and left her heady with their mix. In the Vale, the villagers would be awake now, about to begin their day's work. Breakfast would be underway, the succulent aroma of the foods that were cooking escaping through windows thrown wide to catch the warmth of the day. Later, when the morning chores were done, the village families would gather for stories and games on an afternoon that too seldom came this time of year, anxious to take advantage of its ease and recapture for at least a brief time the memory of the summer gone.

I wish I were there to share it, she thought. I wish I were home.

The morning slipped quickly away, its passing lost in the warmth of the sun and the memories and the dreams. Ridgelines and mountain slopes came and went, and ahead the deep forests of the lowlands beyond the Wolfsktaag began to appear in brief glimpses through the humped peaks. By noon, the bulk of the range was behind them, and they were starting down.

It was shortly thereafter that they became aware of the Chard Rush.

It began as sound long before it could be seen—a deep, penetrating roar from beyond a wooded ridge that broke high and rugged against the sweep of the Eastland sky. Like an invisible wave, it surged toward them, a low and sullen rumble that shook the rutted earth with the force of its passing. Then the wind seemed to catch it, magnifying its intensity until the forest air was filled with thunder.

The way forward leveled off, and the timber began to thicken. Atop the ridge head, freezing spray and a deep, rolling mist masked all but the faintest trace of distant blue from a noonday sky now lost far above the tangled branches of the forest trees with their damp, moss-grown bark and earth-colored leaves shimmering bright with wetness. Ahead, the trail sloped upward once more through clusters of rock and fallen timber that loomed spectrally out of the haze like frozen giants. And still there was only the sound, massive and deafening.

Yet slowly, as the trail wound on and the ridgeline grew close, the mist began to dissipate beneath the thrust of the wind as it raked down across the summit of the land, out of the Wolfsktaag to the lowlands east. The bowl of the valley opened before them, its wooded slopes dark and forbidding in the shadow of the mountain peaks beneath a line of ridges colored gold with sunlight. And here, at last, the source of the sound was discovered—a waterfall. An awesome, towering column of churning white water poured wildly through a break in the cliff rock and tumbled downward hundreds of feet through clouds of mist and spray that hung thick across the whole of the western end of the valley, downward into a great river that twisted and turned through rocks and trees until it was lost from view.

In a line, the three riders drew their mounts to a halt.

"The Chard Rush." Allanon pointed to the falls.

Brin gazed down wordlessly. It was as if she stood at the edge of the world. She could not describe what she felt at that moment, only what she saw. Below, barely a hundred yards distant, the waters of the Chard Rush crashed and swirled down rock and through crevice in a magnificent, breathtaking spectacle that left her filled with wonder. Far beyond the valley into which the waters fell, the distant Eastland spread to the horizon, shimmering slightly through the windblown spray of the falls, colored like a painting faded and worn with age, its clarity muted. A steady mist washed over the Valegirl's dusky face and whipped through her long black hair and forest clothing like a light rain. She blinked the water from her eyes and breathed deeply the cold, hard air. In a way she could not explain, she felt as if she had been born again.

Then Allanon was motioning them ahead, and the three riders began working their way down the inside slope of the wooded valley, angling toward the break in the cliff face where the falls dropped away. Single file, they wound through brush and slanted pine that clung tenaciously to the rocky soil of these upper reaches, following what appeared to be a worn, rutted pathway that ran down past the falls. Rising clouds of mist enveloped them, damp and clinging against their skin. The wind died behind the rim of the ridgeline, the sound of its shrill whistle lost in the muffled roar of the falls. Sunlight dropped away into shadow, a false twilight settling over the forestland through which they passed in gradually deepening waves.

Finally they reached the base of the falls and continued along the dark pathway that had brought them there to emerge at last from mist and shadow into warm sunlight. They rode eastward along the banks of the river through deep grass still green and fresh beneath a scattering of pine and yellow-leaved oak. Gradually the roar of the falls subsided and the air grew less chill. In the trees about them, birds flew in sudden bursts of color.

Life had come back again to the land. Brin sighed gratefully, thinking how relieved she was to be clear of the mountains.

And then abruptly Allanon reined his horse to a stop.

Almost as if the Druid had willed that it should be so, the forest about them went still—a deep, layered silence that hung over everything like a shroud. Their horses came to a halt behind his. Valegirl and highlander stared at the big man and then at each other, surprise and wariness in their eyes. Allanon did not move. He simply sat there astride his horse, rigid against the light, staring ahead into the shadows of the forest trees and listening.

"Allanon, what . . . ?" Brin started to ask, but the Druid's hand lifted sharply to cut her short.

At last he turned, and the lean, dark face had drawn tight and hard, a look within the narrow eyes that neither Valegirl nor high-

lander had ever seen. In that instant, without understanding why it was that the feeling had come over her, Brin was suddenly terrified.

The Druid did not speak. Instead, he smiled—a quick, sad smile—and turned away. His hand beckoned them after, and he started ahead into the trees.

They rode only a short distance through a scattering of trees and dying scrub to where a small glen opened before them beside the banks of the river. There Allanon again drew his mount to a halt and this time dismounted. Rone and Brin followed him down. Together they stood there before the horses, looking out over the glen into a deepening stand of trees beyond.

"What's wrong, Allanon?" Brin finished the question this time.

The Druid did not turn. "Something comes. Listen."

They waited, motionless beside him. So complete was the silence now that even the sound of their own breathing was harsh within their ears. Brin's premonition whispered anew in her mind, come from the rain and the gray of the Dragon's Teeth to find her. Fear stroked her skin with its chill touch and she shivered.

Suddenly, there was a sound, faint and cautious—a soft rustling of dried leaves as something moved among them.

"There!" Rone cried, his hand pointing.

Something came into view through the trees on the far side of the glen. Still hidden within the gloom, it stopped suddenly, catching sight of the three who watched it. For long moments, it stayed frozen within its shelter, invisible eyes staring out at them, a silent shadow within the dark.

Then, with swift and certain intent, it stepped from the trees into the light. The chill that had settled within Brin turned instantly to frost. She had never seen anything like the creature that stood before them now. It was man-shaped in appearance, raised upright in a half-crouch, its long arms dangling loosely before it. It was a big, strong creature, lean and heavily muscled. Its skin was a strange reddish color, drawn tight against its powerful body; it was hairless except for a thick ruff that grew about its loins. Great, hooked claws curled from its fingers and toes. Its face lifted toward them, and it was the face of some grotesque beast, blunt and scarred. Gleaming yellow eyes fixed upon their own, and its snout split wide in a hideous grin to reveal a mass of crooked teeth.

"What is it?" Rone Leah whispered in horror.

"What was promised," Allanon replied softly, his voice strangely distracted.

The reddish thing came forward a few steps further to the edge of the glen. There it stopped and waited.

Allanon turned to the Valegirl and the highlander. "It is a Jachyra, a thing of another age, a thing of great evil. It was locked from the lands by the magic of the creatures of faerie in a time before the dawn of Man—in a time even farther back than that in which the Elves created the Forbidding. Only magic of equal power could have set it free again."

He straightened and brought his black robes close about him. "It appears that I was wrong—the Mord Wraiths did anticipate that we might come this way. Only within a place like these mountains, a place where the magic still lives, could a thing like the Jachyra be set loose again. The Wraiths have given us an adversary far more dangerous than they to overcome."

"Suppose we find out how dangerous," Rone suggested bravely and drew forth the ebony blade of the Sword of Leah.

"No." Allanon caught his arm quickly. "This battle is mine."

The highlander glanced at Brin for support. "It seems to me that any battle to be fought on this journey must be fought by all of us."

But Allanon shook his head. "Not this time, Prince of Leah. You have shown your courage and your devotion to this girl. I no longer question either. But the power of this creature is beyond you. I must face it alone."

"Allanon, don't!" Brin cried suddenly, grasping his arm.

He looked down at her then, the worn face and the eyes that penetrated past all that she would hide a mask of sad determination. They stared at each other, and then without quite knowing why she did so, she released him.

"Don't," she repeated softly.

Allanon reached to touch her cheek. At the far side of the glen, the Jachyra gave a sudden, sharp cry that shattered the silence of the afternoon—a cry that was almost like a laugh.

"Let me come with you!" Rone Leah insisted, again starting forward.

The Druid blocked his way. "Stand fast, Prince of Leah. Wait until you are called." The black eyes fixed those of the highlander. "Do not interfere in this. No matter what happens, stay clear. Give me your promise."

Rone hesitated. "Allanon, I cannot . . ."

"Give me your promise!"

The highlander stood before him defiantly for an instant longer and then reluctantly nodded. "I promise."

The Druid's eyes turned back to the Valegirl one last time, a lost and distant look in the gaze they gave to her. "Keep you safe, Brin Ohmsford," he whispered.

Then he wheeled about and started down into the glen.

XXV

◆

Sunlight spilled from out of the cloudless blue afternoon sky to etch sharply Allanon's tall, shadowy form as it passed against the backdrop of the forest color. Warmth and sweet autumn smells lingered in the air, a teasing whisper to the Druid's senses, and across the woodlands a soft and gentle breeze blew down through the trees to ruffle the long, black robes. Within its banks of still summer-green grasses, the river of the Chard Rush glimmered azure and silver, its gleam reflected coldly in the tall man's eyes.

He was conscious of nothing now but the sleek, reddish-skinned form that crept catlike down the far slope of the glen's shallow bowl, yellow eyes narrowed, muzzle curled back in anticipation.

Please come back! Brin cried out the words in the silence of her mind, rendered voiceless by the horror of the familiar premonition that had returned suddenly to haunt her and dance in wild glee at the edges of her sight.

It was this that the premonition had warned against!

The Jachyra dropped down upon all fours, muscles rippling in corded knots beneath the taut skin as slaver began to form about its mouth. Spikes rose along the length of its spine and flexed with the movement of its body as it crept to the floor of the sunlit glen. Muzzle lifting toward the dark figure across from it, the monster cried out a second time—that same, hideous howl that rang like maddened laughter.

Allanon drew to a halt a dozen yards from where it crouched. Motionless, he faced the creature. On the hard, dark face there appeared a look of such frightening determination that it seemed to the Valegirl and the highlander that no living thing, however evil, could stand against it. Yet the Jachyra's frenzied grin merely broadened; more hooked teeth slipped into view from out of its drawn muzzle. There was madness in the yellow eyes.

For a long, terrible instant Druid and monster faced each other in the deep silence of the autumn afternoon and the whole of the world about them ceased to be. Again the Jachyra's laughter sounded. It stepped sideways—an odd, swinging movement. Then, with terrifying suddenness, it lunged for Allanon. Nothing had ever moved so fast. Little more than a blur of reddish fury, it sprang clear of the earth and tore into the Druid.

Somehow it missed. Allanon was faster than his attacker, slipping aside as swiftly as a shadow gone with night. The Jachyra flew past the Druid, tearing into the earth beyond as it landed. Whirling with scarcely a moment's pause, it sprang at its prey a second time. But already the Druid's hands were extended, blue fire bursting forth. The fire ripped into the Jachyra, throwing it backward in midair. It struck the ground in a tangled heap and still the fire tore at it, burning and searing and thrusting the beast back until it came to a jarring halt against a great oak.

Astonishingly, the Jachyra was back on its feet almost at once.

"Shades!" Rone Leah whispered.

It came at Allanon again, dodging and twisting past the Druid fire that flew from the other's fingers. Raging, it flung itself at the tall man with the deadly quickness of a snake. The blue fire hammered into it, flinging it away, but it caught the Druid with the claws of one hand, tearing into black robes and flesh. Allanon staggered back, shrugging at the impact of the blow, the fire disappearing into smoke. In the tall grass a dozen feet away, the Jachyra came back to its feet once more.

Cautiously, the two antagonists circled each other. The Druid's arms and hands extended guardedly before him, and the dark face was a mask of fury. But in the grasses through which he stepped, droplets of his blood streaked the deep green crimson.

The Jachyra's snout split wide once more, an evil, maddened grin. Trailers of smoke curled from the reddish skin where the fire had seared it, yet the monster seemed unharmed. Iron muscles rippled as it moved, a sleek and confident dance of death that led its intended victim on.

Again it attacked, a swift, fluid lunge that carried it into the Druid before the fire could be brought to bear. Allanon's hands fastened on the wrists of the beast, holding it upright so it could not reach his body. The crooked teeth snapped viciously, trying to fasten on the tall man's neck. Locked in this position, the two surged back and forth across the glen, twisting and squirming in an effort to gain the advantage.

Then, with a tremendous heave, the Druid flung the Jachyra over backward, lifting it off its feet and throwing it to the earth. Instantly the blue fire burst from his fingers and engulfed the monster. The Jachyra's cry was high and terrible, a frenzied shriek that froze the whole of the woods about it. Pain was in that cry, yet a pain that sounded of something inexplicably gleeful. The Jachyra leaped from the column of fire, twisting to free itself, its powerful red form steaming and alive with small bits of blue flame. It tumbled over and over through the grasses, a maddened and raging thing, consumed by an ever darker fire that burned within. It came to its feet yet again, hooked teeth gleaming as its muzzle drew back, yellowed eyes bright and ugly.

It likes the pain, Brin realized in horror. It feeds on it.

Behind her, the horses snorted and backed away from the scent of the Jachyra, pulling against the reins secured in Rone Leah's hands. The highlander glanced back worriedly, calling to the animals, trying unsuccessfully to calm them.

Once again, the Jachyra came at Allanon, darting and lunging through the blaze of Druid fire that burned into it. It almost reached the black-robed figure, claws ripping, and again Allanon stepped aside just in time, the blue fire thrusting the creature away in a burst of power.

Brin watched it all, sickened by the struggle but unable to look away. A single thought repeated itself in her mind, over and over. The Jachyra was too much. The Druid had fought so many terrible battles and survived; he had faced awesome creatures of dark magic. But the Jachyra was somehow different. It was a thing ignorant and incautious of life and death, whose existence defied all nature's laws—a creature of madness, frenzy, and purposeless destruction.

An ear-shattering shriek broke from the Jachyra's throat as the monster flung itself at Allanon again. The horses reared in fright, the reins tearing free of Rone's hands. Desperately, the highlander sought to recapture them. But the instant they pulled free, the horses bolted wildly back toward the falls. In a matter of seconds, they had disappeared into the trees beyond.

Rone and Brin turned back to the struggle below. Allanon had thrown up a wall of fire between himself and his attacker, the flames darting out at the Jachyra like knives as the creature sought vainly to break past. Purposefully the Druid maintained the wall, arms extended in rigid concentration. Then suddenly the arms dropped downward in a sweeping motion, bringing with them the wall of fire. Like a net it dropped across the Jachyra and the beast was consumed. It disappeared entirely for an instant, lost in a raging ball of flame. Twisting and turning, it sought to escape, but the fire clung to it tenaciously, held fast by the Druid's magic. Try as it might, the Jachyra could not shake free.

Brin's hand fastened on Rone. Perhaps . . .

But then the Jachyra bolted sharply away from Allanon and the open grasses of the glen, into the forest trees. Still the flames clung to it, but already the fire was beginning to dissipate. The distance between Druid and beast was too great, and Allanon could not maintain his hold. Howling, the monster flung itself into a stand of pine, shattering limbs and trunks, throwing fire everywhere. Wood and pine needles splintered and flamed, and smoke rolled out of the shadows.

At the center of the glen, Allanon's hands dropped away wearily. At its edge, Brin and Rone waited in hushed silence, staring at the smoky gloom into which the beast had disappeared. The forest was still once more.

"It's gone," Rone whispered finally.

Brin did not reply. Voiceless, she waited.

A moment later, something moved within the burned and darkened stretch of pine. Brin felt the cold that had settled deep within her flare sharply. The Jachyra stepped out from the trees. It glided to the edge of the glen, muzzle split wide in that hideous grin, yellow eyes gleaming.

It was unharmed.

"What manner of devil is this?" Rone Leah whispered.

The Jachyra crept back again toward Allanon, its breath harsh and eager. A low, anxious whine broke from its throat, and its snout lifted as if to catch the Druid's scent. On the long grass before it, a trace of the big man's blood dappled the green a bright scarlet. The Jachyra stopped. Slowly, deliberately, it bent to the blood and began to lick it from the earth. The whine turned suddenly deep with pleasure.

Then it attacked. In a single, fluid motion, it gathered its hind legs beneath it and flung itself at Allanon. The Druid's hands came up, fingers extending—too slow. The creature was upon him before he could call forth the fire. They tumbled down into the long grass, rolling and spinning, locked together. So quick had the attack come that the monster was atop Allanon before Brin's sharp cry of warning could reach his ears. Blue fire flared at the tips of the Druid's fingers, searing the wrists and forearms of his attacker as they grappled, but the fire had no effect. The Jachyra's claws ripped into Allanon, tearing through cloth and flesh, ripping downward into bone. The Druid's head jerked back, pain flooding across the dark face—a pain that went beyond physical hurt. Desperately, the Druid sought to dislodge the beast, but the Jachyra had gotten too close and there was no room for leverage. Claws and teeth tore at Allanon, the corded body of the monstrous attacker holding its victim fast to the earth.

"No!" Rone Leah screamed suddenly.

Tearing free of Brin as she sought to restrain him, the Prince of Leah charged down into the glen, the ebony blade of his great broadsword grasped tightly in both hands. "Leah! Leah!" he cried in fury. The promise he had given the Druid was forgotten. He could not stand back and watch Allanon die. He had saved him once; he could do so again.

"Rone, come back!" Brin screamed after him futilely.

Rone Leah reached the struggling figures an instant later. The dark blade of the Sword of Leah lifted and swept downward in a glittering arc, cutting deep into the neck and shoulders of the Jachyra, driven by the force of magic, tearing through muscle and bone. The Jachyra reared back, a frightful howl breaking from its throat, its reddish body snapping upright as if it had been broken from within.

"Die, you monster!" Rone cried in rage as he caught sight of the torn and bloodied figure of Allanon beneath.

But the Jachyra did not die. One corded arm swung about sharply and caught the highlander across the face with stunning force. He flew backward, hands releasing their grip on the Sword of Leah. At once the Jachyra was after him, howling all the while in maddened delight, almost as if the greater pain pleased it in some foul, incomprehensible way. It caught Rone before he fell, seized him in its claws and flung him the length of the glen to lie in a crumpled heap.

Then it straightened. The dark blade of the Sword of Leah was still buried in its body. Reaching back, the Jachyra wrenched the sword free as if the blow had meant nothing to it. It hesitated an instant, the blade held before its yellow eyes. Then it hurled the Sword of Leah from it, into the air high above the waters of the Chard Rush, to fall into their grasp and be carried from sight like a piece of deadwood, bobbing and spinning in the swift current.

The Jachyra spun back around toward the fallen figure of Allanon. Astonishingly, the Druid was on his feet again, black robes shredded and stained dark with his blood. Seeing him risen, the Jachyra seemed to go completely berserk. Howling in fury, it sprang.

But this time the Druid did not try to stop it. Catching the Jachyra in midleap, his great hands closed about its neck like a vise. Heedless of the claws that tore at his body, he forced the monster backward to the ground, the hands squeezing. Shrieks rose out of the Jachyra's damaged throat and the reddish body twisted like a snake that has been pierced. Still the Druid's hands crushed inward. The muzzle split wide, teeth snapping and ripping at the air.

Then abruptly Allanon's hands released and jammed downward into the open maw. They thrust deep into the monster's throat. From the clasped fingers blue fire ripped downward. Convulsions shook the Jachyra, and its limbs flung wide. The Druid fire burned through its powerful body, down into the very core of its being. It struggled to break free for only an instant. Then the fire broke out of it from everywhere, and it exploded in a blinding flash of blue light.

Brin turned away, shielding her eyes against the glare. When she looked back, Allanon knelt alone atop a pile of charred ash.

Brin went first to the unconscious Rone, who lay sprawled in a twisted heap at the back edge of the glen, his breathing shallow and slow. Gently she straightened him, feeling carefully about his limbs and body for signs of breakage. She found none and, after wiping clean the cuts on his face, she hurried down to Allanon.

The Druid still knelt within the ashes that had been the Jachyra, his arms folded tight against his body, his head lowered against his chest. His long black robes were shredded and soaked with his blood.

Slowly Brin knelt beside him, a stricken look on her face as she saw what had been done to him. The Druid lifted his head wearily, hard eyes locking on her own.

"I am dying, Brin Ohmsford," he said quietly. She tried to shake her head, but his hand lifted to stop her. "Hear me, Valegirl. It was foretold that this should be. In the Valley of Shale, the shade of Bremen, my father, said to me that it should be. He said that I must pass from the land and that I would not come again. He said that it would happen before our quest was done."

He winced with sudden pain, his face tightening in response. "I thought that perhaps I could make it otherwise. But the Wraiths . . . the Wraiths found a way to set free the Jachyra, knowing perhaps . . . at least hoping that I would be the one it would encounter. It is a thing of insanity. It feeds on its own pain and on the pain of others. In its madness, it wounds not just the body, but the spirit as well. There is no defense. It would have torn itself apart . . . just to see me destroyed. It is a poison . . ."

He choked on the words. Brin bent close, swallowing back the hurt and fear. "We must dress the wounds, Allanon. We must . . ."

"No, Brin, it is finished," he cut her short. "There is no help for me. It must be for me as it was foretold." He glanced across the glen slowly. "But you must help the Prince of Leah. The poison will be in him as well. He is your protector now . . . as he said he would be." His eyes shifted back to her own. "Know that his sword is not lost. The magic will not let it be lost. It must . . . find its way to mortal hands . . . the river will carry it to those hands . . ."

Again he choked on the words, this time doubling over sharply against the pain of his wounds. Brin reached out and caught him, held him upright, close against her.

"Don't talk anymore," she whispered, tears filling her eyes.

Slowly he pulled away from her, straightening. Blood coated her hands and arms where she had held him.

A faint, ironical smile flickered on his lips. "The Wraiths think that I am the one they need fear—that I am the one who can destroy them." He shook his head slowly. "They are wrong. You are the power, Brin. You are the one that . . . nothing can stand against."

One hand fastened on her arm in a grip of iron. "Hear me well. Your father mistrusts the Elven magic; he fears what it can do. I tell you now that he has reason to mistrust it, Valegirl. The magic can be a thing of light or a thing of dark for the one who possesses it.

It seems a toy, perhaps, but it has never been that. Be wary of its power. It is power like nothing I have ever seen. Keep it your own. Use it well, and it will see you safely through to the end of your quest. Use it well, and it will see the Ildatch destroyed!"

"Allanon, I cannot go on without you!" she cried softly, shaking her head in despair.

"You can and you must. As with your father . . . there is no one else." His dark face lowered.

She nodded dumbly, barely hearing him, lost in the jumble of emotions that raged within her as she fought back against the inevitability of what was happening.

"The age passes," Allanon whispered and the black eyes glistened. "So must the Druids pass with it." His hand lifted to fall gently on hers. "But the trust I carry for them must not pass, Valegirl. It must remain with those who live. That trust I give now to you. Bend close."

Brin Ohmsford leaned forward until her face was directly before his. Slowly, painfully, the Druid slipped one hand within the shredded robes to his chest, then brought it forth again, the fingers dipped into his own blood. Gently he touched her forehead. Holding the fingers to her flesh, warm with his lifeblood, he spoke softly in a language she had never heard. Something of his touch and of the words seemed to seep into her, filling her with a rush of exhilaration that swept across her vision in a surge of blinding color and then was gone.

"What . . . have you done to me?" she asked him haltingly.

But the Druid did not answer. "Help me to my feet," he commanded her.

She stared at him. "You cannot walk, Allanon! You are too badly hurt!"

A strange, unfamiliar gentleness filled the dark eyes. "Help me to my feet, Brin. I will not have to walk far."

Reluctantly she wrapped her arms about him and eased him from the ground. Blood soaked the grasses upon which he had knelt and the mass of ashes that had been the Jachyra.

"Oh, Allanon!" Brin was crying freely now.

"Walk me to the river's edge," he whispered.

Slowly, unsteadily, they stumbled across the empty glen to where the Chard Rush churned swiftly eastward within its grass-covered banks. The sun still shone a brilliant gold, warm and friendly as it brightened the autumn day. It was a day of life, not of death, and Brin cried within that it could not become so for Allanon.

They reached the bank of the river. Gently the Valegirl let the Druid settle once more into a kneeling position, his dark head lowered against the sunlight.

"When your quest is done, Brin," he said to her, "you will find me here." His face lifted to hers. "Now stand away."

Stricken, she stepped slowly back from him. Tears ran down her face, and her hands made pleading motions to the slouched form.

Allanon stared back at her for a long moment, then turned away. One blood-streaked arm lifted toward the waters of the Chard Rush, stretching out above them. The river went still instantly, its surface as calm and placid as that of a sheltered pond. A strange, hollow silence descended over everything.

A moment later the center of the still water began to churn violently and from the depths of the river rose the cries that had come from the waters of the Hadeshorn—high and piercing. They sounded for but an instant, and then all was still once more.

On the river's edge, Allanon's hand dropped to his side and his head bowed.

Then the spectral figure of Bremen rose from the Chard Rush. Gray and nearly transparent against the afternoon light, the shade rose to stand upon the river's waters, ragged and bent with age.

"Father," Brin heard Allanon call softly.

The shade came forward, gliding motionlessly on the still surface of the river. It came to where the Druid knelt. There it bent slowly downward and gathered the stricken form in its arms. Without turning, it moved back across the water, Allanon cradled close. It stopped again at the center of the Chard Rush, and beneath it the waters boiled fiercely, hissing and steaming. Then it sank slowly back into the river, and the last of the Druids was carried from sight. The Chard Rush was still an instant longer, and then the magic was ended and it began to churn eastward once again.

"Allanon!" Brin Ohmsford cried.

Alone on the riverbank she stared out across the swift-flowing waters and waited for the reply that would never come.

XXVI

AFTER CAPTURING JAIR AT THE FALL OF THE DWARF FORTRESS of Capaal, the Mwellret Stythys marched him north through the wilderness of the Anar. Following the twists and turns of the Silver River as it wove threadlike through trees and brush, over cliffs, and across ravines, they passed deep into the forestland and the darkness that lay close about. All the while they traveled, the Valeman was kept gagged and leashed like an animal. Only at mealtimes was he freed of his bonds so that he might eat, and the cold reptilian eyes of the Mwellret were always upon him. Gray, rain-filled hours slipped away with agonizing slowness as the march wore on, and all that had been of the Valeman's life, his friends and companions, and his hopes and promises, seemed to slip away with them. The woods were dank and fetid, infused by the poisoned waters of the Silver River with rot and choked by dying brush and trees clustered so thickly that the whole of the sky was screened away by their tangle. Only the river gave them any sense of direction as it flowed sluggishly past, blackened and fouled.

Others passed north in those days as well, bound for the deep Anar. On the wide road that ran parallel to the Silver River, which the Mwellret cautiously avoided, caravans of Gnome soldiers and their prisoners trekked in steady procession, mired in mud and laden with the pillage of an invading army. The prisoners were bound and chained—men who had fought as defenders at Capaal.

They stumbled past in long lines, herded like cattle, Dwarves, Elves, and Bordermen, haggard, beaten, and stripped of hope. Jair looked down on them through the trees above the roadway over which they traveled and there were tears in his eyes.

Armies of Gnomes from Graymark also traveled the road, southbound in great, unruly masses as they hastened to join those tribes already advancing into the lands of the Dwarf people. Thousands came, grim and frightening, their hard yellow faces twisted with jeers as they called to the hapless prisoners that marched past them. Mord Wraiths came, too, though no more than a handful, dark and shadowed things that walked alone and were avoided by all.

The weather turned worse as the journey wore on. Skies turned black with thunderclouds and the rain began to fall in steady sheets. Lightning flashed in brilliant streaks and booming peals of thunder rolled the length of the sodden land. Autumn's trees drooped and matted with the wet, the colored leaves sinking and falling into the mire, and the ground turned muddied and uncertain. A gray and dismal cast settled down across the forestland, and it seemed as if the skies pressed against the earth to choke its life away.

Jair Ohmsford felt as if that might be so as he trudged helplessly through the wilderness brush, pulled on by the leather bindings gripped in the hands of the dark-robed figure before him. Cold and wet sank deep within him. As the hours passed, exhaustion began to take its toll. A fever settled in, and, as it did so, his mind began to wander. Flashes of what had brought him to this sorry state mingled with childhood memories in garbled bits of still-life that hovered briefly within his stricken mind and disappeared. Sometimes he was not entirely lucid, and strange and frightening visions would wrack him, stealing through his thoughts like thieves. Even when he was free momentarily of the effects of the fever, a dark despair colored his thoughts. There was no hope for him now, it whispered. Capaal, the defenders that had held her, and all of his friends and companions were gone. Images of them in the moment of their fall flashed in his mind with the blinding clarity of the lightning that crackled overhead through the canopy of the trees: Garet Jax, pulled deep into the gray waters of the Cillidellan by the Kraken; Foraker and Helt, buried beneath the wall of stone rubble brought down by the dark magic of the walkers; Slanter, running heedlessly down the underground corridors of the fortress before him, never looking back, never seeing. Even Brin, Allanon, and Rone appeared at times, lost somewhere deep within the Anar.

Sometimes thoughts of the King of the Silver River would come to him, clear and strangely poignant, filled with the wonder and the mystery of the old man. Remember, they whispered in soft, anxious tones. Do not forget what you must do. But he had forgotten, it seemed. Tucked within his tunic, hidden from the prying eyes of the Mwellret, were the gifts of magic the old man had bestowed on him—the vision crystal and the leather bag with the Silver Dust. He had them still and he meant to keep them. But somehow their purpose was strangely unclear, lost in the swell of the fever, hidden in the wanderings of his mind.

Finally, when they stopped for the night, the Mwellret saw that he was taken with fever and gave him a medicine to drink, mixing the contents of a pouch at his waist with a cup of dark, bitter ale. The Valeman tried to refuse the drink, wracked with the fever and his own sense of uncertainty, but the Mwellret forced it down him. Shortly after, he fell asleep and slept that night untroubled. At dawn he was given more of the bitter potion; by dusk of the second night, the fever had begun to subside.

They slept that night within a cave on a high ridgeline overlooking the dark curve of the river, dryer and warmer than they had been on previous nights, free of the extreme discomfort that had plagued them in the open forest. It was on this night that Jair again came to speak with his captor. They had finished their meal of ground roots and dried beef and drunk a small measure of the bitter ale; now they sat facing each other in the dark, huddled down within their cloaks against the night's chill. Without, the rain fell in a slow, steady drizzle, spattering noisily against trees, stones, and muddied earth. The Mwellret had not replaced the gag in the Valeman's mouth as he had done the past two nights, but had left it loose about his neck. He sat watching Jair, his cold eyes glittering, his reptilian face a vague shadow within the darkness of his cowl. He made no move, nor did he speak. He simply sat and watched as the Valeman crouched across from him. The minutes slipped by, and at last Jair grew determined to engage the creature in conversation.

"Where are you taking me?" he ventured cautiously.

Slitted eyes narrowed further, and it was then the Valeman realized that the Mwellret had been waiting for him to speak. "We go into the High Benss."

Jair shook his head, not understanding. "The High Bens?"

"Mountainss below the Ravensshorn, Elfling," the other hissed. "Sstay for a time within thosse mountainss. Put you in the Gnome prissonss at Dun Fee Aran!"

Jair's throat tightened. "Prison? You plan to lock me in a prison?"

"Guesstss of mine sstay there," the other rasped, laughing softly.

The Valeman stiffened at the sound of the laughter and fought back against the fear that washed through him. "Why are you doing this to me?" he demanded angrily. "What do you want from me?"

"Hss!" A hooked finger pointed. "Doess the Elfling truly not know? Doess he not ssee?" The cloaked form hunched closer. "Then lissten, little peopless. Hear! Ourss wass the gifted peopless, lordss over all the mountainss' life. Comess to uss the Dark Lord many yearss gone passt now, and a bargain wass sstruck. Little Gnome peopless ssent to sserve the Dark Lord if he leavess our peopless be, lordss sstill within the mountainss. Doess thiss, the Dark Lord, and in hiss time passsess from the earth. But we endure. We live!"

The crooked finger twisted slowly. "Then comess the walkerss, climbed from the dark pit of the Maelmord, climbed into our mountainss. Sserve the magic of the Dark Lord, they ssay. Give we up our homess, they ssay. Give we up the little peopless that sserve uss. Bargainss mean nothing now. We refusse the walkerss, the Wraithss. We are sstrong alsso. But ssomething done to uss. We ssicken and die. No young are born. Our peopless fail. Yearss passs, and we weaken to a handful. Sstill the walkerss ssay we musst go from the mountainss. At lasst we are too few, and the walkerss drive uss forth!"

He paused then, and the green slitted eyes burned deep into the Valeman's, filled with rage and bitterness. "Left me for dead, did the walkerss, the Wraithss. Black thingss of evil. But I live!"

Jair stared at the monster. Stythys was admitting to him that the Mwellrets in the time of Shea Ohmsford had sold to the War-lock Lord the lives of the mountain Gnomes so that they might be used to fight against the Southland in the aborted Third War of the Races. The Mwellrets had done this in order to preserve their lordship over their mountain kingdom in the Ravenshorn. It was as Foraker had told him and as the Dwarf people had suspected. But then the Mord Wraiths had come, successors to the power of the dark magic of the Warlock Lord. The Eastland was to be theirs now, and the Ravenshorn would no longer belong to the Mwellrets. When the lizard things had resisted, the Wraiths had sickened and destroyed them. So Stythys had indeed been driven forth from his homeland to be found by the Dwarves and brought into Capaal . . .

"But what has all this to do with me?" he demanded, a sinking suspicion settling through him.

"Magicss!" the Mwellret hissed instantly. "Magicss, little friend! I wissh what you posssesss. Ssongss you ssing musst be mine! You have the magicss; you musst give them to me!"

"But I can't!" Jair exclaimed in frustration.

A grimace twisted the other's scaled face. "Can't, little friend? Powerss of magicss musst again come to my peopless—not to the Wraithss. Your magicss sshall be given, Elfling. At the prissonss you sshall give them. You will ssee."

Jair looked away. It was the same with Stythys as it had been with the Gnome Sedt Spilk—both had wanted mastery over something that Jair could not give them. The magic of the wishsong was his, and only he could use it. It would be as useless to the Mwellret as it had been to the Sedt.

And then a chilling thought struck him. Suppose that Stythys knew that? Suppose that the Mwellret knew he could not have the magic, but that he must make use of it through Jair? The Valeman remembered what had been done to him in that cell in Capaal—how the Mwellret had made him reveal the magic . . .

He caught his breath. Oh, shades! Suppose Stythys knew—or suppose that he even suspected—that there were other magics? Suppose he sensed the presence of the vision crystal and the Silver Dust?

"You can't have them," he whispered, almost before he realized what he was saying. There was a hint of desperation in his voice.

The Mwellret's reply was a soft hiss. "Prissonss will change your mind, little peopless. You will ssee."

Jair Ohmsford lay awake for a long time after that, gagged and hobbled once more, lost in the darkness of his thoughts as he listened to the sounds of the rainfall and the breathing of the sleeping Mwellret. Shadows lay all about the entrance to the little cave; without, the wind blew the storm clouds above the sodden forest. What was he to do? Behind him lay his quest and his shattered plans for saving Brin. Before him lay the Gnome prisons of Dun Fee Aran. Once locked within their walls, he might never come away again, for it was certain that the Mwellret meant to keep him there until he had revealed what he knew of the secrets of the Elven magic. But he would never give up those secrets. They were his to use in service to the King of the Silver River in exchange for the life of his sister. He would never give them up. Yet he sensed that, despite his resolve and whatever strength he could muster to resist his captor, sooner or later Stythys would find a way to wrest those secrets from him.

Thunder rumbled in the distance somewhere, rolling across the forestland, deep and ominous. More ominous still was the despair of the Valeman. It was a long time before exhaustion overcame him and he at last fell asleep.

. . .

Jair and the Mwellret resumed their march north with the coming of dawn on the third day, plodding through rain, mist, and sodden woods, and at midday they passed into the High Bens. The mountains were dark and rugged, a cluster of broken peaks and crags that straddled the Silver River where it washed down out of the high forestland below the Ravenshorn. The two climbed into their midst, swallowed by mist that clung to the rocks until at last, as the day waned and the night began to fall, they stood upon a bluff overlooking the fortress of Dun Fee Aran.

Dun Fee Aran was a sprawling, castlelike complex of walls, towers, watches, and battlements. The whole of the fortress had a gray and dreary cast to it as it materialized out of the rain before them, one that would have been there, Jair sensed, even in the best of weather. Wordlessly, they trudged from the trees, the tall, cloaked Mwellret leading the hobbled Valeman, and passed through the brush and scrub of the bluff face into the sodden camp. Gnome Hunters and retainers of all ranks and standings plodded past them across the muddied grounds, cloaked and hooded against the weather and caught up in their own concerns. No one questioned them. No one gave them a second look. They passed over stone parapets and walkways, over walls and causeways, down stairs, and through halls. The night began to deepen and the light to fail. Jair felt as if the world were closing in about him, shutting him away. He could smell the stench of the place, the closed and fetid reek of cells and human bodies. Lives were expended here without much thought, he sensed with a chill. Lives were locked away within these walls and forgotten.

A huge, blocklike structure loomed before them, windows no more than tiny slits through the stones, doors ironbound and massive. They entered this building and silence closed about them.

"Prissonss, Elfling," Jair heard the Mwellret whisper back at him.

They traversed a maze of dark and shadowed corridors, hallways filled with doors whose bolts and hinges showed rust and cobwebs undisturbed by the passage of time. Jair felt cold and empty as he watched row after row of these doors pass away. Their boots echoed dully in the silence, and only the distant sound of iron clanging and stone being chiseled came otherwise to his ears. Jair's eyes scanned dismally the walls that rose about him. How will I ever get out of here? he wondered in the silence of his mind. How will I ever find my way?

Then a torch flared before them in the corridor, and a small cloaked form came into view. It was a Gnome, aged and ruined, yellow face ravaged by some nameless disease so loathsome that Jair pulled back against the leather ties that bound him. Stythys advanced to where the Gnome stood waiting, bent over the ugly little man, and made a few cryptic signs with his fingers. The Gnome replied in kind; with a brief motion of one crooked hand, he bade them follow.

They went deeper into the prisons, the light from the world without all but lost in the twist of stone and mortar. Only the torch showed them the way, burning and smoking through the blackness.

They stopped at last before an ironbound door similar to the hundreds they had passed before it. Hands twisting roughly about the metal latch, the Gnome wrenched its bolt free. With a grating screech, he brought the heavy portal open. Stythys looked back at Jair, then pulled at the leash and brought him forward into the room beyond. It was a small, cramped cell, empty save for a pile of straw bundled in one corner and a wooden bucket next to the door. A single tiny slit cut into the far wall let through a sliver of gray light from without.

The Mwellret turned, cut free the bonds that tied Jair's hands and slipped loose the gag that bound his mouth. Roughly, he shoved the Valeman past him onto the bed of straw.

"Thiss iss yourss, Elfling," he hissed. "Home for little peopless until you tell me of the magicss." The crooked finger pointed back to the hunched form of the Gnome behind him. "Your jailer, Elfling. He iss mine, one who sstill obeyss. Mute he iss—doess not sspeak or hear. Ssongss of magicss usseless on him. Feedss and tendss you, he doess." He paused. "Hurtss you, too, if you dissobeyss."

The Gnome's ravaged face was turned toward the Valeman as Stythys spoke, but revealed nothing of what the mind behind it thought. Jair glanced about bleakly.

"Tellss me what I musst know, Elfling," the Mwellret whispered suddenly. "Tellss me or never leavess thiss plasse!"

The cold voice hung with a hiss in the silence of the little room as the yellow eyes bore deep into the Valeman's. Then Stythys wheeled away and strode back through the cellroom door. The Gnome jailer turned as well, crooked hands gripping the ironbound door by its latch bolt and pulling it firmly shut.

Huddled alone in the dark, Jair listened until the sound of their footfalls had disappeared.

The minutes slipped away into hours as he sat motionless within the cell, listening to the silence and thinking of how hopeless his position had become. Smells assailed his nostrils as he sat there, rank and harsh, mingling with the sense of despair that coursed relentlessly through him. He was scared now, so scared that he could barely bring himself to think. The thought had never crossed his mind before in all the time that had passed since he had abandoned his home in Shady Vale, fleeing from the Gnomes that hunted for him, but now for the first time it did.

You are going to fail, it whispered.

He would have cried then if he could have made himself do so, but somehow the tears would not come. Perhaps he was too frightened even for that. Think about how you will escape this place, he ordered himself. There is always a way out of everything.

He took a deep breath to steady himself. What would Garet Jax do in this situation? Or even Slanter? Slanter always had a way out; Slanter was a survivor. Even Rone Leah would have been able to come up with something.

His thoughts drifted for a time, wandering through memories of what had been, sidestepping effortlessly into dreams of what might somehow yet be. All of it was fantasy, false rendering of truths twisted in the madness of his own despair to become what he would have them be.

Then at last he made himself rise and walk about his tiny prison, exploring what he could already see was there, touching the damp, cold stone, and peering at the shaft of gray that slipped through the airhole from the skies without. He journeyed all about the cell, studying to no particular purpose, waiting for his emotions to still themselves and his thoughts to settle.

Suddenly he decided to use the vision crystal. If he were to have any sense of what time remained to him, he must discover what had become of Brin.

Hurriedly, he brought the crystal and its silver chain out from their place of concealment within his tunic. He stared down at the crystal, cupped gently within his hands. He could hear the old King's voice whispering to him, cautioning him that this would be the means by which he could follow Brin's progress. All he need do was sing to it . . . .

Softly, he sang. At first, his voice would not come, choked with emotions that swam restlessly through him still. Yet he hardened himself against his own sense of uncertainty, and the sound of the wishsong filled the tiny room. Almost at once, the vision crystal brightened, sharp light flaring outward into the gloom and chasing the shadows before it.

He saw at once that it came from a small fire, and Brin's face was before him, obviously studying the flames of a campfire. Her lovely face was cupped in her hands. Then she looked up and seemed to be searching. There were signs of strain and worry, and she looked almost haggard. Then she looked down again and sighed. She shuddered slightly, as if repressing a sob. All of her that Jair could see seemed to be given over to despair. Whatever had happened to her had obviously been unpleasant . . .

Jair's voice broke as worry for his sister flooded through him, and the image of his sister's frowning face wavered and vanished. The Valeman stared down in stunned silence at the crystal cupped in his hands.

Where, he wondered, was Allanon? There had been no sign of him in the crystal.

Leaves in the wind, the voice of the King of the Silver River whispered in his mind. She will be lost.

Then he closed his hands tightly about the vision crystal and stared sightlessly into the darkness.

XXVII

NIGHT HAD SETTLED DOWN ACROSS THE FORESTS OF THE
Anar when Brin Ohmsford saw the lights. They winked at her like
fireflies through the screen of the trees and shadows that stretched
away into the dark, small, elusive, and distant.

She slowed, her arms wrapping quickly about Rone to keep
him from falling as he stumbled to a halt beside her. An aching
weariness wracked her body, but she forced herself to hold the
highlander upright as he fell against her, his head drooping to her
shoulder, his face hot and flushed with the fever.

"... can't find where ... lost, can't find ..." he muttered inco-
herently and the fingers of his hand gripped her arm until it hurt.

She whispered to him, letting him hear her voice and know she
was still there. Slowly the fingers relaxed their grip, and the fevered
voice went silent.

Brin stared ahead at the lights. They danced through forest
boughs still thick with autumn leaves, bits and pieces of brightness.
Fire! She whispered the word urgently, and it pushed back against
the despair and the hopelessness that had closed in about her in
steadily deepening layers since the march east from the Chard Rush
had begun. How long ago it all seemed now—Allanon gone, Rone
so badly wounded, and she alone. She closed her eyes against the
memory. She had walked all that afternoon and into the night, following the run of the Chard Rush eastward, hoping, praying that

it would lead her to some other human being who could help her. She didn't know how long or how far she had walked; she had lost track of time and distance. She only knew that somehow she had managed to keep going.

She straightened, pulling Rone upright. Ahead, the lights flickered their greeting. Please! she cried silently. Please, let it be the help I need!

She trudged ahead, Rone's arm looped about her shoulders, his body sagging against hers as he stumbled beside her. Tree limbs and scrub brushed at her face and body, and she bent her head against them. Putting one foot before the other with wooden doggedness, she went forward. Her strength was almost gone. If there was no help to be had here . . .

Then abruptly the screen of trees and shadows broke apart before her, and the source of the lights stood revealed. A building loomed ahead, shadowed and dark, save for slivers of yellow light that escaped from two places in its squarish bulk. Voices sounded from somewhere within, faint and indistinct.

Holding Rone close, she pushed on. As she drew nearer, the building began to come into focus. A low, squat structure with a peaked roof, it was constructed of timbers and sideboards on a stone foundation. A covered porch fronted a single storey with a garret, and a stable sat back away from the rear of the building. Two horses and a mule stood tied to a hitching post, heads lowered to crop the drying grass. Along the front of the building, a series of windows stood barred and shuttered against the night. It was through the gaps in the shutters that light thrown by oil lamps had escaped and been seen by the Valegirl.

"A little farther, Rone," she whispered, knowing that he didn't understand, but would respond to the sound of her voice.

When she was a dozen feet from the porch, she saw the sign that hung from the eaves of its sloping roof: ROOKER LINE TRADING CENTER.

The sign swayed gently in the night wind, weathered and split, the paint so badly faded into the wood that the letters were barely legible. Brin glanced up at it briefly and looked away. All that mattered was that there were people inside.

They climbed onto the porch, stumbling and tripping on the weathered boards, to sag against the door jamb. Brin groped for the handle, and the voices within suddenly went still. Then the Valegirl's hand closed about the metal latch, and the heavy door swung open.

A dozen rough faces turned to stare at her, a mix of surprise and wariness in their eyes. Trappers, Brin saw through a haze of smoke and exhaustion—bearded and unkempt, their clothes of worn leather and animal skins. Hard-looking, they clustered in groups about a serving bar formed of wood planks laid crosswise on upended ale kegs. Animal pelts and provisions lay stacked behind the counter, and a series of small tables with stools sat before it. Oil lamps hung from low-beamed ceiling rafters and cast their harsh light against the night shadows.

With her arms wrapped about Rone, Brin stood silently in the open doorway and waited.

"They's ghosts!" someone muttered suddenly from along the serving counter, and there was a shuffling of feet.

A tall, thin man in shirt-sleeves and apron came out from behind the counter, head shaking slowly. "If they was dead things, they'd have no need to open the door now, would they? They'd just walk right on through!"

He crossed to the middle of the room and stopped. "What's happened to you, girl?"

Brin realized suddenly, through the haze of fatigue and pain that assailed her, how they must appear to these men. They might well have been something brought back from the dead—two worn and ragged things, their clothing damp and muddied, their faces white with exhaustion, hanging onto each other like straw-filled scarecrows. A bloodied strip of cloth had been bound about Rone's head, but the rawness of the wound showed through. On his back, the scabbard that had once held the great broadsword lay empty. Her own face was soiled and drawn, and her dark eyes haunted.

Spectral apparitions, they stood framed in the light of the open doorway, swaying unevenly against the night.

Brin tried to speak, but no words came out.

"Here, lend a hand," the tall man called back to the others at the counter, coming forward at once to catch hold of Rone. "Come on now, lend a hand!"

A brawny woodsman came forward quickly, and the two ushered the Valegirl and the highlander to the nearest table, placing them on the low stools. Rone slumped forward with a groan, his head sagging.

"What's happened to you?" the tall man repeated once again, helping to hold the highlander in place so he would not fall. "This one's burning up with fever!"

Brin swallowed thickly. "We lost our horses in a fall coming down out of the mountains," she lied. "He was sick before then, but it's grown worse. We walked the riverbank until we found this place."

"My place," the tall man informed her. "I'm a trader here. Jeft, draw a couple ales for these two."

The woodsman slipped behind the counter to an ale keg and opened the spigot into two tall glasses.

"How about a free one for the rest of us, Stebb?" one of a group of hard-looking men at the far end of the counter called out.

The trader shot the man a venomous look, brushed back a patch of thinning hair atop a mostly balding pate, and turned again to Brin. "Shouldn't be in those mountains, girl. There's worse than fever up there."

Brin nodded wordlessly, swallowing against the dryness in her throat. A moment later the woodsman returned with the glasses of ale. He passed one to the Valegirl, then propped Rone up long enough to see that he sipped at the other. The highlander tried to grasp the glass and gulp the harsh liquid down, choking as he did. The woodsman moved the glass away firmly.

"Let him drink!" the speaker at the end of the bar called out again.

Another laughed. "Naw, it's wasted! Any fool can see he's dying!"

Brin glanced up angrily. The man who had spoken saw her look and sauntered toward her, his broad face breaking into an insolent grin. The others in the group trailed after, winking knowingly and chuckling.

"Something the matter, girl?" the speaker sneered. "Afraid you . . . ?"

Instantly Brin was on her feet, barely aware of what she was doing as she snatched her long knife from its sheath and brought it up in front of his face.

"Now, now," the woodsman Jeft interceded quickly at her side, pushing her gently back. "No need for that, is there?"

He turned to face the speaker, standing directly before him. The woodsman was a big man, and he towered over the men who had come down from the end of the counter. The members of the group glanced at one another uncertainly.

"Sure, Jeft, no harm meant," the offender muttered. He looked down at Rone. "Just wondered about that scabbard. Crest looks like a royal seal of some type." His dark eyes shifted to Brin. "Where you from, girl?"

He waited a moment, but Brin refused to answer. "No matter." He shrugged. With his friends trailing after him he moved back down the counter. Gathering close to resume their drinking, they began conversing in low tones, their backs turned. The woodsman stared after them for a moment, then knelt down beside Brin.

"Worthless bunch," he muttered. "Camp out west of Spanning Ridge masquerading as trappers. Live by their wits and the misfortune of others."

"Been drinking and wasting time here since morning." The trader shook his head. "Always got the money for the ale, though." He looked at the Valegirl. "Feeling a little better now?"

Brin smiled in response. "Much better, thank you." She glanced down at the dagger in her hand. "I don't know what's wrong with me. I don't know what I was . . ."

"Hush, forget it." The big woodsman patted her hand. "You're exhausted."

Beside him, Rone Leah moaned softly, his head lifting momentarily, his eyes open and staring into space. Then he slipped down again.

"I have to do something for him," Brin insisted anxiously. "I have to find a way to break the fever. Do you have anything here that might help?"

The trader glanced at the woodsman worriedly, then shook his head. "I've not seen a fever as bad as this one often, girl. I have a tonic that might help. You can give it to the boy and see if it brings the fever out." He shook his head again. "Sleep might be best, though."

Brin nodded dumbly. She was having trouble thinking clearly, the exhaustion folding in about her as she sat staring down at the dagger. Slowly she slipped it back into its sheath. What had she been thinking she would do? She had never harmed anything in her entire life. Certainly the man from west of Spanning Ridge had been insolent, perhaps even threatening—but had there been any real danger to her? The ale burned warmly in her stomach, and a flush spread through her body. She was tired and strangely unnerved. Deep within, she felt an odd sense of loss and of slipping.

"Not much room in here for sleeping," the trader Stebb was saying. "There's a tack room in back of the stable I let the help use in the trapping season. You can have that. There's a stove and bed for your friend and straw for you."

"That would be fine," Brin murmured and found to her astonishment that she was crying.

"Here, here." The burly woodsman put an arm about her shoulders, blocking her away from the view of those gathered along the serving counter. "Won't do for them to see that, girl. Got to be strong, now."

Brin nodded wordlessly, wiped the tears away, and stood up. "I'm all right."

"Blankets are out in the shed," the trader announced, standing up with her. "Let's get you settled in."

With the aid of the woodsman, he brought Rone Leah back to his feet and walked him toward the rear of the trading center and down a short, darkened hallway that ran past a set of storage rooms. Brin shot a parting glance at the men gathered about their ale glasses before the serving counter and followed after. She didn't much care for the looks directed back her way by the ones from west of Spanning Ridge.

A small wooden door opened out into the night at the back of the building, and the trader, the woodsman, Rone, and Brin moved toward the stable and its tack room. The trader slipped ahead, quickly lighted an oil lamp hanging from a peg on one wall, and then held wide the tack room door to admit the others. The room beyond was clean, though a bit musty, its walls hung with traces and harness. A small iron stove sat in one corner, shielded by a stone alcove. A single bed sat close beside it. A pair of shuttered windows stood against the night.

The trader and the woodsman laid the feverish highlander carefully on the bed and covered him with the blankets stacked at one end. Then they fired the iron stove until its wood was burning brightly and carried in a pallet of fresh straw for Brin. As they were about to leave, the trader placed the oil lamp on a stone ledge next to the stove and turned briefly to Brin.

"Here's the tonic for his fever." He passed a small, amber-colored bottle to the Valegirl. "Give him two swallows—no more. In the morning, two more." He shook his head doubtfully. "Hope it helps, girl."

He started through the doorway with the woodsman in tow. Then once more he turned. "There's a latch on this door," he declared, pausing. "Keep it drawn."

He closed the door softly behind him. Brin walked over and drew the latch into place. From just without, she could hear the voices of the trader and the woodsman as they talked.

"A bad lot, that Spanning Ridge bunch," the woodsman muttered.

"Bad as any," the trader agreed.

They were silent for a moment.

"Time for me to be on my way," the woodsman said. "Several hours back to the camp."

"Safe journey," the trader replied.

They started to move away, their words fading.

"You'd best watch yourself with that bunch inside, Stebb," the woodsman advised. "Watch yourself close."

Then the words died away completely and the two were gone.

Brin turned back to Rone within the silence of the tack room. Propping him up carefully, she forced him to take two swallows of the tonic provided by the trader. When he had taken the medicine, she laid him down again and covered him up.

Then she took a seat next to the stove, wrapped herself in her blanket, and sat back wordlessly. On the wall of the little room, cast by the solitary flame of the oil lamp, her shadow rose up before her like a dark giant.

The charred stump of still-burning log collapsed with a thud inside the stove as the ashes beneath it gave way, and Brin woke with a start. She had dozed, she realized, but didn't know for how long. She rubbed her eyes wearily and glanced about. The tack room was dark and still, the flame of the oil lamp faint and lonely in a gathering of shadows.

She thought immediately of Allanon. It was difficult still for her to accept that the Druid was gone. An expectation lingered within her that at any moment there would come a sharp knock upon the latched door and his deep voice would call to her. Like a shadow that came and went with the passing of the light—that was the way that Rone had described him that last night before the Druid died . . .

She caught herself sharply, strangely ashamed that she had allowed herself to even think the word. But Allanon had died, pass-

ing from the world of mortal men as all must, going from the Four
Lands in the arms of his father—perhaps to where Bremen kept
watch. She thought about that possibility for a moment. Could it
be that he had indeed gone to be with his father? She remembered
his words to her: "When your quest is done, Brin, you will find me
here." Did that mean that he, too, had locked himself into a limbo
existence between the worlds of life and death?

There were tears in her eyes, and she wiped them hurriedly
away. She could not permit herself tears. Allanon was gone, and she
was alone.

Rone Leah stirred restlessly beneath the heavy blankets, his
breathing harsh and uneven. She rose slowly and moved to where
he lay. The lean, sunburned face was hot, dry, and drawn tight
against the fever that ravaged his body. He shivered momentarily as
she watched, as if suddenly chill, then went taut. Words whispered
on his lips, their meaning lost.

What am I to do with him? the Valegirl asked herself helplessly.
Would that I had my father's skill. I have given him the tonic provided by the trader. I have wrapped him in blankets to keep him
warm. But none of it seems to be helping. What else am I to do?

It was the Jachyra's poison that was infecting him, she knew.
Allanon had said that the poison attacked not just the body, but the
spirit as well. It had killed the Druid—and while his wounds had
been so much worse than Rone's, still he was Allanon and much the
stronger of the two. Even the lesser damage suffered by the highlander was proving to be more than his body could fight.

She sank down next to his bed, her hand closing gently about
his. Her protector. She smiled sadly—who would now protect him?

Memories slipped like quicksilver through her mind, jumbled
and confused. They had gone through so much to reach this lonely,
desperate night, she and Rone Leah. And at what terrible cost.
Paranor was gone. Allanon was dead. Even the Sword of Leah, the
one real piece of magic they possessed between them, was gone. All
that was left was the wishsong.

Yet Allanon had said the wishsong would be enough . . .

Booted feet shuffled softly on the earthen floor of the stable without. Blessed with the Elven senses of her forefathers, she caught the noise where another might have missed it. Hurriedly, she dropped Rone's hand and scrambled to her feet, her weariness forgotten.

Someone was out there—someone who didn't want to be heard.

One hand crept guardedly to the haft of the long knife sheathed at her waist, then dropped away. She could not do that. She would not.

The latch on the door jiggled softly and caught.

"Who's there?" she called out.

A low cursing sounded from just outside, and abruptly several heavy bodies slammed into the tack room door. Brin backed away, searching hurriedly for another way out. There was none. Again the bodies slammed into the door. The iron latch gave way with an audible snap and five dark forms came crashing into the room, the faint light of the oil lamp glinting dully off drawn knives. They gathered in a knot at the edge of the shadows, grunting and mumbling drunkenly as they faced the girl.

"Get out of here!" she snapped, anger and fear racing through her.

Laughter greeted her words, and the foremost of the intruders stepped forward into the light. She knew him at once. He was one of those from west of Spanning Ridge, one of those the trader Stebb had called thieves.

"Pretty girl," he muttered, his words slurred. "Come on . . . over here."

The five crept forward, spreading out across the darkened room. She might have tried to break past them, but that would have meant leaving Rone and she had no intention of doing that. Again, her hand closed about the long knife.

"Now, don't do that . . ." the speaker whispered, edging closer. Suddenly he lunged, quicker than the girl would have thought after having drunk so much, and his hand fastened about her wrist, yanking it away from the weapon. Instantly the others closed in, hands grasping her clothing, pulling her to them, pulling her down. She fought back wildly, striking out at her attackers. But they were much stronger than she and they were hurting her.

Then something within her seemed to snap as surely as had the latch on the tack room door when broken. Her thoughts scattered, and everything she was disappeared in a flash of blinding anger. What happened next was all instinct, hard and quick. She sang, the wishsong a new and different sound than any that had gone before. It filled the shadowed room with a fury that whispered of death and mindless destruction. Her attackers staggered back from the Valegirl, eyes and mouths widening in shock and disbelief, and hands coming up to cover their ears. They doubled over in agony as the wishsong penetrated their senses and crushed in about their minds. Madness rang in its call, frenzy and hurt so bitter it could almost be seen.

The five from west of Spanning Ridge were smothered in the sound. They fell against one another as they groped for the door that had brought them in. From their open mouths, shrieks came back in answer to the Valegirl's song. Still she did not stop. Her fury was so complete that reason could find no means to stem it. The wishsong rose, and the animals in the stable kicked and slammed wildly against their stalls, crying out their pain as the girl's voice ripped at them.

Then the five at last found the open doorway and stumbled from the tack room in maddened desperation, curled over like broken things, shaking and whimpering. Blood ran from their mouths, from their ears, and from their noses. Hands covered their faces, the fingers knotted into claws.

Brin saw them anew in that instant as the blindness of her fury left her. She also saw the trader Stebb appear suddenly from the darkness as the intruders ran past, a look of horror in his face as he, too, stopped and backed away, hands held frantically before him. Reason returned in a rush of guilt, and the wishsong died into stillness.

"Oh, shades . . ." she cried softly and collapsed in stricken disbelief.

Midnight came and went. The trader had left her alone again and gone back to the comfort and sanity of his own lodgings, his eyes frightened and haunted. In the darkness of the forest clearing that sheltered the Rooker Line Trading Center, all was still.

She sat curled close to the iron stove. Fresh wood burned in it, snapping and sparking in the silence. She sat with her legs drawn up against her chest, her arms wrapped about them like a child lost in thought.

But her thoughts were dark and filled with demons. Fragments of Allanon's words lay scattered in those thoughts, whispering of what she had for so long refused to hear. The wishsong is power—power like nothing I have ever seen. It will protect you. It will see you safely through your quest. It will destroy the Ildatch.

Or destroy me, she answered back. Or destroy those about me. It can kill. It can make me kill.

She stirred finally, cramped and aching from the position she had held for so long, her dark eyes glistening with fear. She stared through the grated door of the iron stove, watching the red glare of the flames as they danced within. She might have killed those five men from west of Spanning Ridge, she thought despairingly. She would have killed them, perhaps, had they not found the door.

Her throat tightened. What was to prevent that from happening the next time she was forced to use the wishsong?

Behind her, Rone moaned softly, thrashing beneath the blankets that covered him. She turned slowly to find his face, bending close to stroke his forehead. His skin was deathly pale now, feverish, hot, and drawn. His breathing was worse as well, turned shallow and raspy, as if each breath were an effort that sapped him of his strength.

She knelt beside him, her head shaking. The tonic had not helped. He was growing weaker, and the poison was working deeper into his system, draining him of his life. If it were not stopped, he was going to die . . .

Like Allanon.

"No!" she cried softly, urgently, and she gripped his hand in hers as if she might hold back the life that seeped away.

She knew in that instant what she must do. Savior and destroyer—that was what the shade of Bremen had named her. Very well. To those thieves from west of Spanning Ridge, she had been destroyer. Perhaps to Rone Leah she could be savior.

Still holding his hand with her own, she bent close to his ear and began to sing. Softly, gently the wishsong slipped from her lips, floating like invisible smoke through the air about them both. Carefully, she reached out to the sickened highlander, probing for the hurt he felt, searching out the source of the poison that was killing him.

I must try, she told herself as she sang. I must! By morning he will be gone, the poison spread all through him—poison that attacks the spirit as well as the body. Allanon had said it was so. Perhaps, then, the Elven magic can find a means to heal.

She sang, sweet and lingering tones that wrapped the highlander close about and brought him to her. Slowly, he began to cease his shivering and thrashing and to become still beneath the calming sound. He slipped down into the blankets, his breathing growing steadier and stronger.

The minutes slipped away with agonizing slowness as the Vale-girl sang on and waited for the change she somehow sensed must come. When at last it did, it came so suddenly that she nearly lost control of what she was about. From the ravaged, wasted body of Rone Leah, the poison of the Jachyra lifted in a red mist—dissipating out of the unconscious highlander to float above him, swirling wickedly in the dim light of the oil lamp. Hissing, it hung above its victim for an instant as Brin interposed the magic of the wishsong between its touch and the body of Rone Leah. Then slowly it faded into nothingness and was gone.

On the bed beside her, sweat bathed the face of the Prince of

Leah. The drawn and haggard look was gone, and the breathing was steady and even once more. Brin stared down at him through a veil of tears as the wishsong died into silence.

I have done it, she cried softly. I have used the magic for good. Savior this time—not destroyer.

Still kneeling beside him, she buried her face in the warmth of his body, her arms holding him close. In moments, she was asleep.

XXVIII

THEY STAYED ON FOR TWO DAYS AT THE ROOKER LINE TRAD-
ing Center, waiting for Rone to regain strength enough to resume
the journey east. The fever was gone by morning and the highlander
was resting comfortably, but he was still entirely too weak to attempt
to travel. So Brin asked permission of the trader Stebb to keep the
use of the tack room for one day more, and the trader agreed. He
provided them with food for their meals, rations of ale, medicines,
and blankets, and he refused quickly all offers of payment. He was
happy to be of help to them, he assured the Valegirl. But he was
uneasy in her presence and he never quite managed to let his eyes
meet hers. Brin understood well enough what was happening. The
trader was a kind and decent man, but now he was frightened of her
and of what she might do to him if he refused help. He would probably have helped her out of his basic generosity, but fear had added
urgency to his impulse. He obviously felt that this was the quickest
and most expedient way to get her out of his life.

She remained for the most part within the confines of the little
tack room with Rone, seeing to his needs and talking with him of
what had befallen them since the death of Allanon. Talking about
it seemed to help; while both were still stunned by what had happened, the sharing of their feelings brought forth a common determination that they must go forward to complete the quest that

the Druid had left to them. A new closeness developed between them, stronger and more certain in its purpose. With the death of Allanon, they now had only each other upon whom to rely and each felt new value in the other's presence. Alone together in the solitude of their tiny room at the rear of the trader's stables, they spoke in hushed tones of the choices that had been made to bring them to this point in their lives and of those that must yet be made. Slowly, surely, they bound themselves as one.

Yet despite their binding together in spirit and cause, there remained some things of which Brin could not bring herself to speak, even to Rone Leah. She could not tell him of the blood that Allanon had taken from his own ravaged body to place upon her— blood that in some way was meant to pledge her to him, even in death. Nor could she tell Rone of the uses to which she had put the wishsong—once in fury to destroy human life, a second time in desperation to save it. She could speak of none of these things to the highlander—in part because she did not fully understand them, in part because the implications frightened her so greatly that she was not sure she wanted to. The blood oath was too remote in purpose now for her to dwell upon, and the uses of the wishsong were the result of emotions that she promised herself she would not let get away from her again.

There was another reason for not speaking to Rone of these things. The highlander was troubled enough as matters stood by the loss of the Sword of Leah—so troubled, in fact, that it seemed he could think of little else. He meant to have the sword back again, he told her over and over. He would search it out and reclaim it whatever the cost. His insistence frightened her, for he seemed to have bound himself to the sword with such need that it was as if the weapon had somehow become a part of him. Without it, she guessed, the highlander did not believe that he could survive what lay ahead. Rone felt that without it he must surely be lost.

All the while she listened to him talk of this and thought about how deeply he seemed now to depend on the magic of the blade, she pondered as well her own dependence on the wishsong. It was just a toy, she had always told herself—but that was a lie. It was anything but a toy; it was magic every bit as dangerous as that contained in the missing Sword of Leah. It could kill. It was, in fact, what her father had always said—a birthright that she would have been better off without. Allanon had warned her as he lay dying: "The power of the wishsong is like nothing I have ever seen." The words whispered darkly as she listened to Rone. Power to heal; power to destroy—she had seen them both. Must she be as dependent on the magic as Rone now seemed to be? Between her and the Elven magic, which was to be master?

Her father had fought his own battle to discover the answer to that question, she knew. He had fought it when he had struggled to overcome his inability to master the power of the magic contained within the Elfstones. He had done so, survived the staggering forces it had unleashed within him, and then cast it aside forever. Yet his brief use of the power had exacted its price—a transmutation of the magic from the Elfstones to his children. So now, perhaps, the battle must be fought yet another time. But what if this time the power could not be controlled?

The second day drifted into night. The Valegirl and the highlander ate the meal brought to them by the trader and watched the darkness deepen. When Rone had grown weary and rolled into his blankets to sleep, Brin slipped out into the cool autumn night to breathe smells that were sharp and clean and to lose herself for a time in skies grown bright with a crescent moon and stars. On her way past the trading center, she caught sight of the trader as he sat smoking his pipe on the empty veranda, his high-backed chair tilted against the rail. No one had come by for drinks or talk that evening, so he sat alone.

Quietly, she walked over to him.

"Evening," he greeted hastily, sitting forward a bit too quickly in the chair, almost as if he were poised to flee.

Brin nodded. "We will be leaving in the morning," she informed him and thought she detected a look of immediate relief in his dark eyes. "But I wanted to thank you first for your help."

He shook his head. "No need." He paused, brushing back his thinning hair. "I'll see to it that you have some supplies to get you through the first few days or so."

Brin didn't argue. It was pointless to do anything other than simply to accept what was offered.

"Would you have an ash bow?" she asked, thinking suddenly of Rone. "One that could be used for hunting when we . . . ?"

"Ash bow? Got one right here, as a matter of fact." The trader was on his feet at once. He ducked through the doorway leading into the center and emerged a moment later with a bow and quiver of arrows. "You take these," he pressed. "No charge, of course. Good, solid weapons. Belong to you, anyway, since they were dropped by those fellows you chased off." He caught himself, and cleared his throat self-consciously. "Anyway, you take them," he finished.

He set them down in front of her and dropped back into his chair, fingers drumming nervously on the wooden arm.

Brin picked up the bow and arrows. "They don't really belong to me, you know," she said quietly. "Especially not because of . . . what happened."

The trader looked down at his feet. "Don't belong to me, either. You take them, girl."

There was a long silence. The trader stared past her resolutely into the dark. Brin shook her head. "Do you know anything of the country east of here?" she asked him.

He kept his eyes turned away. "Not much. It's bad country."

"Is there anybody who might know?"

The trader didn't answer.

"What about the woodsman who was here the other night?"

"Jeft?" The trader was silent for a moment. "I suppose. He's been a lot of places."

"How would I find him?" she pressed, growing increasingly un-comfortable with the man's reticence.

The trader's brows knitted. He was thinking about what answer he should give her. Finally, he looked directly at her. "You don't mean him any harm, do you, girl?"

Brin stared at him sadly for a moment, then shook her head. "No, I don't mean him any harm."

The trader studied her a moment, then looked away. "He's a friend, you see." Then he pointed out toward the Chard Rush. "He's got a camp a few miles downriver, south bank."

Brin nodded. She started to turn away, then stopped. "I am the same person I was when you helped me that first night," she said quietly.

Leather boots scuffed against the wooden planks of the porch. "Maybe it just don't seem that way to me," came the response.

Her mouth tightened. "You don't have to be afraid of me, you know. You really don't."

The boots went still and the trader looked down at them. "I'm not afraid," he said, his voice low.

She waited a moment longer, searching futilely for something more to say, then turned and walked into the dark.

The following morning, shortly after daybreak, Brin and Rone departed the Rooker Line Trading Center for the country that lay east. Carrying foodstuffs, blankets, and the bow supplied by the trader, they bade the anxious man farewell and disappeared into the trees.

It was a bright, warm day that greeted them. As they made their way downriver along the south bank of the Chard Rush, the air was filled with the sounds of forest life and the smell of drying leaves. A west wind blew gently out of the distant Wolfsktaag, and leaves drifted earthward in lazy spirals to lie thick upon the forest ground. Through the trees, the land ahead could be seen to run on in a gentle sloping of rises and vales. Squirrels and chipmunks scattered and darted away at the sound of their approach, interrupted in their preparations for a winter that seemed far distant from this day.

At midmorning, Valegirl and highlander paused to rest for a

time, sitting side by side on an old log, hollowed out and worm-eaten with age. In front of them, barely a dozen yards distant, the Chard Rush flowed steadily eastward into the deep Anar; in its grasp, deadwood and debris that was washed down from out of the high country twisted and turned in intricate patterns.

"It's still hard for me to believe that he's really gone," Rone said after a time, eyes gazing out across the river.

Brin didn't have to ask whom he meant. "For me, too," she acknowledged softly. "I sometimes think that he really isn't gone at all—that I was mistaken in what I saw—that if I am patient, he will come back, just as he always has."

"Would that be so strange?" Rone mused. "Would it be so surprising if Allanon were to do exactly that?"

The Valegirl looked at him. "He is dead, Rone."

Rone kept his face turned away, but nodded. "I know." He was quiet for a moment before continuing. "Do you think that there was anything that could have been done to save him, Brin?"

He looked at the girl then. He was asking her if there was anything that *he* could have done. Brin's smile was quick and bitter. "No, Rone. He knew that he was going to die; he was told that he would not complete this quest. He had accepted the inevitability of that, I think."

Rone shook his head. "I would not have done so."

"Nor I, I suppose," Brin agreed. "Perhaps that was why he chose to tell us nothing of what was to happen. And perhaps his acceptance is something we cannot hope to understand, because we could never hope to understand him."

The highlander leaned forward, his arms braced against his outstretched legs. "So the last of the Druids disappears from the land, and there is no one left to stand against the walkers except you and me." He shook his head hopelessly. "Poor us."

Brin glanced down self-consciously at her hands, folded in her lap before her. She remembered Allanon touching her forehead with his blood as he lay dying and she shivered with the memory.

"Poor us," she echoed softly.

They rested for a few minutes longer, then resumed their journey east. Barely an hour later, they crossed a shallow, gravel-bottomed stream that meandered lazily away from the swifter flow of the main channel of the Chard Rush back along a worn gully. They caught sight of a single-room cabin that sat back in among the forest trees. Built from hand-cut logs laid crosswise and caulked with mortar, the little home was settled in a clearing upon a small rise that formed a threshold to a series of low hills sloping gently away into the forest. A handful of sheep and goats and a single milk cow grazed in the timber behind the cabin. At the sound of their approach, an aged hunting dog rose from his favorite napping spot next to the cabin stoop and stretched contentedly.

The woodsman Jeft stood at the far side of the little clearing, stripped to the waist as he cut firewood. With a sure, practiced swing downward of the long-handled axe, he split the piece of timber that stood upright on the worn stump that served as a chopping block. Working the embedded blade free, he brushed aside the cloven halves before pausing in his work to watch his visitors approach. Lowering the axe-head to the stump, he rested his gnarled hands on the smooth butt of the handle and waited.

"Morning," Brin greeted as they came up to him.

"Morning," the woodsman replied, nodding. He seemed not at all surprised that they were there. He glanced at Rone. "Feeling a bit better, are you?"

"Much," Rone answered. "Thanks in part to you, I'm told."

The woodsman shrugged, the muscles on his powerful body knotting. He gestured toward the cabin. "There's drinking water on the stoop in that bucket. I bring it fresh from the hills in back each day."

He led them down to the cabin porch and the promised bucket. All three took a long drink. Then they seated themselves on the stoop, and the woodsman produced pipe and tobacco. He offered the pouch to his guests, but they declined, so he packed the bowl of his own pipe and began to smoke.

"Everything fine back at the trading center?" he asked casually.

There was a long silence. "I heard about what happened the other night with that bunch from Spanning Ridge country."

His eyes shifted slowly to Brin. "Word has a way of getting around a lot quicker than you'd think out here."

The Valegirl held his gaze, ignoring her discomfort. "The trader told us where to find you," she informed him. "He said you might be able to help us."

The woodsman puffed on the pipe. "In what way?"

"He told us that you know as much as anyone about this country."

"I've been out here a long time," the man agreed.

Brin leaned forward. "We are already in your debt for what you did to help us back at the trading center. But we need your help again. We need to find a way through the country that lies east of here."

The woodsman stared at her sharply, then slowly removed the pipe from between his teeth. "East of here? You mean Darklin Reach?"

Both Valegirl and highlander nodded.

The woodsman shook his head doubtfully. "That's dangerous country. No one goes into Darklin Reach if they can avoid it." He glanced up. "How far in do you plan to go?"

"All the way," Brin said quietly. "And then into Olden Moor and the Ravenshorn."

"You're mad as jays," the woodsman announced matter-of-factly and knocked the ashes from the pipe, grinding them into the earth with his boot. "Gnomes and walkers and worse own that country. You'll never come out alive."

There was no reply. The woodsman studied their faces in turn, rubbed his bearded chin thoughtfully, and finally shrugged.

"Guess you've got your own reasons for doing this, and it's none of my business what they are. But I'm telling you here and now that you're making a big mistake—maybe the biggest mistake you'll ever make. Even the trappers stay clear of that country. Men disappear up there like smoke—gone without a trace."

He waited for a reply. Brin glanced briefly at Rone and then back at the woodsman once more. "We have to go. Can you help us?"

"Me?" The woodsman grinned crookedly and shook his head. "Not me, girl. Even if I was to go with you—which I won't, 'cause I like living—I'd be lost myself after the first day or so."

He paused, studying them shrewdly. "I suppose you're set on this?"

Brin nodded wordlessly, waiting.

The woodsman sighed. "Maybe there's someone else who can help you then—if you're sure this is what you want." He blew sharply through the stem of his pipe to clean it, then folded his arms across his broad chest. "There's an old man named Cogline. Must be ninety by now if he's still alive. Haven't seen him for almost two years, so I can't be sure if he's even there anymore. Two years ago, though, he was living up around a rock formation called Hearthstone that sits right in the middle of Darklin Reach—formation that looks just like a big chimney." He shook his head doubtfully. "I can give you directions, but the trails aren't much. That's wild country; hardly anything human living that far east that isn't Gnome."

"Do you think he would help us?" Brin pressed anxiously.

The woodsman shrugged. "He knows the country. He's lived there all his life. Doesn't bother coming out more than once a year or so—not even that the last two. Stays alive somehow in that jungle." The heavy brows lifted. "He's an odd duck, old Cogline. Crazier than a fish swimming through grass. He might be more trouble than help to you."

"We'll be all right," Brin assured him.

"Maybe." The woodsman looked her over carefully. "You're a pretty thing to be wandering off into that country, girl—even with your singing to protect you. There's more than thieves and cowards out there. I'd think on this before you go any further with it."

"We have thought." Brin came to her feet. "We're decided."

The woodsman nodded. "You're welcome to take with you all the water you can carry, then. At least you won't die of thirst."

He helped them refill their water pouches, carrying a fresh bucket of water from the spring that ran down out of the hills behind his cabin, then took several minutes more to give them the directions they needed to reach Hearthstone, scratching a crude map in the earth before the stoop.

"Look after yourselves," he admonished, offering each a firm handshake.

With a final word of farewell, Brin and Rone hitched up their provisions across their backs and walked slowly from the little cabin into the trees. Behind them, the woodsman stood watching. It was clear from the look on his bearded face that he did not expect to see them pass that way again.

XXIX

THEY JOURNEYED THROUGH THAT DAY AND THE NEXT, FOL-
lowing the twists and turns of the Chard Rush as it wound steadily
deeper through the forests of the Anar and crossed into Darklin
Reach. Rone was gaining in strength, but he had not yet fully recovered, and progress was slow. After a brief meal on the second
evening, he went directly to sleep.

Brin sat before the fire, staring into the flames. Her mind was
still filled with unhappy memories and dark thoughts. Once, before she felt herself growing sleepy, it seemed that Jair was with her.
Unconsciously, she looked up, seeking him. But there was no one
there, and logic told her that her brother was far away, indeed. She
sighed, banked the fire, and crawled into her blankets.

It was not until well into the afternoon of the third day following their departure from the Rooker Line Trading Center that Brin
and Rone caught sight of a singular rock formation that loomed
blackly in the distance and knew that they had found Hearthstone.

Hearthstone was a dark, clear silhouette against the changing colors of autumn, its rugged pinnacle dominating the shallow,
wooded valley over which it stood watch. Chimneylike in appearance, the formation was a mass of weathered stone carved by nature's fine hand and shaped with the passing of the years. Silence
hung starkly over its towering shadow. Solitary and enduring, it

beckoned compellingly from out of the dark sea of the vast, sprawling forestland of Darklin Reach.

Standing at the crest of a ridge, staring out across the land, Brin felt its unspoken whisper call out through her weariness and her uncertainty and experienced an unexpected sense of peace. Another leg of the long trek east was almost over. The memories of what she had endured to reach this point and the warnings of what yet lay ahead were strangely distant now. She smiled at Rone and the smile clearly caught the highlander by surprise. Then, touching his arm gently, she started downward along the shallow valley slope.

The barely discernible line of a trail snaked down through the wall of the great trees. As the sun moved steadily toward the western horizon, the forest closed about them once more. They picked their way carefully over fallen logs and around jagged rock formations until the thickly grown slope leveled off at its base. Within the forested canopy of the valley, the pathway broadened and then disappeared altogether as the dense scrub brush and fallen timber began to thin. Warm afternoon sunlight flooded softly through the cracks and chinks of the interwoven branches overhead and lighted the whole of the darkened woodland. Dozens of wide, pleasant little clearings pocketed the valley forest and lent a feeling of space and openness. The earth grew soft and loose, free from rock and carpeted with a layer of small twigs and leaves that rustled gently as the Valegirl and the highlander walked across them.

There was a sense of comfort and familiarity to this little valley that was foreign to the wilderness that lay about it, and Brin Ohmsford found herself thinking of Shady Vale. The life sounds, insect and animal, the brief traces of movement through the trees, sudden and furtive, even the warm, fresh smell of the autumn woods—all were similar to that distant Southland village. There was no Rappahalladran, yet there were dozens of tiny streams meandering lazily across their path. The Valegirl breathed deeply. No wonder the woodsman Cogline had chosen this valley for his home.

The travelers passed deeper into the forest, and time slipped slowly from them. Now and again they caught brief glimpses of Hearthstone through the webbing of the dark forest limbs, its towering shadow black against the blue of the sky, and they pointed themselves toward it. They walked in silence, worn and anxious to be done with the day's long march, their thoughts concentrated on the terrain ahead and the sounds and sights of the forest.

At last Rone Leah came to a stop, one hand fastening guardedly on Brin's arm as he peered ahead.

"Hear that?" he asked quietly, after listening for a moment.

Brin nodded. It was a voice—thin, almost inaudible, but clearly human. They waited a moment, gauging its direction, then began walking toward it. The voice disappeared for a time, then returned, louder, almost angry. Whoever was speaking was directly ahead.

"You had better show yourself and right now!" The voice was high and strident. "I've no time for games!"

There was some muttering and cursing, and the Valegirl and the highlander looked at each other questioningly.

"Come out, come out, come out!" the voice shrilled, then trailed off in an angry murmur. "Should have left you back on the moor . . . if it wasn't for my kind heart . . ."

There was more cursing, and the sound of someone crashing through the underbrush reached their ears.

"I've a few tricks myself, you know! I've got powders to blow the ground right out from under you and potions that would tie you in knots! Think you know so much, you . . . Let's see you climb a rope! Let's see you do that! Let's see you do anything besides cause me trouble! How would you like me to leave you here? How would you like that? Wouldn't think yourself so smart then, I'll wager! Now get out here!"

Brin and Rone stepped through the screen of trees and brush blocking their view and found themselves at the edge of a small clearing with a wide, still pond at its center. Across from them, crawling aimlessly about on his hands and knees was an old man. He scrambled to his feet at the sound of their approach.

"Ha! So you've decided . . . !" He stopped short as he saw them. "Who are you supposed to be? No, never mind who you are. It doesn't make a twig's difference. Just get out of here and go back to wherever it was you came from."

He turned from them with a dismissive gesture and resumed crawling along the forest's edge, his skeletal arms groping left and right, his thin, hunched body like a twisted bit of deadwood. Great tufts of ragged white hair and beard hung down about his shoulders, and his green-colored clothes and half-cloak were tattered and worn. The Valegirl and the highlander stared blankly at him and then at each other.

"This is ridiculous!" the old man stormed, directing his wrath at the silent trees. Then he looked around and saw that the travelers were still there. "Well, what are you waiting for? Get out of here! This is my house, and I didn't invite you! So get out, get out!"

"This is where you live?" Rone asked, glancing about doubtfully.

The old man looked at him as if he were an idiot. "Didn't you just hear me say so? What else do you think I'd be doing here at this hour?"

"I don't know," the highlander admitted.

"A man should be in his home at this hour!" the other continued in something of a scolding tone. "As a matter of fact, what are *you* doing here? Don't you have homes of your own to go to?"

"We've come all the way from Shady Vale in the Southland," Brin tried to explain, but the old man just stared blankly at her. "It's below the Rainbow Lake, several days' ride." The old man's expression never changed. "Anyway, we've come here looking for someone who . . ."

"No one here but me." The old man shook his head firmly. "Except for Whisper, and I can't find him. Where do you think . . . ?"

He trailed off distractedly, turning again from them as if to resume his hunt for whoever it was that was missing. Brin glanced doubtfully at Rone.

"Wait a minute!" she called after the old man, who looked around sharply. "A woodsman told us about this man. He told us he lived here. He said that his name was Cogline."

The old man shrugged. "Never heard of him."

"Well, maybe he lives in some other part of the valley. Maybe you could tell us where we might . . ."

"You don't listen very well, do you?" the other interrupted irritably. "Now I don't know where it is that you come from—don't care either—but I'll wager you don't have strange people running around your home, do you? I'll wager you know everyone living there or visiting there or whatever! So what makes you think it's any different with me?"

"You mean this whole valley is your home?" Rone demanded incredulously.

"Of course it's my home! I just told you that half a dozen different times! Now get out of it and leave me in peace!"

He stamped one sandaled foot vehemently and waited for them to go. But the Valegirl and the highlander just stood there.

"This is Hearthstone, isn't it?" Rone pressed, growing a bit angry with this cantankerous oldster.

The fellow's thin jaw stiffened resolutely. "What if it is?"

"Well, if it is, there is a man living here by the name of Cogline—or at least there was up until two years ago. He'd been living here for years before that, we were told. So if you've been out here for any length of time, you ought to know something about him!"

The old man was silent for a moment, his craggy brows tightening in thought. Then he shook his wispy head firmly. "Told you before, I never heard of him. No one around here with that name now or any other time. No one."

But Brin had seen something in the old man's eyes. She took a step closer to him and stopped. "You know the name, don't you? Cogline—you know it."

The old man stood his ground. "Maybe I do and maybe I don't. In any case, I don't have to tell you!"

Brin pointed. "You're Cogline, aren't you?"

The old man erupted in a violent fit of laughter. "Me? Cogline? Ha-ha, now wouldn't that be something! Oh, I would be talented, indeed! Ha-ha, now that's funny!"

Valegirl and highlander stared at him in amazement as he doubled over sharply and fell to the ground, laughing hysterically. Rone took Brin by the arm and turned her toward him.

"For cat's sake, Brin—this old man's crazy!" he whispered.

"What did you say? Crazy am I?" The oldster was back on his feet, his weathered face flushed with anger. "I ought to show you just how crazy! Now you get out of my house! I didn't want you here in the first place, and I don't want you here now! Get out!"

"We didn't mean any harm," a flustered Rone tried to apologize.

"Get out, get out, get out! I'll turn you into puffs of smoke! I'll set fire to you and watch you burn. I'll . . . I'll . . ."

He was jumping up and down in uncontrollable fury, his bony hands knotted tightly into fists, his tufted white hair flying wildly in all directions. Rone came forward to calm him.

"Stay away from me!" the other fairly shrieked, one thin arm pointing like a weapon. The highlander stopped at once. "Stay back! Oh, where's that stupid . . . ! Whisper!"

Rone glanced about expectantly, but no one appeared. The old man was beside himself with anger now and he whirled about, shouting into the forest darkness and flinging his arms about like windmills.

"Whisper! Whisper! Get out here and protect me from these troublemakers! Whisper, drat you! Will you let them kill me? Should I just give myself over to them? What good are you, you fool . . . ! Oh, I never should have wasted my time on you! Get out here! Right now!"

The Valegirl and the highlander watched the antics of the old fellow with a mixture of wariness and amusement. Whoever Whisper was, he had apparently decided some time back that he wanted nothing to do with any of this. Yet the old man was not about to give

up. He continued leaping about hysterically and shouting at nothing. Finally, Rone turned again to Brin.

"This is getting us nowhere," he declared, keeping his voice
purposely low. "Let's be on our way—look about on our own. The
old man's obviously lost his mind."

But Brin shook her head, remembering what the woodsman
Jeft had said about Cogline: an odd duck, crazier than a fish swimming through grass. "Let me try one more time," she replied.

She started forward, but the old man turned on her at once.
"Wouldn't listen to me, is that it? Well, I gave you fair warning.
Whisper! Where are you? Get out here! Get her! Get her!"

Brin drew up short in spite of herself and looked about. Still
there was no one in sight. Then Rone stalked past her, gesturing
impatiently.

"Now look here, old man. Enough is enough. There's no one
else out here but you, so why don't you just stop this . . ."

"Ha! No one else but me, you think?" The old man leaped into
the air with glee and landed in a crouch. "I'll show you who's out
here, you . . . you trespasser! Come into my house, will you? I'll
show you! Whisper! Whisper! Dratted . . . !"

Rone was shaking his head hopelessly and grinning when all of
a sudden the biggest cat he had ever seen in his life appeared from
out of nowhere right in front of him, no more than half a dozen
yards away. Dark gray in color with spreading black panels on its
flanks that ran upward across its sloping back, a black face, ears, and
tail and wide, almost cumbersome-looking black paws, the beast
measured well over ten feet and its massive, shaggy head rose even
with his own. Corded muscles rippled beneath the sleek fur as it
shook itself lazily and regarded the highlander and the Valegirl with
luminous, deep blue eyes that blinked and narrowed. It seemed to
study them for a moment, then its jaws parted in a soundless yawn,
revealing a flash of gleaming, razor-sharp teeth.

Rone Leah swallowed hard and stayed perfectly still.

"Ah-ha! Not so funny now, I'll wager!" the old man gloated and
began chuckling merrily, his thin legs dancing about. "Thought I

was crazy, did you? Thought I was just talking to myself, did you? Well, what do you think now?"

"Nobody meant you any harm," Brin repeated as the big cat looked Rone over curiously.

The old man edged forward a step, his eyes brightening beneath the tufted hair that hung down about his wrinkled forehead.

"Think he might like you for supper? Is that what you think? He gets hungry, old Whisper does. The two of you would provide him with a nice bedtime snack! Ha! What's the trouble? You look a little pale, like you might not feel so good. That's too bad, too bad now. Maybe you ought to . . ."

The grin vanished suddenly from his face. "Whisper, no! Whisper, no, wait, don't do that . . . !"

And with that, the big cat simply faded away and was gone, much as if he had evaporated. For a moment all three stared wonderingly at the space he had previously occupied. Then the old man stamped his foot angrily and kicked at the empty air in front of him.

"Drat you! You quit that, you hear me! Show yourself, you fool animal or I'll . . . !" He trailed off wrathfully, then looked over at Brin and Rone. "You get out of my house! Get out!"

Rone Leah had had enough. A crazy old man and a disappearing cat were more than he had bargained for. He wheeled without a word and stalked past Brin, muttering for her to follow. But Brin hesitated, still not willing to give it up.

"You don't understand how important this is!" she exclaimed heatedly. The old man stiffened. "You cannot just turn us away like this. We need your help. Please, tell us where we can find the man called Cogline."

The old man regarded her silently, his sticklike body hunched and bent, his shaggy eyebrows knitting petulantly. Then abruptly he threw up his hands and shook his white head in resignation.

"Oh, very well—anything to get rid of you!" He sighed deeply and did his best to look put upon. "It won't help you a whit, you understand—not a whit!"

The Valegirl waited wordlessly. Behind her, Rone had turned

back again. The old man cocked his head, reflecting. One thin hand ran quickly through the tangled hair.

"Old Cogline is right over there at the foot of the big rock." He waved his hand almost casually in the direction of Hearthstone. "Right where I buried him almost a year ago."

XXX

BRIN OHMSFORD STARED FIXEDLY AT THE OLD MAN, DISAPpointment welling up inside and choking back the exclamation forming in her throat. One hand lifted in a helpless gesture.

"You mean that Cogline is dead?"

"Dead and buried!" the truculent oldster snapped. "Now be on your way and leave me in peace!"

He waited impatiently for the Valegirl and the highlander to go, but Brin could not bring herself to move. Cogline dead? Somehow she could not accept that he was. Would not word of that death by some means have gotten back to the woodsman Jeft or to others who lived in the forests that lay about the Rooker Line Trading Center? A man who had lived for as long as Cogline had in this wilderness, a man known to so many . . . ? She caught herself. Possibly not, for woodsmen and trappers often stayed apart for months at a time. But who then was this old man? The woodsman had made no mention of him. Somehow it was all wrong.

"Let's go, Brin," Rone called to her gently.

But the Valegirl shook her head. "No. Not until I'm sure. Not until I can . . ."

"Get out of my house!" the old man repeated once again, stamping his foot petulantly. "I have put up with enough from you! Cogline is dead! Now if you're not gone from here by the time I . . ."

"Grandfather!"

The voice broke sharply from out of the wooded darkness to their left where, in the distance, the rugged pinnacle of Hearthstone loomed blackly through the interwoven branches of the silent trees. Three heads jerked about as one, and the forest went suddenly still. Whisper reappeared to one side of them, his blue eyes luminous, his great, shaggy head raised and searching. The old man muttered to himself and stamped his foot one time more.

Then there was a soft rustling of leaves and the mysterious speaker appeared, stepping lightly into the clearing. Brin and Rone turned to each other in surprise. It was a girl, barely older than Brin, her small, supple form clothed in pants and tunic and wrapped loosely in a braided short cloak of forest green. Long, curling ringlets of thick, dark hair hung down about her shoulders, softly shadowing a sun-browned, faintly freckled pixie face that was strangely beguiling, almost compelling in its look of innocence. It was a pretty face, and while not truly beautiful in the way of Brin's, appealing nevertheless with its uncomplicated freshness and vitality. Dark, intelligent eyes mirrored frankness and honesty as she studied the Valegirl and the highlander curiously.

"Who are you?" she asked in a tone of voice that suggested that she had a right to know.

Brin glanced again at Rone and then back to the girl. "I'm Brin Ohmsford from Shady Vale and this is Rone Leah. We've come north from our homes in the Southland below the Rainbow Lake."

"You have come a long way," the girl observed. "Why are you here?"

"To find a man named Cogline."

"Do you know this man, Brin Ohmsford?"

"No."

"Then why do you look for him?"

The girl's eyes never left hers. Brin hesitated, wondering how much she should tell her. There was something about this girl that warned against lying, and Brin had not missed the way in which her sudden appearance had quieted the old man and brought back the disappearing cat. Still, the Valegirl was reluctant to reveal the whole of her reason for their being at Hearthstone without first finding out who she was.

"We were told that Cogline was the man who best knew the forestland from Darklin Reach east to the Ravenshorn," she replied guardedly. "We were hoping he would offer his services on a matter of great importance."

The girl was silent for a moment, apparently considering what Brin had told her. The old man shuffled over to where she stood and began fidgeting.

"They're trespassers and troublemakers!" he insisted vehemently.

The girl did not reply nor even look at him, her dark eyes still locked into Brin's, her slim form motionless. The old man threw up his hands in exasperation.

"You shouldn't even be talking with them! You should throw them out!"

The girl shook her head slowly then. "Hush, grandfather," she cautioned. "They mean us no harm. Whisper would know if they did."

Brin glanced quickly at the big cat, who was stretched out almost playfully in the tall grass bordering the little pond, one great paw flicking idly at some hapless insect flying past. The great oval eyes shone like twin beacons of light as he glanced over at them.

"That fool animal won't even come when I call him!" the old man groused. "How can you depend on him?"

The girl looked at the old man reprovingly, a hint of defiance crossing her youthful features. "Whisper!" she called softly and pointed at Brin. "Track!"

The big cat suddenly came to his feet and without a sound padded over to Brin. The Valegirl stiffened as the beast's black muzzle sniffed tentatively at her clothing. Cautiously, she started to step back.

"Stand still," the girl advised her quietly.

Brin did as she was told. Forcing herself to remain outwardly calm, she stood frozen in place as the huge animal sniffed downward along her pant leg in a leisurely fashion. The girl was testing her, she realized—using the cat to see how she would react. The skin on the back of her neck prickled as the muzzle pushed at her. What should she do? Should she continue just to stand there? Should she touch the beast to show that she was not afraid? But she *was* afraid, and the fear was spreading all through her. Surely the animal would smell it, and then . . .

She made up her mind. Softly, she began to sing. The words hovered in the dark stillness of the evening, floating in the quiet of the little clearing, reaching out, touching like gentle fingers. It took only a few moments for the wishsong's magic to weave its spell, and the giant cat sat back on its haunches, luminous eyes on the Valegirl. Blinking in sleepy cadence to the song, he lay docilely at her feet.

Brin went still. For an instant, no one spoke.

"Devils!" the old man shrilled finally, a shrewd look on his weathered face.

The girl came forward wordlessly and stood directly in front of Brin. There was no fear in her eyes, merely curiosity. "How did you do that?" she asked, sounding puzzled. "I didn't think anyone could do that."

"It's a gift," Brin answered.

The girl hesitated. "You're not a devil, are you? You're not one of the walkers or their spirit kin?"

Brin smiled. "No, nothing like that. I just have this gift."

The girl shook her head in disbelief. "I did not think anyone could do that to Whisper," she repeated.

"They're devils!" the old man insisted and stamped his sandaled foot.

Whisper, meanwhile, had come back to his feet and moved over to Rone. The highlander started in surprise, then shot Brin an imploring look as the beast pushed his black muzzle against him. For a moment longer Whisper sniffed the highlander's clothing in curious fashion. Then abruptly the great jaws opened and fastened loosely about his right boot and began to tug. What remained of

Rone's composure began to slip rapidly away, and he tried to pull free.

"I think he wants to play with you," the girl announced, a faint smile forming on her lips. She directed a knowing look at the old man, who merely grunted his displeasure and moved several paces further away from them all.

"Well . . . could you . . . make sure?" Rone gasped in exasperation, struggling valiantly now to keep his feet as the great cat continued to pull and tug vigorously at the worried boot.

"Whisper!" the girl called sharply.

The huge creature released his grip instantly and trotted to her side. She reached out from beneath the short cloak and rubbed the shaggy head roughly, her long dark hair falling down about her face as she leaned forward to place her head close to his. She spoke softly to him for a moment, then glanced back at Brin and Rone.

"You seem to have a way with animals. Whisper is quite taken with you."

Brin cast a quick glance at Rone, who was struggling to pull his boot back in place on his foot. "I think Rone would be just as happy if Whisper didn't take to him quite so much," she observed.

The girl smiled broadly then, a hint of mischievousness flashing briefly in her dark eyes. "I like you, Brin Ohmsford. You are welcome here—both you and Rone Leah." She extended a slim brown hand in greeting. "I am Kimber Boh."

Brin accepted the hand, feeling in its grip a mixture of strength and softness that surprised her. She was surprised, too, when she caught sight of a brace of wicked-looking long knives strapped to the girl's slim waist beneath the short cloak.

"Well, they're not welcome as far as I'm concerned!" the old man snapped from behind the girl, making a gesture of brushing them all aside with a broad sweep of one sticklike arm.

"Grandfather!" Kimber Boh admonished. She gave him a sharp look of disapproval and then turned back to Brin. "You mustn't mind him. He is very protective of me. I am all the family he has, so he sometimes feels . . ."

"Don't be so quick to tell them everything about us!" the old man interrupted, shaking his wispish head in dismay. "What do we know of them? How can we be sure what really brought them here? That girl has a devil's voice if she can back off Whisper like she did! No, you are much too trusting, girl!"

"And you are much too quick to distrust," Kimber Boh replied evenly. Her pixie face tightened with resolve. "Now tell them who you are."

The old man's mouth screwed into a vise. "I'll tell them nothing!"

"Tell them, grandfather."

The sandaled foot stamped petulantly. "Tell them yourself. You think you know so much more than me!"

Rone Leah had come forward to stand next to Brin, and the two glanced at each other awkwardly. Whisper looked up at the highlander, yawned and dropped his massive head back onto his paws. A deep, purring sound rose out of his throat as his blue eyes slipped shut.

Kimber Boh turned to face the Valegirl and the highlander. "My grandfather forgets sometimes that the games he is so fond of playing are not real. One of the games he plays often involves changing who he is. He does this by deciding to bury the old self and start life over. He last did this about a year ago." She gave the old man a knowing look. "But he is who he always was. He is, in fact, the man you have come to find."

"Then he really is Cogline." Brin made it a statement of fact.

"I am *not* Cogline!" the old man insisted heatedly. "He's dead and buried, just like I told you! Don't be listening to what she has to say!"

"Grandfather!" Kimber Boh admonished once more. "You are who you are, and you cannot be otherwise. Pretending is for children. You were born Cogline and that is who you will always be. Now please try to be a good host to your guests. Try to be their friend."

"Ha! I didn't invite them here, so I don't have to be a good host!"

Cogline snapped obstinately, determined to have nothing whatsoever to do with either the Valegirl or the highlander. "As for being their friend, you be their friend if you want—that's up to you!"

Brin and Rone looked at each other doubtfully. It did not appear that they were going to have much luck obtaining help from the old man in finding their way through Darklin Reach.

"Very well, grandfather—I shall be host and friend for the both of us." Kimber Boh sighed. She faced them squarely, ignoring the old man. "It's growing late. You have come a long way and you need food and rest. Home is just a short distance from here, and you are welcome to stay the night as my guests—and my grandfather's."

She paused to consider something more. "In fact, it would be a great favor to me if you would stay. Few travelers come this far east, and even then I seldom have a chance to talk with them. As I said, grandfather is very protective. But perhaps you would consent to talk with me—to tell me something of your home in the Southland. Would you do that?"

Brin smiled wearily. "For a place to sleep and something to eat, I think that is the least we could do."

Rone nodded in agreement, although not without an apprehensive glance at Whisper.

"It is settled then," Kimber Boh announced. She called to the big cat, who rose, stretched leisurely and padded up to her. "If you will follow me, we can be there in a few minutes' time."

She turned, with Whisper beside her, and disappeared back into the forest. The Valegirl and the highlander hitched up their backpacks and followed. As they passed Cogline, the old man refused to look at them, staring at the ground in grim determination, his heavy brows furrowed.

"Dratted trespassers!" he muttered.

Then with a wary glance about, he shuffled after them into the trees. A moment later, the little clearing stood empty.

XXXI

◆

HOME FOR THE GIRL, THE OLD MAN, AND THE DISAPPEARING cat was a pleasant, but very average-looking stone and timber cottage situated in a broad, grass-covered clearing sheltered by centuries-old oak and red elm. Porches ran along the front and rear of the cottage, and the walls were grown thick with flowering vines and bush evergreens. Stone walkways ran from the home through gardens that lay all about—some flower, some vegetable, all carefully tended and neatly drawn. Spruce and pine lined the perimeter of the clearing, and hedgerows ran along the borders of the gardens. A great amount of work had gone into the care and nurture of the entire grounds.

The same care was evident inside the cottage. Neat and spotlessly clean, the sanded wood plank floors and timbered walls gleamed in the soft light of the oil lamps, polished and waxed. Handcrafts of woven cloth and cross-stitch hung from the walls, and bright tapestries draped the rough wooden furniture and windows. Odd pieces of silver and crystal sat upon tables within a broad-shelved hutch, and the long trestle table at one end of the main room had been set with earthenware dishes and crafted utensils. Flowers blossomed from vases and clay pots, some grown from plantings, some cut and arranged. The whole of the cottage seemed bright and cheerful, even with the nightfall, and there was that feeling of a Vale home at every turn.

"Dinner is almost ready," Kimber Boh announced when they had come inside, casting a reproachful glance in Cogline's direction. "If you will seat yourselves, I will put it on the table."

Grumbling to himself, Cogline slid onto the bench at the far side of the table, while Brin and Rone sat down across from him. Whisper padded past them to a braided throw rug situated in front of a wide stone fireplace where a small stack of logs burned cheerfully. With a yawn, the cat curled up before the flames and fell asleep.

The meal that Kimber Boh brought to them consisted of wild fowl, garden vegetables, fresh-baked breads, and goat's milk, and they consumed it hungrily. As they ate, the girl asked them questions of the Southland and its people, eager to hear of the world beyond her valley home. She had never been outside Darklin Reach, she explained, but someday soon now she would make the journey. Cogline scowled his disapproval, but said nothing, his head lowered in unyielding concentration on his plate. When dinner was finished, he rose with a sullen grunt and announced that he was going out for a smoke. He stalked through the door without a glance back at any of them and disappeared.

"You really mustn't mind him," Kimber Boh apologized, rising to clear the dishes from the table. "He is very gentle and sweet, but he has lived alone for so many years that he finds it difficult to be comfortable with other people."

Smiling, she removed the dishes from the table and returned with a container of burgundy-colored wine. Pouring a small amount into fresh glasses, she resumed her seat across from them. As they sipped at the wine and chatted amiably, Brin found herself wondering as she had wondered on and off from the first moment that she had laid eyes on the girl how it was that she and the old man had managed to survive alone in this wilderness. Of course, there was the cat, but nevertheless . . .

"Grandfather walks every evening after dinner," Kimber Boh was relating, a reassuring look directed to the two who sat across from her. "He wanders about the valley a good deal when the late fall comes. All of our work is done for the year, and when winter comes he will not go out as much. His body hurts him sometimes in the cold weather, and he prefers the fire. But now, while the nights are still warm, he likes to walk."

"Kimber, where are your parents?" Brin asked, unable to help herself. "Why are you here all alone?"

"My parents were killed," the girl explained matter-of-factly. "I was just a child when Cogline found me, hidden in some bedding where the caravan had camped that last night at the north edge of the valley. He brought me to his home and raised me as his grand-daughter." She leaned forward. "He has never had a family of his own, you see. I'm all he has."

"How were your parents killed?" Rone wanted to know, seeing that the girl did not mind speaking of it.

"Gnome raiders. Several families were traveling in the caravan; everyone was killed except me. They missed me, Cogline says." She smiled. "But that's been a long time ago."

Rone sipped at his wine. "Kind of dangerous here for you, isn't it?"

She looked puzzled. "Dangerous?"

"Sure. Wilderness all around, wild animals, raiders—whatever. Aren't you a little afraid sometimes living alone out here?"

She cocked her head slightly. "Do you think I should be?"

The highlander glanced at Brin. "Well . . . I don't know."

She stood up. "Watch this."

Almost faster than his eye could follow, the girl had a long knife in her hand, whipping it past his head, flinging it the length of the room. It buried itself with a thud in a tiny black circle drawn on a timber in the far corner.

Kimber Boh grinned. "I practice that all the time. I learned to throw the knife by the time I was ten. Cogline taught me. I am just as good with almost any other weapon you might care to name. I can run faster than anything that lives in Darklin Reach—except for Whisper. I can walk all day and all night without sleeping."

She sat down again. "Of course, Whisper would protect me against anything that threatened me, so I don't have much to worry about." She smiled. "Besides, nothing really dangerous ever comes into Hearthstone. Cogline has lived here all his life; the valley belongs to him. Everyone knows that and they don't bother him. Even the Spider Gnomes stay out."

She paused. "Do you know about the Spider Gnomes?"

They shook their heads. The girl leaned forward. "They creep along the ground and up trees, all hairy and crooked, just like spiders. Once they tried to come into the valley, about three years ago. Several dozen of them came, all blackened with ash and anxious to hunt. They're not like the other Gnomes, you know, because they burrow and trap like spiders. Anyway, they came down into Hearthstone. I think they wanted it for their own. Grandfather knew about it right away, just as he always seems to know when something dangerous is about. He took Whisper with him and they ambushed the Spider Gnomes at the north end of the valley right by the big rock. The Spider Gnomes are still running."

She grinned broadly, pleased with the story. Brin and Rone cast uneasy glances at each other, less sure than ever what to make of this girl.

"Where did the cat come from?" Rone glanced again at Whisper, who continued to sleep undisturbed. "How does he disappear like that when he's so confounded big?"

"Whisper is a moor cat," the girl explained. "Most such cats live in the swamps in the deep Anar, well east of Darklin Reach and the Ravenshorn. Whisper wandered into Olden Moor, though, when he was still a baby. Cogline found him and brought him here. He had been in a fight with something and was all cut up. We took care of him and he stayed with us. I learned to talk with him." She looked at Brin. "But not like you do, not singing to him like that. Can you teach me to do that, Brin?"

Brin shook her head gently. "I don't think so, Kimber. The wishsong was something I was born with."

"Wishsong," the girl repeated the word. "That's very pretty."

There was a momentary silence. "So how does he disappear the way he does?" Rone asked once again.

"Oh, he doesn't disappear," Kimber Boh explained with a laugh. "It just seems that way. The reason you can't see him sometimes is not because he isn't there, which he plainly is, but because he can change his body coloring to blend in with the forest—the trees, the rocks, the ground, whatever. He blends in so well that he can't be seen if you don't know how to look for him. After you've been around him long enough, you learn how to look for him properly." She paused. "Of course, if he doesn't wish to be found, then he probably won't be. That's part of his defense. It's become quite a game with grandfather. Whisper disappears and refuses to show himself until grandfather has yelled himself hoarse. Not very fair of him, really, because grandfather's eyes aren't as good as they used to be."

"But he comes for you, I gather."

"Always. He thinks I am his mother. I nursed him and cared for him when we first brought him back here. We're so close now that it's as if we're parts of the same person. Most of the time, we even seem to be able to sense what each other is thinking."

"He looks dangerous to me," Rone stated flatly.

"Oh, he is," the girl agreed. "Very dangerous. Wild, he would be uncontrollable. But Whisper is no longer wild. There may be a small part of him that still is, a memory or an instinct buried deep inside somewhere, but it's all but forgotten now."

She rose and poured them each a bit more of the wine. "Do you like our home?" she asked them after a moment.

"Very much," Brin replied.

The girl smiled, obviously pleased. "I did most of the decorations myself—except for the glass and silver things; those were brought by grandfather from his trips. Or some he had before I came. But the rest, I did. And the gardens—I planted those. All the flowers and shrubs and vegetables—all the small bushes and vines. I like the colors and the sweet smells."

Brin smiled, too. Kimber Boh was a mixture of child and woman—in some ways still young, in some grown beyond her years. It was strange, but she reminded the Valegirl of Jair. Thinking of it made her miss her brother terribly.

Kimber Boh saw the look that crossed her face and mistook it. "It really isn't dangerous here at Hearthstone," she assured the Vale-girl. "It may seem that way to you because you are not familiar with the country, as I am. But this is my home, remember—this is where I grew up. Grandfather taught me when I was little what I should know in order to protect myself. I have learned to deal with what dangers there are; I know how to avoid them. And I have grandfather and Whisper. You don't have to be worried about me—really, you don't."

Brin smiled at the assurance. "I can see that I don't, Kimber. I can see that you are very capable."

To her surprise, Kimber Boh blushed. Then hurriedly the girl stood up and walked to where Cogline had dropped his forest cloak on the arm of the wooden rocker. "I have to take grandfather his cloak," she announced quickly. "It's cold out there. Would you like to walk with me?"

Valegirl and highlander rose and followed as she opened the door and stepped outside. The moment the latch clicked free, Whisper was on his feet, padding silently through the door after them.

They paused momentarily on the porch of the little cottage, losing themselves in the splendor of the evening's peaceful, almost mystical still-life. The air was chill and faintly damp and smelled sweetly of the darkened forest. White moonlight bathed the lawn, flower gardens, neatly trimmed hedgerows, and shrubs with dazzling brightness. Each blade of grass, soft petal, and tiny leaf glistened wetly, deep emerald laced with frost as the dew of the autumn evening gathered. In the blackness beyond, the trees of the forest rose against the star-filled sky like monstrous giants—ageless, massive, frozen in the silence of the night. The gentle wind of early dusk had faded entirely now, drifting soundlessly into stillness. Even the familiar cries of the woodland creatures had softened to faint and distant murmurs that soothed and comforted.

"Grandfather will be at the willow," Kimber Boh said softly, breaking the spell.

Together, they moved off the porch onto the walkway that led to the rear of the cottage. No one spoke a word. They simply walked slowly, the girl leading, their boots scraping softly against the worn stone. Something skittered through the dry leaves in the dark curtain of the forest and was gone. A bird called sharply, its piercing cry echoing in the stillness, lingering on.

The three moved past the corner of the house now, through groupings of pine and spruce and lines of hedgerows. Then a huge, sagging willow appeared from out of the darkness at the edge of the forest, its branches trailing in thick streamers that hung like a curtain against the night. Massive and gnarled, its humped form lay wrapped in shadowed darkness, as if drawn inward onto itself. There, beneath its canopied arch, the bowl of a pipe glowed deep red in the darkness, and puffs of smoke rose skyward to thin and vanish.

As they passed through the trailing limbs of the willow, they saw clearly the skeletal form of Cogline, hunched over on one of a pair of wooden benches that had been placed at the base of the ancient trunk, his wizened face turned toward the darkened forest. Kimber Boh went directly over to him and placed the forest cloak about his shoulders.

"You will catch cold, grandfather," she scolded gently.

The old man grimaced. "Can't even come out here for a smoke without you hovering over me like a mother hen!" He pulled the cloak about him nevertheless as he glanced over at Brin and Rone. "And I don't need these two for company either. Or that worthless cat. I suppose you brought him out here, too!"

Brin looked about for Whisper and was surprised to find that he had disappeared again. A moment earlier, he had been right behind them.

Kimber Boh seated herself next to her grandfather. "Why won't you at least try to be friends with Brin and Rone?" she asked him quietly.

"What for?" the other snapped. "I don't need friends! Friends are nothing but trouble, always expecting you to do something for them, always wanting some favor or other. Had enough friends in the old days, girl. You don't understand enough about how life is, that's your trouble!"

The girl glanced apologetically at Brin and Rone and nodded toward the empty bench. Wordlessly, the Valegirl and the highlander sat down across from her.

Kimber Boh turned back to the old man. "You must not be like that. You must not be so selfish."

"I'm an old man. I can be what I want!" Cogline muttered petulantly.

"When I used to say things like that, you called me spoiled and sent me to my room. Do you remember?"

"That was different!"

"Should I send you to your room?" she asked, speaking to the old man as a mother would to her child, her hands clasping his. "Or perhaps you would prefer it if Whisper and I also had nothing more to do with you since we are your friends, too, and you do not seem to want any friends."

Cogline clamped his teeth about the stem of his pipe as if he might bite it through and hunched down sullenly within the cloak, refusing to answer. Brin glanced quickly over at Rone, who arched one eyebrow in response. It was clear to both that despite her age, it was Kimber Boh who was the stabilizing force in this strange little family.

The girl leaned over then and kissed her grandfather's cheek softly. "I know that you don't really believe what you said. I know you are a good, kind, gentle man, and I love you." She brought her arms about his thin frame and hugged him close. To Brin's surprise, the old man's arm came up tentatively and hugged her back.

"They should have asked before they came here," he muttered, gesturing vaguely toward the Valegirl and the highlander. "I might have hurt them, you know."

"Yes, grandfather, I know," the girl responded. "But now that they are here, after having made such a long journey to find you, I think you should see why it is that they have come and if there is anything you can do to help them."

Brin and Rone exchanged hurried glances once more. Cogline slipped free of Kimber Boh's arms, muttering and shaking his head, wispish hair dancing in the moonglow like fine silk thread.

"Dratted cat, where's he got to this time! Whisper! Come out here, you worthless beast! I'm not sitting around . . ."

"Grandfather!" the girl interrupted him firmly. The old man looked at her in startled silence, and she nodded toward Brin and Rone. "Our friends, grandfather—will you ask them?"

The wrinkles in the old man's face creased deeper as he frowned. "Oh, very well," he huffed irritably. "What was it that brought you here?"

"We have need of someone who can show us a way through this country," Brin replied at once, hardly daring to hope that the help they so badly needed might at last be offered. "We were told that Cogline was the one man who might know that way."

"Except that there isn't any Cogline anymore!" the oldster snapped, but a warning glance from the girl quieted him at once. "Well then, what country is it that you plan to travel through?"

"The central Anar," Brin answered. "Darklin Reach, the moor beyond—all the way east to the Ravenshorn." She paused. "Into the Maelmord."

"But the walkers are there!" Kimber Boh exclaimed.

"What reason would you have for going into that black pit?" the old man followed up heatedly.

Brin hesitated, seeing where matters were headed. "To destroy the walkers."

"Destroy the walkers!" Cogline was aghast. "Destroy them with what, girl?"

"With the wishsong. With the magic that . . ."

"With the wishsong? With that singing? That's what you plan to use?" Cogline was on his feet, leaping about wildly, skeletal arms gesturing. "And you think me mad? Get out of here! Get out of my house! Get out, get out!"

Kimber Boh rose and gently pulled the old man back down on the bench, talking to him, soothing him as he continued to rant. It took a few moments to quiet him. Then wrapping him once more in the forest cloak, she turned again to Brin and Rone.

"Brin Ohmsford," she addressed the Valegirl solemnly, her face quite stern. "The Maelmord is no place for you. Even I do not go there."

Brin almost smiled at the other's emphasis on her own forbidding. "But I do not have a choice in this, Kimber," she explained gently. "I have to go."

"And I have to go with her," Rone added grudgingly. "When I find the sword again, that is. I have to find the sword first."

Kimber looked at them each in turn and shook her head in confusion. "I don't understand. What sword? Why is it that you have to go into the Maelmord? Why is it that you have to destroy the walkers?"

Again Brin hesitated, this time in caution. How much should she reveal of the quest that had brought her to this land? How much should she tell of the truth that had been entrusted to her? But as she looked into the eyes of Kimber, the caution that bade her keep watch over all that she so carefully hid suddenly ceased to have meaning. Allanon was dead, gone forever from the Four Lands. The magic he had given Rone in order that he might protect her was lost. She was alone, weary, and frightened, despite the determination that carried her forward on this impossible journey; if she were to survive what lay ahead, she knew she must take what help she could find where she might find it. Hidden truths and clever deceptions had been a way of life for Allanon, a part of the person that he had been. It could never be so for her.

So she told the girl and the old man all that had been told to her and all that had befallen her since Allanon had first appeared in the village of Shady Vale those many days gone past. She hid nothing of the truth save those secrets she kept hidden even from Rone, those frightening suspicions and unpleasant whisperings of the powers, dark and unfathomable, of the wishsong. It took a long time to tell it all, but for once the old man was quiet and the girl listened with him in silent wonderment.

When she had finished, she turned to Rone to see if there were anything further that should be said, but the highlander shook his head wordlessly.

"You see, then, that I have to go." She repeated the words one final time, looking from the girl to the old man and back again, waiting.

"Elven magic in you, eh?" Cogline murmured, eyes piercing. "Druid's touch on the whole of what you do. I've a bit of that touch myself, you know—a bit of the dark lore. Yes. Yes, I do."

Kimber touched his arm gently. "Can we help them find their path east, grandfather?"

"East? Whole of the country east is known to me—all that there is, here to there and back. Hearthstone, Darklin Reach, Olden Moor—all to the Ravenshorn, all to the Maelmord." He shook his wispish head thoughtfully. "Kept the touch, I have. Walkers don't bother me here; walkers don't come into the valley. Outside, they go where they please, though. That's their country."

"Grandfather, listen to me," she prodded him gently. "We must help our friends, you and Whisper and I."

Cogline looked at her wordlessly for a moment, then threw up his hands. "Waste of time!" he announced. "Ridiculous waste of time!" His bony finger came up to touch the girl's nose. "Have to think better than that, girl. I taught you to think better than that! Suppose we do help; suppose we take these two right through Darklin Reach, right through Olden Moor, right to the Ravenshorn and the black pit itself. Suppose! What, then? Tell me! What then?"

"That would be enough . . ." Brin started to reply.

"Enough?" Cogline exclaimed, cutting her short. "Not nearly so, girl! Cliffs rise up before you like a wall, hundreds of feet high. Barren rock for miles. Gnomes everywhere. What happens then? What do you do then?" The finger shifted like a dagger to point at her. "No way in, girl! There's no way in! You cannot go all that distance unless you know a way in!"

"We will find a way," Brin assured him firmly.

"Bah!" The old man spat, grimacing. "Walkers would have you in a moment! They'll see you coming halfway up the climb—if you can find a place to make the climb, that is! Or can the magic make you invisible? Can it do that?"

Brin set her jaw. "We will find a way," she repeated.

"Maybe and maybe not," Rone spoke up suddenly. "I don't like the sound of it, Brin. The old man knows the country and if he says it's all open ground, then we ought to take that into account before we go charging in." He glanced at Cogline as if to reassure himself that the old man did in fact know what he was talking about. "Besides, first things first. Before we start off on this trek through the Eastland, we have to recover the sword. It's the only real protection we have against the walkers."

"There is no protection against the walkers!" Cogline snorted.

Brin stared at the highlander for a moment, then took a deep breath. "Rone, we have to forget about the sword," she told him gently. "It's gone and we have no way of finding what's become of it. Allanon said it would find its way again into human hands, but he did not say whose hands those would be nor did he say how long it would take for this to happen. We cannot . . ."

"Without a sword to protect us, we don't take another step!" Rone's jaw tightened as he cut short the rest of what Brin was about to say.

There was a long silence. "We have no choice," Brin said. "At least, I don't."

"On your way, then." Cogline brushed them both aside with a wave of his hand. "On your way and leave us in peace—you with your foolish plans of scaling the pit and destroying the walkers; foolish, foolish plans! Go on, fly on out of our home, dratted . . . Whisper, where have you got to, you worthless . . . Show yourself or I'll . . . Yiiii!"

He shrieked in surprise as the big cat's head appeared from out of the darkness at his shoulder, luminous eyes blinking, cold muzzle pressed right up against his bare arm. Furious at being surprised like that, Cogline swatted at the cat and stalked a dozen yards away beneath the willow boughs, swearing as he went. Whisper stared after him, then walked about the bench to lie down next to Kimber.

"I think that grandfather can be persuaded to show you the way east—at least as far as the Ravenshorn," Kimber Boh mused thoughtfully. "As to what you will do after that . . ."

"Wait a minute—just . . . let's think this through a moment." Rone held up his hands imploringly. He turned to Brin. "I know you have decided to complete this quest that Allanon has given you. I understand that you must. And I'm going with you, right to the end of it. But we have to have the sword, Brin. Don't you see that? We have to! We have no other weapons with which to stand against the Mord Wraiths!" His face tightened with frustration. "For cat's sake, how can I protect you without the sword?"

Brin hesitated then, thinking suddenly of the power of the wishsong and of what she had seen that power do to those men from west of Spanning Ridge at the Rooker Line Trading Center. Rone did not know, nor did she want him to, but power such as that was more weapon than she cared to think—and she loathed the very idea that it could live within her. Rone was so certain that he must regain the use of the power of the Sword of Leah. But she sensed somehow that, as with the magic of the wishsong and the magic of the Elfstones before it, the magic of the Sword of Leah was both light and dark at once—that it could cause harm to the user as well as give him aid.

She looked at Rone, seeing in his gray eyes the love he bore for her mingled with the certainty that he could not help her without the magic that Allanon had given him. That look was desperate— yet without understanding of what he asked.

"There is no way for us to find the sword, Rone," she said softly.

They faced each other wordlessly, seated close upon the wooden bench, lost in the shadowed dark of the old willow. Let it go, Brin prayed silently. Please, let it go. Cogline shambled back to join them, still muttering at Whisper as he squatted warily on one end of the bench and began fiddling with his pipe.

"There might be a way," Kimber said suddenly, her small voice breaking through the silence. All eyes turned toward her. "We could ask the Grimpond."

"Ha!" Cogline snorted. "Might as well ask a hole in the ground!"

But Rone sat forward at once. "What is the Grimpond?"

"An avatar," the girl answered quietly. "A shade that lives in a pool of water north of Hearthstone where the high ridges part. It has always lived there, it tells me—since before the destruction of the old world, since the time of the world of faerie. It has the magic of the old world in its touch and the sight to see secrets hidden from living people."

"It could tell me where to find the Sword of Leah?" Rone pressed anxiously, ignoring the restraining hand that Brin placed upon his arm.

"Ha-ha, look at him!" Cogline cackled gleefully. "Thinks he has the answer now, doesn't he? Thinks he's found the way! The Grimpond has the secrets of the earth all bound up in a pretty package ready to give to him! Just a little problem of telling truth from lie, that's all! Ha-ha!"

"What's he talking about?" Rone demanded angrily. "What does he mean, truth from lie?"

Kimber gave her grandfather a stern look to quiet him, then turned back to the highlander. "He means that the avatar doesn't always tell the truth. It lies much of the time or tells riddles that no one can figure out. It makes a game out of it, twisting what is real and what is not so that the listener cannot decide what to believe."

"But why does it do that?" Brin asked, bewildered.

The girl shrugged. "Shades are like that. They drift between the world that was and the one that will be and have no real place in either."

She said it with such authority that the Valegirl accepted what she said without questioning it further. Besides, it had been that way with the shade of Bremen as well—in part, at least. There was a sense of commitment in the shade of Bremen lacking perhaps in the Grimpond; but the shade of Bremen did not tell all of what it knew or speak clearly of what would be. Some of the truth could never be told. The whole of the future was never unalterably fixed, and the telling of it must always be shaded by what might yet be.

"Grandfather prefers that I have nothing to do with the Grimpond," Kimber Boh was explaining to Rone. "He does not approve of the way the avatar lies. Still, its conversation is amusing sometimes, and it becomes an interesting game for me when I choose to play it." She assumed a stern look. "Of course, it is a different kind of game entirely when you try to commit the avatar to telling you the truth of what it knows when it is really important to you. I never ask it of the future or listen to what it has to say if it offers to tell me. It is a cruel thing, sometimes."

Rone looked down momentarily, then up again at the girl. "Do you think it could be made to tell me what has happened to my sword?"

Kimber's eyebrows lifted. "Not made. Persuaded, perhaps. Tricked, maybe." She looked at Brin. "But I was not just thinking of finding the sword. I was thinking as well of finding a way into the Ravenshorn and into the Maelmord. If there were a way by which the walkers could not see you coming, the Grimpond would know it."

There was a long, anxious silence. Brin Ohmsford's mind raced. A way into the Maelmord that would hide them from the Mord Wraiths—it was the key that she needed in order to complete the quest for the Ildatch. She would have preferred that the Sword of Leah, with its magic and its power, remain lost. But what matter that it was found again if it need not be used? She glanced at Rone and saw the determination in his eyes. The matter was already decided for him.

"We must try it, Brin," he said softly.

Cogline's wrinkled face split wide in a leering grin. "Go on, Southlander—try it!" His soft laughter echoed through the night stillness.

Brin hesitated. At her feet, stretched between the benches, his gray-black body curled close to his mistress, Whisper raised his massive head and blinked curiously. The Valegirl stared deep into the cat's saucer blue eyes. How desperate she had become that she must turn to the aid of a woods girl, a half-crazed old man, and a cat that disappeared.

But Allanon was gone . . .

"Will you speak to the Grimpond for us?" she asked Kimber.

The girl smiled brightly. "Oh, I was thinking, Brin, that it might be better if it were you who spoke to the Grimpond."

And it was then that Cogline really began to cackle.

XXXII

Cogline was still cackling on the morning following when the strange little company set forth on their journey to find the Grimpond. Muttering gleefully to himself, he skittered about through the leaf-strewn forest with careless disinterest for what he was about, lost in the shadowed, half-crazed world of his own mind. Yet the sharp old eyes strayed often to Brin's worried face, and there was cunning and shrewdness in their gaze. And there was always a sly, secretive mirth that whispered in his voice.

"Try it, Southland girl—you must try it, indeed! Ha-ha! Speak with the Grimpond and ask it what you will! Secrets of all that is and all that will be! For a thousand thousand years the Grimpond has seen all of what human life has done with itself, watched with eyes that no other can have! Ask, Southland girl—touch the spirit thing and learn!"

Then the cackle came and he danced away again. Time and again, Kimber Boh chastised him for his behavior with a quick word here, a hard look of disapproval there. The girl found the old man's behavior silly and embarrassing. But this had no effect on the old man and he kept on teasing and taunting.

It was an iron gray, misted autumn day. The sky was packed with banks of clouds from the dark stretch of the Wolfsktaag west to the fading tips of the forest trees east. A cool breeze wafted down from out of the north, carrying in its wake dust and crumbling leaves that swirled and stung the face and eyes. The color of the woodlands was faded and worn in the morning light, and the first hint of winter's coming seemed to reflect in their gray cast.

The tiny company traveled north out of Hearthstone with Kimber Boh in the lead, somber and determined; Brin and Rone Leah following close behind; old Cogline danced all about them as they walked; and Whisper ranged far afield through the dark tangle of the trees. They passed beneath the shadow of the towering rock that gave to the valley its name and on from the broad, scrub-free clearings of the sheltered hollow into the wilderness beyond. Deadwood and brush choked the forestland into which they journeyed, a thick and twisted mass of woods. As midday approached, the pace slowed to a crawl. Cogline no longer flitted about like a wild bird, for the wilderness hemmed them all close. They worked their way carefully ahead in a line. Only Whisper continued to roam free, passing like a shadow through the dark mass of the woods, soundless and sleek.

The terrain had grown even more rugged by noontime, and in the distance the dark edge of a series of ridgelines lifted above the trees. Boulders and craggy drops cut apart the land through which they passed, and much of their progress now required that they climb. The wind was blocked away as the ridgelines drew nearer, and the forest smelled of rot and must.

Then, at last, they climbed free of a long, deep ravine and stood upon the crest of a narrow valley, angling downward through a pair of towering ridgelines that ran north until they were lost in a wall of mist.

"There." Kimber pointed into the valley. A thick stand of pine surrounded a lake, its waters only partially visible within a blanket of mist that swirled and shifted with the currents of the wind.

"The Grimpond!" Cogline cackled, his fingers stroking Brin's arm lightly, then slipping away.

They passed through the maze of pine trees that choked the valley's broken slopes, winding their way steadily downward to where the mist stirred sluggishly above the little lake. No wind seemed to reach them here; the air had gone still, and the woodland was

quiet. Whisper had disappeared entirely. Broken rock and pine needles lay scattered over the ground on which they walked, and their
leather boots scraped and crunched with their passing. Though it
was midday still, the clouds and mist screened away the light so
completely that it appeared as if nightfall had set in. As she followed
after the slight figure of Kimber Boh, Brin found herself listening to
the silence of the forest, searching through the shadows for some
sign of life. As she listened and searched, an uneasiness grew within
her. There was indeed something here—something foul, something
hidden. She could sense it waiting.

Deep within the pines, the mist began to descend about them.
Still they went on. When it seemed they must surely disappear
into it completely, they stepped suddenly from the trees into a
small clearing where aged stone benches ringed an open fire pit, its
charred logs and ash black with the dampness.

On the far side of the clearing, a rutted trail led away again into
the mist.

Kimber turned to Brin. "You must go alone from here. Follow
the trail until you reach the edge of the lake. The Grimpond will
come to you there."

"And whisper secrets in your ear!" Cogline chortled, crouching
next to her.

"Grandfather," the girl admonished.

"Truth and lies, but which is which?" Cogline cackled defiantly
and skipped away to the edge of the pines.

"Do not be frightened by grandfather," Kimber advised, her
pixie face a mask of concern as she saw Brin's troubled eyes. "No
harm can come to you from the Grimpond. It is only a shade."

"Maybe one of us should go with you," Rone suggested uneasily, but Kimber Boh immediately shook her head.

"The Grimpond will only speak with one person, never more.
It will not even appear if there is more than one." The girl smiled
encouragingly. "Brin must go alone."

Brin nodded. "I guess that settles it."

"Remember my warning," Kimber cautioned. "Be wary of what you are told. Much of it will be false or twisted."

"But how am I to know what is false and what is true?" Brin asked her.

Kimber shook her head once more. "You will have to decide that for yourself. The Grimpond will play games with you. It will appear to you and speak as it chooses. It will tease you. That is the way of the creature. It will play games. But perhaps you can play the games better than it can." She touched Brin's arm. "This is why I think you should speak to the Grimpond rather than I. You have the magic. Use it if you can. Perhaps you can find a way to make the wishsong help you."

Cogline's laughter rang from the edge of the little clearing. Brin ignored it, pulled her forest cloak tightly about her, and nodded. "Perhaps. I will try."

Kimber smiled, her freckled face wrinkling. Then she hugged the Valegirl impulsively. "Good luck, Brin."

Surprised, Brin hugged her back, one hand coming up to stroke the long dark hair.

Rone came forward awkwardly, then bent to kiss Brin. "Watch yourself."

She smiled her promise to do so; then, gathering her cloak about her once more, she turned and walked into the trees.

Shadows and mist closed about her almost at once, so utterly that she was lost a dozen yards into the stretch of pine. It happened so quickly that she was still moving forward when she realized that she could no longer see anything about her. She hesitated then, peering rather hopelessly into the darkness, waiting for her sight to adjust. The air had gone cold again, and the mist from the lake penetrated her clothing with a chill, wet touch. A few moments passed, long and anxious, and then she discovered that she could discern vaguely the slender shapes of the pines closest at hand, fading and reappearing phantomlike through the swirling mist. It was not likely to get any better than it was, she decided. Shrugging off her discomfort and uncertainty, she walked cautiously ahead, groping with her outstretched hands, sensing rather than seeing the passage of the trail through the trees as it wound steadily downward toward the lake.

The minutes slipped by, and she could hear the gentle lapping of water on a shoreline in the silence of the mist and the forest. She slowed and peered guardedly into the mist, searching for the thing she knew waited for her. But there was nothing to be seen except the gray haze. Carefully, she went forward.

Then suddenly the trees and the mist thinned and parted before her, and she found herself standing on a narrow, rock-strewn shoreline looking out across the gray, clouded waters of the lake. Emptiness stretched away into the haze, and clouds of mist walled her about, closing her in . . .

A chill slipped through her, hollowing out her body and leaving it a frozen shell. She glanced quickly about, frightened. What was there? Then anger welled up within, sharp, bitter, and hard as iron as it rose in retaliation. A fire burned away the cold, flaring through her with ferocious purpose, thrusting back the fear that threatened to overwhelm her. Standing on the shoreline of that little lake, alone within the concealing mist, she felt a strange power surge through her, strong enough, it seemed in that instant, to destroy anything that came against her.

There was a sudden stirring from within the mist. Instantly, the strange sense of power was gone, fled like a thief, back into her soul. She did not understand what had happened to her in those few brief moments, and now there was no time to think on it; there was movement within the mist. A shadow drew together and took shape, dark drawn from the grayness. Risen and formed above the lake's waters, it began to advance.

The Valegirl watched it come, a shrouded, spectral thing that glided in silence on the currents of the air, slipping from the mist toward the shoreline and the girl who waited. It was cloaked and hooded, as insubstantial as the mist out of which it had been born, human-shaped but featureless.

The shade slowed and stopped a dozen feet before her, sus-pended above the waters of the lake. Robed arms folded loosely before it, and mist swirled outward from its gray form. Slowly its cowled head lifted to the girl on the shore, and twin pinpoints of red fire glimmered from within.

"Look upon me, Valegirl," the shade whispered in a voice that sounded like steam set loose. "Look upon the Grimpond!"

Higher the cowled head lifted and the shadows that masked the being's face fell away. Brin stared in stunned disbelief.

The face that the Grimpond showed to her was her own.

Jair stirred awake in the dank and empty darkness of the Dun Fee Aran cell in which he lay imprisoned. A thin shaft of gray light slipped like a knife through the tiny airhole of the stone-walled cu-bicle. It was day again, he thought to himself, trying desperately to trace the time that had passed since he had first been brought there. It seemed like weeks, but he realized this was only the second day since his imprisonment. He had neither seen nor spoken with another living thing save the Mwellret and the silent Gnome jailer.

Gingerly, he straightened and then sat upright within the stale gathering of straw. Chains bound his wrists and ankles, fixed in iron rings to the stone walls. He had been hobbled by these shackles since the second day of his imprisonment. The jailer had placed them on him at Stythys' command. As he shifted his weight, they clanked and rattled sharply in the deep silence, echoing down the corridors that lay without the cell's ironbound door. Weary despite the long sleep, he listened as the echoes died away, straining for some other sound to come back to him. None did. There was no one out there to hear him, no one to come to his aid.

Tears welled up in his eyes then, flowing down his cheeks, and wetting the soiled front of his tunic. What was he thinking? That someone would come to him to help him escape from this black hold? He shook his head against the pain of his own certainty that there was no help left for him. All of the company from Culhaven were gone—lost, dead, or scattered. Even Slanter. He wiped the tears away roughly, fighting back against his despair. It did not matter that no one would come, he swore silently. He would never give the Mwellret what it wanted. And he would somehow find a way to escape.

Once again, as he had done each time he had come awake after sleeping, he worked at the pins and fastenings of the chains that bound him, trying to weaken them enough to break free. For long moments, he twisted and turned the iron, peering hopefully at their joinings through the dark. But in the end he gave it up as he always gave it up, for it was useless to pit flesh and blood against smith-forged iron. Only the jailer's key could set him free again.

Free. He spoke the word within the silence of his mind. He must find a way to get free. He must.

He thought then of Brin; thinking of her, he found himself wondering at what he had seen when last he had looked within the mirror of the vision crystal. How strange and sad that brief glimpse had been—his sister sitting alone before a campfire, her face twisted in strain and despair as she stared out across the forestland. What had happened to Brin to cause her such unhappiness?

Self-consciously, his hand strayed to the small bulk of the crystal where it lay hidden beneath his tunic. Stythys had not found it yet, nor the bag of Silver Dust, and Jair had been careful to keep both hidden within his clothing whenever the Mwellret was about. The creature came to him all too frequently, slipping soundlessly from the dark when the Valeman least expected it, stealing from the shadows like some loathsome wraith to wheedle and cajole, to promise, and to threaten: Give to me what I ask and you will be set free . . . Tell me what I want to know!

Jair's face hardened and set. Help that monster? Not in this world, he wouldn't!

Swiftly, he lifted the silver chain and its stone from within his tunic and held it lovingly within the cupped palms of his hands. It was the sole tie he had with the world beyond this cell, his only means of discovering what Brin was about. He stared at the crystal, and his mind was decided. He would use it one time more. He would have to be careful, he knew. But just a moment was all that was required. He would call up the image and then banish it quickly. The monster would never be the wiser.

He had to know what had become of Brin.

With the crystal cupped in his hands, he began to sing. Soft and low, his voice called forth the dormant power of the stone, reaching into its murky depths. The light slowly rose from within and spread outward—a flood of whiteness that brightened the terrible gloom and brought an unexpected smile to his face.

Brin! he cried softly.

The image came to life—his sister's face suspended within the light before him. He sang, steady and slow, and the image sharpened. She stood before a lake now. The sadness on her face had turned to shock. Stiff and unmoving, she stared out across the gray and misted waters at a cloaked and hooded apparition that hung upon the air. Slowly the image turned as he sang, swinging about to where he could see the face of the apparition.

The wishsong wavered and broke as the face drew near.

The face was Brin's!

Then a furtive rustling sound from across the darkened cell turned Jair's stomach to ice. Instantly, he went still and the strange vision faded. Jair's hands closed about the vision crystal, desperately drawing it down within his tattered clothing, knowing even then that it was already too late.

"Ssee, little friend, you have found a way to help me," a cold, familiar reptilian voice hissed.

And the cloaked form of the Mwellret Stythys advanced through the open cell door.

On the shore's edge at the lake of the Grimpond, there was a long, endless moment of silence, broken only by the soft lapping of the gray waters as they washed against the rocks. The shade and the Valegirl faced each other in the gloom of mist and shadow like voiceless ghosts called forth from another world and time.

"Look upon me!" the shade commanded.

Brin kept her gaze steady. The face the Grimpond wore was her own, drawn, haggard, and ravaged with grief, and where her own dark eyes would have been, twin slits of crimson light burned like coals. Her smile taunted her from the shade's lips, teasing with insidious purpose, the laughter low and evil.

"Do you know me?" came the whisper. "Speak my name."

Brin swallowed against the tightness in her throat. "You are the Grimpond."

The laughter swelled. "I am you, Brin of the Vale people, Brin of the houses of Ohmsford and Shannara. I am you! I am the telling of your life, and in my words you shall find your destiny. Seek, then, what you will."

The hissing of the Grimpond's voice died into a sudden roiling of the waters over which it hung suspended. A fine, thin spray exploded geyserlike into the misted air and showered down upon the Valegirl. It was as cold as death's forbidden touch.

The Grimpond's crimson eyes narrowed. "Would you know, child of the light, of the darkness that is the Ildatch?"

Wordlessly, Brin nodded. The Grimpond laughed mirthlessly and glided closer. "All that is and all that was of the dark magic traces to the book, bound by threads that close you and yours tight about. Wars of Races, wars of Man—faerie demons, all one hand. Like rhymes of the voice, all are one. The humankind come to the dark magic, seeking power that they cannot hope to make theirs— seeking then death. They creep to the hiding place of the book, drawn by the lure, by the need. One time to the face of death, one time to the pit of night. Each time they find what they seek and are lost to it, changed from moral self to spirit. Bearers and Wraiths, all are one. And the evil is one with them."

The voice faded. Brin's mind raced, thinking through the mean-

ing of what she had been told. One time to the face of death . . .
Skull Mountain. Past and present were one, Skull Bearer and Mord
Wraith—that was the Grimpond's meaning. They were born of the
same evil. And somehow, in some way, all of it was bound together
in a single source.

"The dark magic made them all," she said quickly. "Warlock
Lord and Skull Bearers in the time of my great-grandfather; Mord
Wraiths now. That is your meaning, isn't it?"

"Is it?" the voice hissed softly, teasingly. "One of one? Where
lies the Warlock Lord now, Valegirl? Who now gives voice to the
magic and sends the Mord Wraiths forth?"

Brin stared at the apparition wordlessly. Was it saying that the
Warlock Lord had come back again? But no, that was impossible . . .

"That voice is dark when it speaks to humankind," the Grimpond intoned in a singsong hiss. "That voice is born of the magic,
born of the lore. It is found in different ways—by some in printed
word, by some . . . in song!"

Brin went cold. "I am not of their kind!" she snapped. "I do not
use the dark magic!"

The Grimpond laughed. "Nor does any, Valegirl. The magic
uses them. There is the key of all that you seek. There is all you need
know."

Brin struggled to understand. "Speak more," she urged.

"More? More of what?" The shade's misted form shimmered
darkly. "Would you have me tell you of the eyes—eyes that follow
you, eyes that seek you out at every turn?" The Valegirl stiffened.
"Love sees you in those eyes when they are the eyes that command
the crystal. But dark intent sees you likewise when the eyes are
sightless and born of your own birthright. Do you see? Are your
own eyes open? Not so the eyes of the Druid when he lived, dark
shadow of his time. They were closed to the greatest part of the
truth, closed to what was apparent, had he thought it through. He
did not see the truth, poor Allanon. He saw only the Warlock Lord
come again; he saw only what was as what is—not as what could be.

Deceived, poor Allanon. Even in death, he walked where the dark magic willed that he should—and when he came to his end, he was seen a fool."

Brin's mind spun. "The walkers—they knew he was coming, didn't they? They knew he could come into the Wolfsktaag. That was why the Jachyra was there."

Laughter swelled and echoed in the silence of the mist. "Truth wins out! But once only, perhaps. Trust not what the Grimpond says. Shall I speak more? Shall I tell you of your journey to the Maelmord with the clown Prince of Leah and his lost magic? Oh, so desperate he is to have that magic, so much in need of what will destroy him. You suspect it will destroy him, don't you, Valegirl? Let him have it, then, so that he might have his wish and become one with all who shared that wish before and passed into death. His is the strong arm that leads you to a similar fate. Ah, shall I tell you of how you, too, shall come to die?"

Brin's dusky face tightened. "Tell me what you will, shade. But I will listen only to the truth."

"So? Am I to judge what is true and what is not, where we speak of what is yet to be?" The Grimpond's voice was low and taunting. "The book of your life lies open before me, though there are pages yet to write. What shall be written shall be written by you, not by words that I may speak. You are the last of three, each to live in the shadow of the others, each to seek to be free of that shadow, each to grow apart therefrom and then to reach back to the ones who went before. Yet your reach is darkest on the land."

Brin hesitated uncertainly. Shea Ohmsford must be the first, her father the second, she the third. Each had sought to be free of the legacy of the Elven house of Shannara from which all were descended. But what did that last part mean?

"Ah, your death awaits you in the land of the walkers," the Grimpond hissed softly. "Within the pit of dark, within the breast of the magic you seek to destroy, there shall you find your death. It is foreordained, Valegirl, for you carry its seeds within your own body."

The Valegirl's hand came up impatiently. "Then tell me how to reach it, Grimpond. Give me a way into the Maelmord that will shield me from the eyes of the walkers. Let me go to my death quickly, if you see it so."

The Grimpond laughed darkly. "Clever girl, you would seek to have me tell you forthright what you have truly come here to discover. I know what brings you hence, child of the Elfkind. You can hide nothing from me, for I have lived since all that was and will live for all that is to be. It is my choice to do so, to stay within this old world and not to be at peace in another. I have made playthings of those of flesh and blood who are my sole companions now, and none have ever broken past the guard I place upon myself. Would you know the truth of what you ask, Valegirl? Beg it from me, then."

Anger welled up within her at the Grimpond's boastful words, and she stepped to the very edge of the gray lake waters. Spray hissed warningly from out of the mist, but she ignored it.

"I was warned that you would play this game with me," she said, her own voice dangerous now. "I have come far and have endured much grief. I have no wish to be teased now by you. Do not press me, shade. Speak only the truth. How am I to reach the pit of the Maelmord without the walkers seeing where I come?"

The Grimpond's eyes narrowed sharply, flickering deep red as the silence between the two lengthened. "Find your own way, Brin of the Vale people," the Grimpond hissed.

Rage exploded inside Brin, but by sheer force of will she held it in check. Wordlessly, she nodded in acquiescence, then stepped back and seated herself upon the shore, her cloak pulled close about her.

"You wait to no purpose," the shade sneered.

But Brin did not move. She composed herself carefully, breathing in the damp air of the lake and drawing her thoughts close about her. The Grimpond stayed suspended above the waters of the lake, unmoving, its eyes turned toward her. Brin let those eyes draw her close. A serene look came over her dusky face, and the long black hair fanned back. It does not yet see what I will do! She smiled inwardly, and the thought was gone an instant after it had come.

Then softly, she began to sing. The wishsong rose into the midday with sweet and gentle words from the lips of the girl seated upon the lakeshore, to fill the air about her. Quickly, it reached out and bound the misted form of the Grimpond, weaving and twisting with its magic. So startled was the shade that it did not stir from its resting spot, but hung suspended within the web of the magic as it slowly drew tighter. Then, for the barest second, the Grimpond seemed to sense what was happening to it. Beneath its gathered robes, the lake waters boiled and hissed. But the wishsong swiftly swept all about the imprisoned form, wrapping it away as if it had become a chrysalis.

Now the Valegirl's voice came quicker and with more certain intent. The shrouding of the first song, the gentle, womblike wrapping that had bound the Grimpond without his seeing, was gone. A prisoner now, as surely as the fly caught within the spider's web, the shade was to be dealt with as its captor chose. Yet the Valegirl used neither force of arms nor strength of mind against this being, for she had seen that such would be useless. Memories were the weapons she called to her aid now—memories of what had once been, of what had been lost and could never be regained. All came back once more within the wishsong's music. There was the touch of a human hand, warm and kind. There was the smell and taste of sweetness and light and the sensation of love and joy, of life and death. There were all these and others, lost to the Grimpond in its present form, barely remembered from the life long since gone.

With a cry of anguish, the Grimpond sought to evade the old sensations, shimmering and roiling in a cloud of mist. Yet it could not escape the magic of the song; slowly, the sensations caught it up and held it, and it was given over to their memories. Brin could feel the shade's emotions come again to life, and within the memories exhumed, the Grimpond's tears flowed. She sang steadily. When the shade was hers completely, she hardened herself against her own pain and drew back what she had given.

"No!" the apparition howled in dismay. "Give them back, Valegirl! Give them back to me!"

"Tell me what I would know," she sang, the threads of the questions weaving through her song. "Tell me!"

With frightening suddenness, the Grimpond's words came pouring out as if released with the anguish that tore its forgotten soul. "Graymark bridges the Maelmord where it lies within the Ravenshorn—Graymark, the castle of the Wraiths. There lies the way that is sought, a maze of sewers that runs from its halls and chambers deep beneath the rock on which it stands, to empty into a basin far below. Enter through the sewers, and the eyes of the walkers will not see!"

"The Sword of Leah," Brin pressed harshly. "Where can it be found? Tell me!"

Anguish wrenched the Grimpond through and through as she touched him in taunting strokes with the feel of what had been lost. "Spider Gnomes!" the shade cried desperately. "The blade lies within their camp, snatched from the waters of the Chard Rush, gathered in by the nets and snares they keep fastened to its banks!"

Abruptly, Brin drew back the magic of the wishsong, filled with the memories and the sensations of the old life. She drew it clear in a swift, painless rush, freeing the imprisoned shade from the trappings that had bound it. The echoes of the song lingered in the stillness that hung across the empty lake, dying into a single haunting note that rang in the midday air. It was a note of forgetfulness—a sweet, ghostly cry that left the Grimpond as it had been.

There was a long, terrible silence then. Slowly Brin rose to her feet and stared full into the face that was the mirror of her own. Something deep within her howled in dismay as she saw the look that came upon that face. It was as if she had done this to herself!

And the Grimpond realized now what had been done. "You have tricked from me the truth, dark child!" the shade wailed bitterly. "I sense that you have done so. Ah, black you are! Black!"

The shade's voice broke, and the gray waters boiled and steamed. Brin stood frozen at the edge of the lake, afraid to turn away or to speak. Inside, she was empty and cold.

Then the Grimpond lifted its robed arm. "One last game then, Valegirl—something back from me to you! Let this be *my* gift! Look into the mist, here beside me where it forms—look closely now! See you this!"

Brin knew then that she should flee, but somehow she could not. The mist seemed to gather before her, swirling and spreading in a sheet of gray that lightened and smoothed. A slow, shimmering motion rippled across its surface like still water disturbed, and an image formed—a figure, crouched low within a darkened cell, his movements furtive . . .

Jair snatched back the vision crystal, thrusting it deep within his tunic, praying that the shadows and the gloom hid from the Mwellret what it was that he did. Perhaps he had been quick enough. Perhaps . . .

"Ssaw the magicss, Elfling," the harsh voice rasped, dashing his hopes. "Ssenssed all along that the magicss were yourss. Sshare them with me, little friend. Sshow what you have."

Jair shook his head slowly, fear mirrored in his blue eyes. "Stay away from me Stythys. Stay back from me."

The Mwellret laughed—a low, guttural laugh that echoed in the emptiness of the cell and the long corridors beyond. The creature swelled suddenly within the dark robes, rising up against the dim light like a monstrous shadow.

"Threatenss me, ssmall one? Crussh you like a tiny egg if you usse the magicss on me. Sstay quiet now, little friend. Look into my eyess. Ssee the lightss."

Lidded, scaled eyes glimmered, cold and compelling. Jair forced his own eyes down, knowing that he could not look, that if he did so he would belong once again to the creature. But it was so hard not to look. He wanted to see into those eyes; he wanted to be drawn into them and the peace and serenity that waited there.

"Ssee, Elfling," the monster hissed.

Jair's hand closed about the small bulk of the vision crystal until he could feel the edges cutting into his palm. Concentrate on the pain, he thought frantically. Don't look. Don't look!

Then the Mwellret hissed angrily and one hand lifted. "Give to me the magicss! Give them to me!"

Voiceless, Jair Ohmsford shrank back from him . . .

The Grimpond's robed arm came down sharply and the screen of mist dissolved and was gone. Brin lurched forward desperately, stepping off the rock-strewn shoreline into the gray waters of the lake. Jair! That had been Jair in the images! What was it that had happened to him?

"Did you enjoy that game, Brin of the Vale people?" whispered the avatar harshly, the waters roiling once again beneath where it hung. "Did you see what has happened to your precious brother whom you thought safe within the Vale? Did you see?"

Brin fought back against the rage that welled up within her. "Lies, Grimpond. You tell only lies this time."

The shade chuckled softly. "Lies? Think what you wish, Vale-girl. A game is only a game, after all. A diversion from the truth. Or is it truth revealed?" Robed arms drew close, the mist swirling. "Dark you are, Brin of Shannara, of Ohmsford, of history spawned. Dark as the magic with which you play. Go from me, now. Take what you have learned of the clown prince's magic and the passage to your death. Find what you seek and become what you surely will! Get you gone from me!"

The Grimpond began to fade back into the gray mist that rolled behind it over the lake's murky waters. Brin stood transfixed upon the shoreline, wanting to hold the shade back, but knowing that this time she could not.

Suddenly the shade paused in its retreat, red eyes narrowing into slits within the mist robes. Brin's own face leered back at her, a twisted mask of evil. "See me as you are, Brin of the Vale people. Savior and destroyer, mirror of life and death. The magic uses all, dark child—even you!"

Then the Grimpond disappeared back into the wall of the mist, its laughter soft and wicked in the deep silence. Soundlessly, the grayness closed about it and it was gone.

Brin stared after it a moment, lost in a gathering of fears, doubts, and whispered warnings. Then slowly she turned and walked back to the trees.

XXXİİİ

◆

Dark and forbidding, the Mwellret Stythys advanced through the gloom of the little cell, and Jair backed slowly away.

"Give to me the magicss," the monster hissed, and the crooked fingers beckoned. "Releasse them, Elfling."

The Valeman retreated further into the shadows, the chains that bound his wrists and ankles dragging. Then the cell wall was pressing into his back and there was nowhere left to go.

I cannot even run from him! he thought desperately.

A soft scraping of leather boots on stone sounded from the cell entry and the Gnome jailer appeared from the corridor beyond. Head lowered into shadow, the hooded form passed silently through the open doorway into the room. Stythys turned at the other's approach, cold eyes glittering with displeasure.

"Ssent not for little peopless," the Mwellret muttered darkly, and the scaled hands motioned the Gnome away.

But the jailer paid no heed. Mute and unresponsive, he shuffled past the lizard creature as if he had not seen him and came directly toward Jair. Head still lowered, hands tucked deep into the folds of the ragged cloak, the Gnome slipped wraithlike through the dark. Jair watched his approach with mingled surprise and uncertainty. As the little man came closer, the Valeman shrank back in repulsion against the stone of the cell wall, the iron of his chains clanking as he raised his hands defensively.

"Sstand away, little peopless!" Stythys rasped, angry now, and his scaled body drew itself up menacingly.

But the Gnome jailer had already reached Jair, a hunched and voiceless thing as he stood before the Valeman. Slowly the cowled head lifted.

Jair's eyes went wide. The Gnome in the ragged cloak and hood was not the jailer!

"Need a little help, boy?" Slanter whispered.

Then a black-clad form leaped from the shadowed corridor without, and the slender blade of a long sword pressed up against the throat of an astonished Stythys, forcing him back against the cell wall.

"Not a sound from you," Garet Jax warned. "Not a twitch. Either, and you'll be dead before you finish!"

"Garet, you're alive!" Jair exclaimed in disbelief.

"Alive and well," the other replied, but the hard gray eyes never moved from the Mwellret. "Hurry and set the Valeman free, Gnome."

"Just be patient a moment!" Slanter had produced a ring of iron keys from beneath the cloak and was trying each key in turn in the shackles that bound the Valeman. "Confounded things don't fit the lock . . . ah-ha—this one!"

The locks on the wrist- and ankle-bindings clicked sharply and the chains fell away. "Slanter," Jair gripped the Gnome's arm as Slanter stripped away the jailer's ragged cloak and tossed it aside. "How on earth did you ever manage to find me?"

"No real trick to that, boy!" the Gnome snorted, rubbing at the other's bruised wrists to restore the circulation. "I told you I was the best tracker you'd ever met! Weather didn't help much, of course—washed out half the signs, turned the whole of the forestland to muck. But we picked up the lizard's tracks right outside the tunnels and knew he'd bring you here, whatever his intentions. Cells in Dun Fee Aran are always for sale to anyone with the right price and no questions asked. People in them for sale the same way. Lock you away until you're bones, unless . . ."

"Talk about it later, Gnome," Garet Jax cut him short. "You." He jabbed sharply at the Mwellret. "You walk ahead—keep everyone away from us. No one is to stop us; no one is to question us. If they do . . ."

"Leavess me here, little peopless!" the creature hissed.

"Yes, leave him," Slanter agreed, his face wrinkling in distaste. "You can't trust the lizards."

But Garet Jax shook his head. "He goes. Foraker thinks we can use him."

Jair started. "Foraker is here, too!"

But Slanter was already propelling him toward the cell door, spitting in open disdain at the Mwellret as he walked past. "He'll do us no good, Weapons Master," he insisted. "Remember, I warned you."

They were in the hallway beyond then, crouched in the shadows and the silence, Slanter at the Valeman's elbow as Garet Jax brought Stythys through the door. The Weapons Master paused for a moment, listened, then shoved Stythys before him as they started back down the darkened corridor. A torch burned in a wall rack ahead of them; when they reached it, Slanter snatched the brand away and assumed the lead.

"Black pit, this place!" he growled softly, picking his way through the gloom.

"Slanter!" Jair whispered urgently. "Is Elb Foraker here, too?"

The Gnome glanced at him briefly and nodded. "The Dwarf, the Elf and the Borderman as well. Said we'd started this journey together and that's how we'd finish it." He shook his head ruefully. "Guess we're all mad."

They slipped back through the labyrinth passageways of the prisons, the Gnome and the Valeman leading and the Weapons Master a step behind with his sword pressed close against the back of the Mwellret. They hastened through blackness, silence, and the stench of death and rot, passing the closed and rusted doors of the prison cells and working their way back into the light of day. Gradually, the gloom began to recede as slivers of daylight, gray and hazy, brightened the passages ahead. The sound of rain reached their ears, and a small, sweet breath of clean air brushed past them.

Then once again the massive, ironbound doors of the building entrance appeared before them, closed and barred. Wind and rain blew against them in sharp gusts, drumming against the wood. Slanter tossed aside the torch and hastened ahead to peer through the watch slot for what waited without. Jair joined him, gratefully breathing in the fresh air that slipped through.

"I never thought to see you again," he whispered to the Gnome. "Not any of you."

Slanter kept his eyes on the slot. "You have the luck, all right."

"I thought no one was left to come for me. I thought you dead."

"Hardly," the Gnome growled. "After I lost you in the tunnels and couldn't figure out what had become of you, I went on through to the cliffs north above Capaal. Tunnel ended there. I knew if the others were alive, they'd come through just as I had, because that was what the Weapons Master's plans had called for. So I waited. Sure enough, they found each other, then found me. And then we came after you."

Jair stared at the Gnome. "Slanter, you could have left me—left them, too. No one would have known. You were free."

The Gnome shrugged, discomfort reflecting in his blocky face. "Was I?" He shook his head disdainfully. "Never stopped to think about it."

Garet Jax had reached them now, prodding Stythys before him. "Still raining?" he asked Slanter.

The Gnome nodded. "Still raining."

The Weapons Master sheathed the slender sword in one fluid motion and a long knife appeared in its place. He pushed Stythys up against the corridor wall, his lean face hard. A head taller than Garet Jax when first surprised by him in Jair's cell, Stythys had shrunk down again, coiled like a snake within his robes. Green eyes glittered evilly at the Southlander, cold and unblinking.

"Leavess me, little peopless," he whined once more.

Garet Jax shook his head. "Once outside, walk close to me, Mwellret. Don't try to move away. Don't play games. Cloaked and hooded, we shouldn't be recognized. The rain will keep most away, but if anyone comes close, you turn them. Remember, it wouldn't take much to persuade me to cut your throat."

He said it softly, almost gently, and there was a chilling silence. The Mwellret's eyes narrowed into slits.

"Havess the magicss!" he hissed angrily. "Needss nothing from me! Leavess me!"

Garet Jax brought the point of the long knife tight against the other's scaled throat. "You go."

Cloaks wrapped close about them, they pulled open the heavy wooden doors of the darkened prison and stepped out into the light. Rain fell in blinding sheets from gray, clouded skies, blown against the fortress walls by the wind. Heads bent against its force, the four started across the muddied yard toward the battlements that lay immediately north. Scattered knots of Gnome Hunters passed them by without slowing, anxious only to get in out of the weather. On the watchtowers, sentries huddled in the shelter of stonework nooks and bays, miserable with the cold and damp. No one cared anything about the little party that crossed below. No one even gave them a second glance.

Slanter took the lead as the north battlements drew near, guiding them past small lakes of surface water and mudholes to where a pair of iron-grated doors closed away a small court. They pushed through the doors and crossed quickly to a covered entry that led into a squat stone-and-timber watchtower. Wordlessly, the Gnome unlatched the shadowed wooden door and led the way inside.

An anteway lay within, brightened by the light of torches jammed into holders on either side of the door. Brushing the water from their cloaks, they paused momentarily while Slanter moved to the edge of a darkened corridor leading left beneath the battlement. After peering into the gloom, the Gnome beckoned for them to follow. Garet Jax snatched one of the torches from its bracket, handed it to Jair, and motioned him after Slanter.

A narrow hall opened before them, lined with doors that stretched into the darkness ahead.

"Storerooms," Slanter informed Jair, winking.

They stepped into the hall. Slanter slipped cautiously ahead; at the third door, he stopped and knocked softly.

"It's us," he whispered into the latch.

The latch released with a snap, the door swung wide, and Elb Foraker, Helt, and Edain Elessedil appeared. Smiles creasing their battered faces, they surrounded Jair and gripped his hand warmly.

"Are you all right, Jair?" the Elven Prince asked at once, his own face bruised and cut so badly that the Valeman was immediately afraid for him. The Elf saw his concern and dismissed it with a shrug. "Just a few scratches. I found an escape passage, but it opened on a thorn bush. Nothing that won't quickly heal. But you— are you truly all right?"

"I'm fine now, Edain." Jair hugged him impulsively.

Helt and Foraker were battered about the face and hands as well, the result Jair supposed of having the greater part of that battlement wall fall on them. "I can't believe that you're all here!" The Valeman swallowed hard against the knot forming in his throat.

"Couldn't very well leave you behind, now could we, Jair?" The giant Borderman gripped his arm warmly with one great hand. "Yours is the magic that we need to heal the Silver River."

Jair grinned happily, and Foraker stepped close, eyes fixing on the Mwellret. "I see that you were able to bring him."

Garet Jax nodded without comment. While the others had been greeting Jair anew, he had stayed with Stythys, the long knife pointed at the Mwellret's throat.

"Little peopless be ssorry they takess me!" the creature hissed venomously. "Findss a way to make them ssorry!"

Slanter spit distastefully into the earth. Foraker pointed at the Mwellret. "You alone are responsible for what happens to you now, Stythys. Had you not taken the Valeman, you would have been left alone. Since you did take him, you'll have to answer for it. You're going to see us safely out of this place, then safely through the forests north and into the Ravenshorn. Steer us wrong just once, and I'll let Slanter do to you what he'd like to have done in the first place."

He glanced at the Gnome. "And remember, Stythys, he knows the way as well, so think carefully before you attempt any deception."

"Let's be gone from here!" Slanter growled anxiously.

With the Gnome leading, the little band passed down the narrow hall through a series of still smaller corridors and arrived at the foot of a winding stone stairway. Slanter put a finger to his lips in warning. In single file, they began to climb. From somewhere above, faint and distant yet, the guttural sound of Gnome voices reached their ears. A small wooden door stood closed at the top of the stairs. Slanter paused momentarily, listened, then cracked the door and peered out. Satisfied, he beckoned them through.

They stood in a massive armory, its floor piled with stacks of weapons, armor, and provisions. Gray light filtered down through high, barred windows. The chamber was empty, and Slanter led the way hurriedly toward a door set into the far wall.

He was almost there when the door abruptly swung open from the opposite side, and he found himself face to face with an entire squad of Gnome Hunters.

The Gnomes hesitated, seeing first Slanter, then the odd gathering of faces that followed after him. It was when they caught sight of Foraker that their hands flew to their weapons.

"No luck this time, boy!" Slanter howled, flinging himself protectively in front of Jair.

The Gnome Hunters came at them in a rush, but already the dark figure of Garet Jax was moving, the slender sword darting. Down went the foremost of the attackers, and then Foraker was beside the Weapons Master, his two-edged axe thrusting back the rest. Behind them, Stythys turned and broke for the door through which they had come, but Helt was on him like a cat, bearing him to the floor. They skidded into a stack of pikes, and the pikes tumbled down about them in a clash of wood and iron.

The Gnome Hunters stood and fought before the open door a moment longer as Garet Jax and Foraker pressed in on them. Then, with a howl of anger, they broke and fled. The Weapons Master and the Dwarf gave chase as far as the doorway; but seeing that pursuit was pointless, they turned quickly to help the struggling Helt. Together, they hauled Stythys back to his feet, the Mwellret hissing venomously, his scaled body swelling until he rose above even the giant Borderman. Holding the lizard firm, they dragged him to where Slanter and Jair stood peering down the corridor without.

From both ends of the corridor, cries of alarm answered those of the fleeing Gnome Hunters.

"Which way do we run?" Garet Jax snapped at Slanter.

Wordlessly, the Gnome turned right, away from the fleeing Hunters, moving down the corridor at a quick trot and motioning the others to follow. They came after him in a knot, Stythys urged on by the long knife Garet Jax held against his ribs.

"Sstupid little peopless!" the Mwellret rasped in fury. "Diess here in the prissonss!"

The hall divided before them. To the left, a gathering of Gnomes caught sight of them and charged with weapons drawn. Slanter wheeled and took the little company right. Ahead, a Gnome Hunter darted from a doorway, but Foraker bowled him over without slowing, banging the fellow's helmeted head against the stone block walls with jarring force. Cries of pursuit rose up all about.

"Slanter!" Jair cried suddenly in warning.

Too late. The Gnome had stumbled into the midst of a swarm of armed Hunters that had burst unexpectedly from an adjoining hall. He went down in a tangle of arms and legs, crying out. Thrusting Stythys at Helt, Garet Jax went to his aid, Foraker and Edain Elessedil a step behind. Weapons glittered sharply in the gray half-light and cries of pain and anger filled the hall. The rescuers swept into the Gnomes, thrusting them back from the fallen Slanter. Garet Jax was like a cat at hunt, fluid and swift, as he parried and cut with the slender sword. The Gnomes gave way. Aided by Edain Elessedil, Slanter struggled to his feet once more.

"Slanter! Get us out of here!" Elb Foraker roared, the great, two-edged axe before him.

"Ahead!" Slanter coughed and staggered forward.

Surging through the Gnomes that still barred their way, the little company raced down the corridor, dragging the reluctant Stythys with them. Gnome Hunters sprang at them from everywhere, but they threw back the attackers with ferocious determination. Slanter went down again, tripped by the haft of a short spear thrust before him. Instantly Foraker was there, broadax hammering at the attacker and one hand dragging Slanter back up. The cries from behind them became a solid roar as hundreds of Gnomes flooded the hallway about the armory door and gave chase.

Then they were in the clear for a moment, bounding down a flight of stairs, cutting back beneath the flooring to a passageway below. A broad rotunda opened before them, its windows and doors neatly spaced about, closed and shuttered against the weather. Without slowing, Slanter wrenched open the door closest and led the little company back out into the rain.

They were in another court, walled and gated. The rain blew wildly in their faces, and thunder rolled across the High Bens. Slowing his pace, Slanter led the way across the court to the gates, pushed them open, and stepped through. An outside stairway circled downward to a line of battlements and watchtowers. Beyond, the dark shadow of the forest pressed close about the walls.

Boldly, Slanter led the company down the stairs and onto the battlements. Gnome Hunters clustered about the watchtowers now, alerted that something had happened within the fortress. Slanter ignored them. Head lowered, cloak wrapped close, he motioned the others into a passageway beneath the battlements. Within the concealment of their shadow, he gathered the company about him.

"We're going right through the gates," he announced, his breath ragged. "No one talks but me. Keep your hoods up and your heads down. Whatever happens, don't stop. Quick, now!"

There was no argument, not even from Garet Jax. Cloaks drawn close and hoods in place, the company slipped from the shadows once more. With Slanter leading, they followed the battlement walls beneath the watchtower to a pair of iron-barred, open gates. A cluster of Gnome Hunters stood talking before them, heads bent against the weather, sharing a flask of ale. A head or two lifted at their approach, and Slanter waved, calling out something in the Gnome tongue that Jair could not understand. One of the Hunters drew away from his fellows and stepped out to meet them.

"Keep moving," Slanter whispered over his shoulder.

A few scattered shouts from behind them had reached the ears of the Gnome Hunters. Startled, they looked back into the fortress to discover what had happened.

The little company marched past them without slowing. Instinctively, Jair tried to shrink down within his cloak, tensing so badly he stumbled and almost went down before Elb Foraker caught him. Slanter stepped apart from the others as they came past the watch, blocking away the eyes of the Gnome who had thought to detain them. He spoke angrily with the fellow, and Jair caught the word Mwellret in the conversation. They were clear of the Hunters now, all save Slanter, passing beneath the battlements and through the open gates. No one stopped them. As they hurried from Dun Fee Aran into the darkness of the trees, Jair slowed and looked back anxiously. Slanter still stood within the arch, arguing with the watch.

"Keep your head down!" Foraker urged, pushing him ahead.

He went into the rain-soaked forest, following reluctantly after the others, and the walls and towers of the fortress disappeared behind him. They pressed on a few minutes longer, weaving their way through the scrub and trees, Elb Foraker in the lead. Then they stopped, gathering beneath a monstrous oak, its leaves fallen and matted into the earth about it in a carpet of muddied yellow. Garet Jax backed Stythys against the gnarled trunk and held him there. They waited in silence.

The minutes slipped by. Slanter did not appear. Crouched down at the edge of the little clearing that encircled the old oak, Jair peered helplessly into the rain. The others spoke in hushed tones behind him. The rain fell steadily, spattering in noisy cadence on the earth and forest trees. Still Slanter did not appear. Jair's mouth tightened with determination. If he did not come in the next five minutes, the Valeman was going back for him. He would not leave the Gnome—not after what Slanter had done for him.

Five minutes passed, and still Slanter did not appear. Jair rose and looked questioningly at the others, a cluster of cloaked and hooded figures in the dark and the rain.

"I'm going back," he told them. Then a rustling noise brought him about and Slanter emerged from the trees.

"Took a bit more talking than I thought it would," the Gnome announced. "They'll be after us quick enough." Then he saw the look of relief on Jair's face and stopped. "Thinking of going somewhere, boy?" he guessed rightly.

"Well, I . . . no, I guess not now . . ." Jair stuttered.

A look of amusement spread over the Gnome's rough face. "No? Still planning on finding your sister, aren't you?" Jair nodded. "Good. Then you are going somewhere after all. You're going north with the rest of us. Get moving."

Motioning to the others, he turned into the trees. "We'll ford the river six miles upstream to throw off any pursuit that lasts that long. River's deep there, but I guess we can't get much wetter than we are."

Jair permitted himself a brief smile, then followed after the others. The peaks of the High Bens rose before them, misted and gray through the trees. Beyond, still far to the north and hidden from view, the mountains of the Ravenshorn waited. It might yet be a long way to Graymark, the Valeman thought, breathing in the cool autumn air and the smell of the rain, but for the first time since Capaal he felt certain that they were going to get there.

XXXIV

BRIN SPOKE LITTLE ON THE JOURNEY BACK FROM THE GRIM-
pond to Hearthstone. She needed to sort through and decipher the
meaning of all that the shade had told to her, for she knew that her
confusion would only grow greater with the passage of time. Pressed
by her companions to tell all that the Grimpond had told to her, she
revealed only that the missing Sword of Leah was in the hands of
the Spider Gnomes and that the way to enter the Maelmord without
being seen was through Graymark's sewers. After saying that much,
she begged them to forbear from any further questioning until they
had returned to the valley, then gave herself over to the task of re-
considering all that she had been told.

The strange image of Jair in that darkened room with the
cloaked form advancing so menacingly toward him was foremost
in her mind as she began the task of sorting through the puzzle
given her. In spite and anger, the Grimpond had conjured up that
image, and she could not believe that there was any truth in what
she had been shown. The cloaked form was neither Gnome nor
Mord Wraith, and those were the enemies that sought the Ohmsfords. It angered her that she had stayed to watch the image play itself out before her, teasing her as the Grimpond had intended that it
should. Had she any sense, she would have turned away at once and
not let herself be taunted. Jair was safe in the Vale with her parents
and their friends. The Grimpond's image was but a loathsome lie.

And yet she could not be entirely certain.

Unable to do anything further with that concern, she pushed it aside and turned her thoughts to the other mysteries that the Grimpond had given her. There were many. Past and present were joined in some way by the dark magic, the shade had hinted. The power that the Warlock Lord had wielded in the time of Shea Ohmsford was the power wielded in her own time by the Mord Wraiths. But there was more to the Grimpond's meaning. There was mention of some tie between the Wars of the Races and the more recent war her father and the Westland Elves had fought against the Demons of the faerie world. There was that insidious suggestion that while the Warlock Lord had been destroyed by the magic of the Sword of Shannara, he was not really gone. "Who now gives voice to the magic and sends the Mord Wraiths forth?" the Grimpond had asked. Worst of all was the shade's sly insistence that Allanon—who through all his years of service to the Four Lands and her people had always foreseen everything—had this time been deceived. Thinking that he saw the truth, he had let his eyes be closed. What was it the Grimpond had said? That Allanon saw only the Warlock Lord come again—that he saw only what was past.

What do you see? the shade had whispered. Are your eyes open?

Frustration welled up within her, but she brought it quickly under control. Frustration would only serve to blind her further, and she needed to keep her vision clear, if she was even to begin to comprehend the Grimpond's words. Suppose, she reasoned, that Allanon had indeed been deceived—an assumption that was difficult for her to accept, but one that she must accept if she were to puzzle through what she had been told. In what way could that deception have been worked? It was evident enough that the Druid had been deceived in his belief that the Wraiths would not anticipate their coming into the Eastland through the Wolfsktaag or that the Wraiths could not follow them after they left the Vale. Were these deceptions only bits and pieces of some greater deceit?

Are your own eyes open? Do you see?

The words whispered again in her mind, a warning that she did not understand. Was the deception of Allanon in some way her own? She shook her head against her confusion. Reason it through, she told herself. She must assume that Allanon had been deceived somehow in his analysis of the danger that confronted them in the Maelmord. Perhaps the power of the Mord Wraiths was greater than he had supposed. Perhaps some part of the Warlock Lord had survived the Master's destruction. Perhaps the Druid had underestimated the strength of their enemies or overestimated their own strength.

She thought then of what the Grimpond had said about her. Dark child, he had called her, doomed to die in the Maelmord, the bearer of the seeds of her own destruction. Surely that destruction would come from the magic of the wishsong—an inadequate and erratic defense against the dark magic of the walkers. The Mord Wraiths were victims of their magic. But so, too, was she, the Grimpond had said. And when she had heatedly replied that she was not like them, that she did not use the dark magic, the shade had laughed and told her that none used the magic—that the magic used them.

"There is the key to what you seek," he had said.

That was another puzzle. It was certainly true that the magic used her as much as she used it. She remembered her anger against the men from west of Spanning Ridge at the Rooker Line Trading Center and how Allanon had shown her what the magic could do to those trees so closely intertwined. Savior and destroyer—she would be both, the shade of Bremen had warned. And now the Grimpond had warned her, too.

Cogline whispered something at her side, then danced away as Kimber Boh told him to behave. Her thoughts scattered momentarily, and she watched the old man slip into the forest wilderness, laughing and chittering like one half gone into madness. She breathed the cool afternoon air deeply, seeing the shadows of early evening beginning to slip down about the land. She found herself missing Allanon. Odd that she should, for his dark and formidable presence had been small comfort to her in the days that she had traveled with him. But there had been that strange kinship between them, that sense of understanding, and of being in some way similar . . .

Was it the magic they shared—the wishsong and the Druid power?

She found tears forming in her eyes as she pictured his broken form once again, slumped down within that sunlit glen, bloodied and torn. How terrible he had looked to her, stricken by impending death, his hand lifting to touch her forehead with his blood . . . A lonely, worn figure in her mind, steeped not so much in Druid power as in Druid guilt, he had bound himself by his father's oath to purge the Druids of the responsibility they bore for unleashing the dark magic into the world of Men.

And now that responsibility had been passed to her.

Afternoon faded into evening, and the little company passed down out of the Anar wilderness into the valley of Hearthstone. Brin ceased to puzzle over the words of the Grimpond and began to think instead of what she was to tell her companions and what she was to do with the small bit of knowledge that she had gained. Her own lot in this matter was fixed, but not so that of the others—not even Rone. If she were to tell him all that she had been told by the Grimpond, perhaps he could be persuaded to let her go on alone. If it was predetermined that she must go to her death, perhaps she could at least keep him from going to his.

An hour later they were gathered together before the fireplace in the little cottage, drawn up in covered chairs and on benches— Brin, the old man, the girl, and Rone Leah. The warmth of the flames danced off their faces as the night settled down, cold and still. Whisper slept peacefully upon his rug, his giant body stretched full-length before the fire. Invisible most of the day on their journey to and from the Grimpond, the moor cat had reappeared on their return and promptly curled up in his favorite resting spot.

"The Grimpond appeared to me in my own image," Brin began quietly as the others listened. "It took my face and taunted me with what it said I was."

"It plays those games," Kimber said sympathetically. "You must not be bothered by it."

"All lies and deceits! It is a dark and twisted thing," Cogline whispered, his sticklike frame hunched forward. "Locked within its pool since before the loss of the old world, speaking riddles no man could hope to unravel—or woman either."

"Grandfather," Kimber Boh cautioned gently.

"What was it that the Grimpond had to say?" Rone wanted to know.

"What I have told you," Brin replied. "That the Sword of Leah is in the hands of the Spider Gnomes, pulled from the waters of the Chard Rush. That the way into the Maelmord without being seen by the walkers is through the sewers of Graymark."

"There was no deceit in this?" he pressed.

She shook her head slowly, thinking of the dark way in which she had used the wishsong's magic. "Not in this."

Cogline snorted. "Well, the rest was lies, I'll wager!"

Brin turned to him. "The Grimpond said that death would come to me in the Maelmord—that I could not escape it."

There was a hushed silence. "Lies, just as the old man says," Rone muttered finally.

"The Grimpond said that your death awaits you there as well, Rone. It said that we both carry the seeds of that death in the magic we would wield—yours in the Sword of Leah, mine in the wishsong."

"And you believe that nonsense?" The highlander shook his head. "Well, I don't. I can look after the both of us."

Brin smiled sadly. "But what if the Grimpond's words are not lies? What if that part, too, is truth? Must I bear your death on my conscience, Rone? Will you insist on dying with me?"

Rone flushed at the rebuke. "If I must. Allanon made me your protector when I sought to be so. What manner of protector would

I be if I were to abandon you now and let you go on alone? If it is predetermined that we should die, Brin, then let that not be on your conscience. Let it be on mine."

Brin had tears in her eyes again and she swallowed hard against the feelings coursing through her.

"Girl, girl, no crying now, no crying!" Cogline was suddenly on his feet, shuffling over to where she sat. To her surprise, he reached up gently and brushed the tears away. "It's all games with the Grimpond, all lies and half-truths. The shade predicts everyone's death as if it were blessed with special insight. Here, here. What can a spirit thing know of death?"

He patted Brin on the shoulder, then scowled inexplicably at Rone, as if the fault were somehow his, and muttered something about dratted trespassers.

"Grandfather, we must help them," Kimber said suddenly.

Cogline wheeled on her, bristling. "Help them? And just what is it that we've been doing, girl? Gathering firewood?"

"No, I don't think that, grandfather, but . . ."

"But nothing!" Crooked arms gestured impatiently. "Of course we're going to help them!"

Valegirl and highlander stared at the old man in astonishment. Cogline cackled shrilly, then kicked at the sleeping Whisper and brought the cat's whiskered face up with a jerk. "Me and this worthless animal—we're going to help all we can! Can't be having tears like those! Can't be having guests wandering all over the place with no one to show them the way!"

"Grandfather . . ." the girl started to interrupt, but the old man brushed her aside.

"Haven't had a run at those Spider Gnomes for some time now, have we? Good idea to let them know that we're still here in case they think we've moved out. Up on Toffer Ridge, they'll be—no, not this time of year. No, they'll be down off the ridge to the moor with the season's change at hand. That's their ground; that's where they'd take a sword like that if they pulled it from the river. Whisper will track it for us. Then we'll turn east, skirt the moor, and cross to the Ravenshorn. Day or two, maybe, all told."

He wheeled back again. "But not you, Kimber. Can't have you out and about in that country. Walkers and all are too dangerous. You stay here and keep the home."

Kimber gave him a hopeless look. "He still thinks of me as a child. I am the one who should worry for him."

"Ha! You don't have to worry for me!" Cogline snapped.

Kimber smiled indulgently, her pixie face calm. "Of course I have to worry for you. I love you." She turned to Brin. "Brin, you have to understand something. Grandfather never leaves the valley anymore without me. He requires the use of my eyes and my memory from time to time. Grandfather, don't be angry with what I say, but you know that sometimes you are forgetful. Besides, Whisper will not always do what you tell him. He will disappear on you when you least want him to, if you try to go alone."

Cogline frowned. "Stupid cat does that, all right." He glanced down at Whisper, who blinked back at him sleepily. "Waste of my time trying to teach him differently. Very well, I suppose we'll all have to go. But you keep out of harm's way, girl. Leave that part to me."

Brin and Rone exchanged hurried glances.

Kimber turned to them. "It is settled then. We can leave at dawn."

The Valegirl and the highlander stared at each other in disbelief. What was happening? As if it were the most natural thing in the world, it had just been decided that a girl barely more than Brin's age, a half-crazed old man, and a sometimes disappearing cat would retrieve for them the missing Sword of Leah from some creatures they had labeled as Spider Gnomes and then afterward guide them into the mountains of the Ravenshorn and Graymark! Gnomes and walkers and other dangerous beings would be all about—beings whose power had destroyed the Druid Allanon—and the old man and the girl were acting as if none of that really made any difference at all.

"Kimber, no," Brin said finally, not knowing what else to say. "You can't go with us."

"She's right," Rone agreed. "You can't even begin to understand what we'll be up against."

Kimber Boh looked at each of them in turn. "I understand better than you think. I told you before—this land is my home. And grandfather's. We know its dangers and we understand them."

"You don't understand the walkers!" Rone exploded. "What can the two of you do against the walkers?"

Kimber held her ground. "I don't know. Much the same as you, I'd guess. Avoid them."

"And what if you can't avoid them?" Rone pressed. "What then?"

Cogline snatched a leather bag belted at his waist and held it forth. "Give them a taste of my magic, outlander! Give them a taste of a fire they know nothing about at all!"

The highlander frowned doubtfully and looked at Brin for help. "This is crazy!" he snapped.

"Do not be so quick to dismiss my grandfather's magic," Kimber advised, with a reassuring nod to the old man. "He has lived in this wilderness all of his life and survived a great many dangers. He can do things you might not expect of him. He will be of great help to you. As will Whisper and I as well."

Brin shook her head. "I think this is a very bad idea, Kimber."

The girl nodded her understanding. "You will change your mind, Brin. In any case, you really don't have a choice. You need Whisper to track. You need grandfather to guide you. And you need me to help them do that."

Brin started to object once more, then stopped. What was she thinking? They had come to Hearthstone in the first place because they needed someone to guide them through Darklin Reach. There was only one man who could do that, and that man was Cogline.

Without Cogline, they might wander the wilderness country of the Anar for weeks—weeks that they did not have. Now that they had found him and he was offering them the help they so desperately needed, here she was trying to refuse it!

She hesitated. Perhaps she had good reason for doing so. Kimber appeared to her as a girl whose heart was greater than her strength. But the fact remained that Cogline was unlikely to go anywhere without her. Did Brin, then, have the right to put her concern for Kimber above the dictates of the trust which she had been given by Allanon?

She did not think so.

"I believe the matter is decided," Kimber said softly.

Brin looked at Rone one final time. The highlander shook his head in helpless resignation.

Brin turned back and smiled wearily. "I guess it is," she agreed and hoped against reason that it had been decided correctly.

XXXV

---◆---

THEY DEPARTED HEARTHSTONE AT DAWN OF THE FOLLOWING day and journeyed northeast through the forestland toward the dark rise of Toffer Ridge. Travel was slow, as it had been during their trek north to the Grimpond. The whole of the wilderness beyond the valley between the Ravenshorn and the Rabb was a treacherous maze of craggy ravines and drops that could cripple the unwary. With packs strapped tightly across their backs and weapons secured about their waists, Brin, Rone, Kimber Boh, and Cogline wound their way cautiously ahead on a warm, sweet-smelling autumn day filled with sound and color. Only occasionally visible, the shadowy form of Whisper kept pace in the trees about them. The members of the little company felt rested and alert, much more so than they should have, since their discussion of the previous night had not ended until early morning. They knew that lack of sleep would catch up with them eventually, but for now, at least, they were filled with the tension and excitement of their quest, and all traces of weariness were easily brushed aside.

Not so easily dismissed, however, were Brin's feelings of uncertainty about taking along Kimber and Cogline. The decision had been made, the pledge given, and the journey begun—yet still the uncertainty that had troubled her from the first would not subside. Some doubts and fears would have been there in any case, she supposed, fostered by her knowledge of the dangers that lay ahead and by the haunting prophecies of the Grimpond. But such doubts and fears would have been for her and for Rone—Rone, whose determination to stand with her in this was so strong that she had finally accepted that he would never be persuaded to leave her. The doubts and fears would not have been, as they were now, for the old man and the girl. All of their reassurances notwithstanding, the Valegirl still thought neither strong enough to survive the power of the dark magic. How could she see it otherwise? It made no difference that they had lived all these years within the wilderness of the Anar, for the dangers they would face now were not dangers made of this world and time. What magics or lore could they hope to employ that would turn aside the Mord Wraiths when the walkers were next encountered?

It frightened Brin to think of the power of the Mord Wraiths being turned against the girl and the old man. It frightened her more than anything that she could imagine might happen to her. How could she live with the knowledge that she had permitted them to come on this journey, if it were to end in their deaths?

And yet Kimber seemed so certain of herself and of her grandfather. There was neither fear nor doubt in her mind. There was only her self-assurance, determination, and that unshakable sense of obligation toward Brin and Rone that motivated her in what she had undertaken to do for them.

"We are friends, Brin, and friends do for each other what they see needs to be done," the girl had explained in the late hours of the previous night when all talk had drifted into weary whispers. "Friendship is a thing sensed inwardly as much as a thing pledged openly. One feels friendship and becomes bound by it. It was this that drew Whisper to me and gained me his loyalty. I loved him as he loved me, and each of us sensed that in the other. I have sensed it with you as well. We are to be friends, all of us, and if we are to be friends, then we must share both good and bad in our friendship. Your needs become mine."

"That's a very beautiful sentiment, Kimber," she had replied.

"But what if my needs are too great, as they are in this instance? What if my needs are too dangerous to share?"

"All the more reason that they *must* be shared." Kimber had smiled somberly. "And shared with friends. We must help each other if the friendship is to mean anything at all."

There really wasn't much to be said after that. Brin might have argued that Kimber barely knew her, that she was owed no obligation, and that this quest she had been given was hers alone and not the responsibility of the girl and her grandfather. But such arguments would have meant nothing to Kimber, who saw so clearly the relationship between them as one of equals, and whose sense of commitment was such that there could be no compromise.

The journey wore on and the day slipped past. It was a savage timberland through which they passed, a rugged mass of towering black oaks, elms, and gnarled hickories. Their lofty, twisted limbs stretched wide like giants' arms. Through the bones of the forest roof, skeletal and stripped of their leaves, the sky shone deep crystal blue, with sunshine streaming down to brighten the woodland shadows with friendly patches of light. Yet the sunlight was but a brief daytime visitor to this wilderness. Here, only the shadows belonged—pervasive, impenetrable, filled with a subtle hint of hidden dangers, of things unseen and unheard, and of a phantom life that came awake only when the light was completely gone and the forestland lay wrapped in blackness. That life lay waiting, concealed silently within the darkened heart of these woodlands, a cunning and hateful force that resented the intrusion of these creatures into its private world and would snuff them out as a wind would a candle's small flame. Brin sensed its presence. It whispered softly in her mind, worming past the slender thread of confidence lent her by the presence of those who traveled with her, warning her that when nightfall came again, she must be very careful.

Then the sun began to drop below the western skyline and dusk to settle over the land. The dark line of Toffer Ridge loomed before them, a rugged and uneven shadow, and Cogline took them through a twisting pass that breached its wall. They walked in silence, fatigue now beginning to slip through them. Insect sounds filled the darkness, and high above them, lost in the tangle of the great trees, night birds sent forth their shrill calls. Ridgeline and wilderness forest tightened about them, closing them away in the darkened pass. The air, warm all day, grew hot and unpleasant, and its smell turned stale. That hidden life which waited within the woodland shadows came awake and rose up to look about . . .

Abruptly, the timber broke apart before them, sloping sharply downward through the ridgeline into a vast, featureless lowland shrouded in mist and lighted in eerie glow by stars and a strange, pale orange gibbous moon that hung at the edge of the eastern horizon. Sullen and dismal, the sprawling bottomland was little more than a shadowed black mass of stillness that seemed to open into the earth like some bottomless canyon where Toffer Ridge slipped away into the mist.

"Olden Moor," Kimber whispered softly.

Brin stared down at the moor in watchful silence. She could feel it staring back.

Midnight came and went, and time slowed until it seemed to cease all passage. A hint of wind fluttered enticingly across Brin's dust-streaked face and faded away. She looked up expectantly, but there was nothing more. The heat returned, harsh and oppressive. She felt as if she had been shut within a furnace, its unseen fires snatching from her aching lungs the very air she needed to survive. In the bottomland, the autumn night gave nothing back of its cooling promise. Sweat soaked Brin's clothing through, ran down her body in distracting rivulets, and coated her worn countenance with a silver gray sheen. Muscles cramped and knotted wearily. Though she shifted about frequently in an effort to relieve the discomfort, she quickly found there were no new positions to be tried. The ache simply followed. Swarms of gnats buzzed annoyingly, drawn by the moisture from her body, biting at her face and hands as she brushed at them uselessly. All about her, the air reeked of rotting wood and stagnant water.

Crouched in the concealing shadows of a clump of rocks with Rone, Kimber, and Cogline, she stared downward along the base of the ridgeline to where the camp of the Spider Gnomes lay settled at the edge of Olden Moor. A jumble of makeshift huts and burrows, the camp stretched between the base of Toffer Ridge and the darkness of the moor. A scattering of fires burned in its midst, their sullen, ragged light barely penetrating the gloom. The crooked, bent shadows of the camp's inhabitants passed through the muted glare. The Spider Gnomes, their strange and grotesque bodies covered with gray hair, were naked to the elements as they skittered about in the withered long grass on all fours, hunched and faceless. Large groups of them gathered at the edge of the moor, shielded from the mist by the flames as they chanted dully into the night.

"Calling to the dark powers," Cogline had informed his companions hours earlier, after first bringing them to this hiding place. "A tribal people, the Gnomes—the Spider folk more so than any. Believe in spirits and dark things that rise from other worlds with the change of seasons. Call to them for their own strength, do the Gnomes—hoping at the same time that strength doesn't turn against them. Ha! Superstitious stuff!"

But the dark things were real sometimes, however, Cogline told them. There were things within Olden Moor as dark and terrible as those that inhabited the forests of the Wolfsktaag—things born of other worlds and lost magics. They were called Werebeasts. They lived within the mists, creatures of dreadful shapes and forms that preyed upon body and mind, snaring mortal beings weaker than they and draining away their lives. The Werebeasts were not imaginary, Cogline admitted grimly. It was against their coming that the Spider Gnomes sought to protect themselves—for the Spider Gnomes were the Werebeasts' favorite food.

"Now, with the autumn's change to winter, the Gnomes come down to the moor to call out against the rise of the mists." The old man's voice had been a harsh whisper. "Gnomes think the winter won't come or the mists stay low if they don't. A superstitious folk. Come here like this each fall for nearly a month, whole camps, whole tribes of them—just migrate down off the ridge. Call out to the dark powers day and night so that the winter will keep them safe and keep the beasts away." He grinned secretively and winked. "Works, too. Werebeasts feed off them for that whole month, you see. Eat enough to carry them through the winter. No need to go onto the ridge after that!"

Cogline had known where the Spider people would be found. With the fall of night, the little group had traveled north along the base of the ridgeline until the Gnome camp had been sighted. Then, as they hunched down within the concealment of the rocks, Kimber Boh had explained what must happen next.

"They will have your sword with them, Rone. A sword such as that, pulled from the waters of the Chard Rush, will be considered a talisman sent to them by their dark powers. They will set it before them, hoping it will shield them from the Werebeasts. We must discover where it is housed and then steal it back from them."

"How will we do that?" Rone had asked quickly. He had talked of little else for the whole of their journey there. The lure of the sword's power had claimed him once more.

"Whisper will track it," she had replied. "If given your scent, he can follow it to the sword, however well concealed. Once he has found it, he will return to lead us in."

So Whisper had been given the highlander's scent and dispatched into the night. He had gone soundlessly, fading into the shadows, lost from view almost instantly. The four from Hearthstone had been waiting ever since for his return, crouched down in the humid dark and the fetid dampness of the bottomland, listening and watching. The moor cat had been gone a very long time.

Brin closed her eyes against the weariness that seeped through her and tried to block the sound of the Gnomes chanting from her mind. A dull, empty monotone, it went on ceaselessly. Several times, while she listened, there had been screams from close to the mists—shrill, quick, and horror-stricken. Almost at once, though, they had ceased. Still the chanting went on . . .

A monstrous shadow detached itself from the dark right in front of her, and she started to her feet with a small cry.

"Hush, girl!" Cogline yanked her down again, one bony hand slipping tightly across her mouth. "It's only the cat!"

Whisper's massive head materialized then, luminous blue eyes winking lazily as he padded up to Kimber. The girl bent down to wrap her arms about him, stroking him gently, whispering in his ear. For several moments she spoke with the moor cat, and the cat nuzzled and rubbed up against her. Then she turned back to them, excitement dancing in her eyes.

"He has found the sword, Rone!"

Instantly Rone was beside her. "Take me to where it can be found, Kimber!" he begged. "We will have a weapon then with which to face the walkers and any other dark thing that might serve them!"

Brin fought back against the bitterness that welled up suddenly within her. Rone has forgotten already what little good the sword did him in Allanon's defense, she thought. He was consumed by his need for it.

Cogline called them close, while Kimber spoke a quick word to Whisper. Then they began their descent into the camp of the Gnomes. They crept down off the rise on which they had hidden, crouched low against the shadow of the ridgeline. Light from the distant fires barely touched them here, and they slipped swiftly ahead. Warnings nudged Brin Ohmsford's restless mind, whispering to her that she must turn back, that nothing good lay this way. Too late, she whispered back. Too late.

The camp drew closer. In the gradual brightening of the fires, the Spider Gnomes grew more distinct, crouched forms creeping about the huts and burrows like the insects for which they were named. They were loathsome things to look upon, all hair and sharp ferret eyes, bent and crooked forms drawn from some best-forgotten nightmare. Dozens of them slipped about, emerging from and then disappearing into the gloom, chittering in a language less than human. All the while, they continued to gather before the wall of mist and chant in hollow, toneless cadence.

The moor cat and his four companions crept soundlessly along the perimeter of the camp, circling toward its far side. The mist drifted past them in trailing wisps, broken free of the wall that hung motionlessly over the empty reaches of the moor. It was damp and clinging, unpleasantly warm as it touched their skin. Brin brushed at it distastefully.

Ahead, Whisper drew to a halt, his saucer eyes swinging about to find his mistress. Sweating freely now, Brin glanced about, desperately trying to get her bearings. The darkness was filled with shadows and movement, the warmth of the autumn night, and the drone of the Spider Gnomes chanting before the moor.

"We must go down into the camp," Kimber was saying, her voice a soft, excited whisper.

"Now we'll see them jump!" Cogline cackled gleefully. "Stay clear of them when they do!"

At a word from the girl, Whisper turned down into the Gnome encampment. Slinking soundlessly through the mist, the giant cat moved toward the nearest gathering of huts and burrows. Kimber, Cogline, and Rone followed, crouched low. Brin trailed behind them, her eyes searching the night.

To her left, things moved at the fringes of the firelight, crawling through a mass of rocks and slipping into the tall grass. Others appeared further out to their right, lurching toward the sound of the chanting and the wall of mist. Smoke from the fires drifted into Brin's eyes now, mingling with trailers of fog, stinging and sharp.

And suddenly she could not see. Anger and fear rose within her. Her eyes teared and she brushed at them with her hands . . .

A shriek broke suddenly from the darkness, rising above the drone of the chanting and freezing the night about it. A Spider Gnome leaped from the shadows before them, frantically trying to escape the giant moor cat that had suddenly appeared in its path.

Whisper sprang ahead with a roar, knocking the flailing Gnome aside as if it were a bit of deadwood and scattering half a dozen more that blocked the way. Kimber raced beside the giant cat, a slight, swift figure in the dark. Cogline and Rone followed, each howling like men gone mad. Desperately, Brin ran after all of them, struggling to keep pace.

Led by the moor cat, the little company charged down into the very center of the encampment. Spider Gnomes flew past them, hairy, crooked shadows that chittered, howled, and leaped for cover. The company raced past the nearest bonfire. Cogline slowed, grappling with the contents of a leather bag secured about his waist. He produced a handful of black powder and threw it squarely into the flames. Instantly, an explosion rocked the bottomland as the fire geysered skyward in a shower of sparks and burning fragments of wood. The chanting before the wall of mist died away as the shrieks of the Gnomes in the camp intensified. The four dashed past another fire, and again Cogline threw the black powder into the flames. A second time the earth beneath exploded, filling the night with a flare of brightness and scattering the Spider Gnomes everywhere.

Far ahead, Whisper sprang upward through the firelight like a massive wraith, gaining the summit of a crudely constructed platform that rose close to the wall of mist. The platform splintered and collapsed with a crash, toppled by the weight of the beast, and a collection of jars, carved wooden objects, and glittering weapons spilled to the ground.

"The sword!" Rone cried out above the din of shrieking Gnomes. Knocking aside the wiry forms that sought to block his way, he charged ahead. An instant later, he was next to Whisper, snatching from the fallen treasures a slim ebony blade. "Leah! Leah!" he cried, brandishing the Sword of Leah triumphantly above his head and forcing back a handful of Gnomes that came at him.

Explosions erupted all about them now as Cogline fed the black powder into the Gnome fires. The whole of the bottomland was lighted in a yellow glare that surged skyward out of blackened, charred earth. Grass fires burned everywhere. Smoke and mist thickened and rolled across the encampment, and everything began to disappear into it. Brin ran on after the others, forgotten in the excitement of the battle, falling farther and farther behind. They had abandoned the toppled platform now and turned back toward the ridgeline. Little more than dim forms in the haze of smoke and mist, they could barely be seen.

"Rone, wait!" Brin cried out frantically.

Spider Gnomes raced past her on all sides, chittering madly. A few reached for her with their hairy limbs, their crooked fingers fastening on her clothing and tearing at it. Wildly, she lashed out at them, breaking free and running on to catch the others. But there were too many. They were all about her, grasping. In desperation, she used the wishsong; the strange, numbing cry flung them back from her with howls of dismay.

Then she fell, sprawling face forward in the tall grass, dirt flying into her eyes and mouth. Something heavy sprang atop her, a mass of hair and sinew wrapping itself tightly about her. She lost control of herself in that instant, fear and loathing consuming her so that she could no longer reason. She staggered to her hands and knees, but the unseen thing still clung to her. She used the wishsong with all the fury that she could muster. It burst from her throat like an explosion, and the thing on her back simply flew apart, shredded with the force of the magic.

Brin whirled then and saw what she had done. A Spider Gnome lay broken and lifeless against the rocks behind her, curiously small and fragile-looking in death. She stared at the shattered form and for one brief instant she felt an odd, frightening sense of glee.

Then she thrust the feeling from her. Voiceless, horror-stricken, she turned and ran blindly into the smoke, all sense of direction lost.

"Rone!" she screamed.

She fled into the wall of mist that rose before her and disappeared from view.

XXXVI

◆

IT WAS AS IF THE WORLD HAD FALLEN AWAY.

There was only the mist. Moon, stars, and sky had vanished. Forest trees, mountain peaks, ridgelines, valleys, rocks, and streams were all gone. Even the ground over which Brin ran was a dim and shapeless thing, its grasses a part of the shifting gray haze. She was alone in the vast and empty void into which she had fled.

She stumbled to a weary halt, her arms folding tightly against her body, the sound of her breathing harsh and ragged in her ears. For a long time, she stood within the haze and did not move, only vaguely aware even now that she had become turned about in her flight from the bottomland and run into Olden Moor. Her thoughts scattered like blown leaves, and though she snatched frantically at them, trying to hold them back and gather them together, they were lost almost instantly. A single clear, hard image remained fixed before her eyes—a Spider Gnome, twisted, broken, and lifeless.

Her eyes closed against the light and her hands clasped into fists of rage. She had done what she had said she would never do. She had taken another human life, wrenching it away in a frenzy of fear and anger, using the wishsong to do it. Allanon had warned her that it could happen. She could hear the whisper of his caution: "Valegirl, the wishsong is power like nothing that I have ever seen. The magic can give life, and the magic can take life away."

"But I would never use it . . ."

"The magic uses all, dark child—even you!"

It was the Grimpond's warning and not Allanon's that mocked her now, and she thrust it from her mind.

She straightened. It was not as if she had not known somewhere deep within that she might someday be forced to use the wishsong's magic as Allanon had warned. She had recognized the possibility from the moment he had shown her the extent of its power in that simple demonstration of the trees intertwined in the forests of the Runne Mountains. It was not as if the death of the Spider Gnome came as some shocking and unexpected revelation.

It was the fact that some part of her had enjoyed what she had done, that some part of her had actually taken pleasure in the killing, that horrified her.

Her throat tightened. She remembered the sudden, furtive sense of glee she had felt on seeing the Gnome's shattered form, realizing that it was the wishsong that had destroyed it. She had reveled for that single instant in the power of the magic . . .

What kind of monster had she let herself become?

Her eyes snapped open. She had not *let* herself become anything. The Grimpond was right: You did not use the magic—the magic used you. The magic made you what it would. She could not fully control it. She had discovered that in the encounter at the Rooker Line Trading Center with the men from west of Spanning Ridge and had promised herself that she would never lose control of the magic like that again. But when the Spider Gnomes had come at her as she fled through their encampment, such control as she had thought to exercise had quickly evaporated under the flood of her emotions and the confusion and urgency of the moment. She had used the magic without any real presence of mind at all, but had simply reacted, wielding the power as Rone Leah would wield his sword, a terrible, destructive weapon.

And she had enjoyed it.

Tears formed at the corners of her eyes. She could argue that the enjoyment had been momentary and tinged with guilt and that her horror at its being would prevent it from reoccurring. But the truth

could not be avoided. The magic had proven to be dangerously un-
predictable. It had affected her behavior in ways she would not have
thought possible. That made it a threat not only to her but to those
close to her, and she must guard carefully against that threat.

She knew that she could not turn aside from her journey eastward to the Maelmord. Allanon had given her a trust, and she knew
that, despite everything that had happened and all that argued
against it, she must fulfill that trust. She believed that even now.
But even though she was bound by the need she saw, she could yet
choose her own code of being. Allanon had intended that the wishsong be put to a single use—to gain Brin entry into the pit. She must
find a way therefore to keep the magic to herself until it was time to
call upon it for that intended use. Only once more would she risk
using the magic. Determined, she brushed the tears from her eyes.
It would be as she had sworn. The magic would use her no more.

She straightened. Now she must find her way back to the others.
She stumbled forward again, groping ahead through the gloom, her
direction uncertain. Trailers of mist slipped past her, and in their
meandering movement she was surprised to discover images. They
crowded about her, drawn from the haze into her mind and out
again. The images began to take the shapes and forms of memories
resurrected from her childhood. Her mother and her father passed
before her, larger in memory than in life in their warmth and secu-
rity, gentle figures that sheltered and loved. Jair was there. Shadows
slipped through the strange, empty half-light, ghosts of the past. Allanon might be one of those ghosts, come from death to the living.
She looked to find him, half-expecting . . .

And suddenly, shockingly, he was there. Come from the mist
like the shade he now was, he stood barely a dozen yards distant,
gray haze all about him, swirling like the Hadeshorn stirred to life.

"Allanon?" she whispered.

Yet she hesitated. The shape belonged to Allanon, but it was the
mist—only the mist.

The shadow that was Allanon slipped back into the gloom—
gone, as if it had never really been. Gone . . .

And yet there had been something, after all. Not Allanon, but something else.

Swiftly, she glanced about, searching for the thing, sensing somehow that it was out there, watching her. Images danced again before her eyes, born on the trailers of mist, reflections of her memory. The mist gave them life, a magic that entranced and lured. She stood transfixed in their wake and wondered momentarily if she were indeed going mad. Such imaginings as she was experiencing were certainly indicative of madness, and yet she felt herself clearheaded and sure. It was the mist that sought to seduce her, teasing her with its musings, playing with her memories as if they were its own. It was the mist—or something in the mist!

Werebeast! The word whispered from somewhere back in her consciousness. Cogline had warned of the mist things as the little company had crouched within the rocks on the ridgeline overlooking the camp of the Spider Gnomes. Scattered all through Olden Moor, they preyed on beings weaker than they, snaring them, draining away their lives.

She straightened, hesitated, then slowly began to walk ahead. Something moved in the mist with her—a shadow, dim and not fully formed, a bit of night. A Werebeast. She hastened on, letting her feet take her where they would. She was hopelessly lost, but she could not stay where she was. She must keep moving. She thought of those who had left her behind. Would they be searching for her? Would they be able to find her in this wall of mist? She shook her head doubtfully. She could not depend on that. She must find her own way out. Somewhere ahead, the wall of mist would fade and the moor would end. She must simply walk until she was out of it, free of its numbing haze.

But what if it would not let her get free?

Her memories came to life once more in the trailers of mist that swirled about her, teasing and seductive. She walked faster, ignoring them, aware that somewhere just beyond her vision the shadow kept pace. A chill settled through her at the awareness of the other.

She tried to envision the thing that followed her. What manner of creature was the Werebeast? It had come to her as Allanon—or had that merely been a trick of the mist and her imagination? She shook her head in voiceless confusion.

Something small and wet skittered away from beneath her feet, flitting off into the dark. She turned away from it, moving down a broad incline into a vast, marshy bowl. Muck and swamp sucked at her boots, and wintry grasses slapped at her legs, clutching. She slowed, sensing the unpleasant give in the ground, then backed away toward the rim again. Quicksand lay at the bottom of that bowl and it would draw her down and swallow her. She must stay clear of it and follow the harder, dryer earth. Mist swirled thickly all about, obscuring her vision as she sought to see her way clear. Still she had no sense of direction. For all she knew, she had been traveling in a circle.

She tramped on. The mists of Olden Moor swirled and thickened in the deep night about her, and shadows moved through their dampened haze—Werebeasts. There was more than one of them trailing her now. Brin stared out at them, following their quicksilver movements as they swam like fish through twilight waters. Grimly she quickened her pace, slipping through the marsh grass, keeping to the high ground. They still came after her. But they would not have her, she swore in silent promise. She belonged to another fate.

She hastened onward, running now, the pumping of her heart and blood a dull pounding in her ears. Anger, fear, and determination all mingled as one and drove her forward. The moor rose before her gently, and she scrambled to the center of a small rise thick with long grasses and scrub. Slowing, she glanced about in disbelief.

The shadows were everywhere.

Then a tall, lean figure appeared from out of the mist before her, wrapped in a highlander's cloak and bearing a giant broadsword strapped across its back. Brin stiffened in surprise. It was Rone! Arms lifted from out of the robes, reaching for her, beckoning her close. Willingly she started toward the highlander, her hand stretching to take his.

And then something stopped her.

She blinked. Rone? No!

A red veil fell across her vision, rage sweeping through her as she recognized the deception. It was not Rone Leah she saw. It was again the Werebeast that tracked her.

It came forward, a shimmering and fluid apparition. Robes and sword fell away, bits of the mist through which it passed. Nothing of the highlander was there now, but only a shadow, huge and changing. Swiftly it drew together, a massive body crouched on thick, clawed hind legs, great forearms crooked and bristling with shaggy hair, and a head wrinkled and twisted about jaws that split to reveal whitened teeth.

It rose up through the mist, twice her size, swathed in the moor's haze. Soundless, it bent its head and snapped at her, a mass of hair and scales, muscle, spiked bone, teeth, and slitted eyes. It was a thing born of darkest nightmares, one Brin might have dreamed in the anguish of her own despair.

Was it real? Or was it simply born out of the mist and the wanderings of her imagination?

It made no difference. Forsaking the oath she had taken only minutes earlier, she used the wishsong. Hardened with purpose, maddened by what she saw, she called it forth. She was not meant to die here within Olden Moor at the hands of this monster. This one further time she would use the magic—on a thing whose destruction did not matter.

She sang, and the wishsong froze in her throat.

It was her father who stood before her now.

The Werebeast slouched toward her, form shifting and changing in the haze, jaws slavering in anticipation of how the Valegirl's life would sate its needs. Brin staggered back, seeing now her mother's dark and gentle face. She called out in desperation, a wild, anguished cry that seemed locked in the silence of her mind.

Back came an answering cry, calling her name. Brin! Confusion swept through her; the cry seemed real, but who . . . ?

"Brin!"

The monster loomed over her, and she could smell the evil of it. But the wishsong stayed locked in her throat, imprisoned by the image she retained of its power tearing into her mother's slim form, leaving it broken and lifeless.

"Brin!"

Then a frightening roar shattered the stillness of the night. A sleek shadow flew out of the mist, and five hundred pounds of enraged moor cat crashed into the Werebeast, flinging it back from Brin. Teeth and claws slashing, the cat tore into the monstrous apparition and both went tumbling headlong through the deep grasses.

"Brin! Where are you?"

Brin stumbled back, barely able to hear the voices over the sounds of the battle. Frantic, she called back to them. An instant later Kimber appeared, darting through the haze, her long hair streaming out behind her. Cogline followed, shouting wildly, his crooked body struggling to keep pace with the girl.

Whisper and the Werebeast surged back into view, lunging and feinting. The moor cat was the stronger of the two; although the mist thing sought to break past, it was blocked at every turn. But now other shadows were gathering in the darkness beyond, huge and shapeless, ringing them all close about. Too many shadows!

"Leah! Leah!"

And then Rone was there, his slim form bolting through the mass of shadows, sword lifted. Eerie, green incandescence swirled about the ebony blade. The Werebeast cornered by Whisper whirled instantly, sensing the greater danger of the sword's magic. Thrusting away from the moor cat, the monster leaped at Rone. But the Prince of Leah was ready. His sword arced down, knifing through the mist into the Werebeast. Green fire flared sharply through the night, and the mist thing exploded in a shower of flames.

Then the light died away, and the night and the mist returned. The shadows that had gathered in the darkness beyond melted back into the void.

The highlander turned, the sword dropping forgotten at his side. He came quickly to Brin, his face stricken.

"I'm sorry, sorry," he whispered. "The magic . . ." He shook his head helplessly. "When I found the sword again, when I touched it . . . I couldn't seem to think of anything else. I picked it up and I ran with it. I forgot everything—even you. It was the magic, Brin . . ."

He faltered, and she nodded into his chest, hugging him close. "I know."

"I won't leave you like that again," he promised. "I won't."

"I know that, too," she replied softly.

But she said nothing of her decision to leave him.

XXXVII

---◆---

IT WAS THE THIRD DAY AFTER LEAVING THE PRISONS AT Dun Fee Aran before Jair and the little company from Culhaven reached the towering mountain range they called the Ravenshorn. Unable to use the open roadways that ran close to the banks of the Silver River as it wound south out of the mountains for fear of being seen, they were forced to traverse the deep forests above, picking their way at a slower pace through the tangled wilderness. The rains finally ceased on the second day out, slowed to a drizzle by midmorning, and turned to mist by noon. The air warmed as the skies cleared, and the clouds drifted east. When darkness slipped across the land, the moon and stars became visible through the trees. Their pace was slow, even after the rains had subsided, for the saturated earth could not absorb all of the surface water that had gathered, and the ground was muddied and slick with it. Stopping only for short periods of time to rest and eat, the company did its best to ignore the poor travel conditions and resolutely pressed ahead.

The sun appeared on the third day, brilliant and warm, filtering down in friendly streamers through the forest shadows, returning bits and pieces of color to the sodden land. The dark mass of the Ravenshorn came into view, barren rock rising up above the treeline. All morning they worked their way toward it, then on through the noonday, and by midafternoon they had reached the lower slopes and were starting up.

It was then that Slanter brought them to a halt.

"We have a problem," he announced matter-of-factly. "If we try to cross through these mountains, it will take us days—weeks, maybe. Only other way in is by following the Silver River upstream to its source at Heaven's Well. We can do that—if we're careful—but sooner or later we will have to pass right under Graymark. Walkers will see us coming for sure."

Foraker frowned. "There must be some way we can slip past them."

"There isn't," Slanter grunted. "I ought to know."

"Can we follow the river until we're close to Graymark and then cross into the mountains?" Helt asked, his big frame lowering onto a boulder. "Can we come at it from another direction?"

The Gnome shook his head. "Not from where we are. Graymark sits on a cliff shelf that overlooks the whole of the land about it—the Ravenshorn, the Silver River, everything. Rock is barren and open—no cover at all." He glanced at Stythys, who sat sullenly to one side. "That's why the lizards like it there so well. Nothing could ever creep up on them."

"Then we'll have to go in at night," Garet Jax said softly.

Again Slanter shook his head. "Break your neck if you try it. Cliffs are sheer drops all the way in and the paths are narrow and guarded. You'll never make it."

There was a long silence. "Well, what do you suggest?" Foraker asked finally.

Slanter shrugged. "I don't suggest anything. I got you this far; the rest is up to you. Maybe the boy can hide you with his magic again." He lifted his eyebrows at Jair. "How about it—can you sing for half the night?"

Jair flushed. "There must be some way to get past the guards, Slanter!"

"Oh, it's no problem for me." The Gnome sniffed. "But the rest of you might have some trouble."

"Helt has the night vision . . ." Foraker began thoughtfully.

But Garet Jax cut him short, beckoning to Stythys. "What suggestion would you make, Mwellret? This is your home. What would you do?"

Stythys let his lidded eyes narrow. "Findss your own way, little peopless. Sseekss another'ss foolissh aid. Leavess me be!"

Garet Jax studied him a moment, then walked over to him wordlessly, gray eyes so cold that Jair stepped back involuntarily. The Weapons Master's finger lifted and came to rest on the Mwellret's cloaked form.

"You seem to be telling me that you are no longer of any use to us," he said softly.

The Mwellret seemed to shrink back within the robes then, slitted eyes glittering with hate. But he held no power over Garet Jax. The Weapons Master stood where he was, waiting.

Then a low hiss escaped the lizard's mouth and its forked tongue licked out slowly. "Helpss you if you ssetss me free," he whispered. "Takess you where no one sseess you."

There was a long silence as the members of the little company glanced at one another suspiciously. "Don't trust him," Slanter said.

"Sstupid little Gnome cannot help you now," Stythys sneered. "Needss my help, little friendss. Knowss wayss that no other can passs."

"What ways do you know?" Garet Jax asked, his voice still soft.

But the Mwellret shook his head stubbornly. "Promisse firsst to sset me free, little peopless. Promisse."

The Weapons Master's lean face showed nothing of what he was thinking. "If you can get us into Graymark, you go free."

Slanter's face wrinkled with disapproval, and he spit into the earth. Standing with the others of the company, Jair waited for Stythys to say something more. But the Mwellret seemed to be thinking.

"You have our promise," Foraker interjected, a hint of impatience in his voice. "Now tell us what way we must go."

Stythys grinned, an evil, unpleasant smile that appeared to be almost a grimace. "Takess little peopless through Cavess of Night!"

"Why, you black . . . !" Slanter exploded in fury and came at the

Mwellret in a rush. Helt caught him about the waist as he tried to push past and hauled him back, the Gnome yelling and struggling as if he had gone mad. Stythys' laughter was a soft hiss as the members of the little company closed about Slanter to keep him back.

"What is it, Gnome?" Garet Jax demanded, one hand fastening about Slanter's arm. "Do you know of these caves?"

Slanter wrenched himself free of the Weapons Master, though Helt still maintained his grip. "The Caves of Night, Garet Jax!" the Gnome snarled. "Death bins for the mountain Gnomes since the time they fell under the rule of the lizards! Thousands of my people were given over to the Caves, thrown within and lost! Now this . . . monster would do likewise with us!"

Garet Jax turned quickly back to Stythys. The long knife appeared as if by magic in one hand. "Be careful of your answer this time, Mwellret," he advised softly.

But Stythys seemed unperturbed. "Liess from little Gnome. Cavess are passsagess into Graymark. Takess you beneath the mountainss, passt the walkerss. No one sseess."

"Is there truly passage in?" Foraker asked Slanter.

The Gnome went suddenly still, rigid in Helt's firm grip. "Doesn't matter if there is. The Caves are no place for the living. Miles of tunnels cut within the Ravenshorn, black as any pit and filled with Procks! Have you heard of Procks? They are living things, formed of magic older than the lands—magic from the old world, it's said. Living mouths of rock, all through the Caves. Everywhere you walk, the Procks are there in the cavern floor. One wrong step and they open, swallowing you up, closing about you, crushing you into . . ." He was shaking with fury. "That was the way the lizards disposed of the mountain Gnomes—pushed them into the Caves!"

"But the Caves do offer a passage through." Garet Jax turned Foraker's question into a statement of fact.

"A passage useless to us!" Slanter exploded once more. "We can't see to find our way! A dozen steps in and the Procks would have us!"

"Havess not me!" Stythys cut him short with a hiss. "Mine iss the ssecret of the Cavess of Night! Little peopless cannot passs, but my peopless know the way. Prockss cannot harm uss!"

They were all still then. Garet Jax stalked back to stand before the Mwellret. "The Caves of Night run to Graymark beneath the Ravenshorn—safe from the eyes of the walkers? And you can lead us through?"

"Yess, little friendss," Stythys rasped softly. "Takess you through."

Garet Jax turned to the others. For a moment no one spoke. Then Helt gave a quick nod. "There are only six of us. If we are to have any chance at all, we have to reach the fortress unseen."

Foraker and Edain Elessedil nodded as well. Jair looked at Slanter. "You're all fools!" the Gnome exclaimed bitterly. "Blind, stupid fools! You can't trust the lizards!"

There was an awkward silence. "You don't have to go any farther, if you don't want to, Slanter," Jair told him.

The Gnome stiffened. "I can take care of myself, boy!"

"I know. I just thought that . . ."

"Well, keep your thoughts to yourself!" the other cut him short. "As for not going any farther, you'd be better off taking that advice yourself. But you won't, I'm sure. So we'll all be fools together." He glanced darkly at Stythys. "But this fool will be keeping close watch, and if anything goes wrong in this, I'll be there to make certain the lizard doesn't see the end of it!"

Garet Jax turned back to Stythys. "You'll take us through then, Mwellret. Just remember—it will be as the Gnome says. What happens to us happens as well to you. Don't play games with us. If you try . . ."

Stythys' smile was quick and hard. "No gamess with you, little friendss."

They waited until nightfall to resume their journey, then slipped down out of the rocks above the Silver River and turned north into the mountains. Light from the gibbous moon and stars brightened the dark mass of the Ravenshorn as it rose about them, great barren peaks towering against the deep blue of the skyline. A worn pathway ran parallel to the riverbank through a scattering of trees and brush, and the little company from Culhaven followed it in until the forestland south was lost from view.

All night they walked, Helt and Slanter in the lead, the others following in cautious silence. The dark peaks drew steadily closer about the channel of the Silver River to wall them in. Save for the steady rush of the river, it was oddly silent within these peaks, a deep and pervasive stillness wrapping about the barren rock as if Mother Nature cradled her sleeping child. As the hours slipped away, Jair found himself growing increasingly uneasy with the silence, staring about at the massive walls of rock, peering into the shadows, and searching for something he could not see yet sensed was there, watching. The company chanced upon no other living creature that night, save for the great cliff birds that winged silently overhead across their nocturnal haunts, and still the Valeman sensed that they were not alone.

A part of this feeling sprang, he knew, from the continued presence of Stythys. Trailing, he could see the black figure of the Mwellret immediately in front of him. He could feel the creature's green eyes constantly shifting to find him, watching him, waiting. Like Slanter, he did not trust the Mwellret. Whatever promises Stythys might have made to aid them, Jair was certain that behind it all lay a ruthless determination to gain mastery over the Valeman's Elven magic. Whatever else happened, the creature meant to have that power. The certainty of it was frightening. The days he had spent walled away in the prisons at Dun Fee Aran haunted him like a specter so terrible that nothing could ever entirely banish it. It was Stythys who was responsible for that specter, and Stythys who would see life breathed back into it once more. While Jair now seemed free of the Mwellret, he could not shake the feeling that in some insidious way the creature had not lost control of him entirely.

But as night lengthened into early morning and weariness blunted the sharp edge of his doubt and his fear, Jair found himself thinking instead of Brin. In his mind he saw her face again as he had seen it twice so recently in the vision crystal—once ravaged as she experienced some unspeakable grief, once awestruck as she looked upon the twisted image of herself in the form of that shade. Glimpses only, those two brief visions, and nothing in either could tell the Valeman what had come to pass. Much had befallen his sister, he sensed—some of it frightening. An empty feeling opened within him as he thought of her, gone so long now from the Vale and from him, on a quest that the King of the Silver River had said would cause her to be lost. It was odd, but in a sense she seemed already lost to him, for the distance and the time that separated them was strangely magnified by the events that had transpired since last he had seen her. So much had happened, and he was so far from what and who he had been.

The emptiness grew suddenly into an ache. What if the King of the Silver River had misjudged him? What if he were to fail and Brin be lost to him? What if he were to come to her too late? He bit his lip against such thoughts, swearing fiercely that it would not be so. Deep ties bound him to her, brother to sister—ties of family, of a life shared, of knowledge, understanding, and caring, and most of all ties of love.

They marched on through the dark of early morning. With the first light of dawn, Stythys took the company up into the rocks. Moving away from the Silver River where it churned dark and sluggish in its channel, they passed deep into the cliffs. Trees and scrub disappeared and barren rock stretched away on all sides. Sunlight broke east above the mountain's edge, a brilliant, blinding gold that flared through the cracks and splits of the rock like fire. They climbed toward that fire until suddenly, unexpectedly, their ascent took them into a cliff's dark shadow and they stood at the entrance of an enormous cavern.

"Cavess of Night!" Stythys hissed softly.

The cavern yawned before the little company like an open maw, jagged rock split and twisted about the passageway like teeth. Wind blew down across the mountain heights, and it seemed as if it whistled at them from out of the Caves. Lengths of dull, whitish wood lay scattered about the entry as if stripped by age and weather. Jair looked closer and froze. The lengths of wood were bones, splintered, broken, and bleached of life.

Garet Jax placed himself before Stythys. "How are we to see anything in there, Mwellret? Have you torches?"

Stythys laughed, low and evil. "Torchess not burn in the Cavess, little friendss. Needss the magic!"

The Weapons Master glanced back momentarily at the cavern entrance. "And you have this magic?"

"Havess it, indeed," the other answered, arms folding within the robes, body swelling slightly. "Havess the Fire Wake! Liess within!"

"How long will this take?" Foraker asked uneasily. Dwarves were not fond of closed places, and he was less than anxious to venture into this one.

"Passs through Cavess quickly, little friendss," Stythys reassured rather too eagerly. "Takess you through in three hourss. Graymark waitss for uss."

The members of the little company glanced at one another and at the cavern entrance. "I'm telling you, you can't trust him!" Slanter warned yet again.

Garet Jax produced a length of rope and tied one end about himself and the other about Stythys. Testing the knots that bound them, he slipped free the long knife. "I will be closer to you than your shadow, Mwellret. Remember that. Now take us in there and show us your magic." Stythys started to turn, but the Weapons Master yanked him about. "Not too far in. Not until we see what you can do."

The Mwellret grimaced. "Sshowss little friendss. Come."

He slouched toward the monstrous black entry to the Caves, Garet Jax a step behind him and the rope about their waists binding them as one. Slanter followed them at once. After a moment's hesitation, the others of the little company also followed. Sunlight fell away as the shadows about them deepened, and they passed into the stone maw and the darkness beyond. For a few moments, the dawn's faint light aided them in their progress, silhouetting the shapes of walls, floors, jagged stalactites, and clustered rocks. Then quickly even that small light began to fail, and the blackness swallowed them.

Now they were practically blind, and their steps faltered to a ragged halt, the scraping of leather boots on rock a rough echo in the cavern's silence. They stood in a knot and listened to the echo die. The sound of dripping water reached their ears from somewhere deep within the blackness ahead. And from deeper still came the unpleasant sound of rock grating against rock.

"Ssee, little friendss," Stythys hissed suddenly. "All iss black in the Cavess!"

Jair glanced about uneasily, seeing almost nothing. Beside him, Edain Elessedil's lean Elven face was a faint shadow. There was a curious dampness to the air, a clinging wetness that stirred, though there was no wind, and seemed to wrap and twist about them. It had an unpleasant feel, and it smelled of rot. The Valeman wrinkled his nose in distaste, realizing suddenly that it was the same smell that had been present in Stythys' cell at Capaal.

"Callss now the Fire Wake!" the Mwellret rasped, startling the Valeman. "Lissten! Callss now the light!"

He cried out sharply, a kind of grim, hollow whistle that sounded of bone scraping, rough and tortured. The whistle rang through the blackness, carrying deep into the caverns. It echoed, long and mournful, and then the Mwellret repeated it a second time. Jair shivered. He was liking this whole idea of the Caves less and less.

Then abruptly the Fire Wake came. It flew at them through the darkness like a gathering of brilliant dust, bits of iridescent fire whirling and sailing on wind that wasn't there. Scattered through the blackness as it darted toward them, it drew together in a rush before the Mwellret's outstretched hand, tiny particles swirling in a tightened ball of light that cast its yellow glow outward to brighten the shadows of the Caves. The members of the little company stared in astonishment as the Fire Wake gathered and hung suspended before Stythys, and against their faces the strange glow flickered and danced.

"Magicss of my own, little friendss," Stythys hissed triumphantly. The snouted face turned to find Jair, green eyes gleaming in the whirling light. "Ssee how the Fire Wake obeyss?"

Garet Jax stepped quickly between them. "Point the way, Mwellret. Time slips from us."

"Sslipss quickly, it doess," the other rasped softly.

They pressed on into the darkness, the Fire Wake lighting their path forward. The walls of the Caves of Night rose higher about them, lost finally in shadowed gloom that even the Fire Wake could not penetrate. From out of the gloom, the sound of their footfalls fell back upon them in strange, sullen echoes. The smell grew worse the deeper in they went, turning foul the air they breathed and forcing them to take shortened breaths to avoid gagging. The passageway split and divided before them into dozens of corridors intertwined in an impossible maze of tunnels. But Stythys did not slow, choosing without hesitation the tunnel he would have them follow. The glowing dust of the Fire Wake danced on before him.

Time dragged past. Still the tunnels and passageways wore on, endless black openings in the rock. The smell grew even worse, and now the sound of grating rock was no longer distant, but unpleasantly close at hand. Then suddenly Stythys drew to a halt at an entrance leading into a particularly massive cavern, the Fire Wake dancing close as his hand lifted.

"Prockss!" he whispered.

He cast the Fire Wake from him with a snap of his wrist and it flew into the cave ahead, lighting the impenetrable blackness. The members of the little company from Culhaven stared in horror at what the light revealed. There, dotting the whole of the cavern floor, were hundreds of jagged, gaping fissures that opened and closed as if mouths engaged in some hideous chewing, the rock grinding hatefully in the dark. Sounds came from within those mouths—gurgling rushes, rendings, deep groaning belches of liquid and crushed stone.

"Shades!" they heard Helt whisper then. "The whole cave is alive!"

"Musst passs through," Stythys announced with an ugly grin. "Little peopless sstay closse."

They stayed practically on top of one another, pale faces gleaming with sweat in the light of the Fire Wake, eyes fixed on the cavern floor before them. Again Stythys led, Garet Jax a step behind, Slanter, Jair, Edain Elessedil, and Helt in a line following, and Foraker trailing. They made their way in a slow, twisting path into the midst of the Procks, stepping where the Fire Wake showed the black mouths not to be, their ears and minds filled with the sounds those terrible mouths made. The Procks opened and closed all about them as if waiting to be fed, hungry animals that sensed the presence of food. At times they closed so tightly that they seemed a part of the cavern floor that was solid, no more than thin lines in the roughened stone. Yet they could open quickly, snatching away the seemingly safe ground offered, ready to swallow anything that ventured above. But each time one lay hidden on the path ahead, the Fire Wake showed the members of the company where it waited and guided them carefully past.

They passed from that first cavern into another and after that into another. Still the Procks were with them, dotting the floor of every cave and passageway so that none was safe to traverse. They moved slowly now, and the minutes dragged away in a seemingly endless passage of time. Weariness set in as their concentration intensified, each knowing that a single misstep would be the last. All the while the Procks opened and closed about them, grinding in gleeful anticipation.

"There is no end to this maze!" Edain Elessedil whispered once in frustration to Jair.

The Valeman nodded in helpless agreement. Foraker pressed close behind now, and Helt brought up the rear. The Dwarf's bearded face was soaked with sweat and his hard eyes were glittering.

A concealed Prock opened suddenly, almost at Jair's feet, its black maw yawning. Frantically, the Valeman jerked away, stumbling into Slanter. The Prock had been right next to him and he hadn't seen it! He fought back against the wave of disgust and fear that swept over him and set his jaw determinedly. It would not be much longer. They would be clear soon.

But then, as they were passing through yet another cavern, through yet another maze of Procks, Stythys did what Slanter had warned all along he would do. It happened so quickly that not even Garet Jax had time to act. One moment they were all together, easing past the hideously grinding fissures; in the next, the Mwellret's hand flicked suddenly backward, casting the Fire Wake directly into their faces. It came at them in a flare of brilliant light, scattering. Instinctively they turned away, shielding their eyes, and in that instant Stythys moved. He leaped past Garet Jax and Slanter to where Jair crouched. Snatching the Valeman about the waist with one powerful arm, the lizard creature slipped a wicked-looking knife from somewhere beneath the dark robes where he had kept it hidden and pressed it close against his captive's throat.

"Sstay back, little friendss!" The Mwellret hissed, turning to face them as the Fire Wake again gathered before him.

No one moved. Garet Jax crouched barely two yards away, a black shadow poised to spring. The length of rope still bound him to the Mwellret. Stythys kept the Valeman between them, the knife glittering in the half-light.

"Foolissh little peopless!" the monster rasped. "Thinkss to usse me againsst my will! Sseess now what liess ahead for you?"

"I told you he couldn't be trusted!" Slanter cried out in fury.

He started forward, but a warning hiss from the Mwellret brought him to a halt instantly. Behind him, the others of the little company stood frozen in a tight circle—Helt, Foraker and Edain Elessedil. All about them the Procks continued to grind steadily, stone grating on stone.

Garet Jax shifted from the crouch, gray eyes so cold that Stythys' arm tightened further about Jair. "Let the Valeman go, Mwellret," the Weapons Master said softly.

The blade of the knife pressed closer against Jair's throat. Jair swallowed and tried to shrink away from it. Then his eyes met those of Garet Jax. The Weapons Master was fast—faster than anyone. It was when he had confronted the Gnome Hunters who had taken Jair prisoner in the Black Oaks that he had first shown how fast he could be. And the same look he had worn then was now in the lean, hard face—a calm, inscrutable look where only the eyes spoke of the death that was promised.

Jair breathed a deep, slow breath. Garet Jax was close enough. But the knife at the Valeman's throat was closer still.

"Magicss belong to uss, not to little peopless!" Stythys rasped in a quick, anxious whisper. "Magicss to sstand againsst the walkerss! Little peopless cannot usse it, cannot usse uss! Sstupid little peopless! Crussh you like bugss!"

"Let the Valeman go!" Garet Jax repeated.

The Fire Wake danced and glimmered before the Mwellret, a whirling cloud of shimmering dust. Stythys' green eyes drew into slits of hatred, and he laughed softly.

"Letss you go insstead, black one!" he snapped. He glanced quickly at Slanter. "You, little Gnome! Cut loosse thiss tie that bindss me to him!"

Slanter looked at Garet Jax, then looked back again. His eyes shifted for just an instant to find Jair's. The Valeman read there what was expected of him. If he hoped to get out of this alive, he was going to have to do something to help.

Slowly Slanter came forward, a step at a time, slipping the long knife from his belt. No one else moved. Jair steadied himself, fighting back against the fear and repulsion that coursed through him. Slanter came closer, another step. One hand reached for the slackened rope that bound the Mwellret to Garet Jax. Jair went perfectly still. One chance was all he would get. Slanter's hand closed about the rope and the knife lifted to the hemp.

Then Jair sang—a quick, sharp cry that Slanter recognized at once. Dozens of gray, hairy spiders clustered on Stythys, crawling over the arm that held the knife to Jair's throat. The Mwellret jerked his arm away with a howl, beating it wildly against his robes in an effort to dislodge the things that clung to it. Abruptly the Fire Wake scattered in a wide circle, taking back the light and throwing everything into shadow.

Cat-quick, Slanter threw himself on Stythys, burying his long knife in the arm that gripped Jair about his waist. That arm, too, jerked away, and Jair tumbled to the roughened stone, free again. Shouts rose from the others of the little company as they charged forward to pull him clear. Stythys flew backward onto the cavern floor, Slanter clinging to him, Garet Jax leaping after. A long knife appeared in the Weapon Master's hand as he sought to cut through the rope that bound him to the Mwellret. But he was yanked off balance as the rope snapped taut. He lost his footing and skidded to his knees.

"Slanter!" Jair screamed.

The Gnome and the Mwellret stumbled through the maze of Procks, clawing wildly at each other. The Fire Wake continued to rise as Stythys' control over it slipped away, and the entire cavern was rapidly falling into shadow. Another few seconds and no one would be able to see anything.

"Gnome!" Foraker cried in warning, breaking away from the others to where the two forms struggled.

But Garet Jax was quicker. He leaped like a shadow from the gloom, his footing regained. The long knife severed the rope about his waist with a single cut. Procks grated and snapped in response to the sounds above, dark maws working madly. Stythys and Slanter were directly in their midst, squirming closer, slipping . . .

And then Garet Jax reached them, flinging himself across the remaining space that separated them, his iron grip fastening on Slanter's leg. With a yank, he tore the Gnome free from Stythys' claws. Clothing shredded and ripped, and a frightful hiss burst from Stythys' throat.

The Mwellret tumbled backward, thrown off balance. Beneath him, a Prock's black maw gaped open. The lizard seemed to hang suspended for an instant, clawed fingers grasping at the air. Then he fell, disappearing from sight. The Prock closed and there was a sudden shriek. Then the black fissure began to grind, a terrible crunching, and the whole of the cavern was filled with the dreadful sound.

Instantly the Fire Wake scattered and fled back into the gloom, taking with it the precious light. The Caves of Night were plunged into darkness once more.

It was several minutes before anyone moved again. They crouched where they were in the blackness, waiting for their eyes to adjust to the absence of light, listening to the sounds of the Procks grinding all about them. When it quickly became apparent that there was not even the smallest amount of light to allow their eyes to adjust, Elb Foraker called out to the others and asked them to respond. One by one, they called back, faceless voices in the impenetrable dark. All were there.

But they knew that they were not likely to be there for long. The Fire Wake was gone, the light they so desperately needed to show them the path forward. Without it, they were blind. They must attempt to move through the maze of Procks using little more than instinct.

"Hopeless," Foraker announced at once. "Without light, we cannot tell where the passages open before us and we cannot choose our path. Even if we escape the Procks, we will wander in these Caves forever."

There was a hint of fear in the Dwarf's voice that Jair had never heard before. "There has to be a way," he murmured quietly, as much to himself as to the others.

"Helt, can you use the night vision?" Edain Elessedil asked hopefully. "Can you see to find a way through this darkness?"

But the giant Borderman could not. Even the night vision must have some light to aid it, he explained gently. In the absence of all light, the night vision was useless.

They were quiet then for a time, bereft it seemed of even the smallest hope. In the darkness, Jair could hear Slanter's rough voice

admonishing Garet Jax that he should have known better than to trust the lizard, as Slanter had told him. Jair listened and seemed to hear Brin speaking to him as well, telling him that he, too, should have listened. He brushed the whisper of her voice from his mind, thinking as he did so that, if the wishsong served him as it did her, he could call back the Fire Wake. But his song was only illusion, a pretense of what was real.

Then he thought of the vision crystal.

Calling excitedly to the others, he fumbled through his clothing until he found it, still tucked safely away, dangling from its silver chain, and he brought it forth into the cup of his hands. The crystal would give them light—all the light that was needed! With the crystal and Helt's night vision to guide them, they would yet get clear of these Caves!

Barely able to suppress the excitement that coursed through him, he sang to the gift of the King of the Silver River and called forth the magic. The brilliant light sprang up, flooding the cavern with its glow. Brin Ohmsford's face appeared within it, dark, beautiful, and worn, rising up before them in the gloom of the Caves of Night like some wraith come forth from another world. Grayness surrounded the Valegirl, gloom all too reminiscent of their own, close and stifling. Wherever she was as she looked past them to her own future, it was no less hostile a place than their own.

Cautiously, they rejoined one another, gathering about the light of the crystal. Joining hands as children might on a walk through some dark place, they began to move forward through the maze of Procks. Jair led, the light of the vision crystal sustained by his voice, scattering the shadows before them. Helt followed a step behind, sharp eyes scanning the cavern floor for where the Procks lay hidden. Behind them, the others followed.

They passed from that cavern into another, but this new cavern was smaller and the proper choice of passage less difficult to discern. Jair's song lifted, clear, strong, and filled with certainty. He knew now that they were going to escape these Caves, and it was because of Brin. He wanted to cry out in thanks to her image as it floated before him. How strange that she should come like this to save them!

Closing his ears to the sounds of the Procks as they grated stone on stone, closing his mind to everything but the light and the vision of his sister's face as it hung suspended before him, he gave himself over to the wishsong's magic and passed on through the darkness.

XXXVIII

I⊤ TOOK THE REMAINDER OF THE NIGHT FOR BRIN AND HER rescuers to work their way clear of Olden Moor. They would not have done so even then without Whisper to guide them, but the big moor cat was at home in the bottomland, and neither the mist nor the shapeless, mired earth gave him pause. Choosing their pathway with instincts that the moor could not deceive, he led them south toward the dark wall of the Ravenshorn.

"We would have lost you to the moor without Whisper," Kimber explained to the Valegirl after they had found her again and begun their march south. "It was Whisper who tracked you through the mist. He is not misled by appearances, and nothing of the moor can fool him. Still, it was fortunate that we reached you when we did, Brin. You must stay close to us after this."

Brin accepted the well-intentioned rebuke without comment. There was no point in discussing the matter further. Her decision to leave them before they reached the Maelmord was already made. It merely remained for her to find the right opportunity to do so. Her reasons were simple. The task entrusted to her by Allanon was to penetrate the forest barrier that protected the Ildatch and to see to it that the book of dark magic was destroyed. She would do this by pitting the magic of the wishsong against the magic of the Mael-mord. Once she had wondered if such a thing were even possible. Now she wondered not if such a thing possible, but if such a thing would prove cataclysmic. The power of the magics unleashed would be awesome—a match not of white magic against dark as she had once envisioned, but a match of magics equally dark in tone and effect. The Maelmord was created to destroy. But the wishsong, too, could destroy, and now Brin knew that not only would the potential for such destruction always be there, but that she could not be assured of being able to control it. She might vow to do so. She might swear her strongest oath. But she could never be certain that she could keep that oath—not anymore, unless she forbore all use of the wishsong. She could accept the risk to herself; she had done that long ago when she had decided to come on this quest. But she could not accept the risk to those who traveled with her.

She must leave them. Whatever fate she was to suffer when she entered the Maelmord, her companions must not be there to share it with her. You go to your death, Brin of Shannara, the Grimpond had warned. You carry within you the seeds of that destruction. Perhaps that was so. Perhaps those seeds were carried in the magic of the wishsong. But one thing was certain. The others of the little company had risked themselves enough for her already. She would not have them do so again.

She thought about it all night as she trudged on wearily through the bottomland, remembering what she had felt in the times she had used the wishsong's magic. The hours slipped past, and the Werebeasts did not come to haunt them again that night. But in the mind of the Valegirl, there were demons of another sort.

By dawn the little company was clear of Olden Moor and found itself in the foothills bordering the southern mountains of the Ravenshorn. Wearied from their long march up from Hearthstone and the events of the night past and wary of traveling farther in daylight when they might easily be seen, the five took refuge in a small copse of pine in a lea between two ridgelines and fell asleep.

They resumed their journey with the return of nightfall, traveling east now, following the high wall of the mountains where it brushed up against the moor. Trailers of mist wound through the trees of the forested lower slopes, a spider's web across the pathway as the travelers passed silently by. The mountain peaks of the Ravenshorn were huge and stark, barren rock lifting out of the forestland to etch sharply against the sky. It was an empty, still night, and the whole of the land about seemed stripped of life. Shadows lay across the cliffs, forests, and the moor's deep mists. In their pooling darkness nothing moved.

They rested at midnight, an uneasy pause where they found themselves listening to the silence as they rubbed aching muscles and tightened boot straps. It was then that Cogline chose to talk about his magic.

"Magic it is, too," he whispered cautiously to Brin and Rone, almost as if he feared that someone might be listening. "Magic of a different sort than that wielded by the walkers, though—born not of their time nor the time when Elves and faerie folk had the power, but of the time between!"

He bent forward, eyes sharp and accusing. "Thought I knew nothing of the old world, didn't you, girl?" he asked Brin. "Well, I have the teachings of the old world, too—passed down to me by my ancestors. Not Druids, no. But teachers, girl—teachers! Theirs was the lore of the world that existed when the Great Wars caused such destruction to mankind!"

"Grandfather," Kimber Boh cautioned gently. "Just explain it to them."

"Humphh!" Cogline grunted testily. "Explain it, she says! What is it that you think I do, girl?" His forehead furrowed. "Earth power! That's the magic I wield! Not the magic of words and spells—no, not that magic! Power born of the elements that comprise the ground on which we walk, outlanders. That is the earth power. Bits and pieces of ores and powders and mixings that can be seen by the eye and felt by the hand. Chemics, they were once called. Developed by skills of a different sort than the simple ones we use now in the Four Lands. Most of the knowledge was lost with the old world. But a little—just a little—was saved. And it is mine to use."

"This is what you carry in those pouches?" Rone asked. "This is what you used to make those fires explode?"

"Ha-ha!" Cogline laughed softly. "They do that and much more, Southlander. Fires can be exploded, earth turned to mud, air to choking dust, flesh to stone! I have potions for all and dozens more. Mix and match, a bit of this and a bit of that!" He laughed again. "I'll show the walkers power they haven't seen before!"

Rone shook his head doubtfully. "Spider Gnomes are one thing; the Mord Wraiths are something else again. A finger points at you and you are reduced to ash. The sword I carry, infused with the Druid magic, is the only protection against those black things."

"Bah!" Cogline spit. "You'd best look to me for your protection— you and the girl!"

Rone began to phrase a sharp retort, then thought better of it and simply shrugged. "If we come up against the walkers, we shall both need to offer Brin whatever protection we can."

He glanced at the Valegirl for confirmation, and she smiled agreeably. It cost her nothing to do so. She already knew that neither of them would be with her, in any case.

She pondered for a time what Cogline had told them. It troubled her that any part of the old skills should have survived the holocaust of the Great Wars. She did not like to think it possible that such awesome power could come again into the world. It was bad enough that the magic of the world of faerie had been reborn through the misguided efforts of that handful of rebel Druids in the Councils of Paranor. But to be faced with the prospect that the knowledge of power and energy might again be pursued was even more unsettling. Almost all of the learning that had gone into that knowledge had been lost with the destruction of the old world. What little had survived, the Druids had locked away again. Yet here was this old man, half-crazed and as wild as the wilderness in which he lived, in possession of at least a portion of that learning— a special kind of magic that he had resolved was now his own.

She shook her head. Perhaps it was inevitable that all learning, whether born of good or bad intention, whether used to give life or to take life away, must come to light at some point in time. Perhaps it was true both of skill and of magic—one born of the world of men, the other of the world of faerie. Perhaps both must surface periodically in the stream of time, then disappear again, then surface once more, and so on forever.

But a return now of the knowledge of energy and power, when the last of the Druids was gone . . . ?

Still, Cogline was an old man and his knowledge was limited. When he died, perhaps the knowledge would die with him and be lost again—for a time, at least.

And so, too, perhaps it would be with her magic.

They walked east for the remainder of the night, picking their way through the thinning forestland. Ahead, the wall of the Ravenshorn began to curve back toward them, turning north into the wilderness of the deep Anar. It rose up from out of the night, a towering, dark band of shadow. Olden Moor dropped away behind them, and only the thin green line of the foothills separated them from the mountain heights. A deeper silence seemed to settle over the land. It was in the crook of the mountains where they turned north, Brin knew, that Graymark and the Maelmord lay concealed.

And there I must find a way to be free of the others, she thought. There, I must go on alone.

The first trailers of sunrise began to slip into view beyond the mountain wall. Slowly the skies lightened, turning from deep blue to gray, from gray to silver, and from silver to rose and gold. Shadows fled away into the receding night, and the broad sweep of the land began to etch itself out of the dark. The trees grew visible first, leaves, crooked limbs, and roughened trunks drawn and colored by the light; then rocks, scrub, and barren earth, from foothills to bottomland, took form. For a time, the shadow of the mountains lingered, a wall against the light, lost in darkness not yet faded. But finally that, too, gave way to the sunrise, and the light spilled down over the rim of the peaks to reveal the awesome face of the Ravenshorn.

It was a stark and ugly face—a face that had been ravaged by time and the elements and by the poison of the dark magic sown within it. Where the mountains curved north into the wilderness, the rock had been bleached and worn—as if the life in it had been peeled away like skin to leave only bone. It rose up against the skyline, thousands of feet above them, a wall of cliffs and ragged defiles burdened with the weight of ages gone and horrors endured. On the hard, gray emptiness, nothing moved.

Brin lifted her face momentarily as the wind brushed past. Her nose wrinkled in distaste. An unpleasant smell rose up from somewhere ahead.

"Graymark's sewers." Cogline spit, ferret eyes darting. "We're close now."

Kimber slipped ahead of them to where Whisper sniffed tentatively at the odorous morning air. Bending close to the great cat, she spoke softly in his ear—just a word—and the beast nuzzled her face gently.

She turned back to them. "Quickly now, before it gets any lighter—Whisper will show us the way."

They hurried forward through the new light and receding shadow, following the moor cat as he guided them along the twist of the foothills to where the Ravenshorn bent north. Trees and scrub fell away completely, grasses turned sparse and wintry, and the earth gave way to crushed stone and shelf rock. The smell grew steadily worse, a rank and fetid odor that smothered even the freshness of the new day's birthing. Brin found herself choking for breath. How much worse would it be once they had found their way into the sewers?

Then the hills dropped away sharply before them into a deep valley that was lost in the shadow of the mountain wall. There, sullen and still, lay a dark lake of stagnant water, fed by a stream that seeped down through the rocks from a broad, blackened hole.

Whisper padded to a halt, Kimber at his side. "There." She pointed. "The sewers."

Brin's eyes strayed upward along the ragged line of the peaks, upward thousands of feet to where the mountain wall cut its jagged edge against the golden dawn sky. There, still hidden from view, lay Graymark, the Maelmord, and the Ildatch.

She swallowed against the smell of the sewers. There, too, lay the fate that was to be hers. Her smile was hard. She must go to meet it.

At the entrance to the sewers, Cogline unveiled a bit more of his magic. From a sealed packet buried in one of the pouches he wore strapped to his waist, he produced an ointment that, when rubbed into the nostrils, deadened the stench of the sewers' poisonous discharge. A small magic, he claimed. Though the smell could not be obliterated entirely, it nevertheless could be made tolerable. Fashioning short-handled brands from pieces of deadwood, he dipped the ends into the contents of a second pouch and they emerged covered with a silver substance that glowed like oil lamps when introduced into the cavern's darkness—even in the absence of any fire.

"Just a little more of my magic, outlanders." He chuckled as they stared wonderingly at the flameless torches. "Chemicals, remember? Something the walkers don't know anything about. And I've a few more surprises. You'll see."

Rone frowned doubtfully and shook his head. Brin said nothing, but decided quickly that she would be just as happy if the opportunity to test those surprises never arose.

Torches in hand, the little company moved out of the dawn light into the tunnel darkness of the sewers. The passageways were wide and deep, the liquid poison discharged from the halls of Graymark and the Maelmord flowing down a worn, rutted channel that cut through the tunnel floor. To either side of where the sewage flowed, there were stone walkways that offered footing broad enough for the company to pass upon. Whisper led the way, luminous eyes blinking in sleepy reflection against the light of the torches, splayed feet padding soundlessly on the stone. Cogline followed with Kimber, and Brin and Rone brought up the rear.

They walked for a long time. Brin lost track of how long a time it was, her concentration divided between picking her way through the half-light and thinking of her promise to find a way to go down into the Maelmord without the others. The sewer wound upward through the mountain rock, twisting and turning like a coiled snake. The stench permeating the passage was almost unbearable, even with the aid of the repellant that Cogline had provided to ease their breathing difficulties. From time to time, sudden drafts of cold air blew down from above them, clearing the smell of the sewage— wind from the peaks into which they climbed. But the drafts of fresh air were few and brief, and the smells of the sewers were always quick to return.

The morning slipped away, the hours lost in the endless spiral of their ascent. Once they came upon a massive iron grate that had been dropped across the passageway to prevent anything larger than a rat from entering. Rone reached for his sword, but a sharp word from Cogline brought him up short. A gleeful cackle breaking from his lips, the old man motioned them back, then produced yet another pouch—this one containing an odd, blackish powder laced with something that looked to be soot. Dabbing the powder on the bars of the grate where they joined the rock, he touched the treated spots quickly with the flameless torch and the powder flared a brilliant white. When the light died away, the bars had been eaten completely through. At a stiff nudge, the entire grate collapsed onto the cavern floor. The company went on.

No one spoke as they climbed. Instead, they listened for the sound of the enemy that waited somewhere above—the walkers and the things that served them. They heard nothing of these, but there were other sounds that echoed through the empty passageways— sounds that came from far above and were not immediately identifiable. There were clunks and thuds, as if heavy bodies had fallen, scrapes and scratchings, a low howling, as if a hard wind slipped down through the tunnels from the mountain peaks, and a hissing, as if steam escaped some fissure in the earth. These distant sounds filled and thus magnified the otherwise utter silence of the sewers. Brin found herself searching for a pattern to the sounds, but there was none—except, perhaps, for the hissing, which lifted and fell with a peculiar regularity. It reminded Brin, unpleasantly, of the Grimpond's rise from the lake and the mist.

I must find a way to go on alone, she thought one time more. I must do so soon.

Tunnels came and went, and the climb wore on. The air within the sewers had grown steadily warmer with the passing of the day, and beneath their cloaks and tunics the members of the little company were sweating freely. A kind of peculiar mist had begun to filter down through the corridors, clinging and grimy, filled with the sewers' smell. They brushed at it distastefully, but it drifted after them, closed about them, and would not be moved away. It grew thicker as the climb progressed, and soon they were having difficulty seeing farther than a dozen feet ahead.

Then abruptly the mist and gloom cleared before them, and they stood upon a shelf of rock that overlooked an immense chasm. Down into the mountain's core the chasm dropped, disappearing into utter blackness. The members of the little company glanced uneasily at one another. To their right, the passageway curved upward into the rock, following the trench that carried the sewage from the Mord Wraith citadel. To their left, the passageway ran downward a short distance to a slender stone bridge barely a yard in width that arched across the chasm to a darkened tunnel that bore into the far cliff face.

"Which way now?" Rone muttered softly, almost as if asking himself.

Left, Brin thought at once. Left, across the chasm. She did not understand why, yet she knew instinctively that this was the path she must choose.

"The sewers are the way." Cogline was looking at her. "That's what the Grimpond said, wasn't it, girl?"

Brin found herself unable to speak. "Brin?" Kimber called to her softly.

"Yes," she replied finally. "Yes, that is the way."

They turned right along the shelf, following it up along the sewage channel, trudging back again into the blackness. Brin's mind raced. This isn't the way, she thought. Why did I say it was? She took a sudden gulp of air, forcing her thoughts to slow. What she sought was back the way they had come, back across the stone bridge. The Maelmord was back that way—she could sense it. Why, then, had she . . . ?

She caught herself roughly, the question answered almost as quickly as it was asked. Because this was where she would leave them, of course. This was the opportunity that she had looked for since Olden Moor. This was how it must be. The wishsong would aid her—a small deceit, a little lie. She sucked in her breath sharply at the thought. Even though it would betray their trust in her, she must do it.

Softly, gently, she began to hum, building the wishsong a stone at a time into a wall of non-seeing, creating in her place and in the minds of her companions an image of herself. Then abruptly she stepped away from her own ghost, flattened herself against the stone wall of the passageway, and watched the others walk past.

The illusion would only last a few minutes, she knew. She sped back down the sewer tunnel, following the cut and weave of the rock. The sound of her breathing was ragged in her ears. She reached the shelf, hastened to where it narrowed, and turned onto the stone bridge. The chasm yawned blackly before her. A step at a time, she inched out onto the bridge, picking her pathway across. There was silence in the gloom and mist that swirled about, yet she felt somehow that she was not alone. Her mind hardened against the brief surge of fear and doubt, and she withdrew deep into herself, passionless and cold. Nothing could be allowed to touch her.

At last she was across the bridge. She stood within the entrance to this new tunnel for a moment and let the feeling return. A brief thought of Rone and the others passed through her mind and disappeared. She had used the wishsong against them now as well, she thought bitterly. And though it might have been necessary, it hurt her deeply to have done so.

Then she wheeled abruptly toward the stone bridge, pitched the wishsong to a quick, hard shriek and sang. The sound echoed in fury through the black, and the bridge exploded into fragments and dropped away into the chasm.

Now there could be no going back.

She turned into the tunnel and disappeared.

The sound of the shriek penetrated up into the sewer tunnel where the others of the little company still picked their way through the gloom.

"Shades! What was that?" Rone cried.

There was a moment's silence as the echo died away. "Brin—it was Brin," Kimber whispered in reply.

Rone stared. No, Brin was right next to him . . .

Abruptly, the image the Valegirl had created in their minds faded into nothingness. Cogline swore softly and stamped his foot.

"What has she done . . . ?" the highlander stammered in confusion, unable to finish the thought.

Kimber was at his side, her face intense. "She has done what she has wanted to do from the beginning, I think. She has left us and gone on alone. She said before that she did not want any of us to go with her; now she has made certain that we do not."

"For cat's sake!" Rone was appalled. "Doesn't she understand how dangerous . . . ?"

"She understands everything," the girl cut him short, pushing past him down the tunnel's passage. "I should have realized before that she would do this. We must hurry if we are to catch up with her. Whisper, track!"

The big moor cat leaped ahead effortlessly, gliding back down the sewer tunnel into the shadows. The three humans hurried after, slipping and stumbling through the mist and gloom. Rone Leah was angry and frightened at the same time. Why would Brin do this? He did not understand.

Then abruptly they were back upon the stone shelf, staring out across the chasm to where the bridge fell away into the dark, broken at its center.

"There, you see, she's used the magic!" Cogline snapped.

Wordlessly, Rone hurried forward, stepping out onto the jagged remnant of the bridge. Twenty feet away, the other end jutted from the cliff face. He could make that jump, he thought suddenly. It was a long way over, but he could make it. At least he must try . . .

"No, Rone Leah." Kimber pulled him back from the precipice, reading at once his intentions. Her grip on his arm was surprisingly strong. "You must not be foolish. You cannot jump so far."

"I can't leave her again," he insisted stubbornly. "Not again."

The girl nodded solemnly. "I care for her, too." She turned. "Whisper!" The moor cat padded up to her, whiskered face rubbing her own. Softly she spoke to the cat, stroking him behind his ears. Then she stepped away. "Track, Whisper!" she commanded.

Wheeling, the moor cat darted onto the bridge, gathered himself and sprang into the air. He cleared the chasm effortlessly, landed on the far end of the shattered bridge, and disappeared into the darkened tunnel beyond.

There was concern reflected in Kimber Boh's young face. She had not wanted to separate herself from the cat, but Brin might have greater need of him than she, and the Valegirl was her friend. "Guard well," she whispered after.

Then she looked back again at Rone. "Now let us also try to find a way to reach Brin Ohmsford."

XXXIX

---◆---

IT WAS NEARLY NOON OF THE SAME DAY WHEN JAIR AND HIS companions emerged once more from the Caves of Night and found themselves on a broad shelf of rock overlooking a deep canyon between the mountain peaks of the Ravenshorn. The peaks were so close that they shut away all but a narrow strip of blue sky far above where the company stood, lost in a gathering of shadows. The shelf ran left along the mountain face for several hundred yards and then disappeared again into a cut in the cliffs.

The Valeman stared upward wearily, following the lift of the mountains against the noonday sky. He was exhausted—drained physically and emotionally. He still clutched the vision crystal in one hand, its silver chain dragging against the shelf rock. They had been in the Caves since sunrise. For a good part of that time, it had been necessary to use the wishsong to project the light of the crystal so that they might find their way clear. It had taken every ounce of strength and every bit of concentration that he could muster to do that. In his mind, he could still hear the sound of the Procks, stone grating on stone, a whisper now of what had been left behind in the darkness of the caves. In his mind, he could also still hear Stythys' final scream.

"Let's not stand where we can be so easily seen," Garet Jax said softly and motioned him left.

Slanter caught up with them, glancing about doubtfully. "I'm not sure this is the way, Weapons Master."

Garet Jax did not turn. "How many other ways do you see?"

Silently, the members of the little company edged down along the rock shelf to the cut in the cliff face. A narrow defile stretched away before them, twisting into the rock and disappearing into shadow. They moved through it in a line, their eyes darting upward guardedly along its roughened walls. A draft of icy air brushed against them, blown down from the heights. Jair shivered with its touch. Numbed by the horrors of the Caves, he welcomed even this unpleasant feeling. He could sense that they were now close to Graymark's walls. Graymark, the Maelmord, Heaven's Well were all near at hand. His quest was almost ended, the long journey done. He felt a strange compulsion to laugh and cry at the same time, but the weariness and the ache in his body would let him do neither.

The defile wound on, slipping deeper into the rock. His mind wandered. Where was Brin? The crystal had shown them her face. But it had shown them nothing of where she might be. Gray mist and gloom had surrounded her in a dreary and desolate place. A passageway, perhaps, similar to their own? Was she, too, within these mountains?

"You must reach Heaven's Well before she reaches the Maelmord," the King of the Silver River had warned. "You must be there for her."

He stumbled and nearly went down, his concentration drifting from the task at hand. He righted himself hastily and shoved the vision crystal back into his tunic front.

"Watch yourself," Edain Elessedil whispered at his elbow. Jair nodded and went on.

Anticipation began to build within him. An entire army of Gnomes guarded Graymark's battlements and watchtowers. Mord Wraiths walked its halls. Things darker still might lie in wait within, sentinels against intruders like themselves. Their company was but six in number. What hope had they against so many and such power? Little, it would appear; and yet, while it should have seemed altogether hopeless to the Valeman, it did not. Perhaps it was the faith that the King of the Silver River had shown in choosing him for this quest—a demonstration of the old man's belief that he could somehow find a way to succeed. Perhaps it was his own determination, a strength of will that would not let him fail.

He shook his head gently. Perhaps. But it was also the character of the five men who had elected to come with him and had sustained him. It was Garet Jax, Slanter, Foraker, Edain Elessedil and Helt—come from the Four Lands to this final, terrible confrontation, an enigmatic mixture of strength and courage. Two trackers, a hunter, a Weapons Master, and a Prince of the Elves had traveled different life-paths to reach this day, and none might live to see its end. But here they were. Their bonding to Jair and to the trust that had been given him transcended the caution and reason that might otherwise have caused them to give greater consideration to the obvious danger to their own lives. It was so even with Slanter. The Gnome had made his choice at Capaal when he had turned his back on a chance to flee north to the borderlands and the life from which he had strayed. All were committed, and in that commitment there was a unity that seemed almost indomitable. Jair knew little of his companions. Yet one thing he knew with certainty, and it was enough: whatever was to happen to him this day, these five would stand by him.

Perhaps that was why he was not afraid.

The defile widened again before them and sunlight streamed down from a new broadened skyline. Garet Jax slowed, then dropped into a crouch and eased ahead. One lean arm beckoned them after. Hunched down against the rocks, they crept forward until they were beside him.

"There," he whispered, pointing.

It was Graymark. Jair knew it instantly without need of being told. The fortress sat high upon a cliff face that curved away before them. It rested upon a broad shelf of rock that jutted sharply outward against the noonday sky. It was a grim and massive thing. Battlements, towers, and parapets rose upward from stone block walls hundreds of feet high, like spikes and blunted axe-heads reaching into the cloudless blue. No pennants flew from the tower standards; no colors draped the casements. The whole of the fortress had a flat and wintry cast to it even in the brilliant light of the sun; the stone had a sullen, ashen tone. What windows there were were small, pinched openings covered over with bars and wooden shutters. A single narrow roadway wound upward against the mountainside— little more than a ledge cut into the rock—ending at a pair of tall, ironbound gates that fronted the complex. The gates stood closed.

They studied the stronghold wordlessly. There was no sign of anyone. Nothing moved.

Then Jair caught sight of the Croagh. He could see only pieces of it lifting from behind Graymark, a rugged arch of stone that seemed almost a part of the towers and the parapets of the complex. Curling back upon itself like some suspended stairway, it threaded its way skyward until it ended high upon a solitary peak that rose above those surrounding it.

Jair caught Slanter's arm and pointed to the peak and the slender ribbon of stones that joined to it.

"Yes, boy—the Croagh and Heaven's Well." The Gnome nodded. "All that the King of the Silver River has sent you to find."

"And the Maelmord?" Jair asked quickly.

Slanter shook his head. "On the other side of the fortress, down within a ring of cliffs. There the Croagh begins its climb, wrapping about Graymark as it passes, then rising on."

They were silent again, their eyes fixed on the fortress. "Doesn't seem to be anyone in there," Helt murmured after a moment.

"What's in there wants you to think exactly that," Slanter observed dryly, easing back on his heels. "Besides, the walkers prefer the dark. They rest for the most part during the day and move about at night. Even the Gnomes that serve them here soon begin to live like that and don't show themselves when it's light. But make no mistake. They're in there, Borderman—walkers and Gnomes both. And a few other things as well."

Garet Jax was studying the mountain trail that wound upward to the fortress entrance. "That is the way they would expect us to come." He spoke more to himself than to the others. "On the trail or by scaling the cliffs." He glanced left to where the shelf they stood upon curved down among the rocks and disappeared back into the mountains through a narrow tunnel. "Maybe not this way, though."

Slanter touched his arm. "The tunnel connects to a series of passageways that leads upward into the fortress cellars. That's how we'll go."

"Guarded?"

Slanter shrugged.

"I'd feel better if we could find a way to climb the Croagh from out here," Foraker muttered. "I've seen enough of caverns and tunnels."

The Gnome shook his head. "Can't be done. Only way to reach the Croagh is through Graymark—right through the walkers and whatever serves them."

Foraker grunted. "What do you think, Garet?"

Garet Jax continued to study the fortress and the cliffs about it. His lean face was expressionless. "Do you know the way well enough to take us safely through, Gnome?" he asked Slanter shortly.

Slanter gave him a dark look. "You ask a lot. I know it, but not well. Went through it once or twice when I was first brought here, before this whole thing began . . ."

He trailed off abruptly, and Jair knew that he was remembering how he had chosen to come back to his homeland to be with his own people and been sent by the walkers to track the Druid Allanon. He was remembering and perhaps regretting momentarily how he had let things get turned about.

"Fair enough," Garet Jax said softly and started ahead.

He took them down through the rocks to where the shelf opened into the tunnel that led back under the mountain. There, out of sight of Graymark, concealed within the shelter of a gathering of massive boulders, he beckoned them close.

"Do the walkers always rest during the daylight hours?" he asked Slanter. It was close and hot within the clustered rocks, and there was a fine sheen of sweat on his brow.

The Gnome frowned. "If you are asking whether we should go in now rather than when it is dark, I say we should."

"If there remains time enough to do so," Foraker interjected. "Midday is gone, and darkness comes early in the mountains. We might be better off to wait until tomorrow when we have the use of a full day. Another twelve hours or so can't make that much difference."

There was a moment's silence. Jair glanced skyward, his eyes scanning the ragged edge of the cliffs. Another twelve hours? An uneasy suspicion tugged at his mind in warning. How far had Brin gotten? The words of the King of the Silver River repeated themselves once again: "You must reach Heaven's Well before she reaches the Maelmord."

He turned quickly to Garet Jax. "I'm not sure we have twelve hours left. I have to know where Brin is to be certain. I have to use the crystal again—and I think I had better use it now."

The Weapons Master hesitated, then rose. "Not here. Move into the cave."

They slipped through the darkened opening and groped their way back into the gloom. There, huddled close about, the others waited patiently as Jair fumbled through his tunic for the vision crystal. He had it in a moment's time, gripping it by its silver chain as he pulled it forth. Cupping it gently in his hands, he wet his lips and fought back against the fatigue that bore down against him.

"Sing to it, Jair," he heard Edain Elessedil encourage softly.

He sang, his voice low and whispered, wearied by the strain to which he had put it in leading them safely through the Caves of Night. The crystal began to glow and the light to spread . . .

Brin paused in the gloom of the tunnel through which she stole. She had a sudden sense of being watched, of eyes following after her. It was as it had been on entering the Dragon's Teeth and again on leaving—as if someone watched her from a great distance off.

She hesitated, her thoughts frozen, and a flash of insight whispered to her. Jair! It was Jair! She took a deep breath to steady herself. There was no logical explanation for such a conclusion—it was simply there. But how could that be? How could her brother . . . ?

In the tunnel behind her, something moved.

She had come some distance from the causeway, a slow and cautious passage through darkness with the aid of Cogline's flameless torch. She had neither seen nor heard another living thing in all that time. She had come so far without sensing other life that she had begun to wonder if perhaps she had been mistaken in taking this tunnel.

But now there was something there at last—not ahead of her as expected, but behind. She turned guardedly, the feeling of being watched forgotten. She thrust the torch forward and started in shock. Great, luminous blue eyes blinked at her from out of the gloom. Then a massive whiskered face pushed its way into the circle of her light.

"Whisper!"

She spoke the moor cat's name with a sigh of relief and dropped to her knees as the beast came up to her and rubbed its broad head against her shoulder in friendly greeting.

"Whisper, what are you doing here?" she murmured as the cat dropped down on his haunches and regarded her solemnly.

She could guess readily enough the answer to that question, of course. Discovering her absence, the others must have backtracked to the stone bridge. Being unable to follow farther themselves, they had sent Whisper after her. Or rather, Kimber had sent Whisper, for Whisper answered only to the girl. Brin reached out and rubbed the cat's ears. It must have cost Kimber something to send Whisper on like this without her—as close as they were, as much as the girl relied on him. As was her nature, she had chosen to give the moor cat's strength to her friend. The Valegirl's eyes misted, and she put her arms about him.

"Thank you, Kimber," she whispered.

Then she rose, stroked the cat for a moment and shook her head gently. "But I cannot take you with me, can I? I cannot take anyone. It is much too dangerous—even for you. I promised myself that no one would be exposed to whatever it is that waits for me, and that includes you. You have to go back."

The moor cat blinked up at her and remained where he was.

"Go on, now. You have to go back to Kimber. Go on, Whisper." Whisper didn't move a hair. He simply sat there, waiting.

"So." Brin shook her head again. "As determined as your mistress, I guess."

She was left with no other choice; she used the wishsong. She sang softly to the cat, wrapping him close about with her words and music, telling him that he must go back. For several minutes she sang, a gentle urging that would not injure. When she was done, Whisper rose to his feet and padded back down the corridor, disappearing into the dark.

Brin watched him until he was out of sight, then turned and started ahead once more.

Moments later the darkness began to dissipate and the gloom to lighten. The passageway, narrow and close before, broadened and lifted in seconds so that her small light could no longer reach to the walls and ceiling. But now there was light ahead that rendered her own unnecessary, filling the passageway with dusty gray brightness. It was the sun. Somewhere close at hand, the tunnel was opening back into the world without.

She hurried forward, Cogline's flameless torch dropping to her side. The passageway turned upward, a stairwell honed and shaped from the tunnel rock rising far ahead into a massive, open-air cavern. She went up the stairs quickly, her weariness forgotten, sensing that her journey was nearing its end. Sunlight spilled down into the cavern above, silver streamers thick with swirling bits of dust and silt that danced and spun like living things.

Then she reached the last step, walked clear of the tunnel onto the broad ledge that lay beyond, and stopped. Before her, a second stone bridge spanned a second chasm, this one twice the size of the first, rugged and massive. It dropped away down the mountain rock thousands of feet into an abyss so deep that even the sunlight streaming down through crevices in the cavern ceiling could not penetrate its blackness. Brin peered downward, her nose wrinkling against the stench that wafted up. Even with Cogline's salve to numb her sense of smell, she felt nauseated. Whatever lay at the bottom of the pit was much worse than what passed through Graymark's sewers.

She glanced across the stone bridge to what waited beyond. The cavern stretched back into the mountain several hundred feet, then opened into a short, high tunnel. Yet it was not a tunnel so much as an alcove, she thought—hewn by hand, shaped and smoothed, with intricate symbols carved into the rock. Light streamed down at its far end, and the sky stretched away in a dim and hazy green.

She looked closer. No, it was not the sky that stretched away. It was a valley's misted wall.

It was the Maelmord.

She knew it instinctively, as if she had seen it in a dream and remembered. She could feel its touch and hear its whisper.

She hastened forward onto the bridge, a broad arched causeway some two dozen feet in width with wooden railing posts pegged into its rock and linked with chains. She moved forward quickly, passed the apex of the arch, and started down.

She was almost across when the black creature rose suddenly from a deep crevice in the cavern floor a dozen feet in front of her.

Muttering irritably, Cogline shuffled to a halt, Rone and Kimber crowding close behind him. Ahead, the sewer bisected into a pair of tunnels, each exactly like the other. There was no indication of which offered passage to wherever it was that Brin had now gone. There was nothing to suggest that either was the better way to go.

"Well, which do we follow?" Cogline demanded of Rone.

The highlander stared at him. "Don't you know?"

The oldster shook his head. "No idea. Make your choice."

Rone hesitated, looked away, then looked back again. "I can't. Look, maybe it doesn't make any difference which one we follow. Maybe both end in the same place."

"Sewer tunnels run *to* the same place, not *from* the same place! Any fool knows that!" the old man snorted.

"Grandfather!" Kimber admonished sharply.

She edged forward between them, scanning the tunnels in turn, studying the blackened waters that flowed through the grooved channels cut into each. At last she stepped back, shaking her head slowly.

"I cannot help you," she confessed, as if somehow she should have been able to do so. "I have no sense of where either leads. They appear the same." She looked over to Rone. "You will have to choose."

They stared at each other for a moment like frozen statues. Then Rone nodded slowly. "All right—we'll go left." He started past them. "At least that tunnel seems to run back toward the chasm."

He hastened into the sewer corridor, his flameless torch held firmly before him, his face grim. Cogline and Kimber looked at each other briefly and hurried after.

The black thing rose from the split in the cavern floor like a shadow come alive out of night's dreamworld and crouched down before the bridge. It was human in look, though as hairless and smooth as if sculpted from dark clay. Hunched over until it rocked forward on its long forearms, it was still taller than Brin. There was an odd, shapeless quality to its limbs and body, as if the muscles beneath lacked definition—or as if there were no muscles there at all and it not a thing of flesh. Sightless, deadened eyes lifted to find hers, and a mouth as ragged and black as the creature's skin yawned in a deep, toneless hiss.

The Valegirl froze. There was no way to avoid the creature. It had clearly been placed there for the purpose of guarding the bridge, and nothing was to pass it. Probably the Mord Wraiths had created it from the dark magic—created it, or called it to life from some nether place and time, as they had done with the Jachyra.

The black thing advanced a step, slow and certain, dead eyes staring. Brin forced herself to stand where she was. There was no way to know how dangerous this creature was, but she sensed that it was dangerous enough and that, if she turned or backed away, it would be on her.

The creature's black maw split wide and its hiss filled the silence. Brin went deathly cold. She knew what would happen next. And that meant that once again she was going to have to use the wishsong. Instantly her throat tightened. She did not want to use the Elven magic, but she could not let this monster reach her, even if it meant . . .

Abruptly the black thing attacked, lunging forward from its half-crouch. The swiftness of the thing caught her by surprise. It was hypnotic. The wishsong stuck in her throat, her indecision freezing it away. The moment hung suspended like a knot in the thread of time, and she waited for the impact of the blow.

But the blow never came. Something came streaking from behind her in a sudden blur of motion, caught the black thing in midleap, and hammered it back. Brin staggered away, dropping to her knees. It was Whisper! The spell of the wishsong had not been strong enough to counteract the command of his mistress; Whisper had shaken the magic and come after her!

The antagonists went down in a tangled heap, claws and teeth ripping. The black thing was caught completely by surprise, having seen only the girl. Hissing with rage, it struggled to dislodge the moor cat from its back where the great beast had fastened himself in a death grip. Over and over they tumbled along the length of the bridge, the moor cat's jaws tearing at the monster's neck and shoulders while the massive black form hunched and thrashed convulsively.

Brin remained frozen with indecision a dozen yards away at the center of the bridge. She must do something, she told herself.

This was not Whisper's fight—this was hers. She flinched at the fury of the struggle, a small cry escaping her lips as the battle between the two took them perilously close to the railing, shaking the iron chains. She must help! But how could she? She had no weapon save for the wishsong, and she could not use the magic. She could not!

She surprised herself with the intensity of her declaration. She could not use the wishsong because . . . because . . . Rage and fear flooded her, mixing with confusion to hold her bound. Why? She howled the question within her mind, a cry of anguish. What was wrong with her?

Then abruptly she was moving forward, edging her way to the far side of the stone arch, away from the combatants. She had made her decision—she would flee. It was she whom the black thing sought. Seeing her run, the thing would follow. And if she were quick enough, she would make the Maelmord before it . . .

She stopped. Ahead where the cavern floor stretched away to the arched opening, she caught sight of something new as it emerged from the creviced rock.

A second creature!

She went perfectly still. The passage opening to the daylight and the valley beyond was too far—and the black thing stood directly in her line of flight. Already it was coming for her. It lifted from the rock, then lumbered toward the bridge on all fours, its blackened maw gaping. Brin backed away. She must defend herself this time. The fear and uncertainty ripped through her. She must use the wishsong. She must!

The black thing hissed and reached for her. Again, she felt her throat knot.

And again, it was Whisper who saved her. Breaking free of the first creature, the cat whirled and catapulted violently into the second, knocking it away from the girl. Scrambling up again, Whisper turned to meet this new enemy. The black thing came at him with a rasping howl, vaulting high into the air. But Whisper was too quick. Sidestepping deftly, the big cat slashed at his attacker's exposed underbelly. Chunks of dark flesh ripped free, yet the monster did not slow. It thrust itself clear with a lunge, dead eyes fixed.

Now the second creature was joined by the first. Warily, they began closing on the moor cat. Whisper dropped back guardedly, keeping himself in front of Brin, his thick fur bristling until he looked twice his normal size. Crouched down on all fours, the black things feinted with quick rushes, moving fluidly from side to side with an ease that belied their bulky appearance. Carefully, they worked to find an opening in the big cat's defenses. Whisper held his ground, refusing to be drawn out. Then both creatures came at him at once, teeth and claws ripping angry furrows through fur and flesh. Whisper was thrown back against the chains of the bridge railing, his powerful body nearly pinned there by the ferocious charge. But he fought his way clear with a surge, slashing savagely at the black things, screaming his hatred of them.

The circling began once more. Panting heavily, his sleek gray coat streaked with blood, Whisper slipped back into his defensive crouch. The attackers had forced him against the bridge railing, away from Brin. They ignored the Valegirl now, their lifeless eyes fixed on the cat. Brin saw what they intended. They would come at Whisper again, and this time the chains would not break the force of their rush. The moor cat would be thrown back over the edge and fall to his death.

The moor cat also seemed to realize what was happening. He lunged and feinted, trying to skirt the edges of the circle, trying to regain the center of the bridge. But the monsters maneuvered quickly to cut him off, keeping him trapped against the railing.

Brin Ohmsford's chest knotted with fear. Whisper could not win this fight. These creatures were too much for him. He had shredded both with wounds that should have crippled them, yet they did not seem affected by the injuries. Their flesh hung in tatters, yet they did not bleed. They were enormously strong and quick—stronger and quicker than anything born of this world. They had obviously been created by the dark magic, not by nature's hands.

"Whisper," she breathed, her voice cracked and dry.

She must save him. There was no one else to do so. She had the wishsong and the strength of its magic. She could use it to destroy these creatures, to obliterate them as surely as . . .

The trees intertwined in the Runne Mountains . . .

The minds of the thieves from west of Spanning Ridge . . .

The Gnome . . . shattered . . .

Tears ran down her cheeks. She could not! Something interposed itself between her will and its execution, held her back from her intended purpose, and froze her resolve with indecision. She must help him, but she could not!

"Whisper!" she screamed.

The black things jerked erect, half-turning. Abruptly Whisper lunged in a feint that froze them in their tracks, then whirled sharply to his right, gathered himself and vaulted them both with a tremendous leap. Landing at a dead run, the moor cat raced for the center of the bridge and Brin. The black things were after him instantly, hissing in fury, tearing at his flanks in an effort to bring him down.

A dozen feet in front of Brin, they succeeded. All three tumbled to the causeway in a raging tangle of teeth and claws. For a few desperate seconds, Whisper held them both. Then one gained his back and the second tore free. It hurtled past the struggling cat toward Brin. The Valegirl threw herself to one side, sprawling down upon the bridge. Whisper screamed. With the last of his strength, he threw himself into the girl's assailant, the second creature still clinging to his back like some monstrous spider. The force of his lunge carried all three into the chains of the bridge railing. Iron links snapped like deadwood, and the black things hissed gleefully as Whisper began to slide from the bridge into the chasm.

Brin came to her knees, a cry of rage and determination wrenched from her throat. The restraints that bound her fell away, the indecision and uncertainty were shattered, and her purpose freed. She sang, hard and quick, and the sound of the wishsong filled the heights and depths of the cavern rock. The song was darker than any she had sung before, a new and terrible sound, filled with fury that surpassed all she had believed herself capable of knowing. It exploded into the black things like an iron ram. They surged upward at its impact and their lifeless eyes snapped back. Limbs clawing, black mouths wide and soundless, they were flung away from Whisper, back away from the safety of the bridge, and into space. Convulsing like blown leaves, they fell into the abyss and were gone.

It was done in an instant. Brin went silent, her dusky, worn face flushed and vibrant. Again she felt that sudden, strange sense of twisted glee—but stronger this time, much stronger. It burned through her like fire. She could barely control her excitement. She had destroyed the black things almost without trying.

And she had enjoyed it!

She realized then that the barrier that had interposed itself between her will and its execution had been one of her own making—a restraint she had put there to protect against what had just happened. Now it was gone, and she did not think it could be put back again. She had sensed that she was losing control of the magic. She had not understood why, only that it was happening. Each use had seemed to bring her a little further away from herself. She had tried to resist what was being done to her, but her efforts to forbear use of the magic had been thwarted at every turn—almost as if some perverse fate had willed that she *must* use the magic. By using it this time, she had embraced it fully, and she no longer felt that she could struggle against it. She would be what she must.

Slowly, gingerly, Whisper padded over to where she knelt, pushing his dark muzzle against her face. Her arms came up to wrap about the big cat gently, and tears ran down her cheeks.

Jair Ohmsford's voice died away in a ragged gasp, and the light of the vision crystal died with it. The face of his sister was gone. A deep silence filled the sudden gloom, and the faces of the men gathered there were white and drawn.

"Those were Mutens," Slanter whispered finally.

"What?" Edain Elessedil, seated next to him, looked startled.

"The black things—that's what they're called—Mutens. The dark magic made them. They guard the sewers below Graymark..." The Gnome trailed off, glancing quickly at Jair.

"Then she is here," the Valeman breathed, his mouth dry and his hands tightening about the crystal.

Slanter nodded. "Yes, boy, she's here. And closer to the pit than we."

Garet Jax rose swiftly, a lean, black shadow. The others scrambled up with him. "It seems we have no time left us and no choice but to go in now." Even in the half-light, his eyes were like fire. He reached out to them, palms upward. "Give me your hands."

One by one, they stretched forward their hands, joining with his. "By this we make our pledge," he told them, a hard and brittle edge to his voice. "The Valeman shall reach the basin at Heaven's Well as he has sworn he would. We are as one in this, whatever happens. As one, to the end. Swear it."

There was a hushed silence. "As one," Helt repeated in his deep, gentle voice. "As one," the others echoed.

The hands fell away, and Garet Jax turned to Slanter. "Take us in," he said.

XL

---◆---

THEY WENT UP THROUGH THE mountain PASSAGEWAYS TO the cellars that lay below Graymark like the Wraiths they shunned. With the aid of torches they found stored in a niche at the tunnel entrance, they crept through the gloom and the silence to the bowels of the fortress keep. Slanter led them, his rough yellow face bent close to the light, his black eyes bright with fear. He went quickly and purposefully, and only the eyes betrayed what he might wish hidden of himself. But Jair saw it, recognized it, and found that it mirrored what lurked now within himself.

He, too, was afraid. The anticipation that had earlier given him such strength of purpose was gone. Fear had replaced it, wild and barely controlled, racing through him and turning his skin to ice. Strange, fragmented thoughts filled his mind as he worked his way ahead with the others through the tunnel rock, his nostrils thick with the smell of musted air and his own sweat—thoughts of his home in the Vale, of his family scattered across the lands, of friends and familiar things left behind and perhaps lost, of the shadow things that hunted him, of Allanon and Brin, and of what they had come to this dark place and time to do. All jumbled and ran together like colors mixed in water, and there was no sense to be made of any of them. It was the fear that made his thoughts scatter so, and he tightened his mind and his resolve against it.

The passageways wound upward for a long time, crossing and

recrossing, a puzzle maze that seemed to lack beginning or end. Yet Slanter did not pause, but led them steadily on until at last they came in sight of a broad, ironbound doorway fastened to the rock. They came up to it and stopped, as silent as the tunnels through which they had come. Jair crouched down with the others as Slanter put one ear to the door and listened. In the stillness of his mind, he could hear the beat of his body's pulse.

Slanter rose and nodded once. Carefully, he lifted the latch that held the door closed, fixed his hands on the iron handle and pulled. The door swung open with a low groan. A stairway rose before them, disappearing beyond the circle of their torchlight into blackness. They began to climb, with Slanter leading them once more. A step at a time, slow and cautious, they made their way up the stairwell. Gloom and silence deepened and wrapped them close about. The stairwell ended, opening upward through a stone block floor. The soft scrape of someone's boot on the stairs echoed harshly through the darkness above, disappearing far away into the silence. Jair swallowed against what he was feeling. It was as if there was nothing up there but the dark.

Then they were clear of the stairs and within the gloom. Voiceless, they stood close about the opening and peered into the gloom, torches held forth. The light could not penetrate to walls or ceiling, but there was a clear sense of a chamber so huge that they were dwarfed by it. They could discern at the edges of their torchlight the shadowed outline of crates and barrels. The wood was dry and rotting, its iron bindings rusted. Cobwebs lay over everything, and the floor was thick with dust.

But in the carpet of the dust, splayed footprints marked the passing of something that was clearly not human. It had not been all that long since whatever it was had ventured down into the lower levels of Graymark, Jair thought chillingly.

Slanter beckoned them ahead. The members of the little company moved into the gloom, groping their way forward from the open stairwell, the dust stirring beneath their boots and rising in soft clouds to mix with the light of their torches in a hazy glare.

Mounds of stores and discarded provisions appeared and were left behind. Still the chamber ran on.

Then suddenly the entire floor rose half a dozen steps to a new level and stretched away from there into darkness. They went up the stairs in a knot, walked ahead twenty yards or so, and passed into a monstrous, arched corridor. Iron doors, barred and sealed, appeared on either side as they pushed forward. Blackened torch stubs sat within their iron racks, chains lay in piles against the walls, and multilegged insects scurried from the light to the seclusion of the gloom. A stench hindered breathing and choked the senses, emanating in waves from the cellar stone.

The corridor ended at yet another stairway, this one curling upward like a snake coiled. Slanter paused, then began to climb. The others followed. Twice the stairway wound back upon itself, then opened into another corridor. They followed this new passageway several dozen yards to where it branched in two directions. Slanter took them right. The passageway ended a short distance farther on at a closed iron door. The Gnome tested the latch, tugged futilely, and shook his head. There was concern on his face as he turned to the others. Clearly he had hoped to find it open.

Garet Jax pointed back down the corridor, the unasked question in his eyes. Could they backtrack and go the other way? Slanter shook his head slowly, the answer in his eyes. The Gnome did not know.

They hesitated a moment longer, eyes locked. Then Slanter pushed past, motioning for the others to follow. He led them back down the passageway to where it divided. This time he took them left. The second corridor wound farther than the first, passing stairwells, niches cloaked in shadow, and numerous doors, all closed and barred. Several times the Gnome paused, undecided, then continued on. The minutes slipped away, and Jair began to grow increasingly uneasy.

Then at last the passageway ended, this time at a pair of massive iron doors so huge that Slanter was forced to reach upward to seize the handles. They gave with surprising ease, and the door on the right swung silently in. The members of the little company peered through guardedly. Another chamber lay beyond, huge and cluttered with stores. But the gloom dissipated somewhat here, chased by a thin, gray light that slipped downward through tiny slits in the walls that were cut close against the chamber's high ceiling.

Slanter gestured toward the slits, then to the far wall of the chamber where a second pair of iron doors stood closed. The others understood. They were within Graymark's outer walls.

With Slanter in the lead, they passed cautiously into the room. No dust lay upon these floors; no cobwebs draped its crates and barrels. The stench still hung upon the air, stifling and rank, but it now seemed carried as much from without as held by the closure of the walls. Jair wrinkled his nose in distaste. The smell might well kill them before the dark things found them out. It was as bad as . . .

Something scraped softly in the shadows to one side. Garet Jax whirled, daggers in both hands, crying out in warning to the others.

Too late. Something huge, black, and winged seemed to explode out of the shadows. It rose against the half-light, its leathered body spreading outward like some monstrous bat. Teeth and claws gleamed, a flash of ivory, and a fierce shriek broke from its throat. It was on them so quickly that there was no time to defend against it. It flew at them in a rush, swept past the leaders, and came at Helt. It caromed into the giant Borderman, winged limbs flailing, and its shriek turned to a frightening hiss. Helt staggered back with a howl, then got both hands on the black thing, and thrust it from him violently, flinging it across the room into a pile of stores.

Garet Jax leaped forward, and the daggers flew from his hands, pinning the thing to the wooden crates.

Slanter had reached the far end of the room and wrenched wide one of the iron doors. "Get out!" he howled.

They raced swiftly from the chamber, one after the other, until all were clear. Slanter shoved the open door closed with a grunt and threw the iron bolts into their fastenings. Shaking, he collapsed back against the door.

"What *was* that?" Foraker gasped, his black-bearded face shiny with sweat and his heavy brows knit fiercely.

The Gnome shook his head. "I don't know. Something the walkers made of the dark magic—some sentinel, perhaps."

Helt was down on one knee, his face buried in his hands. Blood seeped through his fingers in small trickles of scarlet.

"Helt!" Jair whispered and started forward. "Helt, you're hurt . . ."

The Borderman lifted his head slowly. Angry slashes crisscrossed his face. One eye was swollen and already beginning to close. He dabbed at the wounds with his tunic sleeve and motioned the Valeman back. "No, they're just scratches. Nothing bad."

But he was wincing with pain. He came to his feet with an effort, bracing himself against the wall. There was an uneasy look in his eyes.

Slanter had moved away from the door and was glancing about furtively. They were at the center of a narrow corridor that ran to a pair of closed doors at one end and to a stairway opening to daylight at the other.

"This way!" he beckoned, moving quickly toward the light. "Hurry—before something else finds us!"

They started after him, all save Helt, who was still leaning against the passage wall. Jair glanced back and slowed. "Helt?" he called.

"Hurry on, Jair." The big man was still dabbing blood from his face. Then he pushed himself off the wall and started after. "Go on, now. Stay close to the others."

Jair did as he was asked, conscious that the Borderman was following and conscious, too, that Helt was having difficulty doing so. There was something very wrong with him.

They reached the end of the corridor and went up the stairs in a rush. The eerie stillness of the fortress was broken by the sound of other feet and voices, jumbled, distant and indistinct. The shriek of the winged thing had given warning that there were intruders within the keep. Jair's mind raced wildly as he bounded up the long stairway with the others. He must remember that he had the wish-song for protection—that he could use it effectively only if he remembered to keep his head . . .

Something hissed past his face, and he stumbled and went down. An arrow shattered on the stairway wall. Helt was next to him at once, pulling him up again. Arrows flew all about them as Gnome Hunters appeared in the corridor below and on parapets above. The companions were within Graymark's walls, but their enemies knew it now and were converging. Scrambling to the top of the stairs, Jair wheeled right after the others along a line of battlements that overlooked a broad inner courtyard and a maze of towers and fortifications. Gnomes appeared from everywhere, weapons in hand, yelling wildly. A handful lay crumpled on the battlements ahead, brought down by Garet Jax as the black-clad Weapons Master cleared the way forward. The six darted along the battlements to a tower stairwell where Slanter brought them to a halt.

"The drop-gate—there!" He pointed across the courtyard to an iron-barred portcullis that stood raised over an arched entry leading through a massive, stone block wall. "Quickest way for us to reach the Croagh!" His yellow face grimaced as he fought for breath. "Gnomes will realize what we're about in a moment. When they do, they'll bring down the gate to trap us. But if we can get there first, we can use the gate to cut them off instead!"

Garet Jax nodded, oddly calm in the midst of the moment's fury. "Where is the wheelhouse and winch?"

Slanter pointed again. "Beneath the gates—this side. We'll have to jam the wheel!"

Shouts and cries broke from all about them. In the courtyard below the Gnomes began to come together.

Garet Jax straightened. "Quick, then—before they are too many for us."

The little company raced down the tower stairwell, Slanter leading. At the lower end, they crossed through an anteway, dark and

closed, to a single door that opened into the courtyard. All across
the yard, Gnome Hunters turned to face them.

"Shades!" Slanter gasped.

They broke for the gate in a rush.

Brin Ohmsford climbed slowly to her feet, one hand resting lightly
on Whisper's massive head. The cavern was still again, empty of life.
She stood for a moment at the center of the stone bridge and looked
across the chasm to where daylight brightened the tall, arched alcove leading out. She rubbed Whisper's head gently, conscious of
the welts and angry furrows left from his terrible battle with the
black things, feeling the hurt that he had suffered.

"No more," she whispered softly.

Then she turned forward. She left the bridge quickly, without
looking back, and began to cross the cavern floor toward the alcove.
Whisper went with her, padding silently behind, saucer blue eyes
gleaming. Without turning, she knew that he was there. Cautiously,
she scanned the creviced rock for signs of the black things or other
horrors wrought by the dark magic, but there were none. Only she
and the cat remained.

Minutes later she reached the alcove with its high, smooth
walls sculpted from the stone and carved with the intricate designs
she had seen earlier. She paid them little heed, moving at once to
the opening and to the daylight beyond. She had only one objective
now.

The opening passed away behind her and she stood once more
in sunlight. It was midafternoon, the sun gone westward toward
the treeline, its brightness dimmed by mist and clouds that floated
shroudlike across the whole of the sky above. She was on a ledge
overlooking a deep valley surrounded by a cluster of barren, ragged
peaks. There was an odd, dreamlike tone to the setting of mountains,
clouds, and mist. The whole of the valley was bathed in a shimmering, leaden cast. She looked slowly about and then upward behind

her. There, balanced upon the rock above, was a solitary, dismal fortress. Graymark. Winding down from its heights and from far above that, beyond where she could see, was the stone stairway of the Croagh. It wound past her ledge, touched briefly, then spiraled down into the valley.

It was upon the valley that her gaze at last came to rest. A deep, shadowed bowl, it fell away from the light until its lower depths were lost in misted gloom. The Croagh wound down into this darkness, into a mass of trees, vines, scrub, and choking brush, grown so thick that the light could not penetrate. This forest was a twisted and knotted wilderness and it seemed to have neither beginning nor end, but to be contained in its rampant growth only by the rock walls of the peaks.

Brin stared. It was from here that the hissing sound came, the one that she had heard earlier in the sewers. It was like breathing. She squinted against the glare of the gray half-light. Had she seen . . . ?

In the bowl of the valley, the forest moved.

"You are alive!" she said softly and hardened herself against what that realization made her feel.

She stepped far out onto the ledge, to the very edge where the stem of the Croagh joined to it. Crude stairs had been cut into the rock, and she stared down their length to where they disappeared at a bend in the stone. Then she looked past again to the valley below.

"Maelmord, I am come to you," she whispered.

Then she turned back to Whisper. She knelt beside him and rubbed his ears tenderly. Her smile was sad and gentle. "You must go no farther with me, Whisper. Even though your mistress sent you to keep me safe, you must go no farther. You must stay here and wait for her to come to you. Do you understand?"

The cat's luminous eyes blinked and he rubbed against her. "Protect my way back again, if you would protect me at all," she told him. "Perhaps it will not be as the Grimpond has foretold—that I shall die here. Perhaps I will come back again. Keep the way safe for me, Whisper. Keep your mistress and my friends safe. Do not let

them follow. Wait, and when I have done what I must, I will come back to you if I am able. I promise you that I will."

Then she sang to the cat, using the wishsong not to persuade or to deceive this time, but to explain. In images that would carry to the moor cat's mind, she let him feel what she wished and made him understand what it was that she must do. When she was done, she leaned forward and hugged the big cat close for a moment, nestling her face in the coarse fur and feeling the warmth of the beast seep through her, taking from that warmth a measure of new strength.

She rose and stepped back. Slowly Whisper sank down on his haunches and forepaws until he was stretched out facing her. She nodded and smiled. He was taking up guard of her path down. He would do as she wished.

"Good-bye, Whisper," she told him and stepped upon the Croagh.

The stench that had risen from the chasm behind her rose anew from the steamy depths of the valley below. She ignored it, gazing out momentarily over the cliffs to where the light of the sun brightened above the horizon. She thought of Allanon then and wondered if he could see her—if perhaps he might in some way be with her.

Then she took a deep breath to steady herself and started down.

XLI

♦

As one, the six who had come from Culhaven broke from the shelter of the tower door and raced into the courtyard beyond. Screams of warning rose up about them, and the Gnomes converged from every quarter.

At the center of the maelstrom, Jair watched the battle unfold with curious detachment. Time fragmented, and his sense of being slipped from him. Hemmed close about by the friends who sought to protect him, he floated in their midst, voiceless and ephemeral, a ghost that none could see. Earth, sky, and the whole of the world beyond these walls were lost, along with all else that had ever been or would ever be. There was only now and the faces and the forms of those who fought and died in that yard.

Garet Jax led the charge, darting through the Gnomes that rushed to bar his passage, swift and fluid as he killed them. He was like a black-clad dancer, all grace, power, and seemingly effortless motion. Gnome Hunters, gnarled and worn from countless battles, threw themselves in front of him with frenzied determination, their weapons hacking and cutting with lethal force. They might as well have been trying to contain quicksilver. None could touch the Weapons Master, and those who came close enough to try found in him the black shadow of death come to claim their lives.

The others of the company fought beside him, no less driven in their purpose and only a shade less deadly. Foraker flanked him on one side, the Dwarf's black-bearded face ferocious as he swung the great double-edged axe and attackers scattered with howls of dismay. Edain Elessedil flanked him on the other, a slender sword flicking snakelike and a long knife parrying counterblows. Slanter stayed close behind them all, long knives in both hands, a hunted look in his black eyes. Helt brought up the rear, a giant shield, his wounded face bleeding again and frightening to look at, a great pike snatched from an attacker thrusting and cutting all who tried to slip past his guard.

A strange sense of exhilaration flooded through Jair. It was as if nothing could stop them.

Weapons flew past from every direction, and the screams of the wounded and dying filled the gray afternoon. They were in the center of the courtyard now, the castle wall rising up before them. Then a sudden blow struck the Valeman, staggering him with its force. Stunned, he looked down and found the tip of a dart protruding from his shoulder like a peg hook. Pain lanced from the wound through his body, and he went rigid with shock. Slanter saw him stumble and was next to him in an instant, arms wrapping about him to hold him up, pulling him after the others. Helt roared with fury and used the long pike to hammer back the Gnomes that sought to rush forward to seize them. Jair squeezed his eyes shut against the pain. He was hurt, he thought in disbelief as he staggered forward under Slanter's guidance.

The drop-gate loomed ahead. There were Gnomes in its shadow now, rushing about wildly and calling out in warning. The doors to the blockhouse slammed shut and iron winches began to turn. Slowly, the drop-gate started down.

Garet Jax leaped forward, so quickly that the others could barely follow. He reached the gate in seconds, thrusting into the Gnomes who held there. But the winches continued to turn in the blockhouse, iron chains unwrapping. The drop-gate was still coming down.

"Garet!" Foraker screamed in warning, nearly buried in a rush of Gnome attackers who came at him.

But it was Helt who acted. He charged through the Gnome Hunters, pike lowered, sweeping them aside like leaves scattered in a fall wind. Blows rained down upon him, but he shrugged them aside as if they were not felt and went on. Gnome archers trained their fire on the giant Borderman from the walls behind. Twice he was struck; the second time, he staggered to his knees. Still he went on.

Then he was before the blockhouse, his giant frame slamming into the closed doors. The doors buckled with a crunch and flew apart, and the Borderman was within. He hurtled into a knot of defenders, flinging them from the machinery like dolls, his massive hands closing about the winch levers to pull them tight again. The drop-gate slowed and stopped in a grinding of chains and gears, its teeth barely ten feet from the ground.

Garet Jax scattered the Gnomes who remained before the gate, and Slanter and Jair stumbled through into a shadowed court beyond. For the moment, at least, the court was empty. Jair collapsed to one knee, feeling the searing pain from his wound flare outward with the movement. Then Slanter was in front of him.

"Sorry boy, but I've got to do this."

One gnarled hand fixed on his shoulder and the other on the dart. With a wrench, the Gnome pulled the dart free. Jair screamed and almost lost consciousness, but Slanter held him upright, jamming a wad of cloth down into his tunic front and binding it fast against the wound with his belt.

Beneath the drop-gate, Garet Jax, Foraker and Edain Elessedil stood in a line against the advancing Gnomes. A dozen paces beyond, still within the blockhouse, Helt pulled free the winch levers once more. Again, the drop-gate started down.

Jair blinked through the tears brought by the pain. Something was wrong. The Borderman was making no attempt to come after them. He was leaning heavily against the machinery, watching as the gate descended.

"Helt . . . ?" Jair whispered weakly.

He realized then the Borderman's intent. Helt meant to bring down the drop-gate and jam it from the other side. If he did so, it would leave him trapped there. It would mean his certain death.

"Helt, no!" he screamed and jerked to his feet.

But it was already done. The gate came down, slamming into the earth with the force of its release. The Gnome defenders howled with rage and turned on the man within the blockhouse. Bracing himself, Helt threw the whole of his great strength against the winch levers and wrenched them from their fastenings, wrecking the machine.

"Helt!" Jair screamed again, trying to pull free of Slanter.

The Borderman staggered to the blockhouse door, long pike held before him. Gnomes came at him from everywhere. He bent and swayed against their rush, but for an instant he withstood them. Then they swarmed over him and he was gone.

Jair stood frozen behind the gates as Garet Jax came back to him. Roughly, the Weapons Master turned him about and pushed him away. "Go!" he snapped. "Quickly, Jair Ohmsford, go now!"

The Valeman stumbled from the gate, still stunned. The Weapons Master kept pace at his side. "He was dying already," Garet Jax said. Jair's head jerked about, and the gray eyes fixed on him. "The winged thing in the storeroom poisoned him. It was in his eyes, Valeman."

Jair nodded dumbly, remembering the look the Borderman had given him. "But we . . . we might have . . ."

"We might have done many things were we not where we are," Garet Jax cut him short, his voice calm and icy. "The poison was lethal. He knew he was dying. He chose this way to finish it. Now, run!"

Giant Helt! Jair remembered the big man's kindness to him during the long journey north. He remembered his gentle eyes. Helt, about whom he had known so very little . . .

Head lowered to shield his tears, he ran on.

At the edge of the Croagh, midway down its length where it joined to the rock shelf on the cliffs below Graymark, Whisper listened as the sounds of the battle being fought above him grew more fierce. Stretched full-length upon the shadowed stone, he kept watch for the return of Brin or the coming of his mistress. His hearing was keener than that of any human, and he had caught the sounds long ago. But the sounds did not threaten him, and so he kept his vigil and did not move.

But then a new sound reached his ears, a sound not from the battle being fought within Graymark, but from something close at hand. Footfalls sounded on the stone steps of the Croagh—soft and furtive. The moor cat's head lifted. Something was coming down. Claws scraped against the rock. Whisper's head dropped down again, and he seemed to disappear into the stone.

The seconds slipped past, and then a shadow appeared. Whisper's narrowed eyes caught the movement, and the big cat stayed frozen. One of the black things crept down the stairs of the Croagh—one like the things that he had fought within the caves of the mountain. Down the stone walkway it slipped, dead eyes staring as if sightless. It did not see Whisper. The moor cat waited.

When the monster was less than half a dozen steps from where he crouched, Whisper sprang. He hurtled into the black thing before it even knew he was there, a silent blur of motion. Arms flailing, the creature flew from the Croagh to drop like a stone into the valley below. Balanced at the edge of the stairway's long spiral, Whisper watched the thing fall. When it struck, the entire forest about it convulsed in a frenzy of limbs and leafy trailers. It had the unpleasant look of a throat swallowing. Finally, it went still.

Whisper backed from the Croagh, ears flattened in a mixture of fear and hatred. The smell of the steamy jungle rose to assail the cat's nostrils, and he coughed and spit in distaste. He padded back upon the rock shelf.

Then a new sound brought him about with a low snarl. Other dark forms stood upon the Croagh above him—two more of the black things and behind them a robed figure, tall and hooded. Whisper's saucer blue eyes blinked and narrowed. It was too late to hide. They had already seen him.

Soundlessly he turned to meet them, dark muzzle drawing back.

Jair Ohmsford and his companions raced through shadows and half-light deep within the fortress of Graymark now. They ran down hallways thick with the stench of must and sewage, corridors of rusted iron doors and crumbling stone, chambers that echoed with their footfalls, and stairways worn and broken. The castle of Graymark was a dying place, sick with age and disuse and rotten with decay. Nothing that lived here gave tolerance to life; those within found comfort only in death.

And it seeks my death, Jair thought as he ran, his wound throbbing painfully. It seeks to swallow me and make me a part of it.

Ahead, the dark form of Garet Jax darted swiftly on, a wraith that beckoned. The gloom about them lay empty, silent and waiting. The Gnomes had been left behind; the Mord Wraiths had not appeared. The Valeman fought back against the fear that coursed through him. Where were the Wraiths? Why hadn't they seen them yet? They were here within the keep, hidden somewhere within its walls, the things that could destroy minds and bodies. They were here and they must surely come.

But where were they?

He stumbled, fell against Slanter, and almost went down. But the Gnome held him up, one stout arm coming quickly about him. "Watch where you step!" Slanter cried.

Jair gritted his teeth as pain flooded outward from his shoulder. "It hurts, Slanter. Every step . . ."

The Gnome's blocky face turned from his own. "The pain tells you that you're still alive, boy. Now run!"

Jair Ohmsford ran. They raced down a curving hall, and ahead there was the sound of other feet running and voices calling out. Gnomes had come another way and were searching for them.

"Weapons Master!" Slanter warned urgently, and Garet Jax skidded to a halt. The Gnome beckoned them into an alcove where a small door opened onto a narrow stairway that disappeared upward into blackness.

"We can slip above them this way," Slanter panted, leaning wearily against the stone block walls. "But a moment for the boy, first."

Quickly, he pulled the cork from his ale pouch and lifted the spout to the Valeman's lips. Jair drank gratefully in a series of deep swallows. The bitter liquid burned through him; almost at once, it seemed to ease the pain. Leaning back against the wall with the Gnome, he watched as Garet Jax slipped ahead along the stairway, searching the darkness above. Behind them, Foraker and Edain Elessedil stood guard at the stairway entrance, crouched down within the shadows.

"Better now?" Slanter asked him shortly.

"Better."

"Like that time in the Black Oaks, eh? After you'd taken that beating from Spilk?"

"Like then." Jair smiled, remembering. "Cures everything, that Gnome ale."

The Gnome laughed bitterly. "Everything? No, boy—not what the walkers will do to us when they catch us. Not that. Coming for us, you know—just like they did in the Oaks. Coming from the shadows, soundless black things. I can smell them!"

"It's just the stench of the place, Slanter."

The Gnome's rough face lowered, as if he had not heard. "Helt— gone just like that. Wouldn't have thought we would lose the big man so quick. Bordermen are a tough breed; trackers tougher still. Wouldn't have thought it would happen so quick with him."

Jair swallowed. "I know. But it will be different for the rest of us, Slanter. The Gnomes are behind us. We'll get away, just as we have done before."

Slanter shook his head slowly. "No, we'll not get away this time, boy. Not this time." He pushed clear of the wall, his voice a whisper. "We'll all be dead before it's done."

Roughly, he pulled the Valeman up after him, made a quick motion back to Foraker and Edain Elessedil and started up the

stairs. The Dwarf and the Elf followed at once. They caught up with
Garet Jax several dozen steps ahead, and together the five climbed
into the blackness. Step by step, they made their way forward, with
a small glimmer of light from somewhere above as their only guide.
Within Graymark's walls, it was like a tomb meant to hold them
fast. Jair let the thought linger momentarily, desperately aware of
his own mortality. He could die as easily as Helt had died. It was
not assured, as he had once believed, that he would live to see the
end of this.

Then he brushed the thought away. If he did not live, there
would be no one to help Brin. It would end for both of them, for
there could be no hope for her without him. Therefore, he must live,
must find a way to live.

The stairway ended at a small wooden door with a barred window. It was through this window that the daylight slipped down
into the darkness where they crouched. Slanter pressed his rough
yellow face tight against the bars and peered out into what waited
beyond. From somewhere close, the cries of their pursuers rang out.

"Have to run for it again," Slanter said over his shoulder. "Ahead,
through the great hall. Stay close!"

He threw open the wooden door, and they burst into the daylight beyond. They were in a long corridor, high-ceilinged and raf-
tered, with narrow, arched windows cut into its length. Slanter took
them left, past alcoves and doorways draped in shadow, shells of
rusted armor on pedestals, and clusters of weapons hung against
the stone. The cries grew stronger, and it seemed as if the company
were running toward them. Then suddenly the cries were all about
them. Behind, only yards back, a door flew wide and Gnome Hunters poured through. Howls of excitement burst from their throats,
and they turned to give chase.

"Quick!" Slanter cried.

A shower of arrows whistled past them as they charged onto
a threshold fronting a pair of tall, arched wooden doors carved in
scroll. Slanter and Garet Jax flew into the doors, the others only a
step behind, and the doors snapped at their bindings and sagged

open. The company rushed through, tumbling over one another down a long stairway. They were within the great hall that Slanter had sought, a massive chamber bright with daylight that poured through high, barred windows. Beams, aged and cracked by time's passage, ran crosswise overhead, buttressing a cavernous ceiling canopied over rows of tables and benches scattered across the floor beneath in disarray. The five from Culhaven regained their footing hurriedly and raced through the tables and benches, dodging the debris frantically. Behind them, their pursuers burst into the room.

Jair followed Slanter right, conscious of Garet Jax close ahead on the left and Foraker and Edain Elessedil trailing. His lungs burned and the wound in his shoulder throbbed painfully once again. Arrows and darts hissed wickedly past, thudding into the wood of the benches and tables. Gnome Hunters were appearing all about them now.

"The stairs!" Slanter screamed frantically.

Ahead, a long, curving stairway wound upward toward a balcony, and they broke for it in a rush. But several Gnomes reached it first, fanning out across the lower steps, cutting off their escape. Garet Jax went directly for them. Springing atop a trestle bench, he skidded its length and dove into their midst. Somehow he kept his feet on landing, like a black cat striking out at the harried Gnomes. With long knives in both hands, he slipped past their cumbersome pikes and broadswords and slew them one by one, as if they were but helpless targets. By the time the others of the company reached him, all but a few lay dead, and those few had scattered.

Garet Jax wheeled on Slanter, blood streaking his lean face. "Where is the Croagh, Gnome?"

"Through the hallway beyond the balcony!" Slanter barely slowed to answer. "Quick, now!"

They were up the stairs in a rush. Behind, a cluster of new pursuers closed on the stairs and bounded after. Halfway up, the Gnomes caught them. The Weapons Master, the Dwarf, and the Elf turned to fight. Slanter pulled Jair a dozen steps further on to shield him. Gnome broadswords and maces swung high, and there was a fearful clash of metal. Garet Jax staggered back, separated from the others by the press of attackers. Then Elb Foraker went down, his head laid open to the bone by a deflected blade. He struggled to rise, blood streaming down his bearded face, and Edain Elessedil leaped to his aid. For an instant, the young Elf held the attackers at bay, his slender sword darting. But a pike pierced his sword arm. As his guard dropped, one of the Gnomes brought a mace down against his leg. The Elf toppled over with a scream of pain, and the Gnomes were on him.

For an instant it appeared as if they were all finished. But then Garet Jax was there once more, his black-clad form hurtling into the attackers and flinging them back. Down went the Gnome Hunters, dying in astonishment, dead almost before they knew what had killed them. The last of the Hunters fell, and the members of the little company were alone once more.

Foraker stumbled over to where Edain Elessedil writhed in pain, his gnarled hands reaching down to feel the injured leg. "Smashed," he breathed softly and exchanged a knowing look with Garet Jax.

He bound the leg with strips of his short cloak, using shattered arrows for splints. Slanter and Jair hastened down the steps to rejoin them, and the Gnome forced some of the bitter ale he carried down the Elf's throat. Edain Elessedil's face was white and drawn with the pain as Jair bent over him. The Valeman saw at once that the damaged leg was useless.

"Help me get him up," Foraker ordered. With Slanter's aid, they carried the Elf to the top of the stairs. There they propped him up against the balustrade and knelt before him.

"Leave me," he whispered, grimacing as he shifted his weight. "You have to. Take Jair on to the Croagh. Go quickly."

Jair looked hurriedly at the others. Their faces were grim and set. "No!" he cried out angrily.

"Jair." The Elf's hand closed tightly about his arm. "It was agreed, Jair. We pledged it. Whatever happens to the rest of us, you must reach Heaven's Well. I can no longer help you. You must leave me and go on."

"What he says is true, Ohmsford—he can go no farther." Elb Foraker's voice was oddly hushed. He put his hands on the Valeman's shoulders, then slowly came to his feet, glancing in turn at Slanter and Garet Jax. "I think that maybe I've gone as far as I can go, too. That sword cut has left me too dizzy for long climbs. The three of you go on. I think I'll stay here."

"Elb, no, you can't do that . . ." the injured man tried to object.

"My choice, Edain Elessedil," the Dwarf cut him short. "My choice as it was yours when you chose to come to my aid. We have a bond, you and I—a bond shared by Elves and Dwarves as far back as anyone can remember. We always stand by each other. It's time for me to honor that bond."

He turned then to Garet Jax. "This time the matter of my staying is not open to argument, Garet."

A scattering of Gnome Hunters appeared at the far end of the hall. They slowed guardedly, calling back to others that followed.

"Hurry, now," Foraker whispered. "Take Ohmsford and go."

Garet Jax hesitated only a moment, then nodded. His hand reached out to grip that of the Dwarf. "Luck, Foraker."

"And you," the other answered.

His dark eyes met those of the Gnome momentarily. Then wordlessly, he placed an ash bow, arrows, and the slender Elf blade by Edain Elessedil's side. In his own hands, he gripped the double-edged axe.

"Go now!" he snapped without turning, his black-bearded countenance fierce and set.

Jair held his ground defiantly, eyes darting from the face of the Weapons Master to that of Slanter. "Come, boy," the Gnome said quietly.

Rough hands fastened on the Valeman's good arm and propelled him along the balcony. Garet Jax followed, gray eyes cold and fixed. Jair wanted to scream in protest, to say that they could not leave them, but he knew that it would do no good. The decision had been made. He glanced over his shoulder to where Foraker and the Elven Prince waited at the stairway's edge. Neither looked toward him. Their eyes were on the advancing Gnome Hunters.

Then Slanter had them through a doorway into another hall and hastening down its length. Cries of pursuit sounded once more, scattered and distant save in the direction from which they had fled. Jair ran silently at Slanter's side and fought to keep from looking back.

The hallway they followed ended at an arched opening. They passed through into gray, hazy daylight, and the walls of the keep were left behind. A broad courtyard spread out before them to a railing. Beyond, the cliffs and the fortress dropped away into a valley; out of the valley, a single thread of stone spiraled upward past the courtyard's edge. High and then higher it rose, to wrap at last about a solitary peak far above.

The Croagh, with Heaven's Well at its summit.

The three who remained of the little company from Culhaven hurried forward to where the stairway and the courtyard joined and began to climb.

XLII

---◆---

HUNDREDS OF STEPS PASSED AWAY BENEATH BRIN'S FEET AS she descended the stone stairway of the Croagh into the pit of the Maelmord. The slender ribbon of stone spiraled downward, winding from Graymark's leaden towers into the mist and steamy heat of the jungle below, a narrow and dizzying drop through space. The Valegirl traversed it with wooden steps, her mind numb with fear and weariness and wracked with whispers of doubt. One hand rested lightly on the stone railing to give her some sense of support. In the west, the clouded sun continued to pass slowly behind the mountains.

Through the whole of her descent, her eyes remained fixed on the pit below. A dim and hazy mass when she began, the Maelmord sharpened in clarity with each step taken. Slowly, the life that lay rooted there took shape and form, lifting away from the broad backdrop of the valley. The trees were huge, bent, and hoary, warped somehow from the way that nature's hand had shaped them. And within their midst were massive stalks of scrub and weed, grown to disproportionate size, and vines that wound and twisted over everything like snakes without heads or tails. The color of this jungle was not a vibrant, spring green, but a dull and grayish color that bore the cast of something dying with the freeze of winter.

Yet the heat was awesome. To Brin, the feel of the Maelmord was like a day in hottest summer when the ground had cracked, the grass browned, and the surface water dissipated to dust. The terrible stench of the sewers had its life-source here, rising from the earth and the jungle foliage in sickening waves, hanging in the still afternoon air, and gathering like fouled soup in the bowl of the mountain stone. At first, it was almost unbearable, even with Cogline's salve still thick within her nostrils. But after a time, it grew less noticeable as her sense of smell was mercifully dulled. So, too, it was with the heat as her body temperature adjusted. Heat and stench lost the edge of their unpleasantness, and there was only the stark and blasted look of the pit that could not be blocked away.

There was the hissing, too, and there was the rise and fall of the foliage, as if it were a body breathing. There was the certainty that the whole of the valley was a thing alive, a solitary being for all of its disparate parts that could act and think and feel. And while it had no eyes, still the Valegirl could feel it looking at her, watching and waiting.

But she kept on. There could be no thought of turning back. It had been a long and arduous journey that had brought her to this place and time, and much had been sacrificed. Lives had been lost and the character of those saved was forever changed. She, herself, was no longer the girl she had been, for the magic had made her over into something new and terrible. She winced at the admission she could now freely make. She was changed, and the magic had wrought it. She shook her head. Well, perhaps it was not change, after all, that she had experienced, but merely insight. Perhaps learning of the frightening extent of the wishsong's power had but shown her what had always been there and she was who she had always been and had not changed at all. Perhaps it was simply that now she understood.

The musings distracted her only slightly from the Maelmord's bulk as it drew close now with the final twist in the stone stairway of the Croagh, marking the end of her descent. She slowed, staring fixedly downward into the mass of the jungle beneath, seeing the twisted maze of trunks, limbs, and vines shrouded in trailers of mist and the rise and fall of the life that rooted there, its breath hissing in steady cadence. Within the ravaged breast of the pit, no other life gave evidence of its existence.

Yet somewhere within that tangle, the Ildatch lay hidden.

How was she to find it?

She stood upon the Croagh two dozen steps from its lower end, with the Maelmord swelling softly all about her. She looked out across it in confusion, fighting down the repulsion and fear that coursed through her and trying desperately to stay calm. She must use the wishsong now, she knew, as she had been told by Allanon that she could. The trees, brush, and vines of this jungle were like those trees twisted close about each other within the forests above the Rainbow Lake. The wishsong could be used to make them part. A pathway could be made.

But where should that pathway lead?

She hesitated. Something within her advised caution, whispering that the wishsong's power was to be used a different way this time—that strength alone would not be enough. The Maelmord was too large, too overpowering to be mastered in that way. Guile and cleverness must be employed. This thing was but a creation of the same magic that she wielded, all of it descended through the ages from the world of faerie, from a time when magic was the only power . . .

She cut short the thought, her eyes lifting toward the sky once again. The sunlight warmed her face in a way far different from that of the heat of the pit. There was life in its warmth and brightness. It called to her with such strength of purpose that, for an instant, she felt an inexplicable and frantic need to run back.

She jerked her eyes away, forcing her gaze to settle again upon the steamy depths of the jungle. Still she hesitated in her descent. The way was not yet clear to her, not yet certain. She could not proceed blindly into the maw of this thing. She must first discover where it was that she was going and where it was that the Ildatch lay concealed. Her dusky face tightened. She must understand the thing. She must look within it . . .

The words of the Grimpond mocked her, a whisper that teased slyly from the deep recesses of her memory: Look within, Brin of Shannara. Do you see?

And suddenly, startlingly, she saw everything. It had been told to her at the Valley of Shale, but she had not understood. Savior and destroyer, Bremen had named her, risen from the Hadeshorn to summon Allanon. Savior and destroyer.

She leaned weakly against the stone railing as the impact of it struck her. It was not within the Maelmord that she must look to find her answers—not within the pit.

It was within herself!

She straightened then, her dark face savage with the certainty of what she knew. How easy it was going to be for her to pass into the Maelmord and to find what she sought! There was no need for her to force a path within this being that kept watch over the Ildatch—no need, even, to search the Ildatch out. There would be no struggle here, no confrontation of magics.

There would instead be a joining!

She descended the final steps of the Croagh until she stood at last at its end. The roof of the jungle above her seemed to close suddenly about, shutting away the sunlight, leaving her wrapped in shadows, heat, and the unbearable stench. But it no longer bothered her to be here. She knew what it was that she had to do, and nothing else mattered.

Gently, she sang. The wishsong rolled forth, low, hard, and eager. The music flooded the massive tangle of limbs, vines, rampant brush. It stroked and soothed with a deft touch, then wrapped about and cloaked with warm reassurance. Accept me, Maelmord, it whispered. Accept me into you, for I am like you. For us, there is no difference of kind. We are the same, our magics joined. We are the same!

The words that whispered in the music should have horrified her, but they were strangely pleasing. Where once the wishsong had seemed but a marvelous toy with which she might amuse herself— a toy to play with color and shape and sound—the vastness of its use had at last revealed itself to her. It could be anything. Even here, where evil lay strongest, she could belong. The Maelmord was created to prevent anything from entering that was not in harmony with it. Even the strength inherent in the wishsong's magic could not overcome the basic purpose of its existence. But so versatile was the magic that it could forsake strength for cunning and make Brin Ohmsford appear kindred to whatever might stand against her. She could be in harmony with the life in this pit—and she could do so for as long as it might take to reach what it was she sought.

Exhilaration soared through her as she sang to the Maelmord and felt it respond. She was crying, so intense was the feeling that bound her to the music. The jungle swayed in response about her, its limbs bending and its vines and scrub curling like snakes. The music she sang whispered of the death and horror that gave life to the valley. She played a game with it, immersed within her self-creation so that she could be thought nothing less than what she wished to appear.

She drifted deep into herself, bound up in the song she sang. Allanon and the journey that had brought her were forgotten, as were Rone, Kimber, Cogline, and Whisper. Barely remembered was the task she had come to complete—to find and destroy the Ildatch. The release of the magic brought again the strange and frightening sense of glee. She could feel her control slipping away, just as had happened when she had used the wishsong against that Spider Gnome on Toffer Ridge and the black things in the sewers. She could feel the threads of herself unraveling. But she must risk it, she knew. It was necessary.

The breathing of the Maelmord rose and fell more quickly now and the hissing was more intense. It wanted her, had need for her. It found in her a vibrant piece of itself, the heart of the body that lay rooted there, missing for so long, but now returned. Come to me, it hissed. Come to me!

Her face alive with excitement and need, Brin passed from the Croagh into the jungle beyond.

"There has got to be an end to these sewers, for cat's sake!" Rone was insisting to Kimber and Cogline as he stepped clear of the tunnel passage into the cavern beyond. It seemed to him in his frustration that they had been stumbling about in the sewers of Graymark forever.

"There doesn't have to be anything of the sort!" Cogline snapped back, as disagreeable as ever.

But the highlander barely heard, his attention focused instead on the cavern into which they had passed. It was a massive chamber, its roof cracked so that hazy sunlight flooded downward in bright streamers and its floor split down the center by a monstrous chasm. Wordlessly, Rone hurried forward along the chasm's edge, his eyes sweeping toward the stone bridge that spanned it. Beyond the bridge, the cavern stretched away to a high, arched alcove of polished stone, scrolled in some ancient markings and opening into daylight and the green of a misted valley.

The Maelmord, he thought at once.

And that's where Brin will be.

He bounded onto the bridge and crossed, the old man and the girl hurrying after. He was moving toward the alcove when Kimber's sharp cry brought him about.

"Highlander, come look!"

He turned and walked quickly back. She waited for him at the center of the bridge, then pointed wordlessly as he came up. A great section of iron chain forming the bridge railing had snapped and broken. At her feet, streaks of blood lay drying on the stone.

The girl knelt and touched the blood with her fingers. "Not very old," she said softly. "Not more than an hour."

He stared at her in stricken silence, and the same unspoken thought passed between them. His hand came up quickly, as if to ward it off. "No, it can't be hers . . ."

Then a scream rent the air, shrill and terrifying—the scream of an animal filled with rage and fear. It shattered the stillness and their thoughts and left them frozen. It came from beyond the alcove.

"Whisper!" Kimber cried.

Rone whirled. Brin!

He sprang from the bridge to the cavern floor and raced for the alcove's passageway, both hands reaching back across his shoulder for the great broadsword strapped there. He was quick, but Kimber was even quicker. She went past him like a frightened animal, darting from the shadows of the cavern to the alcove and the light beyond. Trailing, Cogline called out in a furious attempt to slow them both, his voice high and shrill with desperation, but his crooked legs too slow to keep up.

Then they were through the alcove and into the light, with Kimber a dozen yards in front of Rone. There was Whisper, locked in battle with a pair of faceless black things on a narrow rock shelf before them, a blur of motion and darkness. Beyond, on a stone stairway that wound downward from the cliffs to the ledge and the valley below—on a stairway that Rone knew at once to be the Croagh—one of the Mord Wraiths stood watching.

At the approach of the girl and the highlander, the Mord Wraith turned.

"Kimber, look out!" Rone howled in warning.

But the girl was already springing to Whisper's aid, long knives appearing in both hands. The Wraith pointed toward the girl and red fire exploded from its fingers. The fire lanced past the girl, missing her somehow, and fragments of rock flew into the air as it struck. Rone sprang forward with a cry, the ebony blade of the Sword of Leah held before him. The Wraith turned toward him instantly, and the fire burst forth a second time. It hammered at the highlander, caught on the blade of the sword, and the whole of the air about him turned bright with flame. The force of the blow lifted him clear of the ground and threw him back.

Then Cogline appeared from out of the caverns, old, bent, and fierce as he screamed at the Wraith in challenge. A little bit of flesh, bone, and cloth, he skittered toward the black-robed form. The walker swung about, pointing. But the old man's sticklike arm whipped forward, and a dark object flew from his hand, hurtling into the Wraith's crimson fire. A tremendous explosion rocked the whole of the mountainside. Flames and smoke geysered skyward from the stem of the Croagh, and bits of shattered rock flew every-where.

For an instant everything disappeared in smoke and silt. Fran-tic, Rone scrambled back to his feet.

"Taste a bit of my magic, you worm food!" Cogline was howl-ing in glee. "See what you can do against that!"

He darted past Rone before the highlander could stop him, dancing about in maddened delight, his sticklike form disappear-ing into the smoke. Whisper's sudden snarl lifted from somewhere ahead, then Kimber's sharp cry. Rone swore in fury and leaped for-ward. Crazy old man!

Directly before him, red fire erupted from the haze. Cogline's thin form flew sideways as if it were a doll flung by an angry child. The highlander set his teeth and hurtled toward the source of the fire. Almost at once, he came up against the Wraith, its black-cloaked form tattered and bent. The Sword of Leah pierced into a burst of red fire, shattering it apart. The Wraith disappeared. Some-thing moved behind him, and the highlander swung about. But it was Whisper who lunged past through a trailer of smoke, the first of the black things clinging to him, the second borne before him in his teeth. Swiftly, Rone struck, the sword cleaving through the creature that hung upon the moor cat's back and stripping it from him.

"Kimber!" he screamed.

Red fire exploded close to him, but he caught it again on the sword. A cloaked form appeared momentarily through the smoke, and he lunged at it. This time the Wraith was not quick enough. Backed against the stone stairway of the Croagh, it tried to slip left, with fire bursting from its fingers. Rone was on it at once. The Sword of Leah came down, and the Wraith exploded into a pile of ash.

Everything went still then, save for the low coughing sound Whisper made as he padded ghostlike through the haze toward Rone. Slowly the smoke drifted away and the whole of the ledge and the Croagh became visible once more. The ledge was littered with broken rock, and an entire section of the Croagh where it joined to

the ledge—where the Mord Wraith had been standing when Cogline had challenged it—was gone.

Rone glanced quickly about. The Wraith and the black things
were gone as well. He wasn't sure what had happened to them—
whether they had been destroyed or merely driven off—but they
were nowhere to be seen.

"Rone."

He whirled at the sound of Kimber's voice. She appeared from
the far side of the ledge, looking small and bedraggled, limping
slightly as she came. Anger and relief flooded through him. "Kimber, why in the name of all that's right and sensible did you . . . ?"

"Because Whisper would have done the same for me. Where is
grandfather?"

Rone clamped his mouth shut on the rest of what he would
have said to her. Together, they scanned the littered rock shelf. They
saw him finally, half buried in a pile of rubble by the cliff side, as
blackened as the ash left by the fires of their battle with the Wraith.
They hurried to him and lifted him clear. His face and arms were
burned, his hair singed, and he was covered with soot. Gently, Kimber cradled the old man's head. His eyes were closed and he did not
appear to be breathing.

"Grandfather?" the girl whispered, her hand on his cheek.

"Who's that?" the old man cried abruptly, startling both the girl
and the highlander. Arms and legs began to thrash. "Get out of my
house, trespassers! Get out of my home!"

Then his eyes blinked and opened. "Girl?" he muttered weakly.
"What happened to the black things?"

"Gone, grandfather." She smiled, relief in her dark eyes. "Are
you all right?"

"All right?" He looked dazed, but nodded resolutely, his voice
becoming stiff with indignation. "Of course I'm all right! Just got a
bit ahead of myself, that's all! Help me up!"

Rone took a deep breath. Lucky to be alive is what you are, old
man, you and the girl, he thought grimly.

With Kimber's aid he pulled Cogline back to his feet and let him test his weight alone. The old man looked like something dredged up from an ash pit, but he seemed uninjured. The girl hugged him warmly and began to brush him off.

"You must be more careful, grandfather," she admonished. "You are not as quick as you used to be. The walkers will have you if you try to run past them again the way you did here."

Rone shook his head in disbelief. Who should be scolding whom—the girl the old man or the old man the girl? What had Brin and he been thinking anyway when they . . .

He caught himself. Brin. He had forgotten about Brin. He glanced toward the Croagh. If the Valegirl had gotten this far, she had almost certainly gone down into the Maelmord. And that was where he must go as well.

He turned from Kimber and her grandfather and hurried across the rock shelf to where it joined with the steps of the Croagh. He was still gripping the Sword of Leah firmly. How much time had he lost here? He had to catch Brin before she got too far ahead into whatever it was that waited in the valley below . . .

Abruptly, he slowed and stopped. Whisper stood directly in his path, blocking the stairway down. The moor cat stared at him momentarily, then sat back on his haunches and blinked.

"Get out of the way!" Rone snapped.

The cat did not move. The highlander hesitated, then started forward impatiently. Whisper's muzzle drew back slightly, and a low growl rumbled in his throat.

Rone stopped at once and looked back angrily at Kimber. "Get your cat out of my way, Kimber. I'm going down."

The girl called softly to the moor cat, but Whisper stayed where he was. Puzzled, she came forward and bent close to him, talking in a low, calm voice, rubbing the massive head about the ears and neck. The cat nuzzled her back and made a soft purring sound, but did not move. Finally, the girl stepped back.

"Brin is well," she informed him with a brief smile. "She has gone down into the pit."

Rone nodded with relief. "Then I've got to go after her."

But the girl shook her head. "You must remain here, high-lander."

Rone stared. "Remain here? I can't do that! Brin is all alone down there! I'm going after her!"

But again the girl shook her head. "You cannot. She doesn't want you doing that. She has used the wishsong to prevent it. She has made Whisper her sentry. No one may pass—not even me."

"But he's your cat! Make him move! Tell him that he has to move! The magic isn't that strong, is it?"

Her pixie face looked up at him calmly. "It is more than the magic, Rone. Whisper's instincts tell him that Brin is right about this. The magic does not hold him; his reason does. He knows that whatever danger waits in the valley is too great. He will not let you pass."

The highlander continued to stare at the girl, anger and disbelief flooding his face. His gaze shifted to the giant cat and back again.

What was he supposed to do now?

Euphoria engulfed Brin, sweeping over her in a warm rush, flooding through her as if it were her life's blood. She felt it carry her down within herself like a tiny leaf borne on the waters of some great river. Sight, sound, and smell meshed and ran in a dazzling mix of wild imaginings, some of beauty and light, some of darkest misshape, all in the ebb and flow of her mind's eye. Nothing was as it had been, but new and exotic and alive with wonder. It was a journey of self-discovery that transcended thought and feeling and was its own reason for being.

She sang, the music of the wishsong the food and drink that fed her, sustained her, and gave her life.

She was deep within the Maelmord now, far from the stairway of the Croagh and the world she had left behind. It was another world entirely here. As she worked to make herself one with it, it reached out to her and drew her in. Stench, heat, and the rot of living things wrapped about her and found in her their child. Gnarled limbs, vines twisted and mottled, and great stalks of brush and weed stroked her body as she slipped past, feeding on the vibrancy of the music, finding in it an elixir that gave back life. From a great distance away, Brin felt their caress and smiled in response.

It was as if she had ceased to exist. Some tiny part of her knew that she should have been horrified by the things that wound about her and rubbed so lovingly against her. But she was given over to the music of the wishsong now, and she was no longer the one she had been. All of the feelings and reasonings that had been hers, that had made her who she was, were masked away by the dark magic, and she was become a thing like that into which she journeyed. She was a kindred spirit, wandered back from some distant place, the evil within her as strong as the evil she found waiting. She had become as dark as the Maelmord and the life that had been spawned there. She was one with it. She belonged.

A tiny part of her understood that Brin Ohmsford had ceased to exist, made over by the magic of the wishsong. It understood that she had let herself become this other thing—a thing so repulsive that she could not have stood it otherwise—and that she would not come back to herself until she had found her way through to the heart of the evil enfolding her. The euphoria, the exhilaration brought on by the frightening power of the wishsong, threatened to steal her away from herself completely, to strip her of her sanity and make her forever the thing she pretended to be. All the strange and marvelous imaginings were but trappings of a madness that would destroy her. All that remained of the one she once had been was that small bit of self that she still kept wrapped carefully within. All else had become the child of the Maelmord.

The wall of the jungle passed away and came about again, and nothing of it changed. Shadows wrapped close about, as soft as black velvet and as silent as death. The whole of the sky stayed screened away, and only the half-light of night's coming penetrated beyond the gloom. All the while that she walked in this maze of darkness and stifling heat, the hissing of the Maelmord's breath lifted from the earth, and the limbs, trunks, stalks, and vines swayed and writhed with the motion. Save for the hissing, there was only silence—intense and expectant. There was no sign of other life—no sign of the walkers, of the dark things that served them, or of the Ildatch that had given them all life.

She went on, driven by that spark of memory she harbored deep within herself. Find the Ildatch, it whispered in its small, empty voice. Find the book of the dark magic. Time fragmented and slipped away until it no longer had meaning. Had she been here an hour? Or more? There was a strange sense of having been here for a very long time, almost as if she had been here forever.

Far distant, almost lost to her in the vast tangle of the jungle, something tumbled from the cliffs above and fell into the pit. She could sense its fall and hear its scream as the Maelmord closed quickly about it, squeezing, crushing, and consuming until the thing was no more. She savored its death, tasted its blood as it was devoured. When it was gone, she longed for more.

Then whispered warnings brushed at her. From a dimly re-membered past she saw Allanon once more. Tall and bent, his black hair gone gray, his lean face lined with age, he reached for her across a chasm she could not bridge, and his words were like sprinkled drops of rain upon a window closed before her. Beware. The wish-song is power like nothing I have ever seen. Use it with caution. She heard the words, saw them spatter on the glass and found herself laughing at the way they fell. The figure of the Druid receded and was gone. Dead, now, she reminded herself in surprise. Gone from the Four Lands forever.

She called him back again, as if his reappearance would serve to remind her of something that she had somehow forgotten. He came, sweeping out of the mists, striding across the chasm that had separated them. His strong hands came down gently to rest upon her shoulders. Wisdom and determination reflected in his eyes, and there was a sense of his never having truly left, but his always having been there. This is not a game you play, he whispered. Never that!

Beware! And she shook her head. I am savior and destroyer, she whispered back. But who am I? Tell me now! Tell me . . .

A ripple in the fabric of her consciousness swept him away, a ghost, and suddenly she was back within the Maelmord. There was a rumbling of uneasiness within the pit, a tone of dissatisfaction in its hiss. It had sensed a momentary change in her and was disturbed. She reverted instantly to the thing she had created. The wishsong rose and swept into the jungle, soothing it, lulling it once again. The uneasiness and dissatisfaction faded.

She slipped ahead again into the nothingness, letting the Maelmord swallow her up. There was a deepening of shadows and a fading of the light. The breathing of the pit seemed to grow heavier. The sense of kinship that the wishsong created between them tightened and left her breathless with anticipation. She was close now—close to what she sought. The feel of it speared through her like a sudden rush of blood, and she sang with renewed intensity. The magic of the wishsong lifted through the gloom, and the Maelmord shuddered in response.

Then the wall of the jungle fell away, and she stood within a massive, shadowed clearing, wrapped close about by trees, brush, and vines. A tower stood at the center of the clearing, ancient and crumbling, lost in the gloom. Walls of stone rose upward toward the forest roof, forming and reforming in a series of spiraling turrets and notched parapets, as stripped and barren in their look as bleached bones. Nowhere did the foliage of the jungle grow upon the tower. As if its touch meant death, the jungle had passed it by.

Brin stopped, the music of the wishsong lowering to a whisper of expectancy as she stared at the tower.

Here! The heart of the evil is here. The Ildatch!

Drawing close the layers of magic that cloaked her, she went to meet it.

XLIII

◆

WOODEN DOORS, WEATHERED AND CRACKED WITH AGE, stood ajar at the tower's dark entry, sagging on hinges broken and rusted with disuse. Wrapped in the music of her song, the Vale-girl passed through. The gloom lay thick within, yet there was light enough by which she might see, a dim and misted glimmer that slipped in thin streamers through cracks and splits in the tower's crumbling walls. Dust carpeted the stone flooring, forming a blanket of fine silt that rose in clouds as the girl's boots pressed down upon it. It was cool here, the heat and the stench of the jungle somehow locked without.

Brin slowed. A hallway wound ahead into shadow. She turned briefly, a warning tug from deep within her bringing her about to stare guardedly back into the mass of the jungle that walled this tower away.

She went on. The power of the magic stirred through her in a flush of sudden heat, and she seemed to float. She passed down the hallway, following its bends and twists, barely aware of the dust as it rose vaporlike from beneath her feet. Once she thought to wonder how it was that no other footprints save hers marked the corridor she followed when surely the Mord Wraiths, too, had passed this way, but the matter faded quickly from her mind.

Stairs rose before her and she began to climb—a slow, endless climb into the center of the tower. Whispers seemed to call out to her, voices that had no source and no identity, but were born of the very air she breathed. All about her, the whispers called. Shadows and half-light mixed and blended. It seemed as if she were soaking into the stone of the tower itself, slipping ghostlike through its chambers, spreading out to become one with it, as she had become one with the Maelmord. She felt it happen, bit by bit, a welcome drawing in of her body. The magic of the song made it happen, still reaching out to the evil that lay hidden there, insinuating her within as if she were truly one with it . . .

Then the stairway ended and she stood on the threshold of a cavernous, domed rotunda that lay gray, shadowed, and empty. Almost of its own volition, the music of the wishsong faded to a whisper, and the voices in the air about her went still.

She entered the room, barely conscious of the movement of her body, still seeming to float as she passed. Shadows crept back from her, and her eyes adjusted to the light. The chamber was not empty, as she had first thought. There, almost lost in the gloom, was a dais; on the dais was an altar. She came forward a step. Something rested on the altar, huge, squarish, and shrouded in a darkness that seemed to emanate from within. She came forward another step. A fierce excitement flooded through her.

It was the Ildatch!

She knew it instantly, before she was certain what it was that she was seeing. This was the Ildatch, the heart of evil. The power of the wishsong filled her and drove through her body with white-hot intensity.

She crossed the room through the raging of her thoughts, twisting down into herself like a coiled snake. The music of the wishsong became a venomous hiss. The room seemed to draw away from her, the walls receding back into shadow until there was nothing in all the world but the book. She climbed the steps of the dais and strode to where it lay closed upon the altar. It was old and worn, its bindings of copper tarnished to a greenish black and its leather covers cracked and soiled—a huge and monstrous tome that looked as if it might have seen the passing of all the ages of mankind that had ever been.

She hovered over it a moment, staring down expectantly, savoring the deep satisfaction she felt at having the book finally within her grasp.

Then she reached down and her hands closed about it.

—Dark child—

The voice whispered softly within her mind, and her fingers froze upon the tarnished bindings.

—Dark child—

The wishsong died into a whisper and was gone. Her throat constricted and sealed the music away, almost before she knew what it was that she had done. She stood in silence before the altar, hands still clasped tightly upon the book. Echoes of the voice lingered fitfully within her mind, tendrils that reached out and bound her so that she could not move.

—I have been waiting for you, dark child. I have been waiting since first you came into being, a baby from your mother's womb, Elven magic's child. Always we have been joined, you and I, by bonds stronger than blood ties, stronger than flesh. Many times we have touched spirit to spirit, and though I never knew you nor knew your way, I knew always that one day you would come—

The voice was flat and toneless, belonging neither to man nor woman, but to something that was both, stripped of all emotion and all feeling, so that there was an emptiness to its whisper that was devoid of life. Brin listened to that voice and went cold to the bone. Deep within, the self that she still sheltered and kept hidden drew back in terror.

—Dark child—

She scanned the shadows of the chamber about her rapidly. Where was the speaker who called to her? What thing was it that held her so? Her eyes shifted in horror to the ancient tome she held. Her fingers were white with the grip they kept, and a burning spread from the leathered bindings.

—I am, dark child. Even as you. I have life. It has always been so. There have always been those who would give me life. There have always been those who would give me theirs—

Brin's mouth opened, but no sound came forth. The burning sensation spread from her hands into her arms and began to climb.

—Know me. I am the Ildatch, the book of the dark magic, born of the age of faerie. I am older than the Elves—as old as the King of the Silver River, as ancient as the Word. Those who created me, those who gave me form, have long since passed from the land with the coming of the worlds of faerie and Man. Once I was but a part of the Word, hidden from sight and spoken only in darkness. I was but a gathering of secrets. Then the gathering took form, written and studied by those who would know my power. There have always been those who would know my power. Through all the ages, I have been there for them and have given my secrets to those who wished them shared. I have made creatures of magic and given power. But never has there been one such as you—

The words echoed in whispers filled with anticipation and promise, and the Valegirl felt them spin like blown leaves through her mind. The burning was all through her now, a tingling like the rush of heat from a furnace as its door is thrown open.

—There have been many before you. Of the Druids were born the Warlock Lord and the Bearers of the Skull. They found in me the secrets that they sought and became what they would. But I was the power. Of men outcast of the races were born the Mord Wraiths, seeds already sown. But again, I was the power. I am always the power. Each time, there is a supreme vision of what must be with the world and with her creatures. Each time, that vision is given shape by the minds of those who would use the power locked within my pages. Each time, the vision proves inadequate and the shaper fails. Dark child, see now a glimpse of what it is that I can offer—

As if of their own volition, Brin's hands carefully opened the book of the Ildatch, and its parchment leaves began to turn. Words whispered from a text in an alien script and language older than

Man, lifting from script to voice, soft and secretive. The Valegirl's mind opened to them, and comprehension of the text came instantly to her. A touch here, a touch there, the secrets of power were revealed to her, dark and terrible.

Then, as quickly as the revelations had come, they were gone again, lingering on in teasing memories. The pages of the book slipped back again, and the bindings closed. Her hands, still fastened on the massive tome, began to shake.

—Only a whisper of what I am have I shown you. Power, dark child. Power that would dwarf that mastered by the Druid Brona and those who followed him. Power that would render meaningless that of the Mord Wraiths who come to me now. Feel that power rush through you. Feel its touch—

The burning flooded through her. She felt herself expand and grow with its rush.

—For a thousand years, I have been used in ways that would dictate the fate of you and yours. For a thousand years, the enemies of your family have called upon my power and sought to destroy what you would keep. All that has brought you to this place and time has been because of me. I am the maker of what you are; I am the shaper of your life. There is reason in all that happens, dark child, and there is reason in this. Do you sense what that reason is? Look within—

A whisper of warning called suddenly to her, and she seemed to remember a tall, black-robed figure with graying hair and piercing eyes speaking to her of that which would deceive and corrupt. She struggled momentarily with the memory, but no name would come and the vision was obscured by the burning that filled her and the lingering echo of the words of the Ildatch.

—Do you not see yourself? Do you not see what you are? Look within—

The voice was cold, flat, and emotionless still, yet there was an insistence to it that wrenched her thoughts away. Her vision blurred, and she seemed to see from without the thing that she had become through the magic of the wishsong.

We are as one, dark child, just as you have wished. There was never any need for the Elven magic, for you are what you are and always have been. That is why we are joined. There are ties born of the magics that make us what we are, for we are no more than the magics that we harbor—you within your body of flesh and blood, I within mine of parchment and ink. We are lives joined, and what has gone before has brought us to now. It is for this that I have waited all these years—

Lies! The word flashed through Brin's mind and was lost. Her thoughts spun in confusion, and her reason scattered. Her hands still gripped the Ildatch as if it held her life within, and she found the words spoken by its disembodied voice oddly persuasive. There were indeed ties that bound them; there was a joining. She was like the Ildatch, a part of it, kindred to it.

She called out the name of the Druid in her mind, struggling to find the memory she had now lost. The burning rose in a fierce rush to carry it away, and again the voice spoke.

—All these years I have waited for you, dark child. From time out of time, you have come to me, and now I belong to you. See what must be done with me. Whisper it back to me—

The words came together in her mind, dark against the red haze of her vision. She sought to scream, but the sound constricted in her throat.

—Whisper what must be done with me—

No! No!

—Whisper what must be done with me—

Tears rose to her eyes and trickled slowly down her cheeks.

I must use you, she answered.

Rone stalked from the Croagh in fury, wheeled, and came back again. Both hands gripped the ebony blade of his sword until the knuckles were white.

"Enough is enough—get that cat out of my way, Kimber!" he

ordered, coming up next to her and slowing as Whisper's massive head swung about to face him.

But again the girl shook her head. "I cannot do that, Rone. He uses his own judgment in this."

"I don't care a whit about his judgment!" Rone exploded. "He's only an animal and he can't make a decision like this! I'm going past him whether he likes it or not! I'm not leaving Brin down in that pit alone!"

Sword lifting, he started for Whisper, but in that instant a deep shudder rippled through the mountain, rising up from the dark jungle of the Maelmord. So strong was the tremor that it staggered the highlander and the girl, causing them to stumble back in surprise. Shaken, they regained their balance and hurried to the edge of the cliffs.

"What's happened down there?" Rone whispered worriedly. "What's happened, Kimber?"

"Walkers, I'd guess." Cogline spit from behind him. "Called up the dark magic to use against the girl, maybe."

"Grandfather!" Kimber was angry this time.

Rone wheeled in rage. "Old man, if anything has happened to Brin because I've been held up here by that cat . . ."

Then he went suddenly still. A line of shadows appeared on the stairway of the Croagh, stooped and shrouded in the fading half-light of the late afternoon. They came one after another, descending from Graymark's leaden walls, winding their way downward toward the ledge where Rone and his companions waited.

"Mord Wraiths!" the highlander breathed softly.

Already Whisper was turning, wheeling into a crouch as he prepared to defend against them. Cogline's sudden intake of breath hissed sharply through the silence.

Rone stared upward wordlessly as the line of dark forms lengthened and advanced. There were too many.

"Get behind me, Kimber," he told her gently.

Then he brought up the sword.

* * *

I must use you . . . use you . . . use you.

The words repeated over and over in Brin's mind, rising in a litany of conviction that threatened to inundate all reason. Yet some tiny semblance of logic remained, screaming at her through the words of the chant.

It is the dark magic, Valegirl! It is the evil that you have come into this place to destroy!

But the touch of the book against the skin of her hands and the burning it brought to her body held her bound so that nothing else could hold sway. Again the voice came to her, wrapping close about.

—What am I but a gathering of wisdom's lessons culled through the ages and bound for the usage of mortal beings? I am neither good nor evil, but simply a thing that is. Learning, recorded and bound—there for any who might seek to know. I take what is given me of the lives of those who work my spells and I am but a reflection of them. Think, dark child. Who have been the ones who would use me? What purposes have they sought to serve? You are not as they—

Brin braced herself against the altar, the book clasped in her hands. Don't listen! Don't listen!

—For a thousand years and longer, your enemies have held me. Now you stand in their place, given the chance to use me as no other has tried. You hold the power that is mine. You hold the secrets that so many have wrongly used. Think what you might do with that power, dark child. All of life and death can be reshaped by what I am. Wishsong joined to written word, magic to magic—how wondrous it would be. You can feel how wondrous it would be if you would but try—

But there was no need to try. She had felt it before in the magic of the wishsong. Power! She had been swept away by it, and she had reveled in its sweetness. When it wrapped about her, she rose far above all the world and all of the creatures in it and she could gather them in or sweep them away as she might choose. How much more, then, could she do—could she feel—if she had also the power of this book?

—All that is would be yours. All. Be what you would and make the world as you know it should be. You could so do much, and it would be as it should with you—not as with those who came before. You have the strength which they lacked. You are born of the Elven magic. Use me, dark child. Find the limits of your own magic and of mine. Join with me. It is for this that I have waited and that you have come. It is what has always been intended for us. Always—

Brin's head shook slowly from side to side. I came to destroy this, came to make an end . . . Within, everything seemed to be breaking apart, shattering like glass fallen to stone. Rushes of blinding heat burned through her, and she felt as if she were a thing apart from the body that sought to hold her.

—I have knowledge to offer that I would give. I have insight that surpasses anything ever dreamed by mortal creatures. It can make you anything you wish. All of life can be made over as it should be, as you see that it should. Destroy me, and all I have is needlessly lost. Destroy me, and nothing of what might come to pass can ever do so. Keep what is good, dark child, and make it your own—

Allanon, Allanon . . .

But the voice cut short her soundless cry.

—See, dark child. What you truly would destroy stands behind you. Turn now and look. Turn and see—

She whirled. A gathering of robed walkers slipped from the shadows like ghosts, tall, black, and forbidding. They filed into the rotunda, hesitating as they caught sight of Brin holding in her hands the book of dark magic. The voice of the Ildatch whispered again.

—The wishsong, dark child. Use the magic. Destroy them. Destroy them—

She acted almost without thinking. Clasping the Ildatch to her protectively, she called forth the power of her magic. It came swiftly, loosed within her like the waters of a flood. She cried out, and the wishsong shattered the tower's dark silence. It went through the gloom of the rotunda, almost a tangible thing. It caught the walkers in a burst of sound, and they simply ceased to exist. Not even ash remained of what they had been.

Brin staggered back against the altar, and within her body the magic of the wishsong mixed with the magic of the book.

—Feel it, dark child. Feel the power that is yours. It fills you, and I am part of it. How easily your enemies must fall before you when that power is called forth. Can you question longer what must be? Think no more that anything different could ever be. Think no more that we are not as one. Take me and use me. Destroy the Wraiths and the black things that would stand against you. Make me yours. Give me life—

Still that part of her locked deep within fought to resist the voice, but her body was no longer her own. It belonged now to the magic, and she was trapped within its shell. She rose through herself, a new being, and that tiny bit of self that still saw the truth was left behind. She expanded until it seemed as if she filled the tiny chamber. There was so little room for her here! She must have the space that waited without!

A long, anguished groan broke from her lips, and she stretched forth her arms, the book of the Ildatch held high.

—Use me. Use me—

Within her, the power began to build.

XLĪV

◆

THE STEPS OF THE CROAGH SPED AWAY BENEATH JAIR'S FEET
as he hastened after Garet Jax and Slanter, and it seemed to him
as he climbed that each step must surely be his last. The muscles
knotted and cramped within his body, and pain from his wound
lanced through him, wearing away at his already failing strength.
He was gasping for breath, his lungs aching, and his sun-browned
face streaked with sweat.

But somehow he kept pace. There was never any question of
doing anything else.

His eyes swept upward along the Croagh as he ran, concen-
trating on the weave of stairs and railing, following the path of the
roughened stone. He was conscious of the cliffs and fortress walls
below him, distant now and fading further, and of Graymark and
the Ravenshorn. He was conscious, too, of the valley all about, en-
cased in mist and the half-light of a dusk that rapidly approached.
Brief images slipped past the corners of his vision and were quickly
forgotten, for none of that mattered now. Nothing mattered but the
climb and what waited at its end.

Heaven's Well.

And Brin. He would find her again in the waters of the well. He
would discover what had become of her, and he would learn what
it was that he must do to help her. The King of the Silver River had
promised him that he would find a way to give Brin back to herself.

His boot slid out from under him suddenly as he stepped on a patch of crumbling stone and he fell forward, his hands scraping as he caught himself. Quickly he pushed back up again and hurried on, heedless of the damage.

Ahead, the other two ran effortlessly on—Garet Jax and Slanter, the last of the little company that had come north from Culhaven. Bitterness and anger flooded through the Valeman. Flashes of light danced before his eyes as he fought for breath momentarily, exhaustion sweeping through him. But they were almost at their journey's end.

The stone spiral of the Croagh swung suddenly right, and the wall of the peak toward which they climbed rose close before them, rugged and stark against the graying sky. Ahead, the stairway ascended to the dark mouth of a cavern that opened back into the heart of the mountain. Less than two dozen steps remained.

Garet Jax motioned for them to wait, then soundlessly climbed the last few stairs to the summit of the Croagh and stepped out onto the ledge. He stood there a moment, his black form framed against the afternoon sky, lean and shadowy. He was like something inhuman, the thought flashed briefly through Jair's mind, like something that wasn't real.

The Weapons Master turned, gray eyes fixing on him. One hand beckoned.

"Hurry, boy," Slanter muttered.

They scrambled up the remaining steps of the Croagh and stood beside Garet Jax. The cavern loomed before them, a monstrous chamber split by dozens of crevices that let in the light from without in dim, hazy streamers. Close about, the shadows gathered, and within their blackness nothing moved.

"Can't see anything from here," Slanter grumbled. He started forward, but instantly Garet Jax pulled him back.

"Wait, Gnome," he said. "There's something there . . . something that waits . . ."

His voice trailed away softly. A stillness settled down about them, deep and oppressive. Even the wind that stirred the mists of the valley seemed to die suddenly away. Jair caught his breath and held it. There was indeed something there—waiting. He could feel its presence.

"Garet . . ." he began softly.

"Shhhhh."

Then a shadow detached itself from the rocks within the cavern entrance, and Jair went cold to the bone. Silently, the shadow slipped through the gloom. It was nothing that any of them had ever seen. It was neither a Gnome nor a Wraith, but a powerfully built creature, almost man-shaped, with a thick ruff about its loins and great, hooked claws at its fingers and toes. Cruel yellow eyes fixed on them, and a scarred, bestial face split wide at its snout to reveal a mass of crooked teeth.

The thing came forward into the light and stopped. It was not black like the Wraiths. It was red.

"What is it?" Jair whispered, fighting to contain the sense of revulsion that swept through him.

The Jachyra gave a sudden cry—a howl that rang through the silence like hideous laughter.

"Valeman, it is the dream!" Garet Jax cried, a strange, wild look crossing his hard face. Slowly he lowered the blade of the sword until it touched the ledge rock. Then he turned to Jair. "Journey's end," he whispered.

Jair shook his head in confusion. "Garet, what . . . ?"

"The dream! The vision that I told you about that night in the rain when we first spoke of the King of the Silver River! The dream that brought me east with you, Valeman—this is it!"

"But the dream showed you a thing of fire . . ." Jair stammered.

"Fire, yes—that was how it appeared!" Garet Jax cut him short. He let his breath out slowly. "Until now, I thought that perhaps—in a way that I could not fathom—I had mistaken what I had seen. But in the dream, as I stood before the fire and the voice that told me what I must do died away, the fire cried out like a thing alive. It was a cry that was almost a laugh—the cry that this creature has given!"

His gray eyes burned. "Valeman, this is the battle that I was promised!"

Before them, the Jachyra dropped into a crouch and began si-
dling forward from the cavern. Garet Jax brought the sword up at
once.

"You mean to fight this thing?" Slanter was incredulous.

The other never even looked at him. "Keep back from me."

"This is a poor idea if ever there was one!" Slanter looked
frightened. "You know nothing of this creature. If it is poisonous
like the one that attacked the Borderman . . ."

"I am not the Borderman, Gnome." Garet Jax watched intently
as the Jachyra approached. "I am the Weapons Master. And I have
never lost a battle."

The cold eyes flickered briefly in their direction and then fixed
once more on the Jachyra. Jair started toward him, but Slanter
grabbed his shoulder roughly and pulled him back again. "No, you
don't," the Gnome snapped. "He wants this fight—let him have it!
Never lost a battle! Lost his mind, that's what he's lost!"

Garet Jax was gliding forward across the ledge to where the
Jachyra had stopped. "Take the Valeman into the cavern and find
the well, Gnome. Do it when the creature comes for me. Do what
you have come here to do. Remember the pledge."

Jair was frantic. Helt, Foraker, Edain Elessedil—all lost in an
effort to get him to the basin at Heaven's Well. And now Garet Jax
as well?

But it was already too late. The Jachyra screamed once and
launched itself at Garet Jax, a blur of motion as it shot across the
ledge rock. It leaped up against the Weapons Master, claws ripping. But the black form slipped aside as if it were no more than the
shadow it resembled. The sword blade cut into the attacker—once,
twice—so quickly the eye could barely follow. The Jachyra howled
and slipped free, circling away for another rush.

Garet Jax wheeled, his lean face fierce, gray eyes bright with
excitement. "Go, Jair Ohmsford!" he cried. "When it comes for me
again—go!"

Anger and frustration tore at the Valeman as Slanter pulled
him away. He would not go!

"Boy, I'm through arguing with you!" Slanter cried in fury.

Again the Jachyra attacked, and again Garet Jax sidestepped the rush, his slender sword flicking. But he was a fraction of a second too slow this time. The claws of the Jachyra ripped through the sleeve of his tunic and into his arm. Jair cried out, pulling free of Slanter.

Slanter spun him about and hit him. The blow caught him squarely on the chin. There was an instant of blinding light, and then everything went black.

The last thing he remembered was falling.

When he came awake again, Slanter was kneeling next to him. The Gnome had pulled him upright and into a sitting position and was shaking him roughly.

"Get up, boy! Get on your feet!"

The words were hard and filled with anger, and Jair scrambled up quickly. They were deep within the cavern now. Slanter must have carried him in. What little light there was came from cracks in the broken rock of the cavern's roof.

The Gnome yanked him about. "What did you think you were doing back there?"

Jair was still dazed. "I couldn't let him . . ."

"Off to the rescue with your tricks, were you?" the other cut him short. "You don't understand anything—you know that? You really don't understand anything! What is it that you think we're doing here? You think we're playing some kind of game?" Slanter was livid. "There's choices been made long before this about living and dying, boy! You can't change that. You don't have the right! All of the others—all of them—died because that was the way it had to be! That was the way they wanted it! And why do you think that was?"

The Valeman shook his head. "I . . ."

"Because of you! They died because they believed in what it was that you had come here to do—every last one of them! Even I would have . . ." He caught himself and took a deep breath. "It would have done a lot of good if you'd gone dashing to the rescue back there and gotten yourself killed, now wouldn't it? A whole lot of sense that would have made!"

He wheeled Jair about and shoved him ahead into the cave. "Enough time's been wasted on teaching you things you ought to know already—time we don't have! I'm all that's left, and I'm not going to be much help to you if the walkers find us now. The others—they were the real protectors, looking out for me as much as for you!"

The Valeman slowed and half turned. "What's happened to Garet, Slanter?"

The other shook his head darkly. "He fights his promised battle—just as he wished." He pushed Jair again and hurried him on. "Find your well quickly, boy. Find it and do what you came here to do. Make all of this madness count for something!"

Jair ran with him and said nothing more, his face flushed with shame. He understood the Gnome's anger. Slanter was right. He had acted without thinking—without consideration for what the others of the little company had given up for him. His intentions might have been good, but his judgment had been poor indeed.

Ahead, the shadows fell away in a haze of graying sunlight that poured down through a massive crevice in the mountain stone. In the floor of the cavern, caught in the half-light, foul black water bubbled up from out of the rock in a broad basin, pumped in some impossible way through thousands of feet of stone from the depths of the earth. Gathering and churning, it gushed through a slot at one end of the basin into a worn channel, then poured through an opening in the mountain wall to tumble to the canyons below, where it began its long journey west to become the Silver River.

Gnome and Valeman slowed cautiously, eyes darting through gloom and hazy spray to the deep niches and corners of the cavern's dark ends. Nothing moved. Only the flow of the blackened waters gave evidence of life, a terrible rush of poison that steamed and boiled as it lifted from the wellspring. All about, the stench of the Maelmord hung like a shroud.

Jair went forward once more, eyes fixed on the basin that was Heaven's Well. How perverse that name seemed to him now as he gazed upon the fouled waters. Silver River no more, he thought dismally, and he wondered how even the magic of the old man could change it back to what it had once been. Slowly, he reached into his tunic front and his fingers closed about the tiny pouch of Silver Dust that he had carried with him all through his long journey east. He slipped the drawstrings free and peered within. The dust lay gathered, like ordinary sand.

And if it were only sand . . . ?

"Quit wasting time!" Slanter snapped.

Jair moved to the edge of the basin, conscious of the sludge that choked the well's dark waters and of the reek. It could not be only sand! He swallowed against that fear, remembering Brin . . .

"Throw it!" Slanter cried angrily.

Jair's hand jerked up, flinging the Silver Dust from its pouch, scattering it in a wide sweep across the surface of the fouled well. The tiny grains flew from the darkness of their container; and in the light of the cavern they seemed suddenly to sparkle and shimmer. They touched the waters and flared to life. A sheet of brilliant silver fire burst from the dark well. Jair and Slanter recoiled, shielding their eyes with their hands, blinded by the glare.

"The magic!" Jair cried.

Hissing and boiling, the waters of Heaven's Well exploded skyward, raining down across the length and breadth of the cavern, showering the two who crouched at the basin's walls. Then a rush of clean air seemed to spring to life, born out of the shower of water. Gnome and Valeman stared in awe and disbelief. Before them, the waters of Heaven's Well bubbled clear and fresh from the mountain rock. The stench and the black, poisoned color were gone. The Silver River was clean once more.

Quickly, Jair took from around his neck the vision crystal and its silver chain. There was no hesitation now. He moved back to the basin and climbed to a small outcropping of rock that overlooked it. He heard again in his mind the King of the Silver River telling him what he must do if he were to save Brin.

His hand tightened on the crystal, and he stared downward into the waters of the basin. All of the weariness and pain seemed to seep away in that single instant.

He threw the crystal and the chain into the basin's depths. There was a blinding flash of light—a flash greater than that created by the scattering of the Silver Dust—and the whole of the cavern seemed to explode in white fire. Jair dropped to his knees in fright, hearing Slanter's harsh cry behind him, and for an instant he thought that something had gone terribly wrong. But then the light fell away into the surface of the basin's waters, and the waters became as smooth and clear as glass.

The answer—show me the answer!

An image spread slowly across the mirrored surface, shimmering like a thing of transparency, then tightening. A tower room appeared, cavernous and flooded with musted, graying light, and there was an oppression that was almost palpable. Jair shrank from what he felt as he watched the room broaden and begin to draw him in.

And then the face of his sister appeared . . .

Brin Ohmsford felt the eyes looking at her, seeing all that she was and would become, then reaching to draw her close. Though wrapped within layers of magic as the power of the Ildatch built within her, she sensed the eyes and her own snapped up.

Stay from me! she howled. I am the dark child!

But that tiny part of her that the magic had not subverted knew the eyes and sought their help. Trapped thoughts broke from their shackles within her mind, fleeing like sheep from wolves that hunted, crying out and striving to reach shelter. She saw them, and the discovery filled her with fury. She reached for the scattered thoughts as they fled and she crushed them, one by one. Childhood, home, parents, friends—the disparate pieces of what she had been before she had found what she could be—she crushed them all.

Her voice found release then in a wail of anguish, and even the aged walls of the dark tower shook with the force of her keening. What had she done? There was pain within her now, brought about by the harm she had caused. A brief moment's insight flooded through her, and she heard the echo of the Grimpond's prophecy. It was her own death, indeed, that she had come into the Maelmord to find—that she had found! But it was not the death that she had supposed. It was the death of self through her entrapment by the magic! She was destroying herself!

But even in the horror of that realization, she could not release the Ildatch. She was caught up in the feel of the magic's power as it built and expanded like flood waters gathering. Before her, she held the book in a death grip, hearing its dispassionate voice whisper in encouragement and promise. Her pain was forgotten. The eyes were swept away. There was only the voice. She listened to its words, unable not to, and the world began to open up before her . . .

At the basin of Heaven's Well, Jair staggered back from the vision of his sister. Was it truly Brin whom he had seen? Horror flooded through him as he forced himself to view again the apparition that the waters had shown him. It was his sister, but twisted into a thing barely recognizable—a perversion of the human being she had once been. She was lost to herself—just as the King of the Silver River had said she would be.

And Allanon! Where was Allanon? Where was Rone? Had they failed her as he had failed her by reaching Heaven's Well too late?

Tears streaked Jair Ohmsford's face. It had come to pass as the old man had warned that it would—everything as he had foreseen. A terrible desperation filled the Valeman. He was all that was left. Allanon, Brin, Rone, the little company from Culhaven, all were gone.

"Boy, what is it that you do?" he heard Slanter call to him. "Get back from there and use what sense . . ."

Jair closed his ears and his mind to the rest of what the Gnome would have told him, his eyes fixing once more on the apparition in the basin's waters. It was Brin that he saw there, however twisted. It was Brin, gone down into the Maelmord, drawn to the book of the Ildatch, subverted somehow by the magic she had come to destroy.

And he must go to her. Even if it were too late, he must try to help her.

He came to his feet again, remembering the final gift of the King of the Silver River. "Once only shall the magic of your wish-song be used to create not illusion, but reality."

He brushed aside the confusion, horror, fear, and despair, and he sang. The music of the wishsong rose up in the stillness of the cavern, flooding the silence and drowning the sudden cries of protest that broke from Slanter's throat. Pain and weariness faded into yesterday as he cried out for the wish. The brilliant white light of the basin waters shimmered again in the air above Heaven's Well, and again the spray geysered skyward.

Slanter staggered away, blinded and deafened. When he finally looked back again, Jair Ohmsford had disappeared into the light.

XLV

◆

THERE WAS A MOMENT WHEN JAIR SEEMED TO STEP OUTSIDE
of himself. He was within the light and yet he was gone from it. He
passed through stone and space like an insubstantial ghost, and the
whole of the land spun wildly about him. Brief images appeared
out of that whirling mass. Slanter was there, his roughened yellow
face staring in shock and disbelief at the empty basin from which
Jair had passed. Garet Jax was locked in mortal combat with the red
monster, his lean face alive with fierce determination and his dark
form bloodied and torn. Gnome Hunters scurried in maddened
confusion through the halls of Graymark, searching frantically for
the intruders that had somehow eluded them. Helt had fallen in the
gatehouse, his body pierced through by sword and pike. Foraker
and the Elven Prince were ringed all about . . .

No more!

He screamed the words, wrenching at them like rooted things
from the music of his song, and the images fell away. He plummeted
downward, racing on the slick surface of the wishsong's cry. He had
to reach Brin!

Below, the tangle of the Maelmord lifted toward him. He could
see its dark mass rising and falling like a thing alive and could hear
the sound of its breathing, a loathsome hiss. Mountain walls swept
past him as he fell, and he watched the jungle stretch out its arms
to gather him in. Panic filled him. Then he plunged into the Mael-

mord; its gaping maw closed about him, the stench and the mist enveloped him, and everything disappeared.

Jair came back to himself slowly. Darkness lay across his vision like a shroud, and his head spun. He blinked, and the light returned. He was no longer falling through the vortex of the wishsong's music or plummeting downward into the tangled dark of the Maelmord. His journey was finished. The stone walls of the tower he had sought to reach surrounded him, aged and crumbling. He stood within them, a part of the vision that the waters of the basin of Heaven's Well had shown him.

"Brin!" he whispered harshly.

A figure turned, ringed in shadows and graying half-light, slight hands clasping firmly a massive, metalbound book.

Brin was a distortion of the woman she had once been, her features twisted almost beyond recognition. All of the exquisite beauty and vibrancy of form had hardened into something that might have been carved from stone. She was an apparition, her color drained away and her slight form skeletal and hunched down against the dark. Horror flooded through Jair. What had been done to her?

"Brin?" he called again, his voice faltering.

Wrapped in the frightening power of the Ildatch magic as it rushed to mix with her own, Brin was barely aware of the solitary figure who stood at the far side of the tower room. He called to her—a soft, familiar call. She fought back for an instant, through the layers of magic that wove about her to the reason that had fled deep within her, and memory returned. Jair! Ah, shades—it was Jair!

But the dark magic tightened again, stealing her back. The power surged through her, washing away all recognition of who it was she faced, bringing her back to the creature she had made herself become. Doubt and suspicion twisted through her, and the empty voice of the Ildatch whispered in warning.

—He is evil, dark child. A deception given life by the Wraiths. Keep him from you. Destroy him—

No, it is Jair . . . somehow he has come . . . Jair . . .

—He would steal the power that is ours. He would make us die—

No, Jair . . . has come . . .

—Destroy him, dark child. Destroy him—

She could not seem to help herself. Her resistance crumbled, and her voice lifted in a frightening wail. But Jair had seen the sudden look of hatred in his sister's eyes, and he was already moving. He sang, his own magic shielding him as he slipped from himself and left behind an image. Even so, he barely escaped her. The explosion of sound that broke from Brin's throat disintegrated the image and the wall behind it instantly and caught him up in the aftershock, throwing him like an empty sack to the stone floor. Dust and silt swirled through the half-light, and the ancient tower rocked with the force of the attack.

Slowly, Jair crawled back to his knees, crouching down within the screen of debris that hung on the air. For an instant, his certainty that he had used the third magic wisely wavered. It had seemed so clear to him when he had first seen Brin in the waters of Heaven's Well. He had known that he must go to her. But now that he had reached her, what was he to do? As the King of the Silver River had foretold, she was lost to herself. She had become something unrecognizable, subverted by the dark magic of the Ildatch. But it was more than that, for not only had she changed, but the magic of her wishsong had also changed. It had become a thing of awesome power, a weapon she would use against him, not knowing who he was, not remembering him at all. How was he to help her when she meant to destroy him?

A moment's time was all that he had to consider the dilemma. He came back to his feet. Allanon might have had the strength to withstand such power. Rone might have had the quickness to elude it. The little company from Culhaven might have had the numbers to overwhelm it. But they were all gone. All those who might have stood by him were no more. Whatever help he was to find, he must find within himself.

He slipped quickly through the screen of smoke and silt. He knew that if he were to be of any use to Brin, he must first find a way to separate her from the Ildatch.

The air cleared before him, and Brin's shadowy figure appeared a dozen yards away. Instantly he sang, the wishsong a sharp humming sound in the stillness, carrying in its music a whispered plea. Brin, it called. The book is too heavy, its weight too great. Release it, Brin. Let it fall!

For a brief second, Brin's hands came down, her head lowering in doubt. It appeared the illusion would work and that she would release the Ildatch. Then a fury swept across her gaunt face, and the cry of her wishsong shattered the air into fragments of sound, breaking apart Jair's plea.

The Valeman stumbled back. He tried again, this time with an illusion of fire, a hiss that scattered flames all about the binding of the ancient tome. Brin screamed, an animal-like cry, but then clasped the book to her as if she might smother the fire against her own body. Her head twisted about, her eyes darting. She was looking for him. She meant to find him and use the magic against him, to see him destroyed.

His song changed again, this time creating an illusion of smoke that billowed in clouds through the chamber. But she would be fooled for only a few moments. He dodged back about the walls of the tower, trying to come at her from a different direction. He sang again, this time sending to her a whisper of darkness, deep and impenetrable. He must be quicker than she was. He must keep her off balance.

He sped about the tower's shadows like a ghost, striking out at Brin with every trick he knew—with heat and cold, with dark and light, with pain, and with anger. Twice she lashed out blindly at him with her own magic, a searing burst of power that threw him from his feet and left him shaken. She seemed confused, somehow uncertain—as if unable to decide whether or not to use the whole of the power that she had summoned. But even so, she kept the Ildatch clasped tight against her, whispering to it soundlessly, grasping it as if it were her life-source. Nothing that Jair tried would make her release the book.

It was no game that he was playing now, he thought darkly, remembering Slanter's scathing rebuke.

He was beginning to tire rapidly. Weakened by his battle to gain Heaven's Well, by his wound, and by the strain of his prolonged use of the wishsong, he was becoming exhausted. He did not have the power of the dark magic to sustain him as did Brin; he had only his own determination. It was not enough, he feared. He slipped back and forth through the gloom and the shadows, searching for a way to break through his sister's defenses. His breathing was labored and uneven; his strength was ebbing away.

In desperation, he used the wishsong as he had used it at Culhaven before the Dwarf Council of Elders to create a vision of Allanon. From the haze that lay over the battered chamber, he brought forth the Druid, dark and commanding, one arm stretched forth. Release the book of Ildatch, Brin Ohmsford! the deep voice admonished. Let it fall!

The Valegirl staggered back against the altar, a look of recognition crossing her face. Her lips moved, whispering frantically to the Ildatch—as if speaking to it in warning. Then the look of recognition was gone. High above her head she lifted the book and her song rang out in a wail of anger. The image of Allanon shattered.

Jair slipped away again, cloaked in a whisper of invisibility. He was beginning to despair. Would nothing help Brin? Would nothing bring her back? What was he to do? Frantically, he tried to recall the words spoken to him by the old man: Throw the vision crystal after, and the answer will be shown you. But what answer had he seen? He had tried everything he could think to try. He had used the wishsong to create every illusion he knew how to create. What was left?

He stopped himself. Illusion!

Not illusion—but reality!

And suddenly he had his answer.

Red fire exploded all about Rone, deflecting from the blade of his sword as he stood against the Mord Wraiths' frightening assault. The walkers crouched on the stone stairway of the Croagh, a line of dark forms winding down out of the cliffs and fortress above, shrouded in smoke and mist against the gray backdrop of the dying afternoon sky. Half a dozen arms lifted and the flames hammered at the highlander, staggering him with their force. Kimber crouched behind him, shielding her face and eyes from the heat and flying rock. Whisper screamed in hatred from beneath the shadow of the stairs, lunging at the black figures as they sought to break past.

"Cogline!" Rone bellowed in desperation, fire and smoke swirling all about him as he sought the old man.

Slowly the Mord Wraiths worked their way closer. There were too many; the power of the dark magic was too great. He could not stand against them all.

"Cogline! For cat's sake!"

A cloaked form broke toward him from the shadows above, fire spewing from both hands. Rone swung the blade about frantically, catching the arc of flame and deflecting it. But the walker was almost on top of him, the sound of its voice a sudden hiss that rose above the explosion. Then Whisper hurtled from his shelter, caught the black thing and bore it away. Moor cat and Wraith tumbled into a fountain of flame and smoke and vanished from view.

"Cogline!" Rone screamed one final time.

Abruptly the old man appeared, crooked and bent, shambling out of the billowing smoke with his white hair flying. "Stand, outlander! I'll show the black ones fire that will truly burn!"

Howling as if gone mad, he flung a handful of crystals into the midst of the Mord Wraiths. They glittered like pieces of obsidian as they tumbled down among the dark forms and were caught in the streaks of red fire. Instantly they exploded, and white-hot flames flared skyward in a burst of blinding light. Thunder rocked the mountainside, and whole sections of the Croagh flew apart, carrying the dark forms of the Mord Wraiths with them.

"Burn, you black things!" Cogline shrilled with glee.

But the walkers were not so easily dispatched. Dark shadows, they swept back through the haze of debris and smoke, and the red fire erupted from their fingers. Cogline screamed as the fire reached him and disappeared. Flames encircled Rone and the girl he sheltered, and the walkers came for them in a rush. Sounding the battle cry of his ancestors, the highlander swung the ebony blade into their midst. Two shattered instantly, turned to ash, but the others came on. Clawed fingers closed about the sword and bore him back.

Then they were all about him.

Worn by the strain that the magic's flow caused within her body and confused by the conflicting emotions that wracked her, Brin stood before the altar on the dais that housed the Ildatch, the book clasped tightly to her. The light failed within the tower room, and the air hung thick with dust and silt. The thing was still out there, the thing that taunted her so, the thing that had taken the form of her brother Jair. Though she sought to find it and destroy it, she could not seem to do so. The magics within her were somehow incomplete—as if for some reason they would not blend. They were one, she knew—the book and she. They were joined. The voice still whispered to her that it was so—whispered of the power that belonged to them both. Why was it so difficult then for her to bring that power to bear?

—You fight it, dark child. You resist it. Give yourself over—

Then the air exploded about her, the magic of the one she hunted bursting through dust and half-light, and dozens of images of her brother filled the chamber. All about her the images appeared, slipping through the haze toward the dais, calling out her name. She staggered away, stunned. Jair! Are you truly here? Jair . . . ?

—They are evil, dark child. Destroy them. Destroy—

Obedient to the voice of the Ildatch, though she recognized still from somewhere deep within that it was wrong, she lashed out with her magic, the sound of the wishsong filling the cavernous room. One by one, the images disintegrated before her eyes, and it was as if she were killing Jair over and over again, destroying him anew with each image shattered. But still the images came, those that remained closing the gap between·them, reaching for her, touching . . .

Then she screamed. There were arms about her, arms of flesh and blood, warm and alive, and Jair was before her, holding her close. He was real, not imagined, but a living being, and he spoke to her through the wishsong. Images filled her mind, images of who they had been and who they were, of childhood and beyond—all that had been in their lives and all that now was. Shady Vale was there, the clustered buildings of the community in which she had grown, the clapboard dwellings mingled with stone cottages and thatched-roof huts, and the people settled back at day's close for an evening meal and the small pleasures that come with a joining together of family and friends. The inn was filled with laughter and small talk, bright with candle and oil light. Her home showed, its walks and hedges folded in shadow, the aged trees colored by autumn's touch and ablaze with fading streaks of sunlight. Her father's strong face was smiling in reassurance, her mother's dark hand reaching to stroke her cheek. Rone Leah was there, and her friends, and . . . One by one the supports that had been stripped from her and so ruthlessly crushed were put back again. The images flooded through her, clear, sweet, and strangely cleansing, filled with love and reassurance. Weeping, Brin collapsed into her brother's embrace.

The voice of the Ildatch lashed out at her.

—Destroy him! Destroy him! You are the dark child—

But she did not destroy him. Lost in the weave of the images that swept through her and tapped deep into a wellspring of memories she had thought lost forever, she could feel the person that she had once been returning. That part of her which had been lost was being put back again. The ties of the magics that had bound her close began to loosen, drawing back and leaving her free.

The voice of the Ildatch was suddenly frantic.

—No! You must not release me! You must hold me close. You are the dark child—

Ah, but she was not! She felt it now, sensed it through the fabric of the lies that she had been persuaded to accept. She was *not* the dark child!

Jair's face lifted before her as if from out of a deep fog. His familiar features blurred and then sharpened, and he was speaking softly to her.

"I love you, Brin. I love you."

"Jair," she whispered in reply.

"Do what you were sent here to do, Brin—what Allanon said you must. Do it quickly."

One final time she brought the Ildatch high above her head. She was not the dark child nor was the book the servant that it had claimed to be. It had said that she would be master of its power, but it had lied. No living thing became master of the dark magic— only its slave. There could be no joining of flesh and blood to the magic, however well intentioned. In the end, any use of it must destroy the user. She saw it clearly now and felt a sudden panic spring from the book. It was alive and it could feel; let it, then! It would have subverted her; it would have drained her life from her as it had drained the lives of so many and turned her into a thing as dark and twisted as the walkers, the Skull Bearers before them, or the Warlock Lord himself. It would have set her loose upon the Four Lands and all who lived within them, to bring the darkness again . . .

With a heave, she threw the book from her. It struck the stone flooring of the tower with stunning force. The bindings shattered, breaking apart. Pages ripped and scattered.

Then Brin Ohmsford used the wishsong. It sounded hard and quick as it caught up the remnants of the book in its power and turned the Ildatch to impotent dust.

. . .

At the edge of the Croagh, on the cliffs below Graymark, Rone felt the clawed fingers of the Mord Wraiths release their grip as if stung by a fire they could not master. The cloaked forms drew back, writhing and twisting against the gray light of the slowly darkening sky. Their voices sounded as one in the sudden silence, a shriek of anguish and terror. All along the length of the Croagh leading down to the ledge where Rone had struggled to hold them, the Wraiths convulsed like shaken rag dolls.

"Rone!" Kimber screamed, pulling him clear of where the foremost of the black things stumbled blindly about.

Flames burst from out of Wraiths' fingers and exploded from their cowled faces. Then, one after another, they disintegrated, falling apart like shattered earthen statues, crumbling and drifting to the stone of the ledge. In seconds, the Mord Wraiths were no more.

"Rone, what happened to them?" the girl whispered harshly, her stunned voice drifting in the stillness.

The highlander's hands still clasped the pommel of the Sword of Leah as he came back to his feet, his head shaking slowly. Smoke and debris drifted in the air across the mountain face, swirling hazily about them. The battered form of Whisper appeared like a ghost out of its curtain.

"Brin," Rone murmured softly in answer to Kimber's question. He shook his head in disbelief. "It was Brin."

And then he felt the first of the earth tremors ripple through the mountainside from the Maelmord.

Exhausted, Brin Ohmsford stared at the blackened stone of the tower floor where the remains of the Ildatch settled in a fine dust.

"Here is your dark child," she whispered bitterly, tears streaking her face.

A deep shudder wracked the tower, rolling out of the earth and spreading through the aged walls. Stone and timber began to sag and crack, crumbling with the vibrations that wrenched at it. Brin's head jerked up, her eyes blinking against the shower of silt and dust that rained down into her face.

"Jair . . . ?" she tried to call to him.

But her brother was slipping from her, flesh and blood dissolving back into the hazy air, an apparition once more. A look of disbelief reflected in the Valeman's face, and it seemed as if he were trying to tell her something. His shadowy form lingered a moment longer in the half-light of the tower's gloom, and then he was gone.

Stricken, Brin stared after him. Great chunks of the tower's stone began to fall about her, and she knew she could not stay. The dark magic of the Ildatch had come to an end, and everything it had made was dying.

"But I am going to live!" she whispered fiercely.

Gathering her cloak about her, she turned and ran from the empty room.

XLVİ

---◆---

THE SİLVER LİGHT FLARED ABOVE THE WATERS GATHERED İn the basin of Heaven's Well and an apprehensive Slanter stumbled back away once more. There was an explosion of shimmering brilliance, a radiance as intense and blinding as the cresting of the sun at dawn, reaching out through the fading of the night. It streaked through the cavern's dark shadows, burst into shards of white fire, and was gone.

Wincing, Slanter looked back again at the stone basin. Standing worn and battered at its edge was Jair Ohmsford.

"Boy!" the Gnome cried, a mix of concern and relief in his voice as he rushed to meet the Valeman.

Jair slumped forward in exhaustion, and the other caught him about the waist. "I couldn't bring her out, Slanter," he whispered. "I tried, but the magic wasn't strong enough. I had to leave her."

"Here, here—just take a moment to catch your breath," Slanter growled as the Valeman stumbled over his words. "Sit here by the basin."

He eased Jair down against the stone wall, then knelt next to him. The Valeman's eyes lifted. "I went down into the Maelmord, Slanter—or at least a part of me did. I used the third magic—the one that the King of the Silver River gave to me to help Brin. It took me into the light and then out of myself—as if there were two of me. I went down into the pit where the vision crystal had shown me Brin. She was there, in a tower, and she had the Ildatch. But it had changed her, Slanter. She had become something . . . terrible . . ."

"Easy, boy. Slow down, now." The Gnome held his gaze. "Did you find a way to help her?"

Jair nodded, swallowing. "She was changed, but I knew that if I could just reach her, if I could touch her and she could touch me—then she would be all right. I used the wishsong to show her who she was, what she meant to me . . . to let her know that I loved her!" He was fighting back the tears. "And she destroyed the Ildatch—she turned it to dust! But when she did, the tower began to crumble, and something happened to the magic. I couldn't stay with her. I couldn't bring her back with me. I tried, but it happened so quickly. I couldn't even manage to tell her what was happening! She just . . . disappeared, and I was back here again . . ."

He dropped his head between his knees, choking. Slanter gripped his shoulders with rough, gnarled hands and squeezed.

"You did the best you could for her, boy. You did everything you could. You can't blame yourself for not being able to do more." He shook his wizened face. "Shades, I don't know how it is that you're still alive! I thought you lost in the magic! I didn't think I'd ever see you again!"

Then he hugged Jair impulsively to him and whispered. "You got more sand than I do, boy—a whole lot more!"

He pulled away then, embarrassed by his action, muttering something about no one really knowing what they were doing in all this confusion. He was about to say something more when the tremors began—a series of deep, heavy rumblings that shook the mountain to its core.

"What's happening now?" he exclaimed, glancing back across his shoulder into the shadows that shrouded the passageway that had brought them in.

"It's the Maelmord," Jair replied at once, pushing himself hurriedly back to his feet. The wound in his shoulder throbbed and ached as he straightened against the basin wall, and he clutched at the Gnome for support. "Slanter, we have to go back for Brin. She's alone down there. We have to help her."

The Gnome gave him a quick, fierce smile in reply. "Of course, we do, boy. You and me. We'll get her out. We'll go down into that black pit and we'll find her! Now here, put your arm about my shoulders and hold on."

With Jair clinging tightly to him, the Gnome began to retrace their steps back through the cavern toward the stairway that had brought them in. Dusk had settled down across the land, and the sun had slipped behind the rim of the mountains. Small slivers of the dying light fell through crevices in the rock to mingle with the twilight shadows as the two companions stumbled resolutely ahead. The tremors continued, slow and steady, a grim reminder that time was slipping from them. Chunks of rock and dirt showered down about them, forming a haze that hung like mist in the still evening air. There was a low rumbling in the distance like the thunder of an approaching storm.

Then they were clear of the cavern once more, passing from its darkened mouth onto the ledge that ran down to the Croagh. In the east, the moon and a scattering of stars were already visible in the velvet sky. Shadows lay in dappled patterns across the ledge face, closing about the last patches of fading light like ink stains spreading on new paper.

In the midst of the shadows and the half-light lay Garet Jax.

Stunned, Jair and Slanter came forward. The Weapons Master lay back against a gathering of rocks, his black-clad form torn and bloodied, the slender sword still gripped in one hand. His eyes were closed, as if he slept. Hesitating, Slanter knelt beside him.

"Is he dead?" Jair whispered, barely able to make himself speak the words.

The Gnome bent close for a moment, then drew back again. Slowly, he nodded. "Yes, boy—he's dead. He finally found something that could kill him—something that was as good as he was."

There was grudging disbelief in his voice. "He looked hard enough and long enough to find it, didn't he?"

Jair did not answer. He was thinking of the times the Weapons Master had saved his life, rescuing him when no one else could. Garet Jax, his protector.

He would have cried if he had been able, but there were no tears left to shed.

Slanter came to his feet and stood looking down at the still form. "Always wondered what it would be that would finally kill him," the Gnome muttered. "Had to be something made of the dark magic, I guess. Couldn't be anything made of this world. Not with him."

He turned and glanced about apprehensively. "Wonder what's become of the red thing?"

Tremors shook the mountain, and the rumbling rolled out of the valley. Jair barely heard it. "He destroyed it, Slanter. Garet Jax destroyed it. And when the Ildatch was shattered, the dark magic took it back."

"Could have happened that way, I guess."

"It did happen that way. This was the battle he had been seeking the whole of his life. It meant everything to him. He wouldn't have lost it."

The Gnome glanced over at him sharply. "You don't know that for sure, boy. You don't know that he was a match for that thing."

Jair looked at him then and nodded. "Yes, I do, Slanter. I do. He was a match for anything. He was the best."

There was a long moment of silence between them. Then the Gnome nodded, too. "Yes, I guess he was."

Again the tremors shook the mountain, reverberating out of the deep rock. Slanter caught hold of Jair's arm and gently turned him away. "We can't stay, boy. We have to find your sister right away."

Jair glanced back at the still form of the Weapons Master one final time and then forced his eyes away. "Good-bye, Garet Jax," he whispered.

Together, Gnome and Valeman hastened to the stairway of the Croagh and started down.

Brin ran through the dim and misted tangle of the Maelmord, free at last of the tower of the Ildatch. Deep tremors wracked the valley floor, shudders that rippled to the peaks of the mountains all about. The dark magic was gone from the land, and with its passing the Maelmord could not survive. The rise and fall of its breathing and the hiss that had whispered of its unnatural life were stilled.

Where am I? Brin wondered frantically, her eyes casting through the gathering shadows. What has become of the Croagh?

She knew that she was hopelessly lost. She had been from the moment that she had fled the tower. Nightfall lay over the whole of the valley, and she was deep within a graveyard where all signs appeared as one and no path showed itself. Through the webbing of limbs and vines overhead, she could see the rim of the mountains that ringed the valley pit, but the stem of the Croagh lay wrapped in darkness against their backdrop. The Maelmord had become an impossible maze, and she was caught within it.

She was exhausted, her strength drained by prolonged use of the wishsong and by her long journey down into the pit. She was lost, and the magic no longer gave her sight. And all about her, the tremors continued to shake the valley floor, forewarning of the destruction of the Maelmord and everything caught within it. Only her spirit remained strong, and it was her spirit that kept her moving now in search of an escape.

The ground sank sharply beneath her feet, giving way with a suddenness that was frightening. Brin stumbled and nearly went down. The Maelmord was breaking up. It was crumbling beneath her, and she knew now that she would be carried with it.

She slowed to a weary halt, gasping for breath. It was pointless to go on. She was running to no purpose, blind and directionless. Even the vaunted magic of the wishsong, should she choose to use it, could not save her now. Why had Jair abandoned her?

Why had he gone? Despair washed through her at the terrible sense of betrayal—despair and unreasoning anger. But she fought back against those feelings, knowing that they were senseless and unfair. Jair would not have left her unless he had been given no choice. Whatever had brought him to her had simply taken him back again.

Or perhaps what she had thought was Jair was not and what she had seen and felt had not even been real. Perhaps it had all been something that in her madness she had dreamed . . .

"Jair!" she screamed.

The echo of her voice broke against the rumblings of the earth and then was gone. The ground sank further beneath her.

Resolutely, stubbornly, she turned and went on. She no longer ran, too wearied to run further. Her dusky face hardened with determination, and she brushed everything from her mind but the need to put one foot before the other. She would not give up. She would go on. When she could no longer walk upright, she would crawl. But she would go on.

Then suddenly a shadow bounded from the tangled dark, huge, lean, and ghostly. It came toward her and she cried out in fright. A massive whiskered face rubbed against her body, and luminous blue eyes blinked in greeting. It was Whisper! She fell against the moor cat in grateful disbelief, crying openly, wrapping her arms about the shaggy neck. Whisper had come for her!

The moor cat turned and started away at once, drawing her with him. She fastened one hand in the ruff of his neck and stumbled after. They slipped through the maze of the dying jungle. All about them, the rumblings grew and tremors shook the earth. Rotted limbs began to crash down about them. Steam smelling rank and fetid geysered from cracks that split the hardened earth. Boulders and slides broke away from the cliffs that walled the valley close and came tumbling through the dark.

Yet somehow they reached the Croagh, its coiled length materializing abruptly out of the gloom, rising from the valley floor into the night. The giant cat bounded onto the stairway with Brin a step behind. The Valegirl scrambled upward, groping her way uncertainly as the rumblings intensified. Massive tremors rocked the Croagh, one following close upon another. Brin was thrown to her knees. Beneath her, the stone began to crack and split. Whole sections of the stairway were breaking off and tumbling downward into the pit. Not yet! she screamed soundlessly. Not until I am free! Whisper's deep roar lifted above the rumblings, and she struggled after the big cat. Below them, giant trees snapped apart like deadwood. The last of the failing twilight died as the sun slipped beneath the horizon and the whole of the land was wrapped in shadow.

And then the cliff ledge was before her again, and she stumbled onto it, crying out to the shadowy forms that closed about her. Arms reached for her, pulling her clear of the crumbling stairs, drawing her back from the precipice. Kimber was hugging and kissing her, her pixie face beaming with happiness and her eyes filled with tears. Cogline was muttering and grumbling, dabbing at her cheeks with a soiled cloth. And Rone was there, his lean, sun-browned face haggard and bruised, but his gray eyes were fierce with love. Whispering her name, he wrapped his arms about her and held her against him. It was then, finally, that she knew that she was safe.

Only moments later, Jair and Slanter came upon them, descending the Croagh from Heaven's Well in their desperate search for Brin. There were astonished looks and exclamations of relief. Then Brin and Jair were clasping each other close once more.

"It *was* you who came to me in the Maelmord," Brin whispered, stroking her brother's head. She smiled through her tears. "You saved me, Jair."

Jair hugged her back to mask his embarrassment. Rone came over and hugged them both. "For cat's sake, tiger—you're supposed to be back in the Vale! Don't you ever do anything you're told?"

Slanter hung back tentatively, eyeing them all with studied suspicion, from the three who persisted in hugging and kissing each other to the spindly old man, the woods girl, and the giant moor cat stretched out beside them. "Oddest bunch I've ever come across," he muttered to himself.

Then the rumblings from the floor of the valley rolled through the mountain rock like thunder, and the tremors shattered apart the whole of the Croagh. It tumbled into the pit and was gone. All of the little company that were gathered on the cliff ledge hastened to its edge and peered through the gloom. Shards of brightness from the moon and stars laced the darkness. In a rippling of shadows, the pit of the Maelmord began to sink. Downward it slipped, downward into the earth as if swallowed by quicksand. Soil, rock, and dying forest crumbled and fell away. The shadows lengthened and drew together until the moonlight could no longer show any trace of what had once been.

In moments, the Maelmord had disappeared forever.

XLVII

Autumn had settled down across the land, and everywhere the colors of the season brightened and shone in the sunshine's warmth. It was a clear, cool day in the Eastland forests where the Chard Rush tumbled down from out of the Wolfsktaag, and the skies were a depthless blue. There had been a frost that morning, and melted patches of it lingered still in the deep grasses and on the hardened earth and moss-grown rocks that lined the riverbanks, mixed with the spray of the channel's foaming waters.

Brin paused at the edge of those waters to gather her thoughts.

It had been a week now since the little company of friends had departed the Ravenshorn. With the destruction of the Ildatch and the fading of the dark magic and all the things that it had made, the Gnome Hunters defending Graymark had fled back into the hills and forestlands of the deep Anar—back to the tribes from which they had been taken. Left alone in the crumbling, deserted fortress, Brin, Jair, and their friends had found the bodies of the Borderman Helt, the Dwarf Elb Foraker, and the Elven Prince Edain Elessedil and laid them to rest. Only Garet Jax had been left where he had fallen, for with the destruction of the Croagh, all passage to Heaven's Well had been cut off. Perhaps it was right that the Weapons Master be left where no other mortal could go, Jair had offered solemnly. Perhaps it should be no different in death for Garet Jax than it had been in life.

They had camped that night in the forests below Graymark, south of where it nestled within the Ravenshorn, and it was there that Brin told the others her promise to Allanon that, when the Il-datch was destroyed and her quest finished, she would come back to him. Now that her long journey into the Maelmord was over, she must seek him out one final time. There were questions yet to be answered and things that she must know.

And so they had all come with her—her brother Jair, Rone, Kimber, Cogline, the moor cat Whisper, and even the Gnome Slanter. They had journeyed with her back down out of the Ra-venshorn, skirted the mountains south along the barren stretches of Olden Moor, crossed again over Toffer Ridge into the forests of Darklin Reach and the valley of Hearthstone, then followed the winding channel of the Chard Rush west until they had reached the little glen where Allanon had fought his final battle. It had taken them a week to complete that journey, and on the evening of the seventh day they had camped at the edge of the glen.

Now, in the chill of early morning, she stood quietly, staring out across the river's flow. Behind her, gathered in the bowl of the little glen, the others waited patiently. They had not come with her to the river's edge; she had not wanted them to. This was something that she must do alone.

How am I to summon him? she wondered. Am I to sing to him? Am I to use the wishsong's magic so that he will know that I am here? Or will he come without being called, knowing that I wait . . . ?

As if in answer, the waters of the Chard Rush went still before her, their surface turned as smooth as glass. All about, the forest grew silent, and even the distant drone of the falls faded and was gone. Gently, the waters began to seethe, rippling and frothing like a stirred cauldron, and a single clear, sweet cry lifted into the morn-ing air.

Then Allanon rose out of the Chard Rush, his tall, spare frame erect and robed in black. He came across the still waters of the river, his head lifting within the shadow of the cowl and his dark eyes hard and penetrating. He did not look the way Bremen had appeared; his body seemed solid rather than transparent, free from the mists that had cloaked his father's shade and free from the death shroud that had wrapped the old man close. It was as if he still lived, Brin thought suddenly, as if he had never died.

He drew close to her and stopped, suspended in the air above the waters of the river.

"Allanon," she whispered.

"I have waited for you to come, Brin Ohmsford," he answered her softly.

She looked closer, seeing now the faint glimmer of the river's waters through the darkness of his robes, shimmering gently, and she knew then that he was truly dead and that it was only his shade that stood before her.

"It is finished, Allanon," she told him, finding it suddenly difficult to speak. "The Ildatch is destroyed."

The cowled head inclined faintly. "Destroyed by the power of the Elven magic, shaped and colored by the wishsong. But destroyed as well, Valegirl, by a power greater still—by love, Brin; by the love that bound your brother to you. He loved you too much to fail, even though he came too late."

"Yes, by love, too, Allanon."

"Savior and destroyer." The black eyes narrowed. "The power of your magic would make you both, and you have seen how corrupting such power can be. So terrible is the lure and so difficult to balance. I gave you warning of that, but such warning as I gave was not enough. I failed you badly."

She shook her head quickly. "No, it was not you who failed me. It was I who failed myself."

The Druid's hand lifted from within the robes, and she found that she could see through it. "I do not have long, so hear me well, Brin Ohmsford. I did not understand all that I should have of the dark magic. I deceived myself—just as the Grimpond told you. I knew that the magic of the wishsong could be as my father had warned—both blessing and curse—and that the holder could therefore become both savior and destroyer. But you possessed reason and heart, and I did not think the danger so great as long as those qualities stood by you. I failed to realize the truth about the Ildatch and that the danger of the dark magic could go beyond those created to wield it. For the true danger was always the book—the subverter of all who had come to use the magic from the time of the Warlock Lord to the time of the Mord Wraiths. All had been slaves to the Ildatch, but the Ildatch was not merely an inanimate gathering of pages and bindings in which the dark magic was recorded. It was alive—an evil that could turn to its uses by the magic's lure all who sought its power."

Allanon bent close, sunlight streaking through the edges of the dark robes as if they had frayed. "It wanted you to come to it from the beginning. But it wanted you tested first. Each time you used the magic of the wishsong, you fell a bit farther under the lure of the magic's power. You realized that there was something wrong in your continued use of the magic, but you were forced to use it anyway. And I was not there to tell you what was happening. By the time that you had gone down into the Maelmord, you were a thing much the same as all who had served the book, and you believed that this was as it should be. This was what the book intended that you should believe. It wanted to have you for its own. Even the power of the Mord Wraiths was insignificant in comparison to yours, for they had not been born with the magic as had you. In you, the Ildatch had found a weapon that carried more power than any that had ever served it—even the Warlock Lord."

Brin stared at him disbelievingly. "Then it spoke the truth when it said that it had been waiting for me—that there were bonds that joined us."

"A twisted half-truth," Allanon cautioned. "You had become close enough in spirit to what it sought that it could make you believe that such was so. It could convince you that you were indeed the dark child of your fears."

"But the wishsong could have made me so . . ."

"The wishsong could have made you . . . anything."

She hesitated. "And still can?"

"And still can. Always."

Brin watched the robed figure move closer still to where she stood. For a moment, she thought that he might reach out to draw her to him. But, instead, the lean face lifted and looked beyond her.

"My death was foretold at the Hadeshorn. My passing from this life was assured. But with the destruction of the Ildatch, the dark magic must pass as well. The wheel of time comes around, and the age ends. My father is set free at last, gone to the rest that had been so long denied him, bound no longer to me or to his pledge to the races of the Four Lands."

The cowled head lowered to her once more. "And now I go, also. No Druids shall come after me. But the trust that was theirs resides now with you."

"Allanon . . ." she whispered, shaking her head.

"Hear me, Valegirl. The blood that I placed upon your forehead and the words I spoke at its giving have made it so. You are the bearer of the trust that was mine and my father's before me. Do not be frightened by what that means. No harm shall befall you because of it. The last of the magic lives now within you and your brother, within the blood of your family. There it shall rest, safe and protected. It shall not be needed again in the age that is to come. The magic will have no useful place within that age. Other learning will be a better and truer guide for the races.

"But, heed. A time will come, far distant and beyond the lives of generations of Ohmsfords yet unborn, when the magic will be needed again. As with all things, time's wheel will come around once more. Then the trust I have given you will be needed, and the children of the house of Shannara will be called upon to deliver it. For the world that will one day be, do you keep that trust safe?"

"No, Allanon, I do not want this . . ."

But his hand lifted sharply and silenced her. "It is done, Brin Ohmsford. As my father did with me, I have chosen you—child of my life."

Voiceless, she stared up at him in despair.

"Do not be afraid," he whispered.

She nodded helplessly. "I will try."

He began to draw away from her, his dark form fading slowly as the sunlight brightened through it. "Put the magic from you, Brin. Do not use it again, for there no longer is need. Be at peace."

"Allanon!" she cried.

He drifted back across the Chard Rush, the waters roiling gently now beneath him. "Remember me," he said softly.

He sank downward into the river, down through the silver waters, and was gone. The Chard Rush rolled on once more.

On the shore's edge, Brin stared out across the water. There were tears in her eyes. "I will always remember you," she whispered.

Then she turned and walked away.

XLVIII

---◆---

SO IT WAS THAT THE MAGIC FADED FROM THE FOUR LANDS
and the tales of the Druids and Paranor passed into legend. For a
time, there would be many who would insist that the Druids had
been formed of flesh and blood and had walked the land as mortal
men and as the protectors of the races; for a brief time, there would
be many who would argue that the magic had been real and that
terrible struggles had been waged between good and evil sorceries.
But the number of believers would dwindle as the years passed. In
the end, nearly all would vanish.

On the same morning that Allanon disappeared from the
world of men for the final time, the little company bade farewell to
one another. Surrounded by the colors and smells of autumn, they
embraced, said good-bye, and departed for their own lands.

"I will miss you, Brin Ohmsford," Kimber announced solemnly,
her pixie face determinedly resolute. "And grandfather will miss
you, too, won't you, grandfather?"

Cogline shuffled his sandaled feet uneasily and nodded without looking at the Valegirl. "Some, I guess," he admitted grudgingly.
"Won't miss all that crying and agonizing, though. Won't miss that.
Course, we did have some fine adventures, girl—I'll miss you for
that. Spider Gnomes and the black walkers and all. Almost like the
old days . . ."

He trailed off, and Brin smiled. "I'll miss both of you, too. And

Whisper. I owe my life as much to Whisper as to the rest of you. If he hadn't come down into the Maelmord to find me . . ."

"He sensed that he was needed," Kimber declared firmly. "He would not have disregarded your warning if he had not sensed that need. I think there is a special bond between you—a bond beyond that created by your song."

"Don't want you coming back again without telling me first, though," Cogline interrupted suddenly. "Or until I invite you. You don't come into peoples' homes without being asked!"

"Grandfather." Kimber sighed.

"Will you come to see me?" Brin asked her.

The girl smiled and glanced at her grandfather. "Perhaps, some day. For a time, I think I'll stay with grandfather and Whisper at Hearthstone. I have been away long enough. I miss my home."

Brin came to her and hugged her close. "I miss mine as well, Kimber. But we'll meet again some day."

"You will always be my friend, Brin." There were tears in her eyes as she buried her face in the Valegirl's shoulder.

"And you will be mine," Brin whispered. "Good-bye, Kimber. Thank you."

Rone added his good-byes to Brin's, then walked over to stand before Whisper. The big moor cat sat back on his haunches regarding the highlander curiously, saucer blue eyes blinking.

"I was wrong about you, cat," he offered grudgingly. He hesitated. "That probably doesn't mean anything to you, but it means something to me. You saved my life, too." He stood looking at the moor cat for a moment, then glanced ruefully back at the others. "I promised myself I'd say that if he brought Brin safely out of the pit; but I still feel like an idiot standing here talking with him like this, for cat's . . . for . . ."

He trailed off. Whisper yawned sleepily and showed all of his teeth.

A dozen yards away, Jair was feeling something of an idiot himself as he faced Slanter and struggled to find expression for the jumble of emotions rushing through him.

"Look, boy." The Gnome was gruff and impatient. "Don't make so much work out of this. Just say it. Good-bye. Just say it."

But Jair shook his head stubbornly. "I can't, Slanter. It's not enough. You and I, we've been together one way or another right from the first—right from the time I tricked you with the snakes and locked you in that wood bin."

"Please don't remind me!" the Gnome grumbled.

"We're all that's left, Slanter," Jair tried to explain, folding his arms protectively across his chest. "All that way we came, you and I and the others—but they're gone and we're all that's left." He shook his head. "So much has happened, and I can't just dismiss it with a simple 'good-bye.'"

Slanter sighed. "It's not as if we'll never see each other again, boy. What's the matter—you think I'll end up dead, too? Well, think again! I know how to take care of myself—said so yourself once, remember? Nothing's going to happen to me. And I'd bet a month of nights in the black pit that nothing will ever happen to you! You're too confounded sneaky!"

Jair smiled in spite of himself. "I guess that's quite a compliment, coming from you." He took a deep breath. "Come back with me, Slanter. Come back to Culhaven and tell them what happened. It should come from you."

"No, boy." The Gnome lowered his rough face and shook his head slowly. "I won't be going back there again. Gnomes won't be welcome in the Lower Anar for a good many years to come, no matter their reasons. No, I'm for the borderlands again—for now, at least."

Jair nodded, and there was an awkward silence between them. "Good-bye then, Slanter. Until next time."

He stepped forward and put his arms about the Gnome. Slanter hesitated, then patted him roughly on the shoulders.

"Now see, boy—that wasn't so bad, was it?"

Nevertheless, it was a long time before he broke away.

.   .   .

It was more than a week later when Brin, Jair, and Rone arrived once more in Shady Vale and turned onto the cobblestone walkway that led to the front door of the Ohmsford home. It was late afternoon, and the sun had already slipped behind the hills, leaving the forest cloaked in shadows and half-light. The sound of voices drifted through the still autumn air from homes scattered about, and leaves rustled through the long grass.

Before them, the windows of the cottage were already lighted against the evening gloom.

"Brin, how are we going to explain all this?" Jair asked for what must have been the hundredth time.

They had passed through the stand of flowering plum, by now almost entirely leafless, when the front door swung open and Eretria came rushing out.

"Wil, they're home!" she called back over her shoulder and hurried to embrace both of her children and Rone in the bargain. A moment later Wil Ohmsford appeared as well, bent to kiss both Brin and Jair, and gave Rone a warm handshake.

"You look a bit tired, Brin," he observed quietly. "Did you and your brother manage to get any sleep while you were in Leah?"

Brin and Jair exchanged a quick glance, while Rone smiled benignly and began studying the ground. "How was your trip south, father?" Jair changed the subject quickly.

"We were able to help a lot of people, fortunately." Wil Ohmsford scrutinized his son carefully. "The work kept us away much longer than we had intended or we would have come for you in Leah. As it was, we just returned last night."

Brin and Jair exchanged another quick glance, and this time their father saw it at once. "Would either of you like to tell me now who that old man was you sent?"

Brin stared. "What old man?"

"The old man with the message, Brin."

Jair frowned. "What message?"

Eretria stepped forward now, a hint of displeasure in her dark eyes. "An old man came to us in the outlying villages south of Kaypra. He was from Leah. He had a message from you telling us that you had gone to the highlands and that you would be away for several weeks and not to worry. Your father and I thought it strange that so old a man would be serving as messenger for Rone's father, but . . ."

"Brin!" Jair whispered, wide-eyed.

"There was something familiar about him," Wil mused suddenly. "It seemed to me that I ought to have known him."

"Brin, I didn't send any . . ." Jair began, then cut himself short. They were all staring at him. "Wait . . . just wait right here, just . . . for a moment," he sputtered, stumbling over the words as he edged past them. "Be right back!"

He dashed past them into the house, down the hallway, through the front room, and into the kitchen. He went at once to the stone hearth where it joined the shelving nooks and traced his way down to the third shelf. Then he moved the loose stone from its niche and reached inside.

His fingers closed over the Elfstones and their familiar leather pouch.

He stood there for a moment, stunned. Then gripping the Stones in his hand, he walked back through the house to where the others still waited on the cobbled walkway. With a grin, he produced the pouch and its contents and displayed them to an astonished Brin and Rone.

There was a long moment of silence as the five stared at one another. Then Brin took her mother with one arm and her father with the other.

"Mother. Father. I think we had better all go inside and sit down for a while." She smiled. "Jair and I have something to tell you."

TERRY BROOKS is the *New York Times* bestselling author of more than thirty books, including the Dark Legacy of Shannara adventures *Wards of Faerie, Bloodfire Quest,* and *Witch Wraith;* the Legends of Shannara novels *Bearers of the Black Staff* and *The Measure of the Magic;* the Genesis of Shannara trilogy: *Armageddon's Children, The Elves of Cintra,* and *The Gypsy Morph; The Sword of Shannara;* the Voyage of the *Jerle Shannara* trilogy: *Ilse Witch, Antrax,* and *Morgawr;* the High Druid of Shannara trilogy: *Jarka Ruus, Tanequil,* and *Straken;* the nonfiction book *Sometimes the Magic Works: Lessons from a Writing Life;* and the novel based upon the screenplay and story by George Lucas, *Star Wars®*: Episode I *The Phantom Menace.*™ His novels *Running with the Demon* and *A Knight of the Word* were selected by the *Rocky Mountain News* as two of the best science fiction/fantasy novels of the twentieth century. The author was a practicing attorney for many years but now writes full-time. He lives with his wife, Judine, in the Pacific Northwest.

shannara.com
terrybrooks.net
@officialbrooks

ABOUT THE TYPE

This book was set in Minion, a 1990 Adobe Originals typeface by Robert Slimbach (b. 1956). Minion is inspired by classical, old-style typefaces of the late Renaissance, a period of elegant, beautiful, and highly readable type designs. Created primarily for text setting, Minion combines the aesthetic and functional qualities that make text type highly readable with the versatility of digital technology.